PRAISE FOR THE WAY OF EDAN

In *The Way of Edan*, Philip Chase has written a highly accomplished first novel. The storytelling is top-notch. There's a gravitas in the writing that put me in mind of Tolkien, with definite shades of Katherine Kerr, along with John Gwynne. This is a novel born of love for the story.

— MARK LAWRENCE

What a wonderful read! Prose that is smooth and accessible, a world with a weight and depth to it, and a gripping and emotional story. There's a lot to love here. Lovely to see the Anglo-Saxon influences that gave me a real sense of time and place, and the storytelling was done with a deft, assured hand.

— JOHN GWYNNE

The Way of Edan encompasses an expanding war driven by voracious religious fanaticism. Young heroes emerge, bonded by loyalty, in an age of ripening prophecy. Traditional fantasy readers will find elves with a fresh spin expanding the familiar bounds of individuality, and women, old and young, who wield magic in positions of power.

— JANNY WURTS

An impressive debut novel. Chase deftly weaves mystery and action with profound world-building. Deeply realized and compelling

— IAN ESSLEMONT

PRAISE FOR THE WAY OF EDAN (CONTINUED)

A classic feeling tale about connection. Connection to each other, to the earth, and to the creatures that live in it, as well as connection to life and death. A story that feels familiar, yet very much belonging to Philip Chase. I loved my time with it.

— MERPHY NAPIER

Gemmell's characters have invaded the landscape of Tolkien in this immersive, addictive, poetic read. An instant classic that will have fantasy and historical fiction fans desperate for more.

— ED FROM THE BROTHERS GWYNNE

Every element of storytelling comes together to weave an engaging and immersive story that is an absolute joy to follow.

— WILL FROM THE BROTHERS GWYNNE

A spectacular debut reminiscent of Ken Follett and Tad Williams.

— MIKE FROM MIKE'S BOOK REVIEWS

PRAISE FOR THE WAY OF EDAN (CONTINUED)

Every word is worth savoring in *The Way of Edan*, the masterful debut epic fantasy from Philip Chase. Lyrical and evocative . . . the most perfectly conceived and executed debut fantasy that I have read since *The Name of the Wind* by Patrick Rothfuss.

— JOHN MAURO FOR GRIMDARK MAGAZINE

This is a marvelous debut penned by a seemingly veteran author with a lot of love for the genre. A magnificent mix of classic and modern . . . it is a lyrical and traditional epic fantasy oozing with mythical quality due to its world-building. *The Way of Edan* might become my favorite fantasy debut of the year.

— PETRIK LEO FOR NOVEL NOTIONS

The Way of Edan is a compelling debut fantasy novel rich in setting, lore, history, and song. Well-seasoned fantasy readers may notice nods to Tolkien, *Beowulf*, and medieval sources, but the incorporation of Buddhist-inspired magic and enigmatic elf portrayals provides a razor-edge balance between beauty and peril. Refined and impactful prose immerses the reader into intimate character conflicts amidst an expanding holy war and into explorations of faith, doubt, duty, loyalty, and particularly empathy.

— JOHANNA FROM JOHANNA READS

RETURN TO EDAN

Book Three of The Edan Trilogy

PHILIP CHASE

Created with Vellum

ACKNOWLEDGMENTS

Well, here we are . . . And *here* we would not be without the family, friends, colleagues, and students who have encouraged me over the years. Once again, I wish to acknowledge the supportive community of friends I have been so fortunate to know on BookTube. You all have helped me in ways I cannot even begin to express, and my gratitude is immense!

It has been wonderful working with Kyra Gregory and Jack Shepherd on the cover art and cover design, respectively. Also, Jack's map of Eormenlond will never fail to make me smile.

Finally, I am certain that no one has ever had a better Nemesis than I have. Of course, how many nemeses can cast fireballs? Thank you for all your illuminating help on these books, A.P. Canavan!

For Reshma

Outer Isles
Hemeldowns
Frost Bay
North Downs
Hrones Sea
Beoroth
hwitwater
The Mark
Farwick
Northweald (Iltharwyn)
Norfast
Rimdale
Wolvendon
folkwater
folkmere
withweald
Kinsford
Birch Bay
Southweald (Iltharwyn)
DWEORG BARROWS
The Dweorghlithes
anrod
Erinstone
theodamar
Woodburg
Torrlond
ORMETBERG
Bay of Haylon
Hasumere
Gorifaen Hills
Belzlan
Sundering Sea
Torrhelm
Derwyn
Caergilion
Gadomiel
glas
BALNOR PASS
Harith
gilion
Iarfath
Marar Mtns
Culvor Sound
maranant
Adanon
Asdralad
Bay of Ethradan
Palahon
Dirgal
Dwarioth
Isles of Yaladir
Gulf of Gath
Kiriath
Halion Sound
Firdal
Isthmus of Lod
Yalawyn
Hormenlond
or
Andumedan
25 50 75 100 150 200 300
scale in miles

Enga Isle
holm
Savage Sea
Ironwood
The Wildlands
SIRUKINN'S WALL
Amlar Mtns
Edwend Downs
Sea of Morthul
kuralas
Slith (The Great Fen)
nurgleth
Nahan
Shohan
diadas
Sildharan
Shinan
Holurad
sannodi
Golzar
ulnodi
lannad
Orudwyn
Kelzaon
Sundara
Gulf of Bahan
Glirdan
Tinubor
N
W
E
S

CONTENTS

PROLOGUE

Work never ended. Not, at least, until you died. When you died, someone else would do the work. That was one thing Oran had figured out in his nine years. After dipping the rag back in the bucket and squeezing the dirty water out of it, he forced the tired muscles in his skinny arm to resume wiping the table. Ever since Father died, he had been working.

He figured it was the same everywhere. Having never set foot outside his home village of Vilwan, he could not say for sure. It was a little corner of the mighty kingdom of Sildharan, which was one of a number of kingdoms in Andumedan. He knew that much, but life likely was the same everywhere — at least for most people.

Of course, there were those few who did not have to work because they found ways to make other people do it for them. Like Baras, who was mouthing off as usual at the corner table with a group of his men and laughing too loud over his ale. Oran frowned as he glanced over at the big man with his fancy clothes. After Father died, Baras started coming more often to the Queen's Inn, even though his big house on his estate was not in the village. He did not like the way Baras looked at Mother, leering at her while ordering her about. Everyone else pretended not to see, but Oran saw.

Oran started when Baras caught him looking and, seeing the boy's fear, gave that predator's smile of his. Frowning to cover his shame, Oran gazed back down at his table and kept wiping. He dropped the rag in the bucket of dirty water again and bent down to wring it out. He squeezed hard. His hands shook as the water trickled and ran down them and dripped into the bucket until the dripping lessened and slowed and then stopped, and he was sure no one could have squeezed more out of it.

The front door banged shut. At first Oran did not think much of it since it was getting close to dinner, when many of the villagers would show up to drink and eat and gossip. But then he noticed something odd. The room had grown quiet, and even Baras had shut his mouth. Oran looked up from his rag and bucket to see who had come in.

Something was not right with the man who stood inside the door. He had pale skin, like the Ilarchae slaves that used to toil in Baras's nearby fields before they all ran away, killed a lot of people, and joined the great battle up north near Thulhan. And his hair wasn't just yellow like some of the Ilarchae, but it was silvery-white like an old man's. The strange thing was the rest of him didn't look so old. More like a young man — younger than Father had been. But the thing that was most wrong with him was his eyes, which were blue. Staring back at all the people gazing at him, they seemed confused and even frightened, like he was gawking at a demon. Oran found he could not look away from them.

"Well, now, what have we here?" Showing his teeth in a sneer both threatening and eager, big Baras rose from his chair, and his five men sitting near him stood up too. They scowled at the man.

The stranger just blinked and looked around like he hadn't heard a thing.

Baras's sneer became a hard scowl. "You an Ilarchae? Or one of them fucking Torrlonders?" His hand reached toward the sword he wore at his hip, and he stepped a couple paces towards the newcomer. The other five men followed him.

The strange man shut his eyes tight for a moment like he was hurting somewhere. Then he opened them again and looked at Baras. "I . . . I seem to be lost." He spoke in a funny, fancy way, like a nobleman. Oran had heard nobles talking in the inn a few times, even a real sorcerer once, but this man didn't look like any noble.

Baras pulled his blade, which whispered out of its scabbard. "Fucking right you are. You're a long way from home, Torrlonder. You may speak High Andumaic, but I know a fucking Torrlonder when I see one."

The stranger tilted his head like he was thinking hard about something but could not quite figure it out. "I came for food. I do not think I am . . . a Torrlonder."

Baras stepped closer to the stranger, and the other men moved closer behind him. They all had daggers out, and it looked like they were ready to use them. It made Oran want to run out of the room, but his legs would not move and his chest tightened, and he could not look away. Baras glared down at the stranger and sneered again. "Way I see it, you're a deserter from their army. A fucking coward deserter. Running away won't save you, Torrlonder. You went the wrong way. Your friends all scarpered back to Caergilion and Adanon, where they'll have their hands full. But *you* won't be joining them." He closed in on the stranger and raised his sword.

Oran winced, but the stranger did not flinch from the coming blow. He did not move. He did not even look scared anymore. His eyes were wide, and he was smiling as if he had just heard the best news of his life. "Caergilion?" He whispered the word like it was important.

Baras was still holding his sword up. He frowned as if he was trying to puzzle out something, and his lips started moving, but no sounds came out for a while. "Who . . . what are you?"

"*Caergilion*," said the strange man again. He ignored Baras. "Yes. That is where I'm going."

"Who are you?" Now Baras was the one who sounded afraid, which made Oran grin. His five men were motionless too. Eyes bulging wide, they were all starting to whimper. Everyone else in the inn gawked — some holding cups and spoons to their open mouths as if frozen in the act of drinking or eating — and did not move from their seats. Oran hardly dared to breathe.

The stranger looked at Baras, and his smile disappeared. "Thank you. In return for your help, I will give you something."

"Please," said Baras, whose voice had grown high and thin. "Please." He sounded like he was going to cry, and still his limbs did not move.

The stranger glanced at Oran, and the smile he gave was gentle. The boy decided he liked this odd man, so he smiled back. The man nodded.

That was when the feeling came to Oran. It was the happiest thing he had ever felt, and his body tingled all over. It was like he was floating or flying, or swimming in light, and his grin grew bigger and wider. The whole room grew bright and beautiful, and it felt like somewhere he had never been, like he was floating above the whole world, which was somehow part of him. A distant part of his mind reflected that he would never forget that feeling for the rest of his life, no matter how long or hard it was.

Baras's sword clanged on the floor. He seemed to be feeling something else. The big man was shaking all over his body and sobbing. His hands clutched his face, and he bent over before falling down and rolling up into a ball while he kept crying. He gasped and seemed like he was choking, but then a long and loud wail, the howl of some miserable lost animal, came from him, and everyone was gawping at him. His whole body kept trembling as he wailed again and again.

"I'm sorry!" was the first thing Baras screamed that Oran could understand. It was long and drawn out. Wheezing and breathing hard, the big man got onto his knees and looked up at the stranger, who peered down at him with no expression. "I'm so sorry." His cheeks glistened with tears, and snot ran from his nose to his lips. "I'm sorry." His head swiveled around in jerky movements as he looked around at everyone in the inn like he was terrified of them all. "I'm sorry. All of you. I'm sorry." His eyes fell on Oran for a moment, and then he glanced down at the floor. "I'm . . . so sorry." It was little more than a whimper. A thread of drool hung from his lip and vibrated as his body starting shaking again, and he sobbed and cried and clutched his hair.

The stranger looked down at Baras and smiled, but it was only a little smile and his eyes were sad. He turned around and walked toward the door.

"Wait." Baras held out one trembling hand toward the stranger, like he was begging for something.

The newcomer turned around again and looked at Baras.

"Please." The big man sniffed, and a sob shook his body. "I will buy you food. You are going to Caergilion? Please. Let me help you. Let me do something. Anything. Food. A horse. Silver. You'll need passage on a ship. Let me give you silver. All my wealth is yours. Only please let me help. I must . . . be clean. Let me be clean."

The stranger was silent for a moment before he nodded. "Food and a horse. Enough silver for passage on a ship. As for the rest, there is work for you here."

Baras sobbed and started crying again, only now he was smiling. "Yes. Yes. Oh, yes. It shall be. You will see. You all will see." Everyone was still staring at the big man, who was weeping and grinning like a madman.

"Who are you?" asked Vinaj, one of the five men behind Baras. He was crouching and gazing at the stranger with his hands shielding his face, as if the man were too bright to see.

Baras held out both hands palm upwards towards the stranger. He was beaming like he beheld the most beautiful vision in the world. "He must be the Prophet. The one they spoke of, who descended on the dragon and stopped the Torrlonders. The Prophet of Edan."

I
FISHING

A wave groaned and crashed on the rocks below Seren, misting her with cool drops that awakened goosebumps on her bare arms, before it foamed and eddied into the next grounding wave. Salty air laden with the scents of seaweed and fish entered her lungs until she released her breath with a smile. Another wave rumbled toward the rocks, and behind it the crest of another formed as the water tumbled over itself, and after it countless others would lumber landward before bashing into the rocks in a never-ending, rising and ebbing moan. At least something in this world was dependable. She gazed south at Crag Isle, a dark mass of rock jutting out of Culvor Sound some three furlongs away. "Ready, losers?"

On her right, Len grinned. "You might not win this time. Tob's been practicing. Haven't you?" He elbowed the other boy on his ribs and winked at him.

Tob rolled his eyes. "What's the point, anyway? We already know she'll win."

Seren put her hands on her hips. "You'll never get anywhere thinking that way."

Tob shrugged. "Don't want to get nowhere. I'll stay here and guard the fish while you two race."

Len scoffed. "Not so fast. I need you so I won't come in last."

"The fish will keep just fine. No one's coming here to bother them," said Seren. She nodded at her two friends. "Now, are you two ready?"

Tob let out a long sigh. "Fine." He took off his shirt, exposing his stocky chest. Len, all skin and bone, followed suit. Both boys bundled their shirts and tossed them next to the cordwain shoes, nets, and three baskets of fish they had stowed behind a large rock.

Seren smiled at them. "Losers carry the winner's basket and . . ."

Tob held up a palm. "No need to say the rules. We know."

"I have to keep you two honest."

Len's eyebrows shot up. "Keep *us* honest? You're the one who tricks us into carrying your basket every week."

"Not a trick. It's a fair contest."

"That you always win." Tob's shoulders slumped forward.

"Fine. Tell you what: This time I'll give you a head start. I'll wait and count to ten after you jump in."

"How do we know you'll count all the way to ten?" Len squinted at her and frowned.

"You can't count that high anyway, so you'll just have to trust me. Besides, if I don't jump in with you two clods, I'll have to wait for the next wave, won't I?"

"In that case," Len spat in his hand and held it out to Seren, "challenge accepted."

Tob shrugged. "Alright. I guess."

Seren grinned at the pair of them and grasped Len's hand before shaking it.

Len returned her smile. "I'll enjoy watching you carry my basket and gear for a change."

"Not a chance."

"Easy to talk. Prove it."

"I will." Keeping her voice casual, almost bored, she gestured with both hands towards the edge of the rocks, below which another wave hit and splashed. "After you."

Len and Tob took their positions over the pool where they always started their race and waited for the next wave to break. After it collided with the rocks and sprayed them, they took in a deep breath while the wave eddied, and then they dove. Two splashes, and they disappeared beneath the turbulent sea. When the surface calmed for a moment, their bodies appeared as shadows under the translucent water like two big fish darting out into the sound. They needed to swim down low enough lest the next wave pick them up and bash them into the rocks. The next wave rolled in over them, and they disappeared until their heads and backs surfaced right alongside each other. Their arms began whirling and their feet kicking in little splashes as they made a line for Crag Isle. Seren smiled at them, and then the wave hit.

She closed her eyes, sucked in air, and dove. The sea received her, cooling her flesh, surrounding her, and turning from roar into blurry pulse as her arms and legs cut through it. The rest of the world receded: the war and disease, the daily worries of the farm, and the constant threats from both occupiers and rebels. All of that belonged to the land, and for this brief moment, she was a creature of the water, with no thought but to move and flow.

She broke the surface and swam with smooth strokes in the direction whither she knew Crag Isle awaited her. The burn of her muscles and the rhythm of her breaths were her companions, and she welcomed them like old friends. In truth, she wished Crag Isle were further out from shore so this could go on much longer, even forever. Nothing could be less complicated than aiming herself toward some far point on the horizon, some distant promise, and heading for it for the rest of her life. A clean line. A clear goal. A purpose to it all . . .

She hardly noticed passing Tob and Len's thrashing forms. She wasn't racing them in truth, but something else. Something she could never outswim or outrun. It was almost a source of regret when she glanced up from her strokes and noticed Crag Isle looming before her. Her body made a slight correction in its course, heading for the dark patch of rock to the right of the island's center, just above where the water lapped the sheer, rocky side of a cliff.

Crag Isle was not truly an island. It was more like a chunk of tortured rock rising above the water's surface, a piece of the sea's floor heaved up to steal a taste of the air. A resting spot for birds, it had no harbor or place for landing a boat, only faces of weathered rock that disappeared in the sound. But Seren and her two friends knew a secret about Crag Isle.

She swam straight for the cliff's face. A few feet before colliding with it, she took in a deep breath and dove under the surface. The thrum of the water filled her ears, and she embraced the peace of the briny darkness. With her arms extended before her, she felt ahead. Where solid rock should have greeted her hands, there was only black emptiness. She kicked and wiggled forward, and her hands brushed against gritty rock at her sides. As the current tried to suck her out of the tunnel, she grasped slimy handholds on the rock and pulled her body forward.

Down here the water had its own heartbeat, and the tunnel she dragged herself through was an artery with a pulse that tugged at her. Inch by inch she made her way forward, feeling her way through the darkness. When the pressure on her lungs was building to the point of discomfort, a blurry source of light appeared above her. Straightening her body, she placed her feet on rock, squatted, and kicked up.

Cutting through the water with her arms, she breached the surface, gasped, and inhaled. Her ears popped and adjusted to the sounds of her own splashing and the water slapping on rock walls. Somewhere outside, a seagull cried, its voice thin and distant. The heart of Crag Isle was a cave, the secret place only she and Len and Tob knew about. A small hole in the roof far above her permitted a column of sunlight to illuminate the cave, glistening off the wet walls and piercing the greenish surface of the water bobbing around her. She swam a few feet to a shelf of rock, hauled her body up, and sat there dripping and smiling as she waited for Len and Tob.

TOB DRAGGED HIMSELF UP FROM THE WATER, GASPING AND dripping. Seren and Len each grasped a hand and heaved him up. He sat with slumped shoulders on the rock shelf and sighed. "Last again."

"Nice of you two to show up. I've nearly dried off waiting for you."

"You've done no such thing." Len looked at Seren with a frown, his eyes flitting down to her chest for the briefest moment before they widened as if he were startled. He looked away at the wall of the cave and swallowed. "Just got here, more likely."

She glanced down at her soaked shirt sticking to her body. She could well imagine her mother putting an end to her swimming contests with Len and Tob. That is, if she knew about them. Perhaps she would quit before Ma found out. *Things are changing, and it isn't fair to Len.* She heard her mother scolding her and hated how the imaginary voice was right. She pulled the cold garment away from her chest with a sigh. Less and less of her childhood remained.

"Any word from your brother?" asked Len.

He would never have asked the question back on the mainland, where such things were spoken of not even in a whisper, but in the barest nod or a lingering gaze. Here in the womb-like space of Crag Isle, with the outside world far away, they could put away all masks and speak as they wished.

"Not in a long while," said Seren.

A silence followed. The three of them listened to the soft lapping of the water as they sat on the shelf of rock inside the cave. Tob tossed a pebble, and it disappeared with a plop.

"I heard the rebels ambushed a Torrlonder patrol just outside Gadomiel." Len glanced at Seren.

She nodded and kept looking at the play of light on the water. "Yeah. Killed a score of them."

"Any losses?"

"Always are."

"Yeah."

Another silence.

"Reckon they can win?" Len looked at Seren and waited for her to answer.

Tob threw another pebble, which plopped and sank down into the darkness under the water.

Len still gazed at Seren, who listened to the cry of the seagulls and the moan of the waves outside, where a world of fear and loss beckoned. Somewhere out there in the midst of it was her big brother, a thought that violated even the security of the cave within Crag Isle.

She swallowed the lump in her throat and squeezed back tears, but the cave grew blurry all the same.

"Don't know." She did not say what she really thought.

Tob cleared his throat. "You two heard about the plague up by Belglam?"

Seren grinned and wiped her eyes with the back of her hand. Her friend was trying to change the subject, steer it away from something too raw. Leave it to Tob to switch from war to disease.

"Yeah," said Len. "My uncle was trading up near there. Came back with stories about fevered people bleeding out of open wounds. People lying outside to die, and no one to help them. Whole villages wiped out. Just what we needed on top of the Torrlonders. It's like Caergilion's cursed."

"Shit." Tob threw another pebble, and the water swallowed it.

Seren let out a long sigh. "That about sums it up. Not much right with the world just now. We'd best head back to it." She conjured up a smile. "You two will need some extra time to carry my gear and basket."

THE COASTAL PATH SEREN, LEN, AND TOB FOLLOWED RAN UP AND down rugged hills that presented bare, rocky faces to Culvor Sound and overlooked little stony bays. In some places, green clad hills marched straight into the water, over which seagulls and other birds wheeled as they made their plaintive cries. The wind whipped the three companions' clothes and hair, and the sun glistened off the ever restless water with its constant moan. For most of their walk they saw little other than distant white specks of grazing sheep, but after cresting one of the knolls, they glimpsed figures atop another rising. Even at that distance, the figures' grey kirtles were visible, and their helms and spears gleamed. The three friends stopped where they were.

"Torrlonders." Tob's mouth was hanging open.

"A score of them. A full patrol." Len looked behind them.

"Not a good idea to run." Seren's jaw tensed, and her hands balled up into fists. "They've seen us. We'd look suspicious, and they'd come after us."

"What do we do?" asked Len.

"Just keep walking. Act normal." She gave him a grim smile. "Or at least as normal as you can manage, Len."

"Very nice. We're about to die, and she makes a jest at my expense."

"Like I said: normal."

Seren gathered her basket of fish from Tob and her net from Len, and the two boys continued to carry their baskets and nets as they approached the Torrlonder patrol marching towards them. When they were within hailing distance, the three friends looked down at the ground in front of them and stopped speaking. Up ahead, the Torrlonders were laughing and jesting in the Northern Tongue. They too ceased speaking, and Seren could feel their eyes fixed on her and her two friends as they approached. She stepped off the path to make way for them, gaze fixed on the dirt. Len and Tob stood beside her in the same posture.

The Torrlonders' heavy boots ground little stones into the soil of the path, and their byrnies and gear clinked. Seren dared to hope the soldiers would march by and ignore them. When they were only a few feet away, close enough for her to smell the leather of their boots and the oil on their byrnies, one at their head called out, "Halt."

The clinking stopped, and the same deep voice said, "Koel, ask those boys if they've seen any rebels."

Seren knew Koel, the son of a local minor nobleman who had gone over to the Torrlonders, and she had no wish to speak with him. So she looked up and answered in the language of the occupiers, "My lord, we saw no one."

Len and Tob shifted their feet back a bit. They could not have known what Seren said since they spoke only Ondunic.

The leader of the Torrlonders, a big man with two red stripes on his shoulder above Torrlond's ensign, frowned at her as he rested his hand atop his sheathed sword's pommel. Beneath his red-crested helm, his eyes were blue, and his nose was crooked like he had broken it more than once. His blond beard was greying on the chin, making him look more grizzled and fierce. He was everything Seren feared most in the world, and he gazed straight down at her.

"You speak the Northern Tongue, boy?"

"Yes, my lord."

"Unusual in these parts. Where'd you learn?"

"Up in Gadomiel. My father used to take me to help trade wool and fish. Northern Tongue came in handy, what with all the foreigners. I got to know a few Torrlonder traders. They helped me learn. Of course, that stopped after . . ." She bit her tongue, but the thought was there, hanging in the air. *After you bastards came and ruined everything*, she finished in her head.

The big Torrlonder grunted and nodded like he knew what she was thinking. He glanced at Len and Tob, who appeared like two frightened rabbits ready to disappear down the first hole they could find. "What about these two?"

Seren looked back at her two friends and smiled. "They don't understand a word we say."

The soldier squinted at the two boys like he did not quite believe her, and then he turned back to Seren. "Alright, boy. You sure you seen no rebels around here? There's reports of them in the area."

"Yes, my lord. I'm sure. We fished all morning. No one came on the path. Until we saw you."

He grunted again, and he began to turn toward his men when another voice called out, "That one's no boy, my lord." It was Koel, who was smirking at Seren. "Are you a boy, you little half-breed?"

"What?" The big Torrlonder turned and frowned down at her.

She stared at Koel. He had always been a slimy, self-important arseling, and now she had a new reason to dislike him. "I never said I was."

"But you let me think you were a boy." The big man's eyebrows lowered over those blue eyes, which threatened violence.

"Let's teach her how to be more ladylike, lieutenant." This came from another of the Torrlonder soldiers. Like the rest of them, he was leering at her.

"It's dangerous to lie to us, girl." The big Torrlonder's fist tightened on the grip of his sword, and he stepped forward.

Seren shrank back a pace. Her heart began to thunder in her chest. "I . . . I didn't mean to. Seemed safer."

Another of the soldiers slid forward and licked his lips. "Reckon it's time for a lesson, lieutenant? She won't lie again after that."

The big man took his hand off his sword and raised his fist. "No."

The other soldiers froze and then scowled, but they said nothing.

For a moment, the big lieutenant's eyes widened as he stared at Seren. His jaw muscles bunched and worked like he was grinding his teeth. He did not take his blade-like gaze from her as he said, "I told you lot: none of that shit when you're under my command. We got rebels to find, and that means staying alert." His face softened into a half smile as he addressed her in a quiet voice. "Take better care, girl. There are bad people loose in these parts, and you never know who you'll run into."

He did not wait for an answer as he turned to his men. "Form up. Let's go."

As the soldiers marched by the three friends, several of them sneered at Seren with eyes that groped and threatened. One of them was the traitor Koel. The three of them did not move until the patrol was well past. Seren let out a long sigh.

"That was close." Len's voice and his hands were shaking. "What did he say to you?"

"I'll tell you on the way. Let's head home."

SEREN SAID GOODBYE TO LEN AND TOB WHEN SHE TURNED AWAY from the coastal path to head inland toward her family's farm. She walked alongside a stream running through their land before it emptied through a narrow gully into the sound. Tied to a shrub on the bank of the stream, one of her father's old cockleboats bobbed and waited. The old man had started using them less, complaining about his knees and hips. Seren suspected the real reason was he did not like to stray far from home anymore, as if, upon his return, it might be gone along with all he built over the years. Everything seemed less permanent these days.

Still, as long as they lived and breathed, the little valley waiting ahead of her was their home. She and Da and Ma and . . . Well, Allon was not there. Of all the things the Torrlonders had brought to Caergilion, her brother's absence was perhaps the worst.

She gazed ahead at the farmstead, where smoke rose from their home's stone chimney before the wind shredded it and tugged it away. The barn too was fashioned from stone, though it was a bit less snug than the farmhouse. Still, her father had built it solid. He always said anything worth making was worth making well.

But Seren's little smile disappeared as she approached her home. Several dozen figures were swarming all over the farmstead, most of them going into and out of the barn. They were carrying sacks of something. Even though her basket of fish was growing heavy, she picked up her pace.

As she approached, she recognized one of the men who were stealing the grain and produce from her family's barn and loading it onto horses. An old friend of Allon's, he had joined the rebels around the same time her brother had. "Iwan son of Iban, what in the name of the Mother's tits do you bastards think you're doing?"

Carrying a large sack on his back, Iwan had the decency to look ashamed as he gazed down at the ground. "Sorry, Seren. We're seizing these goods for Moradoc, son of Malruan, rightful ruler of Caergilion."

Seren's mouth hung open a moment before the words came pouring out. "Is that what they told you to say? You've never seen Prince Moradoc in your life, you oaf, so how can you seize anything for him?"

"*King* Moradoc. Mind your tongue, girl."

Seren looked towards the new voice, which belonged to a thin, tall man in leather armor whom she did not recognize. He had hard eyes that glared at her, and his hand rested on the hilt of his sword.

Seren clutched her basket tighter and glared right back at him. "King or prince: Makes little difference to me which title you use to steal our food."

Rage in his eyes, the stranger snarled and advanced on Seren with his hand raised.

Seren shrank back, but Iwan dropped his sack and stepped in between them with his palms raised. "This is Allon's little sister. Well, his half-sister, anyway."

The tall man's hand lowered, and he smirked at Seren. "That so? He'd better teach the little bitch some manners, then."

Iwan turned to Seren. "Don't make this any uglier than it needs to be. We've all got sacrifices to make until we drive the Torrlonders out. Your brother's inside. Best go see him before we head out."

Seren could not suppress her smile. "Allon's here? In the farmhouse?"

Iwan nodded, and she turned toward her home with the intention of running at a full sprint. But a pair of hands wrenched her to a halt by grasping her basket. The tall man looked down at her. "We'll be needing this too." Before she could object, he yanked it hard out of her hands, and she jerked forward, almost falling in her futile effort to hold on. He began walking away, and Seren nearly ran at his back with her fists ready. But her brother was inside, and the rebels would not linger for long. She debated a moment and then yelled, "At least give me my net back so you can steal from me again, you twelve-way bastard thief!"

The man turned around and gazed at her, and Seren was half sure he would draw his blade. Instead, he sneered at her, picked the net out of the basket, and threw it on the ground before turning away again. She scurried over to collect it and ran by Iwan, who was shaking his head and half smiling.

When she opened the farmhouse door, she squinted until her eyes adjusted to the dim light streaming in the two half-shuttered windows. Arms crossed, her father sat at the table glaring at another man sitting opposite him. From the angry brow lowered on her grey-haired father's face, she could tell it was not a conversation she should interrupt. Another clue was the two men who stood over her father with hard gazes and their blades out. Somehow it all made Da seem smaller and older.

The middle-aged man who faced him at the table wore chainmail and a steel breastplate as well as a sword at his side. A helm rested before him on the table, and he looked at Da with a dispassionate gaze, as if in judgement. Though she had never seen him, Seren was sure she knew who this man was: Imrys, commander of the local rebels. Said to have been a nobleman from somewhere closer to Iarfaen and a distant relative of the king, Imrys managed to preserve a certain elegance even with the rough life he must have been living. Behind the commander stood her brother Allon.

None of the men glanced at Seren, but her father must have observed her entrance as he said, "Go on, commander. Why don't you slay me in front of my daughter? You're as bad as the Torrlonders."

Allon grimaced at Da's words and looked down at the floor.

Commander Imrys's gaze did not falter or change. After a deep breath, he spoke in a calm voice. "Your son's service guarantees your safety this day. But do not test my patience. I have explained our need to you, and if it is in my power to restore what is yours after King Moradoc takes his rightful throne, I give you my word I will do so."

"And will your word feed my family this coming winter?" Da switched his gaze to Allon, but the latter kept his eyes lowered.

The commander frowned. "We're all making do as we can. I've ordered my men to leave you enough stores to survive."

"Survive? And how will we do that when the Torrlonders find out you took food and supplies from our farm? Makes no difference you stole it at sword point. The Torrlonders will call us sympathizers. Insurgents. You well know it. And then where will we be? How will we *survive* then?"

Allon shook his head. "Da, you must tell them we forced you. That you struggled, but we . . ."

"Don't call me that!" Da's hands clenched the armrests of his chair, and the rage in his eyes shoved Allon back a step. "I have *no* son. I have no son." The old man withered in his chair and covered his face with his hands.

A figure came in from the other room, where the family slept. Even dressed in a plain grey frock, Ma commanded the attention of every man there. Seren was used to men allowing their gazes to linger a little too long on her mother. Approaching middle age, she was still beautiful in a way Seren knew she would never be. She stepped close to Allon, whose wild eyes told of his grief, and put her hand on his shoulder. Somehow the gesture soothed everyone in the room.

"Allon. Be on your way, and do what you must. If you can, stay safe and return when you've finished." Somehow, even though he was not her true-born son, Ma had always found it easy to show affection to

Allon — and more of it than she ever did to Seren. Many times she had made peace between him and Da, as she was doing now in her quiet, insistent way.

Allon sighed and gave Seren's mother a gentle smile. Then he nodded and turned to go. On his way out, he looked down at Seren before embracing her. After he released her, he mussed her hair and left without a word. Seren knew it was too hard for him to speak, and she couldn't get a word past the lump in her throat either.

Commander Imrys rose from his chair. "We'll take our leave, then. May the Father and Mother protect you. Pray to them for the return of our rightful king."

The others followed him out, leaving Seren, Da, and Ma to the silence of their reduced circumstances.

THAT EVENING, THEY SAID LITTLE DURING THEIR MEAL. SEREN HAD to keep reminding herself not to talk about Allon the whole time. She wanted to know where he was, what he was doing, and how he was faring, but Da's scowl warned her it would not have done to mention her brother, and so her unspoken thoughts hung in the air. Afterwards, she helped her mother clean up. A wooden cup she knocked over while clearing the table clattered on the floor, making a louder noise than it ought to have.

Her mother frowned at her. "Heed what you're doing. It's not as if you're clumsy. The Mother knows where your mind is half the time — it's for sure not on what's right in front of you."

Seren bent over to pick up the cup. "I was thinking . . ."

"Clumsy I could put up with, but it's like you do it on purpose."

"I don't." She handed the cup to her mother and frowned back at her.

Her mother put one hand on her hip. "And don't make ugly faces at me, girl. Do you want to help around here or not?"

Before she knew what she would say, Seren's mouth opened to unleash a torrent of angry words, but her father's voice stopped her short.

"Not tonight." He held up one palm where he was still sitting at the table and gazed at Seren with his brow lowered, but then a gentle smile crossed his face. "Peace." Rising from his chair, he walked into the sleeping room and returned with his fiddle and bow. "We'll clean up later."

Seren waited while Da sat back down to pluck and tune the strings with quick twists of the pegs, and even Ma stopped what she was doing to sit down next to him at the table, watching him with a quiet grin. Seren liked it when her mother looked at Da that way, which was rare enough these days. Her breaths came a bit slower and deeper, and she rolled her shoulders as the tension eased out of her tired body.

Da slid the bow along the strings to test them. The true sound buzzed alive and pierced the air with its raw vibrations, and he teased out a few little trills to awaken his thick fingers. By the time he started playing the introduction to "The Lost Maid of Derwyn," Seren had her own smile ready for Da and Ma.

The fire cracked and spat in the corner, where most of its smoke rose up the chimney into the darkness outside. Seren's parents gazed at her while the sweet and sorrowful rhythms from Da's fiddle snaked around the room, enfolding them and closing them off from all the troubles of the world. He was a skilled player, and the lilting tune weaved around them until its notes seeped into them, carrying away their slightly swaying bodies. When the introduction neared the right moment, Seren took in a breath, held it until Da paused, and, when he plunged on again, let her clear voice soar. The strings yielded the melody to her soprano even as they entwined it with a melancholy harmony.

In an early month of spring
When the wakened birds all sing
And I wandered from the fields of my old farm,
I approached a forest glade
Where I spied a pretty maid,
And I never dreamt that she would do me harm.
In the middle of the green
Where she thought she was unseen
'Midst the dew and flowers she released her charm.
Her sweet body swayed and danced

And my hapless heart she lanced.
Little knowing, I embraced the coming harm.
Well, her hair was dark as night,
In her eyes dwelled elvish light,
And a bracelet bright bedecked one lovely arm.
There was little else she wore,
A light shift and nothing more,
For in dancing in the wood she saw no harm.

Da's fiddle and Seren's voice embraced the little family in their darkened farmhouse as she continued to sing the story of the lost maid, a mysterious woman with no family or history she would reveal. It was, of course, a tale of doomed love and tragic consequences, for the folk of Caergilion seemed to know no other kind of story. But there was great beauty in it, and Seren knew her performance brought out that sublime sorrow for her Da and Ma, keeping away — though only for a short spell — the real troubles of their lives. For that she was grateful, at least for this one evening.

2

BETRAYAL

Betrayed him. He betrayed *him. Now he sits there preening and gloating, thinking he's won. But I'll see justice done.* Edan's *justice.*

The High Priestess Colburga knelt before Aldmund's tomb in Torrhelm's Temple of the Way. Memories pricked at her. On so many auspicious occasions she had witnessed her mentor, the holiest man she had ever known, standing atop this very tomb, performing the rites and leading the faithful in their worship of Edan. There were times when it hit her anew, as if she had forgotten the terrible loss and needed reminding again and again, ripping open the wounds of the mind. Hers had been sleepless nights and slow, grey days since that fateful, evil day in Sildharan. All their glorious dreams of the Kingdom of the Eternal's fulfillment had turned to ashes.

Somehow she must keep faith. Picturing the man who had led her and taught her everything, she drew strength from his image, which no one could wipe from her mind. Though mention of his name was forbidden, the faithful would never forget.

Her lower lip trembled, but she could give no voice to her grief. Alone in the vast sanctuary, she glanced up at the shadows high above her in the temple's ribbed dome. In the middle of the dome, where a stone framework held the round window, sunlight pierced the temple's dimness in a long column that ended atop the black, circular tomb. From that brightness she took hope, and in it she felt the warming presence of her lord.

More times than she could count, Colburga had come before this tomb to pray to Edan. Her creaky knees were beginning to feel the strain of all those years of praying, and of course she was not a small woman. It was a different burden that weighed her down now, however. Though she assumed the posture of a supplicant, her mind was too restless and angry for prayer. It was past the point of prayer anyway. She knew what she must do to serve Edan and her true lord, the greatest supreme priest since Aldmund himself.

She would be the instrument of righteous vengeance. Vengeance for her martyred leader, the Supreme Priest Bledla.

She could do nothing to King Earconwald for the moment. Soon enough, justice would find the corrupt murderer who called himself king through the illusion of worldly power. First, she needed to eliminate Earconwald's greatest support. That arrogant, scheming, whoremongering betrayer who called himself supreme priest: He would pay for his treachery.

Footsteps echoed behind her. Her body stiffened, and she took a deep breath. The footsteps neared her, and another white-robed form knelt beside her.

Colburga glanced at the loathsome little man next to her with his pointed beard. He gazed at the tomb as if in reverent contemplation, but the only thing he revered was the gratification of his perverted desires. She told herself once again how necessity forced her into this alliance, at least for the present. *It is what my lord Bledla would have done were he in my place. He never flinched from the duty to use the tools at hand in the performance of Edan's will.*

She looked back at the tomb and spoke in a hushed voice. "Will he be alone this evening?"

The High Priest Morcar kept his gaze ahead. "There will be only two guards."

"You'll have to handle them if they move to interfere. I'll deal with Joruman."

At this he turned toward her and raised a questioning eyebrow. "Are you certain? It might become violent. I could . . ."

Her scowl silenced him. "No more pretending, Morcar. I lack the patience for it. I may be a woman, but we both know the gift is stronger in me than it is in Joruman. And far stronger than it is in you. If he's stupid enough to resist, I will overpower him. Just keep the guards out of it. I have no wish to spill *innocent* blood."

He nodded. "As you wish."

"And what of Widhelm, Nothgar, and Edulf?"

"Our fellow high priests are all away."

"*Don't* call them that. They are no more high priests than he is the supreme priest. They are all three his lickspittles and nothing more."

Morcar gave his mocking smile. "Whatever title you wish to grace them with, they are away at their posts now. Widhelm has departed for Etinstone, Nothgar occupies my old place in South Torrlond, and Edulf, our new High Priest of Justice, will be tucked away in the dungeons."

"You're sure?"

"I wouldn't risk it otherwise."

She gazed at the little man for a spell. "No, you wouldn't."

He blinked at her, and then he grinned again. "You think me a coward, perhaps something worse. I prefer to see myself as a survivor."

"You are a high priest consecrated to perform the will of Edan."

Morcar shook his head. "You know what I am. As you said: no more pretending. I'm in this because Joruman is a threat to us both — for different reasons, I grant you, but nevertheless he is our common foe. You are the best chance I have at surviving, and I have been useful to you. I will be useful to you, and I expect you to remember that."

She peered down at the pathetic worm. "I will forget nothing. You'll have what you asked for."

He looked down at the floor so that she saw only the top of his bald head. His shoulders drooped. "Good. I'm tired of it all. Tired of clawing for every little advantage in the game of power. Of fearing for my life. I want out. Just leave me in charge of the monastery here in Torrhelm, and I'll trouble no one." He looked up at her and gazed in her eyes. "Tonight, we'll get it over with."

She clenched her jaw. *I know why you wish to keep your charge of the monastery, you filthy little man.* But she needed him. She nodded and relaxed her white-knuckled fists. "Yes. We'll finish it. We will be the instruments of Edan's justice. Blessed be the Eternal."

"THE SUPREME PRIEST WILL SEE YOU NOW," SAID THE WHITE-KIRTLED guard. He and the other guard gave a slight bow and moved to let Colburga pass. Morcar shuffled in behind her. Once they were within the chamber high up in the royal castle Sigseld, Morcar shut the door in the faces of the guards, and then he nodded and smiled in encouragement at Colburga. She took a deep breath and released it slowly. They were alone in the room with its only occupant, the man who called himself supreme priest.

With the late evening coming on, a lamp on the table and a small army of candles — far more than Bledla ever would have used — illuminated the chamber. Reading one of the dusty old tomes from the shelves, Joruman sat at the table in the room's center. Though the traitor had filled other rooms with items of luxury and decadence, little had changed about this part of the supreme priest's quarters. Thick volumes still filled its shelves, and the Book of Aldmund occupied its prized place alongside the seeing crystal on the table. But in Bledla's absence the room felt empty, a mockery of what it had been and what it ought to be.

Joruman looked up from his reading and shut the book. "Ah, Colburga and Morcar. Welcome to you both. You wish to discuss the provisions for the monastery? Is anything unsatisfactory?" His lips oozed into one of his oily grins.

Everything is unsatisfactory, you traitor and heretic. How I detest your smirk. She moved forward, and Morcar stayed behind her to keep an eye on the door. She clasped her hands together to keep them from trembling. *I am Edan's servant. My lord Bledla, I will never forget.* "We have come here to . . ." The words sounded too weak as they strained out of her throat, which was tight with emotion.

Joruman's brow rose in curiosity. "Yes?"

She cleared her throat. "We have come here to *convict* you, Joruman."

The man's smile broadened as if she had told a great jest. "Convict me? Of what?"

Her breaths grew quick and labored, and sweat broke out on her cold flesh as her heartbeat stammered. She reminded herself that, even though she had always been a healer and violence did not come to her naturally, she was the most powerful person in the room. Most of all, justice and Edan were on her side. She stood taller and said in a clear, strong voice, "Heresy. Corruption. Treason."

The words hung in the air, and a long silence seized the room. To her satisfaction, Joruman's smile disappeared. Rising from his chair, he gazed at her. "Very serious charges. But your authority for making them is doubtful at best."

"We come by the authority of Edan."

"Really now? He didn't mention it to me."

"Do not mock. You *will* answer for your crimes and sins."

"Will I?" He looked behind her. "What about you, Morcar? You have accompanied the high priestess to lay these charges at my feet?"

"I'm afraid so." His voice was cringing, but at least he gave the right answer.

"I see. And where is your evidence?" The false supreme priest sneered, but his arrogance only hardened Colburga's resolve.

She took another step forward. Her body was no longer shaking as certitude won over fear. The first steps on the uphill path to righteousness were always the hardest, but Edan would lend strength to those who gave themselves over to Him. "You have convicted yourself."

"Indeed? How have I done that?"

"With these proclamations of yours."

"I've given several. Which do you mean?"

"All of them. Conferring divine status on that debauched king. Ordaining *him* the head of our faith. You have bargained away your soul for power, Joruman."

The infuriating man smirked at her again. "Well, so much for heresy. What of corruption?"

"You lie with women and discard them. You give away holy offices for favors and bribes. You barter with the Way, the one true faith, like a fevered gambler, as if it were your personal possession to fulfill your sick desires."

"I see. And what was the last? Treason, I think you said."

Colburga's teeth ground together as she strode toward Joruman. She unleashed her wrath, and Edan's righteousness surged in her. The pretender's eyes widened, and he backed up a pace, causing her snarl to morph into a fierce, triumphant smile. The longed for moment had finally come. Vengeance and justice at last. "You *betrayed* our true lord, the Supreme Priest Bledla. For this I execute you, Joruman. For this you *will* die."

Her power awakened. Joruman winced and cowered as he held his hands over his face and began rushing a counter spell. Too late. Colburga was stronger in the gift, and she was already singing the song of origin as blue currents of wizard's fire buzzed and sparked and writhed around her hands, illuminating the room with eerie light. Edan's strength coursed through her — she was the embodiment of His righteous wrath. "Alakathon indomiel ar galathon anrhuniae! Vortalion marduniel im . . ."

Streaks of white light exploded in her mind when something heavy thudded into the back of her head, crunching the bones in her neck. The wizard's fire winked out as the room teetered, and the floor smacked into her knees. She tasted the iron tang of blood, and a sharp pain seized her tongue, which she must have bitten. Trying to clutch onto her bearings, she willed her mind not to slip into unconsciousness. But she fell over onto her left side and rolled onto her back, where she stared up at two forms looming over her. "I trusted you," she whispered to the smaller one.

Morcar shrugged. "Your mistake." He was holding the Book of Aldmund with both hands. The blasphemous little worm must have clubbed her with it.

Joruman held out something to him. "Put this in her mouth. Quickly." Morcar threw the Book of Aldmund on the table.

She tried to resist, to roll away to give her time to summon her power again. If she could gather her thoughts and seize the gift . . . But her head hurt so much, and it slipped out of her grasp even as Joruman held her arms and Morcar sat hard on her stomach, making her grunt and knocking the wind out of her. The little vermin shoved a cold, metallic object into her mouth, in which pain blossomed when several teeth cracked, and she gagged as the foreign object tore down her throat. Jaw clenched, he leered down at her. "Hurry up. She's strong."

With her mouth blocked, her breaths came in quick gasps out of her nose, from which snot dribbled. She hated how desperate she sounded. She bit down on the funnel Morcar had jammed in her mouth, and agony jabbed through her broken teeth and gums. The taste of blood filled her mouth. Joruman's knees dug into her arms until she thought they might break. If the guards heard her . . . She tried to force a scream from her throat, but only a sickly gag gurgled and spluttered out.

Joruman's face appeared upside down, and he held a flask in one hand. He unstoppered it and tilted it over the funnel, and a clear liquid poured out. She struggled to wiggle free, but those knees just ground harder into her arms, and Morcar's hands gripped her aching head. Arching her spine and kicking her feet in the air, she could find no purchase and failed to dislodge the revolting man sitting on her. The liquid ran down the funnel into her throat, which she tightened as a last act of resistance. But Joruman pinched her nose hard, and some instinct betrayed her, making her swallow it even as she gagged and a few drops spattered out. Whatever the vile fluid was, it seeped into her body against her will, spreading into her organs and tissues until it wrapped around her mind with strange warmth.

Joruman peered at her with an assessing frown, and some of the pressure eased off her arms. "The effects are rapid," he said to Morcar.

The latter nodded and removed the funnel from Colburga's mouth, causing her to gag once again and wheeze for air, which rushed into her torn, bloody throat. She reached for the gift, but her head was growing fuzzy, and even the blind panic that had seized her seemed to slip away. The detachment she floated in was almost pleasant compared to the terror of a few moments ago. She wondered what disgusting things they wanted to do with her, but she could not find the rage she was supposed to feel.

Joruman and Morcar grew blurry as the room swam and dimmed, with only the candles providing little points of flickering light. Even though the pressure eased off her stomach, she could no longer command her body to move. She wanted to scream, to say anything, but only a low animal moan emerged from her throat, and drool crept down the side of her cheek.

"Took you long enough," said Joruman's voice, which seemed strangely remote. "You were supposed to knock her out before she sang the song of origin."

"I did it the first chance I got. You saw her looking at me, didn't you?"

"Did she look at you? Or were you simply weighing your options right up to the last moment?"

"No. No, it just wasn't easy. I'm not used to hurting people."

"Not grown women, anyway. Eh, Morcar?"

"I . . . I don't hurt them. Not like . . ."

"Never mind. I don't want to hear the sordid details of your hobbies."

"Anyway, she hadn't finished the spell. I did as you bade me." Morcar's words veered and wavered, echoing and growing fuzzier.

"Hmm. I suppose you did. And I had something waiting even if you hadn't, but it would have killed her. At any rate, you'll have your reward. Call in the guards and . . . them to bind and gag her. Emphasize . . . need her alive, but they must . . . she cannot speak or move."

"I thought you said the mixture . . . prevent her . . . and using the gift."

"And so it will. She'll . . . But one can never be too cautious. Can one?"

Morcar chuckled. "Of course."

Hoping she would never awaken, Colburga slipped into darkness and heard no more.

WATER PLOPPED FROM THE LOW CEILING INTO GREASY PUDDLES, which Joruman avoided as he walked with a torch in hand. Moisture also seeped down the rough rock walls of the tunnel. A white-kirtled guard led the way carrying his own torch, which cast wavering shadows as its flame sputtered.

Repressing a shiver, Joruman glanced at the guard. "Not our most elegant accommodations, are they?"

The guard's stare was blank for a moment, as if he were endeavoring to determine whether the supreme priest was jesting. "No, my lord." Without so much as blinking, he bowed his head and continued on his way.

Joruman rolled his eyes. The guard's piety and lack of imagination had likely been his primary qualifications for this cheerless post. *No room for irony or humor in the minds of the pious.*

Truth to say, the supreme priest did not mind the company, even as lackluster as it was. He had never much liked the timeless darkness of the dungeons, and he could foresee an age when they would no longer be necessary. Crude and primitive, they were the mark of everything wrong with the Way — an institution riddled with brutal and illogical superstitions that hindered progress and relied on corporal punishment, mutilation, and murder to enforce conformity. He would begin the process of transforming all that.

But first, he must use the tools he had inherited, such as his taciturn companion. He smiled at the man. "Tell me . . . What is your name?"

Likely unaccustomed to such interest from his superiors, the man hesitated. "Oswald, my lord." He bowed again.

"Oswald. Tell me, what is your greatest desire?"

The guard frowned as if afraid to give the wrong answer. "To live with the Eternal, my lord."

"Indeed. Thank you, Oswald." *Just another way of wanting to live forever. But wanting something is not how one gets it. We must move from fear and superstition to action.* He was too clever to force tremendous changes in institutions at once. That would instigate a backlash. Instead, he would subtly introduce ideas that would erode the basis of the superstitions, at least among the most intelligent. Perhaps the masses would always need something to cling to, making them irrelevant to the future, which belonged to those possessing a higher state of consciousness.

Either way, when the old faith shriveled, he would have a framework of new suppositions and theories in place. Instead of fearing death and cringing behind delusions in the guise of doctrines, he would lead the worthy into ways of fighting mortality, perhaps even defeating it. That boy, the latest Prophet of Edan, had been right about one thing back in Thulhan: The Way was in truth obsolete. If only there were a means to capture and harness the power within Dayraven. *Now that would be truly useful.*

But there were other endeavors closer to hand, and as he made his way along the dark and damp dungeon tunnel, Joruman gave a nervous, eager smile when he thought of the important task before him. All his other duties and worries receded: sending priests to Rimdale to help Duke Siric with his propaganda against Norfast, the running of the monastery, the maintenance of the faith throughout Torrlond, and appeasing that idiotic king, who had finally departed for the south to quell the rebellions there.

At last he was about to find out. He would test Ishdhara's theories and the spell she claimed would work. Of course, the ancient sorceress had never used the spell herself, but she expressed belief in its authenticity and efficacy. Joruman had the courage and the vision to find out. If it did work, he was on the verge of something tremendous in his quest, for which he would need great power.

"My lord, we've arrived." The guard lifted his torch to illuminate a door at the corridor's end in front of them. The tantalizing presence of the gift pulsed in great measure behind the door. "The High Priest Edulf and the High Priest Morcar await you with the prisoner."

For a moment, the supreme priest hesitated. He frowned as he thought of the terrible price Colburga would pay. In the ancient text, Ishdhara had written of the possibility of great pain and, if the victim survived, madness. He was not interested in hurting anyone. But Colburga had tried to kill him, and he needed a subject. The relentless woman had placed herself in his path, and this was better than simply ending her and wasting would she could still offer. *One life matters naught in the face of what I can accomplish.* He nodded with more confidence than he felt. "Very good, Oswald. Unlock the door and return to your post."

After the guard obeyed, Joruman opened the door and entered a small chamber lit by several torches in sconces. Next to a wooden table at the prison cell's center sat Morcar and Edulf. The latter was squinting and smiling through his grizzled beard at the white-robed woman lying on the table gagged and chained. Like his predecessor, the latest high priest in charge of the dungeons had a nasty cruel streak and enjoyed humiliating the helpless and those weaker than he was, so Joruman was not surprised at his expression. What was surprising was that Colburga was awake. But, to judge by the blank expression in her eyes, she had little idea what was happening. *Probably for the best.*

He settled his torch in an empty sconce near the doorway. "How long has she been awake?"

Edulf grinned, revealing gaps in his grey teeth. "Not long, my lord."

The gag over Colburga's mouth was tight, and her face appeared paler than normal. Was there distress behind her vacant stare? Raising one questioning eyebrow, Joruman looked over at Edulf and Morcar. "Did you follow my orders? No harm was to come to her."

Morcar leaned away from his fellow high priest as he rolled his eyes. "Don't look at me."

Edulf grinned at Morcar and shrugged. "Always hated the old bitch. Shame to waste an opportunity like this, but yeah, I followed your orders to the letter. Wouldn't have taken anything you wanted anyway." His grin widened.

Joruman suppressed a sneer of disgust. "No, I suppose you wouldn't have." He shook his head and considered berating the man for his sadism, but he held his tongue. *Am I any less cruel in what I'm about to take from her? Perhaps not, but it's for a higher purpose.* Anyway, he needed the man's support for now. An imperfect tool was still a tool. He brought his mind back to the task at hand and took a deep breath, focusing on the powerful presence of the gift in Colburga, which was inaccessible to her in her present state.

Edulf spat on the floor as he gazed at the former high priestess, whose head lolled to the side. "Will it kill her?" He and Morcar looked at the supreme priest, and something more than curiosity gleamed in their eyes.

You want to know exactly what I'm doing. Ambitious in your own vicious ways, aren't you? That's what makes you exploitable, I suppose. "It may. Even if it doesn't, she'll have no trace of the gift remaining. And her mind may not be the same. Since the effects are not entirely known, we must regard this as an experiment. It may be dangerous, in fact, to anyone in the room. Thus, for your safety, I require that you leave."

Morcar and Edulf looked at one another, and Edulf's quick grin betrayed their suspicions about Joruman's true reason for their absence. Joruman smiled back at the pair of them. *Of course I'm not sharing what I'm about to do with you two.*

"Yes, my lord," they said together as they bowed.

"The pair of you will remain down the hall in your private chamber, Edulf. I want you within calling distance should I need your assistance." *And I want you together as well since you trust each other even less than you trust me.*

"Yes, my lord."

"I'll notify you when I've finished. Shut the door behind you."

Once they departed and the door clicked shut, Joruman sat in one of the chairs next to Colburga. Her head was turned toward him, and he looked into her glazed eyes. They shifted toward him, and then they blinked.

His brow lowered, and he frowned as he leaned forward. "You can understand me, can't you?"

Her blue eyes blinked again.

"You shouldn't even be awake yet. You *are* a strong-willed one, aren't you?" He smiled at her. "Still, I imagine you're feeling quite groggy."

Her head jerked the slightest bit, and her eyes did not seem quite as blank as he at first thought.

"You're struggling to cut through the fog, aren't you? Let me guess: You want to access the gift? Somewhere in all that dimness, there's a voice screaming to get through. How you must hate me."

He leaned back in his chair and studied her for a while, steepling his fingers. "You might be surprised to learn I don't hate you. Indeed, I even respect your singleness of purpose and your power. Too bad you wasted it all on idiocy."

Her head jerked again.

"Touched a nerve, did I? Well, even then, we needn't have been enemies. Had you been content with your devotion to your faith, I would have left you in your place. But you decided to come after me, didn't you? In the name of the true faith, or some such nonsense. Or was it just vengeance you wanted?"

An unintelligible moan came from behind the gag, and a single tear tracked down the side of her cheek.

Joruman raised his eyebrows. "I see. You always had it hard for him, didn't you? Perhaps you're not as different from me as you suppose. The difference is I choose not to hide, not to lie about what's in front of me."

Her head began trembling.

"I'll grant that Bledla had great power. You as well. But even the greatest power is futile if you lack the vision and courage to embrace what is real. We've lied to ourselves for so long. People have. And people like you have tortured and murdered the few who have the sense to stop lying. To question. To seek the truth, not some consoling fantasy about a place where everything will be put right by a stern but benevolent father. The Kingdom of the Eternal. Look around you: No such thing exists. This is a world with one ruler: death. I've known this since I was a boy, since . . ."

He paused and fidgeted with the garnet ring on the pinky finger of his right hand. "At any rate, we fear it. Not being. Darkness. Nothingness. So we hide behind a make believe father who will comfort the ignorant children long after our fleshly parents have succumbed. The fear of death lies behind everything: faith, desire, greed, procreation, and every institution we've ever built in a futile effort to keep it away, distract ourselves, or at least hide from it. But it's everywhere. Death pervades life. The only rule is to kill before you're killed. We're no different from the other animals in this world." After a long sigh, he stroked his beard and leaned forward as he gazed into her eyes. "But I'm going to put a stop to that. The first step is to face it unflinching. The next, to understand it. At least, I shall begin the process and take it as far as I can."

Her head shook, and her stare grew more conscious, more intense.

"Oh, you don't believe me? Perhaps, then, it won't console you to know that I'll put your power to great use after all. The gift, Colburga. I'm going to use it to find out the truth. But I need enough of it, and you're going to help me."

A long moan, almost a growl, emerged from under the gag.

"It's nothing personal, I assure you. In fact, I apologize for your treatment." He gestured at the chains holding her. "None of this would have been necessary. The mixture you swallowed will keep you numb for some time yet and, I might add, will prevent you from accessing the gift. But I must satisfy people like Edulf and Morcar if I'm going to use them. These are the tools I have, willing and unwilling. It could have been so much more civilized. But, of course, you're the one who tried to kill *me*, aren't you?" He shook his head with regret that he did not entirely feign.

There was no question now: Hate burned in her eyes.

"I've no wish to hurt anyone. In fact, I aim for nothing less than the end of pain. For that, there must be some unfortunate sacrifices, and, at any rate, I cannot allow you to interfere any longer. Know this, Colburga: Your power will contribute to something far greater than your petty faith. We are progressing towards something, and there will come a day when all faiths will wither away, for there will be no more use for them. It may be that only a few who are worthy enough will see that day, and if necessary we will step on the rest of you to reach our goal. But we will become something far greater than your Edan. You may not understand it, but at least you will have the opportunity to contribute toward it." He swallowed in his throat, and then he released a sigh. "I'm sorry. Truly, I am. But if you understood, you would know why I cannot regret what I'm about to do to you."

Colburga snarled, and her eyes narrowed. The chains clinked as she made an effort to pull at them.

"Yes." He nodded. "You're right. It's time."

Joruman rose from his seat and held his hands over Colburga's body. Summoning his power, he left the world of forms and illusions for the realm of origins, where he savored the eternal and the true vision that accompanied it. Power rushed into him, and the clarity of mind he experienced gave him absolute confidence. Like a divine observer, he stood remote from all the emotions even as he perceived his eagerness and Colburga's violated fury. The perfect logic and the keen sight of the gift transcended all. He gazed down at the woman, took a deep breath, and began:

Druanil ecthonias an dharian gadalathon,
Abu mihil inghanias ni rakhyon abhularon.
Vardas diagol im parthas akwinway,
Shardas inkhathol an ghalas khalithway.

He repeated the spell numerous times, each time chanting it with greater intensity. All the while, he focused on the sense of the gift in Colburga, which was immense — slightly larger than it was in him. His awareness coalesced around it, and it grew apparent that the gift, though woven throughout Colburga's consciousness, was also something separate from her. His theories were correct. Since he dwelled in the realm of origins, this observation was not so much triumphant as serene, a source of assurance. He forged ahead, continuing to chant the song of origin.

His power, the energy that inhabited him, began to wrap around the sense of the gift in the woman chained beneath him. It was not her consciousness that he touched — not the identity that thought of itself as Colburga — but the power in her, which was a separate thing. Like the meeting and blending of light from two different sources, the gift in him met the gift in her.

In an intricate, slow dance, he used the song of origin to draw her power toward his until the two began to mingle. It lifted from her and spread out, circling and drifting toward him. Taking a deep breath, he raised his palms outward to receive it. Through the song of origin, he could perceive the minutest particles of his power linking with hers, setting off a tingling sensation that he knew to be tiny explosions caused by the fusion of the two energies. Before his eyes in the world of forms, the tiny explosions winked in and out of existence as blue sparks, glittering until they resembled a mist of shifting light.

As he chanted, the energies coalesced — or perhaps it would have been more true to say they recognized their sameness and leapt toward one another, for they were of one common source, what he thought of as Edan. Edan was not an entity but the underlying energy in all things. The gift was the closest thing to Edan's mind, the deliberate and purposeful expression of the underlying energy, which endlessly groped toward life and death, formation and dissolution, in infinite directions. The gift allowed the truest vision of the world and what lay beyond it, and it presented the ability to manipulate it. When he had enough of it, he would discover if the underlying energy offered a way beyond death and dissolution, a way out of the cycle.

More and more of the gift in her merged with the gift in him, and he perceived the swelling of his power as the bluish light grew more animated. Everything was happening as he had hoped. All his years of speculation and research had led to this moment. Even within the equanimity of the realm of origins, the awe and wonder of this discovery moved him to let out a deep, satisfied sigh followed by a slight smile.

But then something pulled at him, a tug of resistance, producing a twinge of pain that had no center but spread throughout his consciousness. He looked down. Colburga's eyes were narrowed in hate-filled concentration, and they focused on him. Her hands were balled into tight fists, and her entire body trembled with effort. Had the gag not covered her mouth, no doubt he would have seen the snarl twisting her lips. She was fighting. Somehow, she was overcoming the mixture clouding her mind to find and hold on to the sense of the gift within her. With the tenacity of a wild boar, she was pulling her energy back from him.

Joruman shook his head at her impossible stubbornness. He glanced at the door and suppressed the little stab of panic that invaded the realm of origins, and then he doubled his efforts. Colburga's eyes clenched closed, and she growled. Her growl grew in intensity and pitch until it became a muffled scream behind the gag. His chant grew louder and faster, and beads of sweat formed on his flesh as he concentrated on pulling the gift away from her grasp.

It became a struggle for supremacy, but it made no sense that the woman could even be awake now, much less resisting with such wild fury. Ongthew's mixture was supposed to last far longer than this. Over the years, he had tested it numerous times on several subjects — even on himself — and it had never failed. Fortunately, he reminded himself, since Colburga was gagged, she could not utter a spell. *One can never be too cautious, indeed.*

But she could, evidently, hold on to the gift with such fierceness that he nearly recoiled. This was not how the procedure was supposed to happen. He grimaced and chanted with more intensity, ignoring the sweat dripping from his brow. As more blue sparks filled the air, her energy wrenched back toward him, and Colburga's head twisted back as she screamed again. He would have her power no matter what. He must have it.

The woman's back arched up, and the chains that held the iron bands on her wrists and ankles snapped tight. Her body shook with her tremendous struggle, and blood trickled out of her nose, dribbling down her cheeks to patter on the table beneath her. Her muffled scream filled the cell. The energy they vied for began to glow brighter in the space between them. Waves of bluish light warped the air, and he squinted as it swelled, cleansing all shadows from the cell and bathing Colburga's form in brightness. Chanting with still greater intensity, the supreme priest grimaced and vowed to have her power. He tasted it. He needed it. He had to have it for what he would accomplish, and the ignorant bitch had no right to stop him.

A sudden explosion of white erupted, and Joruman staggered backwards until the wall slammed into his back, forcing out a grunt before he slumped to the floor. When he closed his eyes, swirls of red swam before him, and he shook his head in a futile effort to rid his mind of them. His trembling hands touched his face. When he opened his eyes, he could see his hands, though they were dim and seemed to belong to someone else. The red afterglow still danced before him. There was a vacuum in the cell, a gaping void where something was missing. Colburga's power: He could no longer sense it. It was gone. All that remained were the echoes of her agony, fury, and hatred of him branded in his mind forever. No longer detached, he shook his head in a futile effort to dismiss her emotions.

On the table lay her still form. Joruman groaned and winced as he raised himself and then walked over to the table. He steadied his rapid breaths. The woman's eyes were wide open, staring vacantly at the ceiling, and streams of blood had run from her nose to puddle under her head. Her wrists and ankles were raw where she had strained against the iron bands holding her.

"Shit." He buried his face in his hands and let out a long sigh. All that power was gone. A waste. There was even a pang of guilt for Colburga's life. *Would she have regretted slaying me? I think not.* Still, he could not shake the feeling that, with this death, he had entered into something deeper. *I must not look back. The goal is too important. Sacrifices must be made.*

He shook his head. Perhaps not a complete waste. There were lessons here, and he would learn from them. Most of all, his theories were correct. The gift was separate from its wielder, and it could be excised and gathered to increase his power and arm him for the challenges lying ahead. He simply needed to be smarter the next time he tried the spell.

The door clicked, and after it squeaked open, Morcar and Edulf appeared in the cell's doorway. Joruman stood straighter but kept staring at the dead woman beneath him.

"My lord?" said Morcar. "We felt a great pulse of power, and then nothing. After the long silence, we thought it best to check on you."

The supreme priest slowly turned his gaze on the pair, keeping his expression flat. "Your concern is touching." He smirked. "The results of the experiment were mixed, but promising enough to move forward. Colburga is dead. We need a new subject."

Morcar frowned. "My lord? A new subject?"

No looking back. "Yes. Someone with the gift, but not nearly as powerful as she was. We have no captive enemy sorcerers, and therefore it must be one of our own. Someone expendable, whom no one will miss. Also, someone unsuspecting. In short, a loner and an idiot."

Edulf revealed his decaying teeth in a broad grin. "I know just the man."

3

SEEKERS

"The tension is spreading. You can taste it. It will erupt in panic soon." Sequara wished otherwise, but she spoke from experience. From the saddle of her steed she stared ahead at the flat brown of the wheat fields extending ahead on either side of the road.

"Aye." Orvandil rode beside her, saying little but exuding a calm and strong presence, much the way Karad used to.

She thought of her old bodyguard and what fate must have greeted him back in Asdralad. His was far from the only ghost haunting the sorceress. Half her mind was on her island kingdom all the time, and the other half on Dayraven. There was little left of it to spare for Sildharan, but she felt a pang of sorrow for its people.

Sildharan was falling apart, lurching toward the turmoil that precedes destruction. The Ilarchae were gaining ground, grinding down the Sildharae forces, which retreated closer and closer to Thulhan. The barbarians of the Wildlands controlled the kingdom's entire north, and the few gory stories to trickle out of there were not assuring. Years of brutal slavery yielded bloody vengeance, and Sequara was not sure who, if anyone, deserved the most sympathy.

"I'm tired," she confessed while glancing at her companion. "Tired of war. Of death."

The Thjoth turned to her and, to judge by the almost pained look in his eyes, seemed on the verge of his own confession. Instead, he kept to a nod of agreement.

Sequara, however, was not finished. "I wish we could have left this place, like King Vols and King Fullan did." Having done their part to stop Torrlond, the Thjoths and Ellonders had left Sildharan, and Naitaran's arrogance had done little to entice his allies to stay. Too late had the fool realized his error in underestimating the Ilarchae and thus sealed his kingdom's doom.

"One last task here." Orvandil looked ahead with grim determination.

It was Sequara's turn to answer with silence. She dreaded what could happen if they did not find Dayraven. Mixed with that dread was her guilt. Why had she not foreseen his disappearance? What state was he in? She clung to his memories within her mind and refused to believe he might be gone forever.

Not wishing to allow her thoughts to wander in the silence, she took up the conversation again. "That task grows harder. The refugees will begin arriving here as early as the morrow."

"Might be sooner."

The battle-weary citizens of Thulhan were fleeing south and spreading around the countryside. Even in the villages Sequara and Orvandil had ridden by, the people had heard about what was happening close to their chief city. The hard, lingering stares they gave to strangers passing through spoke of their dread over the imminent future.

The frightened villagers were not inclined to be helpful, but Orvandil's presence had been persuasive in eliciting the few directions they needed. Sequara too could have convinced them to speak with a small show of sorcery, but she was glad to be spared the need. Power was a curse, and she hoped to see a day when she would never need to use hers to force anything from anyone. Unlikely, and in the near term, impossible. Duty loomed before her, and she could not deny its call with futile wishes. *Will I ever be a healer again?*

She released a long sigh. "Do you think this will be the one?"

Orvandil appeared to be grinding his teeth as he thought about his answer. "Hope so. We'll find out soon."

Rumors had spread about the Prophet of Edan visiting one of the nearby villages and producing some sort of miracle. The accounts varied and even contradicted each other in several respects. In one version, the Prophet emitted a bright light that burnt sinners to a crisp but left the blessed survivors cleansed and filled with grace. In another, he shattered the swords of his assailants without speaking a word, and they went down on their knees, begging to become his disciples before he ascended to the sky. Sequara did not trust many of the details, but the stories all pointed to the same thing: Dayraven.

No other could be the Prophet they spoke of, and the few sightings of him on the day he disappeared from Thulhan agreed that he had left the city from the south. After gathering as much information as she and Orvandil could, they concluded the most likely location of the village the Prophet had visited to be Vilwan. Something had happened there. It had to have been Dayraven, and, with all the power coursing through him, it was imperative that they find him. Not only was he at risk, but, if he lost his struggle with the being dwelling in him, anyone within miles was in great danger.

She still shuddered at the memory of the vast force that had erupted from him during the Battle of Thulhan. Her heart beat faster even thinking she might be nearing him. She swallowed and shook her head at the combination of guilt, dread, and hope roiling within her. If she had been free to choose him over Asdralad, perhaps he might have remained in control. *I'm so sorry, my love.* Even now she was torn in two, and grief waited whichever way she turned. Releasing a long sigh, she stared down at her leather saddle and the horse's muscled neck beneath her.

"Not far now," said Orvandil. The tall Thjoth was gazing ahead at the horizon, where a dark smudge waited for them alongside the road. The flat brown landscape to either side of it stretched out forever, fields of grain as far as the eye could see. The only break in the monotony was far off to the west, where the distant Osham Mountains hovered like a vast lavender-grey wall beneath white-splotched peaks.

"Must be Vilwan. We'll have word of him. Might even be there still." He urged his steed to a canter with his heels.

He did not sound convinced. Sequara did not trust her voice to remain steady, so she only nodded and commanded her horse to follow.

THE VILLAGE OF LITTLE HOMES CLUSTERING BY THE DUSTY ROAD WAS large enough to boast a decent-looking inn, whither Sequara and Orvandil rode since that was the most likely place for tidings. Like most structures in the rural parts of Sildharan, the inn was built of the local stone, which varied between light brown and reddish in hue. Its wide windows with open shutters invited in the breeze on the hot summer day. Above the wooden door hung a sign portraying either a robed woman or a feminine man with a crown. As a few nearby villagers gazed at them, Sequara and Orvandil alighted from their steeds and tied them to a post outside the doorway. The sorceress stepped forward first. Since the Thjoth could speak little Andumaic, she would do the talking. It was best for Orvandil to just look intimidating by standing behind her and frowning.

"It's the end of times, friends!"

Sequara removed her hand from the latch on the door and turned around. A man wearing a worn brown robe approached from the road. He was big, but not nearly as big as Orvandil. Thick stubble covered his jaw, and dust caked his bare feet. His eyes were wide but somehow vacant, and his lips were parted in a slight smile — the look of a fanatic or a lunatic.

"The final days draw near. But fear not. The Prophet has spoken, and all will be well."

Sequara stepped closer to the man. "Did the Prophet come here?"

The man folded his hands before him as if in prayer. "Yes. Yes, he came here. And he spoke to *me*, sinner that I was." He trembled all over his body. His eyes filled with moisture, and when he blinked them, a tear spilled down his cheek.

"What did he tell you?"

The strange man smiled and nodded. "First, he showed me. Oh, I have no words to tell you what he showed me. I saw . . . I saw . . ." He shook his head. "No, it's no use. I don't have the words. But then he gave me the message." The man stared and grinned at Sequara as if waiting for her to ask the right question.

"What is the message?"

"He said" — the man's voice dropped to a reverent whisper — "'There is work for you here.'" He continued to stare as his head bobbed in a rapid nod.

Sequara and Orvandil glanced at each other, and the Thjoth, who could not have followed the conversation, raised one of his eyebrows as if questioning the man's sanity.

"Don't you see?" pursued the man. He opened his arms in a wide gesture. "He spoke not only to me, but to everyone. 'There is work for *you* here.'"

Sequara narrowed her eyes at him. "That was his message?"

"Yes. And I have found mine. I gave it all away. Every last bit. And I've never been so free." He looked up to the sky and held his palms toward it. "So free."

"That's . . . a very fine thing. Did he say anything else?"

The man ignored her question. "You must find yours. Give no thought to anything else. It's so simple and true, the most pure message from the Prophet of Edan."

"Alright." Sequara nodded. "I'll look for it. But can you tell us anything else? What did the Prophet look like? Where did he go?"

"He was . . ." The strange man glanced at Orvandil, and he squinted and frowned when he looked back at the sorceress. "But why are you asking these things?"

"We wish to find him. To find our work."

He stood straight and shook his head slowly. "No. You're lying. I can tell. You have some other purpose." He looked at the Thjoth again. "Are you seeking to hurt him?"

"No. He is our friend."

"Then why did you ask me what he looks like?"

"We're trying to help him. But first we must find him."

"The Prophet needs no help."

Sequara stifled her frustration. "Then it is we who are in need of help. Will you tell us where he went?"

The man stared at her for a long moment before he grinned and shrugged. "The Prophet goes where he will. I know not where he is." He turned his back on them and walked back down the street, gesturing with his arms and screaming to no one and everyone, "The end is coming! Prepare yourselves!"

Sequara let out a long sigh.

"What did he say?" asked Orvandil in the Northern Tongue.

"Dayraven was here. But the fool won't tell me where he went."

"Might be someone else knows. Let's go inside."

They turned back to the door, which was open. A boy stood there gazing at them.

"Hello," said Sequara. She tried to smile at the boy, a thin little fellow with dark, knowing eyes. He put her in mind of her brother's children, the way they looked at her with a mixture of curiosity and fear. "Is this your inn?"

The boy stared a bit longer before answering. "It's Mother's. I help her."

Sequara nodded. "I'm sure you do. What's your name?"

"Oran."

"Oran." She smiled again and squatted down with her hands on her knees so that her eyes were level with his. "Can you help us? We're looking for . . ."

"Are you a sorceress?"

Sequara's smile faded, and she gave a slight nod. "I am. How did you know?"

"'Cause you talk fancy. I heard one sorcerer here before. Here in the inn. The Queen's Inn, it's called. You sound a lot like him."

"Well, Oran. Perhaps you can help us. We're looking . . ."

"For the Prophet. I heard you talking to Baras."

"Baras?"

"Fellow in the brown robe going on about the end and all. Hasn't been himself since the Prophet came. Which is a good thing. Are you really his friends?"

Sequara swallowed the lump in her throat. "Yes." The word came out with more vehemence than she had intended.

The boy stared at her, and then he smiled. "I believe you. Baras never trusted nobody. But he's much better than he used to be."

"You mean, before the Prophet came. What happened here? What did he do?"

Oran thought for a long moment and scratched his head. "Hard to say. But it felt real nice. Just being near him, it felt all clean and good. Especially when he looked at me. It was like floating somewhere bright . . . Sounds stupid, I know. I can't really tell you, but it changed everyone. Especially Baras. He used to . . . Well, he was going to kill the Prophet. Him and his men."

"How did the Prophet stop them?"

"Just stood there." The boy shook his head. "Maybe he showed us all . . . showed us what we look like."

Sequara nodded and smiled. "Yes, he can do that. Can you tell me what *he* looked like?"

"You mean on the outside?"

"Yes."

The boy shrugged. "He wasn't from here."

"Was he a young man? Light skin, like my friend here?"

"Yes. But he wasn't so big. And his hair was silvery white."

She thought for a moment. "Yes, it had begun to change. After . . ." She looked back at the boy. "Was he wearing a brown robe with a white tunic and black trousers?"

"Yes. That's how he was."

The sorceress took a deep breath and let it out slowly. "This next one is important, Oran. Do you know where he went?"

The boy smiled. "Caergilion."

Sequara was too stunned to close her mouth. The excitement of knowing where Dayraven was intending to go competed with dread at how far away it was. "Are you sure?"

"Yes."

"Did he say why?"

Oran shook his head. "No. That's just where he said he had to go. But he didn't remember it until old Baras said something — after he said the Torrlonders had all gone to Caergilion. He wasn't no Torrlonder, but that's when the Prophet remembered. Seemed important.

Baras gave him everything he needed. Before he gave away everything else, that is."

"What did Baras give him?"

"A horse, silver and all."

"So he rode away?"

"Yes."

"Which way did he go?"

"South. We all saw him go. Said he wanted to ride through Golgar and Sundara and find a ship on the coast for Caergilion. Didn't want to ride north. Said there was something sad up there."

Sequara let out a long sigh. "There is something sad up there, Oran. Tell your mother and the other villagers it likely won't be long before the Ilarchae defeat the Sildharae army. They'll come from the north. You must find somewhere to hide. You must bring enough food and water with you to survive. Prepare now, and leave as soon as you can. Will you tell her all that?"

The boy looked at her with his serious eyes before he nodded. "I'll tell her."

"Thank you, Oran. May the Mother and Father protect you." She stood up and turned to Orvandil. Switching to the Northern Tongue, she said, "We've got to tell the others we've found his trail. Let's go."

THULHAN WAS WRITHING AND BURSTING APART, THE LAST REMNANTS of order giving way to chaos. Great swaths of the once proud city were already charred ruins after the destruction the dragons had wrought. New fires burned and plumes of dark smoke billowed as looters, rioters, and fleeing citizens overwhelmed the few soldiers still posted in the city. Beneath the screams throbbed the ominous sound of the Ilarchae army — now less than a league away — chanting one of its death songs. Like the boom of thunder announcing the arrival of a terrible storm, it was scaring the piss out of the Sildharae, who were running south in a river of flesh.

Orvandil frowned at the swarming crowd before him, all vying to hasten through the south gate in a great exodus. After a hard ride all the way from Vilwan, he and Sequara had to find a path through the gate into Thulhan. Covered with dust and sweat, the last thing he wanted to do was to get mixed up in that churning sea of bodies. But, other than riding down the seething mob with swords flashing, the only way was to force themselves through while leading their horses.

"Let's hope Galdor and Abon have returned," shouted Sequara. It was hard to hear anything over the din of the panicked masses.

He nodded and gestured for her to follow him, and then, pulling his horse behind him, he plunged into the crowd. No doubt sensing the terror all around, the steed neighed and snorted but plodded with him. It was slow going, but he managed to push forward a few inches at a time as the sweaty bodies closed in. The Thjoth was not accustomed to people standing in his way, but the citizens were squeezed up against each other so tightly that many could not move. Anger and fear leapt from their desperate eyes, and many shoved and abused the hapless people stuck in front of them. It was damn near becoming a stampede.

A woman screamed a few feet from him, clutching toward something she could not reach through the press of bodies. Orvandil glanced at where she directed her anguished cries. A small form disappeared beneath uncaring legs and boots. He elbowed aside a man with his free arm, parted two frightened women, and then grabbed a man by his tunic, yanking him back as he was stepping on the child beneath him. With a grunt, Orvandil lifted his body above the press and, as the man's arms flailed, shoved him into a small gap between two other men, where he continued to squirm forward. Straddling the little body beneath him to protect it, the Thjoth bent and scooped up the girl lying stunned on the ground. He held her close to him, and her dark, teary eyes opened wide with fear.

Orvandil smiled to try to comfort the girl, but she only squealed and cried. *A good sign. Nothing broken.* The woman arrived with her arms held out, screaming something he could not understand.

Reckoning she was the mother, he held out the little girl to the woman. She grabbed the child and hugged her to her chest, caressing the girl's hair and squeezing her tight. The little girl buried her face in the woman's chest and bawled. With a tear trickling down her cheek, the woman looked up at him as she smiled and sobbed. "Dhunya. Dhunya," she said.

He knew enough Andumaic to understand that. *Thank you. Thank you.* He smiled back and nodded, and then he turned away, trying not to think about what fate awaited the girl and her mother. Even pushing through the crowd could not keep his mind from conjuring horrific images. Having seen plenty of war, he had enough memories of death and cruelty to draw from, some by his own hand.

Sooner than he expected, the mindless throng began to thin, and his progress quickened. At length, he punched through and yanked his horse out of the seething mass of bodies. After walking forward to where he could move freely, he looked back for Sequara. The sorceress was not far behind him, on the edge of the crowd. She fought her way out and turned around to tug free her steed. The horse emerged, and Sequara turned toward Orvandil, made eye contact, and nodded.

Through scenes of destruction in a city transformed for the worse, they made their way to the royal palace, where they could still hear the screams of the panicked mob by the south gate and, more distant, the death song of the Ilarchae off to the north. A harried and ragged army led by King Naitaran stood between Thulhan and the barbarians, keeping at bay the inevitable assault and fall of the crippled city.

Orvandil frowned. Part of him yearned to join in the battle, to taste the too familiar rush of combat. A perverse voice in his head even hoped the Sildharae army would crumble so the Ilarchae could come pouring into the city, row upon row of worthy foes to cross blades with. They would keep coming and coming until he died or killed them all.

Stupid. He shook his head. He had a more important task, and this was one fight he would have to ride away from. Dayraven needed him, and nothing was more important than that, unless it were the countless lives at risk if his young friend succumbed to the power within him. Sequara and Galdor had explained it all to him, Gnorn, and Abon, but he only needed the chilling memory of the Battle of Thulhan to convince him of the extreme danger lurking within Dayraven.

A perimeter of guards with worried faces still protected the remnants of King Naitaran's grand residence, in which many soldiers wounded in the Battle of Thulhan still lay. The Sildharae lieutenant in charge of the checkpoint near the main gate recognized them and waved them into Thulhan's last sanctuary. The shrill screams of the vicious, frightened, and crazed mobs still entered that space, and smoke drifted by and stung their eyes. But the air felt less thick as they neared the cobbled courtyard next to the stables. Once they had given their horses over to a guard to be stabled and fed, Sequara turned to Orvandil. "I sense Galdor. He's inside. I'll find him and Abon."

"I'll fetch Gnorn. We can meet here and set out after Dayraven."

The sorceress gazed at him for a moment with a thoughtful frown on her face. "Bring Gnorn here, then." She turned away, leaving Orvandil to wonder what she left unsaid. He set out for where he knew he would find the Dweorg.

THE SAME PANIC THAT GRIPPED THE STREETS STRAINED AT THE discipline of the soldiers and healers scurrying around the palace. Orvandil tried to stay out of their way as he strode down hallways toward a large inner courtyard. He entered a ruined cloister and skirted piles of rubble and debris. Blackened craters in the cobbled yard marked where sections of the palace tower had collided with the ground after the dragon fire engulfed it, sending it toppling down in blazing chunks that exploded on impact into a hail of deadly shards.

The metallic pinging of hammer on steel sounded from across the courtyard. Orvandil headed toward the noise, which ceased as he drew near. A lone figure occupied one of the outdoor forges. Seeming oblivious to the Thjoth's approach, he bent his stocky body over whatever it was he was laboring on with a pair of pliers. With his byrny draped over an anvil, Gnorn appeared to be repairing links in it. The scar across the Dweorg's nose and cheek stretched as he smiled down at his work with no trace of the usual sorrow in his eyes. Orvandil grinned. His friend looked happiest behind a forge.

"You've kept busy."

Gnorn looked up and his smile broadened, deepening the web of wrinkles around his eyes. "Indeed I have. What news?"

"We found Vilwan. Dayraven had stopped there, but he's on a horse now and headed south. Seems to be making for Caergilion."

The Dweorg tugged on his thick beard with his sooty hand and squinted. "Caergilion?"

"Aye. A boy there told us, and Sequara reckons he's right. I'll tell you about it later. Time to go."

Gnorn gazed skyward and scanned his surroundings with a frown, as if taking note of the distant sounds of war and chaos for the first time. "Hmm. I suppose it is." He turned his back to Orvandil and paced toward a shelf beneath an open shed. "But first, remove that piece of rubbish planted in your scabbard."

"The sword?"

"If that's what you'd like to call it."

The Sildharae blade made a metallic whisper when he unsheathed it. It was pretty but not as long or strong as he would have liked. Not entirely for show, but showy enough. Though it was the largest sword he could find, it rattled around in his scabbard. These easterners liked their steel supple and thin.

Gnorn picked up something with both hands from the shelf and turned around, holding out the object toward the Thjoth. "*This* is what *I* call a sword."

From the swirling patterns woven into the gleaming steel, Orvandil could see it was a Dweorg-wrought blade. Worth a large fortune, it was longer and broader than most swords. Along the fuller of the double-edged blade Gnorn had etched neat runes, one of which the Thjoth recognized as the Dweorg's personal stamp. Even the solid cross-guard, grip, and pommel were plain but of the highest craftsmanship.

His mouth hanging open, Orvandil gazed at the weapon. "Impressive. What do the runes say?"

Gnorn's face broke into a huge smile. "They read, 'I am Dragonbane's.'"

The Thjoth looked into his friend's eyes and then shook his head. "You *have* been busy. But I've no way to pay you."

The Dweorg scoffed. "The pleasure I had in making it is payment enough. You won't be breaking that one. Besides, I might have borrowed the steel from King Naitaran's smithies." Gnorn winked.

"Anyway, I needed something to do while I waited for you, and I doubt Naitaran will miss the steel. All that's lacking is a name."

Orvandil let out a sigh and shook his head again as he grinned. He dropped the Sildharae sword, which clanged on the cobbles. Stepping forward, he gripped the weapon Gnorn had forged by the hilt and took a long look at the wavy-patterned steel. Turning away from his friend, he swung the weapon, which whistled as it sliced the air. The weight and balance were perfect. Gazing at the bright steel again, he thought of the task before them: finding their friend, who was lost and needed them. Sequara had said he had given so much of himself that he no longer knew who he was. Dayraven was out there somewhere.

"Seeker."

Gnorn bowed his head and nodded. "Good name."

"FUCK. FUCKING BLOODY FUCK. HELL AND DAMNATION. WHAT ARE we doing here still? Shit shit shit."

The wizard Galdor laughed and turned back to Abon, who had been keeping up a steady stream of curses. "Oh, stop fussing. You know why we're here."

The shaper frowned. "That bloody boy's almost got me killed more than once now. What's worse, he almost busted my harp on one occasion." He adjusted the green bag slung over his shoulder. "Soaked it, he did."

"Really, now, Abon. If it weren't for that boy, we'd be dead. Or, even worse, forced converts to Bledla's Way living in his desolate Kingdom of the Eternal."

"We're all looking likely to be dead soon anyway."

The wizard sighed. *That may be truer than you know, my friend. We must find Dayraven. I should have taken more care of him. Too busy planning with King Fullan. Too wrapped up in grief for Arna. Ah, Edan, I'm too old for such self-indulging sorrow. I must find a way to forgive myself. I must find him.* Galdor gazed around at the soldiers, servants, and healers shouldering each other, lugging the wounded, and running in every direction in the crowded hallway. Most of them were shouting to be heard over the others.

King Naitaran's palace was about to succumb to anarchy, and it was the most orderly place in Thulhan. The screams and snarls of fleeing citizens and gangs of looters at large in the city penetrated within the palace walls. A feral madness had taken over. And beneath it all, dim but looming, was the war song of the united Ilarchae, promising death or worse to all within the city. Naitaran and his soldiers would not hold them back much longer. Worst of all, this was all a mere hiccup in comparison to the destruction Dayraven could unleash, but Galdor thought it best not to mention that.

Behind the wizard, the shaper kept mumbling and cursing. Galdor's brow furrowed as awareness of a powerful presence bloomed and tingled in his mind. Somewhere through the press up ahead, one strong in the gift approached.

He favored Abon with a grin. "Not to worry, my friend. I sense Sequara up ahead. Once we meet her and the others, we'll say a fond farewell to Thulhan. And, once we find Dayraven, to Sildharan as well, one imagines."

The shaper rolled his eyes. "One can always imagine."

"Ah, there she is." Galdor pointed ahead at the sorceress in her black tunic. Wiggling his fingers, he waved at her and gave her a toothy smile.

Sequara fought her way through the scurrying bodies around her and stopped before the wizard. "We found his trail."

"Excellent. Was it in the village we suspected? The one with the slippery name?" He frowned and tapped his forehead with his index finger as he tried to recall it.

"Vilwan. Yes."

"That's it. Well, that is good. As you can imagine, Abon and I found nothing since we were looking elsewhere. How far do you reckon he's got? And, more importantly, where has he got to?"

"He picked up a horse in Vilwan. He's heading for Caergilion."

"Caergilion?"

"He may have remembered something. His friend Imharr has a sister who may be living there, probably a slave, if she's still alive. He told me about her, before . . . He wanted to search for her in Caergilion. To honor a promise."

"If he's remembered that much, perhaps other memories will return as well."

"I don't know. I'm only guessing. I wish I could tell you more. At the very least, he seems to think there's something waiting for him there."

"It's a beginning, and we'll make the most of it."

"Yes." Sequara nodded and looked down.

"Well, we'd best hurry if we're to catch him. Abon was just pointing out that Thulhan has suddenly become less hospitable."

The shaper grunted behind him.

Sequara looked up at the wizard, and for a moment her eyes seemed lost as she struggled to speak. "I . . . I must tell you something."

Galdor stared at her, and then, as the realization hit him, his eyes widened for a brief moment before he smoothed over his countenance. He gave the sorceress a gentle smile and put his hand on her shoulder. "Of course. You must go home. I understand. They need you there. I'll tell the others."

She let out a long sigh, and unshed tears watered up her eyes. "Thank you." She wiped her eyes with the back of her hand and sniffed. She embraced Galdor and buried her face in his shoulder.

Closing his eyes, Galdor stroked her hair and waited. He rocked her gently.

"Find him," Sequara whispered. "Find him and heal him. I could not do this if you were not seeking him."

"I'll do everything in my power." He took a deep breath. "You have my word. How will you reach Asdralad?"

She sniffed again, and then she pulled away. Her face became hard like steel. "I'll ride north and slip into Ellond. I'll find a ship in Ellordor."

The wizard nodded. "No doubt King Fullan will aid you, perhaps furnish you with a ship. You may tell him his chief advisor advises him to do exactly that." He put his hand on his chest and grinned.

"Thank you. That will speed my journey."

His grin slipped away. "But there's a danger an Ilarchae scouting party might run across you before you make it to Ellond."

"More dangerous for them than for me."

He smiled. "True. But I hope you'll avoid them all the same."

She smiled back. "Don't worry. The Ilarchae haven't crossed Quinara Sound, and the Sildharae still hold the lands west of Thulhan. For now. My path should be clear enough. Orvandil will tell you everything we learned in Vilwan. He and Gnorn will meet you in the courtyard by the stables."

"Very good. I'll collect them, and we'll be on our way."

"Tell them. Tell them why. Tell *him* when you find him."

He nodded. "I shall."

She took another step back. "May the Mother and the Father watch over you."

"And you, my dear." He pressed his hand over his heart and gave her a slight bow.

She turned and walked away, leaving the wizard and the shaper standing in the teeming hallway.

Galdor watched her disappear into the crowd as Abon stepped up beside him. The wizard let out a deep sigh and let his smile sag. "They'd better watch over us. With all the power running loose in that boy, we'll need all the help we can get."

The shaper shook his head. "Shit."

4
FALLING

Keevan squinted off to the west, where the orb of an engorged and bloody sun sank behind the smoldering ruins of Thulhan. Swirls of dark dust and smoke drifted in the red and orange sky, stinging and watering his eyes even as their acrid scent seeped into his garb, hair, and skin. The death chant of the Ilarchae smothered the panicked screams of the unfortunate remaining citizens. He could not help wondering if the Mother and Father had abandoned the Sildharae forever. Their chief city, a desolation and an ash-strewn shadow of its former self, was all but lost.

He and the tattered remains of his company had the task of holding the far right flank of King Naitaran's battered army, which was making its last stand in a half circle around the north and east of Thulhan. To the right of the bowman, the line of his fellow ragged and tired soldiers extended only a score or so more men, whereas the line to his left curved into the distance beyond his vision and behind the city. A furlong or so behind him, the River Nurgleth murmured and carried on, indifferent to the groans of his wounded and dying comrades lying nearby — and just as indifferent to the scale of the violence about to unfold. In front of him, less than one eighth of a league away, the vast

Ilarchae horde stood ready for a final push before it swallowed Thulhan.

Gripping his bow tighter, Keevan checked the string for the hundredth time that evening. Still tight. *Twelve good arrows left in the quiver*, he reminded himself. Ilarchae arrows. He had wrenched them from the Sildharae dead — the corpses of his fellow soldiers — after their last encounter, just before they retreated again. The memory of twisting and ripping the glistening, reddened tips free from flesh made him gag again. He would need to use them well. *Should've listened to Mother.* Ahead of him, the Ilarchae host seethed and roared out their cursed song. "Wish they'd quit their damn singing."

"Why don't you go ask 'em." Standing next to the archer, Goshal spat a glob of phlegm that landed an inch from Keevan's boot.

The bowman clamped his mouth shut and held back the first words that came to mind.

Goshal grasped his big sword's grip in his big hand and stepped closer. The heavy infantryman was not going to go unanswered. "Ain't you the fuckin' hero of Sirukinn's Wall? The only survivor and all?"

Keevan rolled his eyes. *Here we go again.*

The bulky man was the best fighter in Keevan's company, but he was also the worst arsehole the bowman had ever met, even when they were not staring at death's grim face. He bent down and extended his muscled neck to shove his face next to Keevan's. "Just how did you survive?" The reek of decay accompanied his sour breath.

The archer's nose wrinkled in disgust, and he turned away. "Save it for the Ilarchae. They'll be along soon enough."

Goshal grabbed him by the collar and jerked him around, forcing the archer to look in his angry eyes. "Mother's tits, boy! I wanna know. We're all about to die here, and you can't share your secret? How'd you do it?"

Keevan blinked and frowned up at the big man. "Just dumb luck. That's all." He grimaced when his voice cracked, and the words were thick in his throat.

The infantryman scowled and shoved him away, causing him to stumble and drop his bow as the arrows clattered in the quiver. "More like you ran away, you little shit."

Keevan straightened out his leather jerkin and sniffed as he picked up his bow. He looked back toward the Ilarchae line.

"You gonna fuckin' run again today, boy?"

The archer faced away from Goshal and tried to control his breaths, which came quick and heavy.

The big man stomped closer again. "Huh? You gonna run, you fuckin' coward piece o' shit?"

Staring ahead, Keevan clenched his jaw and squeezed the grip of his bow.

"Father's wrinkled, hairy balls, boy! You gonna cry? Better start runnin' now. Them Ilarchae are comin' for you."

A series of images came to the bowman's mind: his hand reaching for the quiver, Goshal's startled eyes, and an arrow ripping out the man's throat in a spray of blood. His hand obeyed the impulse and jerked up.

The big infantryman grabbed his wrist before he reached the quiver and held it in an iron grip. "What're you gonna do, coward? Gonna stick me with one o' them Ilarchae arrows before you run?"

Keevan tried to tug his wrist free, but Goshal's grip tightened, and the squeezing began to hurt. The big man showed his rotten teeth in a wide smirk. "Can't run now, can you? Fucking coward. The Ilarchae are comin' for you, and you're stuck. Right here."

"I never ran, you big ugly bastard! It was the captain's last order! Don't know why I'm alive. I shouldn't be, damn you! Won't be for much longer, though, will I? But I'll kill you first, you stupid squinty-eyed moss-toothed dumbfuck!" He jerked around like a puppet while the bigger man held him by the wrist.

"Leave him be, Goshal. The Ilarchae are coming for all of us. And we'll meet them." The sorcerer Halnan approached, tall and intimidating even with his wounds and his frayed dark robe. His eyes had a way of seeing right through a person. He always looked calm, but Keevan had seen him unleash death in the heat of battle. Almakhti, the sorcerous lightning that only the most powerful sorcerers emitted, could strip the flesh from a body's bones and leave little other than a blackened, withered skeleton. Keevan had seen some sights during his brief time as a soldier, but almakhti was one thing he would never grow used to. Such sorcery frightened him. Halnan frightened him, truth be told. One of the most formidable Sildharae sorcerers remaining, the sorcerer had the task of commanding the right flank, and now he levelled his placid but unnerving gaze at his two quarreling soldiers.

Goshal's grip loosened. Keevan's hand dropped to his side, but he stared up at the infantryman and growled. He would not give Goshal the satisfaction of seeing him rub the spot where his wrist felt almost broken. The rest of the nearby men, who had all been watching with blank gazes, looked away and pretended nothing had happened. Perhaps they were too tired to care.

Goshal sneered at the archer and turned away. "Sure thing, m'lord. Just tryin' to get some tips from the hero of Sirukinn's Wall before we all die."

Halnan's bandaged head nodded. With purpled half-circles under his eyes, the sorcerer looked as exhausted as Keevan felt. No one had slept for more than brief interludes for days. "We're not dead yet, and while we breathe, we'll defend Thulhan. Hold your places in line, soldiers. The next man's life is in your hands."

Keevan dropped his gaze from the infantryman's broad back and then glanced at the front line of the Ilarchae again. He sniffed and wiped his eyes to clear them of the film of water that had formed. Twelve arrows left. As tempting as it was, he would not waste one on Goshal. The Ilarchae would soon take care of things for them all anyway.

MUNZIL WATCHED WHILE SURT GAVE THE CHIEFTAINS THEIR ORDERS, all eighty-five of them standing in a circle behind the front lines. The war-leader of the united Folk of the Tribes grinned like a hungry northern bear about to feast on a large fish. The rest gazed at him with rapt eyes. They were going to take Thulhan, a long awaited prize, and they knew it.

"Bolverk. Lead your Raven Eyes in the center of our attack. I give you the greatest number of bowmen, three thousand, since there you will find most of their remaining holy men. If you capture their king, cut out his tongue but leave him alive."

The tall, one-eyed chieftain nodded, giving one of his grim smiles beneath his grey beard. Munzil did not like or trust the war-leader of the Raven Eyes, but he approved of the choice nevertheless. Bolverk, the most cunning among the leaders who served Surt, had been adept at exploiting the bowmen in battle. He had also supported the idea of using arrows in warfare from the beginning, but only Surt could have forced all the others to accept it.

Disdaining the bow as a coward's weapon, the folk of the tribes had never used it for warfare — until Surt changed that. Ever willing to adapt to circumstances and learn from his foes, the great war-leader had grasped that arrows were the only way they would reach the Sildharae holy men and women, who slew many warriors with their magic lightning. Since they did use long bows with great range for hunting, there were plenty of good marksmen among the fighters. But few wished to endure the shame of putting away their swords and axes for any part of the battle, and many had grumbled about the tactic — until it started working and the holy men and women died in numbers.

Munzil, last of the Grey Wolves, smiled as the great man continued assigning the leaders their tasks. *He is transforming us. Forging us into one people. A great people. The Folk of the Tribes.* The vision the gods had bestowed upon him was coming to fruition, and they had found their vessel in Surt. Munzil understood this war against the Sildharae was about much more than conquest. It was the forging of a people. His people. He felt sure the gods had chosen the Folk of the Tribes for a great destiny. Gone were the days of their division, which had led to their enslavement and the disappearance of whole tribes, like the Grey Wolves. *Never again.* Munzil shook his head and returned his attention to Surt, who gave his commands to the war-leader of each tribe.

"Graen. You and your Cleft Skulls will come next."

"Aye, War-leader. We'll crush them!" The big chieftain pounded his chest, rattling the finger bones he had sewn to his armor.

"Ogar."

The noseless warrior nodded, his eyes expressionless above the cold sneer he always wore. "Aye, War-leader."

"Your Night Trolls will follow. I want you picking off any who flee."

"As you say, War-leader."

"Gunburcha."

The chieftain spat and licked her scarred chin. "Aye, War-leader."

"Position your Stone Fists next to Ogar's warriors."

"Done."

"Marg, you will lead the Broad Eagles and the other islanders in the attack from Quinara Sound. Preserve any of the foe's remaining ships."

"We'll take their ships, but none of them will leave alive."

"Good. That leaves only the Fire Dragons. Valdur."

The one-eyed chieftain of the Fire-Dragons' Bear Clan nodded. "Yes, my lord?"

"You will lead our Fire-Dragons to attack the far flank of the Sildharae. Their backs are to the river. Make it red with their blood."

"Aye, my lord."

"Any questions?"

Silence met Surt. The chieftains gazed at him, awaiting their dismissal. Eagerness for the coming battle lit their eyes. *They are all his*, thought Munzil. *Just as I am. We are one people at last. And we are strong.*

The great man unsheathed his huge sword, and a chorus of whispering steel followed as the others tugged their blades out. "Await the signal, then. The gods will witness this day. Death and glory, Folk of the Tribes!"

"Death and Glory!" they all screamed as they brandished their weapons.

TUCKED AWAY ATOP ONE OF THE FOOTHILLS OF THE OSHAM Mountains, Captain Uthron gazed east. Other than a lone rider fleeing from an Ilarchae scouting party towards the border with Ellond, they had spotted nothing unexpected that day. He and his six men had arrived in the late morning and settled on the hill, where they found a perfect view of the smoking ruins of Thulhan with the River Nurgleth bisecting them before its waters reached Quinara Sound. The two armies appeared like milling insects from this far away. They had skirmished, the one falling back until it halted to form a protective ring around the charred bones of the city. A last stand. The other was taking its time before it constricted. But now, beneath the westering sun, the larger army was stirring.

"Not long now," said Tiran beside him. "Sure wouldn't want to be down there. Come to think of it, I'm not too keen on being up here. Feels like our feet are a bit too close to the fire."

Uthron glanced over at him. "Once we see the outcome of the battle, we head back to Golgar and report."

"Thank the Mother and Father." Crouching just beyond Tiran and Sorn, Jwola took a swig from his flask and grimaced before he frowned down at it. "Tired of this horse piss. A proper drink's overdue."

At the end of the line, Deevak poked his head forward. "Any notion why the king's in such a hurry to hear about all this? You ask me, the best thing would be to stay well away and let the savages kill all the bastards."

The captain frowned. "No one asked you. You all know what I know, and it's not our place to question the king's motives."

The scout held up his palms. "Just asking, is all. Not questioning any royal motives. Wouldn't understand them anyway. I know my place."

"Good. All we need worry about is reporting what we see — and not being seen." He and his men had been more than cautious since King Veduir's orders emphasized the secrecy of their mission. Even with the sun behind them, he had commanded the lads to stay low and keep under cover. No one down there had spotted them. He was sure of that.

His men would do their job. He knew them well enough — better than he knew his blood family — to understand that. But Uthron also perceived the rest of the men shared Deevak's worry. Truth to tell, so did he. There had been plenty of rumors about the king's intentions, and his was not the first scouting party to spy on the conflict between the Sildharae and the Ilarchae. Some of the scouts had survived run-ins with the Sildharae too, fueling the rumors that Golgar would take advantage of its old foe's conflict with the barbarians. A fear was growling in his gut, one that had started as soon as he returned from escorting Dayraven to the Wyrmberg and King Veduir had given him his new orders.

Not for the first time, he wondered where the strange young man was now. If he was alive. Like everyone else, the Golgae captain had heard the story of the Prophet of Edan descending from above, riding on Gorsarhad, the eldest and greatest of dragons. According to the tales, he defeated the Supreme Priest Bledla on the field of battle, wrenching away the great wizard's power over the lingworms in a wondrous display of light that washed over the armies. *He did it*, thought Uthron with pride and a renewed sense of wonder about the young man he had guided and befriended. A gentle smile crept onto his face, but it did not last long. No one seemed to know where the Prophet of Edan had gone, and rumors had already sprung up that he had ascended back to the sky, or disappeared in a bright light.

Uthron's attention returned to the massive scene unfolding below. *Dayraven may have delivered the Sildharae from the Torrlonders, but nothing will stop the Ilarchae.* Wherever the lad was, he wished him well.

"What do you think, Spider?" Tiran was looking at Sorn, the silent little man who had earned his nickname by climbing where no one else could.

Sorn did not break his gaze from the two armies below. "Lot of dead people soon."

Even Tiran had nothing to say to that. The other men stirred and looked over at Captain Uthron. He nodded. "Aye." *And I pray to Oruma and Anghara we won't be joining them.*

Munzil hurried to keep up with the long strides of Gorm, chieftain of the Boar Clan of the Fire Dragons, and also Munzil's closest living friend. Gorm had as much as adopted him into the Fire Dragon Tribe, and it was a great honor to fight by the huge chieftain's side, but he knew his true place. He would always be the last of the Grey Wolves. He smiled and nodded to himself. They were on their way to where their warriors were arrayed in the formations Surt had devised, and the big man had a huge grin on his face. "Valdur has honored us. The Sildharae far flank belongs to the Boar Clan."

"We'll be the first to crush them." Skuld walked on the other side of Gorm. Not quite as big as her brother, she still towered over most men. Her smile was even hungrier than the chieftain's.

Munzil well knew how fierce that one was. In every battle she emerged covered in blood — none of it her own. *Glad I'm on her side, but best not step too close when the battle lust is on her.*

Gorm glanced over at his sister. "You will command the very edge of our attack. Push them into the river and destroy their flank."

Her teeth showed as her smile grew bigger and more feral, like a predator about to pounce. "They will die before they reach the river, Brother. Unless they run like cowards."

"Take twenty bowmen and your fifty warriors. Choose three to help you lead."

She nodded, and her jaw muscles bunched as she thought for a moment. "Vitar. He's young but quick, and he will learn from it. Hulga. Her experience will balance his lack, and she leads with a good head." She went silent as they strode forward.

Gorm looked at her and raised an eyebrow. "And the third?"

Skuld gazed past her brother at Munzil, who had always fought under Gorm's command. Her smile was more voracious than ever. "I'll take him."

Munzil's eyes widened, and Gorm released a long and loud laugh.

KEEVAN STARTED AND WINCED WHEN THE ILARCHAE WAR HORNS wailed above their death chant. Their front lines began to march forward, and their singing surged in volume. He wiped his sweaty palm on his tunic before he reached back for the arrows. Grabbing them in his fist, he planted them one by one before him in the dirt, counting out each one. With that ritual he claimed the ground beneath him. He would not move from that spot until the arrows were all spent, and then he would unsheathe the short sword he wore at his hip. When he grasped the twelfth arrow and held it in his trembling hand, he took a deep breath and glanced at his fellow soldiers. He would do as Halnan asked. He would defend his comrades until the end. Even that arsehole Goshal.

Standing next to him, the heavy infantryman caught his gaze. Their eyes locked, and there was an intensity there that Keevan had never seen before. *Ugly bastard. But you're* our *ugly bastard, damn you.* After a moment, Goshal nodded, and Keevan nodded back.

The archer looked out across the land. Those Ilarchae were a lot closer now. *Mother help me. I need to piss.* He swallowed and nocked his arrow.

IN LOCKSTEP WITH HIS FELLOW WARRIORS, MUNZIL MARCHED forward at a steady walk. They sang with joy in their hearts at their freedom and strength and dignity. Those who would have taken those things from them were about to learn the depth of their folly. The gods had put the Sildharae and the other Andumae in their path to awaken the tribes to their greater destiny. Munzil was certain of that, and so he did not hate the Sildharae.

Many of the foe had fought with honor, and those who were about to meet them were defending what was left of their city, their great piles of stone that entrapped them. He respected the common soldiers among the Sildharae, who were not so different from the Folk of the Tribes, he suspected. Only ignorance kept the Sildharae soldiers from recognizing this. They feared and hated the Folk of the Tribes because their masters told them to. They were victims of the vicious hierarchy the Sildharae nobles imposed, just as Munzil's kin had been when the slavers stripped them of their honor and humanity. Civilization was a hungry disease, chewing up and spitting out souls without a care and shackling bodies and minds to a paltry existence. Few reaped the rewards of all that suffering. Perhaps there would be some way to teach this to the survivors among the Sildharae, if there were any. In the meantime, the Sildharae soldiers waited in the path of the Folk of the Tribes with weapons ready. They had no hope of victory, but they waited nonetheless.

The regular formations the Folk of the Tribes marched in were another of Surt's innovations, or at least another example of his willingness to learn from the foe. Of old, the Folk of the Tribes would have lost many warriors by running forward pell-mell in a headlong race to display the greatest courage. *Experience alters the line between courage and foolishness*. Up ahead, the far flank of the Sildharae army crouched in readiness. Soon they would be within bow range. The key would be to find their sorcerers first. That would not prove so hard, though it could be costly.

Just as Munzil gazed forward in search of the telltale signs, blue sparks and currents danced and writhed around a dark-robed figure in a gap among the foe.

"Shields up!" yelled Skuld. "Bowmen ready!"

As one, Munzil and the other warriors in the front line raised their shields, huddled behind them, and spread their legs wide to brace themselves. Behind them, other warriors halted and prepared, and yew creaked as the bowmen nocked their arrows.

A blast of lightning flashed to Munzil's right, filling his vision with brightness littered with the dark forms of twirling bodies before a huge crack tore into his mind. His ears rang even as the pungent odor of burnt flesh nearly sickened him, and he flinched as he remembered to crouch lower just in time. He heard nothing over the high-pitched ringing in his ears, but he felt the arrows whoosh over him as a gust. A moment later, another gust passed overhead from behind him. It was a tactic Surt had devised. The foe would catch most of the first wave of missiles in their shields, but the second would find more targets since it was only natural for them to lower their defenses for a moment to assess the damage. And all the bowmen directed their arrows at one spot: whence the lightning had come.

He shook his head in a vain attempt to rid it of the ringing. The shout from Skuld was indistinct, like he had rags stuffed in his ears, but he knew what she was saying. Like the other warriors around him, Munzil stood up, held his shield before him, and marched at twice the previous speed toward the foe. It was vital to reach them swiftly so the spearmen could launch their larger missiles. Amidst the stench and smoke, he stepped over a charred body — whose it was he did not know. With any luck, the holy man was dead. Perhaps it would take another volley or two. Either way, there would be great slaughter.

. . .

The wet warmth of his piss spread down his thigh and trickled onto his calf. Gaping longer than he should have at Halnan, Keevan had a hard time putting words to his thoughts. *Mother's mercy. That's it then, isn't it?*

The sorcerer's eyes bulged in his head as his reddened, dripping hands clutched at the arrow shaft protruding from his ruined throat. The two soldiers assigned to protect the sorcerer with their shields were already down, each filled with arrows. Halnan stumbled and made a hacking noise, and a gout of blood splattered out of his nose and mouth to stain the lower half of his face. Another volley of arrows buzzed and whistled, and shafts sprouted from Halnan's chest and thigh. The sorcerer collapsed onto one knee. Keevan could have sworn those wide eyes were gazing straight at him before the man went down and twitched. The body went still.

A blur passed, and a man to Keevan's left wheezed and staggered backwards amidst flying drops of blood. When the archer looked behind, Udil lay on his back with a spear through him, his limbs flopping a few times like he was trying to get back up. Wrenching his gaze from his dying comrade, the archer screamed and nocked one of his three remaining arrows. There was time to send off two more before the barbarians slammed into them. The last one was for close range. He picked a target and loosed.

The woman next to Munzil grunted and slumped backward with an arrow buried in one eye. It must have just cleared the rim of Alga's shield — a brilliant or a lucky shot. Just after her slack, blood-spattered face thudded into the ground, another warrior rushed forward to take her place in the shieldwall. Their line was holding firm. But in moments they would crash into the Sildharae, and no amount of discipline could keep the melee from descending into a chaos of steel, sweat, blood, and mud. Just the sort of mess the Folk of Tribes knew best.

Munzil grinned behind his shield and marched forward.

. . .

Even in the safety of his perch overlooking the distant battle, goosebumps covered Captain Uthron's flesh as he looked on. His men kept silent as the flashes of blue almakhti decreased in frequency. Using archers embedded and protected within their ranks, the Ilarchae were picking off the remaining Sildharae sorcerers. The barbarians were not supposed to use bows in battle. They were not supposed to march in ordered ranks either, but someone forgot to tell them that, it seemed. There would be much to tell King Veduir of this battle, and Uthron ground his teeth as he thought of the implications.

There were still several jagged arcs of the sorcerous lightning emitting from the center of the Sildharae army into the opposing Ilarchae ranks, but on the flanks the sorcerers must have gone down — it had been some time since the last flashes lit up the battlefield there. In places the Sildharae line was buckling as the larger army rammed into it, and the battle began to boil with hand to hand combat. The outcome was inevitable. The Sildharae flanks would crumble first, and the Ilarchae would surround the remnants of King Naitaran's army and destroy them — unless the Sildharae fled over the river, the only escape left to them. *A retreat's their only hope. But they say Naitaran's an arrogant bastard.*

"Getting ugly down there, ain't it?" Tiran frowned down at the battle. He and the rest of the men did not blink or turn their gazes from the unfolding spectacle.

Uthron was glad someone had spoken to break the spell of silence and tear him from his thoughts. Of course it would have been Tiran.

"Never seen a pretty battle." Jwola shook his head as he stared at the distant carnage. "And this one's big."

"That's a fact," said Tiran. He scratched his ear and peered down at his fingernail to study what was on it. "Bigger and uglier than your mother's saggy tits."

The other men chuckled.

Jwola scowled at his fellow ranger. "What were *you* doing looking at my mother's tits, anyway?"

Tiran shrugged. "Well, they're nicer than your da's."

Jwola's scowl deepened, and then he broke out in a laugh. The other men joined in. Uthron allowed himself a momentary smile before he looked back down at the battle. By the Mother and Father, it was either laugh or cry. It did not even matter that the Sildharae were their ancient enemy. He supposed it might have been different had he been in the thick of it. From where he witnessed it, though, the display of destruction and death darkened the very landscape and almost stole his breath away.

NEXT TO KEEVAN, GOSHAL ROARED AND RAISED HIS SWORD JUST before he waded into the Ilarchae warriors crashing into their line. Steel clashed, and bodies jerked and swayed as blades sought flesh.

A huge man with his axe aloft hurtled toward the archer. Keevan flinched as he released his last arrow into the man's stomach, cutting off his attacker's scream and buckling him over. He released his own yell as he dropped his bow and fumbled for his short sword. The Ilarchae rose again and grimaced, his eyes wild with anger and pain. Before the huge man brought his axe back up, some mad will propelled Keevan's blade, carving into the man's neck and releasing a rope of blood in its wake. The body toppled back. The archer screamed and plunged forward.

STEEL WHISTLED ABOVE HIS HEAD AS MUNZIL DUCKED AND THRUST his sword up into his opponent's armpit, seeking the gap in the armor. After it bit into flesh, he jammed it in further until he carved through the heart, putting an abrupt end to the man's shrieking and thrashing. The body slid off his blade to join all the other dead and dying, wetting the muddy ground with their hot blood. He heaved his shield up to block another attack, and the shock of steel on wood jarred the bones in his arm. Throwing all his weight behind the shield, he lunged forward and heard a satisfying crunch. A body fell beneath him, and he plunged his blade downward into its chest, whereupon its limbs jerked up and then went still.

He snapped his head up to seek his next opponent. The biggest Sildharae he had ever seen finished off Ulrech by chopping off the warrior's arm and then beheading him in spray of blood. In the short moment when Munzil hesitated to challenge the man, another warrior arrived with blade aloft. The meeting of swords produced a massive clang. The newcomer was as huge as the Sildharae soldier, and when she growled in her fury, Munzil recognized her. He watched in case things went badly, but he knew better than to steal any of Skuld's glory by interfering without cause.

Skuld screamed when she attacked, and the two blades clashed thrice amidst the fighters' blurred movements. After the third ring of steel, Skuld tottered off balance. Her opponent closed in with a hard sweep of his blade. She lurched away from it, but as he advanced his free fist caught her jaw. She grunted, snarled, and charged. The blades crashed and locked, sliding and grating against each other as the two combatants leaned into them and grunted.

Skuld rammed her helm into the man's face, stunning him, and then she thrust her sword upward with so much force that it lifted the big Sildharae off the ground after it impaled him and exploded out his back with a squirt of blood. She roared when she slammed the man into the mud and twisted her blade. A crimson fountain trailed the weapon when she wrenched it free and thrust its tip down into her foe's face, which cratered inward as the man dropped his blade and twitched before going still. The Sildharae were all lying dead, writhing on the bloody ground, or jumping into the river in full retreat. Skuld screamed down at the corpse beneath her and whipped her gaze at Munzil.

The feral madness in her eyes shoved him back a step. *She needs someone else to kill.* When she advanced with her bloody teeth bared in a crazed smile, instinct brought his sword up before him.

RIGHT AFTER THE HUGE WOMAN SKEWERED GOSHAL, SOMETHING slammed into Keevan's side, knocking the breath out of him and sending him reeling until the ground punched his body. When he finished rolling, he inhaled with a wheeze that rattled his aching ribs. He staggered up in time to see the backs of his fleeing comrades leaping in the River Nurgleth, their golden tunics disappearing with splashes. He pivoted around. Strewn all over the battleground were bodies — some lifeless and some twisting around in their final, agonized breaths. Over them trampled and seethed the horde of Ilarchae with a mixture of fury and glee burning in their eyes. Mouth hanging open, he blinked as several yelled and sprinted at him in a furious race to part his head and limbs from his body with their massive blades.

The archer's mind cleared in a hurry. He yelped and scrambled for the river, tripping on a corpse and just keeping his footing, which likely saved him as a spear whistled over him. In a near headlong tumble, he flapped his arms as he plummeted from the top of the riverbank. The splash stung his face, and the cool water embraced him.

For a brief moment, when the clashing steel and groaning and screaming disappeared beneath the river's pulse, Keevan was grateful to it for washing all the blood and sweat and piss off him. He floated and let the current carry him downstream for a while before surfacing and gasping for air. The din of battle returned, and he realized the river was carrying him closer to Thulhan — closer to the hooting and bellowing horde of bloodthirsty, triumphant barbarians who would love to hack apart one more Sildharae soldier, whom they could pluck out of the river like a fish.

Some of the screams grew louder, and two dark objects buzzed by his head before splashing in the water. Arrows. Forcing his aching body into motion, Keevan dove deep and swam for the other side of the river, where many of his comrades were scrambling out onto the bank.

Her mouth still stretched in a mad rictus, Skuld stomped toward Munzil. He backed a couple more steps and held his sword before him. "Hold, woman! It's me! Munzil!"

She let loose a fierce laugh. "Put that blade down, fool. It's your other sword I want."

"What?"

She batted aside his steel, bent down to grasp him, and picked him up in an embrace so tight that he wheezed.

"What are you . . ." he managed to get out in strained voice.

Her lips locked onto his, and her warm tongue forced its way into his mouth, tasting of blood and iron. Shock gave way to pleasure and mild alarm when she bit his lip and growled. Still holding him so that his feet dangled in the air, she disengaged from the kiss to gaze at him. "Tonight, after the victory feast, we will share one tent."

His eyes still wide, he forced a weak smile and nodded.

She grinned. "Good." She dropped him, and he landed so hard that he nearly fell on his arse. "But first we finish this." She pointed toward the battle, which was receding toward the city, and snarled.

Munzil recovered his wits enough to say, "Aye," and he followed when she ran toward the fighting.

PANTING AND GRASPING AT THE WEEDS ON THE FAR SIDE OF THE bank, Keevan hunched on all fours in the mud and tried to pull his body out of the river, which tugged at him and threatened to topple him over. All around him, the pursuing Ilarchae screamed in bloody triumph, and his fellow Sildharae shrieked in terror as their foes slew them. Corpses choked and reddened the water. The barbarians were swarming everywhere, and they had begun climbing out onto the far bank to chase down his retreating comrades. Water splashed, and blades chopped into flesh. Pulling himself forward, he closed his eyes and tried to quiet his noisy breaths. He hoped the high grass would conceal him until his lungs recovered. The panicking part of his mind urged him to run, but he was too tired and sore and dizzy. He would wait until the right moment, maybe until it grew dark enough. The sun was nearly down, and under the cover of . . .

Something latched onto his ankle and with brute strength wrenched him out of the grass. Keevan screamed and clutched onto the gritty mud, which came loose in his hand. An animal yell filled his ears as another huge hand pulled him up by his tunic and flung him backwards. He landed on his back with a splash, and bubbling water filled his nose and mouth. Something heavy crushed his chest, holding him down in the clear shallows of the river, and though his limbs flailed and his back arched with all his remaining strength, he could not breach the surface of the water to suck in the sweet air and alleviate the burning ache in his lungs.

Above the surface of the river loomed the dark, blurry, and wavering form of the huge warrior who was squashing his chest and drowning him. But Keevan's attention lurched elsewhere for a moment. Something hard and heavy occupied his hand. A rock from the riverbank? He swung his rock-wielding fist at the , and it connected hard enough to jar the bones in his hand. Red drops pattered down into the water above his face and dissipated into a floating cloud. The warrior's body collapsed, and the water parted to envelop it as it floated like a silent ghost and sank down on top of Keevan, pinning him to the river's bottom. Hovering so close that Keevan could have kissed it, a bearded face with bulging eyes stared at the archer as bubbles streamed from its gaping mouth. Blood streamed out of a gash in its temple, adding to the surrounding red cloud.

Keevan scrambled and thrashed, and somehow he tipped the body off him enough to get his head above the river's surface. Sitting up, he spat out water and coughed and spluttered, and air finally entered his lungs with a painful rattle and gasp. He clenched his mouth closed and tried to breathe without noise. He was not far from the bank, and the water was not deep. Runny snot dribbled out of his stinging nose as he crawled from under the corpse, which bobbed face down in the water. Though he could not see them over the embankment, warriors all around him were still screaming somewhere nearby. The light was fast failing. He looked down at his hand when he realized he was still clutching the rock. A few strands of straw-colored hair stuck to the blood on it. Keevan shuddered and dropped it in the river.

Through mud that slurped and sucked at his hands and knees, he crawled back to the bank and lay down inside the tall grass, hoping no one would see him until the darkness made it possible to slip away. His breathing began to slow and lessen. He kept as still as he could, suppressing the urge to sneeze with as much ferocity as he had used to fight the Ilarchae. The enemy would not make survival easy. They would be hunting down stragglers like him. He would have to be silent. There would be screams in the night, sudden hands in the darkness. They had all heard about what the barbarians did to their captives. But how would he avoid them? He did not even know where to go, or how many of his comrades survived. Was the king alive? Was there still a

Sildharan for him to defend? Curling up as small as he could, he shut his eyes and waited for darkness. But when he shut his eyes, the ghostly face of that Ilarchae — floating in the water with the gash bleeding out the side of his head — still gazed at him.

CAPTAIN UTHRON RELEASED A LONG SIGH. THE BATTLE WAS ALL BUT over. The Sildharae center had crumbled, losing all semblance of a command structure as thousands of soldiers dove into the river, which ran red as the Ilarchae stabbed and shot and skewered their fleeing foes. With a triumphant roar, the barbarians pursued the hapless Sildharae into the river, and many straggled out onto the other side to continue the chase. Yet another surprise came as someone called the Ilarchae to order, and the warriors obeyed. Forming ranks on the other side of the river, the so-called barbarians began hunting down their foe in a more efficient and organized manner.

"That's downright civilized of them, ain't it?" observed Tiran.

Deevak grunted. "If that's the word you want to use. Anyway, the Sildharae are just about dusted."

"Not quite," said Uthron. "You saw the knot of soldiers around the Sildharae center, where the last flashes of almakhti came from?"

Jwola nodded. "You think their king made it out?"

"I do. On one of those barges that crossed the river. Many of their soldiers slipped through the ruins of the city. Looks like Naitaran had enough sense to plan for a retreat. There was a rearguard there, and a wall of soldiers formed up on the far bank to slow the Ilarchae pursuit."

"I saw it," said Arvan. "They're all dead now."

"Yes, but plenty of others made it," said Jwola. "They did their job."

Tiran spat. "That they did. And I suppose we'll be doing ours."

"Eager to leave?" The captain nodded. "Yes. We're heading back to Golgar, lads. King Veduir will want to hear what's happened here this day. The Sildharae lost badly, but they're not finished."

Tiran wiped at his nose. "They've one more battle in them, I reckon. What do you think, Spider?"

Sorn did not move his hard gaze from the scene below them. "One more."

"And I suppose the king will take an interest in how the Ilarchae fought," said Deevak. "Their unexpected tactics and all."

Ushal nodded. "You can bet your last pair of breeches on that."

Tiran scowled. "Who'd want his stinking breeches anyway?"

"No one," said Deevak with a smile. "As if yours smell any better, you arsehole. But the real question is, what's going to happen after we report to the king?"

Captain Uthron's jaw muscles bunched as he ground his teeth. "Only one way to find out. Let's move out of here." Even as he said it, the feeling that they would be returning to Sildharan, or what was left of it, crept into his gut.

5

LONGING FOR HOME

Her horse snorted, its neck muscles twitching as it struggled up the rocky slope. Squinting into the setting sun, Sequara glanced behind her once again. The six Ilarchae scouts were closing in. Hoping they would give up on their quarry once they crossed into Ellond, she had given them a good chase, but their mounts were fresher than hers. Ellond's territory began somewhere in these rugged foothills, and she reckoned she had already passed into King Fullan's kingdom. The Ilarchae did not know or did not care about such boundaries, and they would catch her soon.

The sorceress shook her head. "Mother's mercy." But mercy was a luxury she could ill afford.

No doubt they thought her a Sildharae escapee, perhaps someone important, else why bother chasing her? Showing patience and determination, they had tracked her for miles. *I'm from Asdralad, you fools. I'm not your foe.* They would have no way of knowing the difference, and they were not likely to stop and inquire.

She sighed and grimaced, and her stomach twisted at the thought of slaughtering her pursuers. One sweep of almakhti, and they would meet a fairly quick death. Her right hand let go of the rein, and she gazed at it. Across her once soft palm in a dark, diagonal line ran the rope burn scar. More times than she could remember, the blue currents of energy had buzzed to life and snaked around her hands before she hurled them into those threatening her. She turned her palm downward and moved her fingers, straightening them as she would when she released the energy. So many had screamed as they burned and died. A moment of terror. The stench of scorched flesh and hair. She clenched her eyes closed and then opened them.

"No."

She was so tired of killing, and these people were not her enemies, even if they did not know it. There was one other way to stop them, though it might be dangerous. It would certainly be unpleasant, but far better than slaying them outright. Her jaw muscles tightened as she gritted her teeth. Waiting ahead was the bare summit of the hill her horse was plodding up. Once she crested it, she would wait for them there.

For a moment, she thought of taking control of the scouts' horses and sending the beasts off. She shook her head. These Ilarchae were stubborn and would likely pursue her on foot, and truth to tell her horse did not have much left in it. Would she be able to outrun them? Even if the Ilarchae did not catch her, sending their horses away could endanger them out here in the wild. It might even be a slower way of killing them. No. She would end this now.

Her mare reached the top of the hill and snorted when she tugged on the reins. Sequara alighted from the saddle and patted the horse's lathered neck. She untied her water flask from a strap on the saddle and unstoppered it. When she drank, the water slid down her dry throat and eased away the grit from the day's dusty travel. Her voice would need to be clear. It had been a hard day of riding, and she twisted to stretch her sore legs and back. Just downslope, the Ilarchae were approaching, though they slowed once they saw her dismount.

Her pursuers also alighted from their steeds. She had heard the Ilarchae preferred to fight on foot. They left the animals behind and began to fan out as they stepped closer. Steel rasped to break the silence when they drew their blades. Their eyes locked onto her.

They crouched as they paced closer. The six Ilarchae appeared smaller than she imagined they would. Some of them were women.

One pointed and spoke, a woman's voice, seeming to give orders to the others with hard, quick words. Even if Sequara had been close enough to make them out, she would not have understood the Ilarchae tongue, but she needed no translation to understand the threat. *Time to begin.*

"Druanil ecthonias di andyon dimniathon. Abu mihil inghanias mi rakhyon inlorathon." At first the sorceress whispered the song of origin, but as the Ilarchae crept closer, she repeated it with more volume until at last she shouted the words. All the while, Sequara's energy dissipated into the realm of origins, and she focused her expanded awareness on her six pursuers. A small part of her detached mind retained an awareness of how dangerous this song of origin was. Few would dare the spell at all, and to use it on six at once was a feat only a small number of those with the gift could accomplish.

Dispassionate and serene, Sequara nodded as her energy seeped into the minds of her six attackers. Several of them jerked their heads around as if seeking the source of a ghostly voice. Their arms all lowered, and they went still, staring ahead with vacant eyes. The wind swept the silent hilltop. The sorceress took in a deep breath. The minds of the six Ilarchae were hers to command if she wished, but she would try to reason with them first.

In a confused babble, the thoughts and garbled memories of four women and two young men rushed into Sequara's mind. All but two of the women had been slaves of the Sildharae. This Sequara knew from the fragments of events, images, and emotions assaulting her. Whippings, rapes, and brandings with searing agony that burned away all thoughts other than a desire for an end. The torment of separation from loved ones. Daily abuse and lives reduced to brutal crudity. More than anything, an abiding hatred for their oppressors, of which they held her to be one, and their fear was a pain that throbbed and pushed outward on her skull. It was all so vivid and overwhelming that Sequara had trouble remembering not to hate herself. That was the terrible risk of entering a person's mind, let alone six at once. Their human kinship made it all the more likely for a sorceress to lose her sense of individuality. If she was not careful, she might never return, and they would all stand on that hilltop like statues until they collapsed in death.

Queen Faldira's training saved her once again. The pain of the Ilarchae lives was hers forever, and for this a sense of guilt and regret bled into her mind, but she gripped onto the serenity of the realm of origins.

I have no wish to harm you, she told them in their minds not with words so much as with images and emotions. *I am not your foe. My home is far away, the island kingdom of Asdralad. I seek to return to it. You must leave me unharmed and return to your people.*

She selected one of the women who had been a slave, the one who had shouted orders before, releasing a portion of the woman's mind just enough to allow her to reply to Sequara. The young woman's head trembled, but the rest of her body remained rigid. Beneath her helm, straw-colored hair tumbled down, and her blue eyes gazed at Sequara, reminding the sorceress a little of Dayraven. The Ilarchae woman could have thought her reply and Sequara would have understood, but she spoke aloud in a simple but fluent form of Andumaic.

"If you're no Sildharae, why come you from their lands?"

Sequara paused and debated a moment before electing to tell the truth. She replied aloud in Andumaic, "I fought against the Torrlonders in the Battle of Thulhan. They invaded my home, and I wanted to weaken them." She gritted her teeth before continuing. "I also sought vengeance. Now I will return to Asdralad to kill any Torrlonders that remain."

The Ilarchae woman gave a fraction of a nod, but her eyes remained angry and hard. "We understand vengeance."

"Then, if I release you, will you leave off this chase and return to your people?"

A long pause. "If we do not?"

"Then you force my hand, and I will slay you."

The Ilarchae woman's eyes moved side to side, examining her companions. She was weighing their odds, and they were not good. The woman's eyes widened when she realized Sequara could hear her thoughts.

The sorceress nodded and spoke in their minds. *You would all die where you stand.*

The Ilarchae woman's lip trembled. "Why have you not slain us?"

"I told you: I am not your foe, and I've no wish to kill you."

"You go to fight the Torrlonders?"

"Yes."

Another long pause, but Sequara heard what the woman would say before the words passed her lips, and she knew she meant them. "They are no friends to us. Go your way, and we go ours."

"Very well. When I release you, turn around and fetch your horses. Ride away without looking back."

Sequara snapped back into the realm of forms. The stiff bodies of her pursuers sagged and wobbled before they regained control of their flesh. Several of them shook their heads and blinked their eyes. The Ilarchae woman who had spoken barked an order before turning around and striding toward her horse. The others glanced at Sequara and then followed their leader. They rode down the hill, back the way they had come.

The sorceress stood gazing at them. When the hoof beats faded into the distance and the riders disappeared behind a hill, she released a long breath. She closed her eyes. The fragmented images of their tortured memories stabbed her mind, interwoven with her fears for Dayraven and the gnawing worry over what had befallen her island home in her absence.

Her hands began to tremble. More ghosts in her head. So many haunted her. Queen Faldira, Urd, and the many souls that perished while defending Kiriath from the Torrlonders, with Karad almost certainly among them. And what of the living, if there were any? What of her brother and his family? She knelt, and the trembling spread to her body. Covering her eyes with her scarred hands, she wept on the barren hill. She did not know if anyone remained on her island home, but she had to get back to Asdralad.

PERCHED BEHIND THE RIPPLED, CONVOLUTED TRUNK OF A LARGE mangrove, Imharr watched the two old women hasten as fast as their old bones would carry them through Asdralad's dark Forest of Yalawyn. In spite of their poor vision, they managed to totter along the raised packed-dirt path meandering between the trees, but he worried that at any moment they would topple into the salty marsh, above which the mangrove trees appeared to hover on their thousands of tangled, snaking roots. The elder of the two women leaned on the younger, who glanced behind them every now and then.

Even someone with good vision could not see far due to the density of the trees and the thick vines descending from their branches, but the sounds of pursuit were not far away. The snapping and breaking of branches punctuated the harsh shouts of the closing Torrlonder soldiers. Further off was the ever present moan of the Great Sea's waves. Imharr flexed his scarred hand, which had remained stiff but still strong — in fact, stronger, and resistant to fire — ever since the day he had plunged Wreaker into a dragon's fiery maw. He grasped the pommel of the sheathed sword — now fitted with its third leather grip — and lifted it just enough to feel its weight before dropping it again. It was a ritual he had acquired to reacquaint himself with his Dweorg-wrought blade before he had need of it, which happened more often than he liked these days.

As the two women pressed on, Imharr looked to his right to make sure his charge was still safe. Runan caught his glance and looked up at him. His dark eyes peered from the shadows beneath his hood, which hid nearly all the curls of the lad's black hair. Recalling a different boy he had taken care of in another life, Imharr thought of Dayraven again and hoped his friend — his little brother — was somewhere safe. The warrior smiled in part at the memory of Dayraven's face and in part to reassure the boy beside him, but the prince's serious gaze did not alter. *The lad's old beyond his years. And he's got his mother's knowing eyes.*

"They're coming." Prince Runan's voice was a mere whisper.

"Yes, Highness. That they are."

"Can I fight them this time?"

"You know the answer to that."

"But you've been training me with the sword. I'm ready."

"I've no doubt of your courage, Highness, but I'm no weaponsmaster. You'll need proper instruction once we've returned to Adanon."

"You're the finest swordsman among us. Everyone says it."

"Well, I can swing a sword. But there are correct forms they teach a noble young fellow like yourself."

"You're noble too, Duke Imharr. Besides, I'd rather learn how to stay alive. You'll teach me that."

Poor lad. Life's seen fit to teach him hard wisdom early. "I'll do the best I can. But it's your mother that has the last word just now, and she bade me keep you safe. Watch and learn, Highness. That's your duty, and mine is to keep you alive."

"Are you afraid?"

He scratched his beard with his silver-hued hand, and then he gave a half smile. "A bit. Only a fool or a liar would say otherwise. But if you're willing to learn, fear's a good teacher."

The prince nodded, but his eyes remained steady.

"We'd best keep quiet now, Highness."

The boy nodded again, and they both looked in the direction whence the Torrlonders were approaching.

Rona had ordered Imharr to bring the prince with him on these forays. More than once he had argued against it, pointing out the lad had barely seen eleven years. But the queen insisted Runan would have to learn to fight in order to reclaim his throne in Adanon one day. He needed to be hard, and if that meant seeing men die, then so be it. For the moment, it would have to be enough to survive here on the island of Asdralad, which the remaining Torrlonders were trying to scour of life.

Imharr reckoned the lad's trials over the past months would have hardened most folk, but it was his older brother's death that had snapped him. That and the desperate flight from the Marar Mountains. And the loss of his father, King Balch. Ever since then, the boyish playfulness Prince Runan had managed to preserve even in his family's exile all over the wildernesses of Adanon and Caergilion had died. Perhaps the queen was right after all.

The Torrlonders' shouts grew louder, as did the clinking of their mail and the clanging of their heavy swords, which produced a few dull thwops as the soldiers chopped through branches and vines in their path. Their din was needless and stupid, but he had learned that some soldiers destroyed out of habit. The Torrlonders seemed to hate everything about Asdralad, but they reserved their deepest anger for the forest. They had even tried burning Yalawyn to flush out the refugees and the canny Asdralae who were native to the forest, but thank the Mother and Father its marshes had thwarted the flames. Its trees sheltered the core of the resistance against the invaders. Queen Rona had organized the resistance and given it a heart, but it all would have been impossible without the forest dwellers' aid.

The crashing and cursing of the soldiers drew nearer. Soon they would enter his line of sight. Imharr gritted his teeth. By the noise they were making, he guessed it was a full patrol of twenty. *Good. There'll be a score fewer of the bastards.* His fingers grasped the pommel of his sword and lifted it a few inches before dropping it again. Next to him, Runan shifted his stance. Imharr looked down at the boy and nodded.

Down the path, the two old women had disappeared. They had accomplished their task of drawing in the soldiers. Having reached their hiding place, they should be safe. Of course, that depended on Imharr doing his job.

The first of the growling Torrlonders burst through the trees, waving their blades and bellowing at their fellow soldiers behind them. The salt marshes had soaked their grey tunics and dark trousers. Many had likely fallen in when the weight of their chainmail and stomping boots collapsed the raised dirt pathways, which left room for two at most to walk abreast. These soldiers hated Yalawyn, which made Imharr smile. Their irritability and their arrogance made them careless.

He glanced one last time at Runan, motioning his palm downward to signify the prince should stay put behind the tree. The boy stared back with his serious eyes and nodded. With that confirmation, the warrior took a breath and his unsheathed his sword, baring Wreaker's blade all the way this time.

Imharr leapt from the mangrove roots to land on the pathway some thirty strides in front of the Torrlonders. His leather armor was much lighter than the clumsy mail the Torrlonders wore, but he was still relieved to land on both feet. It would have been a fine start to this business to fall on his arse or slip into the marsh.

The two leading Torrlonders froze and went silent, gawking at the warrior until the men behind them bumped into them, which unleashed a stream of curses in the Northern Tongue. Once the furor died down, the lead soldiers peered again at Imharr with suspicion narrowing their eyes. Raising his blade before him with both hands, the warrior assumed a wide defensive stance, making clear his intention to let none of the Torrlonders pass but inviting them to try. "Come along, my uglies. Don't be shy."

Perhaps surprised to hear the Northern Tongue spoken fluently by a southerner, the Torrlonder in the lead stared with his mouth open at Imharr. For a short moment the soldiers hesitated, seeming to wait for something more. When nothing happened, the lead soldier spat before he grinned. "Kill him."

The Torrlonders charged.

The pathway afforded only enough room for them to run at Imharr in single file, which was what the warrior was counting on. Not to mention the arrows that began whistling and buzzing from the mangrove trees toward the advancing soldiers.

The arrows hit with metallic pings and wooden thuds when they bounced off mail or dug into shields, but some shafts sprouted from legs and arms, drawing out grunts and curses. Two Torrlonders fell off the pathway and splashed into the marsh. Arrows kept flying from all directions, trapping the soldiers in a deadly hail of flitting missiles as several dozen camouflaged Asdralae woodsmen peeled off the mangrove trunks and emerged from their branches and roots. The Torrlonders hunkered down beneath their shields, but their only hope was to charge through and flee along the pathway. Imharr would make sure they did no such thing.

The lead soldier bellowed and careened toward the warrior, who did not alter his stance until the Torrlonder neared striking distance with his sword aloft. Surging forward with fluid grace, Imharr closed the gap before the man could bring his weapon down. The warrior grasped the wrist of his foe's sword arm and thrust Wreaker with precision over the rim of the man's shield. Bright steel parted the soft flesh of the man's throat, and blood gushed from his open mouth. His eyes bulged with shock as Imharr pulled him aside, and before his corpse splashed into the briny water, the warrior's blade rang as he parried the next Torrlonder's steel.

This soldier was a big man, and his blow jolted the bones of Imharr's arm. The Torrlonder raised his shield and rushed Imharr, attempting to bull him over, but he grunted when an arrow tore through his calf. The man sank down on a knee, and Imharr silenced his agonized scream by shoving Wreaker into his open mouth. Teeth shattered, and bloody gashes split the man's cheeks while the sword's point exited the back of his neck. A fountain of gore trailed Imharr's blade when he slid it out, and the wide-eyed soldier slumped down. Kicking the corpse aside, the warrior prepared for the next soldier, who was the last Torrlonder standing.

Arrows buzzed from several directions, and before the soldier reached Imharr, his body jerked several times as a dozen missiles found their mark in his legs and arms. One pinged when it pierced his helm to burrow in his skull. The man's sword fell from his grasp to splash in the water, and his body teetered as his gaze went blank. Imharr held his fighting posture while the Torrlonder collapsed forward and planted his face on the pathway at his feet.

All was silent for a long moment. Imharr looked back at the tree where he had left the prince. Runan stepped out onto the mangrove's roots and leapt onto the path. The boy surveyed the carnage without blinking, taking in everything just as his mother bade him.

Imharr leaned down and wiped his blade clean on the grey tunic of the Torrlonder at his feet. After he sheathed it, he looked for his Adanese companions to see if any had been wounded or killed.

On the other side of the row of bloody Torrlonder corpses littering the pathway, his four surviving fellow soldiers from Adanon approached. It had been their task to prevent the Torrlonders from retreating, and judging by the number of bodies near them, it had not been easy. Nayan, Gilad, and Val were unhurt, but Dun walked with a slight limp. Imharr released a sigh. He could not afford to lose any of them. Travarr and Lon were gone, both killed a fortnight earlier in a Torrlonder ambush. The losses had been heavy, and not only because they had been like brothers to him, with bonds only surviving combat together could form. They needed every warrior they had to fight the contingent of Torrlonders posted on the island for the purpose of wiping out its remaining inhabitants.

Stepping over the bodies, the four Adanese approached Imharr while the Asdralae woodsmen began salvaging as many arrows as they could. The wound on Dun's thigh appeared superficial, but blood had already soaked his trouser leg.

Imharr nodded toward his friend's wound. "You'll need to clean that first thing when we reach camp."

Dun grinned. "Just a scratch, Duke Silverhand."

"Clean it all the same. Use boiled water and that salve the Asdralae healers make."

Standing a little straighter, Dun cleared his throat. "Yes, m'lord."

Imharr just managed to hold back an ironic smile. He still was not used to being the one in charge, or being thought of as a duke. Someone had to command, and perhaps his long proximity to the queen made him the logical choice. That and the fact that he turned out to be better at killing than most other people. But not so long ago he had been a thrall in the faraway kingdom of the Mark, and he was not much older than his four fellow Adanese. The last months had been a breathless blur of escaping one danger after another, and he still had trouble recalling how he had ended up here, except that it all started on that terrible day back in Adanon when his uncle had commanded him to accompany a wounded King Balch. The memory of parting with his Uncle Anarad was still a heavy burden, one that he never put down. Perhaps that's what grief was: getting used to carrying the weight of another loss.

He glanced back at the prince, who was studying the Asdralae as they wrenched bloody arrows out of Torrlonder flesh and collected Torrlonder steel. *We've all had to grow up fast.* He put a hand on Dun's shoulder and nodded. *I reckon I'm supposed to say something.* "Well done, lads." *Never was much of a speechmaker.*

"Thank you, m'lord," said Dun. The others bowed their heads.

"Bird *sikdaichun kasari* swim, eh?" said an old woman's voice in Andumaic from behind.

Imharr turned around. Having emerged from their hiding place, Jhaia and her younger sister were approaching on the raised pathway. He was learning more Andumaic every day, but Jhaia was harder to understand than any other Asdralae he had ever met, and he could make out only fragments. Even when he could understand the words, they seldom made any sense, as if she could speak only in ancient sayings that depended on some arcane local knowledge to interpret them.

He smiled and answered her in Ondunic, though he knew she could not understand a word of it. "Jhaia, you and your sister were supposed to wait in your hiding place. *Poknos*." The last word he said in Andumaic, hoping it was the right one for "wait" and pointing back down the pathway.

The old woman gave him a toothless grin. "Young fellow this old *halduraamuko chantu garneko*?" And then she laughed.

Imharr shook his head and smiled back. The old woman had saved their lives by bringing them to Yalawyn, where she had grown up as a child. Her extended family had taken in Queen Rona like one of their own. Now, with a fierceness that sometimes blazed in her eyes, she insisted on helping however she could in fighting the invaders who had killed her own queen and destroyed her kingdom.

Jhaia peeked around him, and her eyes widened as she took in all the dead Torrlonders. Her face hardened into a frown, and she nodded.

Imharr nodded back. "Yes, we got them this time. But we'd best leave before their reinforcements arrive in greater numbers." He turned toward Khalan, Jhaia's grandnephew and the leader of this group of Asdralae. The woodsman was leaning over a corpse and working an arrowhead free. "*Jaanos*. It's time to go, friend."

Dressed in greens and browns like the rest of the Asdralae, Khalan plucked out the arrow and looked up at Imharr with his dark eyes before he nodded. "Jaanos, tu." He gave orders in Andumaic, and the rest of the Asdralae formed a line along the pathway for their return to camp.

Imharr let out a relieved sigh. No losses this time, and the prince was safe. *Now, if we could only head home. But there's bound to be a lot more of these cursed Torrlonders in Adanon than here.*

THROUGH THE CITY OF ELLORDOR SEQUARA HAD MADE HER WAY TO Stithfast, King Fullan's palace. She had not expected to admire any northern city, but the graceful spires and domes soaring above Ellordor's many schools of learning and its open cobbled streets lined with trees made her feel almost welcome. Unfortunately, the fact that the kingdom of Torrlond lay just across the Theodamar River muted much of that feeling, but she did not plan to stay long, and things were safe enough at present with Torrlond busy tamping down rebellions in Caergilion and Adanon, not to mention dealing with its internal squabbles. None of that concerned her now, though. All that mattered was that she return to Asdralad.

Once she had gained admittance to Stithfast, a servant of the palace conducted her through hallways, one of which emerged outdoors to a cloister-lined garden with trimmed bushes and a towering, ancient oak at each corner. Beneath one of the cloisters she followed the servant, who led her back indoors through a large wooden door. Down more hallways they paced until the servant left her alone in a large room occupied by a long table, a dozen chairs, a fireplace, and a colorful rug covering the stone floor. Windows allowed in ample sunlight, which highlighted the dust motes floating and spinning above the table.

Shortly after Sequara arrived, another servant entered with a tray holding bread, cheese, a large bowl of fruits, a glass of wine, a bowl of water for washing hands, and a towel. With a bow the servant departed, leaving Sequara to nibble at the food and sip the wine until King Fullan arrived. Though she was hungry enough, she found it difficult to eat while she waited to make her request. She rehearsed what she would say in her head.

At last the door opened, and Sequara rose from her seat. In walked Fullan, looking more rested than she remembered him from their time together during the Battle of Thulhan. He wore simple but elegant and well-made garments: a green cloak over his white tunic and brown trousers, and no crown. Silver had invaded the whiskers on his chin, though the rest of his trim beard was light brown. Behind him came in two other men, both more finely dressed than their king. One was burly and grey-bearded, the other handsome, tall, and young, perhaps Sequara's age. She recognized them from Thulhan as two of the king's earls.

Gazing at the sorceress with his intelligent blue eyes, Fullan walked toward her and took her hand in his, bending slightly to give it a light kiss. He released her hand and gave her a warm smile as he gestured toward his companions. "Lady Sequara, perhaps you remember Earl Ashere and Earl Elfwy. I've just been in conference with them, hence my lateness in attending to you. Since they were the cause of your waiting, they wished to accompany me to apologize and to pay their respects."

The two earls bowed to the sorceress.

Sequara inclined her head in a slight bow towards Fullan. "There's no need for apologies. I recall the earls and their faithful service to you."

"Good. And how was my friend Galdor when last you saw him? Can I expect his return soon?"

"I think not. However, before I parted company from him, he encouraged me to come to you. He was well when I left Thulhan, though that city was on the verge of falling to the Ilarchae."

Fullan frowned and stroked his beard. "That is grave news about Thulhan, especially after so many sacrificed to save the city from the Torrlonders. We'll have to watch what the Ilarchae do." He smiled again. "At any rate, I hope Galdor stays out of harm's way. The old fellow has a habit of stumbling into wherever there's trouble, like a mischievous child. He didn't plan on staying to welcome the Ilarchae, did he?"

"No, your Majesty. He and Abon should have departed before the Ilarchae arrived. They are in the company of Orvandil and Gnorn, seeking Dayraven, who was likely making his way to Caergilion." She looked at the floor and swallowed, hoping the king would not press her with questions or notice her flushed cheeks. Closing her eyes for a moment, she scolded herself for allowing her emotions for Dayraven to surface. When she looked up again, the wrinkles around the king's thoughtful eyes deepened as he smiled.

"Perhaps we may speak more of that later, then. For the moment, may we sit together as friends and hear what brings you to Ellordor?" Fullan gestured at the table. "Or would you prefer to rest before we speak? I've ordered a room prepared for you and a bath."

"Thank you for your kindness, your Majesty, but I'm in some haste, I fear. If I may, I would make my request of you."

"Ah. Then let's sit together and hear it, and perhaps later there'll be time for rest and a more leisurely conversation." The king took the chair next to Sequara's, but the two earls remained standing with their hands folded before them. The sorceress sat down and faced Fullan.

"As you say, your Majesty."

"Please, though you've refused the title of Asdralad's queen until you've restored your kingdom, I regard you as my equal. Call me Fullan."

"Very well." She nodded. "Fullan."

"Good. Now, how may I be of service to you?"

Sequara took a long breath, and it came out as a sigh. "I need a ship. To bring me home."

Fullan blinked, but his countenance did not change. "I see. Do you know what to expect there?"

The sorceress grimaced. "Whatever awaits me, it will not be good. But my duty is to return to my people. I do not ask for anything other than passage to Asdralad."

The king paused for a moment, and then he nodded. "I understand duty. But how could I in good conscience simply conduct you to a place that may be very dangerous?"

The sorceress sat straighter. "I'm not defenseless."

"That I well know, and I would never imply otherwise. I meant that I wish I could do more for you. The truth is we expect more retaliation from the Torrlonders for our role in defending Thulhan once they deal with the southwest and their internal troubles with the disputed succession in the dukedom of Norfast. And then there's the matter of the Ilarchae to our east, which you have mentioned. By all accounts, Sildharan will fall, and then what should we expect from the Ilarchae? Threats surround us, and I can spare few resources to help my friends, no matter how worthy they may be."

"I ask for only one ship. A small one with its crew. I will guide them to a remote part of Asdralad's shore, where they may leave me and depart unharmed."

Fullan stroked his beard and lowered his brow. "It doesn't sit well with me, just abandoning you there. It's likely King Earconwald still has soldiers posted on Asdralad. As formidable as you are, you cannot hope to defeat the Torrlonders on your own."

Sequara's jaw muscles bunched as she clenched her teeth. "If you are unable to help me, I'll find another way there."

The King of Ellond leaned back in his chair and stared at her for a while with his hand on his chin before sighing. "No doubt you would."

The young earl, Elfwy, stepped forward. "Your Majesty?"

Sequara and Fullan turned toward him.

Elfwy cleared his throat and faced his king. "I've been thinking for some time that it might be in our interest to collect intelligence on the Torrlonders' activities. Discovering more about their position in the occupied west should help us to understand how soon we can expect interference from them here in Ellond. If Lady Sequara were willing to do me the honor of serving as my guide, I would gladly sail for Asdralad to check on matters there."

Fullan arched one eyebrow and smiled. "You've a weakness for noble causes, my young friend." He glanced at the sorceress before returning his gaze to the earl. "I could ill afford your absence, but it calms my conscience since I know you'll do your utmost to see her to Asdralad safely. And to *collect intelligence*."

The young earl could not keep a slight grin from his face.

The king turned to the sorceress. "Does that suit you, Lady Sequara?"

She nodded at the young earl. "It suits me well, and I thank you."

Fullan stood, and Sequara followed suit. "Then it's decided. You may take forty of your best soldiers with you, Elfwy. That should be a sufficient escort. Make arrangements to depart on the morrow." He faced Sequara. "And now that the matter is settled, perhaps you would like to rest. Afterwards, I hope you'll join the queen and me for the evening meal. There's much I wish to discuss with you."

"It will be an honor to join you. Thank you, Fullan."

The king's smile was gentle. "Good." He held out his arm. "If you'll come with me, I'll conduct you to your chamber."

She took his arm, and the two earls fell in behind them as they walked out the chamber and down the hallway, where elegantly carved statues stood in niches. It was a pity she could not savor the beauties of the place. Too many fears raced through her mind, which could find no rest. A warm bath and good meal awaited her, but her thoughts dwelled on what she would find in Asdralad.

THERE WAS ONE PROPER CHAIR IN THE ENTIRE CAMP. PLACED IN THE middle of Queen Rona's large hide tent and facing the entranceway, it was an uncomfortable wooden thing with no cushion, but, with all the governing she had to perform, she found herself sitting in the damned thing more often than not. She understood better than any other how appearance mattered, and the chair was the closest thing to a throne in the entire forest of Yalawyn, but she did not have to like it. Still, a sore backside and creaky hip were the least of her worries in keeping together the resistance against the Torrlonders on Asdralad. She was making much greater sacrifices than that. Even as the Asdralae came to her tent to petition and advise her, and as Kulva made a brave attempt at interpreting their words, more than half her mind was on Runan.

My son. Could I bear to lose another? Lelwyn's death broke me in pieces. Only Oruma and Anghara know what's holding me together most days. I'm sorry I couldn't save you, my sweet boy. All I have left — is it vengeance? Is hatred of the Torrlonders what keeps me alive? No. I must live for those boys. For Adanon. For some future I can't see. Oh, Balch. I'm doing my best to make them strong. But it hurts so much, and I so want to hide. For what I'm making you do, Runan, I'm so sorry. But I must teach you strength. Keep him safe, Imharr.

"Your Majesty?"

Standing just to the side of the chair, Kulva was staring at her. How long had the woman been trying to get her attention? Rona put on a slight frown in an attempt to appear regal and decisive while trying to dredge up the last words the woman had spoken. Something about the western perimeter of the forest.

"An increase in Torrlonder patrols on the western perimeter, did he say?" Rona made it sound more like a statement than a question.

Kulva nodded. "I think so, your Majesty."

The Asdralae woodsman who had come to report stood solemnly

before her, his hunting knife sheathed and his unstrung bow serving as a staff.

Rona kept her gaze on the man as she spoke in Ondunic to Kulva. "Thank him for this information, and tell him to see that he eats and rests well here in the camp before he returns to his post."

While Kulva spoke to the man in her broken Andumaic, communicating as much with her hands as with her words, the queen returned to her thoughts. Evening was coming on, and the tent began to darken as the light outside waned. *Where are you, Imharr? Where is my son? What have I done? I can't lose another. Oh, Anghara have mercy, it hurts.*

When her gaze returned to the waking world, she noticed the woodsman was gone. "Are there any more waiting outside, Kulva?"

"No, my lady. He was the last for today."

"May I sit now, Mother?"

Rona turned to Dialch, her youngest son, who had stood on the other side of the chair through all the reports and petitions without saying a word. Just as she commanded him, though it was no easy thing for an eight-year-old boy to do. She forced herself to smile and hoped it would convince him. "Yes, my dear." Standing from her chair, she arched her back to stretch the sore muscles and rubbed her temples in an attempt to clear her head of the tired ache that had been growing inside. "You did very well."

He plopped down on a nearby cushion. "Why must I stand through all that? I'm hungry, and I can't understand what they say."

"You must learn more Andumaic, as Kulva has done. It will help strengthen our bond with the Asdralae, who have done so much to help us."

"Then why don't you speak it?"

"Because I don't speak it well yet, and it wouldn't do for the person in charge to speak poorly."

"So you have Mistress Kulva speak poorly for you?"

On Rona's other side, Kulva snorted and laughed. "You have the right of it, little prince. It's a service I'm happy to perform."

The queen gave the old woman a slight nod. Kulva had become indispensable in so many ways.

Dialch frowned and gazed at his mother with his dark eyes that reminded her so much of Balch. "I still don't see why I have to stand there. I could learn Andumaic outside the tent, with the Asdralae children or the soldiers. I could go around like Runan and fight the Torrlonders."

Rona's heart fluttered, and she hid the sudden surge of fear behind a smile. "You must learn to hear petitions and reports. How to be in charge."

"But Runan will be king. Why doesn't *he* stand in the tent all day to learn how to be in charge?"

"You must learn these things as well."

"In case Runan dies too?"

Rona's mouth opened, but she could force no words out as her throat tightened and her eyes brimmed with tears she dared not shed lest they never cease. She stood, unable to speak or move, gazing at her youngest son as his questioning eyes waited for an answer.

Kulva rushed over to Dialch and knelt next to him. "Now, little prince, you mustn't say such things." The old woman's voice shook a little, but she hid her emotions well as she brushed Dialch's soft cheek with her hand and then kissed it. "Your brother will be fine. He and Imharr and the others will get the better of the Torrlonders. And one day, you'll be able to go home."

"To Adanon?"

Kulva nodded. "Yes, little prince. And you'll see the palace again in Palahon."

He shook his head. "I can't remember it."

Rona finally mastered her emotions enough to trust her voice. "You will when you see it again. When we make it anew. It will be like the old one, but even better."

Footsteps approached from outside, and a moment later a voice said in Ondunic, "Your Majesty, may we have permission to enter?"

It was Imharr. Rona's heart leapt, and she waited a moment to respond in order to steady her voice. "You may."

The tent's entrance flap stirred, and when it parted, her beautiful son entered with Imharr behind him, the warrior's hand resting on the boy's shoulder. She suppressed the powerful urge to kneel at Runan's feet and embrace him, covering him with her tears and kisses.

"You've returned safely, my son."

The prince nodded. "Yes, Mother. Thanks to Imharr and the others. The Torrlonders are dead. The patrol of twenty we found, that is."

"And what of our casualties?"

"None, Mother."

"That is good news."

"Yes."

Still kneeling next to Dialch, Kulva mussed the younger boy's hair. "You see, little prince? Your brother's back, and we're that much closer to home."

Rona smiled at the old woman, who had been away from Adanon far longer than she had. Most of Kulva's life had been lived as a slave far off in the Mark. If she could somehow maintain the strength to smile and hope, then Rona could as well.

The queen turned back to Runan. "I'm glad to see you well. Are you hungry?"

"Yes, Mother."

Rona nodded. "Your brother has worked up an appetite as well. Kulva, take the princes with you to dine while Imharr reports to me. Tell the guards outside to allow no one to disturb us."

Kulva turned her gaze to the floor as she bowed. "Yes, your Majesty." Putting her hands on her knees, she groaned a little as she raised herself. She held her arm out to Dialch. "My little prince, will you kindly conduct this old woman to the mess tent?"

Dialch smiled. "Yes, Mistress Kulva." The boy stood a little straighter and took her arm, and they moved towards the tent's exit. Runan gazed at his mother a moment longer as if he would say something, but when she nodded at him, he joined his brother and Kulva, leaving the tent strangely quiet with their absence.

Rona faced Imharr, who stood at attention in front of her, his arms crossed before him. There was a long silence, which she finally broke. "Thank you. For bringing him back alive. For everything."

Still maintaining his rigid posture, the young warrior nodded. "I serve you the best I can. Always will."

"I know that. Do you know what that knowledge means to me?"

Imharr pursed his lips as he paused. "I've a fair idea, your Majesty."

She frowned as she studied him. "What did I request you to do when we're alone?"

For the first time he relaxed his stance, and his face broke into a big smile. "Sorry. Rona."

She put on her best scowl. "You're not the least bit sorry. Come here."

He stepped closer until he stood before her, leaving a small gap between their bodies and staring into her eyes. His smile relaxed, and she reached up to stroke his cheek, which provided an outlet for the pleasant intensity building between them. When he leaned down, she grasped his head between her hands and pulled him closer. The warmth of his lips surrounded hers, and his whiskers needled her face.

She pulled back and pouted a little, but she held him close as she stared into his eyes. "Kissing you would be even more pleasant without that beard in the way."

He ran his fingers through his beard and grinned. "I'll shave it if you command, your Majesty, though I should warn you it grows back scratchier."

She narrowed her eyes in mock anger. "Rona. Call me Rona."

"A thousand pardons." His grin became even more roguish. "Rona."

"Shut up and kiss me."

"Yes, your . . . mmmm."

Her hungry kisses cut him off. For an ecstatic moment her fears receded, and though the ache of her losses would never leave her, she remembered how the world could give pleasure as well as pain. Life awaited her on the other side of the nightmare she had been living. Perhaps this relationship that had developed between them was not fair to Imharr, who was more than a decade younger than she was and, no matter what she pretended, her subject. But she needed him in so many ways, not least for the life he brought her. She could be strong for everyone else, but she had to keep going somehow, and so she surrendered to him the burden of her love and desire.

She clutched his hair and kissed him while the ecstasy intensified, but, recalling the guards outside, she clasped his exploring hands before surrendering all control. She kissed him for a time as he held her in a long embrace. When she caught her breath and could master her voice, she whispered in his ear, "You'll be guarding my tent tonight, yes?"

He swallowed before answering between heavy breaths, "Yes."

"Good. I'll send Kulva out to keep watch, and when she tells you to come inside, we will lie together for a time."

A brief pause, and his eyes widened. "She knows about us?"

"Of course she knows, my love. But no one else, and that's how it must remain for as long as possible."

"Yes. I know." He lowered his eyes.

She held his chin in her hands and made him look her in the eyes. "With you alone I may be unguarded. Soft. I am yours in a way I was not even for Balch. I need that now, though I've never needed it before. But, because of what I must be, the rest of the world must think me hard, especially those closest to me. I'm so sorry to use you this way, but I . . . need you. I owe it to you to tell you this. When we're together, I want to forget I'm a queen and be a woman. If only for a short space. Do you understand?"

He blinked at her and then nodded. "I understand." His face transformed into a mischievous smile, and the hardened warrior became a handsome young man with an irresistible glint in his eyes. "Rona." The smile quickly disappeared. "But what happens if we ever make it home? I mean, with us?"

She kissed him gently. "When that day arrives, we'll figure that out."

He nodded again. "Alright, then. I'm in way over my head every way I turn, but I'll try my best. I'll need your help at times."

It was her turn to grin at him. "Don't worry on that account. I'll show you tonight."

He flushed a little, which made her almost laugh since she knew he was experienced with women, but then he returned her grin.

"Until tonight, then." Her hand contradicting her words of dismissal, she stroked his cheek and then, grasping his leather armor, pulled him closer to her.

They embraced and kissed one last time before she watched him leave the tent. After he departed, she stared at the entrance flap for a while, almost unaware of how her smile faded and gave way to her customary regal frown.

THE TRUE-DREAM HAD COME TO HER THE PREVIOUS NIGHT WHILE she slept in her chamber in King Fullan's palace back in Ellordor. She could think of little else, even though she was finally on her way to Asdralad. Standing not far from the bow, Sequara grasped the railing of Earl Elfwy's ship and swayed as the ship carved through the waves and sprinkled her with salty spray. Behind her, the square sail billowed and snapped in the wind, luffing as it pivoted. The crew scurried about to tack and keep the ship on course, whereas Elfwy's soldiers slept below deck or sat on benches rolling dice and jesting with one another. They had left behind the Theodamar River some time ago and entered the open waters of the Gulf of Olfi.

Though Sequara usually travelled well at sea, a slight queasiness in her stomach tugged at her, and the sea's fishy scent seemed stronger than usual. But that did not disturb her nearly as much as her memories of the true-dream, which had ripped her out of her sleep back in her chamber in Stithfast.

She had seen a fragment of this true-dream before. During the Battle of Thulhan, when she had succumbed to the arrow wound, she had seen Dayraven lost and alone, not understanding who he was. The dream had torn her out of sleep then too, and she had returned to the battle to find Dayraven nearly consumed by the elf-shard dwelling in him. That fragment was part of a longer vision that invaded her slumbering consciousness the night before. Seared into her memory against her will, it replayed in her mind again and again, each time as vivid as if it were happening before her.

In a rugged coastal landscape Dayraven paced back and forth, his hair and beard all silver, just as the boy at the village inn back in Sildharan had described him. But his hair was also disheveled, and his blue eyes were wild with the fearful madness that afflicts a man who no longer knows himself. In the near distance waited a village perched atop a cliff overlooking the sea, its inhabitants scratching out a living from the water's bounty and from green terraces segmenting the rough hillsides. The scene put Sequara in mind of Sundara's golden coast, but she could not be sure where he was. Not anywhere near her, she sensed. Wherever it was, the village contained life, from which a part of Dayraven withheld himself like a pariah.

A horse grazed not far from him, but he ignored the beast as he walked toward the village and then jerked away from it as if scorched by an invisible fire. He held his head with both hands and grimaced in agony, digging into his temples with his palms and all the while mumbling as if conversing with himself. But Sequara knew what he was speaking to. A bizarre conversation was playing out between him and the elf-shard within his mind. As each voice gained the upper hand, he would swing toward or away from the village.

"Peace. I will grant them peace." When the elf-shard spoke through him, Dayraven's voice was slow and indifferent, and it sent a chill through Sequara.

"No. They don't want that. They fear it, and their fear hurts." The human side, the one that was lost but still managed to hold back the elf-shard, pleaded desperately.

"Then I will put an end to the hurt."

"You don't understand."

"My understanding lies beyond yours."

"No! Let them be. They're here for a purpose."

Dayraven stopped walking and looked up with vacant eyes that gazed somewhere far from the village and the sea beyond it. "I told you. Purpose is an illusion they create for themselves. It cannot last. It is so small and fleeting, a spark that dies in the darkness, before which their minds tremble."

A spasm contorted his face, and he jerked his gaze down to the ground as he crouched. "Yet let them have that at least. You have no right to take it."

Power as vast as the night sky sought to bleed from him, to envelop all before him, but somehow he held it all in as he ground his teeth and growled. He toppled over onto the grass and tucked himself into a fetal position, shaking and mumbling as if in the grip of a seizure. When he finally ceased, he lay still for a long time.

He stirred.

Slowly, he got to his knees. He looked around as if lost. "Where am I?" It was little more than a whimper.

With trembling hands he wiped the tears that stained his cheeks. His gaze fell upon the horse, and his face tilted as if he were struggling to recall what the creature was. "Caergilion," he said in a rough voice. His eyes grew hard with purpose, and he clenched his jaw. "I'm going to Caergilion." Each word was a hammer blow, a victory bought through suffering. He rose and stumbled toward the beast, his weary head hung low. "Why am I alone?"

It was those last words that had awakened Sequara and left a hole in her heart where guilt and sorrow festered.

"It's a fair wind, though it's not directly behind us."

Sequara turned toward the voice that yanked her back to the present. Elfwy approached her and adjusted his cloak before leaning on the railing next to her. Though he commanded his men's respect and moved among them with natural authority, in his few interactions with the sorceress thus far into the morning, he had tripped over himself trying to be courteous. He seemed an earnest and honorable young man, and she supposed most women would have found him attractive. But there was something stiff, even awkward, in his attempts to converse with her that made him difficult, though not unpleasant, to be around. Perhaps it was merely her weariness. He looked at her and smiled, but a concerned frown soon replaced the smile. "Lady Sequara, are you well?"

"Just a little seasick." She swiped the single tear on her cheek with a finger. "And the wind in my eyes. That's all."

The earl nodded and gestured aft. "There's no wind in my cabin, which is ready for you." His eyes widened and cheeks flushed. "I meant . . . That is to say, I've had it prepared for *you*. *I'll* be sleeping below deck with the men. Of course. When it's time to sleep, that is." He winced and pressed his forehead with his fingers. "Oh, Edan's mercy." Though he was her age, he at once looked much younger. He took a sudden interest in the waves. "Very windy today. Indeed."

"Yes." Sequara was not sure what else to say to alleviate his self-inflicted misery.

A long sigh escaped him. "How clumsy." He faced her with a set jaw. "Forgive me, please, Lady Sequara. I'm a soldier by training and disposition. Edan knows, I'm not used to the company of women." He rubbed his trim beard. "Other than my mother." His embarrassed smile soon withered.

She mustered up her own smile to put him at ease. "Then you may treat me as you would her."

His mouth hung open for a moment as if he were trying to respond but could not quite work out what she had said. "Oh. Of course."

"And I thank you for the use of the cabin. As you suggested, I'll retire there for the moment to get out of this wind."

"Oh." He bowed. "Rest well, then."

"Thank you, Earl Elfwy."

She doubted she would be able to rest at all, but she needed to be alone for a while. She would use the meditation exercises Queen Faldira instilled in her to focus on Asdralad. Galdor and the others would find Dayraven and lead him back to himself. They had to. And, unflinching, she would return home to whatever awaited her there.

6

LEAVE-TAKING

It was unlike Len not to show up two weeks in a row. The second time he was absent, Seren and Tob caught their fish in near silence, as if they were intruders who dared not interrupt the moaning of the waves and the cries of the seagulls. They did not even speak about the usual swimming contest out to Crag Isle. When they had filled their baskets, Seren faced Tob with her jaw set in a frown.

"We'd best take a look over at his place."

Tob nodded his agreement.

They did not say much as they carried their baskets along the coastal path that wound up and down the green hills and rocky cliffs. Len was the one who usually did most of the talking, and the fine rain drizzling from the grey sky enclosing land and sea encouraged no conversation. Shreds of concealing mist were their only company. Dripping and laboring under the weight of their full baskets, Seren and Tob trudged along until they reached the last hill before Len's family farmstead. When they crested the hill, they put down their baskets and paused.

"Looks quiet," said Tob.

Seren waited for some sort of movement. Sheep bleated in their pen, and from the barn came an occasional cow's bellow. But not one human soul appeared in the little valley. Since Len's father and uncle ran the farm together, and both had large families, there was almost always someone about doing chores and tending to the animals. The silence was wrong. There was not even smoke coming from the chimney of the stone farmhouse.

Seren picked up her basket. "Come on."

She heard Tob's heavy breathing as he followed her down the hill, but when they reached the bottom and still no one appeared, he halted. "Where are they all? You think the Torrlonders got them?"

The Torrlonders had come in force to fight the rebels in Caergilion, especially Commander Imrys's large band, which included Seren's brother Allon. King Earconwald himself had arrived with them, and folk said he was ordering his soldiers to wipe out entire villages if he suspected a single home sheltered any fighters. The few survivors claimed the king and his men did unspeakable things to the villagers before slaughtering them.

Seren turned around. Her chest was tight, but she told herself there was nothing to fear. If the Torrlonders had been here, there was no sign of them now. "Don't know. But we've got to find out." She faced the farmhouse and called out, "Hello! It's Seren and Tob, come looking for Len. Anyone about?"

Only the drizzle answered, and a cow's distressed low from the barn.

"This ain't right," said Tob from behind, his voice quavering.

"Stay here." Seren set down her basket and strode toward the farmhouse.

"Wait!" Tob huffed up behind her. "I'm coming with you."

In the muddy pathway leading by a stone wall toward the farmhouse were tracks that could not have been more than a couple days old. Seren kept her gaze on them to search for clues, but the rain-filled set of footprints told her little. When they passed the open gate into the farmyard, Tob began tugging on her sleeve.

"What is it?"

Tob's eyes bulged, and his mouth formed a horrified grimace. He pointed at something the wall had kept hidden from their view until they entered the gate.

On the wet ground lay a body facing up, its arms spread out wide. A man.

Tob's breathing quickened into shallow pants. "Shit. He's not moving, Seren. Mother's holy tits. He's dead."

Though her heart was hammering a lot faster than it had been a moment before, Seren moved closer.

"Don't go too close," hissed Tob, who stood frozen behind her.

She gazed at her friend and tried to look a lot calmer than she felt. "I won't. But we need to know what happened here. And we've got to find Len."

Tob swallowed and whimpered. "I can't move. I got to piss."

"Just stay put. Better yet, wait for me outside the gate, and you can piss out there. I'll come straight back."

He nodded. "I'll wait for you, but hurry up." He trembled as he walked back toward the gate, but before he reached it, he turned around. "I'm sorry, Seren."

She smiled for him. "It's alright. But wait for me."

"I will."

Seren crept closer to the dead man. There was something odd about his skin, which appeared waxy and grey. Raw sores seeped all over his emaciated arms and face, and she supposed from the red stains streaking his white tunic that similar wounds covered his entire body beneath his clothing. His open eyes, more yellow than white and webbed with red lines, gazed upward as the rain pattered him. There was no sign of violence or any other wound on the corpse. Her heart fell when she recognized him as Len's father, or what was left of him. "Mother's mercy," she whispered. She remembered what Len had said the last time she saw him. His uncle had traded up north, near Belglam, and seen the plague's victims there. He must have brought home more than goods.

Part of Seren was ready to run from the farmyard and flee with Tob. But she thought of Len, and she knew she would never forgive herself if she did not find him. What if he was alive in there, waiting for help? She gritted her teeth and walked toward the farmhouse door. "Hello? Anyone inside?"

Silence answered her. She stepped within knocking distance. "Hello?" She stared at the door for a long time before she worked up the courage to give it a push. It creaked inward, and Seren gasped.

The stench of the place almost knocked her over, and she jerked back as she grimaced and covered her nose and mouth with her hands. It was a sweet, meaty odor that told of rot and decay. Shadows and darkness dwelled within, and all was still. But the light spilling in the open doorway illuminated a form propped against a water barrel opposite the entrance. Slumped to one side, she was sitting on the floor. The sores had left gaping, leaking holes in her once pretty face, exposing the raw meat within. Her blank eyes stared out the doorway as if some sort of hope might have come from there, but Seren could offer her nothing other than revulsion and naked fear. The woman had been Len's Aunt Nilla, and in her lifeless arms she held what remained of her five-month-old baby daughter, Alma.

Seren gripped her stomach as she suppressed the strong urge to retch. She tried to call out again to see if anyone would respond, but she only gagged, and the words stuck in her tight throat for a long while. "Len," she finally managed, though her voice was so weak and shaky that it died only a few feet away.

Someone might still be alive, she told herself. Summoning a will that came from somewhere outside of her, Seren managed to step inside the doorway, pressing her back against the wall to stay as far as possible from Nilla's corpse. Once past it, she headed through the kitchen toward the sleeping room. A semi-rational voice in her head told her she would find all the sick people of the farmstead in there. Maybe Len was waiting for help.

Through the lifeless kitchen she stalked. Nothing stirred. By the light entering a window, she scanned the room's contents, which appeared abandoned in mid-use. Vegetables rotted on a counter. Flies buzzed around putrid meat. An iron pot hung over the fireplace, in which the last flames had long ago yielded to dead ashes.

Something bumped under the table, startling Seren so much that she cried out with a sharp intake of breath and leapt back. Her body shuddered and her heart pulsed in her ears, and she danced back another few steps when a cat emerged from beneath one of the benches. The creature stared at her for a moment and scolded her with a meow before skittering off for the front door.

Seren rolled her eyes and, placing her hand on her chest, steadied her breathing. “Stupid cat.”

Scolding herself for letting the creature frighten her, she looked back toward the dark entrance to the sleeping room on the other side of the kitchen. No sounds came from within. Easing her way through the rest of the kitchen, she locked her eyes ahead. There was a faint light in the sleeping room, probably coming through its window. Just a few more steps. Seren took a deep breath and approached the entrance. At first she squinted to better see what lay within the room’s dimness, but then her eyes widened in horror.

She froze where she stood, unable to utter a cry and wishing she had remained outside with Tob. On sleeping mats lay the dark forms of a dozen or so corpses, most of them small enough to be children, Len’s siblings and cousins. The terrible, weeping sores that made gaping holes marked their flesh. Resting on the floor in a pool of light from the window, the body nearest the entrance was Len’s.

Her friend’s mouth hung open, the tip of his swollen tongue protruding. His bulging, yellowed eyes seemed to plead for help. He had always been skinny, but now his desiccated skin draped loosely on his angular bones. Wet blood and pus still oozed from the many holes in his flesh.

“Oh, Len.” Tears fountained in Seren’s eyes, blurring her vision, and her body shook with sobs. She sniffled and wiped her face, all the while shaking her head in denial of the scene before her.

Len blinked.

Seren’s crying ceased. She sniffed again and craned her head forward, half in horror and half unsure if she had imagined the slight movement.

Len’s tongue retracted, and his mouth formed the word “go,” but all that came out was a hoarse, gargling death rattle. He lay still.

A chill impaled Seren’s body, an ice-dagger in her guts. She stood paralyzed, mouth agape. A moment later, she was somehow on the other side of the kitchen, shrieking and sprinting for the door. She emerged into the rain and relative brightness of the outdoors and kept running, hardly noticing how she slipped in the mud, until she exited the gate and bent over, breathless, next to Tob.

"What happened? Seren? I near shat my trousers when you screamed. What happened?"

Seren looked at her friend. She replied by buckling over and vomiting at his feet.

Tob tripped back a couple steps. "Ugh! What . . . Are you alright? What happened? Did the Torrlonders murder them?"

Seren's throat and nose burned, and she wiped a thread of drool from her chin. She held her stomach and looked up. "They're dead. They're all . . . dead. Let's go. We've got to tell somebody. It's the plague."

"WHERE'S YOUR MIND, GIRL? WOULD YOU HAVE ME CLEAN THE stalls all by myself?" One hand on her hip, Seren's mother leaned on the shovel she was using to scrape all the dung out of the stalls they kept their cows in.

Seren shook her head and gripped her pitchfork tighter. "Sorry, Ma." The present world returned to her along with the familiar scents of her family's barn: dung, dust, grain, and the fresh straw she was strewing in the stalls. It was hard to concentrate on work. For the last few days, the plague's ravages on her friend and his family had filled her nightmares and daydreams. In addition to the horrors she witnessed at Len's family farm, there was the constant fear for her brother eating at her. The Torrlonder troops had routed the Caergilese rebels, and Oruma and Anghara only knew where they had hidden, or if any of them still lived. But the Torrlonders and their king remained in the area, keeping alive Seren's desperate hope that her brother and some of the other fighters might have eluded the occupiers.

She plodded over to the fresh straw piled beneath the window at the end of the barn nearest the door and jabbed it with the pitchfork. Lifting her burden with practiced skill, she waddled over to the empty stall her mother had just finished scraping out, losing only a couple clumps of straw along the way. She heaved the pitchfork, tossing the straw on the floor before kicking it around. Da had herded the cows out to graze on one of the farm's grassy hillsides, but he would return in a while to lend a hand with the chores.

Her mother approached and stood next to her. Seren paused and looked over her shoulder, expecting another reprimand. But the frown Ma wore was more sad than stern, and when the woman put down her shovel, leaning the handle against the wall of the stall, Seren did not know what to expect.

Ma straightened her dress and held out her arms, wearing an almost regretful half smile as she stared at her daughter. "I'm sorry, my girl. Come here."

Seren stood for a moment and gazed back at her mother before she nodded. She let the pitchfork fall and clang on the floor. When they embraced, she breathed in the familiar scent of her mother's hair as they held each other tight. They were the same height now, but her mother's warm body was a woman's and softer than her daughter's. Seren could not recall the last time they had even touched each other. Memories of her younger years prodded at her, times when her mother enfolded her in warmth that muted the occasional pains of childhood. Her eyes blurred, and a single tear tickled the cheek it tracked down.

Ma took a deep breath and let it out slowly. "You've been through a lot. We all have. Times are dark. We'll work through it. Together. You and Da and me."

Her mother held her by the shoulders to look her in the eyes, and Seren sniffed before she nodded. She tried to think of something to say in return, but her throat was tight, and her mother released her, retrieving her shovel to get back to work. Seren watched her for a moment before picking up her pitchfork and returning to the pile of straw.

The two of them did not get much further in their task before running footsteps approached the barn. Seren and her mother looked up at the same time, just as Da appeared at the barn door. He was breathing hard and clutching his stomach as he leaned over. When he looked up, Seren could see the alarm in his eyes.

"Torrlonders." He managed to say between breaths. "They're coming. Several hundred."

For a moment they all stared at each other.

Ma broke the silence. "Get in the house, Seren."

Da held up a palm. "No. There's no time. They're almost here. Both of you stay in the barn. I'll speak to them. No matter what happens, you stay here. Don't let them see you. Understand?"

Ma hesitated, but after she glanced at Seren, she nodded to Da, who disappeared from the doorway. Seren stood rooted until her mother took the pitchfork from her and set it against the wall. She gripped her daughter's arms and looked at her. Seren had no idea how the woman kept her face so calm. "Listen to me. You'll hide in the stall at the end furthest from the door. Crouch down in the corner, and keep still. Not a sound."

"What about you?"

"I'll be in this one." She pointed at the floor. "If any Torrlonders come in here, you stay hidden no matter what."

Seren stared at her mother. Her eyes had that stubborn look she always wore when she would not budge.

"Promise me, Seren."

Her heart was thrumming harder than it had been at Len's farm, and sweat beaded on her clammy skin. She swallowed. "I promise."

"Good. Now go."

Seren forced her legs to walk down the barn's central aisle until she reached the end. Pausing for a moment, she decided to steal a quick glimpse out the window there. Not far away, her father had taken a position in the muddy farmyard, his hands at his sides and his back to the barn. He seemed small as he faced the huge procession that descended the hillside leading to their farmstead. Unable even to blink, Seren held her breath.

Hundreds of soldiers in grey tunics swarmed all over the hillside, marching toward the little farmstead. Arrayed in straight lines, they walked in unison so that their footsteps pounded the earth with a din that swelled as they approached. Many held long spears with glinting tips, while others carried bows. All of them wore swords at their hips. At least a dozen in the lead rode horses, and one in their midst sat astride a magnificent white steed. His ornate helm and breastplate glittered in the sunlight, and a long red cloak cascaded behind him.

Seren shook her head, desperate with the desire to disbelieve what her eyes told her. It had to be King Earconwald. If half of what folk said of him was true, his presence was worse than a curse.

The King of Torrlond turned in his saddle so that he faced the barn, and Seren ducked under the window lest he see her. She scuttled into the stall her mother had told her to hide in, tucked herself into a corner, and clutched her knees in front of her. She tried to quiet her erratic, gasping breaths. What could Da say to this man that would appease him? What did the Torrlonders want? What would they do to her father if he did not answer them the way they wanted?

Seren closed her eyes and took several deep breaths. When she opened her eyes, her hands stopped shaking. It felt too much like a betrayal to cringe in the barn while her father faced the Torrlonders alone. She crawled back out the stall toward the window. Peeking down the aisle, she saw no sign of her mother and reckoned she was hiding where she said she would. Seren crept the rest of the way to the window, careful not to make a sound, and rose until her eyes cleared the sill enough to see what was happening.

With his head hung low, her father knelt in the mud before King Earconwald of Torrlond, who reined in his steed a few yards away. Soldiers surrounded the king on all sides, and many others fanned out all over the farmstead, their mail clinking as they took positions to watch for some hidden foe. The bulk of the soldiers waited just outside the farmstead in their formations. With her mind sundered in competing halves, Seren crouched beneath the window, almost too terrified to continue gawking but unable to tear her gaze away. The corner of the stall where she was supposed to hide beckoned to her, but she chewed her lip and resolved not to abandon her father.

The king turned and waved at one of the grey-clad soldiers standing nearby. The man stepped forward, and Seren frowned when she recognized him: Koel, the spoiled, weasel-faced traitor who ran around licking the Torrlonders' arses. No doubt he was only too delighted to serve as Earconwald's translator.

"Inform this man why we are here," commanded the king in the Northern Tongue. His voice carried far enough for the troops all over the farmstead to hear.

Koel made a bow so deep he could have almost kissed the mud.

"Yes, your Majesty." The traitor faced Da and switched to Ondunic. "Arlon, son of Trebyn, you are accused of the most grievous crime of betraying your rightful king by aiding those who wrongfully and traitorously rebel against him. If you are found guilty of this charge, you will forfeit all that is yours, including your lands and your life. How do you plead?"

Da looked up at Koel, and Seren wished she could have seen her father's face. "Tell his Majesty I've no idea how I might have betrayed him."

Koel smirked at Da. "Do you deny giving aid to the rebels in the form of food and supplies when they came to your farm?"

Da nodded. "They came here, yes. But what they had of me they took by force, at the point of a sword."

Koel's oily grin exuded a sick pleasure, as if he knew what his victim would say and was ready with his next damning question. "How likely is that when your own son was among them?"

Da sighed and gazed at the ground. When he looked up again, he faced King Earconwald as he spoke. "I don't deny the one who was my son joined Imrys's forces. I forbade him, told him to stay out of it. But the boy disobeyed me, and I reckon that makes him his own man." He looked down at the ground again.

"Well?" asked King Earconwald from atop his steed. "What does he have to say for himself?"

Koel answered in the Northern Tongue. "Your Majesty, he admits the rebels obtained supplies when they came to his farm, and he does not deny his son is among them."

Seren gritted her teeth. *That's not all he said. Tell him the rest, you slinking snake!* At that moment she almost rushed out of the barn to shout in the Northern Tongue the words her father had truly spoken, but she remembered her promise to her mother, and her fear also kept her feet rooted.

The king sneered at her father. "Well, then. Tell him he has a choice: Reveal the location of the rebels, and I will grant him a swift death. If not, we'll wrap him in his own guts before he breathes his last."

"Yes, your Majesty." After bowing to the king, Koel faced Seren's father and said in Ondunic. "Where are the rebels hiding? Tell us all you know, and the king will be merciful. If you don't, you'll earn a painful death."

Da shook his head. "I know naught of them."

Koel smirked and turned toward the king. "He claims he doesn't know a thing, your Majesty."

King Earconwald gazed down, his lowered brow promising anger. "Then perhaps there's someone else on this farm who does know."

"He has a wife and daughter, your Majesty," said Koel with a grin.

King Earconwald's smile was that of a predator cornering its helpless prey, his voice calm but ripe with threat. "Then find them."

"You heard the king!" barked a nearby soldier. "Search the house and the barn. Find the woman and the girl!"

Soldiers scurried into action, one kicking in the door to the farmhouse with two comrades behind him. Three others headed for the barn.

Seren ducked and scuttled for the stall, cursing when her ankle knocked against the wooden divider. Had anyone heard? Her ankle throbbed, and she bit her tongue. Just as she tucked herself in the corner, the soldiers' heavy footsteps at the barn's entrance shattered the silence within. Their chainmail clinked as they walked, and steel rasped when they drew their swords. She tried to quiet her breaths and wiped her sweaty hands on her tunic. Would it be better to surrender herself before they found her?

"What have we here?" said one of the soldiers, and a moment later, Seren's mother cried out.

"Don't touch me," said Ma in Ondunic, her voice quavering.

"We found us a pretty one, didn't we?"

"Don't touch me."

"What the fuck's she saying?"

"Fuck me if I know."

"I'd sooner fuck her."

"Bring her out to the king," said a new voice, a rough one that held authority. "I'll check the rest of the stalls."

"Yes, sir. Come on, pretty. The king wants to meet you."

Feet scuffled, and Ma cried out again, this time with more pain than fear in her voice. Seren gritted her teeth, torn between fury and terror. A pressure in her guts gave her the urgent need to piss. Her tight fists shook, and she almost screamed as the heavy footsteps neared her. Tears came to her eyes, and her body convulsed with the effort not to cry out.

The footsteps grew louder. Seren almost wished she still had the pitchfork, but her hands were shaking so much she doubted she would have been able to hold the damn thing. And what use would it have been against a trained soldier, with hundreds more outside? It was time to give up.

Strangely enough, when Seren lost hope, her fear dissipated. Her body stopped trembling, and while she would not have thought it courage, she decided to meet her captor with as much grit as she could muster. She would not cringe. She would not beg. She would face these men and convict them with her eyes, whence they would witness the truth of their crimes. Just when the Torrlonder emerged into the stall's entrance, she stood up.

He was a huge man. Before him he held the naked steel of his large blade. Beneath his helm was a crooked nose, and grey peppered his blond beard. He frowned down at her for a moment until his bright blue eyes widened with recognition. Noticing the two red stripes on his shoulder, Seren remembered him at the same time: the Torrlonder lieutenant that she and Len and Tob had encountered on their way back from fishing, the one who had warned her to be careful.

He stood motionless for a moment as he gazed at her with an intensity that could have been anger, and then he swallowed. "Get down, girl." His voice grated in a near whisper. "Stay in here, and don't move. You hear me?"

Seren's throat constricted, but she managed to nod.

And then he was gone, his footsteps receding as he walked out the barn and announced to all assembled in the farmyard, "No one else in here."

Another man called out, a bit further away, "There's naught but their belongings in the house, your Majesty."

"Well then," said King Earconwald. "What have we *here*? The wife, or the daughter?" Even where she stood, Seren heard the lust in his voice, and many of the soldiers sniggered.

"She'd be the wife, your Majesty," said Koel in the most sycophantic tone possible.

"Far too lovely for this old piece of leather kneeling here, don't you think? Ask her where the daughter is."

"Yes, your Majesty." Koel switched to Ondunic. "Where's your girl, woman? The one who dresses like a beggar boy."

"I sent her out on errands." Ma's voice quavered. "She's likely catching fish at the shore. Out by Crag Isle."

"She claims the girl's at the shore catching fish," said Koel in the Northern Tongue. "It might be true. I've often seen her there in a particular spot with her friends."

"Is she as fetching as the mother?"

"Not at all. She's a dirty little bitch. She favors the old man."

"A shame," said Earconwald. "Still, it might prove useful to question her. Once we've finished here, you will guide a patrol to the shore to fetch the girl and conduct her to me."

"Yes, your Majesty."

"But now for the business of the present. Tell the man I'll be taking his woman inside their house. When I'm finished with her, I'll slit her throat. Unless he reveals where the rebels are. In that case, the woman will live, provided she pleases me."

Koel began relating the king's words in Ondunic. In the midst of them, Da cried out in anger, and then he grunted in pain. A moment later, he screamed.

Seren had remained standing in the stall, unable to move. The raw distress and agony in her father's helpless scream awakened a wrath in her that urged some sort of action. But fear spoke louder, and what could she do? Anything other than hiding was foolish. Gritting her teeth, she decided she would at least witness what the Torrlonders were doing to her parents. Even with the risk of being seen, that was better than cringing in the stall. She crept up to the window and, holding her breath, looked outside with one eye. To keep her hands from shaking, she gripped the sill.

Three Torrlonder soldiers stood over her father, who lay clutching his stomach and groaning in the mud, while two others held her mother by the arms. Ma wept and struggled as she tried to reach Da, who jerked each time the soldiers kicked him.

"Enough," said Earconwald. "I want him alive. For the moment." He alighted from his steed, which snorted as a soldier hurried to catch the beast's rein. His tall boots squelching in the mud, the king strode up to Ma, who went limp in the hands of her captors and looked down at the ground.

The king examined Ma with a slight frown, as if she were a horse he was considering purchasing. "Stand her up."

The two soldiers obeyed.

"Release her."

When they let go of Ma's arms, Earconwald snatched her face in his hand and forced her to look at him. "First, I must keep my word." He fleered as he stared down at her. "At least this won't have been an entire waste of time."

Ma's sudden movement must have surprised the soldiers, for they were slow to react as she lunged toward the king. She grasped something at Earconwald's hip and then swept her arm toward his face. The king shuddered backwards, his eyes bulging as a bright red line welled on his cheek. His trembling hand went to his face, and he shrieked before screaming, "The bitch cut me!"

"Never again!" shouted Ma in Ondunic, and she advanced on the king, who tripped on his red cloak and fell backwards into the mud as he screeched and covered his face with his hands. Before she reached him, her breath rushed out when a length of sharp steel impaled her from behind, its bloodied tip jutting from her chest. She lurched forward and her arms spread out wide. Seren had not even seen the guard draw his sword.

He slid the blade out of Ma's body. With a red stain expanding on her dress, she dropped the king's dagger before slumping forward to fall in the mud, unmoving.

Thrashing in his muddied cloak, the king rose and yelled again. "She cut me! The whore!" He touched his bleeding cheek and, after wincing, gazed at his trembling hand. He slammed her body with a savage kick, and then he turned on the guards. "How could you let her?" The two of them went down on their knees, and, still holding his cheek, Earconwald slapped the one who held his reddened sword, sending the man down into the mud. The king waved and flapped his hand as if he had hurt it. "You killed her. Fool! You robbed me of my sport."

An old man with three red stripes on his shoulder stepped forward and knelt. "Your Majesty, with your leave, may I plead for the lad? He was performing his duty, protecting you from a threat. I beg your mercy."

Earconwald looked down on the old man with a sneer, as if he wanted to slap him as well. He drew his sword, but the old man knelt without flinching. The king shrieked down at him, and spittle flew from his mouth. But then he stomped over to Da, who was crawling in the mud and reaching a trembling hand toward Ma. Earconwald screamed again as he raised his blade over Seren's father, who gasped when the steel pierced his back. The king withdrew the weapon and thrust it into Seren's father again and again, screaming each time.

Seren was shivering and weeping, and her body slid to the floor. Tears washed her face, and snot ran out of her nose. She wanted to keen, but she bit her tongue so hard she tasted blood, and her body convulsed with the effort to suppress her sobs. She crawled back in the stall, where she continued to hear King Earconwald scream.

"Quarter and mutilate their corpses! Set their heads on spikes in the nearest village! And find the girl. I want her. The little bitch will answer for her parents."

Seren held her breath, but her body shook so hard she feared it would betray her.

The King of Torrlond continued in response to someone. "I'll see a healer when I'm ready, damn you. Burn this place to the ground. Burn it all!"

Soldiers shouted and moved around the farmyard, their heavy boots stomping everywhere. Horse hooves trod in the mud, and one of the steeds neighed. Above the general din someone shouted, "Unpack your tinderbox and light us some torches. There's a good lad."

Not long later, footsteps clomped into the barn, though the general din grew quieter as the main body of soldiers withdrew.

“Where do I stick it?” said a voice.

“How ‘bout up your arse?” said another man. “You got a turd between your ears? The straw. There’s a great big pile of it. Should go up nice.”

“What about the stores?”

“Burn it all. You heard the same as me.”

“Seems a waste.”

“Just hurry it up, and let’s get the fuck out. Unless you want to see the king more pissed.”

“Right. Here goes, then. It’ll go up fast with all this straw about.”

“Let’s go.”

A few crackles preceded a sound like a sudden gust, and Seren knew the pile of straw near the door was alight. The barn’s outer walls were stone, but the frame of the structure was wood, and the stores and hay would go up fast. But she did not dare to move since she could still hear some Torrlonders outside shouting. Not long later, the smoke’s stench began to sting her eyes, and wisps of grey began to fill the stall. By the time she could no longer hear the soldiers, the fire at the other end of the structure was roaring. Smoke darkened the barn, and a reddish glow illuminated it as it billowed. Seren began coughing and choking, and it grew difficult to see even the other end of the stall through the haze. When the heat of the flames began to warm her sweaty skin, her terror of the fire overcame her dread of the Torrlonders.

She exited the stall and stole a quick glimpse down the barn toward the door. Outside the fleeting protection of the stall, the heat was so intense that she flinched as it dried her eyes and baked her skin through her clothes. Flames roiled everywhere, and a loud crack preceded the collapse of a portion of the roof, including a large beam that glowed red and sent blinding sparks streaking toward Seren when it slammed on the floor. There was no escape that way.

Her only hope was the window she had been peeking out of. She coughed as she darted toward it, but smoke was already vomiting forth from it. Her eyes watered and stung, and she felt ahead with her hands since she could see little through the haze. Her palms slapped rock, and then she found the opening and heaved her body up. The sill scraped her ribs as she clambered out, and when a loud rumble signaled the end of the rest of the roof, she scrambled out so fast that she fell head first, sending a sharp jolt of pain to her shoulder and the top of her skull before she rolled on the ground.

Seren groaned and rolled further from the burning structure. Once she crawled out of the smoke into the brightness of the outdoors, she scanned the farmyard for any remaining Torrlonders. No one occupied the yard. The bodies of her parents were also gone.

She rose to her knees and then stood. She forced her feet toward the spot where Earconwald and his soldiers had slain Ma and Da. When she reached it, the only sign that remained of their suffering was the blood soaked into the mud. With her tears flowing freely and her body shaking, Seren looked over at the house, which was also engulfed in flames. Flanked by the two burning structures that had been her only home, Seren stood racked by sobs with her eyes wide in horror and disbelief. She shook her head and whispered, "Da's fiddle."

Sprinting for the burning farmhouse, she entered the door and shielded her face from the heat with her arms. Hungry flames consumed all the contents of her home. A wall of them separated her from the entrance to the sleeping room, where Da always kept the instrument. The heat was so forceful that she could hardly keep her eyes open, and she retreated. She ran outside and scrambled to the other side of the house, where there was a window that opened into the sleeping room. Smoke and flames poured out of it.

Seren stared at the window and shook her head. "No," she tried to say, but it was little more than a whimper, and there was nothing she could do to save even Da's fiddle. Nothing would be left to her. The flames rose higher, and sparks floated on the air as smoke billowed. Coughs and sobs shook her body, and she collapsed into the mud of the farmyard, where she sat and watched the remnants of her world crumble and burn away.

LIGHT BEGAN ITS SLOW SURRENDER TO DARKNESS. CLOUDS VEILED the sky, rendering the gloaming a greyness in which color seeped away.

Night fell. No stars glimmered above, and no moon silvered the landscape. The dark's triumph was complete.

In the mud sat Seren, shivering and dazed, gazing toward the charred ruins that had been her home. When a light drizzle began, even the embers in the midst of the ruins ceased glowing, and no warmth emanated from them. The stench of smoke pervaded everything, including her body, hair, and clothes. Most of her mind was drifting far away, clinging to memories of a family that was no more. She could summon the will to do little more. But a small part of her carried on a rational conversation about survival. She was not certain she wanted to survive. Perhaps she would just lie in the mud until her body starved. That would be easiest.

Even as she thought of that, a will deep within her awoke, and she looked around as if noticing the darkness and the rain for the first time. Her greatest act of defiance against the Torrlonders would be to survive. But how?

She thought of her brother, Allon. Even if he was still alive, she had no way of finding him. Her father's remaining cousins were days away in Gadomiel, his nephew and nieces much further north near Belglam. There were distant relatives in Iarfaen too, but that was a whole world away, little more than a name. Seren's mother had no family she knew of.

What of Tob? Perhaps she could seek shelter with his family. His parents and grandparents were kind people. Of course, her presence would put them in danger. She was sure that lying deceiver Koel would look there for her since he knew of their friendship. No. She would not do that to Tob.

Her teeth began to chatter, and goosebumps covered her flesh. The soaked tunic and trousers she wore could do nothing to keep away the chill of night. She needed shelter, and she needed it soon.

Crag Isle was a perfect hiding place, but it could not protect her from the cold. Besides, Koel and the Torrlonders were looking for her there. If she could hide somewhere else for a short time and find some clothes, blankets, and supplies, perhaps she could make it out to the rocky islet later. Then she could hole up there for as long as needed, eating fish and whatever else the sea provided. So she had two problems: where to shelter for the moment, and where to find the clothes and supplies.

Seren sat straighter. The solution that came to her sent another chill through her shivering body. After word got out about Len's family farm, everyone had declared the place off limits, giving the farmstead over to the plague and hoping it would remain contained there. Some kind or enterprising neighbors had come to take away the suffering animals from the barn and the pen, but no one would enter the farmhouse. The corpses remained unburied, haunting the place with their decay.

No one would seek her there. She would sleep in the barn, covering herself with straw to stay warm. There might even be some sacks that would serve as bedding. When daylight came, she would brave the house to find clothes and supplies. Perhaps some food. Remembering the odor and the horrible sores on the bodies, she trembled harder at the thought of entering the house. But she had gone in there before. Survival demanded that she do it again. She would gather all she found and make her way to Crag Isle the next night.

Formulating a plan gave her the will to rise. Her stiff muscles protested, and cold seized her body all over. Hunched over like an old woman, she tried to shake the chill from her limbs, but her shivering only increased in intensity until it became difficult to stand. The drops of pattering rain were like needles in her flesh, and her head ached and throbbed.

Perhaps if she began walking, her body would warm. In the darkness, however, it was hard to remember in which direction Len's farm lay. A muddy sluggishness congealed in her mind, and she tried to suppress a rising panic to reach the clarity she needed. A great blotch in the darkness must have been the piled remains of the farmhouse. On her other side, the charred ruins of the barn. Her mind crawled toward the correct conclusion. She had to walk through the farmyard and toward the shore to the coastal path. Then head west.

One foot in front of the other, and her journey began. She hugged herself and rubbed her upper arms with her palms, trying to restore some warmth to them. A tight ache grasped her head and seemed to radiate from somewhere inside her. The chattering of her teeth and shivering that convulsed her body only worsened. It grew difficult to walk in a straight line, and she did not trust her balance as she teetered and lurched.

Seren pushed her body to keep going. In the darkness, she became more unsure of where she was going. At the edge of the dullness wrapping her mind, her panic grew. Despair unclenched her trembling jaw, whence a moan escaped. She had to reach Len's farm. She dug in and kept walking, but her progress was slow, and she grew less and less certain of where she was. Perhaps she was meandering in circles. Perhaps she was about to totter over a cliff. Time passed, what seemed like a whole night, but only the monotonous darkness surrounded her, and she felt no closer to an end.

The shivering was getting the better of her, and her skull burned and ached with an inner fire, pounding and throbbing with a pressure that blurred her thinking and robbed her of the clarity she needed. Enough of her mind was left to her to wonder where the fever had come from. In spite of her shivering and the goosebumps covering her flesh, sweat dripped from her hair and face, running in rivulets that mingled with the drops of rain. Her breaths grew hoarse, and her chest felt as if someone had stuffed it with rags.

At last her stiff body could go no further, and she let herself fall, hitting the soft mud with something like relief. The rain jabbed her skin in a hundred places, but she could not even stir or groan in protest. She had reached an end. For a while longer she was aware of her body's trembling, but the darkness crept within her, and at last she surrendered to it.

Awareness returned as the color of blood. Her body was afire with heat, and for a moment she thought she was in the burning barn again, unable to breathe through the thick smoke invading her lungs. She blinked, and through much willpower, she held her eyes open. The red of her eyelids gave way to harsh brightness. She was floating in that brightness. No. Something was carrying her. She could tell from the way her head dangled and rocked to the regular rhythm of steps. And though she was not trapped in a fire, her flesh was stinging all over as if something were consuming it.

She groaned and tried to turn her head to see what was carrying her, but it was too much effort to keep her eyes open, and the space within her skull was a knot of sharp pain that stabbed her.

"Easy, lass," said a voice.

Was it someone she should recognize? Through the haze of pain and the heat of her fever, some dim part of her mind thought she knew the bearer of that voice. It was rough and grating, a man's voice, and somehow she associated it with fear. But why was the man carrying her?

"I'm sorry it took me so long to find you. I came when I could. We must hurry now, but I've no notion where to take you."

As Seren began sinking back down into unconsciousness, she realized why she should fear the man. He was speaking not in Ondunic, but in the Northern Tongue.

The voice grew blurry and distant, but it kept talking. "And *who* would take you in like this? Poor lass. A swift death might be a mercy. Still. Couldn't leave you there on the ground."

What was it she heard in the voice? Regret? Fear?

"Not much doubt. It's the plague that's taken you."

Images of corpses with open sores assailed Seren before she succumbed once again to the darkness. Her last thought was to wonder if she even wanted to emerge again.

7

A GREAT CAUSE

Cursing the witch Urd for the thousandth time, Bagsac rubbed his stiff and sore backside as he paced and waited in the hallway outside the supreme priest's chambers in Sigseld. The long ride to reach Torrhelm from Rimdale had not helped, but the blame in truth lay with that horrid old hag from the Mark. It had been her cunning, heathenish ploy to lure him and his faithful followers into her oak ring, attacking them with birds and then with the herd of elk. He fingered the scar on his nose from a gash one of the birds had ripped open with its beak. The motion moved a nerve in his spine just the wrong way, causing a jolt of pain to shoot up his back and down his leg. The agony originated in the very spot where the elk sent by Urd had struck him. He winced and clutched his arse. One of his watery eyes began a series of involuntary blinks as half his face convulsed and twitched.

The physical pain had been bad enough, but it was his fall from grace that wrought the greatest wound. So displeased had the Supreme Priest Bledla been with Bagsac's failure to slay Urd and her grand-nephew, the boy Dayraven, that he exiled him to a cold, remote village near the North Downs in the Dukedom of Norfast. And the boy had become some sort of dragon-wielding prophet. But *that* was hardly

Bagsac's fault, and he was obeying orders to quietly discourage the rumors about the supposed Prophet of Edan.

In that village in Norfast he had made a sort of peace with his lot, but the war between the deceased Duke Durathror's young heir and Duke Siric of Rimdale over the succession to Norfast had brought more troubles, and when King Earconwald and the Supreme Priest Joruman took Siric's part, the traitorous people of Norfast had booted out all of the Way's priests. Thus, poor Bagsac found himself uprooted once again, a refugee of a sort in Rimdale. Through no fault of his own, hardship dogged him everywhere.

But Bledla was dead now, and so was the pagan witch Urd. He had outlasted those who hurt him, and that was something. In this manner perhaps Edan showed favor to him. He had heard about the witch's fate on the island of Asdralad and what they did to her body. A grin broke out on Bagsac's face, at least until another spasm of pain wracked his backside and forced him into a grimace.

The worst of the pain subsided into the usual dull ache, and, after wiping his eyes, he resumed his pacing up and down the hallway, limping in his hitching gait. His quarters in Rimdale were cramped but out of the way, and no one had bothered him much there. He had his duties to preach on behalf of the Way, always emphasizing the justice of Siric's claim to Norfast, but there were few other demands on his time. He had settled into a quiet life and had begun to think he might live out his days in the northern town.

But then came the summons. Bagsac had no notion why the Supreme Priest Joruman would want to speak with him. Was he going to offer him a chance to redeem himself? He swallowed and shook his head, unsure he would even welcome such an opportunity. Or was he in some sort of trouble? Had he neglected his duties somehow? As he had done during the entire journey to Torrhelm, he ransacked his brain and groped for the answer, but nothing came. Instead, his anxiety increased, just as it had done during the jolting ride, along with the stiffness in his backside. The priest clutched the wiry hair on the sides of his head as he limped along the hallway, muttering to himself.

"What have I done this time? Naught I can think of. Naught, naught, and more of naught. *Why* disturb my peace then, eh? What can he want of me? Ouch!" One hand clamped on his arse. "Damn and confound that old witch. Have I not given enough? Sacrificed my health for the Way, I did. Have I not earned my rest? Argh!" He froze for a moment and then hobbled through the ache. "Edan spare me, and may her heathen bones rot! Which is it, then? Am I the object of displeasure, or is this an opportunity? Must be one or the other." He licked his dry lips. "Displeasure or opportunity? Displeasure. Opportunity. Ouch! Displeasure. Opportunity."

Bagsac stopped pacing and looked up. The two temple guards posted outside the door to the supreme priest's chambers were gawping at him, one with his eyebrow raised in curiosity. Realizing he had been speaking aloud, Bagsac let go of his hair and tried to smile at the guards, but another spasm took over his face, sending his eye into a fit of blinking. The guards glanced at each other and then resumed staring at the priest.

Bagsac frowned and pulled at his white robe, and then he turned around to continue pacing. He stopped short, however, when a presence inserted itself in his mind, much like the itch when he sensed a person watching him from just outside his line of vision. Someone powerful in the gift was approaching from behind the door. This wizard was far stronger than Bagsac was, but not so mighty as to send chills down one's spine, as Bledla had done. He bit his tongue and reminded himself not to utter his former lord's name, which all were forbidden to speak aloud these days.

The door clicked and opened, and the Supreme Priest Joruman stood in the entrance to his chambers. The two guards bowed, reminding Bagsac to do the same, even though the motion sent a jolt down his leg. When he looked up with a grimace stretching his face, Joruman was grinning at him as he toyed with a ring on the little finger of his right hand.

The supreme priest wore a thick gold chain around his neck, allowing it to drape over his white robe. Bagsac knew the man only by reputation, but the rumors spoke chiefly of his brilliance, his cunning, and his ambition. And, of course, his lechery, but those last reports were mere whispers and none of Bagsac's concern. His blond but greying beard was neatly trimmed, and his blue eyes gazed at Bagsac as if searching for some hidden secret, making his grin seem almost hungry. What in Eormenlond could the man want from him?

"Just the fellow I wanted to see. Welcome, Bagsac," said the Supreme Priest Joruman in a cheerful voice.

The priest struggled to rein in one of his eyes, which twitched and fluttered and roved with a mind of its own. He licked his lips before he unleashed the words he had rehearsed all the way from Rimdale. "My lord. Thank you for blessing me with the honor of this summons. I hope I will prove myself your worthy servant."

Joruman's smile grew, revealing his white teeth. "You already have."

Bagsac stared for a moment before replacing his puzzled frown with a nervous smile. "Thank you, my lord." He cleared his throat, but his raspy voice still squeaked when he asked, "May I ask how?"

"By coming here. The reports on you were so . . . emphatic that I decided to take a chance and summon you."

"Reports, my lord?"

"Yes. I can already tell you're just the man I've been needing. You shall have the opportunity to contribute to a great cause."

An opportunity, then. Or so it seemed. The priest hesitated. Why were his lips always so damned dry? He moistened them with the tip of his tongue again as he bowed and then jerked with another knife of pain sliding through his body. "I am your servant. But what great cause might it be, my lord?"

Joruman chuckled. "That you shall know shortly. Accompany me. I have something to show you, and all shall become plain. You must be in need of refreshment after your long journey."

"Yes, my lord. Thank you."

The supreme priest smiled again. "Not at all. This way." He strode past Bagsac and set off down the hallway.

The priest blinked at his back and then limped on his way behind him.

DARK AND COLD WERE THE BOWELS OF SIGSELD DEEP BENEATH THE palace's rocky foundation. Nevertheless, sweat was dripping from Bagsac's brow by the time he reached the bottom of the steps, and his limbs were trembling. Though he had modified his gait to an awkward shamble to avoid grinding the nerve in his arse, he had shuddered several times along the way when agonizing spasms seized his body. Edan only knew how he would climb back up the steps.

For the moment, it was a relief to have the steps behind him, but he wondered through the haze of pain what they were doing in the dungeon. His breaths came as hoarse gasps as he labored to keep up with the Supreme Priest Joruman, who walked before him in a pool of ruddy light from the sputtering torch he held. Bagsac kept a wary eye on the long shadows the wavering flames cast on the tunnel's rocky walls with moisture dripping down them. He tried to step around the water collecting here and there, but the wet had already crept through the leather of his boots, soaking his feet after he stumbled into several hidden puddles on the dark, uneven floor.

Not daring to voice the many questions in his head, he shivered as he followed his lord past the dungeon cells. For his part, Joruman kept his silence. The only sounds were the sure footfalls of the supreme priest, Bagsac's shuffling steps, and the plopping drops of moisture from the ceiling into the puddles.

After making several turns down various corridors, Joruman halted before a door. He turned and, with a large grin across his face, waited for Bagsac to catch up. "Here we are."

Bagsac's eye twitched as he peered around the dark tunnel, and he licked his lips. "Where precisely is *here*, my lord?"

"The dungeons beneath Sigseld, of course. Not the most pleasant venue, but I've brought you here for a little reunion."

"A reunion, my lord?"

"Yes. An old friend is inside. Let's not keep him waiting." The supreme priest turned to the door and, grasping its handle, pushed on it. It creaked inward, and from the growing gap its opening created, warmth and light spilled out.

Joruman moved aside, allowing Bagsac to see into a large chamber lit by torches in sconces. Exuding a musty odor, tomes and scrolls filled the shelves lining the walls of the chamber. In the center of the room waited four chairs around a table, upon which books lay in piles and several lit candles stood in waxy puddles as they cast their light. In one of the chairs sat a man Bagsac did not at first recognize. But when the man looked up from his reading, his eager smirk provoked a memory that momentarily erased the heavier build, grey hair, and wrinkles the years had bestowed on him. An involuntary gasp escaped Bagsac, and his eye galloped into a series of twitches and blinks.

The High Priest Edulf laughed, showing the gaps among his grey teeth. "Hoi, Ginger-twitch! Your hair's not so flaming red anymore. What's left of it, leastways."

Bagsac grimaced at both the surge of pain in his backside and the sudden reappearance of the name Edulf had bestowed on him when they were young apprentices in training at the monastery here in Torrhelm. The man leering at him had made those years as miserable as possible. Edulf had been stronger both physically and in the gift, and he had humiliated Bagsac almost daily to prove that fact to everyone. Unfortunately, many others had followed Edulf's example, transforming Bagsac into the favorite object of their taunts and pranks.

The priest licked his lips and attempted to smile through the ache of memory and the throbbing of his body. "Blessed be the Eternal, High Priest Edulf. I congratulate you on your appointment to such an elevated and holy office."

The Supreme Priest Joruman chuckled. "No need to be so formal, dear fellow. Edulf assures me the two of you go way back. Nothing like the bonds of youth, eh?"

Bagsac licked his lips and racked his brain for an appropriate response, but one of his eyes took it upon itself to reply with a violent spasm.

Edulf stood from his seat and waved them in. "Come in, Ginger-twat!" Such had been one of the many cruel variations he gave the nickname. "Don't just stand there with your mouth hanging open."

After placing his torch in a sconce in the hallway, the supreme priest gestured for Bagsac to enter first, and so the priest forced his stiff limbs into motion to shamble inside the chamber.

Edulf thumped one of the chairs at the table and said to Bagsac, "Plant your arse here! I would hear what the years have made you into, aside from uglier than ever. Ah, but time is kind to no one, eh?"

"No, indeed." Bagsac frowned at the wooden chair, knowing full well how painful sitting in it would be and dreading even more its proximity to his one-time nemesis.

"Go on," said Joruman. "Sit. We're all friends here." The supreme priest took another of the chairs.

"Thank you, my lord." Bagsac bowed and, with a wince and a quick groan, eased his backside down into the chair.

"There we are." Joruman glanced at the high priest, who had not yet sat down again. "Some wine, Edulf. Your finest. An Adanese red, I think, will do. The 1663 vintage is particularly fine. We must properly celebrate your reunion."

The high priest bowed. "With pleasure, my lord." He spun around and walked toward the back of the chamber, where there was a long wine rack.

Bagsac moistened his lips again. "Um, my lord. Uh . . . I do not ordinarily partake. Most wines, I find, disagree with my head."

"Nonsense." Joruman's smile hardened. "A 1663 Adanese is not most wines. You'll find it unlike anything you've tasted before."

A brief paroxysm took over one of Bagsac's eyes. "If you say so, my lord."

There was a pop when Edulf pulled the cork from the bottle he held, causing Bagsac to start, which produced a twinge of agony up and down his body. The high priest chuckled as liquid glugged into a glass.

"So," said the supreme priest, and Bagsac turned back to him. "You must give us the latest tidings. How fares Duke Siric in his efforts against the rebels in Norfast?"

Bagsac hesitated and swallowed. "Not as well as we might hope, my lord. The people of Norfast are stubborn in their treachery. And there's talk that they've appealed to their heathen relations in Grimrik, the bloodthirsty Thjoths, for aid."

"I've heard as much. It won't please King Earconwald, I can assure you. If Siric can't manage on his own, the king may need to send in someone to do the job for him."

"As you say, my lord. We priests are urging the people to support the rightful cause. I myself am out at all hours to make clear Edan's will in the conflict."

"I'm sure you are."

Edulf arrived holding a tray laden with the bottle and three glasses filled with red wine. He placed a glass before the two other men and set the tray down on the table before taking up his own, holding it aloft in expectation of a toast.

The supreme priest rose from his seat, and so Bagsac unfolded his pain-racked body to do the same, which produced a series of clicks and pops in his joints as he stood straight. Joruman raised his glass. "To reunions, and to our great cause."

"Aye!" Edulf took a long gulp.

Joruman eyed Bagsac while taking a draft, and so the priest brought his glass to his lips for a cautious sip. A fruity warmth sprang to life on his tongue. After he swallowed and the liquid slipped down his throat, heat radiated into his chest. It swiftly tingled in his joints and bones, and he exhaled a relaxed breath. Eyes slightly widened, he sniffed at the glass and then tipped it into his mouth for a larger swallow, and this time the warmth extended to his brain, wrapping it inside a pleasant numbness. His stiff body relaxed, and a cautious smile crept to his lips.

"You approve?" asked the supreme priest.

Bagsac's tongue slipped out and tasted the trace of wine on his lip. "Yes, my lord. A most excellent choice. Quite efficacious."

Joruman smiled. "Good. Now sit. We have much to discuss."

All three men took their seats.

"So," began Joruman. "Ill tidings in the north, it seems."

Bagsac broke off from the swig he was taking and swallowed. His head swam a little, and so he gave it a quick shake. "I fear so, my lord. But no doubt Edan's righteous wrath will visit the heathens. Just as it has fallen upon the rebels in Caergilion and Adanon. We hear much of King Earconwald's successes in the south."

The supreme priest seemed to smirk at the mention of the king. "Yes, it's likely the king will strengthen our dominion over the south."

The High Priest Edulf cleared his throat while he refilled his glass. "Earl Ulfred's reports from Asdralad also indicate our forces will have the rebels there subdued soon."

"And then," Joruman paused to raise his eyebrows, "once we consolidate our control over the south, perhaps we will resume our conquest of the east. That is, what's left of it after the Ilarchae have torn it to vulnerable little bits."

Bagsac took another draft and found the warmth and numbness leaching away more of his stiffness. "Is that the great cause for which you've asked me to come?" His tongue felt thick in his mouth, so he made sure to pronounce each word with precision. It would not do for the supreme priest to think him so easily drunk.

Joruman gazed at Bagsac before answering, and his smile was gone. Did the supreme priest guess how quickly the wine was going to his head? "No, dear fellow. The cause you will serve is far greater."

As the numbness spread all the way to Bagsac's fingertips, the room began to tilt and swim. When he tried to put down his glass, the wine sloshed out onto his white sleeve before the glass tipped onto the table. "Oh. Forgive me, my lord. Seems to have gone straight . . . to my head."

One of his eyes began to flicker and shudder, but it slowed at once, and then his eyelids grew inexplicably heavy. He caught his head just as it was nodding into the table. "Feeling . . . a bit overcome . . . I fear. So sorry."

"Pray don't mention it," said the supreme priest's voice, but Bagsac could no longer force his eyes open, and he heard more than felt his forehead knock into the table.

"Oh, Ginger-twitch," said Edulf's laughing voice, distant and blurry in the darkness. "You always were such a fucking idiot."

A TINGLING SENSATION AROSE IN THE SHADOWY PLACE THAT WAS HIS mind. Bagsac struggled to recall where he was as he made a futile effort to open his eyes. As if some sort of glue congealed around his thoughts, he could not command his eyelids to budge. Nearby, a male voice was mumbling a kind of steady chant, but it was too fuzzy to understand. For some reason, he remembered how nervous he was as an apprentice in the monastery, always slower than the other boys to master the songs of origin, ever the object of their mockery and scorn. How he loathed himself in those days. He could admit that now, with so many more significant failures behind him. The tingling in his mind intensified to an unpleasant pricking, and his eyelids finally jerked open on their own.

A blurry greyness greeted him, leading him to conclude something was amiss with his vision. With a major effort of will, he blinked several times to try to focus. A ruddy glow illuminated the greyness, but clarity still eluded him. He seemed to be lying down on some sort of hard surface, a table perhaps. It was hard to tell since there was a strange disconnect between his mind and his body, which felt remote from him. This was not altogether unpleasant since it meant he also did not experience the usual pain that racked his body. All the same, he had a niggling feeling the numbness ought to concern him. Something was not quite right, but his muddled head could not focus long enough to discern what it was.

After a few more blinks, his vision sharpened enough to make out what he was staring at. Above him was the grey stone of a ceiling illuminated by torchlight, which told him little about where he was. But when his other senses began to shake off the stupor, the chanting voice grew clearer. The Supreme Priest Joruman. With that recognition, memories flooded back. He had been with the supreme priest and the High Priest Edulf when that rather strong wine seized his head and made a fool of him. Just when the supreme priest had been offering him some sort of opportunity, a chance to redeem himself.

He winced. It was too embarrassing. Mortifying. Perhaps his worst humiliation yet. He had not even finished one glass, but he had grown lightheaded so swiftly. And, like a clumsy ass, he had stained his white robe when he spilled the wine on the table. Perhaps he could salvage the situation. Groveling had often worked before.

He tried to open his mouth to apologize to the supreme priest for his stupidity, but only a raspy moan emerged. Something was in the way, and he became aware of a discomfort digging into his face. Like the rest of his body, which he still had trouble sensing, his face was numb, but it seemed something was tied around his mouth. A gag of some sort.

What in Edan's holy name?

Joruman's chanting voice grew more distinct. He sang a song of origin, but not one Bagsac had ever heard. The man was repeating it again and again:

Druanil ecthonias an dharian gadalathon,
Abu mihil inghanias ni rakhyon abhularon.
Vardas diagol im parthas akwinway,
Shardas inkhathol an ghalas khalithway.

Bagsac's befuddled mind had trouble making any sense of it. However, sensation was returning to his body, which was creeping back under his control, and he thought he might be able to move to gain a better view of what was happening. Perhaps he would even be able to rise, and then he could remove the thing around his mouth in order to explain himself to Joruman.

Anticipating the pain it would cause in his backside, he focused on moving his splayed arms and legs so he could sit up. At first, his hands and feet only quivered, but with a sudden breakthrough, he nudged them into life. Metal clinked. Something cold and hard encircled his wrists and ankles, holding his limbs in place. What could it mean?

He grunted with the effort to lift the weight of his head enough to see what was happening. His head trembled up a few inches, and, before it thumped back down, he caught a quick glimpse of his white-robed body. It seemed he was chained to a table. Standing over him, the Supreme Priest Joruman had been gazing down at him as he continued the song of origin, and tiny sparks of blue light had blinked into being in the space between them. Stabbing through the haze clouding his mind, a spike of fear accompanied his sudden realization: The wine had been drugged, and he was a prisoner.

The pricking in Bagsac's mind grew more painful, and he grimaced as a tremendous force began to pull at him as if stretching something out of his head. What was the supreme priest doing to him? Against his will, the man was exposing and digging into his naked mind to extract something from him. As the full extent of his helplessness dawned on him, the breaths coming out Bagsac's nose quickened into irregular gasps, and his heart squirmed in his chest. He whimpered behind the gag.

More of the blue sparks leapt into existence, illuminating the ceiling in an eerie glow. A horrible pressure pushed outward from within his skull, as if its contents sought to pour out of him. The agony tore a scream from Bagsac, but the tight gag around his mouth turned it into a muffled shriek. What was happening? This was not right. He had done nothing to deserve such terrible punishment. He ransacked his memories for some reason for it all, but there was nothing. Then again, there had never been a reason for the torture Bagsac had endured over the years. Was this yet another horrible prank? Would Edulf and the others burst through the door and bend over laughing at him? The hurt in his head sharpened, and it became difficult to think through it.

Joruman's chanting intensified in pace and volume, and the blue sparks grew so numerous that they took over the room and morphed into bands of wavering light. Bagsac gawked at the light, which seemed to emerge from his head and stream toward Joruman even as the hideous pressure wrested a long, hoarse wail from his throat. What was this light? What was the man doing to him? Why was he hurting him so? The blue light emanating from him gushed toward Joruman. The pressure in his mind grew enormous. His skull would explode, spattering its contents all over the room. He knew it. Pain and blue light took over everything, obliterating all other thoughts.

Something in him snapped. A different ache filled his mind, the quick jerk of something ripping loose, like a limb, filling him at once with relief from the pressure and panicked, sweaty fear. The bright blue light that had taken over his field of vision winked out and yielded to darkness.

When he opened his eyes, the grey ceiling of the chamber returned, silent and glowing in the torchlight. His body was still. The blue light was gone. So was the pain. In its place was a yawning gap, a cavity in his mind where something had previously resided.

The gift. It was gone. He could no longer feel it. The path in his mind to the realm of origins was closed. In its place was a raw, open wound. He could not sense Joruman's strength any longer. He could no longer feel the insects and organisms nearby. A thousand tiny voices that had accompanied him for as long as he could remember were silent. Gone. Since he was a boy the gift had been part of him, the only friend he had in the world, the only thing that made him special when everything else was wrong and awkward with him. It was like having a limb or any of his other senses stolen from him, chopped away, like having sight his whole life but losing his vision in one horrible, inexplicable moment. Like being flayed and losing the ability to touch. How could he go on after such a loss? Somehow, the gift had left him. Joruman had ripped it from him.

Triumphant laughter overflowed from the supreme priest. "It worked! It worked! I can *feel* the power." The man leaned over Bagsac and gazed down at him with ecstasy gleaming in his widened eyes and exuding from his beaming smile. He curled his hand into a tight fist, which he shook as he bared his clenched teeth. "Already I see with greater clarity. I'm stronger than ever."

Bagsac's sweat-drenched body began to quiver as he frantically searched his mind for the gift. He could not find it. It was gone. He was blind. Senseless. Only the wound remained where it had been amputated from him. The bastard had somehow stolen it. Raped his mind and taken it.

Joruman's smile disappeared, and he frowned in obvious surprise. "You're alive." He did not give much weight to the statement. It seemed a mere observation, as if Bagsac's living or dying were a matter for mild curiosity.

"Well," said the supreme priest. "If anything like sanity remains in there, perhaps you will come to know the great cause for which you have sacrificed. Nothing as fleeting or paltry as a kingdom or a faith. Death, Bagsac. We will conquer it."

Bagsac's trembling increased. He needed to curse the gloating thief who stood over him, to beat him with his fists and tear out his throat with his teeth, tasting his blood. But all he could do was tremble and shriek behind the gag. The chains holding him down clinked as his body shuddered, and his trembling set off a paroxysm of agony that shot from his backside up his spine and down his legs, causing his body to jerk with more violence.

In a ghastly cycle, his body shook and wrenched his frayed nerves with jolts of pain, which set off more trembling and extracted pathetic animal grunts and groans from him. All the while, his eyes twitched and blinked, and his face convulsed in uncontrollable spasms. A bereaved, feral wail ripped through his ragged throat only to die against the muffling barrier of the gag. The chains binding him jangled and clanked as his fitful limbs yanked them taut in turns. At some point his teeth clamped down on his tongue, grinding it and loosing the iron tang of blood in his mouth. His gasping breaths wheezed out his nose, whence snot dribbled out as his body juddered out of control.

But the seizure was nothing next to the confusion of empty space in his mind where the gift had resided. Lost. It was lost. And he was lost without it. A mere husk. A flesh sack emptied of purpose and meaning. Agonized and helpless, all he could do was quake and keen over the death within him.

TWO TEMPLE GUARDS HAULED HIM BY HIS ARMS DOWN THE DAMP, dark hallway while the High Priest Edulf led the way torch in hand. Their rough treatment stretched and jerked his fragile spine, transforming his body into a receptacle of anguish. As his legs dragged through puddles and over rough bumps, every step sent jolts of agony up and down Bagsac's shivering body, and with complete loss of control, he had pissed all over himself. His screams and howls filled the dungeon with piteous echoes. Even if he had not mangled his tongue, he could not have said a rational word through the pain, nor could his mind hold on to any thought in the face of the chasm occupying it.

At length, they stopped dragging him and merely held up his limp form, and in between Bagsac's shrieks came a jingling sound as Edulf fumbled with his keys. A click preceded the groan of old hinges supporting a heavy door.

"Toss the wretch in there," said Edulf's gravelly voice.

One guard seized Bagsac's feet while the other grasped his hands. A gasp escaped him when they raised him, and then they threw him through the open door. The hard floor slammed into his back, knocking the wind out of him, and everything went blood red as waves of agony coursed through him. Every brittle bone in him was a locus of pain, but flames of anguish radiated from his backside. Unable to draw air, he could only tremble with his mouth agape in a silently screaming rictus as he lay on the stone floor, and he welcomed the thought that he might suffocate. But air entered his lungs with a hoarse wheeze, and more gasps followed as red gave way to shadowy dimness. As soon as he had enough breath, he released a long wail.

"Shut up! I'd put an end to your shrieking for good if the supreme priest hadn't ordered otherwise." The door slammed to punctuate Edulf's last words, and the cell went dark. Through his raw throat and bloody mouth, Bagsac screamed again and wished Edulf would defy Joruman on this particular matter.

In the darkness he wept. With his throat sore and ragged, Bagsac could no longer scream, so he resorted to emitting a moaning wheeze every time he exhaled, like some dying animal. His body shivered on the cold floor of his cell. His breath stank of congealed blood, and his body reeked of piss. Long did he lay in such wise.

But the pain of his body abated enough to allow some semblance of rational thought to leak through, and his trembling diminished. When he opened his eyes, he found the darkness was not complete. A dim red line glowed at floor level beneath what he guessed was the door. From that he supposed a torch was burning outside in the hallway. It gave enough light for him to make out the outline of his hands, which quivered before his face.

His hands reminded him that he had been human once, that he had possessed an identity outside all this pain. And that identity had centered on something within him, something that was gone. The pit within his mind opened again, and there the empty darkness greeted him. "Unnnhhhh," he grunted around his ruined tongue. "Unnnnnnhhhhhhh," he rasped louder. His shivering returned with renewed force, and, one after another, he let loose screams that could do no more than gargle and dribble from his open mouth.

In the darkness Bagsac lost all distinction between nightmare and waking, and the passage of days and nights became a distant memory. But at some point he realized he must be awake, and, though his tremors never ceased, his stiff body allowed him to slide his hands along the stone of the floor to explore the space around him. Not far in front of him, his fingers stumbled into a stone wall. When he reached out to his sides he met the same result, except that on his right was a ragged, musty piece of cloth that might have once been a blanket. On his left side his hands upset a metal container, which clanged on the floor. Some part of his mind realized it was for shitting and pissing in. A chamber pot, he recalled. Too bad he had already wet himself more times than he could remember. For some reason this thought made him cackle, but the cackling hurt his sore throat, and he choked on his bloody saliva, sending him into a coughing fit from which it took him a long while to recover.

So. He was in a cell large enough to lie down in, but little larger. A grave.

But he was still alive. He was quite sure of it. This was all a mistake. Someone would come along to let him out. Surely they would realize the mistake. Or perhaps he was sleeping again, and this was just another nightmare.

Oh, but it was so dark in here. He shivered harder, and then he remembered an even darker place. The emptiness in his mind. The terrible gap from which he could not escape. Deeper than any grave, blacker than any nightmare. He grinded his teeth and trembled in a fetal tuck. *Someone let me out! I'm still alive!*

TIME PASSED. IT MUST HAVE. HE HAD MUCH DIFFICULTY RECALLING who he was, and he thought he did not want to recall it. But he could remember a man coming more than once, bearing torch light that stabbed his eyes so much that he covered them with his hands and never got a proper look at the man or the cell that was his grave. Perhaps it was a different man each time. He could not tell since the man never spoke. That was fine since he was afraid of the man, and he whimpered each time he heard his footsteps approaching.

Whoever he was, he would bring water and some thick gruel in a wooden bowl. It hurt his wounded tongue to eat, but the gruel lessened the hollow ache in his belly, and he could swallow it without chewing much. The man would also sometimes take away the chamber pot and return it empty when he came back for the wooden bowl and cup. He was proud he remembered what the chamber pot was for sometimes. But he must have forgotten at other times, for often enough he found he had soiled himself. He could hardly stand his own reek, and stinging sores all over his backside and thighs joined the ache in his bones and the sharp pains that sent him into spasms.

HE COULD NOT BRING TO MIND A TIME BEFORE HE WAS IN HIS GRAVE. There was only the darkness surrounding him and the deeper darkness within him, and he spent all his time hiding from one inside the other. Sometimes he outwitted the darkness, which made him grin and chortle, but not too loudly lest it find him. In other moments it seized him before he could scuttle away, and he wept and gnashed his teeth as his body trembled and sweated in the grip of the darkness within.

FOOTSTEPS APPROACHED, DISRUPTING THE DARK'S MONOTONY, AND the usual dread set him quivering. The door clicked and groaned open, and a torch's wavering light hurt his eyes so much that he cowered as far from it as he could under his ragged blanket. The glow seeped through the weave of the old blanket, and through its holes beams of light spotted his filthy robe. He sneered and whined at the ruddy spots. He did not want the light to find him since it would reveal what lurked in his mind.

He waited for the tap of the wooden bowl and cup on the floor so the light would go away and the door would close, but nothing happened. It seemed the man was just standing there watching him, holding aloft the terrible glow of his torch. The thought of this made him shake even harder, and his eyes blinked as his face convulsed.

"Look at me, Bagsac."

It took him a moment to understand that the man had spoken, and even longer to attach meaning to the sounds. And though he grasped what the man wanted, he remained beneath the blanket, quavering and hoping the man would go away.

"Bagsac. Let me see you."

That voice. He knew it. It belonged to someone. Someone who took something. A chasm in his mind yawned before him, and he grimaced and whimpered as he shook his head to make it go away.

"I wish to help you, Bagsac. I'm sorry this was necessary. If I could make you understand . . ."

Then it hit him. That sound the man was making was his name. He winced and shook his head and moaned. Too many horrible things went with that name. Too many things that reminded him of the pit in his mind. He dodged it and returned to his grave, but why would this man not go away? No one should disturb someone in his grave. His body shuddered even harder.

"I'll see what I can do to help you. I don't know how. Not yet. But I'm . . . I didn't expect . . . You see, along with the gift I took from you, I can sense your pain. It's quite vivid at times. I'm truly sorry. You've been through such suffering. But someone had to pay a price, you see. I'll make great use of it, and later generations will thank you. They'll know of your sacrifice. I swear it. Do you hear me? Damn it, man. Can you understand me?"

He rocked back and forth, and his moan vibrated because his body was shaking so much.

Go away. Go away. Go away. Go away.

"Take that rag off your head and let me see you."

Something ripped the blanket from his grasp, and the light brightened to a gleaming flame that ate his eyes. Covering his face with his hands, he balled up his body and shrieked. "Aaaaiiiieeeeee!"

The man stood there for a long while with his horrible light. He made no sound. Nothing happened.

His screams diminished to a croaky rattle every time he exhaled. The torch's glow was still hurting his eyes and filling them with red even though he closed them as tight as he could. But there was nothing else. He began to wonder if the man was there at all. Perhaps he had gone away but left his light there as a form of punishment. What had he done to deserve it? Perhaps the man had left open the door to his grave. Did that mean he could leave?

He eased his hands away from his face, and the redness grew brighter. Cracking open his eyelids, he shivered and winced as the sharp brightness entered his eyes. He closed them when the pain grew unbearable, but he decided to try again. After several tries, he was able to force his eyelids open for short moments, and he turned his blinking gaze toward the light's source.

The man was there, holding the bright torch. But he was no man. A ghost-demon in a white robe stood over him. He could not make out the face since the piercing flames were too near it, but somehow he knew this monster. It was he that had inserted the void in his mind, and it was he that had thrown him in this grave. He knew it.

"Aaaahhhhhhhhhhh!" He screamed as loud and long as his tattered throat would permit, and he covered his face with his hands again as he tried to squirm beneath the stone floor. When he could draw breath, he screamed again.

He kept screaming until the door banged shut and the light disappeared. For a long time he lay and trembled in the darkness.

When he could think again, he dreaded that the ghost-demon would return to hurt him or take something. *It would, it would, it would.* So he must do something. He must hurt it first. But how? It was so strong and terrible. What could *he* do, a forgotten dead man in his grave? *Forgotten and rotten. Forgotten. Rotten.* There had to be a way, else it would hurt him again and again and again. In the darkness his mind groped.

THE NEXT TIME THE FOOTSTEPS CAME, HE SCRAMBLED UP. IT WAS the ghost-demon returning to torture him. To take away something else. To shove him into the void. It had to be. Stooping over with the pain in his backside, he crouched in his grave, ready to pounce the moment the door opened. In his hand he grasped his improvised weapon. He was shaking and sweating, but he had to do something. He would not let it hurt him again.

Not again. No, never. Never, Never, Never. He shook his head to dispel the darkness threatening to swallow him from within.

Metal grated against metal, and the door clicked. A long groan of the hinges, and the sputtering torchlight slapped his eyes. "Here, now. What are you . . ."

He swung as hard as his tortured body would let him. A loud clang of metal on bone preceded a grunt. Drops of piss and chunks of shit flew everywhere. A body collapsed to the floor in the hallway, something clattered and echoed when it struck the stones, and the light dimmed when the torch dropped.

He blinked and looked down at his hand, which still held the chamber pot he had used as his weapon. Perhaps he should have emptied it first. Much of its contents had spattered all over the doorway, and some dripped on his hand and sleeve. The man lying face up on the floor had some on him too. More importantly, the man did not stir.

He started to cackle at the sight of the man at his feet, but he knew he should not make much noise, and his body shook with the effort to suppress his giggles. It was not the ghost-demon. Just a man who had come with water and gruel. The overturned tray, cup, and bowl lay on the floor right in his doorway with the bowl's contents splattered on the stones. His hollow stomach squirmed and groaned at the sight. Crouching down on all fours, he hurried to lick up some of the gruel to quiet the ache in his belly. The stone was cold and rough on his tongue, but the gruel was warm.

He did not have long, and he knew it. Licking his lips, he looked up from his half-eaten meal, and he groaned as he forced his stiff muscles and popping joints to raise his body. The door to his grave was wide open, and he shivered just a little as he stepped outside it. But he was not so foolish as to think he was free just yet. There were other men, and the ghost-demon was waiting for him down here. He had to find a way out.

The torch on the floor was still burning, and he blinked at it for a moment before gathering the courage to lift it. Though it made shadows dance all around him, he might need it down here in the dark places. Stooping to grasp it, he winced at its brightness and trembled to touch it. But he kept it in his grip, and it sputtered when he rose and stepped around the man's body on the floor. He took his bearings. Every twenty paces or so, torches in sconces illuminated the rough stone of the damp hallway outside his grave. It carried on in both directions further than he could see. Which way should he pick?

He stood indecisive for a long moment, but then, like ghosts whispering in his mind, he thought he heard the dim echoes of voices from one direction, and that decided him. He shuffled off the other way, his bare feet flapping and dragging on the cold stone of the floor and splashing in chilly puddles.

He followed the long hallway past many closed doors, fearing someone would open one and emerge just as he came across it. Presences lurked behind those doors. Were they ghosts? *Not friendly. Not nice.* Perhaps they were other graves, but, hurrying past, he did not stop to listen at them. Every now and then, amongst the drops of moisture plopping in the puddles from the wet ceiling, distant voices entered his awareness. Whenever they brushed up against him, raising goosebumps all over his flesh, he limped faster. Flap, drag, flap, drag, flap, drag went his naked feet.

The hallway ended in a closed door. He stood before it debating whether to turn back. There was a latch on the door, tempting him to pull on it, but he did not know what was behind it. What if the ghost-demon were waiting for him there?

Sudden shouts erupted behind him, startling him into jumping toward the door. The movement sent a shock along his rotting spine and legs, and he trembled. Another voice answered the first shouts. They knew of his escape. *They don't like the dead to leave.* They were coming for him, and they would drag him back to his grave, where the ghost-demon would devour his mind.

He grabbed the door's latch and pulled, wincing as the hinges squeaked. It was dark behind the door, but his torch's light revealed a staircase descending further down. He had thought his grave was at the lowest level of the underworld, but perhaps darkness had no bottom. The shouts grew louder and he hurried inside the door, cackling a little at his cleverness when he carefully shut it behind him. But he must hurry. Surely they would seek him here.

The stairs were not easy for his ruined body to negotiate. He leaned on the damp wall and gimped along, huffing and gasping and cursing himself for every echoing noise he made. The stairs went down and down for longer than he thought possible, but they finally came to a landing that led to another closed door. He might have entered this door, but the stairs also continued downward. *Which way, which way, which way?*

The further into the darkness he descended, the harder it would be to find him. He shrugged and turned to continue down the stairs. It was another long way down, and every step was torture to his pain-racked body, but again the way led to a landing, and this time there were no more stairs beyond the closed door. He stepped onto the landing, and something cold slapped his bare feet with a splash. The stagnant water collecting on the rough floor of the landing reached his ankles.

Cold and wet was the underworld. He shivered as he gazed at the door.

"He must've come down this way. You lads check the second level, and we'll check the third. He can't go far."

He started at the thin voice echoing from the darkness above him. *No, no, no, no.* The men must not catch him. They would do cruel things to him. They would give him to the ghost-demon. The door awaited him. Only through darkness could he escape darkness. He knew it well.

His shivering hand tugged on the door's handle, easing it open as its bottom sloshed through water. He stepped through and used great care to close it without a sound, giggling with muffled snorts all the while. He turned around. The long passage before him contained doorways to graves on both sides. It led on in a slight decline in one direction, well beyond the radiance of his torch into deeper darkness. Perhaps it went on forever.

He hobbled on, and the water splashed and gurgled as he stepped with one foot and dragged the other behind him. Splash, gurgle, splash, gurgle he went. He passed by so many graves, and some of the slime- and moss-covered doors were rotting in the wet. Of course, the underworld would have no end of graves. Straight and down went the passage, and the only change was the water deepened until it reached the hem of his robe, seeping into it and chilling his legs. He pressed on. His progress slowed as the water deepened, even though it seemed to pull him along. Water dripped in thicker drops from the ceiling, plopping all around him and trickling all over the dark stone walls. A thick layer of slippery slime coated the floor, and it oozed around his toes with each step.

By the time the water reached his waist, the downward current was tugging at his legs. Goosebumps covered his shivering flesh, and his teeth chattered. Drops of moisture were pattering on his head from above, reminding him of something that often had happened when he had been alive. He had not thought about rain in a long while. It was something from another life. Without knowing it, he had missed it when he was in his grave. With the memory of rain came a vision of sunlight and a band of faint colors splashed in an arch across the sky. He stood for a moment with his mouth open.

"There's a light up ahead! He's down here, alright!"

The lovely vision disappeared, and he jerked forward, splashing water as he struggled through it. In his chest his heart hammered, and he whimpered at the thought of the men catching him. *Hurry, hurry, hurry.*

His spine ached, and the icy water crept up to his chest. But he had to press on. They were coming. He could hear them sloshing toward him. They were coming.

There were no more doors to graves, but the tunnel kept going downward at a steeper pitch as it constricted, with the ceiling lowering to just a few inches above his head. The water rose to his neck, and his arm ached as he held the torch just above it. Its flames sizzled as they licked the wet ceiling. Up ahead, glistening in his torch's ruddy glow, water lapped against the ceiling, completely swallowing up the narrowing tunnel. He stopped, just keeping his balance as the water tried to tow him forward.

This was the end. There was nowhere to go. They would catch him, helpless and bedraggled and cold, and drag him back to the ghost-demon. They would be so cruel to him after he tried to escape. He whined and shivered, but he could think of no way out. From behind, the glow of more torchlight brightened the tunnel and cast wavering shadows that loomed all around him. The men's splashing grew louder.

"There he is! Get him!"

He lurched forward, but the floor disappeared beneath his feet, causing him to stumble beneath the water's surface with a splash. Cold surrounded him. He opened his mouth to scream, but only a gurgling, bubbling noise escaped his lungs. Everything was dark, and he supposed he must have lost his torch in the water. His feet touched the slime of the floor, and he pushed up. His face breached the surface, but there was a sharp pain when his head bumped the hard rock of the tunnel's ceiling, giving him only a moment to suck in air before he sank again.

Something in the water grabbed him. Not the men, for it was no human grip. Rather, the water's force sucked him along, and he slipped downward. He flailed and thrashed, but his tired, pain-racked body could not resist the current, which shoved him down and down. He stopped struggling and grinned as his body plummeted deeper into the water's black coldness. Perhaps he would find a bottom to the darkness after all.

8
VENGEANCE

"I tell you, Irling: The Mercenary Company of Etinstone has seen better days."

"Aye, Captain." Lieutenant Irling walked next to Ludecan as they made their way to the camp's command tent. The two of them trod along the muddy paths that wove in between clusters of soldiers idling about or occupying themselves with dice or stories.

"Never any good days in the long, undistinguished, and unrecorded annals of our sorry history, but plenty better than this."

"That's the truth, Captain."

Ludecan grunted. "Back in Orvandil's time, we had our moments." He spat. "'Course, we don't talk about him, do we? Seeing as how he's a traitor."

"No, sir. Not a word about Captain Orvandil, Captain."

"Smartest thing he ever did was run away from us."

"Aye, Captain."

Since the Thjoth's absence, the company had drifted from one mess to another. And now *this.* This was as shitty as Ludecan had ever seen. *Captain* Ludecan. He scoffed and rolled his eyes.

He had seen better days too, truth be told, but not in a long while. He turned to Lieutenant Irling, whose virtues included never saying much, making him the perfect confidant. "I ever tell you about my brother, *Earl* Ludwulf?"

Irling squinted and frowned as if searching his memories, and then he nodded. "You might've mentioned him a time or two."

Ludecan spat again. "Fucker never should've wed Ulla. How could I let such a thing go unanswered? He was already getting everything else: title, wealth, and lands as well as our dead old man's eternal favor. Arrogant prick. He knew Ulla and I fancied each other."

"Not very brotherly of him, Captain."

Ludecan grunted. "Well, I had a measure of vengeance." He grinned at the memory. "I made sure *Earl* Ludwulf more than half-suspected his son was mine. Which he is. It was almost worth it, too." His grin withered. If only Ludwulf had not been so effective in ruining his career.

As the younger son, he had always known he would have to make his own fortune, and Torrlond's army was his chosen path. But, through bribery, smears, and the influence of powerful friends, his brother had ensured that no regular company would take him as an officer, or even as a soldier. And so his last remaining option had been a mercenary company. Over the years he had worked his way up to lieutenant, and though he had tried to transfer several times, Ludwulf's hate was relentless. When Captain Orvandil did the sensible thing by abandoning the company, he found himself a captain in Torrlond's army. "Captain of a fucking mercenary company. Misfits, drunkards, and loonies. Always in the thick of it." He shook his head.

"That's us, alright." Irling nodded solemnly.

Ludecan glanced at his lieutenant and gave him a half-smile. ***But my true brothers, nonetheless.*** The dead and the living alike had earned his respect. Unlike the pampered windbag he was going to be listening to in a moment.

DUKE SIRIC'S COMMAND TENT WAS LARGE, CROWDED, AND STUFFY. All fifty captains stood in a circle with their lieutenants behind them as the little fat man sweated in the center and blathered on about Edan's justice and his divine right to the dukedom of Norfast, which languished in the hands of disobedient heathens. No one believed a word of it. Not even Siric himself, like as not. Ludecan suppressed a yawn and grinded his teeth. It all boiled down to one thing: greed. Unsatisfied with the dukedom of Rimdale alone, the bloated little turd simply wanted more. Why was it the ones who already had too much wanted what belonged to other folk?

If it had been up to him, Ludecan would have chucked the whole thing and left the people of Norfast to determine their own future with their young duke. That way everyone could just go on pretending Norfast was a peaceful and happy part of Torrlond. But since he was in the army, and since King Earconwald had decided to favor Duke Siric in the matter, he had little choice. The king had loaned the Mercenary Company and a few other companies from the dukedom of Etinstone to Siric for his campaign. Everyone knew it was a poke in the eye to the king's cousin Duke Ethelred of Etinstone, who did not favor Siric's grab for Norfast. Of course, the vast majority of the captains present commanded companies belonging to Rimdale. They all pretended to swallow Siric's horse dung, but Ludecan knew the difference between a soldier who believed in a cause and one who obeyed because he had little choice.

Dressed as usual in his finest and decked out with ostentatious jewels, the oily duke exuded a garlic scent so strong that Ludecan caught cloying whiffs of it even where he stood. As he harangued his captive audience, Siric waggled his finger, and his jowls wobbled on his reddened face, reminding the captain of an over-ripe tomato.

"We will put an end to the traitors, even if we must scour every inch of Norfast. Our spies have informed us that Durathror's heir is hiding in a village just south of the North Downs. We must find and capture the pretender, and the day is won. Better to capture the boy alive since we may use him in our negotiations with the locals." He shrugged. "But dead will do as well. We begin the march on the morrow. Any questions?"

"My lord, what of the army that flanks us?" It was Sigbert who had spoken, one of the other captains from Etinstone. A sensible veteran. Good soldier. Like Ludecan, several of the other captains nodded at Sigbert's words.

"What of it?" said Siric, frowning as if the question made no sense.

"If we march too far north into their lands, they could surround us and cut us off from our supplies."

Duke Siric scoffed. "A rag-tag gaggle of boys and greybeards. It hardly warrants the title 'army,' don't you think?" He raised one eyebrow and smirked at the captain as if he were schooling a simple child.

The tent went silent. Ludecan observed the other captains' faces, which were grim. It was true that many of Norfast's finest warriors had perished in Sildharan when Bledla's dragons pounced, making no distinction between Torrlonders and their foes. It had been a terrible waste and a colossal miscalculation on someone's part. The official blame lay with the former supreme priest, but many whispered that King Earconwald had known and approved. Such rumors began with the Norfasters who had been in Sildharan with Duke Durathror. Some had escaped to tell the tale, and they reinforced the old men and boys of their dukedom, who had proved stout enough. Their "rag-tag gaggle" had kept Siric's forces back for weeks, harrying them and attacking when least expected. Siric's army was camped halfway between the towns of Rimdale and Norfast, well into the Norfasters' territory. Their foes knew the land well and used that knowledge to their advantage. A wise man would respect them, not dismiss them and try to march through them, as Siric planned.

Captain Sigbert did not answer the duke or say what every man was thinking. His stone face remained unchanged. "And what of the Thjoths? Is there any truth to the tales they will come to aid their kin?"

Siric scowled at the captain. "Rumors only. And even were there truth in them, all the more reason to hasten Durn's capture. Without him, they have no one to rally around. Once we march in, the boy won't evade us. Our victory will be swift."

Several of the captains glanced at one another. Others looked at the ground. Captain Sigbert stared at Duke Siric and frowned.

The duke cleared his throat. "But let us say the Thjoths do come. What then? Are you not men enough to handle undisciplined barbarians? Do you not know how to deal with the brutes?"

"Why don't we ask Captain Ludecan?" That damned idiot Captain Grimulf, a close friend of Ludecan's elder brother, was gesturing at him. "He's something of an expert on Thjoths." Grimulf smirked at Ludecan, and all the other faces in the tent, including Duke Siric's, turned toward him.

Ever since Captain Orvandil had deserted Torrlond's army, Ludwulf had encouraged his friends to talk up Ludecan's association with the Thjoth, as if the dragon slayer's treachery somehow extended to him, his former lieutenant. Ludecan stared at Grimulf and did not relinquish his sharp gaze as he spoke in a flat tone.

"The Thjoths relish surprise. They prefer attack to defense. They seek to hit hard and fast when you least expect it, seizing the advantage. Before you know they've hit you, they strike again. In such manner they often overwhelm superior and more organized forces. Their reputation for violence is well earned, especially when they seek *vengeance.*" *Chew on that, you fucking worm.*

He kept his eyes locked on Grimulf, who sneered at him.

The meaning of the exchange appeared to be lost on Duke Siric, who asked, "That's all very well, but how do we prepare for them? That is, *if* they turn up."

Ludecan turned his gaze toward the fat little man. "We pry our eyes open and keep them that way, my lord. And hope they don't turn up."

Siric's little piggy eyes blinked at Ludecan, and then he pouted. Another silence seized the tent.

"Nonsense," said the duke with a little too much force. "There's nothing to fear from the brutes." He dismissed the Thjoths with a wave of his pudgy hand, and then he looked around at all the captains. "You have your orders. Inform your troops that we march north early on the morrow."

EVEN AS HE CREPT BEHIND THE ROCKS, DUNEYR SMILED AT THE memory of Sivora scolding him in their hall in Valfoss before he set out with the warriors of Grimrik. *"Come back alive or I'll wring your skinny neck myself,"* she had said. He had given her a peck on the cheek, and she had grabbed him by the shoulders and squeezed him in a tight embrace that nearly smothered him. She released him and turned away to hide her tears. *"Get going then, man. Don't keep Vols waiting."*

He brought his mind back to the present, but his smile remained as he gazed at the six Torrlonder scouts who rested their steeds and sat chewing their rations only a couple hundred feet away at the bottom of a small dell. Beyond the dell, row upon row of green hills faded to a hazier grey the further they extended into the distance. The westering sun was only beginning to tinge them with the gilded hue of early evening.

Norfast's landscape was similar to Grimrik's. The land was folded into knolls and vales that sharpened northward into the rugged North Downs. It was well suited to the sheep dotting the steep hillsides and the hardy dwellers of farmsteads who celebrated their half-Thjothic ancestry. Of course, the people of Norfast were Torrlonders too and followers of the Way of Edan, not the old gods. But Duke Siric's greed and King Earconwald's stupidity had led to the Norfasters' persecution by their fellow Torrlonders, and they used their Thjothic heritage as an excuse for it. *If they want a quarrel with Thjoths*, he thought with a grin, *then we'll give them a full-blooded one.*

For a moment longer he studied the scouts and their position. The fools had not posted a lookout, nor had they noticed him or his men, which was just as well since Vols had sent him and the others out with the purpose of taking out as many Torrlonder scouts as possible. *"A blind foe is a stupid foe,"* the king had said. If that was true, the Torrlonders were about to become even stupider.

Duneyr turned to Vili, his Norfaster guide, and nodded. Vili's hair was nearly as red as Duneyr's own, as was his downy beard. The tall young man was capable and clever, and, like many from Norfast, he looked and sometimes even sounded like a Thjoth. Even though the Norfasters spoke the Northern Tongue like everyone else in Torrlond, they included many words in it that were unique to Norfast. Duneyr recognized them as remnants of the Thjothic their ancestors brought with them from Grimrik.

Singling out Halvard, Bodvar, Hakon, and Ekil One-Eye, Duneyr conveyed through hand gestures that the four of them should creep around the Torrlonders' position and cut them off from escape should they try to mount and gallop out the other side of the little valley. The four men set out, and Duneyr waited, counting out the time by steadying his breaths. When he reckoned they were in place, he turned to his other three men and hefted his spear to signify they should be ready to cast. They smiled and nodded. A finger over his lips told them to keep silent. No war cries. Surprise was more important.

His guts fluttered, and the usual rush of blood before battle tingled under his flesh while his heart beat faster. *No point in dwelling on it. Do what needs doing.* A quick nod, and he leapt over the rocks to break into a run. His warriors and Vili fanned out beside him. They covered half the distance before any of the grey-kirtled Torrlonders noticed them. First one cried out and shot up from the rock he was sitting on, spilling his food on the ground, and then the others rose. Horses neighed and screams broke out. His grip tight on the smooth ash of his spear shaft, Duneyr stuttered his steps and heaved. Before their foes' swords were out, he and his men had cast their spears.

Duneyr's missile took one in the shoulder, piercing his mail and shoving him backwards to crash on the ground. Three others cringed to the earth with shafts of ash burrowed in their ribs. The remaining two had their swords out and were facing Duneyr and his lads, who had drawn their steel on the run, when spear tips tore through their chests from behind and jerked them down face forward. Their weapons clanged on the ground next to them. Halvard, Ekil, Bodvar, and Hakon sprinted up from their position, their blades out.

Duneyr gazed down on the bloody scene. The horses snorted and neighed at the scent of battle, but they were picketed and did not try to bolt. Three of the Torrlonders were still alive, gasping and crawling away from the Thjoths with a trail of gore behind each. One of them was the man whose shoulder his spear had pierced. He frowned at them. "Finish them quick," he said in the Northern Tongue for Vili's benefit.

Bodvar raised his axe and beheaded one in a swift, meaty chop. Halvard pierced another through the neck. The man twitched for a moment and went still. The one Duneyr had wounded turned over on his back and raised his hands in supplication. He was young. Probably had not seen even a score of winters. "Please. Spare me. I won't tell no one. Just let me lie here. Take the horses, and I'll just stay put here."

Duneyr thought of his eldest son, who was almost of an age with the Torrlonder. He shook his head. *Never order your men to do anything you wouldn't do yourself.* "I wish I could, lad." He raised his sword.

"Please. I can tell you things."

"That would shame you. Better to die well."

"Edan have mercy!"

Duneyr swept his blade past the boy's hand into his neck, which yielded to the steel with a spray of red that spattered the grass. The Torrlonder shuddered and went still, his blank eyes still gazing up at the Thjoth.

"The gods have no mercy in war," he replied to the corpse beneath him. *Damn me. I shouldn't have spoken to him. Shouldn't have hesitated. I'll see this one's eyes in my dreams.* He turned to his men and said in Thjothic, "We'll take their horses and hasten back to King Vols. The attack will begin soon. If the others have had the same luck we have, the Torrlonders won't even know we're coming."

IT WAS MOVING WELL INTO EVENING WHEN LUDECAN RETURNED from a private conversation with Captain Sigbert through the camp, passing by supply carts, officers' tents, and troops laying out their sleeping mats under the open sky. Shedding gear, preparing dinner, and forming circles to dice, they were beginning to settle in for a bit of rest after a sweaty, dusty day of drills and fruitless scouting.

The camp felt wrong. Missing was the banter that reflected their usual confidence. Torrlond's army was formidable, but the soldiers did not like killing other Torrlonders, especially men they had served alongside. Rumors about what really happened to the Norfasters back in Sildharan had eaten holes in their morale. And even if the loyal captains from the dukedom of Rimdale feigned belief in Siric's cause, the troops that served under them did not bother with such a farce. *This whole damn business just doesn't sit right, and they know it.*

He wove his way back to the portion of the camp where the Mercenary Company of Etinstone had landed. The westering sun was lending a subdued glow to the air, and cook fires were already burning, giving off smoke and the meaty scent of rations. When he closed in on the perimeter of his company's encampment, the soldier on guard duty stood straighter and gave him a sharp salute. *Must be a green recruit.* One of the veterans would have kept leaning on his spear and called out a lazy greeting, or just spat. If the boy lived long enough, he would learn to relax.

It turned out to be Oswin, a wiry little fellow not much wider than his spear. Formerly one of Etinstone's street urchins, he was wary and observant, which was likely how he had managed to survive long enough to make it to the cusp of manhood. Only to be caught stealing bread. Presented with the choice of joining the Mercenary Company or losing a hand, he had decided on the former. Ludecan wondered when he would start regretting his decision. At least he was likely eating better than ever before, which was a sad statement indeed.

"Evening, Oswin."

"Evening, m'lord."

"How went the exercises?"

"Lieutenant Irling drilled us hard, m'lord. That he did."

"Good. Where is he?"

"Yonder by the fire, m'lord."

"Carry on, then."

The captain headed for the fire, around which a group of veterans sat on stones or logs. They were so animated about something they were chatting about, they did not notice his approach, and so Ludecan walked up to them without a noise and listened in. It turned out to be the company's favorite topic of late. *Should've guessed.*

"If you'd 'a seen him like I did, you'd never talk like such a lard-head," said Utred.

"Who's the lardhead? I *seen* him, 'cause I was standing right next to you." Garmund gestured with his hands at Utred's side.

Utred wrinkled his crooked nose and frowned. "You was?"

"Can't remember a damned thing ever since that aglak smacked you in the face with Ingbald's head."

"Shut up. I can so."

"Oh, yeah? What'd we eat for breakfast this morning?"

Utred scratched his ear and frowned. "Uh . . ."

"Same shit we always eat," said Bernred. "But that ain't the point." The big man encompassed them all with a wide gesture of his arms. "We was *all* there. We all seen him come from the sky on the biggest damned dragon in Edan's creation with a great big bloody light all around him."

"That we did." Mull nodded and gazed into the fire. "And after he defeated the most powerful supreme priest in living memory, when the sky went dark, and a mortal terror crept into the bones of every witness, we all cowered the same. Don't one of you tell me you didn't feel it."

Captain Ludecan shivered at Mull's words and the memory they evoked.

"Bah," said Garmund, and he spat into the fire. But he frowned and chewed on his lip and did not look up.

"And we all heard what he said." Sergeant Rhof stared at the others as if challenging any of them to disagree. "There's no denying that."

Sergeant Bosa shook his head. "But what a man *says* he is and what a man *is* ain't always the same thing. We all knew him. How come he weren't no prophet before?"

"Did we know him?" Lieutenant Irling shook his head and half-smiled at the others. "Sometimes I wonder. And don't forget there were signs before. In Hasumere. He saved our skins. And when he took control of the aglak, he didn't say a word. Not like all the other priests and wizards and such. No spell or song. Not a blessed word. I tell you he's different."

"All I know about him," said a voice close to the ground, "is no one's heard a fucking peep from him since Thulhan." It was Hewald. One of the quickest and fiercest fighters Ludecan had ever seen, he had joined the company after Dayraven and Orvandil disappeared in Caergilion, but he had been at the Battle of Thulhan and, like the rest of them, seen Dayraven and the dragon after the lad defeated Bledla. He was lying on the ground near the fire with his eyes closed and his fingers interlaced behind his head. "What kind of a fucking prophet disappears and says not a fucking word? Shouldn't he be telling us Edan's will or something?"

"Might be that ain't how it works," said Utred.

Hewald ignored him. "Tell you what I think: Your old comrade had one over on all of us. He may be a clever wizard, but he ain't no fucking prophet, 'cause there's no such thing. Edan and prophets and the Way. It's all horseshit."

"Mind your tongue, or it's likely to get cut out," said Sergeant Rhof. "Or burned along with the rest of you. There's those not so far off that'd take it amiss to hear such talk."

Hewald yawned and stretched. "The same ones that'd take it amiss to hear *you* jabber about your prophet. 'Sides, I ain't talking to them. We're a fucking mercenary company, so we don't have to pretend to believe anything, long as we kill when they say kill. Faith and prophecies are shit people talk about to get what they want."

"So what'd *he* want, then?" Bernred folded his beefy arms in front of him.

Hewald opened his eyes and frowned. "To stop the war over in Sildharan, I reckon."

Aye, thought Captain Ludecan. *But why? And why did he and Orvandil switch sides?* "Don't you lads have anything else to prattle about?"

The men all started, and some of them stood. Even Hewald sat up.

Garmund smiled. "What do you say, Captain?"

"About what?"

"About the Prophet of Edan, who walked in our midst." He widened his eyes in mock wonder and waggled his fingers before elbowing Utred, who scowled at his friend.

Ludecan thought about the Battle of Thulhan, where he had been one of the thousands to witness Dayraven's descent on the dragon. He brought to mind the strange feeling that had always tickled the back of his mind in the lad's presence, even on the first day he met him and pretended he was going to hang him and his southern friend. Most of all, he recalled gawking slack-jawed as the most fearful wonder he had ever known clutched every inch of his flesh. He had faced death many times in battle, but this was vaster and darker than anything he had ever known, like the end of everything. Even thinking about it raised goosebumps all over him. That day on the battlefield outside Thulhan, even the sight of the mightiest dragon in Eormenlond paled in comparison to the bliss and terror emanating from Dayraven.

He opened his mouth to say something, but just then a horn wailed in the distance. Shouts immediately followed.

"What the fuck's that?" Hewald bolted up.

The men all tensed, some putting their hands on their sword hilts, and those who had not stood before were up.

"Shit. Camp's under attack," said Captain Ludecan. "Get your gear back on and rouse the others. Ready yourselves double-quick and form up!"

The men all scrambled about, and Ludecan strode toward his tent to retrieve his shield. *I told that ass the Thjoths like giving surprises.*

"NOT TOO FAR, LADS!" SHOUTED DUNEYR OVER THE SCREAMS, WAR cries, and clashing of steel. "We're not carving our way through the whole damned Torrlonder army."

So far it had been easy, and the timing was just about right. As the sun was going down, they had caught the Torrlonders unprepared, just as Vols planned. The younger, more eager warriors were moving too far ahead, though. Any further, and they would become too entangled with the foe to retreat when the signal came. Their task was to stir up the Torrlonders, give them a shock, retreat into the gathering darkness, and see if the foe would be foolish enough to follow. Vols and the rest were waiting out there to close the trap. Duneyr turned to the greybeard next to him and pointed to a knot of warriors led by Halvard. "Emund! Put a rein on those lads."

Emund gave a smile that exposed his few teeth, which were as grey as his beard. "A bit too keen, are they? I'll fetch them back." He set off.

Gazing through of the melee, Duneyr spotted Torrlonder formations on their way. These were more organized and ready for combat than the half-dressed, jumbled troops the Thjoths were scything through. He would give the signal soon. He squinted ahead through the gloaming. The sky was beginning to purple, but not far away, he could make out dark masses of warriors led by Grimling, Kialar, Arinbjorn, and Asgrim. Grimling's warriors were too close to the enemy lines, and a company of Torrlonders was heading right for them. The others appeared to be in a good position.

He grabbed Hakon's arm and yanked him. "Get over there and tell Grimling to pull his arse back!"

"On my way," said the young warrior before he sprinted off.

Duneyr turned to another of the men posted near him. A large horn hung from the chain around old Skapti's neck. "Be ready to sound the signal."

WOUNDED SOLDIERS STRAGGLED IN THE OTHER DIRECTION AS Ludecan marched his troops in a wide shieldwall of two rows toward the fighting. Some of the blood-spattered survivors supported or carried others. The shouting and clashing of steel were growing louder, and other formations of troops were converging toward the battle. He searched for the duke's standard so he could send a messenger for orders. It was growing harder to see in the dusk, and Siric's command post appeared to be nowhere. Barring any instructions, he would head straight for the battle to find out what needed doing.

Behind the captain, Oswin asked in a shaky voice, "Who done this?"

"Thjoths, boy," said Hewald. "Can't you hear nothin'?"

"Wh . . . Where'd they come from?"

"Out Duke Siric's fat fucking arse. Who cares? Now we fight."

"But . . ."

"Just stay near me, boy, and don't do nothin' stupid."

Up ahead, as eventide was curtaining the sky, Ludecan caught his first glimpse of the fighting. Men in grey kirtles were stumbling back as tall, light-haired warriors swarmed over them. He turned toward his soldiers, and his blade whispered out of its scabbard before he pointed it toward the battle. "Hold the line! Shields up, swords out!"

A chorus of steel sang as he dropped back to merge into the shieldwall. Hewald was on his left, and Bernred on his right. *Good men to have around.* Lieutenant Irling commanded the second row, and the four sergeants were spread throughout the ranks. "March double-time!" he shouted, and he set the pace for his men. His shield and sword already weighed heavy on his arms, and his breaths came fast as he jogged closer to the fight. *Getting too fucking old for this shit.*

A company linked with Ludecan's on the left, and another on his right. Other companies were not far away. They were just in time. The few Torrlonder defenders remaining in front of them were dying fast or fleeing back. It was time to put a halt to the Thjoths' advance. Hundreds of the tall warriors boiled through the tattered remains of the grey ranks with triumphant screams, cutting down the slow and wounded in their path. They rushed headlong for the Mercenary Company of Etinstone.

"Hold the line!" yelled Ludecan. "Defensive stance until more of our lads come! Halt and wait for them! Lock shields and keep them up!"

Lieutenant Irling and the sergeants repeated his commands, and Ludecan brought his company to an ordered stop. The other companies stood their ground too, awaiting the Thjothic onslaught.

"Aldmund's blessed balls," said Oswin. "They're huge."

"Aye," said Hewald. "But they bleed the same as we do."

The tall warriors of Grimrik came on with their battle cries. Their reddened blades shone in the last rays of the evening sun, which stabbed the field from beneath the clouds.

"Hold the line!" yelled Ludecan.

Steel keened and bodies crunched against shields when the Thjoths slammed into the Torrlonder line. Ludecan and his men swayed backwards, but they held. Screams erupted everywhere, and the captain focused on staying alive, praying his men would be able to do the same and keep their line intact for as long as possible. They needed to give the rest of the camp a chance to organize and counter the assault. A horn sounded in the distance, but Ludecan did not think it was one of theirs. He could not dwell on it, for the battle had reached him.

A big axe crunched on his shield's rim, sending splinters flying and a shock up the captain's arm. "Hold the line!" screamed Ludecan. "Shields up!"

A huge Thjoth roared as his blade sawed the air and whistled like a windmill toward the captain's head. The captain ducked behind his shield and grimaced when steel collided with wood with a loud crack that shoved him back and jarred every bone in his body. Knowing it would shatter at the next hard blow, Ludecan slipped off his shield and grunted as he heaved it at his attacker. It bounced off the man's chest, distracting him long enough to allow the captain to slide in and chop at the man's leg, slicing through muscle and cracking bone. With blood streaming from the gash, the big fellow went down, and his sword clattered on top of him.

Ludecan moved in for the kill, but another Thjoth rushed at him, and he parried to avoid being hacked in two. The blades clanged, and the captain fell back a step as his attacker pressed. He growled as he tried to push back his foe, but then something clutched his leg, and he lost his footing.

The ground punched into his back and he grunted. The Thjoth whose leg he had hacked was digging into his calf with his fingers, spitting and snarling like an enraged beast as he tugged Ludecan closer as if to tear him apart with his teeth. The other one straddled the captain with his blade aloft, and he swung down hard. Ludecan shoved his sword in front of his face, holding tight with both hands. Steel screamed, and the blades locked just an inch from Ludecan's nose. He strained and growled with the effort to keep the Thjoth from carving his face. Red smeared the edge of the man's blade, and a drop pattered on Ludecan's cheek.

A sudden blur crashed into the attacker above the captain, freeing Ludecan to roll over and plunge his blade into the raging mouth of the Thjoth who was dragging him by the leg. The big man's scream choked off when sharp steel shattered his teeth and sliced through his throat to emerge on the other side of his head. Ludecan tugged free his sword, which slurped out of the man's ruined face and emerged dripping with red. He rose in time to see Hewald deliver a flurry of blows to the other Thjoth before catching the man off balance and hacking halfway through his neck with a loud crunch. The Thjoth's head hung at an odd angle as he plunged down like a dropped sack.

Hewald turned toward Ludecan. The captain gave his soldier a brief nod, which the man returned. The tumult of a few moments ago had ceased. Other than the groans of the wounded, there was a strange silence. The Thjoths were making an orderly retreat into the falling twilight. So orderly that he suspected the attack had been a feint. But with what goal in mind?

Ludecan scanned the horizon for threats while Hewald rushed toward a fallen comrade. Except for their few dead, the Thjoths had departed with the same suddenness with which they arrived. From the camp many more companies were marching toward the finished battle.

The captain dropped his sword and released a long sigh. Panting hard, soaked with sweat, and spattered with blood, he put his hands on his knees and leaned down to catch his breath. There were many more corpses on the field in grey kirtles than not. The Thjoths had given much worse than they got, and though the Torrlonders would pursue them, Ludecan knew well they would not catch them. Darkness would enshroud them soon, and no doubt the Thjoths had the aid of the locals to negotiate the benighted landscape. Timed with perfection, this had been a probing attack, a mere test of the Torrlonders' readiness. *And we failed.* It could even be a trap, and those who pursued the Thjoths had best be wary. He was too damn tired to warn them. *Not my problem. I've got my wounded to tend to.*

He staggered over to where Hewald crouched over someone. Ludecan winced when he recognized him. The lad Oswin was lying on the ground gasping and shivering. Hewald had found a stick and a rag to make a tourniquet, which he was twisting around Oswin's arm to stop the stream of blood pumping out of the raw stump where his wrist had been. The younger man was staring at where his hand should have been, and his gasps turned into giggles.

"What's so fucking funny?" asked Hewald.

Oswin did not answer him. Instead, the eyes in his pale, sweaty face met Captain Ludecan's, and he smiled as he trembled. "Could'a saved all that marching. Eh, captain?"

Ludecan grunted and tried to smile back. Lose a hand or join the Mercenary Company of Etinstone. *Shit.* "Try to relax, soldier. Hewald will stop your bleeding, and then we'll get you patched up. There's plenty a one-handed soldier can do. One time there was this fellow in the company who lost a hand. He rigged up a hook tied to his arm. Damnedest thing if he wasn't a better fighter with that hook."

Oswin stared up at him with vacant eyes, his smile sagging only a little.

Hewald stopped twisting the tourniquet and let the arm drop. "Fuck. All bled out. Wasn't much in the poor little bastard. He never belonged here."

Ludecan frowned. *He never belonged anywhere.* "You did what you could. We'll bury him proper. But first let's find others we can save." He turned away from Oswin's corpse.

DUNEYR SAT ON A BENCH IN A VILLAGE INN AT A LONG TABLE IN THE common room. It was a cheerful, bright room with a large fireplace that was vacant save for ashes since sunlight streamed in the windows. Around the table were ranged King Vols and his other chieftains, Arinbjorn, Grimling, Kialar, and Asgrim. Grimling's arm was in a sling, but the others were unhurt from the night's work. Duneyr would not have called it a battle. It was more like a slaughter of dumb animals, for several companies of Torrlonders had marched straight into King Vols's trap. Their cries in the darkness must have alarmed their fellow Torrlonders since the other companies had returned to their camp without engaging the Thjoths and Norfasters awaiting them.

At the table too was young Durn, the rightful Duke of Norfast, and his chief advisors. They were eating their meat and drinking their mead in good spirits, celebrating the victory but also planning their next move against the invading troops.

"We've bloodied their noses, and that fool Siric likely still believes you're up north, my lord," said grey-haired Earl Torf to the young duke. One of the few nobles who made it out of Sildharan alive, he was perhaps Durn's most trusted advisor, and he had already earned Duneyr's respect. "We should keep it that way. Let our men continue to feed his spies with false reports of your whereabouts. In the meantime, with the aid of our brethren under King Vols, we'll keep harrying Siric's troops."

Durn faced King Vols. "What do you say, my lord? May we continue to count on your aid?" No whiskers grew yet on the lad's cheeks, and his voice was just beginning to deepen, but he was tall and broad for his age, as his father had been. But where Durathror had been quick to laughter and anger alike, Durn stayed strangely calm, like a man much older and wiser than his years. His long blond hair was tied back in the manner of the Thjoths, and he gazed at Vols with his bright blue eyes, which spoke of a serenity that could face any storm without blinking. In fact, more than of anyone else, he reminded Duneyr of Orvandil Dragonbane. He had decided to like the lad the moment he met him.

Vols swallowed the mead he had been sipping from his mug, then he wiped his beard with his sleeve. He smiled at Durn before he answered. "You may. We remain in Norfast until your fellow Torrlonders see sense and recognize your title. King Earconwald must realize Siric's ambitions are too costly."

Earl Torf cleared his throat. "Forgive me, King Vols, but as much as it pains me, I must ask of your own ambitions. We are grateful beyond words for your timely help, but if you should claim Norfast for Grimrik, it could lead to a costly and long war. If I may be so bold as to ask, what do you intend?"

The King of the Thjoths nodded. "A man may be both bold and wise, and it's best for friends to speak their minds in the open. I vow to the gods I have no ambitions for Norfast, and neither do my people. In the sacred Thingvang our warriors answered your summons, swearing we would aid Norfast in return for the loyalty Duke Durathror showed us at the Battle of Thulhan. Anything less would invite shame upon us, especially when we are kin. Anything more would be foolhardy. Given our numbers, to rule one realm sundered by the Hrones Sea would be nigh impossible, as our ancestors found when they sailed to these lands. Our goal is to restore Durn to his rightful place, but you must decide how to live with your fellow Torrlonders, for you are also of their blood."

"Fair words," said Randver, the youngest of the young duke's advisors. His father had died in the dragon fire back in Sildharan. "But what do the Thjoths gain from it all?"

Vols's smile grew fierce and eager. "Honor. Glory. And if all goes as we wish, a friendlier neighbor in Torrlond's north than that fool Siric would be."

"What of the present threat to your realm?" asked Durn. "With your warriors here, your lands are exposed to the Torrlonders."

"Only a third of our number has sailed here. Our border with Torrlond is well guarded. Besides that, your fellow Torrlonders are busy with the war in the south. Caergilion and Adanon are far from tamed. You may have larger problems as well. The Ilarchae in the east were not pleased when King Earconwald abandoned them in Sildharan. He'll likely have little time or resources to spare for us."

"Your answers satisfy me, my lord, and again I thank you." Durn bowed his head toward Vols. "But what next?"

Gesturing toward Duneyr, Vols smiled again. "Duneyr noticed a few things during the battle with Siric's troops. He has some ideas I've asked him to share with you all. Listen well, for he's a crafty one, is our Duneyr."

All the faces around the table turned to him, and Duneyr graced them with his own large grin. "My lords, we shall make Siric regret his false claim. By the time we finish with him and his troops, he'll be running back to Rimdale as fast as his chubby little nether-cheeks will take him. I think this will please you . . ."

"VENGEANCE! DAMN THE THJOTHS AND ALL THEIR DESCENDANTS. I shall have vengeance!" Duke Siric's jowls flapped as he shook his pudgy fist. The man's face was so red that Captain Ludecan wondered if he would burst. He half considered poking him with his sword to find out.

He had obeyed the summons to the duke's command tent to report on what he had seen the evening before. As grim as it was, his was likely the best news to come out of the whole disaster. The Thjoths had wiped out four companies, and others had taken significant losses. Ludecan reckoned the Mercenary Company of Etinstone was fortunate to have lost only a dozen men.

By stopping the Thjoths, his lads were responsible for saving Siric's army from a worse mauling. Of course, that had not prevented the duke from ordering the other companies straight into the Thjoths' trap. Many had died in the blazes the Thjoths set alight with flaming arrows shot into fields they had prepared with pitch. The fires had glowed eerily in the night while the maddened, helpless screams of trapped soldiers filled the air.

The Duke of Rimdale pounded the armrest of his chair. "Edan curse the wretched heathens! How dare they come here? How *dare* they? The king will hear of this, and we will punish the Thjoths."

Not bloody likely, thought Ludecan. Earconwald was too busy far off in the south, and even when the King of Torrlond did hear of the disastrous campaign, it was more likely Siric's tender hide that would be in most danger. His ambition to take Norfast, motivated by greed that was exceptional even for a nobleman, had thus far yielded only a catastrophic waste of lives and resources. He reckoned the boy Durn would be in good shape to negotiate fair terms with Earconwald in return for submitting to the king's peace. Then it would be good riddance to this bloated toad for him and the Mercenary Company of Etinstone. He resisted the urge to wrinkle his nose at the garlic stench emanating from the man. "Will there be anything else, my lord?"

Siric gazed at him from his seat with a puzzled pout, as if unable to comprehend words through his rage. He waved his fingers, little sausages encircled by gaudy rings, at the captain in dismissal. "You may withdraw from my presence."

Gladly. Same way I'd withdraw from a bad fart. Ludecan turned his back on the fool and passed by the guards to exit the tent, blinking and breathing a sigh as the brighter outdoor light and cleaner air surrounded him. He would return to his men to check on the wounded. Soon enough they would move out and blunder into some other disaster before it was all over. He shook his head. *Damn Siric and his vengeance.*

9

IN QUEST OF THE PROPHET

Abon frowned at the sad spectacle. The former plantation owner shivered as he stared wide-eyed and told his story. He stank of sweat and smoke, and the once fine silks he wore were filthy. Having tracked the prints Dayraven's horse made to the remains of the plantation, the four companions had found the man hiding in the charred ruins of his abode, what had been a palatial country villa before the Ilarchae slaves destroyed it. He was alone and half-mad, but there was no doubt he had seen Dayraven and spoken to him.

The shaper could understand enough Andumaic to make out what the man was saying, especially since he had been a nobleman and spoke a more formal version of the language. The wretch focused for the most part on Galdor, who, of the four companions, had the best command of Andumaic by far and did most of the speaking for their party. But he also stole occasional glances at Abon and Gnorn, and every time his gaze fell on Orvandil, he flinched as if he had touched a piece of metal fresh from a forge.

Abon wondered if the big Thjoth reminded the man of the Ilarchae. To judge by the state of the plantation, there would be few fond recollections there. The Ilarchae slaves had been thorough in their destruction when they rebelled and headed north to join the Battle of Thulhan. Soon the Ilarchae would return, this time as masters. Fortunately, the hunt for Dayraven was leading the four of them out of Sildharan.

To the north, Shohan had been a seething mess, its citizens rushing about in various stages of panic over the impending arrival of the Ilarchae. People were fleeing in every conceivable direction, but nowhere was there certainty of survival. Amidst the pervasive terror, a few individuals were proclaiming the salvation of the Prophet of Edan. It was the end of times, they insisted, and only the Prophet's message offered a way out. But few agreed on what that message was. *Repent!* some cried. *Give up all possessions and claims*, said others. *Sit and meditate on your end,* said still others. Abon reckoned their end would not be long in coming if they sat and waited for the Ilarchae.

South of Shohan, they had picked up Dayraven's trail again. The lad seemed to have skirted the city and the larger towns and villages, as if not wishing to draw near large gatherings of people. In fact, he seemed to avoid company as much as possible, only entering small villages or farmsteads when he needed water and food.

But the young man made quite an impression wherever he did stop, and the Prophet of Edan's reputation grew the further south they rode. When Dayraven interacted with people, he seemed to show them their truest selves, naked of pretense and delusion. Some of the most common reactions included the deepest, most transcending bliss of their lives; a mortal terror that left them gibbering with guilt and regret; or a potent combination of those things with a resolve to better themselves. There was no doubt which category the former plantation owner fell under. Abon wondered if he had lost his wits before or after his encounter with Dayraven.

"Even when the Ilarchae slaughtered everyone and I hid from them, I was not so terrified as that." The man's eyes shifted toward Orvandil, and he winced at the big man's shadow. "The sky darkened. The sky, I tell you. When he approached . . . One moment it was blue, the next ash grey. And I saw . . . I heard . . . By Oruma and Anghara, it was . . . Death walked in his wake. I could not move. He saw through me. Straight through. I was . . . bare. I could not speak for shame and fear until he commanded me."

"What did he say to you?" The wizard Galdor crouched down to see eye to eye with the man, who huddled in a corner of one of the few rooms in the villa where the ceiling remained. The walls were blackened and pocked. Broken and scorched pieces of furniture lay everywhere. Their boots grinded bits of smashed pottery that littered the floor, upon which dark stains that appeared to be dried blood covered the remains of what had been a magnificent mosaic. The detritus of a once prosperous life. Plenty of light streamed in a broken wall on the far side of the room.

The man blinked, and his lips trembled as if he would speak, but no words came. Finally, he found his voice. "Say? At first, he did not speak to me. He did not use words, that is. But I could hear him in my mind. In my mind, you see?" He stared at Galdor and pointed to his own head. "What he put there. Even now, I see it. Day and night, I see it. It haunts me." He grimaced and clutched his temples.

The wizard frowned at the man and said in a gentle voice, "Try to tell us what he said. It could be important. We need to find him."

The man curled into a ball and covered his face with his hands. Either incapable of answering or unwilling, he whimpered and sobbed as his fingers tore at his hair.

Galdor's frown deepened as he looked up at Abon, and he shook his head. The shaper shrugged. He knew a broken man when he saw one. Sildharan was brimming with them now.

The wizard turned back to the man. "Ofttimes, when a man reveals a thing to another, it loses its power over him. If you tell us, it may haunt you no longer. Or, at least, a little less."

The man trembled and sobbed a moment longer, and then one of his eyes peeked out from between his fingers. "A wicked life. A wasted life."

"Yours?"

The man nodded and looked at the floor. "Everything. Everything I had done. Even when the Ilarchae slaughtered my family, I saved myself. Like a coward, I hid. And before that, all the wicked things . . . My deeds. All weighed. I saw them all. Felt them all. What they did to

. . . people. To my shame. Like a worm exposed when the rock it cowers under is overturned. I could not hide." He shook and sobbed, and Galdor waited awhile.

"And did he then speak?"

"No." The man sniffed and wiped his nose with his dirty silk sleeve. "Not words. But I could *hear* him. In my mind. The voices were there."

"Voices?"

"Within my head. And all around me. Two of them."

"Two?"

"Yes. Both his."

"What do you mean? How could you distinguish them?"

"They . . . debated. In my mind, I heard them. One pitied me. Wished to spare me. The other . . . It was so cold. Dark. Oh, by the Mother and Father, I dare not say." His body trembled, and his head shook back and forth.

Galdor leaned closer to the man and almost whispered as he placed a hand on his shoulder. "Please try. What did the voice say? Was it angry?"

The man's eyes bulged as they stared at Galdor, but Abon sensed he was seeing something far away. "No. Not angry. Indifferent. And it promised the end."

"The end? The end of what?"

The man's head and shoulders shivered, and his eyes returned to the present. He frowned, and a tear tracked down his dirty cheek. "Of life. Everything."

In spite of the heat, an icy finger traced a line down Abon's spine, and even the wizard Galdor remained silent. The shaper thought he knew what this madman was talking about. Though he had passed out from his wounds before Dayraven's arrival at the Battle of Thulhan, he had heard about what everyone saw there. Sometimes he thought he saw it in his dreams. And he had met Dayraven after the battle, sensed the lad battling the thing dwelling in him, the elf-shard, with its fierce desire to break free.

Galdor broke the silence. "And the other voice? The one that pitied you?"

The man released a long sigh, and his whole body shivered. "So much shame. I don't deserve such pity. The Mother and Father know I don't. *This* is what I deserve." He gestured with both hands at the room around them, and then he shook his head and wiped his eyes with his grimy, sooty hands before gazing again at the floor.

"What did the other voice say?"

The man faced Galdor and nodded. "That is the one that spoke to me, I think. In words. He asked only for water for him and his horse. And directions south, through Golgar. He spoke Andumaic. I had thought he was an Ilarchae. His hair was almost white. But he spoke like a nobleman. A sorcerer. Oh, but he was much more than that."

Galdor's smile was sad and did not reach his eyes. "I know."

"The Prophet. He came to *me*. All that's left is to wait."

"Wait for what?"

The man smiled for the first time, but it was a grin of madness. "For death, of course. There's nothing else."

THAT NIGHT, THEY CAMPED IN THE SHADOWS OF THE FOOTHILLS marking the border between Sildharan and Golgar. Abon was glad to stop, for his legs and lower back were weary and sore from all their riding, and a building sense of dread seeped away his will. None of them spoke much. Ever since they had left the plantation, they hardly even looked at each other. *We might see our own thoughts written on each other's faces.* The more they learned of Dayraven, the deeper their dread grew. None of them would say as much, but a darkness was creeping over them. And yet, their task grew more urgent by the moment. Every day the lad was out there alone, the odds of a catastrophic release of power grew greater. The shaper had never seen Galdor so worried.

After laying out his spare cloak to sleep on, Abon peered through the murk to steal a glance at the others, whose forms he could make out under the dim moonlight. With a red glow bathing his wrinkled face, Gnorn was on his knees nursing a fire to life with kindling and wood they had collected while Orvandil tended to the horses. Deep in thought, Galdor sat on a stone and placed his hands on his head. The shaper knew the wizard well enough not to disturb him. He had many memories with the old man, going back to the day Galdor saved his life after zealots of the Way attacked him and left him for dead for nothing more than singing of the old gods. Since then, they had experienced many adventures along with the quiet, unspeakable moments shared by friends who know each other well.

It had been an honor all these years to do the wizard's bidding, and still he owed the old man a great debt. At first, he had done what he could to help Dayraven for Galdor's sake. But he realized with a soft smile that he was seeking the lad now for different reasons. *The boy understood. Best damn listener I ever had. He knew why I sing the old tales. Keeping them alive out of defiance and celebration. And he's my friend, too.*

Abon slipped his harp out of its green sack and, after tuning it, plucked at it absently while thoughts of Dayraven roamed through his mind. When they finally caught up to him, which Dayraven would greet them? Would he know them? And would Galdor be able to help him find his way back? The wizard had admitted all he could do was guess. *He's a good lad*, thought Abon. *Else he would've succumbed to it long ago. Stronger than we all could've guessed. He'll beat it yet.*

Gnorn's fire began to crackle and flames flickered to life, casting the growing red glow on their little camp. Dim as it was, Abon smiled at it and the small comfort it provided. Other than the remote stars far above them and the bone-white sliver of moon, darkness surrounded the vast space outside their camp. But by the ruddy light he could see the faces of his companions, who sat around the fire and faced one another. The wrinkles around Gnorn's eyes deepened when he smiled at Abon. "I'd welcome a song, master shaper. Such a night seems made for one."

Abon nodded and strummed a succession of notes, warming up his fingers, which curled and circled in a blur as they brushed the strings. "Of course. What sort of song?"

The Dweorg frowned for a moment, then he nodded toward Orvandil, who was sitting down beside him. "Let the big fellow decide."

The shaper looked at the Thjoth and plucked out another series of notes, elevating them at the end as if posing a question.

Orvandil gave a half-smile. "A quest."

"A quest." Abon struck the strings, and his fingers pulled forth a martial rhythm. "What sort of quest? One that ends ill?" The tune slowed and softened, but his fingers kept the rhythm going without interruption. "Or one that ends well?" and the notes ascended in triumph.

"Makes no matter." The Thjoth shrugged. "They all end."

The wizard Galdor sat up and returned to the present with a smile. "Sing of Froda when he walked with Sithfar."

Abon returned the smile and nodded, and the rhythm flowing from his harp intensified. Said to be an ancestor of Folcwalda, the king who led his people out of Ellond to found Torrlond, Froda was a hero from the age of legends, when men still encountered the gods. But Froda, who was famed as much for his wits as for his courage, was the only mortal ever to return from a journey with the god Sithfar, whose task was to conduct every soul into the final mystery. He was said to have fulfilled his quest to glimpse what lay beyond the known shores by tricking Sithfar out of his cloak and staff through a bargain and switching places with him. But what he saw on that journey he never revealed, for part of the bargain was to keep his silence, and if he broke that vow he would return to that place. Of all the wisdom he gained on his many travels, that was the one piece he could never share. Many said the madness that at length took Froda came of that festering secret, the great mystery that ate at his mind, and that was what finally claimed his life. Thus, in the end, the god outwitted the trickster.

The shaper strummed out an intricate series of trills and chords, weaving a tone laden with mists and shadows before he returned to a steady rhythm. By the firelight he glimpsed the faces of his three companions, whose eyes were fixed on him, ready for the tale to fill them. Eyes half-closed, he unleashed his word-hoard, his memory, and his voice at once, transporting them all to the age of legends:

The years have all yielded — the yore-days long gone,
The eldest of ages — to an era less bright.
But when gods roamed the ground and guarded the realms
From monsters that murdered, from the malice of wights,
Then warriors wielded the wisdom of old,
They battled and bled. Bold were their deeds.

The fearless fighter, Froda the wise,
Sailed over seas, seeking far coasts,
Marched over mountains, mapping the lands,
From shoals where shining shores meet earth,
To the hallowed heights in the hinterlands.
He wandered the world, the whale-roads he crossed,
Many folk he befriended, Fyrnwita's son,
And with cunning he conquered the kings who beset him.
Gundahar the grim, his grip was strong,
But the fiercest of fighters, Froda the bold,
He outwitted the warlord, and won his way free.
And Vormun devoured the vastest of foes,
The ancient ent — he ended his days
When Froda son of Fyrnwita fractured his skull.
But heavy and hard was that hero's greatest feat
When he sought out Sithfar, the silent god . . .

On Froda's ancient journey the shaper took Galdor, Gnorn, and Orvandil. He sang until the fire dwindled into glowing embers, and when the tale ended, they slept beneath the stars, gathering strength for the task ahead.

THEY HAD CROSSED THE BORDER AND RIDDEN WELL INTO THE PLAIN of Golgar when Galdor began to notice the movements of troops. It had been only a matter of time before some of them accosted their little party. Sitting atop his trotting horse, the wizard squinted into the distance and shielded his eyes from the sun with one hand. Like tiny dots with a dust cloud in their wake, a group of black clad Golgae soldiers was riding toward them across the flat plain. Neither fleeing nor skulking would avail them since trying to avoid their pursuers would only attract more attention. Still, it was a damned nuisance since they were already so far behind Dayraven. *We've got to find the boy soon.*

"Mostlike a scouting party," said Orvandil, who rode next to him. "Thirty riders."

Galdor frowned. "I mislike it. King Veduir is planning something. Something rather stupid, I fear."

Gnorn flicked his rein and edged his sturdy little mountain horse closer. "You think he means to stick his nose in the fight between the Sildharae and the Ilarchae?"

"If he does," said Abon from behind the wizard, "he may find the bite he takes a hard one to swallow."

Galdor pulled on his reins, and the others brought their mounts to a halt beside him. "The hatred between the Golgae and the Sildharae runs deep. But, since there's naught we can do about it, we'd do best to stay out of it. Our immediate concern is what to do about those soldiers." The steeds snorted, and their muscles twitched. Knowing the beasts sensed the approach of other horses, the wizard felt their tension. He let out a long sigh as he watched the Golgae scouts grow closer.

"We can't outrun them," said Abon. "Our horses are tired."

"Might be they'd just like a little chat, eh?" Gnorn winked at Orvandil, whose big hand rested on the pommel of the sword the Dweorg had wrought for him. The Thjoth gave his friend a half-smile.

The wizard stroked his beard for a moment, but then he nodded as he reached a decision. "We'll wait for them and see what they have to say. It's possible they've had word of Dayraven's passing through here." He climbed down from his horse and patted it on the neck. He looked up at the others and smiled. "Care to join me for a quick nap?"

The others dismounted and sat nearby. The wizard lay down in the deep grass with his fingers intertwined behind his head and gazed up at the wind driving wispy clouds across the crisp, azure sky. The same wind hissed through the grass and caressed his face, and bright sunlight glimmered across his vision. Galdor took deep, calming breaths, and his consciousness rode the breeze as his body waited.

The distant pounding of hooves did not take long to grow louder. When the scouting party reached them, the soldiers fanned out on their steeds and surrounded the four companions, their spears poised before them.

Galdor stretched and sat up with a groan. "Greetings!" he said in

Andumaic with his palms raised. "No need to point your spears at us. We are peaceful travelers."

"Who are you, and what are you doing in the kingdom of Golgar?" The soldiers were all wearing silver corselets over their black tunics, and their helms gleamed in the sunlight. The one who had spoken also had a white plume on his helm. Some of their horses neighed and tamped the earth with heavy hooves, and Abon's steed snorted in response.

The wizard stood up, and the others followed. "I am Galdor of Ellond, advisor to King Fullan." He gestured with one hand. "This is Abon, the most eloquent shaper in all of Ellond and beyond. Here is Gnorn, Dweorg of the Fyrnhowes, a loremaster and a weaponsmith of the greatest talent. And the largish fellow is Orvandil Dragonbane, a warrior to have on one's side in any battle and a most excellent Thjoth. And who might you be, sir?"

The lead soldier scowled from atop his steed. "I am Captain Ajay of His Majesty's cavalry. Now that I know who you are, you will tell me why you are here."

"Thank you for asking." The wizard beamed a smile. "You might even be of assistance to us. In fact, we are seeking a friend of ours who has likely passed through here recently. His name is Dayraven of the Mark, but these days he seems to be better known as the Prophet of Edan. Have you heard of him?"

Captain Ajay's eyes widened. "There are tales . . ."

"We would be most grateful to hear them and be on our way. I'm afraid we're in some haste. It's rather urgent that we find him."

The captain's frown hardened again, and he gave a quick shake of his head. "And I'm afraid that cannot be."

"King Veduir granted me permission to pass through Golgar not long ago. I'm certain he would not mind our passage in the least."

"That may be, but I have my orders to conduct all strangers wandering our lands to Lady Savatri." Captain Ajay's mouth formed an almost apologetic smile, and his tone softened. "It may be she'll be able to give you tidings of your friend. She's been gathering information. Many rumors have sprung up, and it's certain someone the people are calling the Prophet passed this way. Some of our soldiers . . . encountered him."

Galdor glanced at his companions. Only Abon might have understood most of the exchange since the others spoke little Andumaic. Yet they were all ready. Orvandil managed a casual posture, but his hand rested on his sword hilt. Gnorn's thumbs were in his belt, not far from his axe. And the shaper stood in his usual place, ready to protect the wizard's back. For the briefest moment, he considered unleashing wizard's fire on the soldiers and galloping away, but he dismissed the thought. *Too much bloodshed already. But there could be so much more if we don't find Dayraven in time.* He smiled once again at the soldier.

"Then I shall consider it a great favor if you would speed our interview with Lady Savatri as much as possible. She's a cousin to King Veduir, yes? She will know who I am."

The captain bowed his head toward Galdor. "As you say, my lord."

THE GOLGAE SOLDIERS HAD DONE A HASTY JOB OF CLEANING OUT the abandoned villa and turning it into their temporary headquarters. Here in Golgar, the Ilarchae slaves had not destroyed or slaughtered as much. They simply disappeared to join their kin up north, leaving many of the Golgae plantations without labor. Without labor, many of the plantations had failed. The overgrown state of the fields and the neglect around the villa were clear enough signs, inviting Lady Savatri to appropriate the place for her own use.

Not that she was the sort to need an invitation. Galdor had never met the woman, but it was his duty to know as much as possible about the noble families of every kingdom, and the reports indicated Savatri was formidable as a sorceress and a powerbroker. She had nearly been Golgar's monarch, but her cousin Veduir narrowly beat her out. Since then she had been one of his greatest supports, and it was said only her hatred for Sildharan rivaled her loyalty to Golgar. Galdor hoped she would prove reasonable.

When Captain Ajay returned from reporting to Lady Savatri to conduct him, Gnorn, Abon, and Orvandil into the large dining hall where she was seated on a dais, his hopes fell more than a little. She had surrounded herself with dozens of soldiers in full battle dress. The hall was bristling with them, and they stood all around the four friends, looking on like impassive statues but clearly ready to draw their blades. The wizard also sensed the gift in the woman, and though she was not quite his match, she was powerful enough. The display of soldiery was perhaps meant to tip the scales in her favor. *She's nervous. Afraid. Something happened here. We must tread carefully.*

The wizard Galdor bowed to Lady Savatri and smiled. "Lady Savatri, it is a pleasure to meet you."

Her stern gaze did not alter. For a noblewoman, she dressed plainly, wearing a thin gold necklace over her maroon robe. She was slender with intelligent eyes that weighed him. Streaks of grey had invaded her dark hair, which she had tied behind her head in a tight bun, adding to the severity of her appearance. "That's a pleasant lie, Galdor of Ellond."

"Perhaps you would prefer to deal in unpleasant truths, then?"

One of her eyebrows arched up, and she smiled, though it did not reach her eyes. "We have little choice in that, I fear."

Galdor sighed. "Very well. We are in some haste, but let us trade questions, and perhaps we may help one another."

"And how would you help us?"

"I would begin with some humble and well-intentioned advice."

"Which is?"

"With your ancient foe in a position of weakness, it might be tempting to strike. Sildharan is crumbling, descending into chaos. This might seem like an opportunity. Yet, I would beg your king to be cautious regarding the conflict between the Sildharae and the Ilarchae. The Ilarchae are angry, and that anger has united them. For the first time they feel their collective power, and it would be wise not to stand in their way."

"King Veduir will do what is best for Golgar."

Galdor hesitated a moment, debating how much to reveal of what he guessed regarding Veduir's intentions. *No time for arguments.* "I pray he will."

Lady Savatri's eyes narrowed as she leaned forward and studied the wizard. "And how do you imagine we might help you?"

Galdor smiled. "Ah. As for that, we are in pursuit of our friend, one Dayraven of the Mark."

One of the nearby soldiers stirred, a man with a captain's plume on his helm. Galdor glanced at him before resuming. "It was Dayraven who defeated the Supreme Priest Bledla during the Battle of Thulhan, forcing the Torrlonders to abandon their conquest of the eastern kingdoms. From the events of that day he became known as the Prophet of Edan. Mostlike you have heard of all this."

"Yes. But why do you seek this so-called Prophet?"

The wizard stroked his beard. "Because he is our friend, and because he may be a danger to himself, and to anyone he comes near. We are hoping to help him."

The woman nodded slowly, and her lips curled in the barest hint of a grin, suggesting she knew more than she was saying. "What is the nature of this danger?"

Galdor cleared his throat. "The truth, my lady, is this: Dayraven's vast power came from an encounter he had with an elf. I understand he met with King Veduir once, before he made his way to the Wyrmberg to master Gorsarhad, the eldest of dragons. No doubt the king would have sensed how much energy was in him. The elf put *something* inside his mind, whence it all comes. Thus far, Dayraven has remained in control, even tapping into the elf's power to defeat the Supreme Priest Bledla. But in using that power, he may have unleashed the elf's will, which doesn't seem to be altogether friendly. I have reason to believe Dayraven is wrestling with the elf for control. From his own strength and goodness, he's kept it from executing its will. But at great cost. He seems to be losing all memory, and perhaps his sanity as well. If they disappear entirely, I fear what may happen."

Lady Savatri's eyes widened. "And what is the elf's will?"

Galdor's voice stuck in his throat, and he swallowed and shivered before forcing out the words. "I had a taste of it during the battle outside Thulhan. It swept over everyone. Thousands of battle-hardened soldiers cowered in the dust. But I was close enough to see into his eyes, and never have I felt such cold. It could have annihilated us all. Blotted the whole city from the face of the land. It was on the verge of doing so, I think, but Dayraven came back. He held it in check."

"Then it desires to destroy us all?"

He thought a moment and then shook his head. "It does not desire. It merely *is*. And what it sees when it looks upon us is fear and pain. Perhaps that is what it responds to."

"And you believe you may be of some help to your friend?"

"We aim to find out. And we had hoped you might have word of his passing through here. We've been tracking him, but it's difficult since he tends to avoid people. We think he's on his way to Caergilion."

"Caergilion?"

"Yes. Though we had hoped to catch him before he reaches it. Now you may understand why we are in some haste."

Her lips formed a hard grin, and she gazed at the wizard but said nothing.

Galdor waited a moment longer. "My lady? Have you tidings of Dayraven?"

Still she said nothing.

The wizard frowned at her. "Many lives could be at stake."

She sat back in her chair and nodded. "I have tidings of your *friend*. The Prophet has indeed passed through here. I lost thirty soldiers to him."

Galdor staggered back a step and put his hand over his chest. "Thirty? Edan's mercy. Dayraven slew thirty men? Then I fear . . ." Gnorn and Orvandil, who could not have understood the conversation as it was in Andumaic, stared at the wizard, their concern evident in their frowns.

Lady Savatri scowled. "I did not say he slew them. I sent them to conduct him to me. They returned unhurt, at least in body, but without their gear and weapons. The fools even set their horses free."

Galdor scratched his head. "I don't understand, my lady. You mean to say they did not bring Dayraven to you?"

"Of course not. They had all lost their wits. Rambling on about leaving behind worldly desires and possessions. All they would speak of was the liberation the Prophet promised. They refused to obey any orders. Just sat there like fools and wouldn't stop yammering about the Prophet and this being the time to repent and take stock."

The wizard found it difficult to suppress his grin. "And what has become of these thirty soldiers?"

Lady Savatri's eyes narrowed as if she suspected Galdor wanted to smile. "They shall remain locked up until they see sense and go back to their duty."

"I see. You must do as you see fit, but I would plead mercy for them. We've seen many individuals Dayraven has influenced, and whatever revelation he gives them seems to have a strong effect. You see why we're in haste." He gave her a slight bow. "If you'll give us your leave, we will resume our task of finding him."

"I do not give you my leave." She stood up from her chair and nodded. At that signal, steel whispered as the soldiers surrounding the four friends drew their blades.

Orvandil put his hand on the hilt of his sheathed sword, and Gnorn reached for his axe.

"Stay," said Galdor in the Northern Tongue as he raised his palms to them. "We will talk our way out of this." He turned back to Lady Savatri and addressed her in High Andumaic. "My lady, we've done you no wrong, and I've told you our purpose without hiding anything. What is it you seek from us? You have no cause to imprison us."

"You shall remain our *guests*, not prisoners, as long as you are willing to wait for King Veduir's decision. I must consult him in the matter of the Prophet, and he will wish to hear what you have to say. So much power on the loose is a grave concern, and we would not wish to have it at our backs."

"But, my lady, have I not made clear our need for haste? Lives may be at stake."

"There are many lives at stake in many places."

"But . . ."

"You have been wise enough in your speech, Galdor of Ellond, but it is clear you guess something of our intentions regarding Sildharan. It is imperative that we keep the element of surprise for as long as possible."

"You can't mean . . ."

"What I *mean* is you will be free to go as soon as I'm certain your freedom poses no threat to us."

"How could you deem our freedom a threat to you?"

"You've just come from aiding Sildharan, have you not?"

Galdor frowned at the woman. "Yes, and you know very well why. We aided Sildharan against the Torrlonders to defend every kingdom in Andumedan from their aggression. I explained all this to Veduir. In the process, I might add, we likely spared Golgar from imminent invasion."

"That is possible. But you're a counselor to a king, are you not? Surely you would be foolish not to suspect the friend of your enemy? I assure you we Golgae have not survived by being overtrusting, particularly in matters concerning the Sildharae."

"Are you suggesting we might go back to Sildharan and tell them of your plans to invade while the Ilarchae are overrunning them? This may be difficult for you to understand, but at the moment, finding and helping Dayraven is far more important than the squabbling of any kingdoms. We simply haven't time . . ."

"I'm *suggesting* you wait here as our guests until either I have determined you can be no threat or King Veduir has given me orders to free you. I will contact him as swiftly as I may to ask his will in the matter. It may be your stay with us will be brief."

Galdor stared at her for a moment, and then he sighed. "One can always hope." He looked around at all the soldiers standing with their blades drawn. *We might get the best of them, but we might not. And it would be a mess either way, and unlikely to speed our journey.* He faced Lady Savatri again. "Very well. We agree to remain as your guests for now. But I *beg* you to hasten."

She nodded and smiled, but the smile was a quick and dry formality. "Excellent. I'll send a message to King Veduir immediately." She gestured toward the white-plumed soldier Galdor had noticed earlier. "Captain Uthron will show you to your room."

DEEP IN THE NIGHT, GALDOR LAY ON HIS BACK ON A STRAW mattress inside the spare but comfortable room where he, Gnorn,

Abon, and Orvandil *guested*. Of course, there were guards outside the door, and, a few moments ago, he had spotted moonlit glints of metal from a patrol of soldiers standing at attention on the ground below their second floor window. Lady Savatri was taking no chances.

As he had advised them to do, his companions seemed to have fallen asleep, at least to judge by Abon and Gnorn's loud snoring and Orvandil's steady breaths. Like it often did, sleep evaded him. *Never been good at taking my own advice.* The wizard hummed softly to himself and let his mind wander where it would. After toying with some memories from his younger years with Arna, Bledla, and the others in the monastery in Torrhelm, his thoughts returned to where they most often settled these days: Dayraven.

What might be left of the young man's mind? Was there enough there still to bring him back? Galdor did not know the truth, and his head's answer differed from his heart's. *Well, my heart's always been the wiser, so perhaps there's hope there.* When he pondered the influence the young man was exerting over the people he met, even his head found reason to hope. *His goodness touches them, leaks into them. He makes them see what they are. Feel what they are. Yearn to be something better. That's not the elf. He must be in there still.* Yet he could not shake the dread looming over him like an axe ready to descend on his neck. He released a long sigh.

Just then a man spoke, his voice muffled by the door to their room. Another man answered, and they went back and forth in what might have been a polite argument. A long silence followed. Galdor had returned to his private thoughts for only a moment before the door clicked and creaked open.

A large form sprang up in the darkness near the wizard, and after a startled moment, he realized Orvandil had never been asleep. In the darkness it was hard to tell, but it seemed the Thjoth held his blade before him in a defensive stance. Galdor's old bones were a bit slower in rising, but when he stood, a man's shadowed form stood in the doorway. When he stepped forward, a bit of moonlight from the window gleamed off his white-plumed helm.

The wizard squinted, but he could not see the man's face. "Captain?"

The man waited to speak, and when he did, he kept his voice to just above a whisper. "Yes. It's Captain Uthron. The one who escorted you to this room."

"How may we help you?" The darkness was thick around Galdor's soft words, and he wondered if this was some sort of test or trap. Yet, something he had seen before in the captain's face, the way he had glanced at them earlier, allowed a small hope to grow.

"It's not me you should be helping. It's Dayraven."

Galdor smiled in the darkness. "You speak as if you know him."

"I do. I and two of my men guided him from Holurad to the Wyrmberg when he sought the dragon. I count him my friend."

Galdor turned to Orvandil and spoke in the Northern Tongue. "It's alright. This man is here to assist us, it seems."

The Thjoth sheathed his sword but remained standing next to the wizard, who turned back to Captain Uthron and resumed speaking in Andumaic. "Then Dayraven is our mutual friend."

The captain hesitated again. "Is he in pain?"

"I suspect he is. In his mind he is waging a terrible battle."

"Can you help him in truth?"

"I don't know. But I will either help him, or I will fail. First, I must reach him."

Another long silence from the captain. Darkness shrouded the man's face, but his stiff posture suggested he was making a difficult decision. He shook his head. "There's something you should know. Soon a large battle will take place. The Ilarchae have cornered the remaining Sildharae troops. Their end is all but certain."

"And what of you Golgae?"

Captain Uthron shifted in the darkness and seemed to glance behind him out the door. "We will be . . . Well, you'll no doubt learn what King Veduir intended after it all comes to pass. Please don't ask me to say more than I must."

"I understand."

"This much I may tell you: Lady Savatri . . . She sees you as a possible threat. She doesn't plan to set you free until after the battle's outcome is clear. I fear that could put you in some danger."

"Our safety is the least concern. A far greater cost could come if no one helps Dayraven."

"I believe you. That's why I'm doing this. That, and because I would do what I can to help him."

"And what exactly do you mean to do?"

The captain released a long sigh. "I will free you. You must follow me and remain silent."

Galdor decided to take the plunge and trust the man. "Very well." He turned toward Gnorn and Abon's sleeping forms. They seemed to be having a snoring competition. "We must wake our two companions. I'm afraid they might very well sleep through the coming battle otherwise." He glanced at Orvandil and switched again to the Northern Tongue. "It seems we'll be departing earlier than expected. Would you kindly stir our friends from their slumber?"

"Gladly."

Though he could not see the Thjoth's face, he knew him well enough to imagine the grim smile he heard in his voice.

"He says to keep as quiet as possible when we cross the courtyard. This is the tricky bit. The guards around the perimeter are all his men, but someone might see us from inside the villa."

Galdor whispered his translation of Captain Uthron's words to Gnorn, Orvandil, and Abon. Uthron had thought through every detail of their escape. He had a hundred men under his command, and he had arranged for those most loyal to him to take the second shift of guard duty that night. So far, every one of the guards had stood rigid and looked the other way as the four friends followed the captain down corridors and stairs. Crouching in a dark doorway that offered a view of the villa's broad courtyard, they were waiting for some sort of signal.

One of the guards, a dark blotch in the murk with hints of steel glinting under the moonlight, stirred on the other side of the courtyard, where there was a high gate in the wall surrounding the villa. He walked to the courtyard's center, paused, and seemed to bow toward them, and then he returned to his post.

"Follow me," whispered Uthron.

He crept along the shadowed side of the courtyard, sticking close to the wall of the villa and ducking beneath the first floor windows, which were all darkened. Galdor and the others followed suit. They passed just behind by several soldiers, who stood as still as if they were made of stone. No one said a word.

At length, they reached the gate, which was already cracked open just enough to allow a man to slip through. Captain Uthron went first, gesturing for them to follow just before he disappeared into the darkness beyond the gate. Galdor was about to go through when Abon put a hand on his arm and pointed at himself. The wizard smiled and nodded. Though he trusted the captain, it was better to allow the shaper his precautions.

Abon stepped through, and Galdor waited a moment before following. He found the captain and the shaper waiting on the other side. Gnorn came next, and then Orvandil squeezed through. Captain Uthron nodded and walked into the high grass, away from the cobbled roadway leading to the gate. He led them across a broad field toward a hillock. They walked up it in silence, and the night breeze soughed through the grass as it fingered their clothes.

Several dark forms waited on the other side of the hillock. They turned out to be two more soldiers and four horses saddled and ready for a journey. The steeds appeared to be the same ones the companions had been riding earlier, including the stout mountain horse Gnorn was more comfortable on.

Galdor turned toward Captain Uthron. "We can't thank you enough. But I fear you'll have difficulty explaining our disappearance to Lady Savatri."

"I'll face that task when I must."

"How might she punish you?"

"That depends on how much of the truth I tell her. At least I don't think my life's in danger. We'll be needing every soldier we've got. She's not an easy one to deceive, though."

"Indeed, I should think not." The wizard stroked his beard. "If you'll permit me, there's something I might do to lessen the severity of her reaction."

The captain took a step backward. "What is it?"

"A bit of sorcery. I'll sing a song of origin and touch your mind. You'll feel it as the gentlest brush, like a feather on your skin. Lady Savatri will sense the traces of my presence in you, and she'll assume I took control of your mind, commanding you to free us in this manner. You needn't even lie to her. Simply tell her you felt compelled to act as you did."

Captain Uthron hesitated in the darkness. "It won't hurt?"

"Not in the slightest."

"Sing your spell, then, and I thank you for it."

"Not at all. This leaves me still deep in your debt."

"No. We're doing this for Dayraven. Tell him, Tiran."

"That we are," said one of the soldiers holding the horses' reins. He nodded toward the other soldier, a short, thin fellow. "Even Spider here insisted. 'Course, he's always been the sentimental sort."

The other man said not a word, but he seemed to nod.

Galdor smiled. "Very well, then. Shall I cast it on all three of you?"

"No," said Captain Uthron. "The consequences for this will fall on me alone." His tone suggested no argument.

"In that case, remain still and let your mind wander wherever you wish. Be aware, however, that I will sense your current thoughts most strongly, so think about something you won't mind me seeing." He waited a moment. "Are you ready?"

"Yes."

So instinctive was the journey into the realm of origins for the wizard that he drifted there with barely a thought, releasing himself to its serenity. He chanted in a soft voice, "Druanil ecthonias di andyon dimniathon. Abu mihil inghanias mi rakhyon inlorathon." He repeated the song of origin several times, each time more loudly than the last, all the while focusing on the man before him.

Captain Uthron's mind lay open to him. Within he perceived the full array of the man's emotions: his strong sense of duty, loyalty to his men, anxiety for Golgar, shame at failing his family by his absence, desire for peace and rest, and, most of all, his hope to do right. But most powerful was a memory he dwelled on, unconsciously strengthening it and even tweaking it as he turned it over in his mind. With the memory came many associations that blurred together: the warmth of the sun in a cold and mountainous place, moist breath misting, the piney scent of a nearby forest, a sense of companionship and sorrow at the parting of ways, and a looming mountain crowned by snow. Before the mountain stood a young man Galdor knew well, staring at him. Dayraven wore thick woolen clothes and a fur cloak to keep warm. The lad appeared a bit haggard, but he was smiling, and in his blue eyes the wizard saw the light of friendship Captain Uthron experienced. *Yes,* he thought. *The lad has a way of touching people like that.*

He broke his contact with Uthron and returned to his body, smiling at the memory of Dayraven and still feeling as if it were his own. "Thank you," he said to the captain, though when he said it, he was not sure if he meant to give thanks for his freedom or for the pleasantness of the memory. Perhaps both.

Uthron only nodded in the darkness.

"Will there be any pursuit?"

"I think not. Lady Savatri will be unable to spare any troops, and we're to move north as swiftly as possible at first light."

"We'll be on our way, then. I wish you and your men well, captain."

"As we do you. Find him. Find him and help him if you can."

FROM HIS SADDLE ORVANDIL GAZED FOR A MOMENT BACK AT THE ford across the River Lannad, which marked their safe passage from Golgar to the kingdom of Sundara. Galdor had told him and Gnorn this was the very spot where Dayraven had parted from him, Abon, and Sequara when they were journeying north to Sildharan. The Thjoth had spotted tracks that might have belonged to Dayraven's horse on both banks of the river. At any rate, a single rider had passed this way heading south perhaps as much as a week ago. In his gut, he believed it had been his friend. There was little chance they would catch Dayraven before he set sail for Caergilion. They had lost too many days in searching for him and in needless delays, like the one Lady Savatri caused. At least that Golgae captain had helped. A brave man. Orvandil knew the cost of betraying a cause to do the right thing.

As he and the others kept their steeds to a steady trot that wore on their legs and backs, he caressed the pommel of Seeker, the blade Gnorn had wrought for him. Thus far he had not needed to use the weapon. There was a time not long ago when he would have itched to find a reason to test it. Back in Golgar it had been close. Part of him had *wanted* to fight those soldiers, but Galdor had talked instead. The strangest thing was he had not minded afterwards. He smiled to himself. *Getting old.* He did not doubt the battle lust would rush into him when the time came, but perhaps, after all the mistakes of his youth, he was finally growing wiser. Not least because of Dayraven.

He was not sure what part he would play in helping the lad. At his father's funeral pyre — at the pyre of the man Orvandil slew in battle — Dayraven had said many people would need Orvandil, including himself. He had seemed wise beyond his years then. Like a prophet. And he had made the Thjoth believe in something more than the next fight. *I'll be there for him. Whatever it takes. Whatever it costs me.*

Gnorn rode up next to him, bouncing on his mountain horse. He looked up at the Thjoth. "You're sure about those tracks? A week old?"

"Aye."

"You don't think we'll catch up to him before he sails, do you?"

"No."

The horses' hooves clopped during a long pause.

"We need to find some traces of him in Sundara. Figure out where he sails from, and where to. *If* he sails."

"Aye."

"Which means," Gnorn grunted and shifted in his saddle, "we've still got a long road ahead."

"Aye."

Another pause, during which Gnorn frowned in thought.

"All these people. The ones he's touched. The followers of the Prophet."

"Aye."

"Are they after the same thing we're after?"

Orvandil thought for a long while. "They're after the Prophet. We're after Dayraven."

The Dweorg grunted in response, and then he groaned and rolled his eyes. "All this riding is wearing out my old arse."

The Thjoth glanced down at his friend. “Toughens you.”

“And I suppose your arse isn’t the least bit sore. Made of iron, eh? Iron-arse. That’s what we ought to call you. Never mind Dragonbane. Should be Orvandil Iron-arse. Ha!”

Orvandil only smiled at the Dweorg and chuckled.

Gnorn ignored him and shook his head. “Makes me almost long to be on a ship.”

“Soon enough.”

“Oh, shut up.”

The Thjoth’s grin was bigger than ever.

“AYE. I RECKON HE’S BEEN HERE.”

Seagulls cried overhead, and the salty scent of the water hovered in the breeze. Gnorn tugged at his beard as he and the others sat atop their horses and gawked at the little fishing village on Sundara’s coast. The place had not been hard to find since folk miles away were talking about it. And not just talking. They had been coming, streaming in like worshippers to a shrine where they would find a cure to any ailment. Surrounding the village’s thirty or so huts, tents and makeshift shelters had sprung up and spread outward all along the coastal cliffs and beaches, covering the land like carrion birds all over a battlefield. Not tens. Not hundreds. Thousands of them.

They had passed more than a few pilgrims on their way here, but the Dweorg had not imagined so many people would leave behind their lives just to see the place where the Prophet set foot. Of course, the tales all said he had performed some manner of miracle in this village called Jitawan, but few of them agreed on the details. Gnorn favored the theory that Dayraven had cured some villagers of some disease. Whatever he did, he had made an impression.

“The question,” said Abon, “is whether or not he’s still here.”

“Most of the tales say he departed. Flew out over the water, or some such thing.” Gnorn sighed. “Mostlike he sailed for Caergilion.”

Galdor nodded. “Quite right. But we’d best find out the truth of it. We need a witness. One of the villagers who saw him here. Let’s walk the horses through the camp." The wizard alighted from his steed, and Gnorn followed suit.

The camp of worshipers and seekers of the Prophet proved to be quieter than the Dweorg had expected. In fact, it was almost eerie, like a place for the dead. Most folk were sitting in or near their shelters, posing in meditation or prayer. Most of the prayers were low mumbles, and he could not understand the ones that were loud enough to hear since he knew little Andumaic. A few pilgrims were speaking to each other in quiet tones, and even fewer spared the four companions a glance. But when people did look at them, Gnorn saw in their eyes and fevered smiles a kind of intensity, a bliss that strained at them and spilled out, the kind of look that suggested they were not in fact seeing anything in the physical world, but gazing in awe at something beyond it.

Few of them could have seen Dayraven in the flesh, but some had, and somehow their fever had spread. What was it in the Prophet they all sought? What were they all waiting for? Gnorn reckoned the answer was in that faraway look they had in their eyes. A yearning for answers beyond the fleetingness and pain of their lives. They had all come here to share this otherworldliness with each other. To bathe in it. To let it purify them.

The Dweorg, who knew and loved Dayraven as a man, tried to return their smiles and nodded at them, but his fingers tightened their grip on the horse's rein as he led it, and his other hand rested on the axe tucked in his belt. He had always known of Dayraven's importance and his kindness. He had felt them on the first day they met back in Torrlond, when the lad touched his heart with his simple and genuine compassion in the midst of that mess with the Mercenary Company of Etinstone. But there was something wrong with all this, with all these people abandoning their lives for something with no solidity. In their reactions to the Prophet, Gnorn perceived the elf's influence. *He may be preventing it from killing them outright, but it's creeping into them all somehow.*

After meandering by all the worshipers and squatters, the four friends halted near the simple village huts, which were only a little solider than the shelters surrounding them. A few hundred yards from the village, a scattering of battered fishing boats waited on the beach. Gnorn stood behind Galdor until the wizard turned around and handed his rein to the Dweorg. "Wait here. I'll speak to one of them."

The wizard walked into the village, and Gnorn watched him approach an old man sitting outside one of the huts mending a fishing net. When Galdor spoke to him, the old man smiled and nodded. They talked for what seemed a long while, during which Gnorn looked behind him and found several pilgrims, a mixed group of men and women, staring at him and the others with appraising looks that suggested the friends might not quite belong there since they were still rooted in the world. A sort of taint in their midst. *How do the crackpots always know you're not one of them?* The Dweorg showed them his teeth in a broad smile. "Hello there. Fine day, isn't it?"

The blank-faced devotees to the Prophet gazed at him a moment longer and, without a word, turned and went their way. Perhaps they had decided the best thing would be to ignore the four companions. Pretend they were not there. That suited Gnorn just fine.

At length the wizard returned. He took his horse's rein from Gnorn and sighed.

"Well?" asked the Dweorg.

The wizard gazed at him, Abon, and Orvandil. "Dayraven's gone."

"Sailed to Caergilion?" asked Abon.

"Mostlike, though our friend over there is convinced the Prophet traveled beyond the world's confines. Apparently, Dayraven did not tell them whither he was bound."

"Can't blame him," said Abon. "Look at all the daft people who followed him here."

"*They* would call themselves blessed," said Galdor with a smile. "Perhaps it's all a matter of perspective. But at least we know this much: Three men went with Dayraven in the largest fishing vessel the village had. The old man says he wishes he had been one of them, one of the chosen. But, he says, his purpose is here, to witness to all who come."

"So," said Gnorn, "we know only that he sailed from here, but not whither he went."

The wizard nodded, and the creases on his forehead deepened as he frowned.

"What now?" asked Orvandil.

Galdor waited a while, stroking his beard as he thought. Finally, he nodded. "We go to Caergilion. We'll need to find a ship."

The Thjoth clapped the Dweorg on the shoulder. "We're ready."

Gnorn released a long breath from his cheeks. "A long sea journey. Dayraven, lad, you'd better be there at the end of it." He shivered, and not just at the prospect of being at sea.

10

THE LOST KINGDOMS

Amidst the screams and agonized wails of the wounded and dying, Munzil grunted and tugged on his sword, its leather-covered hilt slippery with sweat and tacky with blood. The crimsoned blade slid out of the fallen Sildharae soldier's chest as if he were unsheathing it. A wet gasp escaped the man's lips, and his bulging eyes stared into Munzil's as a red stain spread all over his golden kirtle. The soldier's fingers relinquished his sword hilt, and his eyelids fluttered before they finally closed. Gulping in air, Munzil stared at the corpse he had just made. "The gods are finished with you. No more pain."

This battle was over. The Folk of the Tribes had crushed the Sildharae at last. Their bodies littered the battlefield, and blood and soil stained their once splendid golden tunics. A mighty kingdom shattered. A few warriors of the Folk of the Tribes lay among them, but the will of the gods was more than clear from the battle's outcome. It was a hard world where survival depended on ferocity and strength. The so-called civilized kingdoms of Eormenlond had gone soft with luxury, depending on magic and forcing others to do their most difficult labor. But the Sildharae were paying a heavy price. In contrast, Munzil's people were simple but free, honest, and strong. Yet, not for the first time, he wondered if their victories would one day cause the Folk of the Tribes to grow arrogant, flabby, and weak — if their conquests would lead to their eventual downfall. How many kingdoms had ended as victims of their own success? Perhaps it was an endless cycle, and the gods, who gave with one hand while taking away with another, laughed at the mortals doomed to repeat it for their sport. He shook his head, banishing such thoughts as unworthy and a mere excuse to pause and catch his breath.

He put his hands on his knees as his chest heaved with rapid, heavy gasps. *Just a moment to rest. Can't keep up with Skuld, damn her.* The woman had charged well ahead of him, reckless as always of her safety.

When he could breathe without gasping, he looked around and surveyed the rest of the battlefield. Surt's plan had worked perfectly, as always. The dead in their golden tunics were like the leaves littering the ground before winter's chill hardened and covered the land. A few tattered remnants of the Sildharae ranks were fleeing toward the Forest of Orudwyn, exactly where the great War-leader wanted them. Of course, they had little choice since the Folk of the Tribes were herding them toward the ancient, tall trees beckoning in the distance.

Imagining how Skuld would taunt him later that night, he grimaced and jogged ahead to find her.

He soon spotted a group of warriors of the Boar Clan of the Fire Dragons. Among them was a form that was familiar and increasingly dear to him. He released a long breath, surprised at the strength of his relief that she was alive. How would it have been had she been wounded or dead? Was he prepared to lose so much again? *Doesn't bear thinking about now. She's alive, and she's tougher to kill than I am.* He shook his head and slowed his jog as he approached her.

Skuld stood up from wiping her sword on the grass and faced him. Munzil frowned at his lover, glancing at the blood oozing from the long but shallow slash on her forearm. He spoke between heavy breaths and tried in vain to keep the emotion out of his voice. "You went too far ahead. Almost got yourself killed. Again."

She grinned at him, though she was breathing hard too. "Try to keep up, old man."

Just then Munzil noticed Gorm standing over something, and the other members of the Boar Clan gathered behind him. He walked toward them. Skuld followed.

Gorm knelt and frowned at the body lying on its back beneath him. Gore covered it, and at least five large wounds in the chest were seeping. One arm was missing its hand, and one leg was bent the wrong way at the knee. Blood streaked the warrior's face from a deep slash across the forehead, but Munzil recognized Vitar. Red also dribbled down his cheek from his open mouth. Somehow, the lad was still alive, and his eyes gazed up at Gorm as a smile trembled on his face. He coughed, and blood spattered from his throat.

"Tell . . ." A few quick gasps interrupted Vitar. "Surt."

Gorm stroked his braided beard and gazed down at the young warrior. "He'll hear how you died, lad. The singers will spread the tale to all the Folk of the Tribes."

Vitar's eyes searched at his side, toward the spot on the ground where his blade lay, still in the grasp of his severed hand. Gorm knelt down and placed the blade on the lad's chest, by which time Vitar's eyes had glazed over and his fitful gasping had ceased.

The big chieftain stared down at the boy before he reached forward and, in a gentle motion that could not have been more incongruous with the huge man's fierceness in battle, closed his eyelids. "Fighter like him doesn't come often. He might've been one of the greatest of the Fire Dragons. One of the greatest of the Folk of the Tribes."

"He died well," said Munzil. *This is our way. The Folk of the Tribes are warriors above all.*

Skuld stepped forward, her knuckles white as she grasped her blade. "No mourning. We have avenged him."

Gorm stood at his full height, overshadowing the rest of them. His clenched teeth showed when he grinned, and then his gravelly voice rumbled, "Aye. And there'll be time for more vengeance." He brandished his sword. "For Vitar!"

The others yelled their agreement, but Munzil only stared down at the lad's mutilated body. *I must be getting softer with age. The boy died well.* But he could not shake the feeling of loss, and once again he wondered about the price of the destiny the gods had chosen for the Folk of the Tribes.

THE BONE-BENDING PRESSURE ON KEEVAN'S RIBS AND LIMBS WAS immense, and as he gasped for breath, the stench of sweat, viscera, and blood nauseated him. The silent men piled on top of him were not moving, so he grunted and wiggled until the weight shifted a bit, and then he found he was able to crawl out from beneath the corpses. The battle was no longer raging when his head poked out, but the tortured shrieks of the wounded shredded the air. In the distance, a few remaining Sildharae were fleeing toward the forest. Not far away, Captain Kalan lay on the ground, his dead eyes staring at Keevan.

He freed his torso, and then he pulled his legs out one at a time. When he stood and looked down below his waist, he held out his shaking hands and giggled for a moment. It turned out he had not pissed himself this time. The wet warmth down there was blood, a great deal of it, and he was pretty sure it belonged to someone else since his legs still seemed to work. This proved fortunate since a group of Ilarchae screamed and began thundering his way. Weaponless and alone, Keevan decided Goshal, who was long dead anyway, could screw himself. He ran.

Passing groups of Ilarchae that had stopped to chop wounded Sildharae soldiers into tiny bits, Keevan huffed and pumped his legs and arms as fast as they would go. Some of the barbarians looked up and, with furious cries, joined the ones already pursuing him. A spear startled him when its tip dug into the earth beside him and peppered him with a chunk of sod, and he jerked sideways like a puppet. The next spear that landed was not so close, and a few others thunked into the soil far behind him. Keevan had always been a swift runner, and no weapons weighed him down, so he was managing to outdistance the barbarians. Not to mention the terror gripping his heart and willy-nilly flinging his legs one before the other even as his lungs burned.

The Forest of Orudwyn grew closer, and Keevan dared to hope he might make it into the shelter of its trees. He had no idea what he would do if he survived, but that did not matter at the moment. The instinct to live took over his body, and he ran even harder as his hoarse breaths came faster and louder.

The ever-closer trees beckoned, and every fiber of his body strained to join his few fellow soldiers who were already disappearing behind the shadowy forest eaves. His boots pounded the earth, and his legs kept spinning on their own momentum. He was pretty sure if he stopped pumping them, he would collapse in a heap and lie there gasping for breath, so he just kept running.

Closer and closer he came to where the trees basked in the sunlight, and behind them waited shelter and safety. He was gasping and wheezing like a mad donkey, and every muscle of his body protested. But he was so close, only a few more yards now to where the wind whispered in the trembling leaves. As he kept running, he dared to glance behind him, and he smiled.

The Ilarchae had given up and broken off the chase. In the distance, they seemed to be forming a line for some reason. He did not care why, only that he would keep running once he entered Orudwyn and caught his breath. Perhaps he would find some of the others, and they would figure out a way to survive. He turned back toward the forest just before a bright shaft of pain slammed through his stomach and knocked the wind out of him with a sickening crunch, forcing a rasp from his throat as his limbs flopped to a stop.

Keevan's eyes clenched closed, and a flash of red so vivid it tasted like iron — it had accompanied the sudden pain, he realized — faded to black. Buckled over like an old man, he grimaced and tried to suck in air, but nothing would come. His mouth was wide open and his head trembled, but he could not breathe. Whatever had hit him held him up, else he would have fallen. He opened his eyes and looked up into the face of a man, a southerner. The man could have been a Sildharae, but instead of gold, his tunic was black, and on his bright helm the breeze ruffled a white plume.

Golgae, thought some remote part of Keevan's mind. *What's he doing here?*

The man's eyes seemed sad, almost regretful, and Keevan wanted to ask him why he was there. But he could say nothing, for the man's sword was burrowed almost up to the hilt in his stomach, just below his sternum. He must have run straight into the blade. His red blood was leaking down the steel and dripping into the soil. There were footsteps. Hundreds of them. Thousands. An army. A mass of bodies moved nearby, emerging from the forest, and he was pretty sure they were all clad in black. But Keevan did not look away from the eyes of the man who had slain him. Those eyes seemed to apologize for the length of steel slicing Keevan's guts and severing his spine, as if the whole incident were a tragic accident. The funny thing was Keevan's mind was as numb as his body. *Oh, Mother. I won't be scared again.* He was as finished as Sildharan.

Since he could not take a breath to speak, he nodded to let the man know he accepted his apology. The man blinked and then kept staring at him, looking as stricken as if he were the one with the sword through him.

Keevan smiled when the trees and the breeze and clinking of armor and weapons and even the man's sad eyes disappeared, and a white light came for him. He slumped forward, but he never felt his body hit the ground.

Captain Uthron bent over and tugged his reddened sword free of the Sildharae soldier's body, which had fallen on its side and curled up as if the man were taking a nap in the blood pooling on the grass. In his desperation to escape the Ilarchae, the lad had not even seen his death coming. However, the shock in his eyes had given way to acceptance, and he seemed to have nodded to Uthron before he died. The memory of that look would twist in his guts for the rest of his days.

The Golgae captain sighed and frowned down at the life he had just taken before he wiped his blade on the grass. He was following the order not to allow a single Sildharae to live, and he dared not disobey after Lady Savatri's displeasure over the disappearance of Galdor and his companions. The only thing that had saved him was her conviction that the wizard had entered Uthron's mind to engineer the escape. Galdor's ploy had spared him the worst.

But it was not Lady Savatri who compelled him to kill the Sildharae. The order had come from King Veduir, whom he would never disobey or question. Besides, the Sildharae were the ancient foes of the Golgae, and they had slain many of Uthron's ancestors and some of his dearest friends. This was the time to settle old scores and right old wrongs. Finally, the Golgae could avenge their ancestors and shake off the dominance of the Sildharae.

Then why does this feel so wrong? Uthron shook his head.

Steel rang out, and a few agonized screams tore the air. His fellow soldiers were slaughtering the few remaining Sildharae that had fled to the forest. The helpless tatters of their ancient foe's army. There were not many left now. The others who had run into the trees earlier were all feeding the soil with their blood. It had been a sorry fate to run from the Ilarchae only to find the ranks of their oldest foe waiting for them inside the cover of the trees. For a fleeting moment, a sense of relief might have suffused them, only to meet an abrupt and violent end. They never had a chance..

Guessing where the final battle between the Ilarchae and Sildharae would play out, King Veduir had hidden his army inside the forest by night to wait for their moment. There was never any question the Ilarchae would win, but the barbarians must have taken some losses, and even they had to be battle-weary after hammering away at the Sildharae. It was the perfect moment for the fresh troops of the Golgae to sweep in, destroy the Ilarchae, and gain predominance in the east of Andumedan. There was safety in such power, safety the Golgae had never known. Veduir's plan was clever, even wise perhaps, though also ruthless. Sometimes a king had to be ruthless for the sake of his people. Moreover, thus far the plan was working.

Uthron sighed. *Something still feels wrong.*

He recalled Dayraven, who had suffered and tried so hard to avert the deaths of thousands. What would the lad have thought of him shoving his sword into that defenseless Sildharae? *I'm a soldier, damn it.* He swallowed his spit, frowning at the taste of bile in his mouth, and turned toward his men.

"Tiran. My horse. Have everyone mount up and get into formation."

Even Tiran was not smiling, and he glanced at the dead Sildharae curled up on the ground before he nodded. “Yes, my lord.”

Uthron turned back to gaze toward the Ilarchae. The barbarians must have spotted them emerging from Orudwyn. Their most forward warriors were pulling back and massing into formations, or what passed for them among the Ilarchae. There were tens of thousands of them, but fewer than he had expected from observing them earlier on scouting missions. *They must have taken more losses against the Sildharae than we thought. The fewer of them, the better for us.*

He sighed again. How many of those Ilarchae, he wondered, had been slaves toiling under the whip their whole lives on Golgae plantations? Of course, given the chance, how many of those same Ilarchae would kill him or make him a slave? *Mother and Father save us all. It's a twisted world we've made. No matter how many Dayravens come into it, we'll always find ways to harm each other for gain, marring everything for generations.*

Hooves clopped behind him. When he turned, Tiran approached, leading the captain's mount by the rein in one hand and holding his spear in the other. After sheathing his sword, Uthron put his foot in the stirrup and pulled himself up on the saddle, whose old leather creaked under him. He breathed in the earthy, familiar scent of his horse, which nodded and snorted, and the muscles on its neck twitched in readiness. When the captain looked down at Tiran, the soldier handed him up his spear.

“Are the men ready?”

Tiran gave him his crooked smile. “Nearly so, my lord. I reckon a good speech will get them there.”

“I hate speeches.”

“I know. Doesn't have to be long.”

Uthron stared into his soldier's eyes, struggling for words during the brief silence that gathered between them. “Doesn't sit right, does it?”

Tiran glanced back at the men before looking back up at his captain. “I reckon not. Still got to do it, though, don't we?”

The captain nodded. “Yes.” Another silence. “Get to your horse, then, and get them ready for a speech. It will begin soon.”

The soldier nodded and grinned. "Yes, my lord."

Captain Uthron turned his steed and gazed out toward the horde of Ilarchae. They were still gathering into lines, which were taking on more uniformity and discipline. The barbarians had learned much about warfare in their conquest of Sildharan, showing a surprising aptitude for tactics. Whoever was leading them knew his business.

He tightened his grip on the smooth ash shaft of his long spear. His company would not take part in the initial charge, but sweat was still running down his neck and back, and his heart thrummed faster than usual. The king was holding back several companies of cavalry as reserves to ride in when and where needed. While Uthron and his men would not immediately engage with the barbarians, no doubt at some point he and his men would see more than enough of the day's combat. *Perhaps we'll luck out, and our initial charge will break them. They must be weary.*

Behind him, the sounds of his company's preparations had ceased. He frowned and shook his head before turning his steed and spurring it into a trot toward his men, who were lined up on their mounts. He reined in before their center and waited as all their serious eyes turned to him. Which of them would not outlive this day?

Captain Uthron let the silence play out a moment longer before he turned his gaze left and then right, taking in every one of the hundred faces. Some were fairly new to him, but most were men he had long known and trusted with his life. Some he counted his dearest friends, his truest brothers, though he always bore himself as their commander. His men all stared at him and waited. One of their horses neighed, and a few others tamped the earth with their hooves.

Uthron nodded.

"It's an honor to serve as your commander."

"The honor's ours, Captain," said Jwola, and a chorus of affirmative grunts and nods followed.

A quick smile, and Uthron continued. "Thank you. That means everything just now. Because we're here for Golgar. And for each other."

"Damn right!" yelled Ushal with his fist in the air, and the others cried out their agreement.

Uthron swallowed. "I'm not much for words, but you men know what you mean to me." He cleared his tightening throat and paused. Opening his mouth to resume, he found he had to swallow again.

Tiran brandished his spear. "For the captain!"

"For the captain!" they screamed.

Uthron gathered himself and nodded as he looked in their eyes. Taking a few deep breaths, he waited until he could speak without his voice breaking. "Stay in formation until the orders come. When they need us, we'll ride in fast and strike hard. Keep your wits about you, heed your commands, and ward each other's backs. May Oruma and Anghara see us through this day, and may their mercy find the slain."

While the men all cheered, Uthron muttered under his breath, "By the Mother and Father, I hate speeches even more than battles."

The captain turned his horse around lest his men see the single tear tracking down his cheek. Many of them would end this day like the Sildharae boy he had slain. To keep his mind from dwelling on it, he looked off to his right. A few hundred yards away, King Veduir sat astride his black steed, conveying commands to his sorcerers via messengers. Surrounded by his picked bodyguard, the king appeared confident, regal, and resolute. His dark robes billowed in the wind as he sent men off with a point and a nod. Each man bowed low before scurrying to carry out his task. Uthron smiled at the sight. *Can't think what's wrong with me. I'm a soldier. Just follow orders. Take care of what I need to. The king knows his business.*

Veduir stopped giving commands and raised an arm high. A silence spread over the Golgae army. Only the wind hissing in the leaves behind them dared to interrupt it. The king looked across the battlefield toward the foe, his eyes as hard as gems, and his arm descended.

Horns wailed, and a vast roar split the air. Uthron's tears flowed freely, and through blurred vision he watched the Golgae ranks move forward, ordered and steady. Row upon row, company by company, they marched across the field of battle, shaking the earth with their footsteps and hoof beats. Soon their black tunics and gleaming steel covered the land.

But Uthron's gaze searched beyond the Golgae to where their foes awaited them. In the distance, the vast horde of Ilarchae stood in long lines. It was not like them to sit while their opponents took the initiative. There was no tactical advantage to the ground they occupied. Perhaps they truly were weary from the combat with the Sildharae and were giving themselves a rest. That made sense.

Uthron frowned, and his eyes narrowed as he looked upon the quiet, patient army of barbarians. *Damn them. What are they waiting for?* Something twisted in his gut. He shook his head, but he could not rid himself of the feeling. *Something's not right here. But what is it? What are we missing?*

WHEN MUNZIL ARRIVED ALONGSIDE GORM AND SKULD OUTSIDE THE circle of murmuring warriors, Gorm rumbled in his gravelly voice, "Is he here?" Several fighters glanced their way and stepped aside to make room. As the bodies moved out of the way, Munzil moved forward and gained a clear view.

Within the circle, Surt was holding up a dark-skinned Sildharae man by the collar of his robe in a one-handed grip, like a mother cat lifting a kitten by the scruff of the neck. With his free hand, the warleader gave his prisoner a back-handed slap. The man's head snapped sideways, and a tooth spun from his mouth along with a squirt of blood. His head lolled, and his eyes crossed as if he were having trouble focusing. Surt threw him to the ground, and when he hit, he rolled and shrieked in agony. He lay there and clutched his bloody thigh, from which the shaft of an arrow poked out. The wretch grimaced and made a strained wheeze through clenched teeth.

No doubt King Naitaran of Sildharan had seen better days. His long hair was matted, and some of it stuck to the sweat on his dirty face. His once fine robe was torn and stained with filth and blood. Perhaps worse than these things, his army was gone. Annihilated. Wiped out. With no army to defend it, Sildharan was no more, which meant Naitaran was no longer a king. But he was still dangerous. Munzil would have counseled Surt not to play with such fire for long. Put a quick end to him and move on to the gathering Golgae army.

With a great deal of gasping, Naitaran managed to rise to his hands and knees. He wiped his split lip with one hand, and his bloody teeth showed in a snarl when he stared at Surt. Between heavy breaths he hissed, ""Alakathon indomiel ar galathon . . ."

Munzil stepped forward with his sword halfway out of its scabbard, but he should have known Surt would be quicker. In two quick strides he was there, and the tall war-leader's black boot sank into Naitaran's gut with a solid thump, driving the air from the former ruler's lungs with a loud rasp. The man went face down in the dirt, and he lay there tucked in half for a long while before he sucked in a loud, croaky breath.

"You've slain many of our warriors with your lightning song," said Surt as he stood over Naitaran.

The former king's hands trembled, and he gasped out the words again. "Alakathon indomiel ar . . . aaahhhhhh!" The spell morphed into a shriek when Surt stepped on the arrow shaft buried in the man's leg.

Surt frowned down at the man beneath him and shook his head. "No more."

The war-leader turned toward the circle of warriors, searching the crowd until he found Munzil's eyes and gave him a quick smile. "Munzil, my brother. This honor is yours. Come here."

Though a smile had accompanied that deep bass, Munzil hurried to obey the command. He strode over and stood next to Surt. "Yes, my lord?"

The big man put a hand on Munzil's shoulder. "Give me your dagger."

Though the war-leader wore his own dagger, Munzil did not hesitate to unsheathe his and hand it over hilt forward.

"Good. Now take hold of the arrow shaft. If he speaks, twist it. When I tell you to, pull hard on it, but don't pluck it out, and keep pulling until I'm done."

Munzil nodded. "As you say, my lord." He knelt down and, when Surt removed his boot, grasped the arrow shaft. Naitaran's lips were peeled back in a grimace, and he was moaning and seething and shaking all over as he lay on his back. He stank of sweat and piss.

Surt unsheathed the dagger he wore at his hip so that he held one in each hand. He crouched down near Naitaran's head, glanced at Munzil, and nodded. "Now."

Munzil tugged with a slight twist of his wrist and felt the arrowhead shift beneath the flesh of the man's thigh. Naitaran's eyes and mouth gaped open in a long and loud shriek. Surt lunged forward and skewered the man's tongue with Munzil's dagger, turning the shriek into a high-pitched, gargled squeal. Blood dribbled down and dripped from the tip of the dagger onto Naitaran's chin. Stretching the tongue out of the man's face with the flat side of the blade, Surt ignored his unintelligible, grunting pleas. Naitaran's eyes bulged as the war-leader raised the other dagger and sliced it downward, sawing deep within the man's mouth. With a spurt of blood, the pink, fleshy tongue came loose, and it jiggled when Surt raised it over his head on Munzil's dagger to display to his assembled warriors.

A loud cheer went up, during which Munzil rolled Naitaran on his side to vomit the blood that had filled his mouth and throat. The former king of the Sildharae glanced up at Munzil, the eyelids of his unfocused eyes fluttering before they closed and he went limp. *A mercy for him he passed out*, thought Munzil. *We'll need to cauterize his wounds if Surt wants him alive.* Yet, had it been his decision, he would have given the fallen king a quick death.

The Folk of the Tribes roared and cheered more when Surt flung away the mangled tongue. Munzil forced a grim smile. It was just and right, after all. The will of the gods. They had avenged the humiliation of their kin. Never would any of the Sildharae holy men oppress and enslave them again. Not even their king, whose magic was gone along with his tongue since he could no longer sing his spells. In Munzil's mind came a vision of his wife and children, and the lost folk of the Grey Wolves beckoned to him. *Yes,* he said to them in his thoughts, *we have avenged you.* But the vengeance did not taste the way he had anticipated, and he wondered where the gods' will would lead them.

As the cheers washed over them, Surt turned to Munzil and, pointing down with his bloody dagger, said in a voice loud enough to be heard over the din, "This one will not join the other holy men yet. Death is too clean, and the gods have one last use for him. You will remain here to guard him."

Part of Munzil wanted to argue that he should fight in the coming battle, but he was tired, and Surt had seen fit to make this duty an honor. He nodded his agreement just as a warrior emerged from the throng and approached Surt. The woman bowed to the war-leader before speaking. "My lord, Gunburcha sends word. She has arrayed our warriors as you bade her. The Golgae troops are on the march."

"Good. Hasten back and tell her to hold our warriors in place. No one meets the foe until I give the order. We'll join you soon."

"Yes, my lord." She nodded and smiled before she turned and ran, breaking through the throng of warriors, which parted for her.

Surt addressed those gathered around him in a thundering voice, and all the warriors went silent when he spoke. "The time has come. We have tasted some blood. Are you ready for more?"

The warriors roared their answer and shook their weapons.

Surt waited until they quieted. "The Golgae are no different than the Sildharae, and they will share their fate. Folk of the Tribes, the gods are with us. On this day we avenge our kin. On this day we feel our true strength!" He raised his large fist.

Loud cheers erupted, and the assembled Folk of the Tribes thumped their chests and clashed their weapons against their shields.

"Whoever would win glory, find your place in our ranks." The war-leader pointed toward the front line. "There you must await the signal. When it comes, let the gods' fury flow through your blood. Smite the foe, and leave none to tell their tale of woe!"

The loudest roar of all washed over Munzil like a thousand thunderstorms unleashed at once, and his heart soared with his people. He nodded and smiled at them all, at the pride in their fierce, joyous faces. His doubts receded. This was the vision the gods had given him. On this day it would all come to pass.

When the din subsided and the warriors strode off to take their places on the front line, a firm hand grasped his shoulder. Surt handed him his dagger, which he took and sheathed. The big man gazed at him and grinned. "You were right."

Munzil did not need to ask what Surt meant. He recalled the day when he first saw the great man, during the battle when the Fire Dragons defeated the Blood Spears, and knew he was the one. He nodded back at the war-leader and looked up into his eyes.

"All is ready," said Surt. "This is our moment."

"Bolverk and the others are in position?"

"He sent a message this morning. They are ready." Surt's eyes narrowed, and he grinned. "You don't trust him, do you?"

"Bolverk?" Munzil shrugged. "He's a clever, dangerous man. He always led the Raven Eyes with as much cunning as courage."

Surt nodded. "Aye. Courage and cunning. We need both."

Munzil looked at the ground. "That we do."

"Bolverk is one of us, and he serves his purpose well." Surt's eyes hardened, and his grin disappeared.

Munzil knew not to argue with that look. "Yes, my lord."

"That's the lesson you taught us, Munzil. The message the gods gave you. We are one. And we are strong."

Munzil's throat caught, and he did not trust himself to speak, so he gazed at his leader and smiled.

Surt's big hand squeezed his shoulder. "And after we conquer the east, we have another task. The coward Torrlonders betrayed us. The gods gave them no heart for the battle, showing us the way. We will burn their dwellings of stone, and we will tear down their high places. Eormenlond will belong to the Folk of the Tribes."

Knowing it would be as Surt said, Munzil nodded. He watched the great man stride toward the battle, followed by Gorm, Skuld, and other warriors. His brothers and sisters, free and proud. And one. Those Golgae were doomed.

CAPTAIN UTHRON SQUINTED AND BIT HIS LOWER LIP AS HE PEERED into the distance. The front line of the Golgae army would soon march within bow range of the Ilarchae. Still the Ilarchae did not budge, though a few moments earlier, a loud shout had gone up among them. After that, they had gone quiet again as more barbarians fell into line to face the advancing Golgae. What were they waiting for? The question burrowed in Uthron's mind like an itch he could not reach. His horse snorted and tamped the earth as if impatient for action, and the captain tugged on the rein. "Easy, boy." *Must be nerves.*

He glanced over at where King Veduir sat astride his steed. Surrounded by his guards, the king peered ahead with an unwavering expression. A man who knew what to expect. Uthron's orders would come from one of the messengers waiting near the king. Soon. First the chaos of the initial clash, then the king would impose his patterns on the battle. A good commander had a plan, but he could also think on his feet. The smallest adjustment could mean everything. All depended on the chain of command and the training instilled in the soldiers. Numbers were important, but discipline even more so. And Veduir was a great tactician. That was their advantage, along with the power of sorcery, which the barbarians could not match.

A vast roar jerked Uthron's gaze back toward the Ilarchae. It was part thrill, part terror, and part relief to see the barbarians rushing toward the Golgae troops to meet them. He released a long sigh. *Finally. They're doing what they're supposed to.*

Like a monstrous cloud of gnats, the dark specks of thousands of arrows filled the sky. The missiles flew in both directions to descend on the closing armies, which did not surprise Uthron since he had seen the Ilarchae use bows in battle. They had adopted that tactic recently, among other things. But the barbarians would not be shooting down the sorcerers among the Golgae. Having observed their strategies against the Sildharae, King Veduir had determined to keep his most powerful commanders, the handful of Golgae sorcerers who could wield almakhti, in the rear. Like the cavalry reserves, the sorcerers would sweep in to help their troops where needed. In his overall strategy Veduir was bold, but in its execution he was cautious. In holding back his greatest weapons, the most powerful sorcerers among the Golgae, he was waiting for the right moment to exploit his advantage.

At his distance, Uthron witnessed the front lines crash into one another before the din of steel and screams reached his ears. Both armies ceased to advance, and they became enmeshed in one another in a seething, roiling mass. Uthron gripped his spear and his rein tighter. The ground beneath the combatants would soon transform into reddened mud, and the cries of the wounded and dying would vie with the screams of the living. He glanced over at the king once more. Veduir sat unmoving on his mount, gazing and determining where to pour his strength.

Uthron remembered to breathe. *Let it come.*

He looked behind him to check on his men. Arvan caught his eye and smiled at him. But then the young man jerked forward, and his smile morphed into a grimace as his eyes widened. When he slumped sideways and fell from his horse, Uthron caught sight of two arrow shafts buried in Arvan's back. Several other men withered and fell, horses screamed and bucked, and panicked shouts broke out.

Uthron's heart hammered in his chest, and his mouth gaped open. Behind the chaos enveloping his company, a horde of Ilarchae was emerging from the Forest of Orudwyn. Thousands of them streamed out of the shadowed trees like hail from an iron-grey sky, and they were screaming their war-cries. Anger vied with horror as the icy realization clutched his mind: The barbarians had outwitted them, using their own trick. They had been waiting in the forest behind them, and they had snuck up on them when the battle was at its loudest. How the barbarians had hidden so many warriors with so little noise he did not know, but they had severely, even lethally, underestimated the Ilarchae.

A second volley of arrows and spears tore through the captain's men while his mind struggled as if in a nightmare. Deevak screamed with a spear pinning his thigh to his frantic horse. Blood gushed from Ushal's mouth when an arrow shredded his throat. Dozens of them dropped from their frantic horses. Uthron's men were dying. They had to fight back. Before the foe could form a proper line, it was essential to attack.

"Turn! Turn and charge!" he commanded. Before galloping into the fray, he glanced over to make sure King Veduir knew what was happening.

Uthron yanked on his rein, and his steed neighed as it pulled up short. The captain stared with his mouth wide open.

King Veduir swayed in his saddle, one reddened hand grasping the bloody spear tip jutting out of his chest. Three arrows also protruded out of the man's back. His mouth worked as if he were desperate to suck in breaths that would not come. Those eyes full of such confidence and strength moments before stared wide in disbelief around him, where most of his guards lay dead or writhing, pierced by a storm of arrows and spears. Several arrows whistled and sprouted from the muscled rump of Veduir's steed, and the animal screamed as it galloped forward, toppling the monarch backwards. The king slammed into the ground and did not move.

A quick glimpse told Uthron the Ilarchae had known far too much and had been far cleverer than he could have feared. The barbarians had concentrated their attacks on the unguarded backs of every sorcerer. They were all down, their robed bodies full of arrows. The greatest advantage the Golgae had was gone, and so was their chain of command. *We were blinder than the Sildharae. Our arrogance has killed us.*

"Charge!" he screamed. "Fight!" He urged his steed forward, but then a huge crack ripped the air all around him and a white light flashed, causing his steed to skitter to the right. Even as he cursed his horse and brought it under control, a small hope blossomed inside him. *Almakhti!*

Among the Ilarchae ranks was a huge rent where smoking bodies littered the earth. At least one Golgae sorcerer had escaped the initial slaughter. Which one, and where was he? Knowing how vital it would be to protect the sorcerer, Uthron searched desperately in the chaos.

Crackling tendrils of energy answered the captain's second question just before another stream of almakhti snapped and surged into the Ilarchae. Dozens of the barbarians screamed as the terrible power scorched them and flung their bodies like rags, filling the air with the scent of burnt flesh and hair. The energy left a red line of afterglow across Uthron's vision, but he rode toward the sorcerer to protect him.

Not him. Her. As he galloped closer, Uthron gained a clear view of Lady Savatri. She was unhorsed, and an arrow had pierced her shoulder, leaving one hand limp by her side. Somehow, the sorceress was able to maintain the concentration to wield almakhti. She gritted her teeth in a fierce and determined glare, and though Uthron could not hear the words, her lips sang the spell to unleash another wave of death upon the Ilarchae. If she could hang on a little longer, there might be some slim hope of beating back the barbarians.

Energy crackled and writhed around both of her hands, but the brightness erupted from only the unwounded side. Just as it exploded from her hand, arrows fell like rain around her, and half a dozen sprouted from Savatri's chest. The almakhti arced up into the sky to disappear among the clouds as the sorceress staggered backwards and fell.

"No!" yelled Uthron as he raced toward her, weaving between combatants and knocking over a few as his steed's hooves sent up clods of turf. His horse screamed a moment later, and something wet pattered all over him, but he had no time to puzzle over it since his mount was collapsing under him. He had enough presence of mind to jerk his feet out of the stirrups but no time to leap away from the horse. He flailed and fell backwards, waiting for what seemed far too long before something slammed into him to drive the wind from his lungs and fill his head with fragmented brightness.

NAUSEA ACCOMPANIED THE DIM GREY LIGHT THAT CREPT INTO Uthron's awareness. His head felt swollen and raw with pain, a rotten melon ready to burst, and when he turned it, something loose seemed to rattle around inside. The light gathered some focus, and he groaned as shadowy forms took shape in the midst of it. Dark lines of varying thickness reached across his vision, and as they took on more crispness, he realized what they were.

He was lying down and staring up at tree branches. In a forest. A musty, earthy smell accompanied a faint breeze. Light was bleeding down through the branches and fluttering leaves. He squinted as the light seemed to dig through his eyes and pierce all the way to the back of his skull. Stiffness clawed at every tendon and muscle in his aching body, but nothing hurt like his head did. He must have hit it badly.

He was alive. His men were dead.

Before his vision they screamed and tumbled from their panicked horses with arrows and spears impaling their bodies. A tightness in his chest seized his breath. Another image came and sickened him: the young Sildharae he had slain was looking up into his eyes. He was too tired to live. *Mother have mercy. Better I had never awakened.* Far better to just lie there until his pain-racked body starved to death. He thought of his failure — Oruma curse him, his men were all gone — and wondered how and why he should live. He exhaled, and his breath leaked out like a long, slow sigh.

He lay there for a long while, unsure if he had fallen back asleep for a time. The pain and the memories remained, seared into his mind, where they played out whether he wanted them to or not.

From somewhere he summoned the will to stir. He tried to sit up and groaned at the wave of dizziness accompanying the urge to retch.

"Easy, Captain. You took a bit of a knock there," said a familiar voice.

He blinked and turned his head toward it. The man came into focus. "Tiran?"

"Aye. I'm here." He was sitting with his back against a tree trunk. Red stained the raggedy bandage surrounding Tiran's forearm, and another bandage covered one of his thighs.

"You're wounded."

"'Fraid so."

"But alive."

"'Fraid so."

"Thank the Mother and Father. Anyone else?"

"Well, there's Jwola there, but he's a bit worse off than I am."

"Morning, Captain," said Jwola in a strained voice.

Uthron turned his head the other way, gritting his teeth at the dizziness that came with the motion.

Jwola was also sitting and leaning his shoulder on a tree.

"Where are you wounded?"

Jwola nodded toward his calf wrapped in a stained bandage. "There. And . . ." He winced as he shifted his shoulder a bit. "Took an arrow in the back."

"As luck would have it," said Tiran, "his mail and one of his ribs stopped it before it hit anything important. When we dug it out, we found the arrowhead had cracked the rib clean through."

"Must hurt," said Uthron.

Jwola give a sickly smile. "Only when I breathe."

The captain fought through the nausea and the aches all over his stiff body to sit up, splaying his hands out to hold himself steady. He almost fell back down, but he clenched his eyes closed until the dizziness stopped rolling and throbbing through his head. When he opened them, he found dried blood spattered all over his tunic and mail. His horse's blood, not his. He groaned. "I feel a hundred years old. Morning, you said?"

"It's the day after the battle, Captain," said Tiran. "We lost."

"No shit," said Jwola.

Uthron swallowed, dreading the answer to his next question. "Any other survivors?" *All my men. I failed you. Why am I here now?*

"There's Spider," said Tiran.

"Sorn?"

"Who do you think dragged you here? Little bastard didn't even have a scratch on him. He's off looking for horses now."

"And the Ilarchae?"

"The ones that mowed us down from behind were in a hurry to join the main battle. Once they cleared off, Spider found me and Jwola. Dragged us here and told us to stay put for a spell. We weren't in much of a position to argue. He came back after a bit with you slung over his shoulder. Used his knife to dig the arrows out of us, cleaned us with some water out of some skins he found, then he disappeared again."

"His knife? Must've hurt."

"Like an axe up the arsehole, and we still need to clean the wounds proper when we can make a fire."

Jwola spat. "Shit."

"And where is Sorn now?" asked Uthron. "Have you seen him since?"

"It was dark when he came back. Don't know how he found us. Told us the Ilarchae had returned and slaughtered all our wounded." Tiran's voice shook a little, and he cleared his throat before he carried on. "He couldn't save anyone else. Maybe a few others got away. They could be hiding in the forest like us."

There was a long silence that seemed to assert the impossibility of other survivors. Uthron could not muster the spirit to say anything.

Tiran waited and then continued. "After they finished massacring us, they headed north. The whole time we thought they'd find us and finish their business. It was a bit of a rough night. Good that you slept through it. But Spider was right. They all headed off."

"North? Not west? Not toward Holurad?"

"Seems they have other plans. Besides, none of them know where the Hidden City is, do they? The Ilarchae slaves always stayed in the plain to raise crops, so even they couldn't lead the others there."

"Keeping it hidden appears to have been a wise precaution." The captain released another long sigh. *There might still be a reason to live. But my men are gone. I failed them.*

"Always been our way. That's how we survived all these centuries. We'll hole up there until this passes over. No one can assault the Hidden City."

Uthron nodded. *All dead. Nothing can bring them back. I should be with them.* Worse than the ache all over his body and the sharper pain in his head, a hollowness dwelled inside him, a dark and empty space in which he could find no will to care. But Tiran and Jwola and Sorn were alive. They had not failed him, and he had to find it in him to lead them, lest he fall short again.

Once he made that resolution, his next decision became clear in his mind. "So it's back to Holurad. If Sorn finds a horse, he must ride there. The three of us will catch up as we can. We've got to send warning as soon as possible, and we'd just delay him. Reshara must be informed."

"Veduir's heir? The girl?"

The captain nodded. "Our most powerful remaining sorcerer. And our queen now. She may be a girl still, but she's what we've got." He swallowed and closed his eyes as the dizziness sickened him again. The whole thing sickened him, and he was tired and sore everywhere. *Perhaps she'll have more wisdom and less pride than her elders. Otherwise, we might be joining Sildharan among the lost kingdoms.*

II
REBIRTH

Save for the water's gurgle against the ship and the waves groaning on the distant shore, the Bay of Kiriath was quiet. The whole of Halion Sound had been that way, with only the indifferent seagulls circling high overhead. The sapphire water was the same, but the fishing ships and trading vessels laden with textiles were lacking. That had been the first sign of the transformation Sequara was witnessing. The second was the burned out and crumbled buildings that grew visible in what had been Kiriath as the sailors reefed the sail and rowed closer to the ghost city's corpse. Black scorch marks streaked the tan stones, and not one structure appeared whole. The Torrlonders had been thorough in their destruction.

Her gaze drifted upward, toward the hilltop where the palace had stood. A gaping ruin remained. The trees and gardens were gone, and she supposed they must be wind-driven ashes. Asdralad could never again be the home that had nourished her. She knew it. That knowledge chilled her flesh and clogged her lungs, making it hard to draw breath.

She had concealed her emotions upon approaching her home shores from Earl Elfwy and the other Ellonders, his soldiers and sailors. Her heart had pounded in her chest, and her body tried to betray her with its shivers. But she had withdrawn into the realm of origins, and her breaths slowed and steadied as she meditated the way Queen Faldira had taught her.

Yet even in the realm of origins her fury smoldered, waiting for the moment when her feet would touch shore. The Torrlonders were still there, like a disease on the land that needed cleansing. Several of their large ships waited, tied up at the docks. She counted them again. Ten ships. That meant as many as a thousand soldiers, according to Earl Elfwy. Sequara's jaw muscles bunched and lined her cheeks as she ground her teeth. Her fingers drummed on the railing at the ship's bow. Her gaze did not waver from the shoreline.

Thoughts of her brother and his family crossed her mind. She had no idea if they were even alive, or if any living Asdralae remained on the island. If there were some, were they enslaved? Were they in hiding? One thing she knew: She would begin with the Torrlonders. Then, if there was anything left to heal, she would return to her true purpose. She had always been a healer, but the Torrlonders had made her a weapon. Now they would see what that weapon could do.

She closed her eyes, and amidst her fury wafted sweeter, gentler memories, like the scent of flowers on a breeze. She could not keep Dayraven out of her thoughts. He too was part of the island for her. Most of their time together had been in Kiriath, at the palace. It was there, in the place that symbolized all her duties, that she had fallen in love with him, aching with a desire she suppressed day after day, always returning to the intimacy they had known when she called him away from death at the Battle of Iarfaen.

She began to see with his eyes, something that often happened to her whether she willed it or not. The sorrow Dayraven would have felt upon seeing Kiriath this way became hers. Would he have joined her in seeking revenge? Would he have followed her consuming desire to slay the monsters that did this? It mattered little, for he was elsewhere, and his mind was even further away than his body. She shook her head in a vain effort to dispel the ever-present worry for him. She could not mend both Asdralad and him at once, and beneath her anger she shoved the thought that she mostlike would be able to fix neither. *Galdor will find him. He will help him.*

She released her grip on the railing and, avoiding the sailors, made her way aft toward Earl Elfwy, who stood conversing with Lieutenant Eanred. She had assessed Eanred as a sensible and capable veteran who was deeply loyal to Elfwy. The lieutenant also had not hidden his distrust of Sequara and his distaste for their current mission. It was a sentiment many of the soldiers and sailors shared, but none of them dared voice it openly save Eanred, whose bluntness had won Sequara's respect, even if it was grudging. She cleared her throat to make sure they were aware of her approach.

Earl Elfwy turned and gave her a bow, whereas Eanred nodded and frowned at her through his grizzled beard while his lord spoke. "Lady Sequara. Eanred and I were reviewing the disposition of the men once we reach the city."

She gave him a curt nod. "You needn't do this. This change of plans is very generous, but there is great risk. You can still just leave me ashore. King Fullan expected you only to escort me here. You've nearly accomplished that task, and once it's done, you're free to return to Ellond. That would be in the best interest of your men."

"I agree," said Eanred, who continued to frown at her.

Elfwy's face went rigid, and he glanced at his lieutenant. "Their best interest is the same as Ellond's, and it serves our kingdom to aid our neighbors and allies. I aim to see you here safely, not toss you off the ship without a care as to the outcome. That would be wrong as well as stupid. No. No halfway measures."

"I thank you for your concern, but I assure you . . ."

The earl raised his palm to cut her off. "This is the least we can do to see Asdralad restored, little though it may be." He lowered his hand. "You're certain of their numbers?"

Sequara nodded. "I sense only a handful of presences near the docks. Fewer than ten. Six, I believe."

"Those would be soldiers posted to guard their ships. And the rest?"

"Further away — well outside the city ruins — there is a body of hundreds. Two or three hundred, perhaps."

Earl Elfwy's eyes narrowed in concentration. "It must be their home encampment. Those posted at the docks will warn them of our arrival soon enough."

"Good." Sequara clenched her jaw.

Elfwy's eyes widened for a moment, as if he glimpsed the storm of her fury roiling beneath the placid surface. "Anything else?"

"Any other lives are too far away for me to sense."

The young earl nodded. "The rest of the Torrlonders must be inland, which suggests there is someone they are still attempting to control. There must be some active resistance on the island."

Sequara tried to answer him, but she did not trust her voice, and so she limited her response to a nod.

Elfwy favored her with a gentle smile. "I've reviewed what we discussed with the men, and they're ready." His face softened again, and he pleaded with his eyes as well as his voice. "At the very least, let us help you begin the liberation of your kingdom. With luck, you will soon find out where your people are."

Sequara gazed at the handsome and earnest earl and then at the lieutenant with his stoic face. She turned back to Elfwy. The truth was she could use all the help she could get, especially since she did not know what to expect. Not to mention the fact that forty soldiers would attract the Torrlonders' attention more swiftly than one lone woman could. *The sooner they come, the better. If this young earl's sense of honor serves Asdralad, then so be it.* And yet it still seemed wrong to allow Elfwy to drag himself and his men to their deaths.

She gazed at him for a moment. "I intend to rid the island of the Torrlonders or die in the attempt. The latter may be the more likely outcome."

His smile was gentle, not in the least patronizing. "So you've told me. And I believe you. As for me, I intend to see you on shore and allow you time to assess the situation before I depart."

"Very well. But remember one thing: When the Torrlonders arrive, stay out of my way."

TWO OF THE SIX TORRLONDERS GUARDING THE DOCKS WERE GONE long before Earl Elfwy's ship drew near, presumably to warn the encampment of the arrival of a ship they would have recognized as Ellonder as it approached. The other four took off running moments before the ship glided within bow range. They disappeared behind the rubble as the sailors eased the ship in and its side bumped against the groaning dock.

Sequara was the first off the ship, stepping onto one of the new docks the Torrlonders must have built since Queen Faldira had ordered the previous ones burnt to thwart the invaders when they landed. Her boots thudded on the wooden planks, which still smelled freshly hewn. Behind her came the clink of mail and weapons as well as the Ellonders' murmurs. She began walking down the center of what had been Kiriath's main thoroughfare.

A charred, dusty smell lingered among the ruins. Instead of the farmers and fisherfolk who had congregated near the docks to hawk their wares, silence greeted Sequara. Debris littered the pock-marked stone street, and the sorceress's boots grinded bits of rock into it with every step. Amidst the rubble and ruins, all of Kiriath's color had vanished along with its people. The wind kicked up dust and ash and soughed like a ghost.

She rubbed a bit of grit from her eye. It was difficult to recognize where she was, but small remnants of the buildings provided her with clues to her bearings. A piece of wall around a surviving doorframe had belonged to her favorite tailor's shop. A little further down, where the blackened stone had caved inward, had been an inn where one of Kiriath's most renowned singers once dazzled her audiences. The shops and inns were all gone, as were the towers of the noble houses that had loomed so high behind them. The absence of even those towers that she had erstwhile found so imposing tugged at her heart.

Sequara stopped. To her right were the remains of the adjacent temples of Oruma and Anghara. Amidst the charred and broken rubble, she caught glimpses of fragmented green stones, all that remained of the temples' distinctive ancient columns. Those temples had stood there since Asdralad's founding. Within them the sorceress had witnessed countless rituals and felt the divine presence of the Father and Mother. Empty ruins remained. The sun shone into the exposed sacred spaces of the roofless temples. She walked closer to them.

She ceased breathing for a moment. Within the piles of blackened stone were sprinkles of color — bits of dust-covered clothing poking out here and there. Underneath the clothing were the rotting remains of people, her people. A bleached hand reached out of the rubble, nothing but bone now, mostlike pecked clean by birds. It looked so small. Sequara supposed it had been a child's. Along with many others, he or she had died either in the smoke and flames or when the temple collapsed. A few corpses lay just outside where the temple doors had been, as if they had sought to flee the burning buildings but were cut down or shot with arrows when they exited. Sequara could almost hear their screams' echoes in the stones. Her fists clenched.

The Torrlonders had shown no mercy.

Neither would she.

The sound of many footsteps marching in unison interrupted her raging thoughts, and her head slowly turned toward it. They were still distant, but the clinking of armor and weapons rose above the din as they approached. Sequara strode back toward the street's center. Two columns of Ellonder soldiers drew up behind her, one on each side as they flanked her. Elfwy was at the head of the one on her left. When she caught his eye, he nodded. The approaching footsteps grew louder. She faced the direction whence they came and took a deep breath.

When she slipped into the realm of origins, it received her and purged her of impatience and fear. She waited, keeping her face as calm and still as a stone lying in the deepest depths of the Great Sea. She began to chant. "Alakathon indomiel ar galathon anrhuniae. Vortalion marduniel im paradon khalghoniae." At first she murmured the words, but each time she repeated them, the song of origin grew louder and more forceful.

The noise of the approaching Torrlonders surged, and their front ranks appeared, filling the entire width of the littered thoroughfare with grey kirtles behind bright swords and solid shields. Here were the ones that had destroyed her home and slaughtered her people. Still they occupied her land, her island home, and in that moment it did not matter whether they were human or not. For the sorceress, their deeds and crimes had erased their humanity. With their faces shadowed beneath their helms, they embodied the evil that had persecuted her people. They marched closer to her, and she walked closer to them as she kept up her chant, almost shouting the words.

As tendrils of bright blue energy buzzed into life and snaked around her hands and wrists, Sequara increased her pace. The Torrlonders kept coming, and a man in their lead shouted something as he pointed toward her. She broke into a sprint and screamed, "Alakathon indomiel ar galathon anrhuniae! Vortalion marduniel im paradon khalghoniae!"

ELFWY NODDED TO HIS MEN AND JOGGED FORWARD, TAKING CARE TO obey Sequara's desire that they should stay behind her. As Sequara moved toward the mass of oncoming Torrlonders chanting her spell, a stab of panic spread through his chest. In that moment it all made sense. In fact, he had suspected it since they departed from Ellordor, though he had not wanted to admit it. The beautiful sorceress had seemed so full of despair during the whole journey from Ellond, always brooding, seldom smiling, and hardly willing to speak. When she broke into a sprint, she confirmed his worst fear: Her intention all along was to die here on her native soil. She was a powerful sorceress, but no one could defeat so many soldiers alone. It was a tragic waste of so much beauty and power in one person, and his heart recoiled at such a loss.

The Torrlonders grew nearer, marching in unison, confident in the inevitable outcome of this encounter. Elfwy glanced back toward the docks. The chance of escape diminished with every moment, and the idea of abandoning Sequara to her chosen fate flitted through his mind. If madness had taken her, it was no fault of his. He had done his duty. The men would not argue with the order to retreat back to the ship.

Never.

He ran forward just as the wizard's fire began to crackle around the woman's hands. He had thought of grabbing her by the arm to talk sense into her, but she was running too fast, and the wizard's fire suddenly made it seem a poor idea. He kept pursuing her, not looking back to see if his men were keeping up. "Sequara!" he yelled as she screamed her spell. "We can still flee! There are too many . . ."

With a thunderous crack, a blinding bluish-white flash of energy rent asunder the air in front of the sorceress, and Elfwy jerked and staggered backwards. He found his balance and shook his head, trying to regain his vision, across which a red afterglow danced. A high-pitched whine rang in his ears, and all other sounds became fuzzy.

One of his men, Stanwin, stood at his side, but his voice seemed faint and distant. "My lord, are you hurt?"

Elfwy blinked. "Fine. Stay in formation. We'll ward her on both sides."

"I reckon she'll not need much of our help, my lord."

The earl followed his soldier's gaze, and as his vision cleared, he understood the awe in the man's voice. Where the solid shieldwall of Torrlonders had been, dozens of smoking corpses littered the thoroughfare, and tongues of flame still licked some of them. The explosion of energy had strewn their bodies everywhere, tossing them into the rubble on both sides of the street. A few of them groaned and struggled to rise while others screamed in agony. Most lay still. Shouts of command mingled with the screams. It was hard to see through the haze how many Torrlonders were left standing, but there had been so many.

Sequara had stopped advancing. She stood in a wide stance amidst the drifting smoke, awaiting her foe. She extended her hands before her as if preparing to unleash another wave of deadly wizard's fire.

Elfwy nodded. "Like she said, stay out of her way. Move up!"

He noted with approval how his soldiers held their formation as they marched closer to Sequara. They raised their shields, and they turned their alert gazes all around as they gripped their unsheathed swords. Their two lines flanked the sorceress, but the earl made sure to keep the men behind him a healthy distance from her, as did Lieutenant Eanred, who led the other line.

Elfwy gazed through the smoke to where the Torrlonders were reforming their front line. They still had the numbers to surround his forty soldiers, but the city was filled with so much rubble that the only approach that could accommodate the Torrlonders was the thoroughfare they were on. The collapsed buildings on either side formed effective barriers that would allow only a few men through at a time. He and his men would take care of any coming that way, but they would have to be careful of any bowmen the Torrlonders might send.

Someone among the Torrlonders barked commands, and metal clinked as the re-formed front line advanced once more toward the sorceress. Elfwy grinned as Sequara began chanting again, yet the words sounded different from the first spell. The marching footsteps grew louder, and soon enough the front line broke through the haze with their shields raised. Keeping their formation tight, they stepped over the bodies of their slain comrades, some of which were still smoldering.

The sorceress stood still as she faced them all, chanting all the while. Elfwy gripped his sword hilt tighter as the Torrlonders kept coming. Nothing was happening. Had Sequara used up all her energy in the first assault? He looked at her hands for the telltale crackling of energy that preceded wizard's fire, but there was nothing.

The Torrlonders emerged from the smoke and marched close enough that their angry features grew visible beneath their helms. There were so many of them. Their line was several ranks deep, and they occupied the entire thoroughfare. Elfwy glanced back at his men. They had assumed fighting postures, their shields and swords held ready.

Sequara shouted her spell louder than before and lifted her palms. At once, the corpses lying on the street that had been smoldering erupted in roaring, roiling flames. At least a dozen of them exploded into massive conflagrations that swallowed the Torrlonders who had been marching over them. Shrieks broke out, and their discipline shattered as men recoiled and became fuel for the fire.

The engulfing flames ascended into a writhing wall of death, and even at a distance, the heat smacked into Elfwy's exposed face, causing him to wince as he witnessed the horrific deaths of scores of men. The stench of smoke, seared flesh, and burnt hair filled the air along with the Torrlonders' screams. Within the uncanny inferno men flailed and teetered, and a couple of them broke away from the wall of fire to emerge tottering and grasping as they screamed at the pain of the flames eating their flesh. Like blind shadows within the flames, they staggered a few steps towards Sequara before collapsing and succumbing to the consuming fire. This was no clean death. Elfwy wished he could not hear their shrieks, and with an effort he repressed the powerful impulse to retch.

Before the wall of flames stood Sequara's small silhouette, her arms raised as she shouted her spell. Elfwy crouched behind his shield in wonder at how she could withstand the heat, which bent the air in waves and gusted back the woman's hair and tunic. He stepped toward her, thinking to place his shield before her lest the conflagration devour her. But a cry jerked his head back. Stanwin pointed toward the ruins. With fire illuminating and reddening their blades, grey-kirtled Torrlonders were climbing over the rubble. Dozens of them.

"Attack!" yelled Elfwy. "Hit them before they gain the street!"

SEQUARA TOOK A DEEP BREATH AFTER HEALING THE FIFTH Ellonder. He would have bled to death from the wound in his thigh, but she had managed to close it enough to stop the flow. "You'll need to rest several days. The wound will reopen if you strain it." She glanced down at the flesh of her palms, stiffened with drying blood.

The soldier nodded and looked up at her as she sat over him. "Thank you, my lady." His eyes were wet with unshed tears, and his voice was strained. "Thank you." From healing him she knew he had been thinking of his wife and three children, a boy and two girls. The memories of the other four men she had saved still jostled within her. That was one of the things that made healing so difficult and draining, though those memories would fade within days or hours. Only one person's memories had stayed with her, become part of her, after healing him. She shook her head. She could not think of Dayraven now. Not with so much to do here. There were more wounded Ellonders, men who had sacrificed to help her. She began to rise, but the world tilted, and she sat back down again.

"Lady Sequara, you are weary." Earl Elfwy crouched next to her and looked in her eyes, his brow wrinkled in a concerned frown.

"I'm well enough. There are more of your wounded I can help."

"My men have patched them up, and none are in danger of their lives. Rest now. Please."

"How many did you lose?"

The earl looked at the ground. "Six. No more. Thanks be to Edan. And to you."

It would have been none had you abandoned me here. And I might have died in their stead. Six more deaths to lay at her feet. She would never be able to count them all. "I'm truly sorry."

He returned his gaze to her eyes. "I know you are, but they died for a good cause."

"Did they?" The horror of slaying so many men returned to her mind, like vomit forcing its way up. With an effort, she held her composure. Still, the burnt stench of their deaths filled her nostrils, and their torment and fear echoed and bounced around in her skull. What had she allowed the Torrlonders to make her? She did not dare ask the earl how many Torrlonder dead there were.

"The other men believe so. So do I. You're here to free Asdralad. To reclaim it for your people from aggressors."

If there are any of my people left, she finished in her head. She looked at the man's handsome and earnest face, and as she held back her tears, she nodded.

The earl looked away as if to give her a moment to collect herself. "But now you must rest. Gather strength for what comes next. You've won a victory, but I fear it's not over."

"For you it is. I thank you for not only seeing me here safely, but for going beyond your duty to aid me. Return to Ellond now with your men."

Elfwy was silent a short space. "We'll see about that." A gentle smile came to his lips. "I've been talking it over with them. They seem to think that, after that long sea voyage, it would be good to stretch their legs a bit. That would also allow me to collect more intelligence on the Torrlonders for King Fullan."

"I won't have more of your men's deaths on my conscience."

His smile remained even as he shook his head. "Can't be helped, my lady. When you stand in battle next to someone, you form a bond. The men believe your task is theirs now."

"But they could all die. This time we took the Torrlonders by surprise. But there are more of them, and some at least from today must have escaped to warn them. And what if others come to join them? I will not doom your men. You must command them . . ."

Footsteps approached, and Lieutenant Eanred appeared standing next to where his earl crouched. He cleared his throat. "Here to report. Couldn't help overhearing a bit, my lord."

Sequara looked up at him. "I told you to rest. You need time to recover from your wound."

"Your pardon, my lady." The veteran patted his side, where the tip of a sword blade had punctured his byrny. Blood stained the mail around the broken links. "I reckon you patched me up better than you thought. Besides," he nodded at the earl. "Lord Elfwy has the right of it. We'll be finishing what we started here. To a man, we're with you."

Once again she found it hard to speak, so she nodded at Eanred first and then again at Elfwy. *So. More deaths to come.*

THEY MOVED THE FOUR MOST SEVERELY WOUNDED MEN BACK TO THE ship. Earl Elfwy suggested they all sleep aboard it as well, but Sequara refused. She had begun to reclaim Asdralad, and she would not move from her native soil until she finished. So they camped amidst the ruins of the city, not far from the docks.

That night, after succumbing to exhaustion, she dreamt of all the men she slew, and it was only then that she saw them as men. Their agony revisited her afresh, the horror of their painful deaths. Even within her dream she loathed herself for it, and the next moment she was explaining to Queen Faldira why she had to do it. The queen frowned down at her as if she were angry, and she would say no word. She pleaded with her mentor to speak to her and tell her what to do, but the woman only sat in harsh judgment. That was when she realized Faldira was a corpse with bluish rotting flesh, and she awoke with panting breaths. She did not sleep the rest of the night.

Before morning arrived she arose and walked past the guards without a word to them as they bowed to her. In the darkness she stood in the middle of Kiriath's thoroughfare and stared all around her.

The ruins were black, silent shadows, but in her mind they whispered of the men she had burned, and her people who had died there haunted them.

She withdrew into the realm of origins, breathing in all the ghosts and sensing their return to Oruma. In the realm of origins the great weight of her grief at all the deaths did not disappear or even lessen, but she opened herself to them, took them into herself, and weaved them into her. And she understood she would cause yet more before she finished. Her strength in the gift and her years of training and discipline: All of it found its purpose in the present. She had bound herself to this duty when she was a girl, the moment Queen Faldira had chosen her and she embraced that choice.

By the time the Ellonders were stirring, the sun's ruddy light was bleeding over the horizon. Sequara took it as an omen of things to come, and she nodded in acceptance.

"IT'S THE SAME AS ALL THE OTHERS. THE TORRLONDERS AREN'T MEN. They're beasts."

"No. Beasts don't murder like this. They kill to live. This is a sickness of men."

"They've shamed themselves beyond redemption. Soldiers are meant to protect, not . . . this."

Lost in the bitter world of her grief and rage, Sequara half heard the disgust and shock in the words Lieutenant Eanred and Earl Elfwy's other soldiers were exchanging at the sight of yet another Asdralae village massacred, the skeletal and charred remains of its inhabitants strewn on the ground where they died, unburied and anonymous. But they were not anonymous to Sequara. They were her people, the ones she was meant to protect. *If I can no longer protect them, I'll avenge them.*

She knelt with her head hanging down by what appeared to have been a family, with two larger skeletons lying in a futile gesture of protection or mourning over two smaller ones. She did not know if they died by flame or by sword, but their home was ashes all around them. She closed her eyes against the dust and grit that a breeze lifted.

Footsteps approached behind her, crunching on the brittle detritus beneath the ash. "My lady," said Earl Elfwy's voice. "We will find them. The ones that did this. I swear it on my honor."

Sequara lifted her head and nodded. Releasing her spirit into the realm of origins, where her grief diminished to an insistent whisper, she began to chant a song of origin.

"You ask me, we should've left this stinking shithole of an island a long time ago," said Edgar.

"No one asked you." Garulf scanned the horizon for any sign of the sorceress and men accompanying her. Nothing but the browns of Asdralad's torrid landscape met his gaze. Beneath him, his horse snorted, seeming more skittish than usual. But he could see no sign of anyone other than his scouting party of six mounted men. Sweaty, saddle sore, and irritable, they had ridden for the better part of the day under the hot sun searching for the supposed sorceress and warriors that the escapees from Kiriath had reported.

"Why us?" persisted Edgar with one of his favorite themes of late. "Why'd we get stuck here when the rest of Torrlond's army is off winning glory elsewhere?"

"They're doing the same thing we're doing, idiot." Garulf spat. "Killing whoever the king tells us to. That's what soldiers do."

"We follow orders. I know." Edgar sighed. "What do you reckon about this sorceress?"

Garulf could hear the slight tremor of fear in Edgar's voice, and, if even half of what was said about her was true, he did not blame the man. "Something happened in Kiriath, for sure. Our job's to see if we can find out what. Remember, if we see her, we don't engage. Ride hard to go and report."

"Won't have to tell me twice," said Bernwold behind him.

"Right, lads, let's check that rise over there." Garulf pointed off into the distance, but before he could spur his horse, a chorus of shrieks drew his eyes upward.

A large squabble of noisy seagulls was descending toward them, enough to block the sun and cast a swath of shadow over them.

"Shit!" said Edgar, drawing Garulf's attention as he wiped a smear of white from his cheek. "One of them fucking birds just shat on me! Ugh! Stinks like a troll's hairy arsehole." He grimaced as he smelled his fingers.

"Sounds like an improvement for you, Edgar." Bernwold smirked.

Garulf would have laughed, but the sergeant sensed something strange as his gaze returned to the sky. "They're headed straight for us."

"What are they . . ." But the answer to Bernwold's question came before he could finish it.

Not slowing the least in their headlong descent, the gulls slammed into the faces of the Torrlonder scouts, surrounding them in a flurry of feathers and sharp beaks.

"Ah, fuck!" Garulf swatted at the birds assaulting him. Among the deafening shrieks of the birds, he heard the screams of his fellow soldiers, whom he could not see for all the gulls surrounding them. He tried to give the order to ride away, but only a muffled cry emerged as a lunging beak tore at his lip, and he shut his mouth lest the bird burrow inside it. Hot pain lanced through his left eye, which burst when a frenzied gull breached his guard with its dagger-like bill. Garulf tried to grab the creature and crush it as warm fluid streamed down his cheek, but he lost his balance and teetered off his horse. His wrist crunched when he landed on it, but the lancing pain up his arm was momentary as a burst of light erupted in his head with the impact.

When consciousness returned, Garulf was surprised he was alive. A moment later, he wished he was not as he emerged into a world of pain. His head felt swollen, and his face was sticky with his own blood and Edan knew what else. His arm was on fire with agony where it had broken, and each breath sent jolts of pain through his body due to what he suspected were several broken ribs.

He groaned and opened his remaining eye to find a shadowy form standing over him with the sun behind it.

"Tell me where the rest of the Torrlonders are, and I will make your death swift."

It was a woman's voice, and Garulf could hear the steel in it.

"Sorceress," he managed to grate out.

"Where are they?"

Garulf would have shrugged if his body were not so shattered. He reckoned she would find them soon enough anyway, and all he wanted was for the pain to stop. *I'm finished no matter what.* He thought about explaining how all he ever did was follow orders, but the words felt flimsy before he even tried to utter them, and he was in too much agony to bother. "Due south. On the outskirts . . . of the forest."

The figure above him was silent a moment. "Good enough. May the Mother and Father have mercy on you."

I very much doubt they will, was his last thought.

EARL ELFWY ORDERED HIS MEN TO FAN OUT ALONGSIDE THE sorceress with their shields up. Since he knew she would unleash wizard's fire at the foe, he posted no one in front of her to protect her, but he stayed as close to her side as he dared. On her other side stood Lieutenant Eanred, who now regarded the sorceress the same way he did his own daughter. Elfwy released a long breath. At least he and his men might draw away some of the arrows, and he prayed to Edan none would find Sequara.

About six hundred Torrlonders faced them, their backs to the forest. A few days ago, it would have seemed foolhardy, if not absurd, for so few to seek battle with so many. Sequara had changed his perspective. Had he been a gambling man, he would have wagered their chances just about even, but both sides would take losses. Being a soldier, he shouted to his men with steel in his voice, "Time to finish them, lads! Follow Lady Sequara's lead. For Ellond and Asdralad!"

Looking one last time at the beautiful sorceress, he smiled at her and knew he could not have found a nobler cause to die for. *But I'd rather live for her,* he admitted to himself with a touch of shame at his folly.

Sequara screamed her spell, and wizard's fire buzzed to life around her outstretched hands, crackling and writhing in seeming eagerness. He braced himself for the loud bang and the flash of energy. But before that happened, dozens of the Torrlonders withered to the earth, some crying out in agony. Most of the fallen had been in the back rows of their formation. He had less than a moment to puzzle over it before the sorceress unleashed her power.

WITH GRIM SATISFACTION, IMHARR PEERED BETWEEN THE LEAVES and branches to watch the Torrlonder bodies fly in the air when the violent flash of almakhti assaulted them. Conveying his orders through Khalan, the leader of the Asdralae woodsmen, he bade the archers to loose twice more before he led their forces out of the forest. Nayan and Gilad commanded the flanks of their attack, and he took the center. Val stayed behind with Prince Runan to guard the lad. He would have left Dun there too, but, after a long fever, his friend had perished of the infection in his leg wound, leaving only four of Queen Rona's Adanese guards left, including himself.

Imharr was bone weary of watching his friends die, and of watching the Asdralae suffer and die too. That was why he had grown so excited when some of Khalan's scouts reported the arrival of a powerful sorceress who attacked the Torrlonders when she landed in Kiriath, slaying well-nigh three hundred of them. He had not quite dared to believe it, but he and Rona had immediately begun to lay their plans.

The northerners' presence was a small mystery, but, of course, he recognized the sorceress: Sequara, the heir to Asdralad's throne. During her months spent in Adanon leading the Asdralae who fought alongside the Adanese, he had come to know the sorceress well, and he knew how capable she was. Even more vivid in his memory was the intimacy of the journey he and the others shared with her when the sorceress saved Dayraven and brought him away from the Battle of Iarfaen.

They had feared Sequara dead. But when Imharr saw her, for the first time since the Torrlonders had taken the island, hope kindled inside him. There had been no time or opportunity to coordinate anything with the sorceress and her party, but the Torrlonders had awaited her in just the right place.

Imharr unsheathed his blade and brandished it. "Attack!" he screamed in Andumaic, and three Adanese emerged from the forest at the head of more than four hundred Asdralae fighters. Armed with farming tools and weapons scavenged from the Torrlonders, they ranged in age from lads scarce grown enough to call men to greybeards with their best days long behind them. None had been warriors before the Torrlonders came, but what they lacked in experience they more than made up for in their fierce desire to rid their home of invaders and murderers.

"Freedom!" someone among the Asdralae cried, and as the word spread among the others, Imharr too took it up. Succumbing to confusion at being attacked before and behind, the Torrlonders abandoned their disciplined formation. A burst of almakhti shattered the air and washed the color from the world. Steel clashed. Men screamed their death cries. "Freedom!" he yelled for Asdralad and Adanon as he guided his blade past a Torrlonder's shield and sliced open his exposed neck.

AMIDST THE WRECKAGE OF BATTLE AND THE ODOR OF ALMAKHTI-seared bodies, Sequara slumped to the ground and knelt there. All the living Asdralae fighters nearby went to their knees and faced her, seeming to wait for her command. Her people. They were alive. Too stunned for anything else, she finally allowed her tears to come, and they swelled into sobs that shook her body. She sat and wept, too exhausted to care who witnessed her.

It was over.

Hundreds of corpses littered the ground, most of them wearing grey kirtles. So much death. She would never rid herself of its stench. According to Earl Elfwy's reckoning, save for a few possible stray patrols, this had to have been the last of the Torrlonders on Asdralad. And, at the last, her people had come. They were alive. Yalawyn had sheltered them, thanks be to Oruma and Anghara.

She tried to speak or at least smile at them as they waited on their knees, but more tears came from a seemingly endless reservoir, all the grief and loss she had known ever since the Torrlonders began their War of the Way. This included the loss of herself, the woman she had wanted to be and her story she had created and cultivated for so long, for she had slain so many that she could never see herself as a healer again. That woman was as dead as the many soldiers she had killed.

And yet, hers were tears of relief too. She had not failed her people. A success she could never call it, for so many Asdralae had died. But she had returned to protect them or die trying, and at the end of it, she lived to know she had not failed but had fulfilled her duty.

Knowing herself too weary to heal anyone, she allowed the tears to flow. There was no more left of her. She had nothing else to give. And so her spirit bathed in the cleansing tears. For how long she sat there she knew not, but at length she grew aware that someone knelt near her.

She rubbed her eyes and looked up at Elfwy. A cut on his cheek bled freely, but she was glad to note he seemed otherwise unhurt. He smiled at her, and then he held out his hand. She nodded and smiled back, and then she took his hand in hers. No words passed between them. They needed none, and nor would they have served them. In his blue eyes she saw the acknowledgement of all they had been through in the last days together, and she knew she would not have accomplished her task without him and his men.

"Lady Sequara," said a new voice in strangely accented Andumaic.

Sequara let go of Elfwy's hand and looked up at the newcomer, in whose eyes she saw the hardened look of a man who knew what it meant to kill in order to survive. The warrior's familiarity jarred her at first, perhaps because he was leaner than she remembered him, even from those dark days in Adanon and Caergilion, which haunted them both and bonded them. But his scarred sword hand still had the silver hue that it had taken on after she healed it from the touch of dragon fire. "Imharr?"

"Yes." He glanced at Elfwy with a slight frown before facing her again and smiling, but she could not recall his smile ever seeming so sad. "It's good to see you," he said in the Northern Tongue.

Sequara wiped her wet cheeks with the back of her hand and sniffled. "You are well met this day, Imharr. Dayraven would take great joy from knowing you're alive."

He directed another glance toward Elfwy for a moment before he smiled back at her and nodded. "Is he well?"

The sorceress looked down at the ground before answering. "He lives. I . . . would know otherwise." She swallowed before continuing. "We must speak of him, you and I."

Imharr nodded. "And so we shall. But I see you are weary. If you would allow me, my lady, I will conduct you to our camp inside Yalawyn. Many of your people have survived within its shelter. Queen Rona will be eager to speak with you."

In that moment, with a sense of both guilt and relief, she knew who had held the remnants of her people together in her absence. "Yes," answered Sequara, and her voice sounded drained even to her. "Take me to Queen Rona."

Amidst the joy, mourning, relief, and tempered celebration of the camp that served as the temporary headquarters of the resistance movement against the Torrlonders, Sequara smiled and watched Queen Rona of Adanon inside the latter's tent. Rona had come to greet Sequara at the periphery of the camp, and there they had embraced with true warmth. There too Jhaia had come, and when the shrunken old woman took her turn to hug Sequara and broke down in tears, the sorceress again wept openly for joy and relief, feeling like a little girl again in the warmth of the embrace. They held each other long. At length, Jhaia grasped her by the shoulders and looked up to her face. She wiped her cheek, sniffled, and said, "My Queen. My beautiful daughter. You've come back. To the same nest the bird always returns."

Jhaia had a saying for every occasion. Sequara smiled at the memory as Rona listened to Imharr's report inside the queen's tent. She and the queen had come to know each other well back when Sequara fought in Adanon, and they shared a deep mutual respect. The sorceress thought of her as a wise elder sister, and she somehow found it easier to speak openly with Rona than she ever had with Queen Faldira, whom she had revered.

Rona sat in the tent's one chair as she spoke with Imharr about the battle in Ondunic, which Sequara could not understand. The warrior seemed to draw to the end of his account after a smile spread across his face. Rona nodded to him and spoke for a moment. Then she gave him a grin suggesting something more familiar than a queen addressing her warrior, speaking words that made Imharr's eyes widen briefly before he bowed to them both and exited the tent.

The queen turned to Sequara, and her grin disappeared for a moment as if she had forgotten the sorceress's presence during her discussion with Imharr. She recovered quickly and smiled once again as she rose from the chair and took Sequara's hand in her own.

"Sit with me," she said in the Northern Tongue, the language the two could speak most fluently with each other. She gestured at two cushions on the floor. "I'm so weary of posing in that chair. Your arrival has, among other things, relieved me of the need for it."

Sequara nodded and sat with her legs folded under her next to Rona, who continued to hold her hand.

Rona looked her in the eyes. "In truth, you've gained us all a great victory. You've won the freedom of your people, my dear."

Sequara let out a long breath. "With much help from Earl Elfwy and the timely appearance of Imharr leading the resistance fighters. But at some cost."

"Imharr tells me thirty-four Asdralae died in the battle, and forty-nine took serious wounds. Each life *is* a terrible cost, but no one would deny the worth of their sacrifices. The Torrlonders are gone. Asdralad is cleansed. Your people are free."

Sequara nodded at Rona's words even as, in her mind, she added more of Elfwy's warriors to the tally of the dead. Twenty-five of the original forty were alive, including the four they had left behind at the ship. "My people. There would be none left had you not been here to organize the resistance. It needed a center, a strategy, and belief. You gave it all those things and more."

"I suppose what happened to us in Adanon was fine training for all that."

"Perhaps. But it also required someone with the right skills and weight of personality. I am deep in your debt."

Rona shook her head. "No. It is I who owed you and Queen Faldira for what you and your people did in Adanon."

Sequara frowned. "Adanon. The Torrlonders still occupy your kingdom as well as Caergilion. And as long as they're there, they remain a threat to us here." She regretted being unable to savor the happiness of the moment and wondered if ruling meant ever foregoing the luxury of contentment.

Rona's face hardened, and her eyes narrowed. "Then let us take the fight to them."

"How?"

"We have the Torrlonders' ships. We have several hundred fighters. We could perhaps scrape together as many as a thousand after combing the island."

"Nowhere near enough to defeat the Torrlonders in Adanon."

"True. But what if the Torrlonders are already struggling to keep control there? What if the resistance in Caergilion and Adanon has carried on without us, and all it lacks is a focus, a spark that will unite their people against the invaders?"

Sequara thought a moment. "The risk would be great. We would have to be sure the people would rally around us. At the moment we know too little. In fact, we're blind."

"Not entirely." At Sequara's puzzled frown, Rona continued. "We would, of course, first send a ship for tidings. But we have good reason to believe the Torrlonders' control in Adanon and Caergilion is not as strong as they would like."

"How do you know this?"

"A wounded Torrlonder we captured before you arrived here. Before he died of his wounds, we tried to save him. In return, he spoke freely and with some bitterness about the lack of reinforcements in Asdralad. He and his fellows seemed to feel abandoned. Their leader here, Earl Ulfred, had been begging the mainland for more soldiers to destroy us, but none ever came. Our captive said it was because the Torrlonders are too busy fighting insurgents in the southwest, and he hinted there was some strife within Torrlond itself. He would say little of that, and he was nearly delirious from fever, but we believe he spoke the truth."

Sequara took a moment to absorb everything Rona was saying. "If he did, it may be our best chance is to sail for Adanon, as you say. Boldness may be our wisest course." A slight wave of nausea hit her, and her hand went to her stomach.

"Are you well?" asked Rona.

"Fine. Just a little queasiness. It's been hitting me since I journeyed from Sildharan. I'm so tired, to speak truly."

Rona's eyebrows lowered in an expression of curiosity, as if she were examining the sorceress in a new light. "Has your appetite lessened of late as well?"

Sequara thought for a bit. "Yes. I've been distracted with everything. Eating is the last thing I think about anymore."

Rona continued to stare at her, and her lips quirked into a slight smile, prompting Sequara to ask, "What is it?"

The smile widened. "Forgive me, my dear, but under which moon did you last bleed?"

"No. That's . . ." Sequara's eyes widened, and her hand went to her belly.

Rona's smile disappeared. "I'm sorry. I shouldn't have pried. It's just that, after carrying a few of her own, there are certain things a woman recognizes. Perhaps you're merely exhausted from all your efforts."

"I'm . . ." Sequara's eyes blinked, and her mouth worked, but no words would come out. Her mind raced back to a beautiful evening by the River Lannad on the border between Sundara and Golgar. They had been journeying north to Sildharan when it happened. It had seemed inevitable, that blissful succumbing to desire that had built in her for so long. *Dayraven.* He flooded her thoughts, and all the emotions that came with him threatened to shatter her composure.

"I'm sorry," repeated Rona. "It was discourteous of me."

Struggling to overcome her embarrassment and bewilderment, Sequara smiled and squeezed Rona's hand. "You're too perceptive. That's all. I hadn't realized myself."

"Perhaps you're not . . ."

"I am." In speaking those two words, she knew she was carrying Dayraven's child. She did not have Rona's experience as a mother, but she was a trained healer. "I was so foolish not to notice."

"Does Dayraven know?"

"He . . ." She gawked at Rona and felt the flush spreading across her face. "How did you know *that*?"

A quick smile from the queen. "It was evident enough when I arrived here. The way you both gazed at and avoided each other."

"You *are* too perceptive. Or was I so obvious?"

"You hid it much better than he did. Of course, we mustn't fault him for that. He *is* a man. But I'm guessing your secret is safe with me."

Sequara's hand went to her belly again. "I never thought . . ." The moment she accepted the truth of her condition, vast emotions began to compete within her. All of her repressed longing for Dayraven invaded her, filling her with a bliss that stretched the boundaries of her identity. It shocked her that she would even consider having a child, let alone feel such giddiness and freedom at the idea.

At the same time, the weight of her duties fell upon her as a physical thing, pushing her shoulders down and bending her spine. She was a queen now. "No ruler of Asdralad has ever wed or had a child. It's forbidden."

Rona gazed at her and gave her a smile that did not reach her eyes. "I know." She put her hand on Sequara's shoulder. "You must decide, then. If you wish to have this babe, you must step down as Asdralad's ruler. *Or*," she said as she held up her index finger, "you may change the rules."

"What do you mean?"

The queen took a breath. "The Asdralad you knew is no more. It's time to build something new. Perhaps the rulers of the new Asdralad will choose to wed and pass the gift on to their children. It's always seemed such a loss to me that they've never done so. Now that most of your ruling families have been wiped out, there will be a great need for those with the gift. You might even say that your having a child is a necessity to keep the gift strong in Asdralad."

"But I could never . . ."

"You are a ruler. The best Asdralad could have. It is the prerogative of rulers to change the rules, so long as it does no harm. All traditions have their origins, but sometimes they come to cause more hurt than good, and then it's time to change them. It seems to me Asdralad would be best off with *you* guiding it. Faldira knew that, and who would dare to question her wisdom? And you might be best able to fulfill your duty with the support that comes of being loved." She smiled. "Sometimes rulers must do things that enable them to keep going. No matter how much we pretend not to be, we are human. It's no crime to have desires. In fact, they may help you to better understand your people."

Sequara sat dazed for a moment. She yearned to believe in what she was hearing, but it ran counter to all her prior assumptions. Though the woman hid it well, she knew Rona's grief over the losses of her husband and eldest son, and yet she could still be an effective ruler and advocate such attachments. "I must think this over. It's too much."

"Of course. Think carefully, my dear. And know that I'm always willing to lend an ear. And to support you when you decide."

"Thank you." As she held Rona's hand, however, a sudden resolution came to her, falling into place with perfect finality. In her heart, she knew where Dayraven was. Having fulfilled her duty to Asdralad, she would find him, and it was fortunate that freeing Adanon and Caergilion coincided with her desire. Her many trials had purged her, and though she did not quite yet recognize the woman emerging from them, she began to embrace this new person with an eagerness she had never felt before. She faced Rona and said with all the conviction welling up in her, "But of one thing let us be certain: We *will* prepare a fleet and find enough fighters to fill every ship. We *will* liberate Adanon and Caergilion. Nothing less would make Asdralad safe."

Rona nodded, her eyes hardening even as she smiled, and the sorceress nodded back.

With the force of prophecy Sequara believed it: They would defeat the Torrlonders in the southwest and send them back to their kingdom, thus securing safety for Asdralad. And in Caergilion, as she had once before, she would find Dayraven.

12
THE RETURN

The small fishing boat's keel sliced into a sandbar not more than fifty feet from where waves groaned and lapped the shoreline, and the hull shuddered as his hand grasped the boat's wooden railing to keep him from pitching forward. Hemming in the small beach, the green hills looming overhead were sheared off by water and wind into rocky cliffs, above which seagulls keened. The heavy breeze was laden with the tang of salt and the rotten musk of seaweed. When a wave smacked the boat's stern, its spray sprinkled his face. He breathed in the air and stretched.

His body was stiff with the confines of the voyage, but it was nowhere near as weary as his mind, which never rested from its constant struggle. Perhaps the conflict would lessen now that he had arrived in the place where he hoped for some sign, or at least a clue. The idea that he had been in this place before niggled at the edges of his awareness, though he could not be certain. Something important had happened here, or would happen. It was all he had: a word and a sense of purpose waiting in the place it represented.

He had reached Caergilion.

His companions had asked him where to put him ashore, and rather than confess he did not know, he asked them to leave him at the first convenient spot. Since they were simple Sundarae fishermen who rarely ventured far from their native waters, none of the three knew the Caergilese shores well. But, when he was a lad, Omong had once sailed with an uncle to this part of Andumedan on a merchant ship. He it was who told them of Culvor Sound, and that if they sailed down it some way, there were small, sandy bays amidst the rugged cliffs where they might approach the land. The large town of Gadomiel, where long ago the merchant whom Omong's uncle worked for traded his goods, lay not far to the north. Once on land, he reckoned he would head for Gadomiel as a likely place to gather tidings, though he dreaded being near so many people. *But if I must find my purpose, I must speak to someone.*

"My lord," said Rahal, "this is as close as the boat may come. May we see you to shore?"

He turned his gaze to the man, whose dark skin had browned even more during the voyage from Sundara, and found the will to smile at him. "You've done enough, my friend. I'll help you push the boat off, and then you must be on your way. If, as you tell me, this land is under occupation, there may be danger here. I would not have you linger."

"Please, lord." Birshan folded his hands before him. "If you won't allow us to stay with you, we would beg one final boon."

A boon. Grant them the only real boon there can be for their kind: the eternal rest, whispered the voice. Its susurration was a chill wind skimming the contours of his raw mind, speaking not in words but in thoughts he knew only too well. He closed his eyes and once again suppressed the power within him. When he opened them, the three fishermen were waiting for his reply. "You must return to your families. Cherish them. Live your lives. Live them well, friends." *Rest, rest, rest*, it seethed.

Omong bowed his head. "We will obey you, lord, though it pains us to part from you. But please. Let our feet touch the land where you will tread. Let us embrace you one final time before we must journey back, and send us away with one final blessing."

A blessing. Give them the blessing of oblivion. Just as the thought's shadowy tendrils brushed along his awareness, the salty wind kicked up as if in sympathy with it, snapping his brown robe and flinging his silver hair before his eyes. *Bless them*, it hissed. A slight shake of his head banished the voice. "I will give you my blessing. But it is only one man's wish for the well-being of his friends."

"Not so, lord Prophet," said Birshan with a smile. "Edan's blessing comes from you. We felt its joy the whole journey."

The bliss of unbeing calls them. They know it not, but they feel it. Bless them. He released a tired sigh. "Edan's blessing you call it. But I have told you: It dwells in *you*. In all of you. It is in the sea, in the sky, in the birds wheeling above us, in the fish you live from, and in the old soil of the land. Most of all, it is in those you should love and cleave to. Open your eyes, my friends, and you will see it."

"Even so," said Rahal, "for the sake of our friendship and our reverence to you, we ask for this final blessing."

Bless them. Bless them. Though it was still late summer, the voice within was a winter wind skimming along bare branches, piercing and fingering his mind. He nodded. "Very well. Let us go to shore. And then I bid you hasten home."

All three grinned, and Omong said, "Thank you, lord Prophet."

He removed his boots and rolled up his dark breeches. Then he took off his robe and bundled up the boots inside it.

Omong approached him holding out a sack. Without asking, he knew what it contained. The last of their provisions: smoked fish, dried bread, hard cheese, and a skin of watered-down wine. They had shared these among themselves as brothers. Otherwise, the boat contained only a barrel of potable water that was still mostly full. "Please, my lord. Wherever it is you go, you'll need somewhat to eat."

He shook his head. "I'll find what I need along the way. You will take this food with you, for you shall have more need of it than I. There will be no argument." *They'll have no need of it if you bless them*, rustled the cold shadow in his mind.

Omong hesitated a moment and then bowed before he stowed away the bag.

He turned to climb over the boat's side. Birshan was already standing in the waves up to his thighs. The fisherman held up his hands, and he lowered his bundled robe to him. He swung his legs over the side and, clinging to the coarse wood with his hands and feet, climbed down before jumping and splashing into the water, which cooled his flesh and soaked his breeches as well as his white kirtle's hem. His toes sank into the gritty sand beneath the water.

For a while he stood within the rough caress of the waves as they splashed against him and nudged him toward the shore. Swelling, rolling, and breaking, wave after wave slapped against him while the sun beat down, warming his face. There was something in the repetition that the icy voice within him responded to. *The endless breath of the world. In and out for eternity. They will never understand until they join it once again. Why not shorten their grief?*

"My lord?" Rahal stood next to him.

He took a deep breath and then smiled. "It's a beautiful day, is it not?"

"Yes, my lord."

He nodded, and they waded through the water to follow Omong and Birshan toward the little beach waiting in the cliffs' shadows.

The waves sucked at their soaked clothes as they emerged from the sea, and when their feet reached the beach, leaving four sets of fleeting footprints in the wet sand, the salty water dripped from them. Birshan handed him his bundled robe. He faced his three friends, who stood in a row waiting.

They knelt and bowed their heads before he could say a word. He would have clasped them as friends and equals, but they expected something else from him.

Bless them.

His hand reached out and hovered over Omong's head. For a moment he held it there, and it trembled.

Bless them.

A white light bled from his hand and emanated from his fingertips. No longer did his fragile flesh mask it. The light grew in intensity until it joined the glare of the sun on the waves and the brightness of the sky. It sought out from him toward these three who fooled themselves every day into believing they were individuals, that they had a will that mattered beyond the next breath. In a moment it could cure them of that illusion and all the pain it evoked. Gone would be all their desires, gone all their pain.

Bless them.

The light swelled toward them to absorb their spirits and reunite them with the fabric of the world, with the underlying energy in all things, with the Edan they so yearned for without understanding why. Soon it would bathe them in eternal peace. Older than time, the shadow behind the light exuded a long and content exhalation. Light and darkness: the primal separation could not keep them apart forever. They were one.

He yanked his hand back, and it trembled as his true voice growled within him, *No.*

The light winked out and flesh returned. Three simple men dressed in worn, wet garments knelt before him on a beach with their heads bowed. He gazed at his hand for a moment — the veins snaking over the bones beneath the skin seemed to belong to someone else — and then he lowered it to touch Omong's head. The touch rooted him once again in the world of forms, and the shadow receded like shreds of mist.

These three were his friends and had showed him kindness and trust. He had no right to take anything from them.

"Edan's blessing upon you. Live well and perform your duties as best you can, foremost among them the love you bear your fellow beings." He repeated the gesture and the words with the other two. Mere words. They wrought no magic, but he hoped they would heed them. He hoped they would live long lives filled with chances to love. There would be pain too, of course. But it would be theirs, part of their story, for without it there was no possibility to love. He smiled at them.

"Rise. Go home now, and share your blessings."

Omong, Rahal, and Birshan stood, each with tears in his eyes. "Thank you, my lord Prophet," Omong managed to stutter. They bent down to touch his feet, a sign of the greatest respect. Though it made him uncomfortable, he allowed them the gesture.

He nodded and said no more.

They turned back toward the boat and waded through the waves. Standing on the beach, he watched their wiry bodies push the boat off the sandbar and clamber up it. They rowed until they lowered the sail and caught the wind, pointing the vessel west to head out of Culvor

Sound and then voyage east, back toward Sundara across the Great Sea. He gazed out toward the horizon until the boat become a small speck on the vast water stretching away forever, and the barest hush within him — he was no longer certain which voice it was — whispered, *They will return to it soon enough no matter what we do.*

A STEEP, ROCKY PATH MEANDERED UP ONE OF THE CLIFFS. He climbed it until he reached the top, producing a pleasant ache in his leg muscles, which he had little used during the sea voyage. His breaths were heavy by the time he paused on top of the coastal knoll to turn and take in his surroundings. Clad in green, hill after hill plunged into the foaming waves until they receded far into the hazy distance. This was a rugged, undulating shoreline battered by wind and water, one that would provide no easy living for those who dwelled along it. Nevertheless, the sea's bounty would ease their lives somewhat, and the small white dots of sheep sprinkled on several slopes suggested the folk had found another means of providing for themselves. Indeed, during the journey here from Sundara, Omong had remarked that much of Caergilion's wealth stemmed from its trade in wool. Or rather, it had before the Torrlonders came.

He wondered a moment where his feet should lead him. Failing any other suggestion, he decided to follow the path snaking along the hills. West or east? He gazed west first. In the distance glinted something metallic, or rather several somethings. A few peaks away, a party of helmed soldiers was heading toward him.

Supposing they must have spotted him, he squinted and shielded his eyes from the sun as he peered at them. They seemed to wear grey kirtles, suggesting they were some of the Torrlonders his fishermen friends had warned him of. A sense of familiarity and foreboding crept into him, but he suspected it had more to do with some memory hiding behind the wall of his amnesia than it did with any current threat. Perhaps these Torrlonders could begin to furnish him with answers. He struck out toward them.

It was not long before he approached them at the crest of a hill. A score of soldiers, most of them big men, clinked in their byrnies as they strode toward him. On their hips they wore swords, and they carried round shields. Their scowling faces bespoke no friendly intentions. The man in their lead, one of the biggest among them, held up a fist, and the whole party halted. The big soldier stared at him and spoke in a loud, gravelly voice.

"You there! Come here, old man."

He understood the words, recognizing they belonged to a language other than the one he had used back in Sildharan, Golgar, and Sundara. Since his skin was lighter in tone like the Torrlonders', he wondered if this tongue the big man had spoken was his native one. It seemed odd to consider it, as if he were making an observation about a stranger. But he was just that: a stranger to himself. Perhaps these Torrlonders could provide some clues for him.

He walked toward them at a steady pace, keeping his gaze firm on the leader. The soldiers facing him shifted a bit in their stances, and several rested their hands on their sword hilts. In their minds, someone unafraid of them was a threat. Recognizing this, he tried to put them at ease by smiling, but their only reaction was to deepen their scowls.

"Look at him. He ain't old at all, lieutenant, though his hair's whiter than my granny's," said a soldier behind the leader. The man was wrinkling his nose in confusion as he stared.

"I'm not blind, Wilstan." The big leader gazed at him with his blue eyes and frowned. He had a crooked nose, and grey had taken over the chin of his blond beard.

"Some kind'a freak," mumbled another of the soldiers.

"Who are you?" asked the leader.

Their words and appearance flooded him with so many associations that danced at the periphery of his mind. When he tried to grasp them, they flitted away.

"Do you understand the Northern Tongue?" The leader used a louder voice and slowed down his speech.

The more words they spoke, the more they seemed to stroke his hidden recollections. They were so familiar, yet there was something different about the way these men talked. He stared at them in fascination and sought his elusive memories.

"Koel, come here," said the leader. Two red stripes on his sleeve set him apart from the others. "Ask him who he is."

A man with darker skin stepped forward. He was smaller than the others, but he wore the same garb. The little man's oily smile revealed his high opinion of himself and low opinion of others. "Ki hwyt ti?"

This language too touched upon his awareness, though in a much more vague and remote way. He did not understand the words, so he shook his head.

"I've come from afar."

It was beyond strange to hear these words, as if someone else had spoken with his voice. Yet something fell into place when he uttered them. *So. This is my native tongue.*

The lot of them had started when he spoke, but then their stances relaxed. They were doing a poor job of covering their fear.

"So you do speak the Northern Tongue." The leader's eyes narrowed as he gazed at him. Beads of sweat stood out on his brow where his helm did not cover it.

"Sounds like a Markman, lieutenant."

The leader glanced backwards. "Shut up, Wilstan. I'm not deaf either." He resumed staring at him. "How about it? You from the Mark?"

He staggered back a step at these last words. Something long dormant in his mind awakened enough for him to sense its presence, but a barrier kept him from grasping it. He stared a moment longer at the one the others called lieutenant.

"I . . . I think I may be. The Mark." He tried out the words, and they rang in his mind. But he still could not access what they pointed towards.

The lieutenant stepped closer, and he loomed over him. His cheeks were flushed, and a growl entered his voice. "Listen here, Markman, or whatever you claim to be. You need to tell us who you are and why you're here. And who was on that boat that sailed away? Speak fast." He held up his index finger, which seemed to be some sort of signal since, a moment later, steel whispered as the soldiers unsheathed their swords.

He stood his ground and looked up into the lieutenant's face.

"Three men, fishermen from Sundara, are on the boat. Birshan, Omong, and Rahal. They are my friends, and they are returning to Sundara."

"And why did Beer-shit, Among, and Rail bring you here?"

"I asked them to."

The lieutenant's face turned a deeper red. "Damn it, man. Don't toy with me. Why are you here, and who in Edan's name are you?" His soldiers stepped forward, and some prowled behind him to surround him.

He gave the man a sad smile. "In Edan's name, you say? So I have been speaking, and yet, until this moment, I've been no nearer to knowing who I am or whence I come. That is why I'm here. In Caergilion."

The leader slowly shook his head. "Enough. If you won't give me proper answers, I'll have to take you in for questioning." He nodded, and his soldiers moved in from all sides.

Bleeding out the barest hint of power from his mind, he reached out to them all and inhabited them. Rigid and wide-eyed, they all froze where they stood. Within they cowered as he surveyed every recess of their minds in less than a moment, knowing each of them as they did not even know themselves. He considered showing them what he saw. *Release them*, whispered his constant companion. *Grant them rest from their toil.*

He looked into the lieutenant's eyes, which bulged as the man stared back in helpless fear. "I have questions of my own, and I thank you, for you've begun to show me some answers, I think."

He tilted his head in curiosity.

Something other than his energy, a tiny lifeform, inhabited the lieutenant and most of his men, including the little dark one who had spoken in the other language. Something foreign to their bodies, something virulent and indifferent to their survival. *Show them the mercy of oblivion. How these fleshlings suffer.* At once, the man's red face and the sweat on his brow made sense.

"You are not well."

The lieutenant's face sagged, and he shook his head, which began to quiver.

"There is a thing inside most of you. You would call it an illness. You are on the verge of much pain and torment. Its early stages have already crept upon you, and after you suffer, it will leave you dead." *Give them the mercy of our embrace. End their torment.*

The leader nodded, and the fear in his mind spiked.

"You've seen what this does, haven't you?" *Show mercy. End it.*

The man nodded again, more vigorously this time. His terror was a rising fever, like the one that was beginning to claim his flesh.

He looked deep into the lieutenant's mind, viewed memories of a dark-haired woman and a girl, almost a young woman now. *Wife and daughter.* They were far away at the moment, but he clung to them. He saw the man's deeds, his attempts to do right by his kingdom and his conscience, and the increasing difficulty of heeding both demands. His worries for his family, for his soldiers, for his kingdom, and even for the people of Caergilion swirled in his mind, and even though he swam against so much despair, he was unprepared to bid it all goodbye. *End all this needless worry and pain.*

He nodded to himself. "It *is* better not to let you suffer."

A bright light emanated from him, the unmasking of the power lurking beneath his flesh. He was only a window to its energy, which reached forth from him and illuminated the men cowering before him. The light bathed them and bleached their features, and they were powerless in their helpless fear. They could neither run nor cry out, but their minds trembled as they beheld a rent in the world they believed they knew. The light claimed them, and all they could do was tremble as it cleansed them.

The light winked out, and a cold breath withdrew. He stood before them, a mortal man wrapped in flesh.

The soldiers all dropped their swords and shields to gawk at their own hands and prod at their faces. The lieutenant collapsed to his knees and stared up at him, and his mouth quivered open.

He tried to smile at the man. "Rise. The thing that was inside you is no more."

"He's right, lieutenant," said another soldier. "I feel better now. Better than I've ever felt in my whole Edan-blessed life. It's gone." That man too went to his knees, and all the soldiers knelt, even those that had not yet perceived the coming of the disease in their bodies.

"You healed us." A tear tracked down the lieutenant's cheek. He did not need to dwell in the man's mind to know his emotions. His relief. The passion with which he yearned for his family. The man remained on his knees.

"You are a good man," he said, and he knew it for true. "You have much to do still."

The lieutenant looked down at the ground, and his rough voice quavered. "Can you do it for others? Heal them of the plague?"

"Yes."

"Then," the lieutenant lowered his voice to a near whisper, "may I take you to . . . someone?" He glanced up with pleading eyes. "Please? If you agree, we must hasten."

He peered down at the man. Perhaps these Torrlonders *were* helping him find his purpose. He had come to Caergilion for a reason. They would show it to him.

He nodded. "Yes. Rise and lead me where you will."

THE LIEUTENANT DISMISSED HIS MEN AND COMMANDED ONE HE called Sergeant Hulm to conduct them back and report to their captain. "Tell him we found a healer," instructed the lieutenant. "And that I'll return with him once I've looked into things a bit. Mind you, all we know of this man is he can save us from the plague. No need for further speculation. You hear me?"

Sergeant Hulm smiled and nodded. "Aye, lieutenant, I understand. Just as you say."

Before they left, the soldiers gave many words of thanks for their healing. Once they set out, the lieutenant led the way in the opposite direction. The two of them walked over several coastal hills until they reached a path leading inland. Along the way they spoke little, but he asked the lieutenant his name.

"Edgelaf, my lord. My friends pare it down to Edge."

"Edge, then."

The lieutenant hesitated a moment. "You needn't tell me yours. I've heard the tales of what happened in Sildharan. You're the Prophet of Edan."

He smiled. "So they tell me."

Another hesitation. "I'd best speak openly of this, my lord. You could be in danger here. King Earconwald is in Caergilion, and I reckon he won't be much pleased with you."

Back east, he had heard stories about what he had supposedly done in Sildharan. Dragons, wondrous magic, the defeat of someone called the supreme priest, and Torrlond's retreat. The stories varied in details, but that was the essence of it. He recalled none of it. "His displeasure matters naught to me."

"As you say, my lord. But if you begin healing folk here, word will spread. He'll hear of you. And if I know him, he won't sit idle."

"I will heal folk. Then let us see."

Lieutenant Edgelaf hesitated a moment and then nodded.

The inland path ended at a small farmstead consisting of a stone house with a thatched roof and a barn, also wrought of the local grey stone. A low wall surrounded the farmstead, and when they approached the gate, someone emerged from the farmhouse and walked toward them.

The lieutenant stopped at the gate, and so he waited alongside him. A stocky lad approached them, one of the bronze-skinned natives of Caergilion. When the boy neared them, he gave a familiar nod to Lieutenant Edgelaf. But when he opened the gate and gestured for them to walk through, he gawked at the Prophet, who quested out with a touch of energy toward the boy.

"This boy has the plague too, though he knows it not. I must heal him."

"Yes," said Edge. "But there's another who needs you first."

"Very well." He turned to the lad. "I will heal you afterwards."

The boy stared at him, his eyes wide and mouth open.

"He can't understand you," said the lieutenant. "Only speaks Ondunic. But we have an understanding. He's a friend of the one we've come for. It was the only place I could find to hide her. Seems his family's kindness would've cost them, had you not arrived."

He led the way to the barn. The boy kept his distance, and when

Lieutenant Edgelaf opened the door and held it, the boy stopped and watched.

The Prophet glanced behind him at where the lad waited.

"He won't come in," said Edge. "They've given her shelter, but they've stayed clear of her. Smart, but not smart enough, I suppose." He entered the barn, and the Prophet followed him.

Windows at either end of the structure let in a small amount of light, but it was still dim and grey inside. The fertile scent of manure and straw was heavy in the air, though the stalls were empty of creatures at the moment. Edge walked past them and the stores in sacks to the barn's other end. This end was dustier as if from long disuse, but the Torrlonder stopped at the last stall and then looked back at the Prophet. The big man swallowed and sniffed back tears. "Can you still help her?"

The Prophet peered into the stall. A Caergilese girl lay in a cot in the corner. Blankets covered her body, but he could see from her hollow cheeks how emaciated she was. There was no movement, no rise and fall of her chest, but when he quested out with his mind, the life within her still pulsed in tiny, slow throbs. The alien thing burned and raged throughout what was left of her body, careless of its host's impending death. Moreover, there was something other than the disease, a thick shadow of agony enveloping her mind.

"You said the people of this farmstead don't go near her."

"Aye. Hard to blame them. Tob's a good lad, and his family's kind. But they know what the plague does."

"Then who has kept her alive?"

Edge looked down, and his foot scuffed away a piece of straw. "I look in on her when I can. Fed her at first. Can only get a few drops of water in now. It's not always easy to get away. The captain's got his suspicions."

"Is this dangerous, what you've done?"

The lieutenant let out a long sigh. "King Earconwald wanted her. She'd done nothing wrong. But he's . . . What he would've done to her, I will not say." He shook his head. "I couldn't just leave her lying there. She deserved someplace decent. It's a small enough comfort. But I've kept it secret. Let's just say it's not something I want spread around."

"Why have you done this?"

Edge stared at him for a moment, and his jaw muscles bunched beneath his beard. "I've a daughter back home. Reminds me of her." He frowned. "I'm a soldier. Served Torrlond well. But I suppose I'm not proud of what we've done here." He looked away. "Might be she's my way of redeeming myself. Just a little."

The Prophet nodded.

Edge looked at him again. "Can you save her?"

The Prophet returned his gaze and gave him a gentle smile. "She's almost gone, but I'll do what I can. It's not only her body. Her spirit has taken a terrible wound."

The Torrlonder growled. "Earconwald. He murdered her parents. Burned down their farm."

He nodded. "If I can't heal her mind, nothing I do with her body will matter. She must want to live for me to help her, or she will drift away. That might be a mercy."

Edge's lower lip quivered, and he looked down.

He reached up and put his hand on the man's shoulder. "I will try."

A DIM LIGHT INVADED THE DARKNESS, STIRRING HER AWARENESS. The light pulsed and grew. She had all but bid goodbye to such light, and its presence surprised her. She rolled away from it, not wanting to have anything to do with it. There was a dull sensation of something unpleasant where the light was, and she had just found some peace. Yet it nudged forward in a shy but steady exploration, like gentle morning rays of sun brushing over grass.

The light waxed into a steady brightness, illuminating her and calling to her. She turned toward it at first in curiosity, but then the terrible pain returned in vivid detail, and for a brief moment she glimpsed the violent deaths of a woman and man. It so distressed her, but the light wanted her to return to the pain, and she recoiled from it as if it burned her. She tried to hide from the light, to burrow deeper into the darkness, but rather than pursue her, as she feared it would do, the light simply waited. She hoped it would go away, but it did not. It remained and called with a dim and gentle but persistent voice.

After a long while, when it did not disappear, she glanced back toward it. Patient and warm, it coaxed her with mild and calm whispers. It meant her no harm. Perhaps she would see what it wanted. She crept back toward it. As she neared it, it grew once more until it shone with an intensity that made her hesitate. It seemed to ask something of her, as if it were posing a question. At the same time, it offered something to her. It seemed kind and comforting. The question and the offer grew clearer. It wished to share her pain if only she would accompany it. This seemed impossible, but it assured her it was not. It soothed her with caresses, and it promised safety. She paused to ponder the offer, and then, deciding to take a chance, she reached out.

The light entered her and took over everything, blinding her until there was only whiteness. After a brief moment of startled fear, she exhaled in wonder. The brightness was bathing her and soothing her. It inhabited her and shared her pain, and though the pain would still be there, the cleansing luminosity assured her she would survive it because it would accompany her. It would always be with her, and she took great comfort from that.

At the same time, though it felt so far away, she recognized warmth and strength flooding her ravaged body. The light burned away the thing that had all but destroyed her withered flesh. With a rush and an ache, the tissues of her body began to awaken and fight again since they had found the energy to do so. That revival also lent vigor to her spirit, and it in turn willed her body to struggle, to grope for life. Body and spirit each heartened the other.

But she was also no longer bound by flesh. Floating in the light, she breathed in and out not with lungs but with her entire being, and the bliss that began as a tiny spark in her expanded until she outgrew her body. Above the world she hovered, and she was in all of it as it was in her, and she accepted all the pain and love the light promised. Comforting her with both solace and the pledge of a place in the world, the light embraced her. She had a purpose, and it called her to fulfill it. Trusting it to catch her in its embrace, she made a decision.

She opened her eyes.

. . .

Blinking against the brightness invading her eyes, Seren waited a moment for them to adjust until she could take a steady look at her surroundings. Her body, at once full of aches and strangely remote from her, lay stretched out and covered by blankets. With a groan and a great deal of exertion, she lifted her right arm, but she did not recognize the stick-thin thing that emerged as the blanket slipped off it. She stared at her emaciated hand in wonder, and then it flopped to her chest.

"Oh, lass," said a gruff voice in the Northern Tongue. "You're alive."

With an effort she turned her head toward the voice, and there was a big Torrlonder kneeling next to her. As exhausted as she was, her first reaction was to startle in terror. But then the crooked nose, greying beard, and blue eyes fell into place, and she remembered the man.

"Easy, lass. You'll be feeling weak for a while. We'll get some water and food into you. Something salty to start with, I reckon. We'll nurse you back."

She tried to speak, but her lips were gummed together, so she wet them with the tip of her tongue and peeled them apart. It was a struggle to form words, as if she had to remind each muscle of her neck and mouth how to do it.

"You saved me." The slow words came one at a time in a thin croak.

A tear tracked down the big man's cheek, and he sobbed once before he answered. "I did what I could." He pointed behind him with his thick thumb. "But he's the one who saved you."

"Edge gives himself too little credit," said a new voice. "He did a brave and good thing."

She tried to pivot her heavy head on a neck that seemed too skinny and weak, and in the end her eyes did most of the work to find the voice's source. A silver-haired man stood behind the big Torrlonder, but by the smooth skin of his face she could see he was young. Pale like the Torrlonders, he had the kindest eyes Seren had ever seen, and she found it impossible to look away from them.

At once she knew: He was the healing, comforting, beautiful light that had called her back.

. . .

He had found his purpose in Caergilion. There was much pain in this land, much suffering. *Grant them the only peace there is.* He ignored the ever present shadow-whispers eeling through his mind. He could help. He would help.

It was this girl — this fragile, traumatized girl who stared at him from what had been her deathbed — who had shown him. When he healed her and inhabited her mind, he had seen the memories of all she had suffered. In the most tender way he could, he had begun to help her recover from those wounds too. They would always scar her spirit, but there was hope. Beyond her memories, too, there was something about her, a sense of deep familiarity, that convinced him he had arrived in the right place. With that familiarity came a feeling of both fulfillment and anticipation. He had much to do here.

You could have ended her pain.

No. I know her. Never had we met ere this day, but I know her. She has shown me what I must do here. She will help me.

The girl's lips quivered, and he could see what effort it cost her to form words. "I know you."

The mirror image of his own thought. This was no chance meeting. "Yes." And then he realized he could understand her words. "You speak . . . the language I speak? The language of the Torrlonders?"

"She speaks the Northern Tongue well," said Edge, who smiled at the girl and nodded.

Yes, he thought. *That is its name.* And then an idea came to him. "Good. I will have need of someone. A person to render my words into Ondunic, for I intend to speak to the people here." He looked into the girl's eyes. "Will you do this for me?"

Her dark brown eyes returned his gaze, eyes so uncanny in their familiarity, and her lips quirked into a small smile. That smile told him her spirit would survive.

"Gladly," she said.

On the grassy slope of a gentle hillside he sat, his legs crossed beneath him. Above the salt-laden wind that teased his hair came the moan of Culvor Sound's waves behind him. Seren sat next to him. She was still very thin, but three days and more healing and strength from him had produced a wondrous transformation in the girl. A long path lay before her, especially to heal her spirit's wounds, but she had set out on it. He smiled at her as he ordered his thoughts, and she returned the smile.

Below them, hundreds of people looked up and waited. They were beginning to trickle in from further away as word spread of one who could heal them of the plague, arriving in carts, on horses, and on foot, sometimes even in the arms of others. He had considered wandering further inland, perhaps to Gadomiel, but staying in one place made it easier for the increasing number of people to find him.

Just as they had in the east, people flocked to him. Pilgrims. What drew them like flies to honey, he had no doubt, was the power within him, the one that sought to end their very existence. It called to them and promised the bliss of release. He knew they did not understand the call and were not in truth ready for what it offered, and so he stood between it and them, and he would use the power to help them instead. The indifferent energy within him could not understand their desperate urge to live their fleeting lives, but *he* could, for he had been one of them. He clung to the faith that their lives had some meaning, or that they could forge some purpose for themselves with enough effort, and as long as he believed it, he would keep suppressing the shadow's compulsions and use its power to aid them.

On their faces were written their troubles, doubts, hopes, and expectations. It all added up to a vast and growing burden, but he could find no better purpose for the power within him than to carry it. With their weary spirits and their plague-racked bodies, they came with the flame of hope still flickering in them. There were pallets scattered among the throng that some had used to carry the worst off to the hillside. Few would need the pallets for their return journey.

Since the sun had risen he had been healing all who came for help. Most of those who waited were native Caergilese, but a few were Torrlonder soldiers as well, those who had been out on patrol when Edge brought him to their picketed encampment. Edge's captain had allowed him to enter, and soon enough he had visited several other Torrlonder companies besides that first one. Just as with the

Caergilese, some of the Torrlonders had been gravely ill from the plague, while others did not even know they were going to be. But no matter their state, they all expressed the same gratitude, and he left them all smiling in wonder.

More than a few of those Torrlonder soldiers stood at the periphery of the crowd he was addressing, ostensibly to keep order and make sure no rebel elements mixed among the natives. But he knew the Torrlonders hearkened to him just as attentively as the Caergilese listened to Seren's translation. His message was a simple one, so simple he could hardly believe the need to say it aloud, and yet people seemed to require hearing it before they could acknowledge what had always been within them. He cherished the naïve and beautiful hope it would change everything if it could sink into enough of their hearts. When he spoke, he paused often to allow Seren to translate, and the girl's voice projected well.

"Some call it Edan. Some Oruma and Anghara. Still others have many names for it, many faces. These are but words and symbols, a groping in the dark for what we all yearn for. My friends, no matter what name we give it, it dwells in us all. In Torrlonders and Caergilese alike. In all of us. And once we recognize the truth of this, once we grasp it with our minds and hearts, the only thing we can do is honor one another. In myself, in my family, in my friends, and, yes, in my foes: in all alike I recognize the god within. And once I recognize this, it becomes impossible to offer anything other than the love due to every living thing."

He paused and considered their faces. In a small number dwelled a measure of acceptance, but in far more there was doubt, and even hostility in a few. Several Caergilese cast wary glances at the Torrlonders, and some of the latter shifted their stances or rested their hands on the pommels of their sheathed swords.

He spread his hands wide, and their attention returned to him. "What does this mean? You may wonder, how do I offer the love this man speaks of? My friends, it is simple, though not always easy. Who are you, and who are those near you? Think a moment." He paused and watched their faces.

"Good. Now, whatever you are — soldier or farmer, merchant or fisher, wife or husband, mother or father, sister or brother — it matters not. What matters is that you perform your duties to the best of your ability and in a way that honors those near you. A true soldier protects the weak and maintains his dignity by serving the people, never bullying or exploiting them — whichever people he may watch over." Several of the Torrlonders cast their glances to the ground. "A true farmer labors to feed those around her. A true merchant never cheats or steals, but honors every bargain. A true fisher blesses her family with sustenance. Wife and husband honor and cherish one another. Mother and father sacrifice for the sake of their children. Sisters and brothers," he paused to take them all in, "Sisters and brothers recognize the god in one another. And I tell you this: You," and he gestured with his hands to take them all in, Torrlonders and Caergilese alike, "you are all sisters and brothers. No matter how hard, it is your duty to find a way to honor and love one another."

He released a trickle of his power and allowed it to seep into them. Dwelling in them all, he became a reflection of them, showing them the blessed wonder of not only who they were, but also their kinship and oneness with their neighbors. Their desires and fears, their joy and despair: In all these were they bound to one another. Torrlonders and Caergilese, they all began to look around at each other. Some gawked in amazement, as if seeing for the first time. Others wept. A few embraced. He knew it would not last for all of them, but it was a step in the right direction. And some would never forget. *It matters naught*, rasped the slithering shadow within his mind. *Whether they listen or not, they will all meet with great pain before the end. Why not spare them?*

He glanced at Seren next to him, and she beamed a smile at him, banishing the voice that tormented him.

He put his hand on her shoulder and smiled back. "Is that not right, little sister?"

Her eyes watered up, and she nodded.

THE PROPHET SPOKE A BIT LONGER, AND AFTER A TIME HE DISMISSED his listeners, exhorting them once more to fulfill their duties and spread the word about what they had heard. They departed filled with purpose and hope, things they had long foregone. The Torrlonders watched them, and some even nodded towards or smiled at the Caergilese passing them by. A few Caergilese returned the gestures. It was a beginning.

One soldier trudged up the slope toward the Prophet and Seren. As he neared them, they stood and smiled.

"Hello, Edge," said the Prophet.

"My lord." The Torrlonder gave a quick bow, then he turned to Seren with a bright smile. "Looking much better, lass." But his smile soon drooped into a frown.

"But *you* look worried," she said.

He nodded. "I am. That's why I came to talk."

The Prophet's smile also faded. "What is it, my friend?"

"It's what I warned you about before. There are those among us who are eager to please King Earconwald. They think to win his favor by telling him of you. Even some Caergilese who serve us."

"Koel," said Seren as if the word tasted bitter.

Edge nodded. "Aye. The scrawny little eel asked for leave to join the king's main fighting force yesterday. From him or someone else, Earconwald will hear of you. He's busy leading the fight up north against the rebels at the moment. It could be some days — not today, and not on the morrow — but it's a matter of when, not if, the king will come for you."

The Prophet nodded. "I am ready for him."

The Torrlonder chewed his lip for a moment and looked uncomfortable. "Not meaning to doubt you, my lord, but just in case, mightn't it be best for Seren to keep out of sight when the king arrives? I've no doubt that worm will be whispering in his ear of her as well."

The Prophet looked at the girl, whose face belied the protest she was about to utter. He held up a hand. "Yes. We'll find someplace for her. But set your mind at rest. I mean to keep not only Seren but all of Caergilion as safe as I can."

"But Earconwald . . ."

"Leave the king to me. Our meeting is meant to be, and his coming will spare me the need to seek him." From a dull whisper, the vast power within him quickened into a sharp and eager hiss, as if sensing an opportunity to free itself. *They will know our mercy.* For once, he did not try to suppress it right away.

The evening light was waning when the Prophet and Seren returned to Tob's family farm. They ate with the family — Tob, his mother and father, and his grandparents — inside the farmhouse. After some talk during which the Prophet kept silent since he spoke no Ondunic, the two of them retired to the barn. The cows filled only three quarters of the stalls, so it had been an easy matter to set up a cot for the Prophet in the stall next to Seren's. The family had insisted that he and Seren should sleep in the little farmhouse, but he found he preferred the openness and peace of the barn. Seren never seemed to consider leaving his side. That was just as well since she still required healing.

He bid her goodnight and lay under the blanket Tob's mother had provided for his cot. After a few deep breaths, he closed his eyes and gave up all thoughts, leaving his mind as still as a pond on a windless dusk. But a small sound nudged his awareness, and when it came again he opened his eyes. Once more it came, a sob suppressed into a gentle sniff, and he realized Seren was weeping. For a moment he thought to give her some privacy, but then he thought better of leaving her alone.

"Seren?"

A sniff and then a long pause. "I'm sorry." Her voice sounded muffled.

"You've done nothing wrong. Would you like to talk?"

Another pause. "Yes."

He rose and, by the dim light seeping in the window, made his way to her stall at the end of the barn and paused at the entrance. She lay on her side in a tuck beneath the blanket so that even her head was covered. He walked to her cot and sat down at the foot.

"I'm here." He said nothing more, waiting and inviting her to speak when she would.

Her head emerged from the blanket, and she wiped her eyes with one hand. She released a long sigh, which ended in a small sob and a shiver. "I miss them."

"Your parents."

"Yes. And Len too. He was my friend. He deserved better."

"Would you like to tell me of him?"

A tiny smile creased her cheeks. "He was always talking. Full of jests. He could make me laugh even when I thought I had no heart for it." Her smile disappeared, and she went still for a while. "I think he loved me."

He nodded at that and waited.

"Ma would've scolded me for saying that." Her smile returned for a moment. "She was always after me about being a proper young lady. I never wanted to hear it. I wanted things to stay the way they were." She looked at him, and in the dimming light he could still make out her face, which had grown almost vacant. "But they didn't."

Friends are fleeting. Family is fleeting. Flesh falls away, hissed the slithering shadows that gathered around and within him. It grew easier to ignore the voice when Seren resumed.

"I suppose it all started when Allon went off."

"Your brother?"

"Yes. He joined the rebels to fight the Torrlonders. Da was so angry."

"And you've had little word of him?"

"We saw him not long before the Torrlonders . . . He and some other rebels came to the farm for food and supplies. I pray to the Mother and Father he yet lives."

"You are close to him?"

"He's my best friend. Always looked after me. When we were little, he kept the other kids from bullying me. He once beat Koel when he found out he'd been taunting me again. Hitting me with a stick and calling me 'half-breed' and such."

"Half-breed?"

"It's what they'd call me when Allon wasn't around. Because of Ma."

"Your mother was not from here?"

She shook her head. "Ma was born in Adanon. She was a slave. Da and his first wife bought her when she was a girl. She grew up on the farm. A while after Da's first wife, Allon's mother, died, Da granted her freedom and asked her to marry him and help him raise his son. Ma was that pretty. Then I came along. Folk around here never quite accepted her as one of them, I suppose, but she worked hard and won their respect." Seren stopped.

He waited.

She took a deep breath. "That's why she always wanted me to be so careful. I never . . ." A sob broke her words, and she sniffed. It was some time before she resumed. "I didn't listen to her very well."

He smiled. "It seems to me most daughters your age don't listen much to their mothers."

"I suppose. But I lost mine, and now . . ." Her tears came again, and she wept for a long time.

He could have calmed her using the power within him, but he sensed she needed those tears, and so he only leaned over and put his hand on her head, gently stroking her hair. Her sorrow was a constriction in his chest and a tightening in his throat. He sat for a long while with her as she shook and cried out her grief, and even as he tried to comfort her, he once again pondered how familiar she seemed, as if he had heard her story before somewhere. He would do what he could to help her and the people of Caergilion. Beyond a doubt, this girl had shown him his purpose.

13
GAIN AND LOSS

The Supreme Priest Joruman took a seat at the round table in his chamber and grinned down at the seeing crystal mounted on its iron base. It had taken him time to discover the secret to wiping the crystal clean of Bledla and investing it with his own presence. Having collected the other six crystals from their various locations, he had invested them as well and attuned them to his servants in places where he most needed them. They were a useful and swift tool for gathering information from afar, and information was the currency of power.

According to the scroll that unlocked the secrets to using the seeing crystals, the Prophet Aldmund himself had wrought them out of dragon's tears. Joruman smirked at the notion. Even if the ancient prophet did have something to do with the crystals' creation, he must have had a jeweler shape them for him. It made sense since a globe was best for yielding the truest image, though it was still far from perfect. From there, Aldmund would have used some lost song of origin to alter the crystals into a receptacle for the energy that came from the gift. In a sense, it was like trapping and freezing wizard's fire in the crystal. The supreme priest gave a grudging nod of respect to his ancient predecessor. He still did not know how the process worked or what song of origin was necessary, but he would find out. Almost certainly, it had been a technique of the Andumae lost to them for generations. It was not the only Andumaic lore Aldmund had revived. There was so much knowledge for him to uncover.

Using the seeing crystal to communicate with one far away required wielding a song of origin to unfreeze the energy within it. The one Joruman stroked was the master crystal, and he had invested all the other crystals with a tiny portion of his energy so that they were all linked to this one. In each of the other crystals he had also used the appropriate song of origin to invest a minute amount of his servants' energy. Only someone who had undergone that attuning ritual could use the crystal, and the users of the other crystals could speak only to him through his crystal, not to each other. It was fascinating lore, especially the investment of energy in the crystals, for he was learning more and more how fluid the gift could be. He wondered if there was a limit to how much of the gift an individual could gather to himself.

He frowned at the thirst within him. The energy he had taken from Bagsac had swollen his power. His heightened abilities included a keener and subtler awareness of the energy inhabiting all living things. It was as if he had never seen color before, but now the world unfolded in its full vividness and splendor. He was most certainly more powerful than any of his high priests or priests. He was mightier in the gift than Arna had been, and mostlike he was approaching the strength in the gift that had existed in Bledla.

And yet, with Bagsac's power had come the nightmares. As if there were a link between him and the wretch, he perceived the man's fear and torment. Often in his waking hours as well they leapt out at him. Even after the man drowned deep down in the dungeons, it felt to Joruman like he was still somehow wallowing in Bagsac's misery. He wondered if there was no ridding him of the echoes of the man's horror. He released a long sigh. *If that is the price, so be it. I too must make my sacrifices to attain the goal. I have given much, and I will give more. There is no price too high to accomplish the enlightenment of humanity and its freedom from fear.* The question eating at him now was whether he required more of the gift to pursue his research. Perhaps he would undertake the ritual once more to ensure that he surpassed Bledla — just as soon as his new power stabilized a bit more and Bagsac's presence faded.

Edulf had been right about the man's naïveté. However, it irked him that Bagsac had gone and drowned himself. He had wanted to study him further and help him as well — if only he could have made him understand the importance of his contribution to Joruman's research. But there was no need to allay the man's torment now. The idiotic guards never even found the priest's body. Most interesting and haunting was what Joruman had sensed within the wretched priest following the ritual. After he had torn Bagsac's power from him with the song of origin, the man no longer gave off the sensation of one with the gift. But neither did he feel like someone without it. Instead, there was a void, a sort of cavity in the man's mind that was palpable. It had been rather macabre, like an open wound seeping darkness, and at the same time fascinating and most worthy of study. Joruman had wished to find a way to heal the hole in Bagsac, unless it was a permanent feature of the man's mind.

It mattered little now. He clenched his teeth and fists and took deep breaths, closing his eyes to savor once again the exhilaration even as the pain he had inherited from Bagsac accompanied it. A tainted boon it might have been, but could he doubt its worth? Secrets of life lay themselves bare to his enhanced perception, and he grasped the fabric of the world with depth that made him scorn his earlier understanding.

The next time he performed the ritual, his power *would* surpass Bledla's. The secrets of life and, yes, even death, would unfold to his mind. He would conquer that last horizon, the distant shore that all of humankind had cringed in fear of for its entire existence. He would usher in a new era of enlightenment and glory such as had never been. *One more time. I must find the right subject.* That would make him indisputably the most powerful wielder of the gift in Eormenlond. Perhaps the most powerful ever.

Save for one, he reminded himself. Dayraven.

He licked his lips and stared somewhere far away. There had been such blinding power there, blazing like the sun, and he could almost taste it even now. But also much instability. Dangerous. He shook his head. Still he remained unable to learn anything satisfactory about the elves. In all the ancient scrolls and tomes he had read, no one claimed knowledge of their origin or purpose. And yet, somehow, this boy had managed to contain the power of an elf within him. At least for a while. Perhaps he was dead. Joruman took long, slow breaths while dreaming of what he could do with such a vast amount of the gift. *True divinity would lie within our grasp.* Not only would such power conquer death, but it would deliver the ability to create whole new worlds.

But what had become of Dayraven? There had been rumors of the Prophet of Edan stirring up things in the east, but reliable information was hard to come by with the Ilarchae on the loose there. Moreover, there had been a long silence regarding him. It did not seem right that the boy would just disappear after defeating Bledla and thwarting Earconwald's ambitions. Something was wrong, and he suspected the instability he had always felt in Dayraven's presence. The boy had lost control of the elf's power and probably perished. Perhaps someone with a stronger grasp of the gift would fare better. He would double his efforts to gather lore on the elves.

At the moment, more immediate matters called for his attention. He caressed the smooth surface of the seeing crystal again. It was time to contact Nothgar.

"Alakathon vindathae ni tiralae inkhathon. Vortalion bardhalae im hinathae dhulgathon."

He let loose a long, satisfied sigh at the release of his power. The master seeing crystal glowed and then swirled with a blue light. At first sluggish, the light quickened and brightened until its glow illuminated Joruman's smiling face and cast dancing shadows about the chamber. Linked to the crystal, his mind fed it with thoughts of the man he wished to summon. Somewhere far away to the south, he knew, an identically shaped crystal stirred alive and called out to the man linked to it.

It was not long before the bearded face of Nothgar, High Priest of South Torrlond, appeared. The lips on his morphing face moved before Joruman heard his voice, which echoed as if it came from the bottom of a well. "My lord, I answer your summons."

"Very good, Nothgar. I wish you to report. What tidings of the south?"

"My lord, I've just had fresh news from our spies in the army regarding King Earconwald's efforts in Caergilion and Adanon."

"And how goes our monarch's glorious campaign?"

Nothgar shrugged. "About as you expected, my lord. Incompetence and stupidity cause many delays and disasters. What could have been a swift victory has turned into a longer matter."

"Any serious setbacks?"

"No, my lord. Our superior numbers and military power guarantee the outcome, but the king will be busy far longer than he wishes. The plague there has also caused great complications. It's spread from Caergilion to Adanon. Some of our troops are among the victims. The king will go nowhere near the affected areas."

"Which no doubt has put him in quite the foul mood. Our Earconwald is not famed for his patience."

Nothgar looked uncomfortable a moment and shook his head. "It's said he's slaughtering the Caergilese in large numbers. Not the rebel fighters — he can't find those — but the villagers across the countryside."

"Winning more admirers, no doubt. So, plenty of needless misery and suffering in the south, and Earconwald is stuck for the moment. Anything else?"

"Yes, my lord. There are rumors coming out of Caergilion. I heard them only this day." The high priest waited a moment.

"What of?"

"I hesitate to trouble you with them since at the moment they're vague, but there's talk of the Prophet emerging in Caergilion, in a remote area far to the west."

"The Prophet of Edan?" Joruman heard the eagerness in his own voice and calmed himself.

"Yes. Yes, my lord. But they are vague rumors only."

"What would he be doing there?"

"I know not, my lord. Supposing the rumors are true."

The supreme priest stroked his beard and nodded. "Find out the truth of them, and report to me as soon as you learn more."

A confused look passed over Nothgar's face for a moment, but he soon recovered. "Yes, my lord. He is important, then?"

"*Power* is important, my dear Nothgar. Tell our spies to find out all they can about the Prophet. If he's in Caergilion, no doubt Earconwald will hear of him too."

"No doubt."

"We well know what Earconwald will do. Like a spoiled child that destroys every trinket he gets his hands on. Such a waste. Far better if we were to find the Prophet first. I want to hear everything you can learn regarding him. Everything. Contact me as soon as you hear anything. Is that understood?"

Nothgar bowed his head. "Yes, my lord. It shall be so."

The Supreme Priest Joruman smiled. "Good. If there's nothing else, you are dismissed."

"Thank you, my lord."

Joruman let go of the link, and Nothgar's wavering face disappeared from the seeing crystal. The blue light faded and winked out, leaving the chamber feeling much darker. The supreme priest sat in his chair, his chin resting on his hand as he thought long and hard. His other hand joined it and toyed with the ring on his little finger, absently twisting it and rubbing the little stone's smooth surface.

At length, he stood up. "So, you may be alive after all."

It was something of a relief. It had never sat well with him that he had tried to arrange Dayraven's death. Most importantly, of course, a great opportunity still existed. He stroked his beard and then rubbed his hands together. With an effort he calmed his breaths, a little startled at just how hungry and excited he was. Bledla had thought the greatest power in the land lay with the dragons. Dayraven had proved otherwise. Gazing at all the books and scrolls lining his shelves, Joruman grinned. "If I can't learn of it anywhere else, perhaps you will help me." So much of the gift already bubbled and roiled within him, but the elf's power called him, for with it he surely would accomplish everything he desired.

. . .

BRIGHTNESS PRIED OPEN HIS EYELIDS, BUT HE SHUT THEM AS SOON AS the sharp, cruel light entered. Long he lay there with them closed, trying to recapture the sweet forgetfulness of his slumber, which claimed him in all too short intervals. Day or night, sleep was the easiest time to escape from the inner darkness he dreaded more than anything. Even his nightmares were better than the waking moments when he failed to elude the gaping chasm in his mind. It was a raw wound oozing shadows from which there was no escape. He yearned for sleep that would never end. But the nasty sun had done its work, and he could no longer ignore the various pains assaulting him from so many quarters at once.

Waking from sleep had become a ritual in avoiding as much pain as possible. He would rise only when the raw ache in his belly outgrew the stiffness of his swollen joints and the jolts up and down his spine and legs. Until then, each moment was an attempt to roll away from one pain only to find another awaiting him.

He groaned as he eased from a tuck on his side to lie on his back. The throbbing in his shoulder and hip lessened, and thousands of little needles pricked his numb arm when the pressure came off it. But just when he released a sigh, agony lurched through his backside, and he gasped as its tremors traveled up his spine and down his leg. This set off a series of convulsions, and his jerking limbs scattered bits of garbage from the pile he had slept on. His face joined in the seizure, which finally ended with a series of twitches in one eye.

He lay still and moaned. Everything ached. Even his skin stung with countless sores. But now that it was all over, the greatest remaining pain was the emptiness eating at his belly. It was time to rise.

Slowly he unfolded his body, and his joints all popped as he moved each quivering limb. With each movement he emitted a series of animal grunts, and only the acidic torture in his stomach kept him going. He gained a position on all fours, and he stared at the filthy, hard ground for a while. The greasy hair growing out the sides of his head hung below his face in clumps. As he took some hitching breaths, his own reek stung his nose. Piss and shit and vomit and filth and sweat and rot and the sticky-sweetness of decomposition: all mixed together in a potent miasma of stench around him. At least it kept people away. He giggled and cackled at the thought until his spine pinched a nerve and sent him into a series of shivers.

With a grimace contorting his features and trembling in every muscle, somehow he made it the rest of the way up. Standing hunched over, he gazed down at his skeletal body covered by the filthy grey robe that smelled even worse than he did. The robe had been another color at one time, but he had hidden that knowledge from himself. It would not do to reach into that hiding place since he knew it would remind him of other things. Better forgotten.

He settled his mind on finding something to stifle the pain in his belly, and he grinned at how skillfully he had avoided the thing that frightened him more than anything else, the thing that did not bear thinking about. It was always waiting for him, but he was crafty, and he had learned to avoid such traps. Most of the time.

He stood in a narrow alley. The rotting garbage was slick and slimy beneath his bare feet. No one bothered him in this alley since the occupants of the two buildings adjacent to it emptied their chamber pots in it from the windows above. He knew what a chamber pot was, and he cackled at the memory of one he had used to escape . . . But no, he never thought about that dark place, his old grave. He shook his head to dispel all the associations before they reminded him of something else, something he could not think of.

The one building next to the alley was full of women who sometimes giggled and sometimes cried in pain and sorrow. A lot of men went in and out of that building. They were mostly men who scared him, and he was careful to avoid their greedy gazes. From the other building also came many noises, mostly shouting and sometimes brawling, and sometimes noises made by stringed things, blowing things, and banging things, usually with a human voice or voices accompanying them. These noises touched his mind in places he did not wish to remember, so he shut his ears to them. Often the men who left that building with all the noises staggered out as if they had forgotten how to walk straight. Those men frightened him too. There was even a man there who sometimes came to the alley and shouted and kicked him until he scuttled away, but it had been a while since that last happened.

That man was bad enough, but no one gave him shivers like the ghosts in white robes that sometimes haunted the nearby docks. Almost always accompanying the ghosts were men wearing clinking metal with bright helms and sharp swords. They were horrible too, but it was the ones in white that sent him whimpering into dark corners to tuck himself in as far as he could burrow, rocking and clenching his eyes closed and holding his hands to his ears. At all costs, those prowling ghosts must not catch him.

His body shuddered at the thought of them, but then a sharp poke inside him reminded him of his hollow belly. It was better to look for something to fill him when the sun was gone and fewer eyes could spot him by the moon's lesser light. But he knew secret ways to slink unseen, and he had discovered the best places to find food.

On a good day, he would find a scrap of something nearby, just behind the building where the men brawled and made noises long after the sun was gone. The man who kicked him often threw things out the back door: bones he could crack open with a rock or his teeth to suck the marrow out of, vegetables or fruit gone soft and smelly with rot, stale bread he could suck on. Sometimes maggots already squirmed in the food, which provided a more filling meal than usual. Once he discovered a real treasure: a chunk of salty cheese that tasted delicious after he scraped the thick, fuzzy layer of bitter blue mold off with his fingernails. For the whole day afterward he had licked at the grit under his nails just to savor the taste that clung to them. Bitter saliva filled his mouth at the thought of that cheese.

Dragging one foot, he shambled back toward the rear of the building and glanced up to make sure the contents of no chamber pots were tumbling his way. He had to be careful when he emerged from the alley lest the man spot him. He had a feeling their uneasy truce depended on him not being seen. And he did not wish to be seen anyway.

He squinted at the brighter light when he reached the alley's end. Poking his head out, he peeked around. No one occupied the space between the backs of the buildings and the backs of the other buildings, the ones fronting the next street up. He waited a moment, and then he crept forward, shuffling one careful step at a time.

His breath caught and his eyes bulged. Near the door that was the destination of his search lay the carcass of a large bird. A whole carcass. Just sitting on the ground for anyone. There might have even been some scraps of meat and cartilage clinging to a few of the bones. He lost all caution and hobbled toward it.

A low growl stopped him. From the shadows of the alley between the other two buildings emerged a stray cur, its hackles raised and yellowed teeth gleaming behind taut lips as it stalked closer to the prize. The outlines of ribs showed beneath its tawny, shabby fur. With ears and tail flattened, its eyes locked onto him, and its growl swelled until a threatening bark punctuated it.

He started and backed up a pace. His hands trembled, but when the pain in his belly prodded him again, he balled them into fists. Fight or flee: that was the choice he faced. Was he not a man? He recalled that he had been. He had possessed the power of speech and even another power that set him apart, but it would not do to think of that just now, and he kept that door closed in his mind. The point was he had a *right* to that carcass.

Licking his cracked lips and swallowing in his dry throat, he shook his head and stared at the snarling dog. Did he not take precedence over this creature? Even in his current state, he must. He set his jaw and stood up to strike a more imposing posture, the effect of which was only slightly marred when his eye twitched in a series of spasms. The time had come. He would seize what was his. He inhaled a deep breath, and then he took the plunge.

He meant to release a primal war-cry, but it sounded more like a strangled croak as he gimped in the closest thing he could muster to a headlong rush toward the carcass.

The stray darted forward and reached it first, scrambling on its claws and exposing its razor teeth in quick jabs while erupting in loud and fierce barks.

He jerked back with a startled cry and just missed being nipped. At the same time, the bones in his arse ground together, and the nerves between them screamed. So did he. With his hand gripping his backside, his limping retreat back to his alley was swifter than his sortie had been. After he reached its safety, he leaned his shoulder against the wall and gasped in wheezing breaths.

Once the ache subsided enough, he shuffled back to take a peek and see if the cur had departed and left him anything. Sitting with its legs around the carcass and tearing at it with its jaws, the mangy beast spotted him and growled with exposed teeth, at which point he darted back into his alley. He was still panting with all the exertion.

He limped back to his sleeping spot and leaned his back on the wall. But he found his legs too wobbly and weak to hold him up, and he slumped down to sit on the filthy ground. He stared forward until a sob creased his face into a grimace. His whole body succumbed to trembles as the sobs racked him, sending snot down onto his upper lip and drool down his bearded chin.

When the sobs ceased, he sat staring at the wall before him, listening to his shallow breaths for a long while.

A shadow enveloped the alley, probably a cloud blocking the sun. Whatever it was, it sent a chill through him. In his despair over losing the carcass, he had been unprepared. The shadow caught him by surprise. He tried to dodge it, to slip away by thinking of something else. It was too late. His eyes bulged, and he sucked in a wheeze of air as it seized him and shoved him to the edge of the abyss. He was naked and trembling before it, the horrible chasm in his mind. He could never escape it, for it was *in* him. It was absence and darkness, a wound that would never heal.

"Unnnnhhhhh." He heard the low animal noise squeezed from his throat, but he could not move, and he could not look away from the void. In the throes of this almighty terror, he forgot all about his hunger and yearned for oblivion.

The Supreme Priest Joruman rose from his seat at the table when the two temple guards escorted the man into his chamber.

"Duke Ethelred of Etinstone, my lord," said one of the guards before they both bowed.

Dressed in well-made but unostentatious garb beneath a green travelling cloak, the stocky man stood between the guards. His eyes narrowed in a wary frown, as if he were assessing the supreme priest and not quite enthusiastic about what he saw.

"Thank you, Ulfbert." Joruman nodded to the guard who had spoken. "You may leave us."

The two guards bowed again before exiting and closing the door behind them.

Joruman smiled at Ethelred and gestured toward one of the chairs at the round table. "Please, Lord Ethelred." He had thought long and hard about this meeting. Ethelred was the king's cousin. After Earconwald, the duke was Torrlond's second most powerful noble. And heir to the throne. He needed an understanding with this man. An alliance, if possible. "Be at ease."

The duke cocked one eyebrow, expressing just how little ease he expected to find here. "Thank you, Lord Joruman." He sat and waited, scowling at the supreme priest and not bothering to mask his distrust.

Joruman sat in the chair nearest him. On the table he had taken care to leave the seeing crystal on its base and the large Book of Aldmund on its stand, obvious signs of his office. Ethelred was said to be a pious old warrior, but he wondered just how deep that piety went. His own impression was that the duke was above all a practical man, and he hoped that assessment would prove correct. He gestured at the bottle of wine and two glasses he had placed next to the Book of Aldmund.

"May I offer you some refreshment? A Caergilese white from the Gorifaen Hills?"

The duke gave a curt nod.

As he uncorked the bottle, Joruman attempted to keep up the conversation, which remained rather one-sided. "You had fine weather for your journey."

Silence met him.

"I trust it passed well." Another twist, and the cork popped out of the bottle, releasing the subtle and pleasant bouquet it had trapped within.

"Well enough."

"And how fares Lady Winberta?" The pale liquid glugged from the bottle and swirled into the glasses while he poured.

"Well enough."

"I see. And your sons?" He handed one glass to the duke.

"The same." Ethelred sniffed at the glass and frowned at it. He did not drink.

"Ethelwulf is the eldest, is he not? Your heir. I hear he's quite the young warrior."

The duke looked Joruman in the eyes. His flat expression was no longer quite a scowl. "Yes."

The supreme priest grinned. "What a fine thing to have a strong heir. It must give one a sense of security."

Duke Ethelred put down his glass and stared at him for an uncomfortable length of time. "Why have you summoned me here?"

Joruman sighed. "Right to business, eh? Alright, then. To begin, the king and I agree the situation in Norfast is untenable. A sorry disgrace, in fact. Since you are a man who prefers to cut straight to the point, here it is: Siric has bungled his campaign against the Norfasters. Badly. And now the Thjoths have become involved. We require an immediate remedy to the situation."

"We?"

"The king and I agree that, while he remains engaged in the south against the rebels there, *you* are best equipped to solve the issue. Your dukedom borders on Siric's, and you are a man of widely respected military talent."

"Why summon me here to tell me that? You could've sent a message and spared me the journey."

"Let's just say I wanted to arrive at my own understanding with you. Man to man. But let us first discuss the issue of Norfast."

Ethelred frowned and shook his head. "At the king's behest, I've already loaned several of my companies to Rimdale. The reports they send me are not flattering of Duke Siric. They do not encourage my further involvement."

"Siric is a bumbling, sycophantic ass."

The duke released a bark of laughter. "On that point we agree. So why should I aid him in his grab for Norfast? The man has no just claim on the land."

The supreme priest raised his eyebrows. "He has his sovereign's blessing for the endeavor."

Ethelred released an impatient sigh and glanced down at the table. "True." The word was almost a growl.

Joruman held up his index finger. "Yet, if someone else were to do the work of subduing the Norfasters, that man would have a stronger influence over the outcome."

"Speak plainly. What are you suggesting?"

"I'm suggesting you obey your king's command. Bring your strength to Norfast and win decisively with your soldiers. But do so in a way that makes Siric as irrelevant as possible. Take charge there. When it's clear the victory is yours, it will complicate Siric's claim, which is, as you have observed, rather tenuous to begin with. Meanwhile, I will be here to counsel the king in a way that is favorable to your influence over the matter."

"Meaning what?"

"Meaning we will work together to persuade Earconwald to grant the dukedom to someone more worthy of it. Perhaps someone who would not forget his debt to us."

Duke Ethelred's eyes narrowed, and he frowned as he stared at the Supreme Priest Joruman. Finally, he nodded. "I will obey my king's command. And if you wish to see justice done in Norfast, I will gladly work with you."

"Excellent. Perhaps you might think of a few candidates you consider worthy of a dukedom. When next we meet, we may discuss our options before we back one."

The duke squirmed a bit in his seat as if uneasy with such conspiring. "I suppose that will be necessary."

Joruman grinned and held up his glass. "To our understanding, then." He tipped it and drank. Swishing the wine around in his mouth before swallowing, he savored the vintage's crisp taste.

The duke took up his glass and raised it before taking a cautious sip.

The two men looked at one another for a moment longer than was comfortable. Duke Ethelred broke his gaze first to put down his glass on the table. "You spoke of the king in the south. What news do you have of his campaign there?"

"Officially? Everything is going according to plan. Earconwald is gilded in glory, and the rebels in Caergilion and Adanon are either cowering in their hovels or dead." Joruman paused. Now that he had offered something to the duke, it was time to test things a bit further. "But let us speak the plain truth between us. The campaign is taking far longer than it should. The rebels are holding out because we underestimate them again and again, and we win no worthy allies because our only policy is to punish and destroy. Some might say arrogance, waste, and lack of competence have mired our efforts."

"Some might say such words border on treason." The scowl had returned to the duke's face.

Joruman inhaled and took the plunge. "Come, now. You know as well as I what is happening down there. Did you really need to ask me?" He took the duke's lack of response for an answer and continued. "Is it treason to suggest effective policy? I assure you, I act in the best interest of the realm. I seek to promote competence, from the lowest to the *highest* offices." He gave Ethelred a meaningful nod.

The duke's hard gaze faltered, and he looked down at the table.

Recognizing his moment, Joruman pressed his point. "*You* know how conquest works. Military superiority is not enough. Riding in and winning dramatic victories gains nothing permanent. To absorb the south, we must have allies there. Locals. And they need an incentive to join us. We require a far more sophisticated approach, and someone in charge with a strong sense of justice. Give people justice and stability, and they will follow you. What good will raping and destroying do us?"

The duke looked up, and from the uncertainty in his frown, the supreme priest realized he had won a point. All knew of Earconwald's proclivities and the wanton destruction he left in his wake. He was a debauched fool, and Joruman could see this knowledge in Ethelred's eyes. Yet he dared go no further just now. Ethelred was a loyal man, and he was likely patient enough to wait to inherit the throne rather than seize it before Earconwald drank himself to death or died in some foolish gesture.

The supreme priest sighed. "No doubt King Earconwald has thought of all these things."

Duke Ethelred seemed to measure him again with his hard gaze. "No doubt." He took another sip of his wine, and then he smacked his lips and looked at Joruman. "Bledla often counseled my cousin."

The words surprised the supreme priest, not least because he had forbidden the use of his predecessor's name. He opened his mouth to issue a polite reminder, but Ethelred held up a palm and interrupted him. "I know you wish his name erased, but I don't give a damn. As you said, let us speak the plain truth between us."

Joruman gave him a slow nod. "Very well."

"Earconwald has no children. When he dies, I or my son *will* inherit Torrlond's throne. I intend that rule to be different from my cousin's. He would have benefited much from listening to Bledla. Oh, I know the man had his own sort of arrogance and blindness, but Bledla *believed* in something. But for their faults, he and Earconwald could have accomplished great things. Since you seek an understanding with me, understand this: If I am king, I will work with the Way to make this realm as great as it can be, but not just for the rulers. You have rightly surmised that justice and stability interest me most. If you share those interests in truth, then we will work together well, both now and in the future. Together, we can accomplish great things. So, I ask you, what do *you* most believe in, Supreme Priest Joruman?"

Joruman took a sip of wine to give him a moment to gather his thoughts. In the midst of them roiled his heightened power along with the echoes of Bagsac's terror and pain. "These are frank words, my lord, and I thank you for trusting me with them. What do I believe in, you ask? Knowledge. I seek knowledge in order to . . . make lives better. To accomplish great things, as you say."

Ethelred's nod was uncertain. "Learning is an important function of the faith."

The supreme priest smiled. "Yes. It is." *It is its only worthy function, and it will be the Way's demise. The rest shall fall away.*

This time the duke's nod had more conviction. "I believe we may work together well, then." He extended his thick hand. "We appear to have our understanding."

Joruman clasped it with his much thinner hand, and the man's calluses rubbed against his smooth palm when they shook on it. "Indeed, we do." *For as long as I need you. You're a good man. Much harder to manipulate than your cousin. However, once I have the knowledge I seek, the kingship, dependent as it is on the whims of lesser and greater men, shall fall away too. The world will change.*

LYING ON HIS SIDE IN HIS GARBAGE PILE NEST, HE PROPPED HIS EYES half open and watched the stream of folk hurrying by the mouth of his little alley. It was the best distraction he had devised, and it could keep his mind occupied for long stretches without any reminders of the sort he needed to avoid. There were so many people, more than there ought to have been in the whole world of the living, and almost none of them looked his way, so busy were they with their tasks and pursuits.

Such invisibility gave him a small sense of coziness, though he was too cunning to be lulled, and a part of his mind was always alert for traps. Since the alley opened out to the street adjoining the river docks, in the daytime there was a constant bustle accompanied by plentiful cries, curses, and shouts. Sailors and longshoremen predominated, but there were also soldiers, servants, and a good sprinkling of the sort of women who lived on one side of his alley.

Today he noticed something different. First, several of the stick-thin street urchins infesting the docks passed his alley in a group, one of the little gangs he had spotted oftentimes before. These homeless boys almost always kept out of the way, finding it safer to blend in than stick out and draw attention. The odd thing was this group had chattered merrily among themselves and walked on the street as if they had the same right to it as everyone else.

Hard on their heels followed another group. That would not have been quite so unusual had not three more groups followed them along with five of the older beggars. They were all headed in the same direction, and the children had talked among themselves in excited voices. He frowned toward the mouth of the alley. What could it mean?

A little later, another group of urchins passed, and the smallest of them paused as he looked down the alley at him. "Oi, Shakes!" piped the boy. "They're givin' away fresh bread today. Plenty for all!" Then he was gone.

He lay there puzzling over what the boy had said. He understood the words well enough and attached the correct meanings to them. But he could not wrap his head around the idea that someone was giving away good bread. His brief time on the streets had taught him one thing: Nothing was free. He scoffed and shook his head. Deciding to stay put, he resumed watching the passersby.

It was not long before his empty belly prodded him. Though he tried to focus on the people's faces and gaits, his mind kept wandering and repeating the boy's words, "fresh bread." He shook his head again. *Fresh bread*, said the little voice. One of his eyes skittered in a series of rapid blinks. *Fresh bread.* He licked his lips, and then he clenched his eyes closed. *Fresh bread.*

His stomach turned upside down and emitted a long groan, and some of the saliva pooling in his mouth dribbled into his beard. He flung his eyelids open and growled. Perhaps it would hurt nothing to investigate. He would just have to be clever enough to stay away from traps.

With a series of groans and pops, he managed to get his joints in motion. When he had risen, he hobbled over to the mouth of his alley. As he peeked out, the people walking by avoided the entranceway, and some wrinkled their noses and scowled at him. He paid them no mind, for something had grabbed his entire attention.

Just a few hundred feet from his alley, a small crowd of urchins and beggars gathered by one of the docks. Because of the press of people between him and the throng of homeless, he did not have a clear view of what they milled around. But several waifish boys and beggars squeezed out of the crowd, grinning at the prize in their hands as they walked away. They each held a whole loaf of bread.

His jaw fell and his eyes widened, and he whimpered as he tried to gather the courage to cross the busy street. There were so many people between him and his glorious meal, or even meals if he chose to hoard it. A tiny, grimy boy wearing nothing but a sack and layers of dirt ran by with one of the loaves. His hands reached toward the disappearing boy's prize, and his tongue snaked out of his watering mouth to lick his crusted lips. He turned back to the crowd and steeled himself. Keeping his gaze glued to the throng of homeless, he stepped out of his alley.

With eyes wide and faces wrinkled in disgust, people in the street parted before him, making his path far easier than he expected. He giggled and rubbed his hands together as he gimped on his way, dreaming of his loaf and anticipating the gummy softness within the crust. Perhaps it was even still warm inside. He could imagine the doughy scent wafting with the steam as he tore it open. More people stepped out of his path, and his smile blossomed. He was so close now.

The smile froze on his face, and he stopped in mid-hobble as he thought he glimpsed something through the press of ragged bodies. A moment later, a beggar turned with his treasure in hand and stepped away, exposing a horrific vision. The thing sitting on a stool and distributing the loaves wore a white robe.

A gargling scream tore out of his throat, and he threw his trembling hands before his face. It took some time for him to command his legs into motion, as if they were stuck to the street cobbles. He pivoted and lurched back toward his alley. Only to slam into something solid that had been behind him. He staggered back a step, almost falling on his arse. When he gazed up at the huge soldier towering over him, he released another raspy shriek.

"See here. What's all this carrying on?" The big soldier grabbed him by the arm.

He screamed as if the touch burned him, but the man was so strong, and he could not shake his way free no matter how he whimpered and struggled.

"Quit your fuss, or I'll knock you one. By Aldmund's holy words, your reek's enough to stun a man."

"Don't hurt him. Bring him here, Eldric. And no cursing," said a gentle but commanding voice.

The soldier spun him around to face the creature in the white robe, who had stood up from his stool. His struggling ceased when courage failed him, and his body went so limp that the only thing holding him up was the soldier, who grasped him by both arms. To his boundless horror, the ghost-demon took a step toward him with a hungry smile lighting up his face. All he could do was whimper with his mouth agape and succumb to his own terrible trembling. He was helpless even to look away.

The demon scratched his beard. "I don't recognize you. What's your name?"

"Aaaaah! Aaaiiii!"

"That's Shakes, m'lord," said a little urchin's voice. "He's new. He don't talk none."

"Shakes? I see. Be gentle with him, Eldric."

"I'm trying, my lord." The soldier grunted as he heaved him up by the armpits like a limp puppet.

The ghost-demon took another step and held out a hand with a loaf in it. "Are you hungry? You've nothing to fear. Here. Let me . . ." His mouth froze open, and he gawked in obvious horror. "Edan's mercy, man. What happened to you? Never have I felt such a wound before."

"Gaaaahhhhh!" The terrible void swooped down upon him, the deep beyond darkness. Looming up like a sudden storm, it mocked him for how puny and foolish he was to think he could ever avoid it. Was it not in him? Was it not the wound at the center of his spirit? It would swallow him and consume him in eternal torment.

He jerked up, snapping the back of his head against something that crunched.

"Aldmund's balls!" came the soldier's muffled curse.

The strong grip on him was gone. At his sudden freedom, he leapt away in a frantic scramble, flailing his skinny limbs faster than he would have thought possible. He paid for the shambling run with jolts of pain up his spine and down his leg that jerked his body every few steps, but he heeded them little as he darted through the crowded street, knocking into startled people and ignoring their angry cries.

It was all a panicked blur. Sometime later, he was panting, whining, and clutching himself in a fetal tuck in a small hole behind a warehouse. Dogs, rats, and small urchins used the hole to gain access to the goods in the warehouse. He did not fit through it, but it was large enough to hide most of him. He shook and moaned as he used every trick he knew to distract his cowering mind.

Fresh bread, said a little mocking voice. Behind it stood a ghost in a white robe.

He gritted his teeth and spluttered at it.

Fresh bread.

He shook his head and clenched his eyes closed.

Fresh bread.

He banged his head on the ground again and again, grunting each time until blood ran down his forehead and onto his face. Chortling at his cleverness, he watched the blood drip and soak into the soil. *Fresh bread.* It was much weaker now. He smacked his head some more until the voice went away. When unconsciousness claimed him, he was grinning beneath his blood mask.

A RUSH OF EXCITEMENT COURSED THROUGH JORUMAN AS HE TRACED the words in the book once again. The light from the many candles he had lit in his chamber tinged the vellum orange-yellow, and he brushed the faded ink with his fingertip. A pleasant breeze drifted in the open window, at times swaying the candle flames and altering the light. Outside was the dark night, but within his chamber a whole world was opening up as he read the Andumaic words for the third time, this time aloud:

"'The truth behind the elves is a matter still shrouded in great mystery. The books of lore preserved from the homeland make little mention of them, and of a certainty, nowhere is there recorded their song of origin. Thus, we may suppose the elves coeval with the songs of origin, meaning they partake of the realm of origins and are not, as such, creatures of time. But such is only conjecture. Here are the facts we may assert: The elves manifest most often in places remote from human touch or relatively immune from human power, such as in deep forests or in bodies of water. In addition, they may take a human form, but they are not limited to such and often take the semblance of some other natural creature, yet they are always said to be beautiful in appearance. Of their original form no one can claim knowledge, but it is likeliest they are in fact formless and take on a shape only to mortal minds, which could not comprehend their true nature and thus construct a thing which they may grasp. In any case, elves produce a singular effect upon anyone who gains a full view of them, which is to say they leave the viewer with a sound body but a privation of spirit. Our most ancient lore refers to this as the death of Anghara, signifying its uniqueness, and it is unlike anything else, even the comatose state that often results from severe injury to the head. One with the gift feels this difference as the complete absence of spirit in the viewer of an elf. Such is the sum of our knowledge. And yet, the temptation to conjecture is strong. The little we know of them suggests that elves are direct manifestations of the realm of origins in our world, perhaps a sort of portal to it. As such, they are nothing less than concentrations of eternity, immune to anything like death as we know it. Their power is, thus, immense, perhaps without limit.'"

Joruman stared at the final two sentences, his face split in a broad grin. After a moment, he shook himself out of his daze and narrowed his eyes, gazing at the book as if assessing it anew while he twisted the ring on his little finger. He had always dismissed *Observations of Ogmos the Wise* as apocryphal. That was why, among the rare and forbidden books in the supreme priest's private library, he had not consulted it ere now. But an instinct had drawn him toward it, and since he had taken it off the shelf and blown the dust off it, he had not put it down.

The hierarchy of the Way had long ago condemned the book as containing numerous heresies, and yet that had not prevented Bledla and his predecessors from keeping a copy in this chamber. Based on the handwriting and the few grammatical errors it contained as well as certain philological changes in High Andumaic, he knew it for a copy of a copy of a copy. Could its author truly have been the great Andumaic sorcerer, father of the eastern dynasties of Sildharan and Golgar?

Then again, what did it matter? The weight of opinion from a reputedly powerful sorcerer like Ogmos was nothing to dismiss, but it was just that: opinion and conjecture. And if the writing did not belong to the great man, it was someone else's conjecture.

And yet . . .

Joruman found himself wanting to believe in Ogmos' authorship. The writing indicated a perceptive and lucid mind, and across the centuries the supreme priest felt a kinship with it. According to legend, Ogmos had been stronger in the gift than all other Andumae on these shores. If that weighty claim were true, the man might have been more powerful than even Bledla had been. The strength of the gift in him would have given him insights unavailable to others, revelations into the true nature of such mysteries as elves. Most compelling were his perceptions regarding those unique creatures, or manifestations. A single paragraph in the thick tome lying open before the supreme priest contained them all. But the words written there resonated so closely with Joruman's instincts and hopes.

He glanced at the last two sentences again and knew the truth of them deep within himself. "Concentrations of eternity, immune to anything like death as we know it. Their power is, thus, immense, perhaps without limit."

The elves were the key. Solve their mystery, and he would achieve everything he desired. As sweet as it was, the power he contained at the moment would someday seem a mere trickle, a pathetic hint of the eternity that could be. There was so much to gain, and he had some notions of where to begin.

He laughed aloud, giddy with new conviction. He could almost fancy himself free of Bagsac's haunting fears. Fists tightened into balls, he nodded to himself. Though he did not know how to carry it all out yet, he knew what he must do.

14
PURSUIT

Rocking with the waves beneath the ship, Galdor leaned on the railing and stared at the rugged hills of Caergilion's northern coast. Somewhere in that land, their pursuit would end and they would at last find Dayraven. He hoped. Terrible urgency was building in him, and he wondered if he was feeding it with his own fears, or if it was a foreboding of some imminent event. Perhaps both.

"Can you sense him, my lord?" Also gazing across the water at the land they were approaching, Abon stood next to the wizard.

Galdor released a long sigh. "I think so. Somewhere in that land ahead of us is a disturbance — distant and yet vast."

"A disturbance? As in the dangerous kind?"

The old wizard frowned. "While in the realm of origins, I feel it like a spider might detect an insect's presence on her web. Only this web is infinite. And the insect a great deal larger than the spider." He shook his head with uncertainty. "There is, I think, great conflict and constant strain, but we are still too far away for me to know their nature or the boy's exact whereabouts."

"Sounds concerning."

Pausing a moment to consider the best response, Galdor raised his eyebrows. "It is a bit concerning how much power is running loose, and in someone so young and inexperienced."

"'A bit concerning?' Something in the way you say it makes me think you really mean 'bloody terrifying'."

Galdor cracked a smile, but it was a brief one. Not for the first time, he wondered how Dayraven had contained it, let alone controlled it long enough to defeat Bledla. The boy had been strong in the gift to begin with, but he doubted power was the reason he had been able to live with the elf in his mind. Perhaps it had been because he had never wanted it in the first place. He had never even considered using it for himself. So much power would have lured most people into dark places. But Dayraven had somehow steered clear of such temptations. It seemed almost too naïve to consider, but Galdor believed it to be true even as he thought it over: Only Dayraven's goodness had kept him alive, had kept the elf from devouring him. But his time would run out, and he had to find the boy before that happened. Or something worse.

"Well, my dear Abon, we shall see. Let us hope we find his trail soon."

The shaper grunted. "Nothing we can't handle, I'm sure. Thousands of Torrlonders running loose, not to mention their ongoing war with the native rebels. And our lad with untold power bleeding out of his mind. And what if the Torrlonders get to him before we do?"

"We'll just have to beat the Torrlonders to him." The old wizard closed his eyes for a moment, not wanting to think of what might happen if they did not.

Galdor shook his head again. Every creak and twinge in his old body asserted itself, and his shoulders almost hunched over with the weight of his cares. Ever since Arna's death he had felt more feeble and tired. Even though they had been apart for so long, it had somehow consoled him to know his beloved had been alive somewhere. Never had he felt such closeness to anyone else, and never had he stopped thinking of him. A part of him had always been with Arna, and with his death that part of him too seemed to have died, leaving the rest of him thin and hollow. *Ah, my dearest friend. How I missed you all those years.*

Finally, I found you again. Only to lose you. And now, I must remain here. Alone.

He released another long sigh. Somehow he would find the energy to do what needed doing. And, in fact, he was not quite alone. He smiled and glanced at Abon. Not far away, Orvandil and Gnorn were wrapped in their cloaks and attempting to sleep on the ship's deck. Two of the companions had slept while two kept watch during the whole voyage from Sundara. They were all solid friends, and their devotion to Dayraven would see them through this.

Footsteps approached from behind him on the wooden deck. He turned to find the ship's captain approaching.

"We reach Belglam soon," said Choor in Andumaic. He leaned over the railing and spat out a wad of the betel leaves he was always chewing, and then he held out his hand. "You can pay me the rest."

Galdor smiled at the Sundarae smuggler and hefted his coin pouch so that it jingled. "As we agreed, you'll have the remaining portion of your silver as soon as we arrive safely." He tucked the pouch under his robe. "No sooner."

The smuggler captain scowled at the wizard for a moment, and then he nodded before sticking more betel leaves in his mouth and stalking away to bark orders at his men.

"Do you trust that man?" Abon squinted as he watched Choor scream and slap one of the younger sailors.

"Not in the least."

"I wouldn't trust him with a copper that belonged to his own mother."

The wizard grinned at his friend. "Nor I. But what choice did we have?"

"None."

Galdor nodded. Choor's ship had been the closest one they could find leaving Sundara's shores for Caergilion. No doubt King Tirgalan would have helped them, but they would have lost more time traveling all the way to Glirdan. After following a tip, they had located the smuggler in a coastal village not far from the one where all the pilgrims waited. Fortunately, he and his crew had been about to make a run to Belglam.

Since the wizard and his friends had no way of knowing where in Caergilion Dayraven would be, Belglam was just as good a place as any. They would simply be four additional passengers on Choor's ship. But that had not stopped the greasy little fellow from charging an exorbitant amount of silver for granting passage to the companions. He justified the price by insisting the risks and the costs had increased a great deal since the Torrlonders took over Caergilion, which was no real argument since he was making the run with or without them. In addition, he had demanded they ask no questions about the cargo below deck, so Galdor did not even know what the man was smuggling. The crew never spoke about it. Whatever it was, he clearly expected it to be worth a great deal of profit, for that was the only thing that motivated a man like him.

"In fact, I suspect our good friend Choor and his lads would have robbed us long ago were it not for their healthy fear of Orvandil."

"Oh? Been reading minds, have you?"

"It doesn't take a wizard to know a thief." He grinned again. "But, yes. In fact, I have, since you asked. He's wondering what might be in your bag besides your harp. Or if the harp might fetch a good price."

"He's seeking up the wrong tree there. My plain harp's only worth something to someone with the skill to play it. And I'll kill the little shit if he touches it."

"Hmmm." Galdor nodded. "I believe you would."

"And what's the thieving sneak make of you?"

"Me? He believes me a helpless old man whose money pouch is too heavy for him."

Abon grunted. "The more fool he."

"Well, the sooner we're rid of his company the better."

"Then we go about finding Dayraven."

"Yes. We'll seek tidings of him in Belglam."

"We'd best take care. The Torrlonders aren't likely to greet any of us with open arms. We'll be stepping into a nest of adders."

The wizard smiled. "Not to worry, my dear Abon. I'll exercise the same caution I always do." He waggled his eyebrows at the shaper.

Abon sighed and shook his head. "That's what I fear."

. . .

Belglam was a large town and trading center in northern Caergilion. In good times, the market squares were alive with activity. Colorful merchants from various lands would shout at each other, mostly in the Northern Tongue but also in Ondunic, Andumaic, and even Thjothic. Many came to trade their goods for Caergilese wool, but all sorts of wares could be found. In good times. Now there were more soldiers than merchants in the markets. And they all spoke the Northern Tongue and wore grey.

For that reason, Galdor had led the others on their way from the docks into town by keeping to the smaller streets and alleys. They avoided the dockside taverns since too many Torrlonder soldiers patrolled there. At one point they had waited in a shadowed alley while a large patrol marched by on the street. It had been a tricky business, but once they reached closer to the town's center, fewer soldiers appeared. When they turned a corner on a quiet street, the wizard nodded and pointed at a sign above the doorway of a two-story building constructed of large exposed timbers and bricks stacked between them. On the sign was carved a wooly sheep next to a shepherd holding a staff.

"Let's hope the keeper speaks the Northern Tongue," said Abon. "None of us knows enough Ondunic to find an outhouse."

"I picked up a bit during my time here and in Adanon," said Gnorn. "So did the big fellow." He nodded at Orvandil.

Galdor lifted his eyebrows. "Enough to have a subtle conversation that would lend us firm knowledge of where to find Dayraven?"

The Dweorg frowned. "Well, I could find an outhouse. I think. But let's hope the keeper speaks the Northern Tongue."

The wizard smiled. "At any rate, in a trading town like Belglam, an innkeeper would be at a serious disadvantage if they did not speak it. There's likely no need to worry, Abon." He nodded toward the door. "Shall we find out?" He started to reach for the latch, but before opening it, he turned to address the others behind him. "Remember, we must be as subtle and quiet as possible here. Leave the talking to me, and watch for my lead."

. . .

When they entered the dim but cozy common room, Abon shadowed Galdor and assessed the place. Natural light filtered in through two windows with thick, cloudy glass, but no candles or torches were lit. Small wonder, for too few persons occupied the room to make it worthwhile to light them. Save for the innkeeper, who stood behind a long counter polishing bottles and glasses no one was using, the place was empty. In addition to the entry they had used, there was one other way in or out, a door at the back of the common room that Abon suspected led to a kitchen and rooms for wayfarers. Perhaps there was a back exit out of the building that way too. The saddest thing about the place was the lack of noise, and the shaper knew at once what it most needed: a good musician. *And for the Torrlonders to fuck off.*

The balding innkeeper at first favored them with the sort of desperate smile a man puts on when he has seen too little business for a long while. But he must have had a good nose for trouble since the smile sagged into a puzzled frown. Abon grinned. A Dweorg, an enormous Thjoth, a half-cracked old man, and an ugly shaper: likely not his everyday sort of patrons.

Galdor leaned on the counter and slapped a silver coin on top of it. He smiled at the innkeeper on the other side. "Ales for my three friends and me, my good man."

A confused stare was the innkeeper's only response.

The wizard straightened up. "Do you not speak the Northern Tongue, then?"

The innkeeper seemed to rouse himself with a slight shake of the head. "Oh, yes. Begging your pardon, sir. I do speak it well."

Galdor faced Abon to give him a ridiculous wink, as if to say, "*Told you so.*" He turned back to the innkeeper, who continued apologizing. "It's just we see few, ah, Torrlonders like yourselves this far into town." His nervous glance at Orvandil and Gnorn made it clear he was not at all certain they were Torrlonders. "Not that it's no honor, sirs. And we're happy for your business. 'Silver spends the same no matter the hand that offers it,' my old Da always used to say."

"We're not Torrlonders," said Galdor with a grin.

"Oh." The relief was evident in the innkeeper's smile.

"We're pilgrims. On a pilgrimage."

"Oh. I see. Well, in that case, if you'd like to find a table, I'll get you those ales, shall I?"

"Thank you. We've had a long journey, and we're quite thirsty."

The wizard selected a corner table with four stools as far from the front entrance as possible, and the friends sat down. Abon took the stool with a clear view of the door and kept a close eye on it.

"Pilgrims?" said Gnorn in a hushed voice. He glanced at Orvandil with an eyebrow cocked in skepticism.

Galdor frowned in irritation. "I'm improvising, Master Dweorg. Have you a better idea? If not, I suggest you . . . Ah, thank you!" The last part he said with a smile to the innkeeper, who approached with four foaming mugs gripped in his hands. They thunked when he set them on the table.

The innkeeper wiped his hands on his apron. "Will there be anything else, then? Perhaps you've worked up an appetite as well?"

"Such was my very thought," said Galdor. "What meal are you serving today?"

"The finest mutton in Belglam is all I can offer you here at the Jolly Shepherd, with some fresh-baked bread and greens roasted with garlic."

"Splendid." The old wizard pointed upward with his index finger to declare the matter was decided. "We'll have that, then."

The innkeeper nodded, but before he turned to go, Galdor held out his hand to stay him. "I wonder if I might trouble you with one other matter." He wiggled his fingers and grinned. "You see, we've come from afar with little reliable information to go on. As I said, we're pilgrims, and we've been seeking someone for a long time. The trail has led us here." On that last word he pointed down at the table. "I wonder if you might confirm whether our sources are correct. Have you, perchance, heard any rumors about one they call the Prophet of Edan?"

"Prophet of Edan?" The innkeeper shook his head. "Not in Belglam, sir."

Galdor's face and shoulders sagged, and Abon repressed a deep sigh of disappointment. All that way for nothing. And how would they find Dayraven now?

The balding man smiled, oblivious to the devastation his news wrought on his guests. "No, sir. You'd be wanting to head south, past Gadomiel. Steer clear of Derwyn Forest along the way. There's been a good deal of fighting betwixt the Torrlonders and the, ah, rebels there. Go all the way to where the coast meets Culvor Sound. That's where you'll find him."

Galdor's eyes widened. "He's there? The Prophet of Edan?"

"Of course. Everyone knows that, unless you've been hiding in a cave somewhere." His smile fell. "Or been detained on a long journey. Begging your pardon, sirs."

Galdor reached up to slap the man's shoulder. "Thank you, my good man. That's excellent. Most excellent. It would have been a shame to have made such a long journey for nothing. And, since you've already been so helpful, perhaps you could also tell us . . . You see, we've heard a great deal about the marvels the Prophet has performed here and there. Have there been tales of any . . ."

"Have there? Only that he's curing everyone of the plague. Lot of folks left here when they heard, carting their sick ones along."

"You don't say?"

"I do say. And a good number of folk have been saying somewhat more . . ."

The conversation receded as Abon stood and stepped away from the table. Frowning, he approached the inn's front door. He thought he had seen a shadow pass by one of the thick-paned windows. He was not sure, but it had seemed like a man, perhaps crouching as he hurried along. But before he took another step, Galdor shot up from his seat.

"Don't touch that door!"

At the same time, the door burst open, and grey-clad soldiers bristling with weapons poured in along with a white-robed priest of the Way. "Kill the heathens!" yelled the priest as he pointed toward the companions.

Abon grabbed the nearest thing to hand, a stool, and tossed it at the

Torrlonders. It crashed into the first two soldiers, halting their headlong rush long enough to give Galdor a chance to finish the song of origin he had begun. "Alakathon indomiel ar galathon anrhuniae! Vortalion marduniel im paradon khalghoniae!" intoned the wizard in a commanding voice behind him, and the shaper knew well enough to duck.

A monstrous bang accompanied a flash of energy, blanching the common room of all color and banishing all shadows for one intolerably bright moment. Glass shattered, wood splintered, and men screamed in a terrible explosion. As he stood up, a ringing invaded Abon's ears. He coughed and peered through smoke and haze at the smoldering Torrlonder corpses strewn all over pieces of rubble. One was the white-robed priest. The door and the entire front of the inn were gone, replaced by a gaping ruin. Smashed bricks, shards of glass, and broken pieces of wood were scattered everywhere in the wake of the wizard's fire. Liquid dripping from a cracked bottle perching sideways on a shelf's edge made a steady tap, tap, tap on the floor. The shaper looked behind him.

The innkeeper stood with his mouth wide open, eyes blinking and bulging in shock as they gawped toward what had been the front of his inn. Galdor, Gnorn, and Orvandil stood next to him. The wizard leaned toward him and asked as he pointed behind him, "Is there a way out the back through that door?"

The innkeeper did not alter his terrified gaze, but he managed a quick nod.

"Sorry for the mess." Galdor produced a quick, toothy smile and dug coins out of his purse before placing them on the table. Abon knew they would be gold, enough for a new inn if the man wanted. The wizard waved a hand at him. "Come along now, Abon. We don't wish to linger."

The shaper caught up to his friends as they were stepping through the door into a dark hallway. Galdor held it open for him. As he passed him, Abon raised an eyebrow. "Subtle and quiet, eh?"

"Oh, shut up."

. . .

ABON'S HARP BOUNCED ON HIS BACK AS HE RAN THROUGH THE MAZE of streets and alleys. When he emerged into a small market square, he knocked over a man, who fell into a street vendor's cart, upsetting a load of melons. Curses and cries followed in his wake, but he did not dare slow down. There had been more Torrlonders outside the inn, and it had not taken them long to discover the four companions. To judge by the hollering and clanking of mail and pounding of boots, a lot more had joined them.

"How'd they know to find us, let alone that we were in Belglam?" asked Gnorn as he huffed behind Abon. They were sprinting through the city in an all-out race for the southern gate.

Abon glanced behind him, beyond the Dweorg. The Torrlonder soldiers were visible, perhaps a hundred of them, shoving aside townspeople and pouring into the square from streets and alleys like a furious grey river flooding the town. "Choor. The little shit's purse must be heavier now," answered the shaper between heavy breaths.

"Never trust a smuggler," said Orvandil up ahead.

"Even if he's a Thjoth?" Gnorn laughed at his own jest.

"Especially if he's a Thjoth," said Orvandil with a chuckle.

"Quiet, you fools!" In the lead, Galdor ducked into an alley. Though the old wizard managed a quick pace, he did not seem too certain of where he was going, and he gasped out his heavy breaths. "We've got to find the blasted gate, and then we've got to figure out what to do when we get there."

They emerged from the alley into a much broader square, at the end of which a large wooden gate waited. Abon thanked all the gods it was open. Word of the pursuit must not have reached the soldiers manning it yet, else they would have closed it. A crowd of people milled near it, but at the moment they were all waiting as a column of mounted Torrlonders was riding into town.

"Time to figure it out," said Gnorn.

Galdor did not stop his sprint. "Each of you grab a horse and ride out. I'll do the rest." The wizard began mumbling a chant the shaper could not hear.

Abon kept running even as he unsheathed his sword. Many faces in the crowd pivoted towards the four companions and the sound of a hundred pursuing soldiers behind them. The Torrlonders on the horses turned towards them with puzzled frowns. A moment later, the puzzlement changed to anger.

"Whatever you're doing, Galdor, do it fast," mumbled the shaper.

The mounted soldiers in the lead of the column spurred their steeds toward the companions. But instead of obeying, the horses neighed and bucked, flinging their shocked riders onto the cobbled square. The same happened throughout the entire column, and the grey-kirtled soldiers began tumbling and rolling all over the square amidst the chaos of their screaming and thrashing beasts.

Abon smiled at Galdor's handiwork even as he spotted the horse he would take. On the way to it, he passed a soldier struggling to his knees and, using the flat of his blade, smacked the man on the back of the helm with a loud ring. He sheathed the sword and, crouching low, grabbed the bucking horse's rein. Emitting a low whicker, the beast went calm at once, allowing the shaper to put his foot in a stirrup and pull himself onto the saddle. He shook his head in wonder at how the old wizard never seemed to run out of tricks.

When he looked about, most of the horses were still in a wild-eyed fury, pounding the cobbles with their hooves and whinnying loudly. Townspeople were screaming and running about, mostly away from the horses, and many were running into the path of the Torrlonders who had pursued the friends from the city, fouling their efforts to reach the commotion. A few of the formerly mounted soldiers were trying to catch their steeds with ill success, whereas others limped away or lay where they had fallen. Galdor was mounted, as was Orvandil. But the shaper did not see Gnorn.

"Curse these long-legged beasts!" yelled the Dweorg, and Abon turned toward his voice.

Gnorn's arms and chest were draped over the saddle of a horse, and as the red-faced Dweorg attempted to haul himself the rest of the way up, his arse poked out while his legs dangled and kicked below him. The confused beast was turning in circles. "Hold still, damn you!" cried Gnorn, unaware of the three Torrlonders rushing toward him with their blades out.

Abon turned his horse about, but by the time he was ready to charge, Orvandil had alighted from his steed and drawn his Dweorg-wrought blade in one fluid motion. In three long strides he was among the Torrlonders.

The Thjoth met them by dodging one blade and parrying another as he positioned himself before Gnorn. In a blur of motion Abon could not follow, Orvandil morphed the parry into a mighty sweep of his blade that carved through one foe's neck. Ropes of blood trailed the steel, and the Torrlonder's head spun before smacking into the cobbles. His gore-spattered companions froze in wide-eyed terror at the bellowing Thjoth and then bolted the other way.

Orvandil sheathed his sword. He turned and grabbed the rein of the horse Gnorn was spinning and cursing on. Once the steed stood still, he seized the Dweorg's belt and, with a loud grunt, half hauled and half tossed his friend into the saddle. Gnorn landed and sat astride the beast with his mouth in a surprised circle.

"Let's go!" yelled Galdor. "Ride out!"

Orvandil leapt onto another horse, and Abon dug in his heels to bring his mount to a gallop. The guards were attempting to close the gate, but dozens of whinnying horses pushed against it as they and the four companions raced out. Like a herd, the horses followed the ones the four friends rode, and, his breath still coming in heavy gasps, Abon once again grinned at Galdor's cleverness in thwarting any pursuit. With the wind whipping his cloak behind him, he took some comfort in the head start they were getting. Still, the Torrlonders would come after them, so they had best put some miles between them.

As the four friends made camp in the darkness of night under the forest cover, Orvandil nodded in acknowledgement of Galdor's cleverness and leadership. Beneath his jests and distracted air was a fierce, powerful, and wise man, a good man to follow. Once they had gained enough distance from Belglam, the wizard bade them each take a fresher, unburdened horse. Then, he had used his power over the beasts to disperse them in groups of four every which way. The Torrlonders would have a fine time puzzling out which tracks to follow.

After that, they had ridden south for the Forest of Derwyn. Despite the innkeeper's warning, Derwyn was the best chance the four friends had to hide from their pursuers and lose them. Also, many soldiers patrolled the road from Belglam to Gadomiel, so they needed a less traveled way to get to Dayraven. They would just have to avoid more Torrlonders, the ones who lurked around the forest in hopes of capturing and destroying the Caergilese rebels it harbored. But these Torrlonders would not be looking for them, at least not until the ones from Belglam arrived.

So far, though they had reached deep into the forest, they had seen no sign of Torrlonders or rebels. They had stopped only when it grew too dark to carry on. They would risk no fire, but at least they had plenty of provisions from the Torrlonders' saddlebags, and they would not go hungry. His three friends and the tethered horses were mere shadows in the darkness, for little moonlight spilled through the silvered canopy to spot the forest floor. Orvandil chewed on some dried meat he had found in his saddlebag and took a swig from a water flask to get it all down in one swallow. "I'll take first watch," he said to the three shadows sitting nearby.

"Very well," answered Galdor's voice. "I'll take second. Wake me in a bit. We'll all need rest for the morrow."

While his three companions wrapped themselves in their cloaks and lay down on the forest floor, the Thjoth eased through brush and leaves, moving with them and stepping on the sides of his boots to maintain his silence. Lest a twig crack under him, he felt out each step before putting all his weight down. A strand of a spider web he must have walked through tickled his nose, but he ignored it. He chose a spot within viewing distance of his friends yet hidden from them. Then, leaning his back against a tree, he stood and waited.

Time passed in the dimness of the forest, which came alive with its night sounds. Insects chirped and buzzed, an owl hooted, and bats flitted about. The Thjoth scratched when a mosquito whined by his ear and brushed his cheek, but he kept still otherwise. He stood straighter when something rustled nearby, but it turned out to be a small forest creature, probably a squirrel, skittering in the dry, brittle leaves of the forest floor.

No matter how many times he brought them back to the task of watching, his thoughts wandered. Osynia, queen of the Thjoths, came to his mind. Vols, his cousin, was a lucky man, and Orvandil smiled at the memory of their three daughters. For years he had carried a dream of Osynia as the young woman he had given his heart to, but what came to him now was the mature, commanding queen he had met back in Grimrik when he and Gnorn journeyed there to rally the Thjoths. He sighed, admitting to himself he loved both images.

There had been other women, like Dalriana back in Asdralad, and he spared a thought for the tavern owner he had shared a bed with in those days. He hoped she had somehow survived the Torrlonder invasion. But he could not muster for her or anyone else the same passion that coursed through his chest when he thought of Osynia. Perhaps it was best he stay away from his homeland for good.

Dismissing his fantasies, he centered his mind on his task: finding Dayraven. He glanced down at the hilt of Seeker, which had proven as fine a blade as he could have hoped for when he beheaded the Torrlonder earlier that day. Gnorn knew his work. Each time Orvandil stroked the hilt or drew the blade to clean and oil it, it was a reminder of his purpose. He acknowledged it was not just for friendship's sake, nor even because of how good the lad was. Dayraven was his redemption. He felt no shame in admitting it. Yet, at the same time, there was another thing that did call up something like shame: Carving through that poor Torrlonder's neck had been a source of grim and deep satisfaction.

To say that he had enjoyed doing it was not even close to the mark. He had *needed* to do it. As brief as the moment had been, it unburdened his deep yearning to fight. All day long he had taken satisfaction from reliving the scene again and again, seeing the man's shocked eyes just before he died, the spatter of blood on his two companions, and the terror in their faces before they bolted. Orvandil had nearly sprinted after them as well, but something — Gnorn's predicament, perhaps — had jerked him back to his duty and his higher purpose of finding Dayraven. There had been so many Torrlonders there to fight, but he had wrenched himself away to flee with the others. Ever since Gnorn handed him Seeker, he had been hankering to wield it in combat. Almost he could have believed the sword whispered of a thirst that needed slaking. Of course, it was not the steel, but rather something deep inside him. Today was just a taste, and one that did not sate his need. If anything, it had whetted his desire to wield the sword again. He longed to find out what more he could do with it.

The Thjoth let out a long sigh. All this chasing after Dayraven was supposed to make him a better man than the killer he had once accepted as his true self. And yet, the quest was bound to put him in places where he would need to fight. Those Torrlonders would have hurt or slain Gnorn, after all. He had done what was needful. But he wished he had been less thrilled to do it. *Might be even Dayraven can't change me. That might be the most hopeless fight I've ever faced.* In his mind he heard a response — it took on Dayraven's voice — to that thought. *It's the most hopeless fights that summon the greatest courage.* Orvandil smiled and nodded.

GNORN PUSHED ANOTHER TREE BRANCH OUT OF HIS PATH AS HE stepped over a fallen log and tugged his horse by the rein. It was slow going through Derwyn, especially while dragging the lanky beasts behind them. Still, given the protests coming from his sore back, arse, and legs, it was better to lead them than ride them, unaccustomed as he was to such tall steeds. And at least the going had sped up a bit. Some time ago, they had come upon a narrow deer path heading roughly south, and so they were keeping to it for the moment. The entire time they had seen no signs of Torrlonders or rebels save the blackened remains of an old campfire. There was no telling who it had belonged to, and it appeared long abandoned. Galdor led them, followed by Abon and then Orvandil. He was bringing up the rear of their little company, which suited him fine since it allowed him to carry on his conversation with Hlokk without anyone bothering about it.

"Not that I fancy traipsing through forests, mind you," he muttered as he swatted an insect away from his face. "But this does seem the safest route."

He looked up towards the sunlight glimmering through the forest canopy and frowned as if considering something.

"Too slow? Perhaps. But the wizard has the right of it. He's one we can trust. It would be much slower still if we had to fight Torrlonders the whole way along the road. Ofttimes the least worst way is best."

A thin branch disturbed by the passing of Orvandil's horse swayed toward him, and he batted it aside with his forearm.

"Of course we'll find him at the end of it. We have to. That's all there is to it."

There was a long pause before he pursed his lips and then murmured, "Now listen, Brother. It'll do no good to voice such thoughts. We'll do what we always have: carry on. Besides, we're close on his trail now. He'll be there. You'll see."

"What are you muttering about back there, Gnorn?" Abon's voice carried from well on ahead.

Gnorn started. He must have been speaking louder than he had thought. "Hmmm? Oh. The bugs. Too many bugs in this forest." He slapped an imaginary one on his cheek.

"They like Dweorg-flesh most," said Orvandil's voice in front of his horse.

Gnorn smiled at his friend. The Thjoth had long known about his conversations with his dead brother. A couple times on the road he had caught him at it. He never said a word. But once, he had looked up after answering Hlokk's voice to see Orvandil staring. The Thjoth's eyes betrayed his sorrow for only a moment before he nodded, and in that nod was acknowledgement of Gnorn's right to grieve in the way he saw fit.

As captain of the Mercenary Company of Etinstone, Orvandil had known Hlokk briefly, but well enough to understand how close the brothers had been. In many ways, the Thjoth had filled some of the gap left by Hlokk's absence, though nothing could replace the bond Gnorn had shared with his brother. Though he was the elder, he could not even remember ever being without Hlokk before the Battle of Iarfaen.

They had been fools back then. He knew it now. His cousin Ilm had been right all along. Seeking their deaths by joining Torrlond's army had been a coward's way out. It had been selfish to abandon his folk. His head hung a bit lower, and he shook it gently. "Yes, Brother, we were wrong," he said in a mere whisper. "We gave in to despair."

In fact, they had so much to live for: communion with and responsibilities toward their people as well as the joys and hardships and the thousand little things that fill everyday life. Dayraven had shown him that. Perhaps someday he would get a chance to apologize to Ilm. He hoped so. There were so many moments when he yearned to see his friends and relations back in Etinstone, where the exiled Dweorgs of the Fyrnhowes clung to an existence in their own segregated quarter. He wondered how they fared.

But this — all this marching, riding, sailing, fighting, running, and seeking — this was his chance, his duty even, to give something back to the lad. He and Hlokk had as much as sworn to take care of him. The memory of their first meeting with the lad and Imharr at the crossroads prodded his mouth into a smile. He would do what he had to do to find him and help him. And one day, when he was too old and fat to traipse through forests, he would write the tale of it all. A true loremaster was not just one who knew all the old histories, but also one who added to them. Dayraven's story would be Gnorn's greatest contribution to the body of knowledge. Always he had looked to the past for answers. But this was different. "Yes, Brother. Our little way of touching the future."

The shrill cry of a bird somewhere off to his left preceded a similar one off to his right. There was something strange about the birds' calls, however. He frowned as he considered it, and when he heard men's voices yelling, he realized they had been no birds at all. He let go of his horse's rein and tugged his axe out of his belt. Up ahead, Orvandil had pulled out his long dagger and was glancing to both sides.

The shouting grew nearer but not more comprehensible, and Gnorn realized it was in Ondunic just when several men emerged from the trees holding bows nocked with arrows. They were pointed at him.

The men were clad in worn garb, mostly in the greens and browns of woodsmen, and they had the dark hair and bronze skin of the Caergilese. They were thin enough for Gnorn to guess they had been living hard and bare lives for a long while.

"Easy now," came Galdor's voice from up ahead. "We're friends. Do any of you speak the Northern Tongue?"

That was when Gnorn heard his own name spoken with a Caergilese lilt. "Captain Gnorn?" One of the archers lowered his bow and approached the Dweorg with a broad smile on his face. "Captain Gnorn ydy er! A Captain Orvandil!"

As it turned out, one of the rebels had served for a time under Daen and Goel, the two men who had led the Caergilese fighters back when Gnorn and Orvandil took charge of the Asdralae in the resistance movement against the Torrlonders in the south. His name was Ban. Though Gnorn did not recognize him, Ban seemed to remember him and Orvandil quite well, which stood to reason since they had been the only Dweorg and Thjoth among the alliance of Adanese, Asdralae, and Caergilese. Daen and Goel had perished in the Torrlonder ambush in the mountains, the same one that resulted in King Balch's capture and Gnorn and Orvandil's flight with Queen Rona and her sons. Ban had survived only because he had been among a handful of men sent out the previous day on a scouting mission.

All this Ban conveyed by another of the Caergilese rebels, Dunal, who spoke enough of the Northern Tongue to make some communication possible. Gnorn also used a tiny bit of his rudimentary Ondunic, though he did not need to locate an outhouse. It was Dunal that Gnorn addressed, but another of the Caergilese seemed to be the one in charge, and the translator kept swiveling back and forth between the rebel leader and the Dweorg, who became the spokesperson for the four friends but also had to keep repeating Galdor's words. It made for a somewhat confusing conversation as they all stood together in the forest.

"Is there any danger? Ask him if there are any Torrlonders nearby," said Galdor.

"Are there Torrlonders nearby?"

Dunal shook his head. "We kill their scouts. Then track you."

The wizard pursed his lips, not quite satisfied with the answer.

"Perhaps we can take that as a 'no'," offered Gnorn.

"Very well. Tell them where we're headed."

Gnorn opened his mouth to speak, but Galdor put his hand on the Dweorg's shoulder. "And ask them if they can help us. Perhaps guide us past any other Torrlonders."

Gnorn nodded and then turned to Dunal. "Can you . . ."

Again the wizard tapped the Dweorg's shoulder. "See if they can even get us to the coast. To Culvor Sound."

Gnorn raised his eyebrows at Galdor.

"Sorry." The wizard smiled. "Well, go on then."

The Dweorg turned once again and opened his mouth, only to feel the hand return to his shoulder.

"Oh, and be sure to find out what they know of the Prophet of Edan. Can they help us reach him?"

He scowled at the wizard. "Is that all?"

"Yes, I should think so." He smiled again. "Have you got it all?"

After much back and forth between Gnorn and Dunal and Dunal and the rebel leader along with further unnecessary encouragement from Galdor, an understanding emerged that the rebels would in fact conduct the four friends safely out of Derwyn. They informed them that the majority of the Torrlonders were south of the forest, closer to where the main body of rebels awaited them.

The main body of the rebels was under the command of a nobleman named Imrys, who fought on behalf of the young rightful king of Caergilion, Moradoc, son of Malruan. It was said that King Earconwald himself led the Torrlonders massed there, and thus it would have been quite unsafe to try to exit the forest from the south. Their small group of thirty men had come north to scout and make sure the Torrlonders were not seeking to come at the rebels from behind and surround them. They were obligated to report back to the main camp, but, in consideration of Gnorn and Orvandil's past efforts on behalf of the rebellion, the leader would detach ten men, including Ban and Dunal, to guide the four companions safely on their way. Once out of the forest and past the main force of Torrlonders, they would be on their own to reach Culvor Sound. Regarding the Prophet of Edan, the rebels seemed to have heard of him, but they were guarded in what they would say, as if they had not quite determined whether he was friend or foe.

"Well, that will have to do." Galdor nodded. "Give them our thanks."

"Our thanks to you," repeated Gnorn.

"Danach," said Dunal to the leader.

"Mae'r ruarch," said the leader with a nod.

"You are welcome," said Dunal in his thick, lilting accent.

"You're welcome," said Gnorn to the wizard with a forced smile, and at last they were on their way.

15

PARABLES, SONGS, AND TRUTHS

The grey clouds that often lingered over Caergilion were a fickle company. On occasion they released an angry downpour, and other times they brooded over the deep greens of the landscape in melancholy indecision about whether or when to shed their tears. Most often they drizzled in a fine mist that was not quite rain, but a constant infusion of moisture. Such, observed the Prophet of Edan, was their state on this day.

He peered down the grassy hillside at the thousands of gazes awaiting him. Sick in body and spirit, they had journeyed from all over Caergilion and even Adanon. From villages and towns, from the coastal fells to the inner plains, they had arrived in expectation of healing and consolation. Not a few were Torrlonder soldiers, who also trickled in from every corner of the lands they had conquered for the same reasons as the others, and perhaps also to seek some means to allay the guilt prodding them from within.

They were all his brothers and sisters. It did not matter where they came from or who they were — they had all congregated here, to the place where he had found his purpose. So swiftly did word of his deeds spread, so dire was their need for hope. And he tried to give it to them. Every day he bled power for those who crowded round him until the thing in his mind grew too hungry, its shadow-whispers too insistent. When he could no longer heal for fear of imparting the ultimate mercy and devouring all their souls, he told them stories.

Thus he hoped to change the world.

There was an interesting thing about stories, he had realized. Tell people a truth in plain words, and they were more than likely to forget it amidst the thoughts and cares of their daily lives. But clothing that same truth in a story allowed people to uncover it for themselves, and having done so, they might keep it in their hearts. Also, he had realized another thing: He liked telling stories. He suspected this had been true of the man he had been before he lost his memory, but he could recall none of the tales that man would have told.

He looked up at the next person he would heal: a white-haired old woman who hobbled toward him, relying on a gnarled stick to steady her steps. In the morning there had been a long line of folk snaking down the hill. He had established a rule that the worst off and the most helpless should be the first in line — the ones who lay on pallets, burning up with plague fever, and the children and elderly. More and more people were streaming in with minor ailments, but these willingly waited their turn, for plenty of them had come in truth just to be in the presence of the Prophet. Caergilese, Adanese, and Torrlonders alike observed the spirit of this rule, and often they even helped one another, giving over their places to someone in a worse state. In spite of her age, this stubborn woman had taken a place near the end of the line, waiting for the morning and the better part of the afternoon.

Realizing she stirred some hidden memory of his, he cocked his head as she approached. She was small and had bound her hair behind her head, and there was something familiar about the way she leaned on that stick. But when she neared and gazed at him with her dark brown eyes, the spell was broken and the familiarity dissipated. She spoke in Ondunic. Standing next to him as always, Seren rendered her words into the Northern Tongue.

"Good afternoon, Prophet. Though your hair is as white as mine, now that I'm close enough, I see you are younger than I thought you'd be." After Seren finished with a quiet giggle, the old woman looked at him with a serious expression, and she seemed to be forming a judgement.

He gently quested out to her with the power within him and smiled. "To tell you truly, sister, I feel both young and old. But you needn't have waited so long. There were those with less need who came before you."

Following Seren's translation into Ondunic, the old woman scoffed. "Nonsense. Just a touch of stiffness in my joints. I came to see if you might help me. Drawing the water of a morning grows a bit tricky, and there are other things I used to do that I can no longer." Seren gave a sad smile as she finished translating. Even she sensed there was more to this old woman's story. The girl had a good understanding of people, and he had come to rely on her.

The Prophet nodded and gazed into the old woman's eyes even as he shared the images and losses that occupied her mind. It was a strange thing to touch the memories of so many others without knowing his own. "My sister. I know why you came. You lost your husband and son many years ago, but the pain is still with you, a hole you cannot fill. The beautiful granddaughter you raised on your own died only a week ago of the plague. And your grandson who joined the rebellion has long been missing. You have cared so much for others, but you have outlived those who should have cared for you."

The old woman staggered, and her body sagged so much he feared she would fall. But, as she had done all those years, she held herself up. "I'm so tired. So tired now." A sniffle broke up Seren's translation.

Mercy, slithered the chilling voice in the shadows of his mind. *Give her the only true rest.* "I know," said the Prophet. And he did know, for her burdens weighed on him and became part of him. "I can heal your body for a time. But I cannot erase the pain of your spirit. What I can do, I will. I will share your pain and embrace you. Will you have it so?"

When Seren finished rendering his words, the old woman waited a while before she nodded.

He nodded back at her. "Come close."

She tottered to him and bowed the head on her withered neck.

He enfolded her in his arms, and the power within him surged as he allowed it to seep out like a consuming brightness. *Let her go*, hissed the power as it wormed through him until it swelled in widening gyres. His mind trembled with the effort to ignore it. *Give her to me*, seethed the shadow towering within him, and he knew it would have its way in the end. Why did he deny it day after day? What was this futile effort of his? Making these creatures his purpose was like holding the rain in his hand. He could cling all he wanted, but they would slip away. They always had, and they always would. *She is mine*.

No, said a man's voice. His voice. *She is not yours. Not yet. She is her own while she breathes, and she wills to live, else she would not have come to me.* He winced as the old woman's agony flooded him. Years of toil and care, all for the sake of love and duty. The ferocity and tenderness whereby she had held on to her dear ones: husband, son, granddaughter, and grandson as well as myriad friends and neighbors. That had not prevented them from leaving her. Love and pain, joy and loss — they were all one, each necessary for the other to exist, like the symbiosis of life and death. Leaving himself wide open, he took it all in, and amidst all the power and brightness within him, he found a place for it. For a moment longer he bathed her in the light. *There will still be those who need you*, he promised her.

When he let go of her, the woman dropped her stick. The swelling and pain in her joints would be absent for a time. Gone too was the plague that had begun to usurp the toughened old body she had pushed so hard over the years. But that was not why her face beamed up at him. She was no longer alone. He had shared her pain and imbibed her losses, making them part of him. During their brief contact, he had become her. She was not alone.

She nodded as she smiled. Tears tracked down the wrinkles of her weathered cheeks. "Yes. I think I'll be able to fetch that water now." Seren also grinned as she translated through her own tears.

More than that, he knew this woman would share the gift of life within her, as she always had. "Go in peace, sister." He turned to Seren. "She is the last for today. Tell them I would speak to them now."

"THERE WERE TWO BROTHERS," HE BEGAN AS THOUSANDS OF FACES looked up at him through the drizzle. He paused to allow Seren to speak in Ondunic, and then further down the slope, there were others who would repeat the words in both tongues so that all could hear.

"They were twins, and their mother loved them both. But they were as different from each other as the sun is from the moon. The elder, who had preceded his brother from the womb by only a short space, was a great warrior. He was strong and fast, and he gained fame from his feats of arms. The younger, on the other hand, was a lover of music and lore. As much as folk admired the elder for his deeds, they loved the younger for his gentleness and perception. They each loved the other in their own fashion, and they both loved their mother without reservation.

"There came a time when an illness carried away their mother to her death. The elder twin sank into grief, and folk said he became grim with his loss. The younger brother too mourned her, but in his own quiet way. For in his wisdom he knew that, as hard as it was, death was right in the end. He reasoned that his mother had lived a long and prosperous life, and so, rather than give in to despair, he celebrated that life. Yet the elder twin took it amiss and reckoned his sibling did not love their mother as he should. He could not see there was more than one way to honor their mother and her memory, and resentment joined grief to eat at his heart.

"The mother had been a wealthy woman, and loving both her sons equally, she had arranged to divide her estate and pass half of it on to each of them. This satisfied the younger twin, but the elder spoke ill of his brother. 'Why should we weaken the family estate for the sake of one who loves his mother so little? I am the elder, and by rights it should all pass to me.' So he told himself.

"Such thoughts took root and festered within him until one day, he took his sword in hand and gathered his friends and came to his brother, whom he began to blame for their mother's death. With his blade pointed at his brother's throat, he claimed all of their mother's estate and told the younger he would either die or from that day become his slave. He justified this by saying the younger twin's response to their mother's death showed his evil character, and he convinced himself he believed these words when he said them.

"The younger twin chose slavery over death, not because he feared the latter, but because of what he foresaw. 'Brother,' said he, 'What you do is wrong. But I will serve you lest you stain yourself with my death. That is a thing from which you could never cleanse yourself.' And so, for years he served his brother without complaint.

"At first the elder brother took great satisfaction from seizing his twin's share of the estate. He saw himself as a great lord, and he even told himself that their mother would have wanted it that way. But as the years passed and his victories in battle accumulated, what at first seemed a minor discontent grew until he could take no pleasure from anything. His life became a mockery, for though he gained praise for his power and wealth, he could never hold on to the brief happiness that came with each acquisition, and he perceived the praise as shallow and empty, mere wind.

"What ate at him most, however, was how content his younger twin always seemed to be. Somehow, even in his state of slavery, he held on to his dignity. Not only that, but he performed every task he was given with diligence and care, thus frustrating the elder brother more since he could find no reason to chide or punish him.

"Finally, the elder twin decided to spy on his brother, hoping to catch him in some treacherous act or at least find out why his lips always seemed on the edge of a knowing smile. And so it was that, one evening, when it was time for the slaves to return to their sleeping quarters, he watched his brother in stealth and saw him clasp some small object in his hand before smiling at it and returning it to his pocket. 'So, he's been stealing from me,' he said to himself. He trailed his brother to the small chamber where he slept, all the while thinking of how he would give him the most lashes allowed under the law before the entire estate.

"After the younger twin entered his chamber, the elder burst in and said, 'Now I've caught you. I know the reason for all your smirks. Turn out your pocket.'

"The younger brother did as he was told and put the object in his twin's outstretched hand.

"The elder looked down at a small, battered tin whistle. 'What is this?' said he.

"The younger twin gave him a gentle smile. 'Our mother gave it to me when we were children. It no longer works, but it has helped me to remember her. Keep it if you like.'

"That was when the elder brother remembered the tin whistle, and how he used to wince when his twin first learned it, and how he had practiced on it for years until he could play it with skill and grace. It had been his first musical instrument.

"Something broke in the elder twin then. He had hardened his heart for so long, but the memories of this tin whistle cracked it until it burst with all the regret and longing his actions had birthed. And he was no longer blind. He perceived how his younger twin had loved their mother, perhaps not in the way he had, but with a depth that could not be measured. Their grief over death was the same, and they faced the same darkness, but each faced it in his own way. He went down on his knees and begged his brother for forgiveness, and he promised to restore all that was his. And it was only from that day that the elder brother began to heal from the loss of his mother, for he had loved her much. But now he understood her from his brother's eyes as well, and so he grew to love her even more."

Just as the Prophet finished his story, the sun sliced through a rent in the clouds and shimmered through the curtain of drizzle, transforming the droplets into a multitude of little jewels suspended in the air and brightening the whole hillside for a fleeting moment. A collective murmur rolled through the congregated people, and many of them looked up and smiled. He had healed them of their infirmities, and he took their smiles as the greatest possible reward. Moreover, beyond the bliss and hope of this one day, he hoped they would hearken to the story.

He did not tell them the elder brother was Torrlond, or that the younger brother was Caergilion. Nor did he say their mother was their god or gods — Edan or Oruma and Anghara, it mattered not. Perhaps they knew, or perhaps they would figure it out. It would not do to say such things in too direct a fashion. But he trusted some would ponder the little tale. And if they pondered it enough, perhaps it would nudge them toward change. Though he was not so naïve as to suppose it would happen with such sudden grace, or that all the terrible pain of Torrlond's occupation of Caergilion could so easily be forgiven, perhaps he could push things a bit closer to the happy ending he had offered in his story. Such, at least, was his hope.

EVENING WAS SETTLING INTO NIGHT WHEN THE TORCH LIGHT appeared at the gate of Tob's family farm. Having just finished his meal within the farmhouse and washed up, the Prophet had been returning to the barn to retire for the night. He watched the party of seven Torrlonders enter the gate and approach the barn. The one who bore the torch at their head was Edge. He recognized the others as men who often appeared when he spoke on the hillside. He had healed all of them of the plague, and each face stirred their dormant memories within him.

"Evening, my lord." The bluff lieutenant bowed his head, as did the other six.

"Hello, Edge. Greetings to you all. To what do I owe the honor of your visit?"

"We're the honored ones, my lord," said another of the Torrlonders.

"Edge?" Seren darted out the barn door and wrapped the big Torrlonder in her skinny arms.

Grinning like a happy bear, he returned her embrace with his free arm. "Hello, my lass." He tousled her hair.

"It's been two days since you last came." She put her hands on her hips and pouted up at him in mock severity.

He looked at the ground and swallowed. "Oh, well. I wish I could come more. I do. But it's hard to get away sometimes."

He did not say the real reason for his absence was his fear of drawing too much attention Seren's way. Sensing this, the Prophet smiled. "Soldiers have many duties."

Edge turned his gaze to him. "That's why we came, in fact." He glanced at the other six men before continuing, as if seeking confirmation in their faces. He nodded and took a deep breath, seeming to gather enough courage to make his next statement. "We've decided something, my lord."

The Prophet gestured toward the door. "Would you like to come inside and tell me about it?"

The lieutenant shook his head. "Might as well have it out right here." He paused a moment and then took the plunge. "We've been thinking. No. That doesn't even half cover it. It's been eating us up."

"What has?"

The big man gestured at himself with his free hand. "This. Soldiering. This damned war. What we have to do. What we've done." He choked on the last word and cleared his throat.

"We can't do it no more, my lord," supplied another of the soldiers. "It just ain't right. You've shown us that."

"We always knew it, truth to tell," said Sergeant Hulm. "You just gave us the courage to see it."

The Prophet nodded calmly. "It is good to know your own hearts."

"So we decided," said Edge, who recovered his gruff voice. "We're going to leave. Deserting is better than staying. Better than being used in ways we can't live with. And for what?"

Seren started as Edge was speaking, backing a pace as if pushed, and there was momentary anguish in her eyes.

Seeing how she recovered her poise in a heartbeat, the Prophet did not think Edge or the others had noticed her reaction. He kept his focus on the soldiers. "So you seven came to tell me this. Are there more soldiers of the same mind?"

The lieutenant nodded. "Aye. Plenty. Almost all the ones you healed, and a good number of others. We're all fed up, but we're the only ones who could get away tonight. We came for your blessing. And then I reckon we'll head for the mountains, disappear for a while until it's safe to head back into Torrlond. So. There it is." He went down on his knees, and the other six followed. "Will you bless us, my lord?"

The Prophet gazed down into his friend's eyes. Sorrow for these men mingled with pride in their courage to act as their conscience bade them. But amidst such feelings grew a foreshadowing of their purpose. Thinking of Seren and the many Caergilese whom he had come to know, he knew what he must say. "You always have my blessing, such as it is, my brothers. And I understand why you have come to your decision, which is honorable. But I would counsel you otherwise. Remain soldiers of Torrlond."

Edge and the others frowned. The lieutenant shook his head. "But we can't do what they ask any longer. There'll soon come a time when Earconwald returns. He'll give orders, command us to do things . . ."

"I know that time will come. I'm waiting for it, and I shall have need of you then. What is more, the people of Caergilion shall have need of you. As soldiers. Even so will Torrlond, your homeland. I have seen this. The moment to show your true hearts will come, and you will know it, my brothers. Soon. It shall be soon. Until then, do as you have done: Protect the people you watch over. This is my counsel only, for I would not have you bound to any duty that destroys your spirit."

They all bowed their heads. "You may only counsel it," said Edge, "but your counsel is a command for me. I will remain."

"Aye," said one of others, and the rest followed.

"Rise with my blessing then, my brothers. We have work to do." The Prophet smiled, but it was not entirely for Edge and the others. He knew what he would do when Earconwald came. To his surprise, even the hungry shadow within him rustled and hissed in assent, and he sensed it was biding its time. *Yes.*

SEREN STOOD BEFORE HER AUDIENCE OF ONE AND POURED everything she had into her song, for whether alone or in a crowd, *he* was the most important audience she could imagine. He lay down on the cot in his stall, his features hidden in shadows. It mattered naught that he would sleep before the song ended. In a sense, that was really the point.

A few days ago, she had begun to sing again, at least when she thought she was alone. But he had overheard her once from outside the barn, and he said her voice was beautiful and soothing. Since then they had begun a ritual wherein he asked her to sing each evening before they slept, and she would comply before going to her cot. By the time she finished her song, he would be lying still, his breaths steady with sleep. She knew he grew weary. Who would not after healing so many people day after day? She sometimes saw the strain in his face, and in those brief moments she feared for him. And so she sang for him, happy to give him the only thing she could: a bit of peace and rest.

The songs were all in Ondunic — the ones her father had taught her. At times she ached with longing to hear his fiddle join her, weaving its mournful, lilting notes with her voice, but she knew it was gone. All burned up in the fire. But she liked to think her father would have been proud of how she sang.

She knew that, as he lay there so quiet and unmoving in the dark, the Prophet could not understand the Ondunic words. Nevertheless, she liked to think that he heard her gratitude and devotion in them.

For this evening she had chosen a tune that was at once deceptively simple and difficult to execute. It was slow and melancholy, even for a Caergilese song. Sung well, it would leave its listeners in helpless tears. Tara's Lay, it was called. It spoke of love and sacrifice, and as she neared its end, her voice balanced on that precarious edge that enraptures those fortunate enough to witness such a thing, just maintaining a delicate dance of control over a precipice of overwhelming emotion:

She watched them ride away as dawn lapsed into day,
With the woman's hands both clasped around him tight.
And nothing did they ween of the pain she bought so keen
When she saved their lives in darkness of the night.
Her wounds all grieved her sore, but nothing hurt her more
Than the baleful ache that flooded through her heart.
Brynad would never know, for she'd never dared to show
Her love, and now they'd ever be apart.
From the bridge she gazed afar, till they passed beyond the scar
Of the hill where she had first beheld him ride.
And when they disappeared, she knew that she had neared
The final breaths her body would abide.
She crawled down to the bank — into the stream she sank
And let the water wash away her blood.
As dawn lapsed into day, it carried her away
Into the cold indifference of the flood.
So Tara breathed her last, and then her body passed
Downriver near where Brynad sat his steed

And when by some strange chance, she fell beneath his glance
He sorrowed, guessing who had served his need.

A strange silence followed the last note. Seren listened until the Prophet's gentle, steady breaths filled the silence and darkness. She rubbed her eyes with her knuckles and thought of turning in to her cot. But something held her feet there. Perhaps it was the outpouring of the song that released her emotions. It had begun earlier in the evening, though. Edge's announcement about leaving had birthed or revived within her a raw fear, a dread that was a palpable weight on her heart. She knew it was not rational, but the fear was that everyone she loved would leave her. She stood motionless, paralyzed by the notion of being alone, as tears trickled down her cheeks.

WITHIN HIS MIND THE SHADOW-WHISPERS HAD GROWN LESS AND less urgent, less ravenous, with every verse of Seren's song. Each note drained away a little more of the terrible drive, and each lift or fall of intonation caressed his spirit. By the end, the darkness within him was the barest whisper, and he almost felt like a normal man. *Sleep*, it seemed to sigh, and whether it meant the eternal sleep or simple rest for a weary body he was not certain. For a fleeting moment, he lay content.

The girl had a wondrous voice, but it was more than just that. He had found her singing the most effective means of calming him, of soothing away the desperate need to seize everyone's pain forever. Though he could not understand the words to Seren's songs, he perceived truths in her singing. In her notes and voice were sorrow and joy and beauty so keen it could wound. It was, he realized, the ultimate argument against the whispers and urgings of the terrible power within him. Those songs told the truth about why people lived. Why they carried on.

But there was another truth shrouded in Seren's passionate voice, a personal one, and he sorrowed at her understandable fear of abandonment, which he had glimpsed earlier that evening. She had been through so much for one so young. Sensing the girl had not returned to her cot, he blinked until he could make out her shadowy form standing in the dimness.

"Seren."

"You . . . You're awake?" Her voice trembled.

"Yes. I was listening to your song."

"Oh. Do you . . . Did you like it?"

"Yes. It's beautiful."

"Thank you." She sniffled. "Have you been awake every night? When I sing?"

"Yes. I don't sleep so much. But I thank you. Your singing does more for me than you may realize."

"I know you're tired sometimes."

"Yes. I am." He sat up and put his bare feet on the hard-packed dirt floor of the stall. "But right now I am thinking of you. The idea of Edge leaving upset you."

"Yes."

"I think we're all afraid to be alone sometimes." He sighed. "Given what you've been through, you would feel that fear more than most. I would too. I would like to help you, if I can, to feel less afraid."

"How?"

"What helps me is to know that those who touch my life become part of me, and I part of them. Even with my memories lost, those I knew before are part of who I am in ways I can't begin to understand. And those I meet from this day forward will be as well. This life is such that we will not always be together in these forms, but I try to keep in mind that everyone I meet stays with me, even when we leave each other's company."

"But you won't leave me, will you?"

The pain in her voice filled him, and he nearly sobbed before mastering his voice to answer her. "Oh, Seren. Those we love are always within us, no matter what. In that sense, I will never leave you. But, one way or another, this body I live in for the moment will not always be by your side."

Silence met him.

He moved to one end of the cot. "Come sit next to me, please, little sister. There's something I must tell you."

She hesitated for a moment before obeying. He felt her small weight press down on the other side of the cot from him. She waited for him to speak.

"It's a hard thing for me to say." He paused. "In coming here, especially in meeting you, I felt for the first time a sense of my purpose. Before that I was so lost. I have much to thank you for. I want you to know that. But there will come a time when my purpose will bring me elsewhere."

"What do you mean?"

"I mean I will need to leave here. Leave Caergilion. Not now, but the time is mostlike not far away."

"But . . . You can't."

"I'm very sorry, but I fear I must."

"You can't leave me." Her last word veered into a sob, and she began to cry. She shuddered but then mastered her voice quickly. "I have no one else. I have nothing."

"Seren . . ."

"I'll come with you. Wherever you're going, I can come. Can't I?"

He sighed. "Where I am going you cannot come. I wish it were otherwise."

"No. You can't leave me." She sniffled again. "Not after . . . You can't leave me alone again."

"You will not be alone. Tob and his family care for you. Edge will be here. Your brother may return."

"No, no, no. You don't understand. Why do you want to leave me?"

He paused to collect his voice. "I don't want to leave you. But I must leave Caergilion to protect it. And you cannot come with me."

"But why?"

He released a long sigh. "Very well. I owe you at least the truth, but you must repeat what I'm about to tell you to no one. Not even Tob or Edge."

"Alright." She sniffled and sat up straighter.

"There is something inside me. A power. It's not me, but it's what I use to heal people. It's what draws them to me. But it wants something else, and I don't know how long I can deny it."

"What does it want?"

Sleep. Give them the mercy of eternal sleep. "It believes the only way to end suffering is to end life."

There was a long silence. "Life? All of it?"

"Yes. At least, all human life. Perhaps it's our awareness that leads to our suffering, though other creatures endure pain too. But we seem to impose so much more suffering on the world, including ourselves."

"So, it wants to kill everyone?" She had stopped crying now.

"Yes."

"Is it . . . here? Right now?"

"It's always with me, sometimes whispering, sometimes more . . . insistent. At this moment it is quieter than usual. But it will return, and each day it grows stronger while I weaken."

Another long silence. "Who are you?"

He grinned in the darkness, but it was a bitter grin. "The Prophet of Edan, I suppose." He shook his head. "I wish I knew. I have no memory of anything before waking up in Sildharan. People there told me stories about some things I had supposedly done. Riding a dragon into a battle, defeating the Torrlonders with a terrible, bright magic. I don't know. Even the things I've done since waking up seem strange to me, like a dream of someone else's deeds."

"But why must you leave?"

"For you. For Caergilion. When Earconwald comes, I will make things right. For that to happen, I must go to Torrlond. I know that now."

"Then why can't I come with you?"

"The power in me . . . It will be very dangerous, little sister. I will not allow you to be near when I unleash it."

"Then, will you come back?"

He waited a time before deciding how to respond. "I will promise one thing if you will promise me something in return."

"What?"

"If I can, I will come back to you. I swear it. But you must promise to remain here, where you'll be safe. I will make Caergilion safe for you before I leave. Do you understand?"

"I think so."

"Do we have an agreement, then?"

She sat for a while, but at length her answer came. "Alright. Yes."

"Good." He looked down at the floor, glad for the darkness. He did not wish for her to see the guilt in his eyes, for he knew one of two things must happen: The power within him would one day consume him utterly, or he would perish when he unleashed it. Either way, he did not expect to come back.

"THIS HAD BETTER BE THE END OF IT, NOTHELM."

King Earconwald spat, half to convey his disgust and half to rid his mouth of the sour taste of last night's drink. Surrounded by elite soldiers sworn to protect their ruler, he gazed toward the battle raging just outside the southern edge of Derwyn Forest. He winced at the general clamor of screams and clashing steel. Even at that distance the din invaded and stabbed his pounding head. He could not quite make out what was happening, but it seemed to him his troops were driving forward, and he reckoned that was good. He took a swig from his wine glass. It was a tasty Caergilese red. *Caergilese red*, he thought. *How appropriate. Yes, their blood will flow today.*

He laughed aloud at his jest, and in the process some of the damned wine slopped out of the glass. Just then he recalled how it had been Moda's favorite, and he shook his head to banish the memory. He looked about and scowled at Earl Nothelm, who was not standing where he was supposed to be. Why would not the damned man stay still? He held up his glass. "More."

Nothelm frowned at him, and for a moment he thought the earl was going to lecture him like a woman again. He thought he had fixed that for good the last time, and he was getting ready to slap the man. But Nothelm turned toward the soldier standing nearby, the one holding the bottle. "The King requires more wine."

Earconwald pressed on his temple and groaned. His Edan-cursed head was still throbbing as it had been all morning. The idiot with the bottle was far too slow as he approached, and for some reason the damnable glass was shaking as the king held it out. "Hurry up." But the glass kept trembling, and the fool was pouring the wine everywhere but in the glass. "Damn you!"

"I'm sorry, your Majesty." The soldier's fear-stricken face looked at Nothelm, who strode forward. "Let me assist you, your Majesty." The earl took both bottle and glass and poured. He held out the full glass.

King Earconwald looked with disgust at the two of them. He could see the old earl's disapproval in his frown, but of course the man feared to say anything. If he had not needed him, and if there had been more men he could trust, he would have been rid of the tedious nag long before. But Nothelm was a good soldier. A useful tool. The sort of man his empire was founded upon. The backbone of Torrlond's power. He had to give him that. "Good soldier," he mumbled as he took the glass.

After he downed it in a few gulps and released a satisfied gasp, his head began to feel more as it should. "A bit better. One more." He held out the glass, and Nothelm refilled it without a word before handing the bottle back to the soldier. This time he took only a small sip. The fools thought he could not handle his drink. Let them see. He would nurse this glass for as long as he liked.

The sounds of battle surged in the distance, and he remembered why they were standing in a field outside a forest so damned early in the morning. "This had better work, Nothelm. I'm sick of this place. Sick of the rain and constant drizzle. Sick of the food. Sick of living in a damned tent. Sick of the damned, ungrateful people." He chortled at his next thought before he voiced it. "Sick of the stringy, dark women with their little tits."

He gestured with his hands in front of his chest, spilling more wine. "Give me a fair-haired, pink-nippled Torrlonder with big ones any day. Eh? You like big tits, Nothelm?" He waggled his eyebrows and guffawed.

The captain of his guard cleared his throat and looked down at the ground, but he said nothing.

The king glanced at the man holding the wine bottle. "What about you, soldier? Are you a big-tit man?"

"I . . . couldn't say, your Majesty. I suppose so, if it please you."

He rolled his eyes. "Edan's balls. What depressing bores I'm saddled with for company." He paused and gazed at the battle, but there were so many damned bodies moving everywhere that it hurt his head, and he was too tired to try to figure out what was happening. He yawned. Then he took a gulp of wine, and somehow the damned glass was empty again. "Enough of this. Just tell me when we've won, Nothelm. And find a big-tittied woman for my bed tonight. A Torrlonder."

He flung his glass behind him and tottered toward his command tent, but then he remembered it was the other way and pivoted. When he did so, something reached up from the ground and tangled his feet, and he began to fall until something caught him. He looked into Nothelm's face, which was so close to his he could feel the old fellow's sigh on his cheek. Something stank like sour wine and vomit, but it might have been his own breath. Nothelm gazed back at him as he held him in his arms. There was something in his eyes. Pity? Disappointment? It disgusted him.

He mustered a vicious grin. "Or better yet, a Thjoth. Get me a Thjothic bitch with a blonde cunt for my bed tonight. We must celebrate our victory!" He pushed away from Nothelm and laughed the whole time he weaved his way back to his tent, sniggering even after he forgot why he had started laughing in the first place.

It was all a chaos of steel and blood and sweat and screams. This was no ambush or skirmish. It was the most savage battle Allon had ever seen, and not only because of its scale, for it was a desperate fight for survival. He plunged his sword into a grey-kirtled soldier's back, and a gout of blood trailed the blade when he yanked it out. The soldier shrieked and went down, one less Torrlonder to gloat over their corpses. But there were so many of them.

Grey tunics surrounded them in every direction. It was over. The Caergilese rebels' last stand, and no one would ever sing of it, for no matter the justice of the cause, the losing side never wrote the chronicles. The moment he had realized the Torrlonders had surrounded their position, he knew it would be the end. But that did not stop him from trying to reach Lord Imrys.

The Torrlonders must have known who the commander was, for they surrounded his position and attacked it no matter how fiercely the rebels fought back. Allon hacked another soldier from behind, nearly chopping his leg off in his attempt to hamstring him. The bone in the man's thigh cracked as the leg folded, and he went down screaming and clutching the gash as blood sprayed from it. The next foe faced him head on, and their blades clashed three times before the man slipped on someone's spilled bowels and fell on his back. Allon rushed on and did not look back.

He swung his sword and chopped again and again, little caring whether it hit steel, wood, or flesh and grunting with feral abandon as he lost awareness of everything but the need to keep wielding his blade. The muscles of his arms ached, and his breaths came in heavy gasps. Blood ran all over him, making his sword's hilt slippery, but he kept hacking at the grey kirtles and bright helms. A part of him wished some blade would descend on him and end it all so he could stop and rest, but nothing touched him. So he kept stabbing and hacking until there were no more grey kirtles athwart his path. And then there was Lord Imrys, still standing amidst a knot of his men.

"This way, my lord!" Allon gestured at the trail of bodies behind him, a small gap in the closing trap of foes. Not far beyond that gap lay the forest, offering the possibility of escape and sanctuary beneath its leaves. A small hope kindled inside him. If they could just reach the trees, they might evade the Torrlonders.

Imrys and the others fought their way over, and the commander nodded at him. "Well done," Allon thought he said, but he could only see his lips move amidst all the tumult and noise, for more Torrlonders were pouring in.

"Go, my lord!" screamed Allon. He turned his back to Imrys so he could fight off the enemy soldiers and give his lord a chance to flee. His blade rang out when it clashed with a Torrlonder's, but the man was off balance, so he kicked his leg from under him and, when he went down hard, plunged steel into his stomach.

"Allon!"

"Go, my lord."

"Come with us!"

Allon spun toward Lord Imrys's voice and saw the man gesturing wildly for him to come. He nodded and began to run towards him.

"Allon!" screamed Lord Imrys again.

A loud crack accompanied the stars that blossomed in his head and the jolt of pain down his neck, and he floated into darkness.

FEELING MUCH BETTER AFTER A HOT BATH AND SOME entertainment to accompany his afternoon meal, Earconwald sat on a chair in his tent with a fresh glass of wine dangling from one hand. He looked up at Nothelm, who stood before him like the tiresome old fool he was.

The king smacked his lips. "The Caergilese whore they sent me for lunch wasn't half bad, but she was no blonde," he observed to the old earl.

"I know naught of that, your Majesty. But perhaps my report will please you."

"Very well, then." He made a lazy gesture of permission with his free hand. "Report."

Nothelm nodded. "Your forces have routed the last significant band of rebels, your Majesty. They are broken. Most of them slain."

"And their commander?"

The earl frowned. "We've not found him among the dead yet. Nor is he captured. A few of the rebels escaped into the forest, but we've sent patrols in to sweep up. If Imrys is in there, we'll find him. But even if he somehow manages to evade us and survive, he'll no longer have much of anything to command. Today's battle was the last of the rebellion in Caergilion, your Majesty. The regular troops posted here can handle things from here on out."

Earconwald took a sip from his glass before he regarded Nothelm. He grinned. "Good. Now, there's only one other thing keeping us in Caergilion, isn't there?"

Nothelm nodded. "Yes, your Majesty." He still wore his disapproving frown, but Earconwald did not care what he thought.

"Did you bring the fellow? The one I asked for?"

"Yes. He's outside. Shall I bring him in?"

"Yes. At once."

"As you say, your Majesty." The old earl gave a stiff bow and exited the tent, and the king smiled after him before savoring a sip of wine.

Nothelm soon returned with distaste wrinkling his face and two guards behind him. Between the guards walked a young Caergilese dressed as a Torrlonder soldier. He was a little weasel of a man, one Earconwald recognized as a minor noble whose family had been useful enough. This particular fellow had served him as a translator and informant several times.

"Ah, Boil. There you are."

The man bowed so low he almost kissed the floor of the tent. He looked up and swallowed before giving a nervous, sycophantic smile. "Koel, your Majesty."

"What?"

"My name is Koel, if it please you, your Majesty." The fellow was sweating where he stood, with drops of it running down his forehead into his face.

Earconwald chuckled. "Such funny little names. Whatever it is, it's time for you to be useful."

"It's an honor to serve you."

"Nothelm here informs me your little rebellion is over."

The man backed up a step and glanced around him as he wrung his hands. "Not *my* rebellion, your Majesty. I'm your loyal subject."

"You're a Caergilese, are you not?" He held up his palm. "No matter. You do much to redeem yourself."

He bowed again. "Thank you, your Majesty."

"Now, let's not waste time. You say you know where to find the man who calls himself the Prophet of Edan?"

"Yes. I know where he preaches." He glanced down at the floor and licked his lips before continuing. "I've heard his false words myself. And I know where he sleeps. Who has helped him. I can give you names."

"They say he's been healing people of the plague. What do you make of that?"

The little man pointed at himself. "I, your Majesty?" He shook his head as if denying something. "I don't know. Perhaps it's some trick to deceive people into rebellion."

"No doubt you're correct. Smart man."

The Caergilese man grinned like a child given a sweet.

"You see," continued Earconwald, "I've met this Prophet of Edan before. I know him. I know where he comes from. And I know how dangerous he is. He's a liar. And a fraud. You may trust me when I say he can be doing nothing good."

"You must be right, your Majesty."

"Of course I am. So we will pay this false prophet a visit." A predatory smirk crossed the king's face. "And the girl you told me of? The one from the farm? Whose bitch-mother did this?" He pointed at his cheek, where the new scar still itched.

"Yes, your Majesty." Koel nodded. "She's with him."

"Good. We won't forget her." He turned to Nothelm and showed his teeth in a fleer. "Perhaps I won't be needing that blonde just yet," and he laughed for a long while at his jest.

16
MORTAL KINGS

By evening the Thjoths and Norfasters were limping in tatters back to their camp in the hills, with small groups of exhausted and demoralized men trickling in from everywhere. Their saving grace was inflicting enough casualties on the Torrlonders to halt their pursuit. But Duneyr knew they could not linger long. They needed to find another place to hide out for a bit and regroup.

Earl Torf appeared ahead walking toward some destination, and Duneyr broke off from his men to go speak to him. The old Norfaster's arm was in a sling, and his face was a mournful sight. Fear gripped Duneyr's heart and squeezed it. If Duke Durn had died in that battle, it was all over, and they had fought for naught. He prayed to all the gods the boy was unscathed.

"Greetings, Earl Torf," he said in the Northern Tongue.

The old man looked up, and he gave Duneyr a weary nod.

"How fares your lord?"

The earl managed a slight smile. "Unhurt, thank Edan. But we took a thorough beating today."

The chieftain breathed out a sigh. "Aye. That we did. The Torrlonders are fighting harder and smarter. Duke Ethelred's a different leader from that fool Siric. But it's not over. We carry on."

"What next, then?"

"I know not, but I expect we'll move on as soon as we treat the wounded. Has King Vols returned?"

"I haven't heard, but I only just arrived myself. The duke ordered me to have my arm looked at by a healer."

"Ah. Likely for the best. Where is Durn?"

The earl pointed with his good hand. "Yonder in his tent. He awaits King Vols there."

"Then that is where I'm bound. I wish you well. We'll fight again another day."

Earl Torf nodded and turned to go on his way.

Duneyr walked through the camp, where the wounded lay groaning and screaming everywhere even as others attended to them. The sounds of defeat. He approached the duke's tent, and the Norfaster guards there waved him in without a challenge.

Within the tent, Durn was listening to young Earl Randver. The tall duke stood leaning over a table with his hands braced on it, the expression on his youthful face calm even as Randver spoke with urgency. Upon Duneyr's entrance, Durn looked up and favored him with a grim smile.

"Welcome, Duneyr. I'm glad to see you alive."

"Not as glad as I am to *be* alive. It's good to see you well, my lord."

"Randver and I were discussing our choices. Given the severity of our defeat, I reckon we need to hole up somewhere and lick our wounds."

In his composure and intensity, the boy so reminded Duneyr of Orvandil Dragonbane that he shivered. And once he filled out his frame, he would be of a similar size. "That would be wisest, I think."

"But we must await King Vols. I would hear his counsel."

"Yes. That is best, but I expect he'll agree with you as well."

Durn nodded, and he made a slight frown. "We lost many good men today."

"Aye. That we did."

"My father would have mourned them."

"I expect he would have."

The young duke's smile was so fierce, it was almost a snarl. "But only after he avenged them."

Duneyr nodded. "Yes. That's the way, my lad. But we'll do it smart. We'll bide our time. It will come, and we'll seize it. But I don't reckon I need to tell you that." He walked closer and crossed his arms before his chest. "I met your father a few times. A great man, just as quick to laugh as he was to roar, and he could be as furious as they come. His was a hot anger, bright and sudden, powerful like a swollen river. Not the sort a man would like to stand in front of. But you, lad, you've got a cold anger. The rarer kind. More like a rising flood. And I'll tell you this: it's the cold sort of anger a wise man fears most. You can stay out of a river's path. But a flood is relentless. It creeps up on you, coming in its own time, but when it does, there's no escaping it."

Duke Durn gazed at Duneyr. At length, he nodded, and the chieftain knew the lad understood.

Someone burst into the tent behind Duneyr, and the chieftain pivoted. It was Hakon, who was breathing hard. Before he spoke, Duneyr could see something was wrong from the blond warrior's troubled eyes.

"Best come quick."

"What is it?"

"King Vols . . . He . . ." Hakon swallowed and gazed around with a desperate expression as if he might find the words he could not voice somewhere in the air. He shook his head and then gestured for them to follow him before exiting the tent.

Along with Durn and Randver, Duneyr trailed Hakon through the camp. Duneyr's chest seemed to tighten with each step, and the sense of dread was a weight that threatened to slow him until he could not move. The camp had already been a grim scene before, but a sort of hush flowed through it in a wave, darkening it further with a layer of silence only the moans of the dying penetrated. Hakon led them past tents and knots of men standing together. The strangest thing was how most eyes turned to Duneyr as he walked past. A few grim faces nodded at him. Denial sprang up in him even as his dread and foreboding grew. He focused on Hakon walking before him until they rounded a tent, beyond which a large throng of warriors gathered around something.

Duneyr's heart fell in his chest. "No." He shook his head, but there was no denying what he saw.

A group of Thjoths held up a body above the press. The body rode over the crowding warriors as if sleeping. But even at a distance, Duneyr could see the blood staining the kirtle and byrny from a wound in the chest. The silence that had seized the camp was emanating from that group of men, from that still body. Hakon had been right. No words could carry the depth of it. King Vols was dead.

The procession made its slow way toward where Duneyr was standing. Warriors cleared the path for the bearers of the slain king, and at their head were the other chieftains: Kialar, Asgrim, and Arinbjorn. Grimling was not there, and Duneyr wondered if the day's battle had claimed that chieftain too. But even that thought did not remain long in his mind, for before him was the overwhelming fact of his lord's death.

The bearers of King Vols stopped when they reached Duneyr. With a closer view, he could see bloody wounds all over Vols's body, and red soaked his entire chest. His eyes were closed. Kialar, Asgrim, and Arinbjorn gazed at Duneyr, and he knew what their eyes were asking of him. *I'm no king,* he thought. *Would that Orvandil were among us.*

They waited for him.

Duneyr took a deep breath. "We'll choose a new king in the Thingvang when we return to Grimrik." He glanced to his side, where Duke Durn stood, staring at him like everyone else.

He returned his gaze to his fellow chieftains. "Before that, we have but one duty."

The silence of sharpened iron met him in their gazes.

"EASY NOW, SERGEANT." CAPTAIN LUDECAN CROUCHED NEXT TO Bosa, a man he had known for as long as he had been in the Mercenary Company of Etinstone, which was a longer time than he cared to think about. They had both been young when they joined. He could not remember what sort of trouble had forced Bosa into the company, but the man had grown into a capable and smart veteran who knew how to stay alive as well as anyone Ludecan knew. All of which could mean nothing in the midst of a battle. *Fate's a fickle bitch*, thought the captain. *And there's not a thing you can do when she comes for you.*

Lying on his back, Bosa groaned and struggled to raise himself, just getting his sweaty head up enough to glance at his body. When he took in his chest and stomach, he rolled his eyes and fell back down.

"Hold still, man. I'm going to patch you up."

The sergeant smiled, exposing his reddened teeth, and a dribble of blood leaked out the corner of his mouth. "No point," he managed to gasp.

Ludecan glanced at the wide puncture wounds in the man's stomach and chest and sighed. He was not certain if an axe or sword had done the work — mostlike a broad-bladed sword wielded by one of those huge Edan-cursed Thjoths — but whatever had done it had broken through the links of the man's byrny and reached deep into his flesh. Most of Bosa's blood had pulsed and leaked out of him before the captain reached him, and it had pooled beneath him, leaving the man as pale as a full moon on a cloudless winter night.

No point. That about summed up everything.

The captain nodded at his sergeant. There had never been any lies between him and his men. At least he could say that. "I reckon you're right, my friend. I'll just keep you a bit of company, then." He sat on the ground next to Bosa.

The sergeant looked up at him, and the man's ruined body trembled with effort as his mouth opened. He kept staring at Ludecan like he wanted to tell him something important.

"It's alright." Ludecan put his hand on his sergeant's brow. His other hand grasped one of Bosa's, which was slick with blood. *How in Edan's fucking creation could it be alright? The man's dying.* Nothing he could say would be adequate for this moment. He knew that. He had been here many times before, every time failing to say or do the right thing. But that did not prevent him from trying. *Damn me for a fool.*

Bosa still gazed at him, and his jaw worked up and down, but only a gargling sound came out of his mouth.

Ludecan squinted and frowned down at the man, straining to listen for Bosa's last words as if they were the most important thing in the world. But the man's hand went slack and his eyes stopped seeing. No more trembling. No more pain.

The captain closed his friend's eyes. The aching muscles in his legs and back complained when he stood up to take a long and weary look at his surroundings. "What a fucking mess." He scowled at the carnage all around him and shook his head. "And we won."

Dead Thjoths lay all over the earth, as did the bodies of many Norfasters, who were supposed to be their fellow Torrlonders. But there were more corpses in the grey kirtles of Torrlond's army than not. Not one of them would profit when this whole argument about who should govern Norfast would be settled. Neither would he, and sure as shit the Mercenary Company of Etinstone would be no better off. Still, today was a victory — the first his side could claim since the miserable campaign began, now that the bloated fool Siric was out of the way. The Duke of Rimdale was still around, and he strutted about and shouted his opinions as if everyone cared. But few paid heed to him now that Duke Ethelred had arrived and taken matters into his hands.

Duke Ethelred was a soldier, and he was a man soldiers could follow. He was also prepared to make the hard decisions. Today's battle had been costly, but it had been necessary. Ethelred had grasped one important fact: His side could afford the losses far more than the Norfasters and Thjoths could. They would win by attrition if they had to. Grind them down. Duke Ethelred was a respectable commander and a sound tactician, but there was little subtlety about this. Perhaps it was the best and quickest way, but it would get messy. *'Messy.' A quaint word for this butcher's bill.* Ludecan grimaced at the lies he told even himself. *How else does a man keep going?*

But they *had* won . . . in a manner of speaking. The important thing was they had forced their foes back this time and shown the willingness to fight and win. The Norfasters and their cousins from Grimrik were far from finished, Ludecan knew, but they had taken a mauling, and they would need to gather themselves before they could even think of mounting an attack. If nothing else, Duke Ethelred had gained the Torrlonders a stronger bargaining position. Bought with the lives of his men, the coinage of war. Such were the politics of power. The captain took one last look at Bosa, and then he returned to his present task of double-checking for any of his men who might survive their wounds. Thus far it had been fruitless.

In addition to the dead, the wounded and dying covered the churned up and reddened ground. Some shrieked out the agony of their last moments, while others, like Sergeant Bosa, went quietly. The place stank of blood and shit, like all fresh battlefields. It was a stench at once familiar and nauseating for the captain. He had smelled it many times, and he should count himself lucky he would smell it again. *Edan curse me. I'm a soldier. I know nothing else.* He pushed himself to move on.

He stumbled past Thjothic and Norfaster dead without a second look, but each time he came to a grey-kirtled corpse, he looked at the face, turning over the body if he had to. Most he did not recognize. A few he did. The field and surrounding hills would take some time to soak in all the blood. The earth would cover all the bones with green grass, and one day no one alive would recall how so many of their kind had lost their lives in this place. For now, though, it looked like some grim kingdom of the dead, with the living who attended them appearing like forlorn wraiths. He sighed when he spotted another of his soldiers. By his own count, the Mercenary Company of Etinstone had lost at least a quarter of its men.

He thought he had seen the worst of it when another sight stopped him in his tracks. Coming at them from behind, at first he had not recognized them, but then he heard Utred's anguished voice scolding someone, and he knew whose body the soldier sat by before he reached them.

Garmund's head lay cradled in Utred's lap, and his body did not stir. The wounds all over the former's arms and chest appeared serious, but it was likely the gash in his neck that finished him. The two of them had always fought like an old married couple. If Garmund thought one thing, Utred was sure of the opposite. If Utred professed a belief, Garmund was quick to disagree. Ludecan could not count the number of times the company had gone to sleep listening to those two bicker, most especially of late about the Prophet of Edan.

Utred looked down at the still face on his lap and wiped his crooked nose with the back of his hand before he sniffled. "Damn fool. Told you a hunerd times afore not to rush too far for'ard. Nothin' good comes o' not listenin'. I was a'screamin' an a'shoutin', but you was too damn smart to look back. Ain't that so?" He shook the head as if expecting a response that Garmund was just too stubborn to give. "Ain't it?"

Captain Ludecan approached and put his hand on Utred's shoulder. "He's gone. Let him go."

Utred looked up at him as if in appeal, and he just stared that way for a while. But he took the captain's hand when he extended it, and after laying Garmund's head on the ground, he stood up.

"I'm sorry," said Ludecan. "Truly I am."

Utred looked at the ground and nodded.

Footsteps squelched in the mud, and the captain looked over at where Lieutenant Irling led Hewald, Bernred, and Mull toward him.

"My lord," said Irling. "We've rounded up all our wounded. We don't expect to lose any others." The lieutenant glanced at Utred and then over at where Garmund lay dead. When his eyes met the captain's, Ludecan nodded.

"Bosa's dead too." The captain turned to Mull. "I reckon that makes you sergeant now, soldier. Congratulations on your promotion."

Mull's eyes widened for a moment, and then he scowled. "Not me, captain. Give it to Hewald."

"Fuck that." Hewald spat. "I'm no fucking sergeant."

Ludecan shook his head at Mull. "You've got seniority."

"What about Bernred, then?"

"Too stupid."

Bernred snorted and cracked a fleeting grin.

Mull turned toward Utred and opened his mouth, but then, seeming to think better of it, he closed it and frowned. "Shit."

"That's settled, then." Ludecan released a sigh. "Let's get back to the wounded and see what needs doing."

"Captain!"

Ludecan turned toward the new voice. It was Sergeant Rhof, who slipped in the mud and stepped over and around corpses as he hurried toward them. When he reached them, he put his hands on his knees while he collected his breath.

Ludecan had sent Rhof for tidings. "Did you find out what the orders are?"

"No, my lord."

"Then why the fuck are you here?"

"Sorry. But I heard something you might want to know. There's talk among the men."

"Well, have it out, then."

Rhof gave a knowing smile and nodded. "They say the king of the Thjoths died in the battle."

"King Vols?" said Bernred.

"No," said Hewald with a wicked grin, "the *other* king of the Thjoths, you fucking lard-ass."

Bernred scowled at him. "Least I ain't got lard for a brain."

Hewald shrugged. "I could open up your fucking skull to find out, but I doubt there's much in there at all."

Bernred growled and stepped toward Hewald.

Captain Ludecan cut the air with his hand. "All of you shut up!"

The men went silent and looked at him, but he gazed only at Sergeant Rhof. "Are you sure of this?"

The sergeant nodded. "As sure as can be. He got cut down. Stabbed through the heart and then some. The Thjoths fought like rabid beasts to get his body, but he was deader than dead when they carried him off."

The captain's shoulders sagged. "Shit."

Rhof's smile turned into a puzzled frown. "What's the matter? Ain't that good news?"

Ludecan gazed at the man. "What do you know about Thjoths, Sergeant Rhof?"

Mull nodded. "They'll fight thrice as hard now. Till they're all dead. Or we are."

HAVING ASSURED HIMSELF HE HAD THOUGHT OF EVERYTHING HE needed for the journey and made all the necessary arrangements for his absence, Joruman strode across one of Sigseld's cobbled courtyards toward the stables. A combination of his power, Bagsac's fears, and his desperate need to find Dayraven seemed to roil from his mind and trail in his wake. Behind him, Morcar hurried to keep up, and behind the high priest marched Ulfbert at the head of ten temple guards creaking in leather armor, their boots clacking on the stones. Light and swift they must travel, so they could wear no mail. In truth, with his enhanced power, the supreme priest had no need of guards, but he supposed a man of his station ought to have at least a minimal entourage to act as servants. As long as they did not slow him down.

"But I don't understand, my lord. Why must you leave Torrhelm in the first place, and why in such haste?" The High Priest Morcar was puffing behind him.

Joruman did not bother to turn towards his high priest. Morcar likely knew more than he was letting on, and he found his feigned ignorance and attempts at cunning tiresome. Such pathetic scheming was far beneath the supreme priest now, but he would not satisfy the worm with more information than he already had. He did not mask the irritation in his voice. "Quit whining. I told you it's a matter of extreme urgency I must attend to myself. I would not leave otherwise."

The High Priest Nothgar had contacted him through the seeing crystal that very morning with tidings that the Prophet of Edan in Caergilion was indeed the same man who had defeated Bledla and stopped Torrlond's army in Sildharan. Furthermore, King Earconwald was journeying toward him with his army in tow. No one knew the king's intentions, but the debauched idiot likely intended to slay the Prophet, and all that blessed power would go to waste. Or, perhaps even more likely, the king would trigger something he would regret, unleashing the elf's power within Dayraven. Joruman did not know what might happen if that occurred, but there was a very real possibility it would put the power of the elf beyond his control and ruin the unique opportunity Dayraven presented. Either way, he had to reach the Prophet of Edan as soon as possible.

"But what will you tell the king?" wheedled Morcar in an all too obvious attempt to solicit more information regarding Joruman's plans.

The supreme priest rounded on his high priest, causing him and the temple guards to make an abrupt halt. "What will I tell him?" He poked Morcar's chest. "I'll tell him I had to commit the foolish act of leaving Torrhelm in the hands of idiots to prevent *him* from committing a far more foolish act. Why do such dull-wits surround me?" His mind was throbbing with power, the thirst for more of it, and a simultaneous terror of it. It all threatened to split open his skull.

"I . . . I'm sorry, my lord. It's only that, with so much instability both within the kingdom and without, it might be a ticklish time to have both the king and the supreme priest absent from Torrhelm."

Joruman took a deep breath. "Look here, Morcar. Matters are in hand. Duke Ethelred has the situation in Norfast under control. If anything noteworthy occurs, all you need do is contact me through the seeing crystal for instructions. It's simple. Just report to me. Is that clear?"

"Yes, my lord. But what of the Ilarchae?"

"What of them?"

"You said there were messages from the east. Our scouts report they are massing in the north of Sildharan, where they're gathering large numbers of ships."

"Perhaps the barbarians wish to take up fishing."

Morcar blinked at him. "My lord, you can't be serious. The Ilarchae have conquered Sildharan and Golgar. With so many of our troops engaged in Norfast and in the south, we're spread thin. Torrlond's northeast is vulnerable. The barbarians' next move could be a grave concern, could it not?"

"Silence!" Joruman jerked up his palm and Morcar winced, but, wishing to maintain his dignity, the supreme priest suppressed the urge to slap the man. There was no time for any of this nonsense. "I tell you the matter upon which I am embarking is far graver than any threat you could imagine, real or conjured. *Nothing* could be graver." He scowled down at the shrinking high priest. "Will you question my judgement or dare to lecture me? Whether in private or, far worse, before my temple guards?"

Ulfbert and the other guards shifted their feet and looked away.

Morcar stared down at the cobbles. "No, my lord. Of course not."

"Then cease your prattling. I told you already: I sent messages to

Duke Weohstan and Duke Heahmund regarding the Ilarchae. Their territories are in the northeast, closest to Sildharan, so they'll have good reason to keep a close watch on the barbarians' movements. And between us and the Ilarchae lies the entire kingdom of Ellond."

"Weohstan and Heahmund." Morcar cocked an eyebrow after he uttered the names. He dared not say more, but there was no need to.

"What? You fear I don't realize the quality of the good dukes? Yes, those two are more accomplished schemers than they are military strategists. But it's a simple task I've given them. Keep watch and report. Simple tasks for simple minds."

Morcar swallowed and gazed down at the ground again while Joruman made the allusion more obvious than necessary by pointing at the high priest's head.

"Besides, there's nothing to fear from the east. The Ilarchae will be a long time in consolidating their conquests, if they can even manage to hold on to them. I know the barbarians. Do you forget I've been among them?" Joruman gave a bitter smile at the memory of his uncomfortable journey into the Wildlands. "Their leader is an impressive fellow, but discipline and unity are new to them, and their divisions will assert themselves again at some point. No doubt they'll begin squabbling over some rocks or bit of mud."

"They conquered Sildharan and Golgar."

"Weak and corrupt kingdoms rotting from within. And you're repeating yourself. Will you waste more of my precious time, Morcar?" The power in him surged and loomed, and the only thing that could rival it was his desire for more. He *needed* to find Dayraven. His breaths came heavy and fast, and sweat oozed from his pores.

The high priest shrank again. "No, my lord. As you say, I'll keep an eye on things here and contact you when there is need."

"Good. I'm certain you won't disappoint me." Joruman did not trust the little pervert, but there was no time for any other arrangements, and his mind could hold nothing else but the dire need to reach Dayraven. Some remote part of him knew Morcar was voicing valid concerns, but nothing else could possibly matter in the face of what was at stake in the south. No threat or amount of wealth or region or kingdom could vie with the severe and consuming need to get to the

Prophet of Edan. With sudden and complete understanding, he knew it deep in his core. The power of the elves: With it, he could accomplish everything. Nothing else mattered.

Morcar bowed. "Blessed be the Eternal, my lord."

The Supreme Priest Joruman grunted and dismissed the idiot and all his tedious questions as soon as he turned to stride toward the stables. On his way there, he twisted the ring on his little finger before donning the supple leather riding gloves he had tucked in his belt. The words of *Observations of Ogmos the Wise* echoed in his head again and again. *Concentrations of eternity, immune to anything like death . . . Power without limit.*

He *had* to reach Dayraven. Like a vast lodestone, the elf's power drew him from afar, whispering of promises of enlightenment and salvation. It was impossible that Earconwald should reach the boy first and ruin everything. *The dissolute moron. He's outlived his usefulness.* Of course, there had been a time when Joruman himself sought Dayraven's death, when the boy was in the way of his plans. He recalled with chagrin how he had arranged for Crida to kill him in battle. Fortunately, the assassin had failed. *To think the boy had once been in my hands.* It was too frustrating to dwell on.

Alas, he could not have known. That time seemed so long ago, before the pursuit of knowledge had opened his eyes to the greater truth. Now that he understood the nature of the gift and what the elves truly were, he knew there might never be another opportunity like the one Dayraven presented. The first thing he had to do was secure the boy somehow. He would need to study the matter, but he was reasonably certain the song of origin he had used on Colburga and Bagsac would extract the elf's power, which seemed to be the same as the gift in its nature, but far vaster. Then it would only be a matter of figuring out how to hold the power. There could be no mistakes like the one with Colburga, whose death still haunted him along with Bagsac's misery.

But the elf's power was something a human mind could contain. Dayraven had proved that much. And if a young man with little knowledge of the gift could hold on to it and even use it for his own ends, how much more could an experienced and knowledgeable wizard like himself accomplish?

He already knew the answer to that question. *Immune to death. Power without limit.* His breaths quickened, and a large grin took over his face at the thought of it.

When he and the guards arrived at the stables, he was pleased to see the stable boys had saddled and readied twelve of the swiftest steeds. The stable master had wanted to prepare a covered carriage for him, but there was no time for such encumbrances, and he had needed to threaten the man to make him understand. No one could grasp the urgency of his journey. *Fools. How could they understand?*

The boy who held his horse gawked up at his face, and his hand trembled as he held out the rein. The supreme priest paused for just a moment, wondering what the lad saw. The boy reminded him of something he did not wish to think about, a time long ago, when there had been little hope and the stench of death had been thick. *Fear not. I'm going to save us.* He gave the lad a nod before placing his boot in the stirrup and pulling himself up onto the saddle.

After he was mounted, Joruman called out to his guards without looking back, "We ride hard."

"Yes, my lord," said Ulfbert.

The supreme priest dug in his spurs, and the horses' hooves clattered on the cobbles as they cantered out of Sigseld. But all Joruman heard were the words of Ogmos the wise. *Immune to death. Power without limit.*

MUNZIL OPENED HIS EYES. MORNING LIGHT WAS CREEPING THROUGH a gap in the entrance flap to Skuld's hide tent. He smiled. Not Skuld's tent. *Their* tent. It was time to begin thinking of himself as part of a family once more. Perhaps, if the gods willed it, Skuld would even bear his children. Nothing would replace the ones he lost, but he believed he was ready to be a father again.

He was lying on his side, his naked body pressed against Skuld's bare back. His arm was draped over the curve of her waist, the hand reaching to cup one of her big breasts, which he began to caress.

Sounding half asleep, she groaned with pleasure. "Take care, little man. If you rouse me, I'll ride you again just as hard as I did last night."

He was still sore from that. He grinned and shook his head before releasing her breast, and then he kissed the back of her head, taking in the familiar scent of her golden hair. Every inch of her was becoming precious to him. He had memorized each scar on her body, which was a haven of milky curves and hard muscle. She was both powerful and, in spite of the fact that she could break him in half, tremendously feminine. Like a warrior goddess. *His* goddess.

Hugging her tight, he placed a hand on her belly, and they lay there for a long while in the comfort of each other's warmth.

"Today's the day," he said, breaking the silence.

Another short silence followed, until she answered him. "Yes." She turned over to face him. Even the scar on her face had become part of her beauty. She grasped his head and kissed him, and they explored each other's mouths with their tongues before she released him and looked in his eyes. "You began all this, my heart's fire."

"The gods began it. I was but their chosen messenger."

"Even so. It's your day as much as anyone's. The fruit of your dream."

"It's *our* day. *Our* dream. The Folk of the Tribes. And Surt has led us to it."

"Aye. He has." She set her jaw, and her eyes narrowed in a dangerous glare. "But *you* began it." She smiled, erasing every hint of anger. "I remember the day you came to us, when I flirted with you."

"*Flirted* with me? You nearly killed me. And you punched me so hard in the gut I buckled over."

She laughed. "I had to measure you. You wouldn't have me mate with a weakling or a coward, would you?"

He laughed too, and they looked in each other's eyes. "No, my warrior goddess. I would have you mate with *me*."

They kissed again, and he decided that he might not be quite as sore as he thought.

. . .

On Sildharan's shore they gathered. Thousands of ships floated in the Gulf of Olfi, for Quinara Sound was too narrow to contain them all. A good number of them were Sildharae vessels, the prizes of conquest. Some of the ships belonged to the coastal tribes, like the White Foxes and the Hawk Claws. Many others came from the island tribes, like the Broad Eagles and the Tall Spears. It was a massive fleet with but one purpose: to convey the Folk of the Tribes to their destiny.

On the land they all stood facing the lapping waves: scores of thousands of warriors from the Fire Dragons, Raven Eyes, Stone Fists, Night Trolls, Cleft Skulls, Strong Axes, Boar Tusks, Bear Fangs, Snow Bears, Bright Shields, Red Swords, Black Elks, and so many more. Some had been slaves, members of lost tribes or those born among Andumae masters into no tribe at all, but that did not matter, for they were in truth all one people now. Among the sea of warriors, the clan totems jutted above the throngs on their long poles. The sea-wind toyed with some of the totems, ruffling feathers and swaying bones, but all else was still. For such a massive gathering, the warriors were rather quiet, emitting only a low rumble of murmurs. They were waiting for the completion of something — a thing even larger than their current gathering, and a thing to which they could not have given a name even though it touched every one of them. Wrapped in fate and the blessing of the gods, they waited.

In their midst, Munzil was also waiting. He too represented one of the lost tribes, the Grey Wolves. But he had found a home among the Boar Clan of the Fire Dragons, and his bond with Skuld was a strong facet of that. He took pride too in belonging to the tribe whence the great War-Leader of the entire Folk of the Tribes came. Never had there been a man of his like, and Munzil swore the singers would pass down Surt's tale forever.

Next to Skuld and her brother Gorm he stood, surrounded by their clan, their tribe, and their people. Theirs was an honored place, for they had a clear view of the immense bonfire that cracked and roared with such intensity that its air-bending heat brushed Munzil's face. The conflagration on the beach was the focal point for the entire gathering. Within the flames were the blackened and charred bones of ninety-nine captured Sildharae and Golgae soldiers. The air was heavy with the scent of their sizzled fat, seared flesh, and burnt hair, and Munzil could still hear the echoes of their screams. Such a huge sacrifice would please the gods, but the greatest moment was only now arriving.

The War-Leader Surt stood before the sacrificial bonfire holding another man by the arm. The prisoner was naked, and a recent beard covered his jaw. In spite of the filth caking his skeletal body, Naitaran, who had once been king of Sildharan, somehow managed to hold on to some dignity as he stared in defiance at the thousands of warriors gazing at him. Next to Surt, he appeared almost a fragile child, though he was tall for one of the Andumae. Robbed of his tongue and magic as well as his throne, the man still held great value as a sacrifice in the gods' eyes. Though he was a humbled mortal who had lost the gods' favor, he had been a mighty king. Munzil reckoned Naitaran knew his end was near when the man glanced over at the bonfire, straightened up, and clenched his teeth as if preparing himself. He was ready to die. But it would not be as simple as burning to death like all the others.

Surt clutched Naitaran by the neck and slammed him face down into the sand of the beach. The War-Leader unsheathed the long dagger at his hip, and then he knelt on top of the former king's back to pin him down. Naitaran's arms and legs began thrashing, but his struggle would do him no good.

Surt brandished his blade. "To Raknar, chief of the gods, victory-wielder, and ruler of war, I give this sacrifice!" His deep voice boomed and carried far, and the thousands of warriors cried out and whooped, their voices erupting and rolling like thunder. When their long cheer ended, Surt's dagger descended and punctured Naitaran's back. The former king shrieked, but his ordeal had only begun.

His arms spattered with gore, the War-Leader sliced through flesh and hacked through bone, and from where Munzil stood he could hear cracking and popping as Surt tugged and severed ribs from the former king's spine, each time eliciting a wail from the prostrate man. All the while, Naitaran gurgled and spluttered, but his arms and legs lost the strength or the will to keep flailing, and all his squirming had ceased. At length, Surt cast aside the dagger and reached inside Naitaran's exposed back. The War-Leader's victim shrieked as his reddened hand emerged grasping a bloody sac, one of the man's lungs. In his fist went again, and he yanked out the matching organ, giving the former king a gruesome pair of wings. Each of them still inflated with every breath that racked the man's agonized frame.

Hoarse gasping escaped Naitaran's ruined body even as Surt grasped it by the neck with one hand and by one of the legs with the other hand. Without much effort, he heaved the body over his head, smiling as blood trickled down onto his face. When Surt turned in a circle to display the sacrifice to the assembled warriors, Naitaran's limbs and head flopped down, and his eyes bulged as his speechless mouth rasped out his agony.

At last, Surt strode over to the bonfire with the sacrifice still raised above him. Before the roaring flames and smoke, his form became a dark, wavering silhouette, but Munzil could see him toss the ruined body into the fire, and then he emerged, smoke curling off him as he smiled at the assembly.

The great man nodded as he beheld them all, his face striped with heat-dried blood. "May the gods smile upon our sacrifices this day. Folk of the Tribes, Sildharan and Golgar have fallen to our blades. So the gods have favored us. And some of us will return to these lands. Their wealth belongs to us, and their people are our slaves. But first, honor and fate demand that we sail west. The Torrlonders betrayed us in war, pretending to befriend us but fleeing during the hour of need. We must avenge their cowardice!"

Shaking their fists and beating their chests, the warriors all shouted and yelled their agreement in a long and deafening cheer.

Surt waited with his arms folded before his huge chest, and then he commanded silence with a narrow-eyed frown. The shouts ceased in a hush that radiated outward until it reached the furthest warriors, and then he resumed. "But it is not only vengeance we seek. Fate too draws us west, for the gods are leading us on, showing us our true strength. Not only the east, but all of Eormenlond will taste our wrath. And, in the end, nothing will be as it was. The Folk of the Tribes will one day rule all these lands, from shore to shore, north, south, east, and west. From weaker people we will take what the gods have given us, for they have shown us the way. Now, my people! Our moment is now, and we will seize it!"

Raising a bloody fist, the War-Leader shouted. Though many of the assembled warriors were too far away to hear his exact words, their scores of thousands of voices joined his. It mattered little whether they heard or not, for the singers would repeat the words. What counted was that they all knew themselves to be one people. One among them was Munzil of the Grey Wolves, the man to whom the gods had given the dream. As he held Skuld's hand and screamed with everyone else, their divine will coursed through him, and he rejoiced.

17
THE PATH OF LOVE

"Oft have I spoken to you of love. As I have told you, it lies in action first, whence the feeling follows. It is a great joy to love a person who returns it. But what if someone meets your love with hate? What if your neighbor persecutes you, beats you, or steals from you? How are you to love?"

The Prophet of Edan paused to give Seren a moment to translate. Once she finished, others further down the hillside conveyed the words to the throng listening below. Thousands of faces looked up at him, many of them nodding as they waited for answers to questions buried deep in their hearts.

"My brothers and sisters, first you must know that the power to answer that hate lies within you. *You* decide what person you will be. You create that person with every choice you make. This is the freedom no one can take from you. Will you allow the hate and injustice of others to twist you into something you do not wish to be? Or will you hold fast to a vision of you as a person who acts with love and honor? When you decide, you have made the first step toward hate or love."

A Caergilese man not far from the front of the crowd stood up. "But how, lord Prophet?" he shouted in the Northern Tongue with only a trace of the Ondunic lilt. "We have lost so much. Our land. Our wealth. Our dear ones. *How* do we love those who hurt us? What must we do? Give away our lives?" He glanced at the Torrlonder soldier nearest him, who stared at the ground.

The Prophet paused to allow Seren and others to translate the question. He nodded toward the questioner, who had sat down again. "This is a fair question, and a needful one. How do you love those who hurt you? Give away your life, you ask? Let me ask a question in return. What would giving away your life serve? In most cases, it would help neither you nor your persecutor. But there may be a time when such a sacrifice is necessary. Will you be prepared for it?" He gave a deep sigh and nodded. "The path of love is not always easy, and it is not always clear, though it will reward you like no other. You may stumble away from it at times, but it is always awaiting your return. It requires courage and determination to stay on it. You must be true to yourself and your deepest beliefs. Most of all, it requires *being* the person you choose to love."

He paused again, and as others conveyed his words, there was a slight stir in the crowd. The next question was written in so many of their eyes.

He smiled. "'What does this mean?' you may ask. How can I *be* another person? Brothers and sisters, you have this power. You have the power to see that which is not before you. What else is it that makes us human but our fancy, the vision of our minds that allows us to journey away from ourselves and what surrounds us? And when we return from such a journey, we behold truths formerly hidden from our eyes. Here is the heart of the matter: To love, you must first seek to understand. You have reached understanding when you perceive that what you do to anyone, you do to yourself."

The translators finished, and he waited a moment longer to let the people soak in this idea. "So. First you *choose* to love. Then, through your inner vision, you *become* the person you wish to love — you try with all your mind to understand the person. What does this person want? Why? What drives this person to commit such deeds? What does this person need, or what would be best for them? Answering such questions requires that you listen. When you begin to listen, then you begin to understand how to love the person. You will know how to *act.*"

The Prophet took a deep breath. This was the crucial link in his hopes. He was trying to prepare the Caergilese. Everything depended on them being able to forgive the Torrlonders someday. "When you act with love, you free yourself from the burden of hate. What is more, by forgiving and loving your persecutor, you give them the chance to free themselves as well, for as much as your persecutor seeks to steal your freedom, they take away their own. Forgive them. Love them. This is the way toward freedom and peace, and it begins in your own heart when you commit to the path of love."

Many of their eyes widened in wonder, and he could see the idea and even the desire to follow the path taking root in their hearts.

Someone slowly stood up. As many eyes turned toward the figure, the Prophet recognized a very old Caergilese man with wispy white hair fringing his head whom he had healed earlier in the day. The old man looked toward the Prophet, who well knew the suffering that had etched every line on his stoic face, and nodded. He stood as straight as he could and, with the attention of everyone in the crowd fixed on him, tottered toward the nearest Torrlonder soldier while silence seized the throng.

Like many of the other Torrlonders, the young soldier stood on the periphery of the gathering. As the seated Caergilese made way for the ancient fellow, the soldier's eyes widened in recognition that he was the target of the old man, whom he awaited. When the ancient one stood before the soldier with the wind tossing his white hair and beard, he raised his chin to look up into the latter's eyes. The soldier, a large man but young enough to be the old one's grandson, loomed over the Caergilese man. Still looking nervous to be the object of such appraisal, he gave a nod that was almost a bow in acknowledgment of the old man's presence.

The entire crowd waited in silence. The old man flung his arms wide, and the soldier flinched before gazing at the fellow with bewildered eyes. Stepping forward, the ancient Caergilese put his withered arms around the big soldier and embraced him.

The Torrlonder gazed down at the bald pate beneath him with

disbelief that gave way to a sad smile of acceptance as the old man held him. The soldier's lip quivered just before his face crumpled, and he returned the embrace as sobs shook his body. The soldier's legs gave way, and, weeping freely, he went down on his knees before the old man and removed his helm. The old Caergilese man, who had suffered and endured far more than the young Torrlonder could know, comforted the latter by placing his hand on his head, his own tears streaming down his wrinkled face.

Next to the Prophet, Seren sniffled, and it was difficult to find a dry pair of eyes in the throng. Caergilese and Torrlonders alike smiled through their tears as they watched the old man and the Torrlonder soldier, who rose once again to embrace the ancient fellow.

The Prophet smiled and nodded as he took it all in, his heart full of such hope that he almost forgot the whisperings of the elf-shard. These were the seeds he planted, and he hoped they would bear fruit and plant other seeds in their turn.

At the sound of a galloping horse, murmurs arose among the crowd. Seeing the direction in which many turned their gazes, the Prophet pivoted around. A mounted soldier crested the hill behind him and was riding toward him with clods of earth flung from the steed's hooves. A Torrlonder soldier in a grey kirtle. Sergeant Hulm.

He awaited Hulm, and by the time the sergeant reached him and dismounted from the lathered horse, Lieutenant Edge and three other soldiers had broken away from the crowd to join them. The five of them and Seren waited for Hulm to catch his breath while those in the throng looked on and whispered to their neighbors, looks of concern and fear replacing their smiles of a moment before.

The sergeant bowed. "My lord, he's here. King Earconwald. And the main body of our forces here in the south. Thousands of troops. Perhaps four thousand. I'm not far ahead of them. Just north of us. They're marching here. Straight *here*." He pointed down, giving further urgency to his words.

Edge grasped his sword's hilt, but the Prophet touched him on the shoulder. "No, Edge. Not that."

"But you told us . . ."

"I counseled you to remain soldiers of Torrlond. Your duty is to protect the people of Caergilion." He glanced at Seren and made sure Edge's eyes followed him.

"But he'll kill you. Earconwald will . . ."

"He'll do nothing to me that I do not wish him to."

"I can't just desert you. It's not in me."

"You are not deserting me. By serving the people of Caergilion, you remain with me. By being true to your hearts, you are true to me and to all of them."

The big man's hand fell away from his sword. "You mean to sacrifice yourself."

"Must I not do what I ask of others?" *Release them*, slithered the shadow in his mind. *Release them all.*

Edge's eyes widened with understanding, and he nodded. "We all have our sacrifices to make. The path of love."

The Prophet squeezed his shoulder. "Just so. When we spoke before, I told you Caergilion will need you, and later Torrlond. These things will come to pass. Be true to your heart, my friend. It is a good one, and it will not lead you wrong." He glanced at the thousands of people behind him. "Begin by leading all these people away. I go to confront Earconwald. Do not fear for me, but keep these people safe. Keep them away from where I go. Do you understand?"

Edge cleared his throat. "Yes, my lord." He looked toward Seren. "We'll see every last one of them to safety."

The Prophet followed his gaze. What he saw left him nearly breathless with a hollow guilt in his chest, but he tried to muster a smile. *I must do this. For her too.*

Seren stood gazing at him, tears welling in her eyes and spilling down her cheeks. "You're leaving me." Her voice faltered as a sob broke through the words.

He stepped forward and embraced her, allowing her to release her anguish in more sobs that shook her body. They stood that way for a while. When she calmed a little, he whispered in her ear. "Remember what I told you, and our promises to each other. Stay with Edge." He grasped her shoulders and looked down at her face until she looked up into his eyes and nodded. He embraced her once more, and then, without looking behind, ascended the hill to begin his path, leaving behind the ones who had given him purpose in order to love them the only way he knew.

Astride his white stallion, King Earconwald led his troops across the hills toward Culvor Sound. The din of hooves and marching feet shook the very earth beneath them. The thousands of grey-kirtled soldiers following in his wake were his mighty sword. As an army, they had once again asserted his right to rule these lands. Every man of it was an extension of his power and majesty.

Next to him rode his guide, Koel, and on his other side rode Captain Nothelm. The king allowed himself a broad grin. He was in a fine mood this day. Finally, he would have his revenge against the boy who had spoiled his conquest of the east. It had been only a delay in the inevitable, but Earconwald did not approve of delays or those who caused them. Dayraven would have no dragons with him this time, no means of threatening the king. True, the boy was a formidable wizard, and perhaps there would be some wizard's fire or some other method of attack. But no wizard could withstand four thousand soldiers. Earconwald's archers, whom he had positioned at the front of his ranks, would bring down Dayraven long before he had a chance to utter a spell. He would dance over the pretender's bloody corpse. His only regret was that he would be unable to prolong the Prophet's death, but he stifled his annoyance at that. Of course, there was a small chance the arrows would only wound him, in which event he would be able to finish off the fellow in a manner more to his liking.

"Prophet of Edan," he scoffed aloud. He swayed in his saddle before he caught himself. That morning he had begun his celebrations early, and the drink had also alleviated the dryness in his mouth and the throbbing in his head. To cover his slip, he looked over at Koel as if he had meant to shift in his saddle. "You say we're nearly there?"

The little weasel grinned at him. "Just a few more hills until we reach Culvor Sound, your Majesty. The place where he preaches is nigh it."

Earconwald grunted and then turned toward Nothelm. "The archers are ready, are they not?" He had been most particular with

Nothelm about the need for the archers to occupy the front line. They would need to release their arrows before the fellow sent any wizard's fire their way. He wondered how many men the boy could slay at once, and then he wondered if he might not wish to ride toward the rear of his army after all, though he would cut a less splendid figure that way.

The old earl stared ahead. "They are, your Majesty."

He tried directing a severe and commanding frown toward Nothelm, but his blinking somewhat ruined the effect as he found it hard to keep looking in one direction. "And the scouts?"

"All your men are in position. The scouts have ridden ahead to follow him should he flee to the coast."

"Ha! The coward. He'll not escape me. I've cornered him." He pounded his saddle with his fist, causing his horse to snort, and then he teetered but straightened up before he fell. A moment later, he turned again toward Koel. "Are we nearly there?"

The little man was squinting as he stared ahead at something. He pointed toward it. "Your Majesty?"

Earconwald peered far ahead until his gaze rested on the top of a rise two hills away. A lone figure upon it walked toward him and his army. It was too distant to see well, but, for some reason he could not explain, a sobering chill suffused his body at the sight. "It's him."

Why had no scouts warned him of the Prophet's arrival? Where were they? The king realized his steed had halted. So too had his entire army behind him. He looked aside at the captain of his guards and made a decisive cutting gesture with his hand. "Nothelm. Order the archers forward."

Nothing happened, and so the king looked to his side. "Nothelm? Did you not hear my command?"

The old earl sat unmoving atop his mount, his eyes wide in shock and his mouth gaping as he gawked toward the lone figure.

"Nothelm? Nothelm! He's only one man, damn you. Order the archers forward, or I'll have you flogged."

No response or change in the earl's countenance.

"Very well. This is the last time I indulge you. I'll strip you of your position and send you home in bloody tatters when this is over. Archers, forward! Archers, I say! Your king commands you!"

Not a soul stirred among his entire army. His troops remained where they stood, like thousands of statues someone had placed in the midst of the green hills. Not a man among them blinked. Not even a horse whickered. The king turned his gaze back toward the hill where the Prophet of Edan approached them. His blood froze in his veins, and the sudden urge to piss pressed upon his bowels. Goosebumps covered every inch of his flesh, and he shivered. He shook his head, trying to dispel the hazy muddle within it from all the wine he had drunk that morning. "Damn it all. What insolence is this?"

From the distant figure emanated a bright light that grew until the king squinted at its intensity and tried to shield his eyes with his hand, and though his panicking mind recoiled from it, he could not look away. Above the Prophet of Edan the sky blackened, becoming a vast, cold void that called out to Earconwald and claimed him. The Prophet was a bright star in the void, but the king was by far most terrified of him, for he was the doorway into the darkness. "No. No! I forbid you to come. I command you to go away!"

Without his bidding, his steed neighed and broke into a gallop, heading straight for the brightness on the horizon. "No! Nooooooo!" he wailed. Bouncing atop the horse, Earconwald grasped its neck and dared not let go as the ground streaked by in a blur. Even if he had not lacked such courage, he knew he would not have been able to release his grip, for an immense will had driven into his quivering mind and possessed it.

RAW POWER EMANATED FROM HIM LIKE A CELESTIAL BEACON. Knowing he would need it to wield the minds of so many men, he had released it the moment he spotted the army in the distance. The eager entity dwelling in his mind exploded, and, riding with it like a feather in the wind, his awareness swelled with it until he was no longer a body. He was the wind, the land, the sea, and the light that suffused them all. In the plants and the living things his consciousness dwelled, including the birds of the air, the sheep on a distant slope, and the small creatures burrowing in the earth and hiding from the vibrations that had been produced by the thousands of soldiers in whom he now commanded stillness.

Each one of the soldiers' minds was a wondrous maze of memories, an organic instrument of such intricate complexity as to be a world in itself, and four thousand of them made up a cosmos. And yet, not understanding their place in the web of beings, they did not know even the smallest portion of their own minds. They were deluded creatures of a fleeting moment, clinging to the ephemeral and unaware of the eternal, and in their delusion they unleashed destruction, pollution, and pain on the world and on themselves. He inhabited them all, experiencing not only their swirling memories but their emotions, chief of which was their terror at the will binding them.

End their fear. The power spoke like a vast storm looming above and around everything. It was the voice of darkness, both inevitable and right. *End their pain*. He could absorb them all, steal away their sorrow forever, leaving behind only the flesh that would return to the soil whence it came. In their smallness and self-imposed isolation, each one could think only of his own importance, but they were nothing more than animated dirt. They always had been, and all he needed to do was remind them of this unmovable fact.

The power in him swelled, darkening the sky as it absorbed more light. He was a breach in the world of forms, collapsing light into him and emitting it as a cold brightness. As he reached forth, every one of the soldiers' minds cowered even as their bodies remained stiff with paralysis. But when he set his power in motion to bring them to a merciful end, the thinnest of threads held it all back. He tilted his head in curiosity.

No, screamed a tiny voice within him. The stubborn mortal in him kept tugging him away from his resolve. Why? He stopped and hearkened to it. *That's not why we're here. Forgiveness. We must forgive them. There is one among them, the most wretched of all, who must be forgiven for the healing to begin. We have come for him.* He frowned as he paused for a moment, and, nodding in quiet admiration of the mortal trapped within him, he could find no argument to answer that voice. Moreover, his patience was endless. And so, he complied with the mortal's desire for the moment. From among the thousands he called forth that one, whose mind quivered in futile resistance.

Under his command, the man galloped toward him on a white steed. The pounding of hooves grew louder as the beast bore its rider across the hills. It was not long before the horse approached with the man shivering and sweating atop it, his mind a diseased and poisoned morass of fear and slavish attachment to the fleeting self he clung to. The horse slowed to a canter and then a trot and then, snorting with its heavy breaths, it came to a stop. The wretch slid off the beast and fell in a heap on the earth, where he trembled and whined as he curled into a ball.

He stared down at the suffering one who counted the pleasing of his pitiful ego above all else, and in so doing lost his capacity to live. *End it*, said the power. *This sickly thing has nothing to live for. No purpose but to destroy itself slowly as it brutalizes others.* He shook his head, and, asserting a measure of control again, the mortal spoke. *It is not our place to judge or punish, only to show. He will be his own judge, his own punishment.* And yet it seemed to him that, with the vast release of power, the mortal part of him had diminished further, another portion of it disappearing into nothingness. It was fading, yielding inch by inch and particle by particle to the infinite and inevitable. He braced himself. For now, there was enough of the mortal left in him to carry through his plan. "All must be forgiven," he said aloud. "Else the healing cannot begin."

He took several steps until he stood over the groveling man. "King Earconwald. I'm told I've met you before, but I fear I do not recall it. It matters little. In the memories of others I have seen you, and that is how I know you. Of course, your thoughts and deeds — at least as you perceive and recall them — are mine as well, but let us not dwell on them. It's the others I wish you to see. You *will* see them, and you will know what you have done."

Earconwald's head jerked up. His eyes bulged in incomprehension and fear, and spittle ran from his open mouth into his beard. He shook his head in denial.

The Prophet of Edan released a sigh. "You must know what you have done. You must feel it as they have felt it. It is the only way. The only way for you to begin. I'm sorry. Your path will be long and hard, I fear, for you have far to go."

He opened the king of Torrlond's mind, a receptacle hitherto empty of concern for anything beyond the momentary desires of its basest portions. It was waiting to be filled with something else. The man gasped as his arms splayed outward and his head wrenched back so that he gazed up at the sky.

The Prophet waited a moment, and then he nodded. *For Seren. And the uncounted others.*

Into the king's awareness the Prophet poured the memories of some of the Caergilese, Adanese, and even Torrlonders whose lives he had brought to ruin. From the people whose bodies and minds he had healed he shared them, moments of agony, fragments of loss and pain. Just as they had experienced their personal tragedies, Earconwald now lived them: the sweaty fear, the wrenching bereavement, the fury of violation and impotence. As these memories were born within the man, the Prophet perceived tiny explosions of energy, leaving in their wake new connections that altered the pathways of the king's mind. In that moment Earconwald forgot who he was, for he was all of those sufferers at once, and he lived through thousands of the thefts, rapes, and murders he and his greed had perpetrated.

A long wail escaped the king's mouth, which gaped in a rictus of agony. When his scream ceased, the man gasped for breath as he knelt and stared ahead with eyes that did not see.

"That is not all of them, of course," said the Prophet. "Perhaps not even one in a hundred of those who have suffered at your hands. Only the ones I healed. Their memories are in me too. I weep every day for them. And you will too."

Earconwald remained on his knees, and he still gazed forward with blank eyes. His face began to tremble, and then his whole body joined in. His hands clutched his temples, and he squeezed his eyes shut just before a cry burst forth from his mouth, opening the floodgates to tears that flowed as he wailed and shook with racking sobs. The king buried his face in the grass as he tore at his hair and pounded his fists on the ground. He ripped off his cloak and writhed and rolled. His nails scratched his face, and he began tearing off his boots and clothes, all the while shrieking and weeping. King Earconwald continued a long while until — naked, dirty, and seeping from the scratches he inflicted on himself — he curled up on the ground and cried tears that washed his face in blood. He made loud and tortured animal sounds, but at length his heaving breaths began to steady, and he lay with his face buried in his hands, still sniffling and weeping.

The Prophet picked up Earconwald's cloak and approached him. "You may not find your voice for quite some time. But I will help you convey your orders to your army."

The king only continued his crying.

The Prophet looked down on him with a sad smile. "It's time for you to go home."

SOMEONE PUT A CLOAK OVER HIS SHOULDERS, AND HE FLINCHED AT the touch. So filthy. He could never cleanse himself of the corpse-stench surrounding him like an aura. It had become part of his flesh. He prayed no one would ever touch him again. The pain stabbed him right up into his guts. Grey-kirtled soldiers had been raping him before they . . . No, they had killed his son and left his tiny body in the middle of the village square, where the crows . . . They blinded his mother after they . . . The king of the Torrlonders himself had come into their home and forced his little sister . . .

Recalling he *was* the king of the Torrlonders, he shivered and curled up tighter. He could form no words, for every time he tried to, another image assailed his mind. They slapped him again and again, and he never knew where the hand would come from or what part of him it would hit. He cowered and howled out his agony, a lost animal in a roiling sea of anguish. And what shredded his mind most of all was the knowledge that *he* had caused it. He would never be clean of it.

Unless . . . He reached toward his side, but then he remembered he had discarded everything when he tore off his clothes, which had burned him with all their reminders of what the man wearing them had done. He glanced up from his crouch to look around. The cloak that someone had placed on his shoulders slid off as he got to his knees. He winced and jerked as more memories assaulted him, but he kept searching. He would silence all these ghosts. No more agony. His breaths became rapid gasps as he sought what he required.

His belt along with the scabbarded sword and sheathed dagger lay only a few feet away. He scrambled toward them on all fours, caring nothing for his nakedness or the pain in his foot when he stumbled on a rock. More images struck him, the torture of thousands inflicted on him at once. Wheezing for breath, he gazed at the dagger in its sheath where it lay in the grass. It was gilded with jewels on the hilt, a thing of pomp and show. But its Dweorg-wrought blade was more than sharp enough to accomplish what he needed — he knew that too well. He shuddered at more memories. Among them, his terrified mother had the courage to grab that very dagger and cut King Earconwald's cheek before one of his soldiers pierced her through with his sword. Her loss was a hot blade through his body, and he gritted his teeth and growled as he fought to retain his purpose.

He shook his head to banish the horrible image, and his hand seized the weapon. Grasping the hilt in his trembling hands, he pulled it free of the sheath. The faint swirls in the shining steel testified to its workmanship, and the blade's gleaming edge seemed to whisper to him. He brought that edge closer to the bare, soft flesh of his upturned wrist. More fragments of memories exploded in his mind, and he flinched from them like blows to his body. He could not hold the dagger steady, for the shaking in his hands had spread to his whole body. His breath wheezed against his clenched teeth, spraying spit as it seethed.

With a scream, he forced the dagger closer to his waiting flesh. Only inches away from his wrist, the quivering steel crept closer. The sharp edge hovered and then touched the vein snaking beneath his sweat-covered skin, nicking it enough for a tiny sliver of red to surface. The flesh would part and give way so easily, allowing the life to seep out with the release of blood.

But with the sting from his small cut arose an intense horror, and he could press the blade no harder. He screamed in rage and terror, trying to force the steel into his skin. The dagger did not budge. He shrieked again and tossed it away, keening a lament at his inability to stop the memories flooding him. It was then that he faced a truth he had long known and repressed: He was a coward. A miserable wretch who could not end his torment because he was too afraid. Afraid of what?

Something touched his shoulder, and he started and jerked away, cringing on the ground. He glanced up at the terrible brightness that was the Prophet of Edan, and then he hid his face in his hands.

"No," said the voice above him. "Your end will not be so easy as that. Rise now, and put on your garments. I will release your men, and you must speak to them."

HE LED THE HORSE BY THE REIN, AND EARCONWALD WALKED BY HIS side, a little behind him. Clothed but still bleeding from the scratches on his face, the king sniffled and shuddered, and every now and then he flinched from some invisible blow. They approached the army of mortals, whose fear and awe the Prophet tasted, until he judged it was time to abandon his control of them.

Though the power within him was reluctant to let go of the four thousand mortals it inhabited, he managed to stifle it down into his innermost recesses, where it soughed and hissed about the sweetness of the long sleep. The human portion of him, which had been fading, seemed to regain a little solidity, and he once again sensed the boundaries of his body as the enormous energy seeped out of the soldiers, leaving him diminished.

He sighed. It was an immense relief to withdraw from so many minds, though the echoes of their memories still rattled around within him, and his shoulders sagged when the burden lifted from him. But he did not leave them without planting seeds of suggestion, which he hoped would grow in strength so that at least some of these men would do their part in the world he hoped they would build. For the moment, the troops began to stir and gaze around them in wonder, but none of them moved closer to him and his companion.

Of course, there was still one mind in which he must keep a subtle presence. Earconwald was far too dismayed and haunted to speak on his own. With a little encouragement, however, he would be able to give orders. They neared the foremost troops, and the two men on horseback at their head dismounted. One was a Caergilese, a little man who still shivered at the darkness he had confronted within him. The Prophet recalled healing him along with Edge and the others when he first arrived in Caergilion. The other was a grizzled veteran of some rank, a man the Prophet recognized from Earconwald's memories, and, having dwelled in his mind, he knew him for a decent and loyal captain. He was the one Earconwald should speak to.

The man — Captain Nothelm, his name was — stared at the Prophet with wide eyes, and, glancing once at Earconwald's dirt and blood-smudged face, went down on his knees. With a rustling and clinking of byrnies, the entire army knelt, each pair of blinking eyes directed toward the Prophet. The echoes of his presence still lingered about the troops like wisps of mist. They could not grasp what they felt, and never could they have explained their wonder, but he knew they would obey him without question. *Command them to embrace the only lasting bliss. Grant them peace*, hissed the insistent power within him.

He closed his eyes and wrenched back control of his mind, but he recognized his mortal will was growing smaller and blurrier than it was wont to be after using the power. Already he had been fading a little more every day, and this release and large expenditure of the energy dwelling in him had cost him. *No*, he answered it when he could hold on to his voice. *These men have a task.* He could have commanded them, yet it was better for the orders to come from their king, and so he prodded Earconwald's mind.

The king of Torrlond shuffled beside him. The man's jaw worked for a moment, and his mouth opened and closed. He cleared his throat and addressed Captain Nothelm. "We return to Torrlond. The Prophet of Edan will accompany us." Earconwald's mouth closed, and he stared with vacant eyes at the ground.

Nothelm looked toward the king as if just realizing he was there. He nodded slowly. "Yes, your Majesty. As you say." He looked back at the Prophet, asking with his eyes for permission to rise and begin their journey.

Forcing a weary smile, the Prophet of Edan nodded. *So it begins. I only hope I can hold on long enough.*

. . .

After long marches during the days, the army camped during the nights. King Earconwald kept to himself in his tent and spoke to no one, though sometimes the sounds of uncontrolled weeping came from within, and so Captain Nothelm took command of the journey back to Torrlond. The Prophet also said little, speaking to the troops and telling them stories when he could, both to ease his mind and to guide them while he had the chance. But his constant struggle against the power within him took most of his concentration during the long marches, and he walked alone, often closing his eyes as he stooped and took little notice of the soldiers who stole awed glances at him.

He knew they could see his struggle, and perhaps too they sensed on some unconscious level the power that thirsted for them and aroused their fascination. *Peace*, it breathed. And there were moments when he began to reach out toward the thousands of men. It would have been so easy to end their longing and their pain forever. The mortal in him managed to snatch back such deliverance, but it grew harder with every occurrence, and each time he feared it would be the last.

If the days were hard, the nights were an eternity of torture. In a simple tent set apart from the rest of the army, the Prophet lay on a sleeping mat and stared upward as he slept not at all. He dreaded slipping off since it might allow the power to escape him. Still, as he wrestled with it, it crested inside him and lusted for the thousands of souls it sensed nearby. *Mercy. Rest.* With clenched teeth, he repeated the words that allowed him to continue: "Forgiveness. Love." Thoughts of Seren, Edge, and the others sustained him too, and he clutched on to their faces in his mind. It had been for their sakes that he made this sacrifice, but compassion for the Torrlonder troops swelled in him as the days went by, and for them too he tried to hold on to his purpose.

But other thoughts and memories swirled within him as well, and these gave weight to the voice that never relented in its demand. *Grant them peace.* Countless images came to him from the minds of the four thousand troops camping without his tent. Their minds seethed with memories of what they had done to the Adanese and Caergilese, the atrocities they had committed against their fellow beings behind the shield of religion and conquest. Many repressed their recollections, whereas others allowed them to gnaw at their minds and picked at them like an itchy scab, and still others, the most twisted and lost among them, lusted after them and longed to create more. The Prophet saw them all — they were part of him since he had inhabited those soldiers.

Such creatures were doomed to create more pain for others and themselves. *Show them mercy.* They would keep stumbling from one act of destruction to the next, scarring the world and inflicting their agony upon it. *Give them rest.* More than anything, they feared to die, the end of the tiny self they believed, in their delusion, to be real and of greater importance than all else. Fools. That fear of death was the source of all they made and destroyed. It was what made them human, the center of their identity. There was only one answer to it. *End the fear.*

The drowning mortal in him struggled to stay above the surface of the immense power, like a shipwrecked man bobbing on the Great Sea. It was claiming him, he knew. Clutching his hands into tight fists, he gritted his teeth and growled, "Forgive. Love." As he lay staring into the endless darkness, he knew the light of each fleeting day would bring less relief than the one that came before.

One foot in front of the other. Taking no notice of the landscape and forgetting how many days he had been marching, he counted out the moments by the steps of his feet and struggled to focus only on them. The army near him was a large presence he tried his best to ignore, though the power within him tugged him toward it again and again. It was not their thousands of marching boots nor the glint of their many weapons and armor that drew him, but the energy within them called to him in urgent whispers, begging to be released from the confines of tortured flesh.

At times he forgot why he struggled against the looming power, but he never ceased, even when he could merely grasp on to the idea of resisting its urges. He kept shaking his head and forcing one foot in front of the other. His shadow wavering before him measured the pace, but it also reminded him of the infinite shadow whence there was no escape. He winced and closed his eyes, opening them every once in a while to make sure of his steps. If he could only keep walking, he might outdistance the consuming need to devour their energy and grant them deliverance.

"My lord Prophet?"

The frightened voice was nearby. He looked up and turned toward it. A young soldier was gazing at him. Amidst the chaos roiling within him, the lad's memories of his family and friends in a village near Etinstone stirred in his mind. There too was his heartbreak at having to leave following his father's death and his lover's betrothal to another. Joining Torrlond's army had been both an escape and a necessity, else his family would have starved. The young soldier was an earnest fellow who had already picked up the pieces after life shattered his hopes. In all likelihood, if he lived long enough, he would need to do so again. And again. And again. Such were mortals' lives. The Prophet returned his gaze for a while before he realized the lad was waiting for him to say or do something.

"Yes?"

The young man swallowed and, looking aside as if regretting his courage in approaching the Prophet, forced the words out. "I beg your forgiveness, my lord. I wondered . . . Are you unwell? Is there aught I can do for you?"

Rest. Rest. Rest. He forced a smile and shook his head. "No need for forgiveness, brother. But there's naught you can do. I thank you all the same." He nodded toward the nearest formation of troops, and, without another word, the awed lad accepted the silent invitation to leave him to his own thoughts and turned away.

The Prophet's gaze lingered on him. "Wait."

The young soldier turned again to face him.

"What is your name?"

A nervous smile. "Dunstan, my lord."

"Dunstan." It was good to put a name to the memories. He nodded and smiled again, this time without so much effort. "Thank you."

The fear left Dunstan's face, and his smile grew into something bright and living. "It was nothing, my lord. I hope to serve you better sometime." After a bow, he turned again to rejoin his fellow soldiers.

The Prophet sighed. *You already have.* He watched the young soldier return to his position among the ranks of the Torrlonders. For at least a brief moment, he had been able to forget . . .

Rest! The power within him surged and tore after the young soldier, smashing free of the Prophet and sending him reeling forward. His body disappeared, and he soared above the entire army, gazing downward at the terrified men. They cowered at the flaring of his brightness as the surrounding light, the very rays of the sun, collapsed into him, leaving the sky a dark mass that promised to swallow them all. Incomprehension and terror warred with wonder and ecstasy, rendering the four thousand soldiers of Torrlond unable to move. The power loomed ever higher in its triumph, and it prepared to envelop its helpless prey in the blessedness of oblivion. He would free them from their prisons of clay, their flesh-cages, so that, as they dissolved, they might know for a brief but blissful moment what they were, before they reunited with the eternal silence.

Summoning them, he spread his arms outward even as he became a bright window, ready to receive them. All four thousand, from the king to the youngest soldier, faced him in obedience to that summons, and as their energy began to separate from their flesh, they forgot the lives and identities they had thought so important only moments before. With terror and ecstasy, they understood their unity with what lay beyond the window. In truth, they had never been anything else, and, on the cusp of their awakening before the final sleep, they prepared to leap through.

"Dayraven!"

He turned toward the screaming voice and the hoof beats accompanying it. A man atop a horse was shouting at him and waving his hand as he galloped closer. The others who had been riding behind him cowered some distance away. They wore the garb of soldiers, but this man was clad in a white robe, which whipped behind him in his charge. Perhaps he was fey, but he seemed braver than all the other mortals, or at least he mastered his fear in a way they did not, for he rode straight toward the light, not needing to be called.

"Dayraven!" he shouted again before he yanked the rein of his lathered horse. The beast neighed as it staggered to a stop, and the man leapt off it, just catching himself as he stumbled. Shielding his terror-widened eyes, he ran toward the brightness. When he reached within a few feet of it, he grimaced and kept his hands before his face, but he did not back away. "Dayraven," he said between heavy gasps. "If you're still in there, I can help you."

"Dayraven?" A faint ripple of recognition passed somewhere deep inside him.

The white-robed man trembled as he nodded. "Yes. *You* are Dayraven. Search my memories. I knew you. I met you, before . . . Before you became the Prophet. Before the elf took over. I can help you. Search my memories, and you will see a glimpse of who you were."

The power reached out and seized the mortal, who gasped and froze in rigid paralysis. Within the vast maze of images dwelling within the white-robed man, the most powerful were of a woman with no face that he longed for and suffered deep anguish over. He had been a boy when he lost her, and the cruelest thing was he could not bring to mind her features. In a great city, there were large and ornate buildings of stone in which stores of knowledge and power waited. There passed countless hours of frustration and occasional triumph while searching through books and conducting experiments. There were the bodies of women he had enjoyed and pretended not to care for as each one failed to fill the ache of loss. There were intricate plans and manipulations to achieve his ends, long journeys that tested his patience, rivals he outwitted and survived, and victory over another man in a white robe, one who had been more powerful than he. He had feared the Supreme Priest Bledla, who had been a powerful madman.

In the last scene he saw the body containing him from the white-robed mortal's eyes. He was standing before a massive dragon of such a dark-red hue that it was almost black, and row after row of awed soldiers from various armies encircled him. He had no recollection of this event from his own eyes, nor did any of his own memories from before Sildharan return to him. But within this white-robed mortal were other memories of the one he called Dayraven, and with the strange and jarring revelation that *he* was this young man the mortal had seen, he began to hear a familiar voice again. "Forgiveness. Love," he said aloud.

Stepping back from the brink, he heaved the terrible power back within him and released the four thousand men back into their bodies. The light returned to the sky, and the chill left the air. As if reborn, the four thousand trembled and gazed around them in wonder at a world they did not recognize.

But the Prophet looked with somber eyes at the white-robed man. "You once tried to have me killed." It was not an accusation — only an observation.

Even as he caught his breath and sweat ran down his brow, the man was grinning and nodding giddily. "Yes. There can be no lies between us. Yes, I did. But it's not too late. I'm here to help you now. So much power. By Edan's splendor, I've touched eternity. You've struggled mightily with it, I can see. But I can bring you back to yourself. And then, we'll defeat it." Still gasping for breath, he put his hands on the Prophet's shoulders and stared in his eyes. "We'll defy death."

IN THE LATE EVENING, AFTER THE SOLDIERS MADE THE CAMP READY, the Prophet sat on a chair in the Supreme Priest Joruman's tent. At times he tightened his grip on the chair's armrest and closed his eyes as he waged a silent battle within him. The power still hungered to put the thousands of soldiers to their final rest, but he was able to contain it by focusing on Seren and the good he might do her by holding on. He looked up after realizing the supreme priest, who held a wine glass as he sat across from him, had been addressing him.

"Dayraven?"

The name still sounded strange, like a boot made for someone else's foot. "Your pardon. There is much on my mind." He glanced down at his own untouched glass of wine.

Joruman's eyes narrowed as he stared at him for a moment. "The elf tries to master you, does it not? What does it want?"

He looked down again and winced as another wave of power battered him.

Joruman held up a palm. "My apologies. There's just so much I need . . . so much I wish to know."

The wave ebbed, and he could breathe again. He nodded. "It's alright." The supreme priest had explained to him as much as he knew about the source of the power within him. Knowing folk called it an elf did little to help him, especially since no one truly knew what an elf was. He released a sigh. "What does it want? It seeks to deliver humankind forever from pain and loss."

"By what means?"

"Death."

The supreme priest sat straight in his chair and took a sip of wine, but his gaze never left the Prophet. "That we must not allow." He held his glass in his right hand, upon which the fingers of his left hand toyed with a ring. "You've kept this force in check for long."

"But I'm losing. Every day more of me disappears, and it grows stronger. Do not doubt its strength."

Joruman shook his head. "Oh, no. Not I. I have tasted it." His eyes took on a hungry look.

"It could shatter me forever anytime it wants to. It always could have. I don't know why it hasn't. But it won't matter soon. There's not much left. I can't hold on much longer. I had hoped . . ." He winced and looked down as the power within him surged in another wave that assaulted his feeble walls, shaking him deep in his core.

Joruman leaned forward. "Yes. Go on."

He took a deep breath. "I had hoped to make peace. Between Torrlond and the south. To show the Torrlonders what the Caergilese and Adanese have suffered. To convince the southerners to forgive you. And to help you understand why you must leave them and their lands. For your good and theirs."

The supreme priest gave a smile that seemed gentle, genuine, and tired all at once, but beneath it he could not conceal his longing. "Not long ago, I would have laughed at such a notion. But, after feeling the power in you, and witnessing what you did to Earconwald . . ."

"I only allowed him to see."

Joruman grinned and raised his glass as if making a toast. "He'll never be the same again, will he?"

"No. I had hoped, if he recovers enough to rule, he might undo some of the harm he caused. But to truly make peace, I need to convince more of you." He gazed into Joruman's eyes and weighed him. Having experienced his memories, he knew him for an intelligent and ambitious man, one who rationalized inflicting pain on others so that he might achieve his end, which he believed more noble and important than anything. Behind it all, a great fear drove him. "Those like you, who wield much power and know what they do, can make the difference. You can increase or decrease the suffering according to your decisions." He shook his head to banish the hissing of the power. "But I'm afraid I won't last long enough."

"And what will happen when it defeats you?"

"In truth, I know not. But if I were you, I would be as far away as possible before that happens."

Joruman's eye's widened, and he took a too casual sip from his wine glass. "I'll take that advice into consideration." A wide grin broke out across his face. "But I don't intend to abandon you."

The Prophet gave him a weary nod. "Before I . . . go, I would ask you to tell me what you know of me. My past. Where I come from."

"Have you not seen my memories of you?"

"Yes, but memories tend to be fragments of images. Feelings. Not always reliable, either."

The supreme priest nodded. "Of course. Well, you come from the kingdom of the Mark, from a remote place. Your father was . . . Let me see. What was his name? Edgar? No. Not quite. Edgil? Yes, that's it. Edgil. A thegn to one of the Mark's earls, I believe. Dayraven, son of Edgil of the Mark."

"And my mother?"

Joruman's eyes looked into his, and in them was a moment of genuine empathy as a strange connection leapt out between them. "I know nothing of her, I fear. I could be mistaken, but I surmise you lost her long ago." The connection evaporated as swiftly as it came, and there was only the man's cunning smile, beneath which he buried his pain. "These things happen."

Recalling the man's boyhood loss, the Prophet nodded. "Yes. They do."

The supreme priest took a sip of wine. "There's little else I know, other than the part you played in defeating my predecessor, which you have already heard about. I apologize. *He* — my predecessor, that is —

might have known a bit more. Of course, I was the one who discovered you, back in Hasumere."

"The fen. I saw that memory."

"Yes." Joruman frowned and looked down. "I was a fool then. Understanding little, I saw you as an obstacle to my goal."

"And what is your goal? What do you want?"

The smile returned, and the supreme priest's eyes flashed. "The same as yours, in a manner of speaking. To defeat death."

The Prophet shook his head. "You cannot." *Rest. Rest. Rest.*

"I refuse to believe that." Joruman leaned forward, and his blue eyes bore into the Prophet's. "There is a way. There's vast power in you."

"I will succumb to it soon. Perhaps in a few days. Perhaps tomorrow. Perhaps before I take another breath."

"No. You've held it in check. You've controlled it. Even used it. If even a small portion of what I've heard of your deeds is true, you've wielded far more power than any other sorcerer or wizard who's ever lived."

The Prophet released a weary sigh. "There's almost nothing left of me. I tell you, it will triumph soon, and woe to those who are nigh when it breaks me."

The Supreme Priest Joruman leaned still closer, and his voice dropped to an urgent whisper. "But what if another takes the burden from you before it defeats you?"

The Prophet's eyes widened as something he had long foregone blossomed in him: hope. But he smothered it as soon as he realized its presence. "I know your purpose. I've seen what you did to the woman and the man."

The supreme priest's face hardened, and he gave a curt nod. "Ah, yes. That. I fear it was necessary . . ."

"Part of the power within you — the gift, you call it — once belonged to another. You wish to take the power in me to fight against death. You cannot do this thing."

Joruman ignored him as his words rushed forth. "There's a song of origin, once known among a few of the Andumae of old. I have recovered it. With it, one wizard might lift away from another the gift and absorb it. I have used it with success. A few complications arose, but nothing I could not manage."

"Even were you to succeed in taking what the elf put into me, what do you think would happen?"

"Of course, with the amount of power, it could be a delicate matter. A willing subject would be far less dangerous, rendering . . ."

"You cannot defeat death with it. Don't you see? It *is* death."

The supreme priest's mouth hung open, and he blinked at the Prophet. But he recovered soon, and he shook his head as his smile returned. "No. You've fought the elf for so long, and I'll admit you must know it in ways I cannot. But in this you're wrong. You must be. It's the only way."

"My brother, you would take my burden from me for the power to defeat death. I know you would dare it. But this is a thing no one can do. Better to leave me on some desolate mountaintop or in the midst of a vast forest or at the bottom of the Great Sea, so that no harm comes to anyone when I lose this struggle."

Joruman stared at him, his desperation to convince the Prophet evident in his eyes, but he was wise enough to hold his tongue. "Very well. You must be weary, and so for now I'll cease to debate the matter with you. But know that my offer stands. The moment you change your mind, I will take your burden from you. You've carried it far enough. And though I can promise nothing, I also hope you will return to yourself once the power is lifted from you. At the very least, we might delay the destruction you fear. And what's more, I promise you this: Whether you take my offer or refuse me, I will work toward your goal of freeing Caergilion and Adanon. I fancy Earconwald will need little convincing in his present condition, and I have some power over many of the dukes of Torrlond."

The Prophet looked into the man's eyes for the truth, and he saw it. "I believe you would."

"Domination over kingdoms matters naught to me. They all come to an end. What I want is the knowledge we require to make *gods* of men. Immortality is within our grasp, my friend."

"And would you give the Caergilese and Adanese the aid they require to rebuild so that peace may last?"

"I would. You have my word."

The Prophet rose from his chair, and his knees ached as they pushed up his exhausted body. *End it all*, whispered the power as it curled around him and tightened its shadowy coils. But its constant refrain took on new meaning, and in spite of his misgivings about the Supreme Priest Joruman, the small hope he had felt moments before rekindled. "I will think on your offer."

Joruman too rose. "Think well on it. I *can* save you. I can save us all." He nodded. "I bid you goodnight."

18
THE BROKEN PROMISE

"By the ancestors' beards," said Gnorn as he tugged on his own, "how are we to find him when there's naught but ghosts lingering in these dismal parts?" The mist and the nearly constant drizzle had weighed down his cloak, and moisture dripped off his helm, nose, beard and anything else that stuck out.

"We'll find him." Orvandil, who had already dismounted, extended his hand up to the Dweorg.

Gnorn clasped his friend's hand and groaned as he wiggled off his horse and plopped onto the ground with a thump and a tinkling of his mail. "My bones ache, and I smell like wet horse. I've had enough of that long-legged beast."

Galdor chuckled. "She's likely had enough of you too. Dweorgs are not light, especially bedraggled ones." The wizard and Abon had already alighted from their steeds and tied them by the wall enclosing the little farmstead. Within waited a barn and a small stone farmhouse. Its dwellers appeared nowhere.

The Dweorg grunted as he and Orvandil tied their mounts by the others. "Where have all the people gone?"

Galdor opened the gate and stepped through. "They're hiding. Something's happened here. Let's see what we can find."

Abon followed the wizard, and Orvandil went through next, their boots squelching in the mud. Gnorn paused and looked around at the deep green hills surrounding them and the creases of little valleys hiding amidst tatters of grey mist. The damp breeze was heavy with Culvor Sound's salty scent. They had followed the coastal path to this farmstead where the Prophet had supposedly stayed. The information had not been easy to come by since they had to avoid the Torrlonders and find a local who could speak the Northern Tongue. An old tinker driving his two mules and cart to Gadomiel had given them directions to this place. The man had been bursting with stories of the Prophet, going on at length in his lilting Caergilese accent about the miraculous healings and the crowds brought to tears by the beauty and wonder of his teachings. He claimed to have stood in the Prophet's presence five days ago in the midst of a large throng, but since then he had been traveling in remote parts. The tinker was the last living soul they had encountered in this abandoned and shrouded landscape.

Gnorn frowned and shook his head. "I mislike this quiet. How do we know this is even the right farmstead?"

"We don't know," said Galdor up ahead without turning around. "But we've got to start somewhere."

The wizard led the way to the stone farmhouse. Gnorn followed through the drizzle behind the others. No signs of life stirred within, while silence answered Galdor's loud knock on the front door. He waited and then knocked again. "Hello? Anyone about?" More silence followed. Turning around, the wizard faced the others with a frown on his face. "Perhaps we ought to take a peek inside. Abon, would you be so kind as to pick the door's lock?"

The shaper unsheathed his dagger and stepped forward. He put his hand on the latch, and there was a metallic click. Abon pushed, and the door swung inward with a creak. The wan daylight spilled inward to reveal the entrance to the simple, rustic interior, beyond which lurked silent shadows and stillness. Drops of moisture dripped from the roof's edge and plopped into puddles, but nothing else made a sound.

Galdor pursed his lips and raised his eyebrows. "That was fast."

Abon shrugged. "Wasn't locked."

"Might be they left in a hurry," said Gnorn.

The wizard nodded. "Well, let's see what's inside." He stepped within.

Abon followed him again. Gnorn and Orvandil glanced at each other before the Thjoth followed the shaper. Standing in the drizzle, the Dweorg hesitated. "There's an ill feeling about all this." Hands on his hips, he gazed up at the farmhouse, and then, sensing movement behind him, he turned around before giving a startled cry.

A troop of Torrlonders was pouring through the farmstead's gate, their swords out as they rushed across the muddy yard toward the farmhouse. At least a score of them.

Gnorn backed up a pace as he plucked his axe from his belt. "Ho! We have company!"

The Thjoth rushed out of the farmhouse door with Seeker already unsheathed. The leading Torrlonders stopped short in their sprint and staggered to a halt. Abon and Galdor emerged next, and the wizard strode out in front, mumbling a spell under his breath.

Sword drawn, one of the Torrlonders stepped forward and called out. Gnorn recognized the stripe of a sergeant on the shoulder of his grey kirtle. "Thieves! Put your weapons down and come peaceable-like, or it'll go hard with you."

"We are not thieves," said Galdor.

"So you broke into that farmhouse just to tidy up, I suppose."

"We did not break in at all. The door was open. We're looking for someone."

"Still thieves. The saddles on those horses mark them clear enough. They belong to Torrlond's army, and you're not in it. So, horse thieves, and unless I miss my guess, mostlike murderers too."

The Torrlonders raised their swords, and Gnorn gripped his axe tighter, sparing a moment to worry over how slippery the drizzle had made the handle. But before any command came, Galdor stepped forward and thundered out a song of origin. "Alakathon indomiel ar galathon anrhuniae! Vortalion marduniel im paradon khalghoniae!" Wizard's fire sprang to life, crackling and writhing around his hands as it formed a focal point of bluish light amidst the dreary and grey scene.

The Torrlonders jerked back, and even Gnorn flinched at the brightness and heat. But to his credit, the sergeant stood his ground.

The wizard's fire winked out, leaving the farmstead and surrounding hills even dimmer than before. Galdor stood in the rain, no longer a harmless old man but a figure of power and authority. "There's no need for you to die, soldier. We're here to find someone, a friend of ours. We *must* find him, and once we do, we shall leave this place in peace. You can even have the horses we borrowed."

The sergeant's wide eyes betrayed his fear, but his voice shook only a little when he spoke. "You're seeking the Prophet, aren't you?"

Galdor nodded and stepped forward. "Yes."

"You say you're his friends?"

"Yes, we are, indeed. We're here to help him. What do you know of him?"

The sergeant frowned and gazed at the wizard for a long while. "We serve the Prophet. If you would know more of him, you'd best come with us."

"How do we know this is not a trap?" Gnorn leaned close to Orvandil as he whispered. They were leading their horses behind Galdor and Abon, who were following the sergeant and his men through the Torrlonder camp.

Orvandil shrugged. "We don't."

Many of the grey-kirtled soldiers in the camp stared at them, and none of their eyes seemed welcoming. They took a muddy path that wove by the many tents as troops drilled and marched all around them. Some of the idle Torrlonders gathered in groups as they leaned over desultory cook fires that spat back at the drizzle. But Gnorn noticed something odd. Instead of gambling and cursing as soldiers were wont to do, the knots of men huddled together as if in some sort of intense and earnest debate. Moreover, though Gnorn could hardly believe his eyes, several groups seemed to be at prayer. "Don't they know they're soldiers, not priests? What ails these men?"

Orvandil gave one of his half-smiles that might have seemed a snarl to one who did not know him well. "The Prophet."

They made their way toward the only permanent structure in the encampment. It was some sort of walled-in villa, which must have once belonged to a Caergilese noble whose home overlooked his lands. Soldiers and messengers streamed in and out of the gate, no doubt conveying orders. The sergeant led them there and halted a few hundred feet from the gate. "My men will tend to your horses. I'll take you inside to meet our leader."

"Which lord or captain is he?" asked Galdor.

The sergeant gave a crooked grin. "He sure ain't no lord."

"What is he, then?"

"Come on in, and you'll see."

SOMETHING WAS DIFFERENT ABOUT THESE TORRLONDER SOLDIERS. Some higher purpose was driving them, and it had created a conflict with their loyalty to Torrlond. In this Galdor sensed the unmistakable presence of Dayraven. Still, he was not about to let down his guard, and, should he need a spell in a hurry, he kept his mind a step away from the realm of origins. With a wary glance around him, he followed the sergeant through the courtyard to the columned portico fronting the building's entrance.

The sergeant led them inside the villa, where it took a moment for Galdor's eyes to adjust to the dimness of the front hall. On one side, a stairway led up, and before them the entrance hall led to a wide corridor containing doors along both sides. Caergilese tapestries on the walls bespoke the former owner's wealth. The wizard made a subtle assessment of his surroundings as the sergeant stopped a soldier on his way out and asked, "Where's Edge?"

The hurrying soldier jerked a thumb backwards as he walked by. "With the captain."

Their conductor turned toward Galdor and gestured with one hand. "This way, my lord."

The wizard and his friends followed the man down the corridor until they reached a closed door near the end. A guard stood outside it.

The sergeant nodded at the guard. "Edge inside with the captain?"

"Aye." He looked over Galdor and the others and then back at the sergeant. "You have business with him?"

"These four claim to be friends of the Prophet. They're looking for him, and they say they're going to help him. The old one's a wizard."

The guard looked again at Galdor, who put on his best pleasant smile. The man did not smile back, but something more than curiosity lit up his eyes. He turned back to the sergeant. "You think it's what we've been waiting for?"

"Don't know. Could be. That's why I wanted to have a word." He nodded toward the door.

"Right." The guard knocked on the door and waited a moment before opening it. "My lord, Sergeant Hulm's here to report. He's brought a wizard and some others who are seeking the Prophet."

"Send them in," said a voice from within.

Sergeant Hulm nodded, and Galdor followed him inside the room. It might have been a simple bedchamber once, but it was furnished with a table upon which several maps and piles of papers lay. A sputtering candle on the table accompanied the pale light streaming in through the open window, providing enough light to see by. Two men who had been leaning over the table looking at the maps stood straight. The three red stripes of a captain marked the one's shoulder, and the other had the two stripes of a lieutenant. The captain was a greybeard with a kindly sparkle in his eyes. The lieutenant was a big man. In a corner on a chair sat a third person — a thin Caergilese teenaged girl, whom Galdor might have easily overlooked had he not been wary enough to make a close inspection of the room before entering it. His three companions came in behind him, and the large lieutenant's eyes widened for a brief moment at the sight of Orvandil. Galdor supposed he did not often see men bigger than he was.

Sergeant Hulm made a slight bow and cleared his throat. "Captain Godwin. Lieutenant Edgelaf. We found these four looking for the Prophet, claiming they wish to help him. The old man's a wizard. I thought it best to bring them here."

Galdor stepped forward. "Captain Godwin. I fear we have little time. It's of dire importance that we find the Prophet."

The old captain smiled. "Your pardon, lord wizard, but in matters of the Prophet, you should address yourself to Lieutenant Edgelaf, not me."

The wizard directed a puzzled look toward the lieutenant. "I'm afraid there's much here I don't understand."

Lieutenant Edgelaf spoke in a gruff voice. "Might be I can clear things up for you. We serve the Prophet."

"We?"

"Almost all the Torrlonders remaining in Caergilion, and many in Adanon. We've been organizing things. Waiting."

"Waiting for what?"

"A sign. The Prophet told us we'd know when. He told us to protect the people of these lands, and that we'd know when to return to Torrlond and serve it. I reckon Sergeant Hulm here was hoping *you* might know something of what the Prophet meant." His eyes narrowed as he gazed at the wizard. "Do you?"

Galdor paused, wondering what the safest answer might be. He decided on the truth. "I fear I don't. We came here to find our friend. The Prophet. Dayraven."

The lieutenant's eyes widened as wonder took over his face. "*That*'s his name? Dayraven?"

In the corner the girl stirred, but Galdor kept his attention on Lieutenant Edgelaf. "Yes. It was, at any rate. We're his friends, and we've come to help him."

"What help do you think he needs?"

Galdor took a deep breath. "There is a vast power in him. No doubt you've felt it. But it's not part of him. It's something foreign to him."

"Foreign?"

"An elf, in fact. Dayraven survived an encounter with an elf, something that has never happened to anyone before. But it put that power in him. There's little time to explain. Suffice to say this vast power is not stable, and though Dayraven, the Prophet, has used it to do much good, it will take over him."

"What are you saying? The Prophet would never hurt anyone."

"*He* would not. But the elf might. I myself have felt its chilling hunger, and its intentions toward humankind are not what we would call friendly. By some miracle — through the good in him, I believe — he's managed to wield the elf's power even after he forgot who he was, but it's only a matter of time before it devours him. When that time comes, when the man utterly yields to the power, it could be very bad for anyone nearby. It could be catastrophic, in fact. That's why we must reach him."

Lieutenant Edgelaf shook his head. "You're saying he would harm others? That he's a danger? I can't believe this."

"I can." All eyes turned toward the Caergilese girl, who had spoken in the Northern Tongue. She stood up. "Before he left, the Prophet told me something." She looked down at her feet and seemed uncertain whether she should continue. "He didn't want me to tell anyone."

Galdor smiled at her while wondering who she was and why Dayraven would have confided in her. But there was time for only the most important questions. "What did he tell you, dear girl?"

Lieutenant Edgelaf took a step toward her. "You don't have to speak if you don't want to, Seren."

When she looked up, Galdor saw the courage in her eyes. She returned the wizard's gaze. "What you say is true. The Prophet told me there was something in him. Some power. He used it to heal people. But he said it wanted to end suffering. To kill everyone. He went to Torrlond to make things right. To help us all. That's what he told me."

Galdor's shoulders sagged, and he wondered how he would find the will and the energy to move from the spot where he stood, let alone trudge up to Torrlond in search of Dayraven. "Edan help us all. He went to Torrlond?"

Lieutenant Edgelaf, who had been frowning at the girl, nodded. "Seems he told Seren more than he told the rest of us, but that all fits, I suppose. He asked us to protect the people here when he left. And that's what we'll do until the time comes."

The wizard looked from the lieutenant to the girl called Seren. "Do you know what he intended?"

Edgelaf answered. "No. He went off to meet King Earconwald and his army . . ."

Galdor staggered back a step. "Oh, Edan's mercy. Earconwald? And an army?"

"Some four thousand troops," said Sergeant Hulm. "I saw them myself."

Galdor took a deep breath. "What happened?"

The lieutenant shook his head. "We don't know. But after he met them, the army turned northward and headed back to Torrlond without a word to us."

"Are you certain? Nothing else?"

"We sent messengers, and they came back with strange tidings. They were not permitted to see the Prophet, but they told us the soldiers in Earconwald's army all seemed to be his followers, somewhat like us. They were marching back to Torrhelm. And the messengers came back with orders for us to stay put. Since that's what the Prophet wanted anyway, here we are. At least for now."

"And what of Earconwald?"

The lieutenant shrugged. "Our messengers never saw him either. They spoke to Earl Nothelm, captain of the king's guard."

"So, as far as you know, Dayraven — the Prophet — is heading for Torrlond in the company of King Earconwald and an army of four thousand."

Edgelaf nodded. "That's about right." He looked uncertain for a moment. "He means to make some sacrifice. I don't know what, but my guess is he'll make peace somehow."

Galdor weighed his options and released a long sigh. It would have been so easy to give up and go home. But Dayraven would need them. What was more, the Torrlonders were in grave danger. "We've got to help him. We must reach him as soon as possible. Before they reach Torrhelm."

"They won't be hard to track," said Abon. "And we can move more swiftly than an army."

"Aye," said Gnorn. "But what do we do once we catch them up?"

"Just so, Gnorn. We must think that over carefully." Galdor turned to Sergeant Hulm. "I'm afraid we'll need to *borrow* those horses a little longer. Unless you could provide us with fresh ones?"

Captain Godwin nodded. "Put their saddles on fresh mounts, sergeant."

The sergeant grinned and winked at Galdor. "Yes, my lord."

The wizard turned to Captain Godwin and Lieutenant Edgelaf. "You have my thanks. You're doing the right thing. I don't know what will happen, but if the Prophet thought you had some purpose here, he must have foreseen something."

"He foresees much, and if you find him, I hope you'll find your fears quieted as well." Edgelaf smiled. "May Edan speed you on your journey."

"Thank you." Galdor turned toward the Caergilese girl, who was staring at him, her eyes serious and penetrating. He smiled at her and, still wondering who she was, gave her a slight bow. "Thank you all. You give me hope. Dayraven has been among you. I can see that. You are his true friends, as are we."

AS THEY MADE THEIR WAY OVER CAERGILION'S GREEN HILLS, Orvandil glanced behind him once again. Just at the moment he expected, the rider was outlined against the sky atop a hillock before he descended into the valley. The Thjoth rode up beside Galdor. "A rider tailing us. Doesn't want to be seen."

The wizard turned his head toward him, his bushy eyebrows cocked in mild surprise. "Really? Do you suppose our Torrlonder friends sent a scout to look after us?"

"If he's a scout, he's not a good one."

"Hmm. Still, perhaps we'd best find out who he is and what he wants."

"Keep riding. I'll loop back, take a look."

The wizard nodded. "Alright. But be careful."

Orvandil smiled at that. "Always."

The Thjoth nodded at Gnorn and Abon before directing his horse away from the others up over a hill and then down into a valley that paralleled the one his friends were riding in. He brought his steed to a trot and headed south until he judged he had come nigh their pursuer, and then he rode back up the hill. When he crested it, he scanned the valley. Disappearing into a stand of trees and then emerging from it, the rider was below and a little ahead of him, unaware of his presence. From that distance, he appeared a small man. Keeping his eyes on the ground, he was still warily tracking Galdor and the others, taking care not to get too close.

Orvandil watched and waited a few moments before directing his horse down the slope. When he reached the bottom, he rode behind their pursuer, keeping his horse to a slow trot. He rode into the shade of the stand of trees, and when he drew near its edge, he tugged on his rein to halt his horse before emerging out into the sunshine.

The rider had stopped just a few hundred feet ahead. At first, Orvandil thought their pursuer must have spotted him and was awaiting him. But then the rider dismounted and attempted to inspect one of his horse's hooves, stooping over to pull up the leg. The horse objected to this procedure with a loud neigh and a sudden jolt that knocked the rider onto her back. *Her* back, the Thjoth supposed, for the scream accompanying the rider's fall had been high-pitched.

Orvandil dismounted and tied his horse to a tree before walking toward the fallen rider, who lay still in the grass. Her horse had shied away from her but had not gone very far and was grazing. She still had not risen by the time Orvandil reached her and stood over her, covering her with his shadow.

Her eyes popped open, and she gave a startled cry before crawling backwards on her elbows and feet through the deep grass. "Stay away. Stay away from me." She fumbled at her side and drew a dagger that she extended before her with a trembling hand.

Orvandil did not move. "The girl from the villa with Lieutenant Edgelaf."

"Don't hurt me. He'll come after you if you do."

"I'm not going to hurt you."

"I know what you are. You're a Thjoth."

"So?"

"So, Thjoths run after people and do unspeakable things to them. Everyone knows that."

Orvandil smiled. "You're the one running after us."

"Well, I . . ."

"Why?"

She pursed her lips and lowered the dagger, and she fixed the Thjoth with her dark eyes. "You're going after the Prophet."

"Yes."

"I'm coming with you."

Orvandil raised an eyebrow. "What if we don't want you?"

"I'll follow you anyway. You can't stop me."

Orvandil nodded. There was courage in this skinny girl. "Does Lieutenant Edgelaf know?"

She glanced down at the ground and shook her head. "No. He wouldn't have let me." She looked up again with defiance in her eyes. "But he's not my father."

"What about your father? And your mother?"

A slight shake of the head, and her eyes took on a haunted look. "Gone."

"Sorry." The Thjoth recalled Edgelaf's protective gaze at the girl. "The lieutenant cares about you."

The girl sighed. "I know. And I hate doing this behind his back. But I have to."

"Why?"

"Because he needs me."

"Who?"

"The Prophet. Dayraven." She said the name like she was trying out the sound of it, but also with great reverence. She went on, and the rest of her words sounded like a confession. "I promised him I'd stay, but he broke his promise first. He never meant to come back at all, did he?"

He gazed at her for a while, and then he shook his head. "Mostlike you're right. But he meant good by it, I don't doubt." He sighed and sank down into a crouch so that his eyes were closer to hers. "I think the same way you do sometimes. That he needs me. Truth is, we need him just as much. More. A lot more." He extended his hand toward the girl and smiled. "I'm Orvandil."

She reached toward him, and after her small hand grasped his big one, he helped her up.

"Seren." She brushed some grass off her tunic.

"What's wrong with your horse?"

"Picked up a stone."

"Let's have it out, then."

GALDOR, ABON, AND GNORN WAITED ATOP THEIR HORSES AS Orvandil and Seren rode up to them. When they reached his companions, the Thjoth fell in beside them and nodded toward the girl. "This is Seren. She's coming with us."

"What?" Abon scowled at him like he had taken leave of his senses. "We can't bring a child with us."

"I won't get in your way," said Seren. "And I can ride fast."

The shaper ignored her. "It's too dangerous." He pointed northward. "There's a fucking army of Torrlonders up ahead, and the gods only know what Dayraven's going to do."

"Abon has the right of it." Gnorn frowned. "It's not wise to bring her close to such peril. We should send her back."

When Seren looked toward Orvandil, he smiled and nodded to her, signaling she should make her own defense.

The girl shook her head at the shaper and the Dweorg. "You can't send me back."

"We bloody well can." Abon pointed at her steed. "She likely stole the horse. The Torrlonders will be after her soon enough."

"I *borrowed* it." Seren raised her eyebrows as she made a conspicuous glance at Abon's mount with the Torrlonder saddle on it, and after she silenced him with the implication, she gazed at the shaper with defiance in her eyes.

Orvandil grinned. The girl had been listening well during their interview with Lieutenant Edgelaf, using Galdor's very word to cover her theft.

Seren continued. "And I hid my tracks well. Edge and the others won't know where I've gone until it's too late."

Gnorn shook his head at Orvandil. "My conscience won't allow it. Some harm may come to the lass."

Seren turned to the Dweorg. "You can't turn me back now. It's just as dangerous for me to ride back alone. What if something happened to me on the way? What would your conscience say then?"

The Thjoth turned his grin on Gnorn and shrugged. "She scored one over you there, friend."

Gnorn's frown deepened. "We'll ride back with her. Make sure she's safe."

"You don't have time, and we all know that." The girl's face took on a more stubborn look as she jutted her chin up. "Like I told Orvandil, I'll follow you no matter what you decide. You'd need to tie me up and strap me to the horse to send me back."

"Don't tempt me, child." Abon turned toward Galdor. "My lord. Tell that mad Thjoth we can't bring this girl with us."

Orvandil turned towards Galdor, who had stayed silent during the debate.

The wizard pursed his lips and stroked his beard as he stared at Seren, and then he broke out in a rich chuckle. "Welcome to our little company, Seren. I have questions for you, and we have much to tell one another. We will gain from your knowledge of Dayraven. Come and ride next to me."

Abon's palm smacked his brow as he shook his head in mute protest, and Orvandil grinned at how the girl had bested them all.

THE WHOLE DAY, WHILE GALDOR CHATTED MERRILY WITH SEREN, Abon rode in sullen, stony silence that he interrupted once in a while to curse and shake his head. When they made a halt, it was none too soon for him. Not far from where the River Glas met the River Gilion, they made camp on a hilltop as twilight was surrendering to darkness. Beneath the long light of the westering sun, the rivers shimmered like narrow, wayward bands of steel etched into the deep green plain stretching out below. While he massaged his horse, Abon made his grumbles loud enough for the others to hear. "It's plain fucking madness. Letting a child tag along. No bloody good will come of it. Mark my words."

No one seemed to be marking his words or paying much attention to him as they prepared the camp, but he kept talking as if his horse at least were an attentive audience. "What do you think she'll do when things get messy? Where's she going to run to? And *who's* supposed to get her out of it? That's what I'd like to know."

The mute horse stared back at him and nodded.

"No. Not me. Wasn't my bloody idea to bring a silly girl along."

The shaper finished tending to his horse, and after taking out a bundle from a saddlebag, he moved toward the crackling fire Gnorn was coaxing to life to lay out his cloak for a place to sleep. The warmth would feel good tonight.

The Dweorg glanced at the shaper. "There's a chill in the night air. Summer's on the wane."

Abon grunted. "Aye. The leaves will be turning up north."

He slipped the strap of the green bag off his shoulder and pulled out his harp. The gut strings would need a good tuning. He began plucking at them and twisting the pegs. When the strings were all true, he looked up. The girl was sitting across the fire from him. Staring at him. No. Staring at his *harp* with a hungry look in her eyes.

The shaper held the instrument a bit closer and scowled at her. "What?"

She broke her trance and looked down. "Nothing."

He strummed the strings and teased out a couple trills, and the girl's eyes darted back to the harp. Frowning down at the instrument, he determined to ignore her as his fingers found a rhythm and he thought about what tale to sing. He had finished a story the previous evening, a hero's adventure, and he was in the mood for something quieter. Perhaps one of the old tales of the gods . . .

He made the mistake of looking up, and the damned girl was still staring at him like she was starving and wanted to eat his bloody harp. Perhaps it was some trick of the fire's light, or perhaps it was the smoke from it, but he thought the girl's eyes had watered up somewhat. The back of her hand went to her eye and wiped her cheek, and she sniffled.

Oh, gods. Abon swallowed the lump of guilt in his throat, but it still suffused him along with a sort of helpless awkwardness, and he was glad the fire's light was already reddening his burning face. Perhaps he had been a bit too harsh, though the gods knew he was right about her being in danger. He turned his gaze away from the girl and played on a few more moments until it became unbearable. The rhythm uncoiled as his fingers stumbled to a stop. "Shit." He rolled his eyes and glanced up at the girl, who looked away and pretended to take a sudden interest in the darkness outside the firelight.

The shaper released a long sigh. *Time to start over.* "Do you play?"

Wiping her eyes again, the girl gawked at him as if unsure he was addressing her. "What?"

"I said, do you play?" He nodded down at his harp.

She shook her head, and the sad-startled look that made him feel like he had just committed a vile crime remained in her dark eyes. "No."

"Oh." He looked down, and his fingers began plucking and looking for the rhythm again.

"The fiddle," she said, and after a long pause, "A little bit."

He grunted and kept strumming, not bothering to look up.

"And I sing."

Something in her voice demanded his attention. He glanced at her, and there was that fearless look he had seen when she defied him and insisted on accompanying them to find Dayraven. There was no trace of tears. He stopped playing again. "You do, eh?"

"Yes. I do. But all the songs I know are in Ondunic."

"Matters not. Songs go deeper and higher than any language. If they're done well enough." He fixed his eyes on her in challenge, and he began playing one of the Caergilese rhythms he had learned over the years. They were all mournful and beautiful, and this was the most complex one he knew.

As he wove the notes and they ascended like the sparks of their little fire into the surrounding darkness, she gazed at him with her dark, serious eyes. At length, she nodded in silent acceptance of his challenge. And then, when he came round to the beginning of the rhythm again, she sang.

Abon had no idea what the Ondunic words meant. Just as he said, however, it mattered not.

As soon as the first notes were born in her lungs and vibrated and swelled from her throat, he knew what he was hearing: the most beautiful, clear, melancholy, and wondrous voice ever to caress his ears. Almost he lost the rhythm it startled him so. But he held on, and he kept playing as the notes cascaded out of her like a mountain spring welling up from some depthless source to play over the rocks. They lapped the crisp night air and enfolded him in their purity. Within that voice were flashes of splendor and the profoundest sorrow, for which it was all the more beautiful. Its sublimity both shattered and cleansed him. Only with an effort and the discipline of many years did he keep from shaking apart and losing himself, and he closed his eyes as he concentrated on giving that voice something close to the accompaniment it deserved and demanded.

Verse after verse spilled out of the girl and soared into the surrounding darkness like flames, challenging it with their clarity and brightness, and even the vast, cold night seemed to hearken, startled out of its eternal indifference. The stars shivered above, anticipating the next notes, which called upon the sliver of bone-white moon to witness. Abon just managed to cling on to the girl's voice and fly with her. Stirred and stretched, he bent all of his long mastery of the harp toward keeping pace until the vibrations his fingers drew from the strings intertwined in a delicate and faultless dance with the girl's singing.

Desiring the perfection of the moment never to end, the shaper lost any sense of how long she sang. Deep within him, down in his very core, that voice struck something — all the ache of loss and desire that filled his little frame — with words he did not know, and yet it was, he recognized, the only tale there was to tell. It was as ancient as the human race, and no matter what tongue gave it new expression, it would always remain the same.

The shaper's eyes stayed closed, and when he realized Seren had sung the last of her song as the echoes of her notes receded like ghostly waves passing over his mind, he found the strength to weave the threads of the rhythm to a gentle close and lay the tale to rest.

Silence.

He opened his eyes. In shocked stillness, Galdor, Orvandil, and Gnorn sat around the fire, their stares fixed on the girl. The Dweorg wiped his wet cheek with his thick hand, and the wizard shook his head in disbelief, his bright green eyes moist even as he smiled sadly. Even the Thjoth's mouth hung open as he gawked at Seren. How could a young lass possess a voice filled with such longing and suffering?

Abon could not bear to look at her. His lower lip trembled. He shuddered and buried his face in his hands, and then he wept like he had not since he was a child.

EARCONWALD'S ARMY TRAVELED WITH GREAT SWIFTNESS, ALMOST AS if fleeing from pursuit. After tracking them for so long, the small company caught their first glimpse of the four thousand troops off in the distance just as the Torrlonders reached the foothills of the snow-capped Marar Mountains near the city of Iarfaen. Abon cursed, knowing full well it would have been better to have caught up with Dayraven before he crossed into Torrlond. The closer they came to Torrhelm, the more difficult it would be to reach the young man and help him.

The army was making for Balnor Pass, the widest and easiest way over the mountains. The shaper wondered if Dayraven would recall the pass or the Battle of Iarfaen. He had played a small role in saving the lad that day. Of course, it would have been impossible without Sequara. Abon spared a thought for the sorceress and hoped she was faring better in her journey than they were.

Their immediate problem was how to get over the mountains to keep following the army. The Torrlonders would have a garrison watching Balnor Pass, but Orvandil and Gnorn insisted there were other ways over the mountains a small party could use. They had found one while fleeing from the Torrlonders with Queen Rona and her company.

It proved no simple matter to lead the horses after the paths grew rocky and steep, and they lost much time in having to retrace their steps more than once, but they ascended the mountains. The air grew cool while their breaths grew shorter and more labored. Even as they sweated while trudging over the rocks, the biting wind chilled their flesh and awakened goosebumps. They all had to make use of the spare cloaks and blankets in their saddle bags, but even then they spent the nights shivering and huddled together for warmth. All the while, from the way Galdor fretted, Abon knew the matter was growing more urgent with each passing moment. The party's spirits dimmed and flickered, but, strangely enough, it was Seren who remained keenest and urged them on. Without her, they would have been a grim, sullen group. Somehow she gave them hope. Perhaps it was her courage. Perhaps it was her faith in Dayraven. Whatever it was, Abon's admiration for the girl grew, not least for her singing as they closed each long day with a song or two.

At length, they began to wander downward from the heights. The crisp air began to warm again, and the rocky paths grew greener and milder as trees began to provide shade from the sun. Abon wondered how far the Torrlonders had come and how difficult it would be to catch up with them. It would have taken some time for the entire army to proceed through Balnor Pass. With luck, they would overtake it within a day or two.

But what if the Torrlonders had pushed ahead even faster than before? They had crossed the length of Caergilion with great urgency, and the fear grew in the shaper's mind that the companions would find themselves too far behind to reach Dayraven before their foes conducted him to Torrhelm. Once he was in the Torrlonders' chief city in a secure place, how would they rescue him?

He was about to give vent to this fear when they crested a foothill providing a clear view of South Torrlond's rolling landscape. Galdor and Seren stopped ahead of him, and he pulled his horse up to them. Below them, spilling out from a narrow vale tucked in the mountains and spreading out like a grey blanket over the undulating hills, Earconwald's army gathered for the march to Torrhelm.

The shaper released a sigh. They were not too late. Now all they had to do was figure out how to reach Dayraven in the midst of that army.

"We need information." Abon crossed his arms. "Before and above anything else, we need to know what's happening with Dayraven. At the moment, we're blind."

"Aye," said Gnorn. "But how do we get it? Should we stroll into Torrlonders' camp and make a friendly inquiry?"

Galdor shrugged. "Why not?" He beamed a smile at the frowning Dweorg. "An excellent idea, dear fellow."

Gnorn wrinkled his nose in disbelief. "What? Surely even you aren't mad enough to walk into a camp of four thousand Torrlonders. They may or may not be under Dayraven's influence, and we don't know how receptive they'll be to visitors. They're Torrlonders, after all, and some might know who we are. What's more, we're not even sure Dayraven is down there with them."

The wizard let out a deep breath, and his smile disappeared as his eyes took on a haunted look. "Oh, I assure you, he's there. I can feel the power in him."

Abon looked at his old friend. "From here?"

Galdor gave a curt nod. "It is vast. And growing." There was a moment of grim silence while the companions took in that information. The same worried look passed over all their faces save Seren's. The girl looked more determined than ever, and that gave heart to Abon.

The wizard broke the silence with another cheerful, if somewhat forced, smile. "But you're quite right, Abon. We need to know what's going on down there. We can't all go in, so perhaps one of us might sneak in."

"Risky," said Gnorn. "Whoever goes will have to wait until night."

"Maybe not."

Everyone turned toward Seren, who had spoken. The girl grinned. "There's a grey kirtle with Torrlond's ensign in my saddlebag. One of us could wear it into the Torrlonder camp."

"Excellent!" Galdor clapped his hands. "Fetch it for us, if you will."

While the girl scampered toward the horses, the wizard continued. "Now, we must decide which of us will don the disguise. We may rule out Seren. Of the rest of us, it should be the least conspicuous." He turned a critical gaze toward Gnorn and shook his head. "No, certainly not." He frowned at Orvandil and wagged his white beard. "Not at all." The old wizard turned to the shaper with a bright smile. "Well, dear Abon, it would appear it's down to you or me."

Abon rolled his eyes. "Alright. I'll go."

"Splendid. There's a good chap."

Seren returned holding up the grey kirtle. On the shoulder was Torrlond's ensign. Two bright-red lines marked a lieutenant's rank, which would draw more attention to the kirtle's wearer. It was also much too large for Abon.

The shaper frowned at the girl. "You stole Lieutenant Edgelaf's horse?"

She glared at him. "*Borrowed.*"

He sighed. "Well, lass, it's better than nothing. You did well. Though it might appear more like a dress than a kirtle on me."

As he approached the marching Torrlonders through the trees, Abon kept tugging the kirtle back up and tucking it into his belt. He had rolled up the sleeves so they would not droop over his hands. Mumbling and cursing, he snuck up to the rear of Earconwald's army, which was still emerging from the forested vale to join the rest of the troops before they all journeyed to Torrhelm. The sounds of marching boots and hooves were not far off, and through the branches and leaves he caught glimpses of the soldiers as their byrnies and helms gleamed in patches of sunlight.

He crouched behind a trunk and paused a moment while he reviewed his plan. He would emerge from the trees and melt into one of the passing groups of soldiers. Simple. He just needed to time it right and hope no one noticed him.

"You there!"

Abon spun around and suppressed a curse.

A group of six soldiers converged on him from the trees. Scouts. He should have known they would be scouring the perimeters of the march. He would need to think fast.

The lead soldier approached him. "What are you doing here? The orders are to stay . . ." His eyes glanced at Abon's shoulder. "Oh. Sorry, lieutenant."

The shaper cleared his throat. "Had to take a shit."

The soldier looked confused for a moment.

Abon shrugged. "It was a bit runny, if you catch my meaning. Must've been those beans last night."

The man's face wrinkled. "Oh. Right."

Abon shook his head. "The shit they make us eat, eh?"

Another of the soldiers nodded. "You got that right, lieutenant."

They all nodded and stared at each other for an awkward moment.

"Well," said Abon. "Best be getting back to my company. You know the orders."

They all straightened up, and the lead soldier gave a sharp nod. "Yes, my lord."

"Well done, lads." Abon turned away from them, rolled his eyes, and breathed a large sigh as he walked out of the trees and fell in next to a group of soldiers. A few of them glanced at him, but after noticing the stripes on his shoulder, they said nothing. Pretending he knew where he was going, the shaper outpaced them and walked ahead.

That, he decided, would be his tactic until the army stopped to make camp for the night. He could not join any company since they would know he did not belong, but if he could keep moving about as if he were heading somewhere important, no one would question him. He kept his ears open for word of Dayraven, but the men said little as they marched, and they all seemed weary from the pace they had been keeping. Every once in a while, with a mumbled curse, he had to hike up his kirtle and tuck it back into his belt.

CAMPFIRES PROVIDED ISLANDS OF WARMTH AND LIGHT IN THE darkness, and they cast their ruddy glow on the faces of the Torrlonders huddled around them. Like the soldiers back in Caergilion, these troops seemed a pious lot. Many of them conducted quiet debates among themselves, and plenty of them muttered prayers. Whatever Dayraven was doing, he had clearly touched these men deeply.

Abon heard several conversations about the Prophet, and one provided him with a good idea of where he was in the camp: in a small tent near the Supreme Priest Joruman's much larger one. Knowing the supreme priest was also in the camp did little to lessen the shaper's anxiety, but he had no difficulty finding the sumptuous tent housing the spiritual leader of the Way of Edan. It was, of course, well guarded, and he had walked past it as if on his way to conduct business elsewhere in the camp.

Of Earconwald the soldiers said little, but from what he heard, Abon gathered something ailed the king, who kept to himself inside his tent. The army's real commander was Earl Nothelm, the captain of the king's personal guard. The soldiers spoke of him in tones of great respect, but it also seemed clear that Nothelm was under orders from the supreme priest, who had taken charge. The shaper tucked away all that information and hoped it might be of some use to Galdor.

After waiting until the campfires died down and the soldiers went to sleep on their cloaks, he made his move. He moved naturally through most of the camp — to do otherwise would call attention to him — but when he drew nigh the supreme priest's tent, he had to be more cautious. There were still plenty of guards about the tent, but Abon found a wagon he could hide under. He slipped beneath it and watched for a while.

Within Joruman's tent was the flickering glow of candles. Over the sound of the guards' pacing and his own breaths, Abon thought he could hear the low tones of conversation emerging from it. He wished he could hear the words, but the number of guards made it impossible to creep closer. The most important thing was to discover which of the small tents nearby was Dayraven's. He watched and waited.

The shaper's patience paid off. When the entrance flap to the supreme priest's tent stirred and a man emerged, he held his breath. The light of the torch the man carried illuminated his face, making his identity unmistakable. Dayraven.

The lad's hair and beard appeared silver-white, but Abon would have known that face anywhere. The shaper smiled as he watched his friend head toward one of the smaller tents, walking by several guards who bowed low to him. Dayraven stuck his torch into the dirt to snuff it out and disappeared inside the tent. Abon nodded to himself. He had to find a way to have a word with the lad. Perhaps they could escape the camp together this night and rejoin Galdor and the others at the meeting place. First, he needed to find a way to Dayraven's tent without being seen.

After a guard walked by, the shaper scuttled out from beneath the wagon and crept in a large circle around the supreme priest's tent. He would come at Dayraven's tent from the other side, which was darker and had fewer guards prowling around. All went well, but, when he was closing in on his goal, he had to duck behind another tent while a guard strode by. The man took no notice of him. He blessed his luck and prayed to all the gods it would hold.

Hardly daring to breathe, Abon slinked from his hiding spot toward Dayraven's tent. He reached it and hid behind it as more guards made their rounds close to its entrance. Sweat trickled down his back as he thought about his friend lying just on the other side of the canvas. Once the guards receded, he ducked down on all fours, making his silent way to the entrance. He knew he would not have long once he reached it, but he also did not wish to startle Dayraven. Staying in a crouch, he whispered into the entrance flap. "Dayraven. It's me, Ab. . ."

Something slammed into his back, and he rolled with another body, both of them grunting until they stopped. Abon lay face down with the large weight of a guard on top of him. The man's knee dug into his back, and he held one of the shaper's arms behind him, wrenching it back. Abon growled as the man shouted, "To the Prophet! Protect the Prophet!"

Many other footsteps arrived at once, and some of the new arrivals bore torches. Others held down the shaper's kicking legs and flailing arm.

"Who is he?"

"Don't know," said the man above him, the one who had tackled him. "I caught him sneaking outside the Prophet's tent."

"An assassin?"

"Like as not. Best question him."

Abon groaned. "I'm not an assassin."

"Who are you then? What company are you in?"

"I'm Ulfnoth. Lieutenant Ulfnoth."

"What company?"

The first thing to come to Abon's panicking head was the company he had actually served in once, however briefly. "The Mercenary Company of Etinstone. Augh! Get off me."

"Mercenary Company of Etinstone? Aren't they up north, fighting in Norfast?"

"He's a liar."

"Who are you? And what are you doing sneaking near the Prophet's tent?"

"Let me see his face," said a new voice. It held authority and the expectation of obedience.

Someone yanked off Abon's helm and wrenched his head back so that it felt like his neck would snap. An involuntary groan escaped his throat. Before him stood a man in a white robe. He could not look up high enough to see the man's face, but he had no doubt who it was.

"An assassin, you say? We must tolerate no threats to the Prophet," said the Supreme Priest Joruman in a tense voice.

Steel whispered as someone unsheathed a blade. Abon's mind screamed at him to struggle even as his heart squirmed in his chest, but too many hands held him down, and the pressure increased on his spine. In his mind flashed a memory of a time long ago in his native Ellond, when followers of the Way had cut him to pieces and left him for dead, giving him the scar he bore across his face, among others. Their cold blades had burned in his flesh. Footsteps approached, and the helpless shaper closed his eyes, wondering where they would cut him first and how long it would take him to bleed out.

"Release him."

The voice was quiet, but it produced an immediate effect. The hands grasping Abon's limbs disappeared, as did the weight on his back. He lay there gasping for a moment, and then, after picking up and donning his helm, he struggled to rise and meet the eyes of his friend, for the voice had been Dayraven's.

Amidst a confusion of torchlights, soldiers in grey kirtles surrounded him and glared at him, but Abon took little notice of them for the moment. His eyes widened at the changes in his friend. The silver hair shone in the ruddy light, and though his face remained the same, terrible suffering haunted the lad's eyes.

"Dayraven," said Abon between heavy breaths. "I've come to . . ."

"Be still. I shall know why you've come and who you are."

The shaper's body went rigid as a vast power flooded his mind, wherein an explosion of light paralyzed him and bleached away all voluntary thought. The fear of dying he had experienced moments before was a small thing next to the infinite horror ripping through him, hissing and screeching a wordless nothingness. The light terrified him down to the very depths of his being, but it also called him toward it, and it seemed an eternity passed as it regarded him in the same manner he might have watched a mote of dust spinning in the sunlight. Helpless, he cringed and trembled before it as it stripped him bare.

The light disappeared, and the shaper's body sagged so much that he almost fell onto his knees. The world returned with the soldiers and the torchlight and the face of his friend, and then it seemed only the briefest moment had gone by while Dayraven entered and ransacked his mind. Abon tried to gather his thoughts, to say something or even give the barest signal in the form of a nod, but he could not begin to master himself. He could only stand there blinking at the man who contained such an indescribable maelstrom of power within him.

The lad gave him the saddest smile he had ever seen, and though he kept his gaze on Abon, he addressed the soldiers around him. "You will allow this man to leave the camp unharmed. He had no ill intentions. Merely a pilgrim. Take his kirtle only, for he is no soldier of Torrlond."

"Very well," said the voice of the Supreme Priest Joruman from behind the shaper. "You heard the Prophet. You three, see the man out of our camp, and take the kirtle."

"Yes, my lord," answered one of the soldiers.

While they pulled the kirtle off Abon, who cooperated by extending his arms, Dayraven continued to stare at the shaper. He heard the lad's voice in his mind. *You were my friend, I know. Thank you for coming for me. But you must flee now. Go far from Torrlond. As far as you can. Tell the others. Tell Seren especially. As she is dear to you, keep her far away. And stay away, for I do not know how long I can hold it back. A very short time, I fear. Stay away, and do not ever come near me again. The time is coming.*

Abon nodded dumbly, and then rough hands seized him and shoved him on his way. They said nothing until they saw him out of the camp, and then they gave him a warning that he would die the next time he attempted such a stunt. When he departed from them without the kirtle but still wearing his byrny and the rest of his gear, he breathed a long sigh and hastened to go meet Galdor and the others, still in uncomprehending shock and wonder over what Dayraven had done to him.

Seren eyed Abon as they passed amidst the choked river of people, carts, horses, dogs, chickens and sundry other animals and modes of transport flooding the cobbled streets of Torrhelm — all screaming, growling, creaking, crying, barking, clucking, and shoving their way through. The shaper was returning to himself, but all the way from South Torrlond, he had been strangely silent, not even cursing or taking out his harp to accompany her singing until last night, when he first seemed close to normal again. That is, he had been silent only *after* he finished babbling about Dayraven and the end of times and all sorts of nonsense about fleeing as far as possible. All his talk had alarmed Galdor and even Gnorn and Orvandil, but Seren had convinced them they had to see through their quest and help Dayraven however they could.

Thus, they had tailed the army all the way to Torrhelm, and Seren had watched as Galdor grew more desperate with each mile. But the plains had offered no chance for them to approach the Prophet, surrounded as he was by an entire army, and the wizard had at length decided their best opportunity to draw near him might come in Torrhelm. He seemed to believe that if he could get close enough, he would be able to reach the Prophet with a spell and perhaps help him. So, they had ridden ahead of the army and entered Torrhelm to wait for their chance. As the miles passed, Seren had watched the monstrosity that was Torrlond's chief city emerge from the plain and the river over which it loomed. The closer they grew to it, the vaster it seemed, with towering buildings casting huge shadows and impossible numbers of people teeming in and out of it on the crowded road.

Now that they were in Torrhelm, Seren felt trapped within its high stone walls. It was nothing like Gadomiel, the nearest thing to a city she had been in before. This was on a scale that was no longer human, and she could not stop gawking up at the tall buildings and flinching from the pressing throng, not to mention the noises and smells that were a constant assault on her senses. At least they had stabled their horses at a dockside inn to make it easier to pass through the streets.

Galdor led them toward King Earconwald's castle Sigseld, a bristling fortification on a hill in the midst of the city. The rumor was that the king, the supreme priest, and the Prophet would all enter it after their journey from the south, and huge crowds had gathered to witness the event. The large numbers of soldiers lining the street providing access to Sigseld's main entrance seemed to confirm the rumor. On both sides of the street, the stone-faced soldiers standing shoulder to shoulder faced the crowd and formed a barrier beyond which they would allow no one, keeping the street clear for the arrival of the kingdom's revered leaders. The people's excitement was especially keen since the famed Prophet of Edan was at one with the supreme priest and king, and this seemed a great promise of things to come for Torrlond. The talk buzzing all around spoke of Edan's favor and the prosperity that was sure to flow into Torrlond.

Seren knew better. All these people had no notion who the Prophet really was. Their ideas about glory and riches and Edan's blessing of their kingdom over all others had nothing to do with the gentle and loving man she knew. But she had faith he would show them why he had come. He would make things right, just not the way all these people expected. And he would never make common cause with such an evil man as Earconwald.

Galdor urged them on until the crowd lining the street grew too thick for him to make headway. He turned back to Orvandil. "Perhaps you could cut us a path, my friend."

The big Thjoth nodded. "Stay close." He put his hand on the shoulder of a man in front of him. The man turned around with a frown on his face and seemed about to object, but then he thought better of it and moved aside to let the big man through. Galdor followed him, and Seren slipped in after the wizard, pushing her way through the flesh and sweaty smell of all the bodies. Gnorn and Abon came last, and the Dweorg kept his hands on Seren's shoulders to stay with her and shield her from the worst of the jostling.

In that manner Orvandil cleared the way until the companions gained a view of the street. A few people stood between them and the soldiers guarding the street's perimeter, but Galdor touched the Thjoth's arm and nodded to signal they were close enough. After that, the wizard began chanting something Seren could not hear over all the noise of the crowd. She supposed it was the spell he needed to use, but she knew little of such things and decided to focus on what she could do. Since she was shorter than the others save Gnorn, she could see less than she would have liked, but by shifting about, she could catch glimpses of the street whereon the procession would pass. There was so much excited chatter among the people that she could hardly hear her own thoughts.

The babble swelled and then erupted into screams that pierced her ears. Moments later, the first of the king's guard rode past with gleaming helms and spears, their horse's hooves clattering on the cobbles. More mounted guardsmen came, and then a thick group of them arrived surrounding a figure.

Seren held her breath as she caught a brief glimpse of King Earconwald, the man who murdered her parents. But he had changed much. The arrogant and pompous villain who had destroyed her family had become a shell of a man who stared ahead with vacant eyes, seemingly oblivious to the shouts of his adoring subjects. The crown and glitter of the garments he wore no longer fit him, as if he were an imposter wearing the king's props. The Prophet must have done something to him, and Seren would have loved to know what.

But she could give it little thought since, as the king disappeared down the street, another group of guards rode up. In their midst were two riders. The one who wore a white robe must have been the supreme priest, but Seren had no eyes for him.

In spite of the screams all around her and her fear of the throng and all the Torrlonder soldiers, and even in spite of the haunted look on his face, Seren could not help but smile when she beheld him. He rode next to the supreme priest, but unlike the leader of Torrlond's faith, the Prophet did not wave at the adoring people. Instead, he stooped in the saddle in weariness, turning eyes that seemed serene on the surface to gaze over the crowd. But Seren guessed at the tension beneath those eyes, and she wanted nothing more than to help him bear the terrible burden that was grinding him down.

Next to her, Galdor chanted more loudly, but Seren could still not make out the foreign sounding words. She glanced at the old wizard, whose eyes were closed with creases of tension across his face. Her gaze turned back to the Prophet, who sat up on his horse as his eyes widened and snapped in her direction.

A wave of power swept through the crowd, which gasped and went silent as one, as if some giant bellows sucked away all the air. The sky overhead darkened, and a fist of fear and awe squeezed Seren's heart, sending ice deep inside her. Beside her, Galdor went boneless and collapsed, but Orvandil caught and held up the old man. In front of her on the street, the Prophet's head lolled as he gripped it in both hands, and he seemed close to teetering off his steed.

The power that had gripped everyone blinked out, and Seren realized she could move and breathe again. Screams broke out in the crowd, soldiers looked everywhere in confusion, and horses neighed and bucked. "To the castle!" yelled the supreme priest over all the commotion. "Get the Prophet inside the castle!" The supreme priest rode close to the Prophet and grabbed his horse's rein, and then he held on as he galloped down the street, pulling the Prophet's horse beside him.

Seren lost sight of them as bodies jostled all around her and soldiers began bludgeoning people, and the screams took on a shriller note of frenzied panic. But she could hear the Prophet's voice in her head, coming as if from afar. *You broke your promise, as I did mine. I'm sorry. So sorry. But you must leave. You cannot help me, and I can't hold it any longer. Flee. Run far away. With all the life left to me, I beg you to flee. Run, Seren. Run. It is taking me now.* The gradually fading voice dimmed to nothing, and he was gone. No trace of his presence remained. The crowd was dispersing everywhere as soldiers growled and shoved the reeling people back with their spears. A few bodies writhed on the ground, clutching wounds where soldiers had struck them, and some lay still in pools of blood.

Seren stood with her mouth hanging open, unable to budge until a strong hand grasped her arm and pulled her away. Gnorn and Abon stood by her, shouting instructions she could not hear while fleeing people shoved her and them. Nearby, Orvandil carried Galdor's limp body and yelled something. It was so hard to listen or even find the will to move.

The Prophet was lost. And so was she.

19
THE CONQUEST

Not far from the mouth of the River Maranant, the invasion fleet from Asdralad came ashore in Adanon. Local rebels had secured a safe perimeter for the landing, but the precaution proved unnecessary as the Torrlonders offered no opposition and were nowhere visible. Sequara's relief at their safe arrival blended with her anxiety over what the Torrlonders were preparing, for surely their foes must have had word of so many ships. She kept her senses wide open for any hint of an attack as the soldiers disembarked from the ships.

From there, the Asdralae and Adanese small army of foresters and farmers began to march northeast. The plan Queen Rona proposed was to make their way up to Palahon, meeting up with more Adanese rebels along the way. Their hope was to draw more fighters to join them and inspire an uprising of the populace against the Torrlonder overlords. The major problem with that plan was what would happen if the Torrlonders descended in force upon them before their ragtag army could build any momentum. Sequara had no doubt as to the outcome should that happen.

They lacked both numbers and experience in open, large-scale conflict. Few, if any, leaders were as cunning and capable as Queen

Rona. Imharr was an able fighter and had proved himself a solid strategist, while Khalan had led the Asdralae well in the forests of Asdralad. Even so, they had no hope of victory in a pitched battle against an organized Torrlonder army. They were taking a huge risk — all or nothing. And yet, the local rebels who had met them at the shoreline had encouraged Queen Rona in her bid to take back Adanon this way. Their intelligence pointed to some dissension among the Torrlonders stemming from the activities of the famed Prophet of Edan.

Those tidings had spread warmth through Sequara — a mixture of intense worry and joy that prompted her hand toward her stomach, a reflex she kept having to hold back lest anyone guess what Rona knew. She scolded herself for being almost giddy with the thought: Dayraven was in the southwest. He had been among the people, and he had done something important here. Thus, the sorceress's hopes for their mission blended with her desire for Dayraven, producing the swirling emotions she bottled beneath an impassive face. Everything pointed to this being the moment to free the southwest from Torrlond's tyranny, but that did not prevent the acidic anxiety in Sequara's stomach from churning as she contemplated her reunion with Dayraven and how she could help him. Besides that, there was the ever present dread of when and how the Torrlonders would show themselves.

Beside her rode Rona, looking eager and strong. Adanon's rightful queen exhibited no inner turmoil at the prospect of gambling everything in one throw to regain her kingdom's throne so that she could one day pass it on to her eldest remaining child, Prince Runan. Sequara observed how Rona kept a regal posture at all times save in private, and the petite woman could be imposing enough, but the sorceress also knew her warmth. Faldira had taught Sequara what it meant to be a queen, but Rona had given her leave to be a woman, not only to accept the humanity within her but to embrace it.

This resolution was still so new and exciting to her that she feared to lose it. She kept telling herself she would find the means both to be with Dayraven and serve Asdralad, should her people accept her that way. Dayraven had been right back in Thulhan: Together, they could contribute much to rebuilding the island kingdom. She ached to change that moment when she responded to him as she thought her duty demanded, but she knew the futility of berating herself, and she bent her thoughts toward how she would find him and help him. For Asdralad's security and the sake of her allies and friends, she needed to help Rona retake Adanon and liberate Caergilion, and then she would be free to seek him. She prayed to Oruma and Anghara the reports of the Torrlonders' strife were accurate. They would need all the luck they could get, but somehow she felt the pull of fate in everything, and she began to tell herself all would come out well.

And yet, like the unending abysses said to cleave the mountains beneath the Great Sea, her fears remained lodged deep within her. What if the Torrlonders defeated them? Why had their foes not appeared to defend their claim to the southwest? She had expected an army of grey kirtles to smash against them at any moment, and though it was a relief to march as far inland as they had without opposition, each mile increased the tension and the dread of sudden attack. The greatest and least acknowledged fear of all was that she would be unable to save Dayraven again — that he would be beyond her, his humanity burned away.

"You appear thoughtful, my lady."

Sequara turned toward Elfwy, who rode on her other side. The young earl managed a smile, though the sorceress sensed the tension beneath it. Interpreting King Fullan's command to see her to Asdralad safely in the most liberal way possible, Elfwy had insisted on continuing to accompany her. His mission, he had said, would be complete only when Asdralad was hers without any danger to her. His men backed him up in this, with Lieutenant Eanred calling it their sacred duty, and they had become almost as devoted to her as Elfwy was.

"Just wondering where the Torrlonders are," she answered with half the truth.

Elfwy nodded, his worry becoming more obvious as he frowned. "Aye. I expected some sign of them at least long before now."

Keeping her face impassive, Sequara returned the nod. She was grateful for all the Ellonder earl and his men had done and for his continued loyalty. But she sighed as she glanced at him atop his horse. Though she could not conceive of why, she feared Elfwy had fallen in love with her, and she felt a measure of guilt for continuing to use him and his men. But they needed every able body they could scrape together, and the twenty-five remaining Ellonders were the best soldiers they had. If guilt was the price of having such able warriors on her side, then so be it. It was not the worst sacrifice she would have made.

She still winced when she thought of how many human beings she had slaughtered. She had killed in battle more times than she could remember, but the carnage that had happened back in Asdralad was something of another order. She had been a vessel of vengeance, a vehicle of deadly power that raged through her and left her empty for days. The scorching flames and searing almakhti glowed and flashed in her nightmares amidst screams and shrieks, and the stench of death would cling to her forever. What had she become? Even if he were himself again, would Dayraven want anything to do with her? Of a certainty, she could never be the healer he had known back in Asdralad. The war had changed her, warped her into a killer, and of that she was more ashamed than anything, though it was duty that had swept her along this path.

The sorceress returned to the present with a shiver that twitched her shoulders. The din of their makeshift army clinking and clanging and stomping all around her accompanied the dust it kicked up. She was glad to be at the head of the long column rather than at the rear, where they could hardly see for all the dirt hovering in the air, covering their clothes and flesh in a fine layer of grit and settling into their noses, eyes, and mouths. She was also relieved it was no longer the high months of summer, for the night breezes at least offered a cool salve. But it was still hot enough in the day that sweat ran down her back, and her horse whinnied from time to time as if inquiring when they might stop. She too would fain have it all over. *Let it end. However it might be, let it be over.*

The sound of galloping hooves interrupted her thoughts as a rider neared her. When the mounted woman drew close — no doubt one of the Adanese rebel scouts — Imharr rode away from the column to meet her. Once they came together, the woman gestured northward and spoke Ondunic in an excited tone. Imharr nodded to her, and then he rode back to convey the tidings to Queen Rona, again in Ondunic. When he had finished, Rona turned to the sorceress.

"The Torrlonders have come to meet us," said the queen of Adanon in the Northern Tongue. "They're only a few miles away."

Fear twisted like a blade in Sequara's gut, and her lungs seemed to constrict. Yet, at the same time, her mind felt strangely numb and remote. The moment had finally come. She realized she was not so much afraid of dying as she was of killing again. "Did she say how many?"

Rona's eyes widened a bit. "Six."

"Six thousand?" This was beyond their worst fears. Her mind raced. They would have to make a rapid retreat and think of another plan, perhaps disperse their forces, else their campaign would end this very day with all their deaths.

Rona smiled, and Sequara wondered if the news had loosened her wits. "No, dear. Six. Only six. And under a flag of truce."

According to the laws of truce, six of them rode to meet the Torrlonders. Accompanying Sequara and Queen Rona were Prince Runan, Imharr, Khalan, and Earl Elfwy. Among the Torrlonders, the highest ranking was a sergeant. The other five were common soldiers. But the most astonishing thing about them was their zeal for the Prophet. The grizzled sergeant, who named himself Beda, spoke for them all.

"According to the Prophet's command, we surrender this kingdom to you in return for our safe passage back to Torrlond."

Even Queen Rona could not conceal her shock as she glanced at Sequara and then gawked at the soldier as if she did not understand or could not believe what he had said. Since the queen seemed at a momentary loss for words, the sorceress spoke the first thing that came to her mind. "These are welcome words, but how do we know this is not a trap?"

Sergeant Beda smiled and nodded, and then he pursed his lips as he thought for a moment. "Understandable you'd be wondering that, my lady. If you knew the Prophet, though, you'd have your answer."

Sequara nodded at that, and she could not help giving a small smile of her own.

Queen Rona recovered her composure and spoke up. "Some of us do know him, sergeant. We would be glad of word of him, but first, perhaps it would help matters if you would explain why you are surrendering, and where your superior officers and nobles are. Why are they not here to offer their peace?"

Sergeant Beda grinned again. "They might've offered you their peace, but they've already left. Once he figured out which way the wind was blowing, Duke Athelgar packed up and ran back to Torrlond. Most of the noble officers went with him, as well as enough soldiers to make sure he'd make it safe. The rest of us were waiting for you."

Rona frowned at him. "Waiting for us?"

"That's what the Prophet told us to do, my lady. He said to protect these lands until the time came. And when we heard your ships had run ashore, we knew it had come." The other soldiers nodded to confirm their sergeant's words.

"But why should you obey the Prophet rather than your officers or your king?" Earl Elfwy kept his hand on his sword's hilt. "Are you not still Torrlonders?"

"Aye. That we are, and we'll be heading home as soon as you all agree to the terms. As for obeying the Prophet, we owe him everything. Many of us would be dead if it weren't for him." The sergeant stood a bit taller and held his head high as if he were about to reveal his proudest achievement. "He laid his hands on me, cured me of the plague when I was a goner and no mistake. But what he really did, mind you, was change me for the rest of my days. Don't see things quite the way I used to. Hard to explain, and I've never been good with words, but I reckon at least a bit of that's spread to all of us."

Sequara was surprised to realize she liked the bluff sergeant. It was not just his devotion to Dayraven, whom he knew as the Prophet. He was a good man — someone's grandfather, someone's father, someone's husband. A man with depth beneath his craggy surface, who felt and loved and was loved. Accompanying this realization was the sickening feeling that, had Sergeant Beda been posted in Asdralad, she would have incinerated him on sight. Screams and crackling flesh and the smell of burnt meat surged in her mind, and she almost retched. She focused on the sergeant again, looked into his eyes, and saw in them that he was speaking the truth.

Queen Rona, however, still did not appear convinced, at least to judge by her frown. “The Prophet commanded you to cede Adanon and Caergilion back to their rightful rulers, and you are doing so in obedience?”

Beda scratched his beard and squinted a moment. “Might be he didn’t say it in so many words, your Majesty, but it’s what he wanted. We all knew it deep down inside. You might say we knew what was right all along, and he helped us to see it. And when word came from Lieutenant Edge, we all agreed.”

“Lieutenant Edge?” Adanon’s queen cocked a questioning eyebrow.

“He’s a sort of leader among us who follow the Prophet. He was his friend. The one who first found him, as I heard it.”

“And your other leaders — Duke Athelgar and all the noble officers — have fled back to Torrlond?”

“Yes, your Majesty. Excepting Duke Uwain. But he’s no Torrlonder, as you know.”

Queen Rona’s brow wrinkled as she glared at the sergeant, who shrank back a bit. “And where is the traitor?” This was the first time Sequara had seen anger flash from the queen, and she was glad not to be its object.

“He’s holed up not far from here in his castle with a few loyal followers. Not enough to offer you much trouble, your Majesty, but I reckon you’d want to deal with him soon.”

“Be assured, Sergeant Beda, we shall.”

Sequara shared Rona’s anger. She had known Uwain and had never liked the man even before the Adanese duke betrayed them to the Torrlonders, causing the deaths of King Balch, Prince Lelwyn, and countless others. But that anger was nothing next to her joy at what Dayraven had done in the southwest. He had freed them. He had made peace possible by conquering Adanon and Caergilion without a single blade, arrow, or drop of blood. She had always known of his beauty, and somehow he had given it to all these people. A tingling eagerness invaded every inch of her flesh. She could no longer wait for word of him, but she calmed her mind and mastered her voice before she spoke to the Torrlonder sergeant.

"And the Prophet? Where is he now?"

Sergeant Beda turned to her, squinted, and sighed. "He's gone, my lady."

"Gone?"

"Went to Torrlond with King Earconwald and the Supreme Priest Joruman along with an army. I reckon he'll fix things up there to make way for us. Leastways, that's my guess. Opinion is somewhat divided, as it were, on the matter, but the answer will come if we wait long enough."

Sequara kept her face rigid and held her stance even as the ground fell from under her. Dayraven had gone to Torrlond, where he was both in danger and a dire threat to everyone around him. She, for one, would not wait to find out why.

NOT A SOUL STIRRED IN THE STOUT STONE FORTRESS THAT WAS DUKE Uwain's ancestral seat. The front gate had been wide open, inviting Sequara and Rona and their followers to enter without opposition. The only creatures greeting them in the eerily silent courtyard were a few scrawny chickens and a forlorn old nag with protruding ribs. The latter gazed toward them with placid, cloudy eyes.

Surrounded by a group of warriors that Imharr led, the sorceress and the queen strode across the courtyard toward the high, iron-banded doors giving access to the largest portion of the fortress. Not a sound came from within. Earl Elfwy and his men formed a wider perimeter around the two women and their party, and each Ellonder kept glancing all around the courtyard and at the empty battlements on the walls above them.

Sequara studied the queen until Rona returned her glance. The sorceress whispered to her companion, "We must be wary here. There is death in the air."

Rona nodded in agreement, and then she turned toward Imharr. "Open it."

Imharr gestured at his men and singled out two. He stood before the group and drew his sword with his silver-scarred hand. His men followed suit, all of them poised for combat. The Ellonders too drew their weapons and widened their stances, but they kept moving their eyes everywhere. The two men Imharr had singled out approached the doors, and each seized an iron ring. At a curt nod from Imharr, they pulled.

The doors creaked outward, and sunlight leaked inward to reveal a large, shadow-filled hall. Imharr and his soldiers rushed inside with clinking mail and pounding boots, after which Elfwy and the Ellonders tightened their circle around the two women. Sequara and Rona waited without until Imharr yelled something in Ondunic. There was no urgency in his voice, but it was taut. Not for the first time, Sequara wished she knew more Ondunic and resolved to learn it. Rona nodded at her, and the sorceress followed the queen inside.

It took a moment for Sequara's eyes to adjust to the dimness. Dust motes spun in the wedge of sunlight illuminating the hall's center. A long table stood there surrounded by benches, and a high chair at one end waited in the gloom, behind which there was a large fireplace containing nothing but a bed of dead ashes. Sconces with unlit torches were mounted on the stone walls and stone columns. Tapestries decorated the walls, but only those the sunlight bathed showed their colors, while the rest appeared grey.

Imharr and his men had fanned out around the hall, but they were all looking in one place: up toward the large wooden rafters supporting the roof. There, dangling above the table, was the hall's only occupant.

Duke Uwain's eyes bulged, and his swollen tongue protruded from his lips. The little man's head was crooked to one side. Sequara reckoned if he had jumped from the rafter on which the rope was tied, he likely died as soon as the noose around his neck snapped it. Or, perhaps he suffered for a while, kicking and thrashing in the air before choking for want of air. It did not bear thinking about. Yet Queen Rona stood there a long while staring at Uwain's corpse with a frown and a fierceness in her eyes.

At length, Sequara leaned closer to Rona. "We should leave this place."

Rona nodded without looking away from the body. "Imharr, have your men cut him down and bury him in an unmarked grave. Then we march to Palahon."

THERE WAS LITTLE OTHER THAN RUBBLE LEFT OF ADANON'S CHIEF city. Hard by the River Maranant, the blackened ruins of Palahon lay alone amidst the broad plain. Bledla's dragons had wrought a most thorough destruction. The stubs of towers gaped open like mouths frozen in the act of screaming. Over the former homes of the mighty and the humble alike, not a single roof remained, and more of the surrounding wall had crumbled than remained standing, though somehow one gate remained, a futile mockery of the fortifications many had once thought invincible. In the middle of it all was a dark heap of stones, the jumbled bones of the royal castle. Save for the moaning wind, nothing stirred within it, as if the Torrlonders had banished all life from that place forever.

All too familiar with the destruction the Torrlonders left in their wake, Sequara looked on Palahon's corpse for a long while until she glanced at her companion. Not heeding Imharr and Elfwy's protests, Queen Rona had insisted on seeing the ruins by herself. She had relented only so far as to allow Sequara to accompany her. And so, the two women had left behind their combined army to ride ahead to Palahon.

The sorceress was glad to be there, if only for friendship's sake. Sitting atop their steeds on a slight prominence amidst the plain that afforded a good view of the distant city's ruins, they stared for a long while without a word passing between them. Rona showed no emotion on her face as she kept her gaze steady on her former chief city and dwelling place. Sequara respected her silence.

At length, Adanon's queen nodded. "*You* know what it feels like, don't you?"

Sequara believed she knew what her friend meant. "The despair. The sorrow. The overwhelming loss of hope that you can find the will to start all over again."

"Yes. All that."

"More than anything, the inability to wrap your mind around all the loss. And yet, you will find a way to begin. Because you must. That is all you need do. Begin. One stone put in its place. Don't think beyond that. And then the next. And the next. Before long, the stones begin to take shape again, and with that shape comes a flicker of hope for the future. A desire to create once again. Perhaps even someday the pleasure that comes with creating. And so it goes on. That is all we can do."

Queen Rona nodded again, and she was silent a long while. "I'm glad you came with me."

The two women remained thus for a length of time until the queen spoke again. "You'll ride north to Torrlond to find him." It was not a question.

Sequara sighed. "Yes. Before I can begin in Asdralad, I will do that. I do not know if I will find hope or despair there, but I will do it all the same."

"My blessing goes with you. You can send Khalan and most of the others back to Asdralad to begin rebuilding. You should have them there to secure the island as well. But take a handful of soldiers with you. The Torrlonders have all left, but you'll find plenty more of them in Torrlond, where most of them will not be followers of the Prophet. It won't hurt to have a few swords guarding your back. I will bid Imharr and a few of his best warriors to travel with you."

"No. You'll have need of every last strong pair of hands, especially Imharr's. And he is devoted to . . . Adanon."

Rona favored Sequara with a wry grin. "He is indeed."

Sequara managed a quick smile in return. "I will go alone to Torrlond. But you're right. I'll send back Khalan with instructions, and I'll return to Asdralad when I can."

"Perhaps Elfwy and his men would accompany you."

Sequara shook her head. "His mission was finished long ago. I'll tell him to return to Ellond and his king."

Rona pursed her lips and nodded. "You may tell him, but he may see it otherwise."

. . .

"Honor compels me to complete what I started, my lady." Earl Elfwy glanced down at the ground and then looked back into Sequara's face. They stood apart from where his men were setting up camp amidst the Asdralae army. Lieutenant Eanred and the others conspicuously refrained from even glancing in their direction. The handsome earl's mouth moved, but he left something unsaid even as his eager eyes expressed it.

"Honor? And what of duty? Your duty to Ellond, and King Fullan?"

"I'm fulfilling the mission King Fullan entrusted to me."

"That mission ended the moment we touched shore in Asdralad. You and your men have given more than you needed to. More than I deserve."

"More than you deserve?" He shook his head. "Not so. I only wish I could give you what you deserve." His face reddened, and he looked down again.

"I cannot in good conscience allow you to continue."

Elfwy fixed her with his gaze again. "Why not? We know the cause we serve. If you say you must go to Torrlond, then I . . . *we* will follow. I may be able to help in more ways than one. My mother is cousin to the wife of Duke Ethelred, the second most powerful noble in Torrlond. If there's something you need there, perhaps . . ."

Sequara took a deep breath. "Earl Elfwy. I must insist. You and your men will head south and sail your ship back to Ellond, where you are no doubt needed."

He held up his palms in entreaty. "I know you don't *need* me. I've seen how powerful and determined you are. Not to mention stubbornly self-reliant. But no one should face such dangers alone. A true person would never allow a friend to do so. And have I not earned your friendship? At least let me claim that."

The sorceress frowned at him. "You have. Of course you have. But you don't understand why I'm going to Torrlond."

"To seek the Prophet, you said."

"Yes, but you don't know *why*."

Elfwy smiled, but it was a sad smile and it did not reach his bright blue eyes. "You forget something. I was there."

"What do you mean? Where?"

"At Thulhan. In the battle, at the end. I'll never forget it. I saw the Prophet of Edan descend on the dragon. I felt the wonder and terror of him, like everyone else. And I witnessed the only person who could have saved us all turn him from whatever demon he had become back into a man. I saw you embrace him."

It was Sequara's turn to look down and redden. "He is . . . dear to me. I have not told you everything. I needed . . ."

The earl shook his head. "There's nothing you need to explain, my lady. I know very well what I'm getting myself, and my men, into." He grimaced and scratched his beard. "I confess I had allowed some hope to grow that you might return certain feelings that have taken root in me. Fool that I am. Edan knows you're blameless in this. You've done nothing to encourage such sentiments." He smiled, and this time the smile brightened his handsome face. "But any service I'm fortunate enough to give you comes with no price, no expectation. I know you'd do the same for a friend."

Touched by his generosity, kindness, and nobility, Sequara swallowed in her throat and nodded when she could find no words to answer him.

"Then it's settled. We accompany you to Torrlond, and you allow us to keep our honor by finishing what we started." Elfwy extended his hand to her.

She shook her head. "I shouldn't allow this. But I may need your help." *And I fear what I may find. Oruma and Anghara help me, in spite of what he says of me, I'm afraid.*

"Then take it. I offer it freely. And let there be no misunderstandings between us." His hand was still waiting for her.

Sequara looked at the hand, and then her gaze shifted to his face. She returned his smile. "Very well." She took his hand, and they shook for a moment before releasing their grip. "But you leave me in your debt."

"Not so. It's only what one ally or friend would do for another. You may have occasion to help Ellond at some point."

"If I do, I'll try to be as faithful as you have been."

Elfwy bowed his head. "At your service, my lady." He smiled again, but his smile could not conceal all his pain, and she wondered if it would have been wiser to refuse him. He was noble and good, and she was using him. *But he's right. I may have need of him and his men.* The guilt was one small burden to add to her great tally. She would pay that price and not look back as she bent all her purpose toward finding Dayraven. She had freed her home. Her people would rebuild. And now, not for duty but to follow her own heart for the first time since she was a child, she would seek something she craved with her whole being.

"THIS IS GOODBYE FOR NOW, THEN," SAID QUEEN RONA. SHE SMILED and embraced Sequara as they stood with Imharr in the queen's command tent outside the ruins of Palahon. When they released one another, the queen looked up at the sorceress and gave her a long, assessing look, like a mother seeing off her daughter and checking to make sure all was in order. "You and Earl Elfwy and his men have all the horses and supplies you need?"

"Yes. Everything is ready."

Imharr cleared his throat. "I and my men will ride north with you as far as Iarfaen."

Sequara nodded. "We'll be glad of your company."

Imharr was to convey a message to the leaders of the Caergilese rebellion, or to the restored Caergilese king, young Moradoc, if he could find him: Queen Rona wished to offer Caergilion aid in rebuilding. It was her hope to forge a new friendship with their neighbor where hatred had once existed. They had proven they could work together during the Torrlonder occupation of their kingdoms, and the queen wished to take advantage of the new peace to broaden their alliance from a necessity to a choice.

Imharr nodded, his cares written plain in his frown.

The sorceress smiled at him. "You're doing the right thing."

The Adanese duke sighed and shook his head. He managed a rueful smile. "Divided loyalties again. We've been here before, haven't we?"

"Your place is here." Sequara glanced at Queen Rona. "Dayraven would understand."

"I know. But I miss him. I wish I could help."

"You'll be of far more use here. Besides, you'll be working to secure the peace that Dayraven made possible. In this you honor him. And, if all goes well, you'll see him again someday."

This time Imharr nodded, and his smile, while still sad, seemed more genuine. "Thank you. Take care of Day, and take care of yourself."

"I intend to." Sequara turned to Queen Rona, perceiving the woman's grief and her strength. "Adanon will thrive again. You'll make a great ruler."

"Until Runan is ready."

In Rona's expression Sequara read her incredible determination. She nodded. "Still, he'd do well to heed you long after he becomes king."

The queen smiled. "I'm afraid I won't give him much choice." She reached up and brushed Sequara's cheek with the tips of her fingers. "And you, my dear. You will rule Asdralad well and wisely. Queen Faldira chose well. But do not fear to make some choices for your own sake. We cannot make so many sacrifices that there's nothing left of us." Her hand reached out for Imharr, who grasped it tenderly with his silver-scarred hand and looked down, almost making Sequara laugh at his newfound shyness. The man was far sadder and wiser than he had once been, and very much in love. Rona grinned at him before facing Sequara again. "How else can we serve our kingdoms?"

Sequara nodded, taking hope from Rona and Imharr's love. "I'll find Dayraven, and I'll do whatever I can to help him. Once that's finished, I'll return to Asdralad and give everything I have to rebuild my home. I hope he will come with me." Her hand went to her belly. "We shall see then."

"You will find fulfillment, I think. And at some future, more peaceful time, perhaps we will meet again and find we have healed along with our kingdoms."

"I hope to see that day."

Rona embraced her again and squeezed. "May the Mother and Father bless you, my dear."

Sequara returned the embrace with just as much warmth. "And you. May their strength and grace fill you and guide you all your days."

20

DISSOLUTION

Munzil crouched behind his shield just before three arrows thumped into its wood in quick succession, nudging his forearm back with each impact. Next to him, Gorm roared out orders he could hardly hear over the din of battle. Arrows whistled, warriors screamed in wrath and pain, and bodies splashed as they struggled and fell. The marshy water at the mouth of the Theodamar River soaked through his boots, and the muck beneath it clung to their soles, making every step forward an effort. The rest of him was sodden and dripping as well since he had fallen face forward when he first jumped from the ship, and he was still spitting out salty grit. A man on his other side sprouted arrows from his shoulder and thigh, and as he groaned and sank down, his blood joined that of all the others clouding the river where it met the Gulf of Olfi.

"Shieldwall! Form the shieldwall!" Gorm's deep, booming voice sharpened, and Munzil scrambled forward to lock shields with the warriors of the Boar Clan of the Fire Dragons, who had the honor of being at the forefront of the first attack on Torrlonder soil. The local Torrlonders had scraped together a decent enough defense, but Munzil could tell they did not have the numbers to hold back the Folk of the Tribes for long. More and more ships were landing behind theirs, and warriors at the height of their battle lust were pouring off them. Most would not get a chance to engage with the foe since the vanguard would make corpses of all their grey-kirtled hosts before long.

They would all get their chance later. No doubt the Torrlonders from these parts had sent messengers further inland, and larger armies would come to offer a better fight. These men shooting their arrows at them would all die whether they stood their ground or not. The bow was not a weapon with which to win glory, but, given their numbers, these local soldiers had kept their honor well enough thus far. Even the Folk of the Tribes had resorted to bows when they had to fight the holy men and women of Sildharan and Golgar.

He glanced down the line both ways to see if he could spot Skuld and was rewarded with a sight of her not far away, towering over the men on both sides of her about a dozen places on his right. With that assurance, he gazed forward and anticipated Gorm's command to march forward. No doubt the huge chieftain was waiting for the shieldwall's completion.

Munzil held his place as more arrows rained on them, but their shields sheltered them from the worst of the storm. An occasional grunt or cry told that one of the missiles had found its intended target, but most of them thunked into wood or splashed into water. At length, Gorm brandished his sword to give the order. "Boar Clan! March to the foe! Give them . . ."

A guttural sound choked out of the chieftain. Munzil turned toward his friend and brother, and he nearly dropped both blade and shield at what he saw.

An arrow shaft jutted from Gorm's throat, and blood oozed down his neck from the hole it had punched through his flesh. A pained growl twisted his reddened face as blood dribbled from his mouth into his braided beard, and it was too obvious he would never finish what he had begun to say. Nevertheless, Gorm thrust his sword forward, signaling the warriors of the Boar Clan should attack.

A series of gasps and a wave of stunned silence met him. Unable to conquer his shock and disbelief, Munzil too could not move or cry out. Gorm had always seemed too massive and solid for anything to hurt him, and he had been not only Munzil's constant companion, but also the foundation of Munzil's acceptance among the Fire Dragons. The chieftain staggered back a pace, splashing and stirring up the water, but he still held out his trembling sword, pointing it toward the foe.

A lone scream of rage and grief tore asunder the silence. Munzil knew whence it came even before he turned toward Skuld. His lover's stricken face turned away from her faltering brother as she finished his war cry, "Boar Clan! Give them death!" Skuld rushed toward the Torrlonders and did not glance back to see who followed.

Releasing a deafening roar, the warriors of the Boar Clan flung themselves toward the foe. Munzil screamed and sprinted toward the waiting Torrlonders, abandoning all caution as well as the safety of the dissolving shieldwall. Red vengeance and fury propelled him. Arrows buzzed by him, and one more slapped into his shield, but he heeded it little. When he left behind the water for the sandy shoreline, his feet quickened their pace in spite of his straining muscles, burning lungs, and heavy breaths. Not far away waited the line of their foes.

A WAVE OF HEAT FROM THE DISTANT FLAMES BRUSHED THE FLESH OF Munzil's face where he stood on the deck. Wood crackled. The reek stung his eyes. The wind shifted, tearing aside the veil of smoke to give him a clear view of the other ships wreathed in greedy fire.

The Folk of the Tribes had placed their few hundred dead aboard the vessels they had come ashore in. They left them with such treasures as they could, sacrificing a few captured Torrlonder soldiers in the place of slaves. Then, according to Surt's command, they set the ships ablaze. All save one. Flames devoured the thousands of vessels, disgorging billowing smoke that climbed and soared into a giant cloud that blackened the sky and hid the sun, casting a vast shadow over sea and land. Within this gloom of day turned night, the fires illuminated the faces of the Folk of the Tribes in eerie shades of red as they witnessed the conflagrations from the shoreline. The world was all heat and flames and fury, like the end of times, when even the gods would succumb to the violence of chaos.

Herein was a message. The Folk of the Tribes would not turn back until they conquered these lands and made their people into slaves. Munzil understood it was more than a gesture. It was a sacred vow.

The last and largest ship waiting to go up in flames was for Gorm. Munzil stood aboard it with a few others, including Surt, Skuld, and the other chieftains of the Fire Dragons. They had already placed Gorm lying face up in the center of the ship, just before the mast. The chieftain's eyes were closed, and he wore the blood-crusted garments and mail he died in, a testament to his most honorable death in battle. He had fought with the arrow in his throat, spraying his foes' innards with huge sweeps of his blade. Just ere the battle ended, he had grasped the shaft and ripped the missile out of his neck, and his life ended with the huge gout of blood that followed.

Returning from his memories of the battle to the present, Munzil gazed in silence. He had no words to express his grief. He reckoned the gods were exacting the price of his people's fate. *Always there's a price. No one knows the bargain the gods give him until his last breath. But with such losses the gods harden the Folk of the Tribes. They will find us keener than ever.* Gorm had been a great warrior and a good man. He had been Munzil's closest friend among the living. His loss was a terrible blow, but he had died in a befitting manner.

The chieftain's large sword lay atop his chest and stomach, beneath his folded arms. The members of the Boar Clan and even the other clans of the Fire Dragons as well as warriors of other tribes had given treasures to pile on the huge warrior: rings, arm rings, necklaces, torques, cups, plates, and coins — gold and silver that blushed in the glow of flames. Munzil had given an arm ring he had worn for years, one that replaced a prize he had won as a warrior of the Grey Wolves. His arm felt bare without it. There too next to Gorm was the boar skull that was the sacred token of his clan. Only the greatest of chieftains earned such a rare honor.

One other joined the tribesfolk aboard the ship. Surt held a Torrlonder, the local commander who had put up such a stout resistance with so few troops. He was an old but solid earl, as they called men of his rank. His face was bruised and bloody with one eye closed shut, and from his labored, wheezing breaths Munzil reckoned he had a couple cracked ribs. He was not small, but next to Surt no one looked big. With both hands and feet tied, he would have had trouble standing without the great war-leader holding him up.

The Torrlonder earl — Munzil did not care to remember his name — gazed with little outward emotion at all the proceedings around him as the chieftains finished piling the clinking treasure on top of Gorm. He must have known what was coming, but he did not beg or whimper. He said nothing. His silence was not resignation, for there was fierceness in his gaze. Munzil admired his courage.

When the chieftains began pouring jugs of oil over Gorm's body and the ship's deck, the Torrlonder earl broke his silence, speaking in the Northern Tongue and glaring at them all. "You savages will all die. You can't hope to . . ."

Surt's fist cracked into the man's nose, causing him to grunt and cutting off whatever he was about to say. As he teetered, Surt's other hand held him up by his collar. Munzil was the only one who would have understood the Torrlonder earl, but that was beside the point.

"Slaves speak not unless spoken to." There was no anger in Surt's voice. The war-leader was simply pointing out a truth.

The thick smoke from the other ships was drifting their way again in the sea breeze and stinging Munzil's eyes. It ascended to the darkened sky, a message — both warning and promise — that the Torrlonders could see from afar. The hungry flames licked and crackled and roiled, exuding heat in air-bending waves that seemed to beckon toward this last remaining vessel. It would soon be time to leave.

When all was ready, Surt nodded to Skuld, the new chieftain of the Boar Clan. Munzil's lover strode toward the Torrlonder earl with a dagger in one hand. She grasped his hair, pulled his head back to expose his throat, and, with a slight snarl on her lips, slit it in a swift motion. A red line appeared on the white neck, and then, as his heart pumped it, the blood sprayed outward to patter on the ship's deck. Surt dropped the body, which crumpled and thumped on the deck and then struggled with feeble twitches as the life poured forth and pooled beneath it.

One-eyed Valdur handed Skuld a lit torch, and they all made their way to the railing on the side closest to shore. They clambered down, but Skuld came last, tossing the torch onto the oiled deck before leaping down to join them. Fire roared to life, and they all watched the ship go up in eager flames. They stood there for a long while, until Surt turned away and the other chieftains joined him. Munzil lingered a while longer, but he said nothing as he stood behind Skuld.

His lover's shoulders shook, but she did not turn around. "Go."

Munzil dropped the hand he had been raising to put on her shoulder. He bowed his head, and then he turned to walk away, leaving Skuld alone to mourn her brother. There was no need to say there would be plenty of opportunity for vengeance.

IN THE DISTANCE TO THE SOUTH, FAR BEYOND THE LINES OF THE Torrlonder army, a white, jagged peak jutted into the sky, a lone giant overlooking the landscape. The Ormetberg. Munzil knew that was its name in the Northern Tongue. Few of his brothers and sisters among the Folk of the Tribes would have shared this knowledge, but they all would have agreed the mountain was a fitting guidepost for their march south to Torrhelm. Few of them too would have ever had a sight of the Torrlonder chief city, though they would have all known it was the greatest pile of stones human hands had ever made in all of Eormenlond. They would humble the Torrlonders by destroying it. Of course, before they reached Torrhelm, they had an army or two to annihilate.

The army facing the Folk of the Tribes across the plain was smaller than Munzil had expected, with not even a quarter as many soldiers as there were warriors among his people. They had learned from captured scouts that the Torrlonders were divided and spread thin, with some conflict in the northwest of the kingdom taking many troops away, and many more stationed in Caergilion and Adanon, far off in the south.

Whatever the cause for the foe's lack of preparedness, this would be a joyous slaughter. And even with the numbers in their favor, Surt was taking no chances. Realizing their superior forces opened an array of options, the war-leader had devised a strategy to outflank the Torrlonders on both sides and destroy them in a pincer movement with the least cost to the Folk of the Tribes. They would even make use of their bows, just as the Torrlonders would do, and Munzil felt no shame in that. Surt was wise. They would forget no lessons, especially the costly ones.

Munzil glanced to his right, where Skuld stood in the line of warriors awaiting the war horn to signal the beginning of the battle. His lover stared ahead toward the Torrlonders, betraying her eagerness with the intensity of her gaze. Her jaw muscles bunched as she clenched her teeth, but otherwise she stood as still and strong as stone. Beyond her, shields up and weapons ready, the hardened warriors of the Boar Clan were arrayed, and beyond them stood the rest of Fire Dragons and then all the other tribes. Munzil smiled.

Skuld seemed to sense his smile or his gaze, for she turned to face him. Her eyes were still red from crying out her grief for her brother, but across her face broke out the first smile Munzil had seen her wear since his death. It was beautiful and fierce. "This day, I dedicate the slain to him."

Munzil returned her gaze, and he gave her a slow nod. "As do I."

"Fight well, then. And try to keep up, old man."

Munzil grinned, and then the war horn tore the air with its long wail. Among the Folk of the Tribes there arose a vast roar, and Munzil's heart soared with it, taking joy in their freedom and strength. They marched forward as one folk toward their foe, to whom Munzil was grateful for giving his people their purpose this day. Their steps shook the very earth.

EARCONWALD LAY IN BED, STARING AT SCENES PLAYING THROUGH HIS mind whether he closed his eyes or not. Sleeping or waking, he saw them, and he was no longer certain if he ever slept at all. He suspected it had been a long time since he really had. He was bone weary, but the visions that ever haunted him allowed him no rest. There would never again be rest for him. He knew that.

Along with the fragments of memories rushed all the associated feelings of despair, helplessness, sorrow, agony, and loss. Sometimes he grew uncertain whether he had lived them in truth or not, or if they were merely terrifying images the Prophet had seared into him. Either way, they were all his now. He could escape neither the images nor the raw emotions, forgetting for long periods who he was amidst the sea of horror swirling in his mind. Yet, even when he could not bring to his awareness his own paltry identity, the sense of overwhelming guilt never left him. For, though he knew not who he was, the memories screaming at him without ceasing would never let him forget that *he* was responsible for them. He was their author and originator. Oftentimes he even saw the man he recognized as himself in them, and these were by far the worst.

So he lay on the bed and whimpered like a lost animal, and his hands shook as they pulled at his beard and hair. His whole body trembled often enough, and he thought he knew why. It wanted drink. He had not touched a glass of wine for days and nights, which were all the same to him now. At first, he had tried to drown himself in drink so that he could stop the assault of memories, but it had only worsened it, unleashing them with a chaotic swiftness that made his heart hammer. He had then tried to kill himself by forcing even more down his gullet, but his body betrayed him by vomiting up everything, leaving him with a throbbing head still full of the images he so dreaded.

There was no escape. Only the unending horror. He was not certain, but perhaps that realization was what had prompted him to wander in here, of all the chambers in Sigseld. To *this* bed. It was stripped of its coverings, and of course the body was long gone, but the furnishings in the room had not changed. Even if they had altered, this place would always remind him of the murder he wrought here.

The deceased Queen Moda's memories did not occupy his mind like so many of the others. Yet, when he could recall who he was amidst all the other scenes of slaying and rape and callous brutality that no creature other than the lowest and worst of humankind would perpetrate, he sometimes saw her face as his hands were clutching her throat and choking the life from her. It was full of fear. Wide-eyed surprise. Yes. Death had surprised her. At the time he had enjoyed it. The erotic sense of power over her. But now he only obsessed over what it must have felt like to her. The helplessness and terror she must have experienced. Perhaps there was relief in there too. Her life with him had never been happy.

But no. Delusions were no longer a luxury he could indulge. He had murdered her. She had not wanted to die. It was that simple.

He lay on her bed just where her body had lain after his hands had crushed her throat, leaving the white flesh of her neck bruised. Her nose had been bleeding too from when he struck her. The bright blood had stood out on her pale face. He could still hear the wine glass shattering on the floor. The bump, bump, bump of her head against the bed's headboard. The gasp from her throat. Her stillness, inviting him to kiss her after he had mastered her — oh, but he had wanted her to live in that moment. Once, as a child, he had smashed his favorite toy in a fit of anger and then cried over its loss. For a moment he had felt that way about Moda, but then came the knock at the door. There stood the tall, white-robed man on the other side. The white robe with blood spreading all over it from where a glittering sword impaled the man.

"Your Majesty?"

Earconwald started and flung himself off the bed to land in a crouch on the rug. He shielded his eyes from the bearded man who had walked into the room without him realizing it. "Who . . . Who are you? What do you want?"

The greybeard dressed like a soldier frowned at him. "It's Earl Nothelm, your Majesty. There are urgent tidings that demand your attention."

"What?"

"Your kingdom is in mortal danger."

"My *kingdom*?"

"Damn it, man. The Ilarchae have invaded Torrlond. They captured or killed Duke Weohstan and Duke Heahmund. Killed or captured, it's all the same with those savages. The dukes' armies are gone. Destroyed."

"What?"

The man tugged at his beard as his face grew red and angry. "The Edan-cursed Ilarchae are marching *here*, your Majesty. To Torrhelm. An army bigger than what we have now protecting the city. A lot bigger."

The trembling took over his body again, and he found he could not speak for all the quivering of his jaw and chattering of his teeth.

"Duke Siric and Duke Ethelred have the closest armies away in Norfast. We must send word to them before it's too late. It may already be too late, but they can raise other troops and arrive in time to relieve us from a siege."

His head shook whether he willed it to or not, and he clutched his temples as a series of horrible memories jabbed him and sent hot pain through his body.

"Our armies in Adanon and Caergilion are too far away to help, but we must recall them all the same. The south is lost, but we've got bigger problems, and we can't count on the troops we have down there in the near term. Which leaves us with what we've got right now. We should be able to hold out here in Torrhelm, but we need someone in charge, damn it."

"Who?" He squeezed out the word, which emerged as a hoarse whisper.

The old soldier sighed, and his shoulders slumped. "Whatever it was the Prophet did to you, and however much you had it coming, we need you back now, your Majesty. Someone has to give the orders. The Supreme Priest Joruman won't speak to me. Refuses to see anyone. He's holed up with the Prophet doing Edan knows what. And *you*. If you won't take command, I'll have to find someone who can."

He flinched from a series of images — tortured bodies, the cries of children, the wailing of mothers. Whatever the bearded soldier had been saying fled from his mind, but he returned to hear the man finish saying something else.

". . . leave me no choice but to call Duke Ethelred here and bid him to take command. For the sake of the kingdom." For some reason, there were tears in the old man's eyes, and he looked more frightened than frightening. His voice began to shake. "When I was young, I was proud to serve your father. And when you came, I gave you everything I had. I never thought in all my years of loyal service to you I'd . . ." He sniffled and frowned. "The kingdom needs a king. Truth is, you've been a terrible one for a long time. I've wasted my life protecting you. I wish it weren't so, but there it is. Ethelred is far more worthy." He paused and squinted as he stared. "Edan damn you, do you even know what I'm saying?"

He shivered, and his head shook without him willing it to.

The old soldier scowled at him in disgust, and he placed his hand on the hilt of the scabbarded sword at his hip. For a fleeting moment he both hoped and feared the man would kill him, but the greybeard only said, "Ethelred will have to decide what to do with you. I'm done." He turned and strode out the door, leaving it open.

Earconwald wished the man had closed the door, but he did not have the courage to get up and do it himself. He believed there might be guards posted out in the hall, but he could not recall if they were there to protect him or to keep him imprisoned. So he curled up on the bed, moaning and rolling from one side to another. He shut his eyes and opened them in succession as he tried to decide which might provide him with a little relief from the relentless storm of memories. In truth, neither closing nor opening them helped.

Earconwald stood high in Sigseld, his white-knuckled hands clutching the stone railing of the balcony adjacent to the queen's chamber. A strong gust tossed his hair back as he squeezed his eyes shut to keep from peering down from the dizzying height and losing the shred of courage he had managed to muster. He steadied his breaths and pried open his eyes again to gaze outward. Torrhelm's usual smoke drifted and hovered about the city, but there was a sense of vulnerability, a waft of panic in the air. Even from as high as he was, Earconwald could perceive it was not business as usual down below, for the citizens had heard of the Ilarchae invasion, which had shaken their customary confidence. Once the barbarians reached the city, there would be no controlling the people. They would die like sheep. *No.* We *will die. We.*

So many souls waiting for death. Was that not the end of it all? The ceaseless memories slamming against his mind testified to this one brutal fact of the world. Cities and kingdoms were naught in the span of the long darkness. Nothing had existed in Eormenlond that did not succumb to it, and nothing ever would.

King Earconwald. King of nightmares and horrors. King of pain and anguish. King of nothing, not even his own mind. He whimpered and gripped the stone railing even more tightly, his hands slippery with sweat. He wore only his white nightshirt, which the wind pushed and bullied, whipping it behind him. With a grunt and a sudden resolve, he hauled his body up with his shivering limbs before he could question what he was doing. And then he was up. On the edge of freedom. His bare feet stood on the cold, rough stone of the railing as he crouched there. He raised his trembling body into a standing position, swaying forward and backward as the wind howled and shoved him. He grimaced when he opened his eyes and beheld the spires and domes glistening far beneath him.

The view from his royal residence had never so terrified and enticed him. On the verge of his kingdom's ruin, he felt the immeasurable weight of his sins like a vast force ready to tug him down, down, down. Yet, for a brief moment, the torturing memories yielded to the world around him, which unfolded with strange clarity.

On the turrets of the palace, blue banners with white-capped silver mountain and golden crown snapped in the breeze. From the oldest sections of the castle to the most recent constructions, Sigseld exuded a grand sense of history and solidity. He knew this for an illusion. Nothing was permanent, and even stone succumbed to wind and rain and ruin.

His ambitions were dust, the folly of swollen pride. Only fear remained. Desperate fear of the memories. Fear that they would go on forever. *Fear and despair are left to me. There is but one way to end it.*

He swallowed as he glanced downward again, and the vertigo made him tipsy as the impossibly distant ground seemed to drop even further away. His body shook with great violence, causing his feet almost to slip off the railing, and the wind provoked goosebumps all over his flesh beneath his nightshirt. Far below, the ant-like people swarmed in the vast maze of busy streets. Merchants and laborers, soldiers and thralls, nobles and whores — none of them knew him. None of them cared. When he became a pulpy mass of blood and guts on the cobblestones awaiting him, none of them would recognize what he had been. But he would serve as a message for them all. His life had been for naught. All lives were nothing and without purpose, except to suffer. There was no center, no meaning to any of it. History was a lie.

Monuments to the past were a mockery. The only future was futility. The only truth was darkness.

Earconwald whined and sobbed as his eyes followed the streets out to the thick walls and towers encompassing the city. The Ilarchae were coming. They would swarm over the walls. They would raze the proud commercial buildings around Great Cheaping with their pretentious columns and large windows. The Temple of the Way and Sigseld would burn and crumble. The barbarians would pillage and destroy the towering homes of West Torrhelm and the slums of East Torrhelm alike. Wealthy and poor would become slaves or food for crows. In the end, it mattered naught which. This mighty kingdom, the once dominant force in Eormenlond, would soon end in destruction, as all things ever had and must.

But at least there was something in all of that: He too would perish, and the nightmares would end. A crazed smile passed over his face, and giddy laughter escaped him as he looked down. The faraway street awaited him, like the light at the end of a long tunnel.

One foot left the railing, shivering and hovering in empty air.

Far below, the hard ground beckoned to him. A few moments of blurry flight, and it would all be over at last. No more torturing memories. This flesh-sack would be broken and empty.

He swayed forward, and then backward. He screamed at his other foot to leave the railing, to leap into the void. Way down at the bottom, it was waiting for him. Freedom.

His whole sweat-drenched body shook, and he shrieked in the face of the howling wind. Collapsing into a ball, he tottered, closed his eyes, and fell.

Backwards. The floor of the balcony smacked into his back, and he grunted as its stones punched the air out of his lungs. His cowardly body had betrayed him again. He curled into a fetal tuck and drooled and wailed as he pulled his hair and beard. Rolling onto his hands and knees, he beat the stone floor with his fists. When his hands hurt too much to carry on, he sobbed and retched for a long while until his breaths calmed into a steady wheeze.

Earconwald looked up and started.

A pair of guards stood at the entrance to the balcony. Beneath their helms, they stared at him with blank gazes. How long had they been there? Had they seen him perched on the railing? If they had, why had they not moved to save him? Was it not their sacred duty to protect him?

Amidst the haunting memories and images of suffering playing out before his eyes, a thought crossed his mind: These men wanted him dead.

There was a time when all dwellers of Torrlond had adored him. His soldiers worshipped him, and his subjects loved him as their communal father. But these men with their dull stares regarded him with no effort to conceal their contempt. They had not shoved him over the edge, true, but they had also not rushed over to save him either. They had *hoped* he would throw himself over and rid them of his repulsive presence.

"I know who you are." Earconwald sneered at them. "You think I don't know, don't you? You're Nothelm's men. He sent you, didn't he? To watch. To watch me die." He shook his head, and his shivering grew so violent that he could no longer speak between his chattering teeth.

Without a word, the two guards turned away and walked back into the queen's chamber, leaving the trembling King of Torrlond alone on the balcony.

DEEP BENEATH SIGSELD, IN THE BOWELS OF THE EARTH, THE Prophet of Edan sat alone in a cell. The cell was small and damp, with tiny rivulets of moisture running down the rough, rocky walls. There was a musty pallet for sleeping on as well as a small table with two chairs. Atop the table burned a sufficient number of candles to illuminate the cell, and several unlit candles lay beside them. On the floor lay chains that were affixed to the wall. Though he had requested this cell, he had no wish to wear those chains. There was also a smaller adjacent chamber with a hole in the floor for relieving himself. He had almost no appetite, but a silent guard came at regular intervals with a trencher of food and a pitcher of clean water. When the guard departed in haste, he always locked the door from the outside, inserting one of his jingling keys into the lock and producing a loud click.

He allowed the fearful guard his little illusion, as if such a thing as a lock could make a difference. As if such a thing as wood or iron or stone could contain him. It would be as easy as a thought to destroy the door, or to seize the guard's mind or his very life, and make his way to the surface, where his fate awaited him. For that matter, he could float through and above this prison in the world of forms as if it did not exist and master every human crawling on the streets above and huddling in the imaginary protection of their homes. Yet the mortal within him strove with all the little shreds left of him to keep from doing these things. The mortal wanted to stay down there for as long as he could. But it would not be long now, even as mortals measured these things, and so he waited.

The mortal, on the other hand, struggled. He strained to pay as little heed to the guard as possible when he came, shutting his senses to the man's emotions, and he ignored the sparse details of the cell. He sat on the pallet with his feet on the cold stone floor, clutching his head in his hands. Deep beneath the land's surface, he was much further from the myriad people milling about in the city above. Torrhelm was teeming with them. Through the tons and tons of rock above him, he could still feel them, though they were somewhat muffled, allowing him to withstand the insistent whispers just a little longer. Their energy tugged at him with a desire older than time, a longing that the fleeting flesh-and-bone vessels containing that energy could never have consciously understood.

Every voice, every emotion was a vibration on the vast web of which they were all a part. Though they knew it not, he and they were one, as they always had been and would be throughout every world and time. It would be so easy to answer their call and remind them. So many souls, and all he needed to do was reach out to end their struggling and suffering. If only they knew what a relief it would be to stop playing the game, to stop hiding from what they were. With every breath they deluded themselves, and only their last would bring them the truth. Even in the depths of this cell, he detected their rising panic as some vast threat approached the city. Life, the breakage of eternity into time, was full of such threats and such fears. He could put a stop to it all for them.

The Prophet's hand rose and trembled, and he gritted his teeth before the hand lurched back to his head and grasped it, as if that flesh could contain what dwelled within. It would not be long now. It had been a magnificent struggle, one that lasted far longer than it should have, but it would end soon. The mortal in him might endure as long as it would take for the hidden sun to rise and fall only a few more times. Perhaps only once more. Perhaps not even that long. And then, he would fulfill his purpose. Once the mortal was gone, he would be free to take them all away.

The mortal had wanted to do otherwise. He had come here to make peace. He had convinced himself he could use the power to help the people of this kingdom to do right — as if there really were a difference between right and wrong, good and evil, light and dark, or life and death — and not only free those they had warred upon, but also to help them rebuild their lives. That would never happen, he knew. It was not in the nature of such creatures. But it suited him to be here, for the mortal's desire had led him to a place where he could bring peace to so many more, and he could bring this large dwelling place, this cancerous growth, back in harmony with the soil, the grass, the trees, the river, and the air.

This city, Torrhelm, was full of souls. It was a concentration of warped energy, a large and complex lifeform composed of so many parts. These agonized parts could not see what they were, so attached were they to their flesh, and their collective agony was what created this place. Each and every one grasped onto the misery, so frightened of what was coming. He would take it all away.

The mortal in him strained with a burst of effort, and his limbs shook as he groaned. It fascinated him. He thought he had understood mortals well enough — their fear, their attachment, their vision little different from that of worms or any of the other creatures they fancied themselves separate from and even superior to. This man, however, did not struggle for his own sake. He fought for some misguided notion that life existed for a purpose, that others deserved a chance to create and pursue what little beauty they could find amidst all the pain their attachments caused. To this idea he had clung with a tenacity that should not have been possible. It was not for himself that he feared, but for all the others. Of course, it was all one. Misguided the mortal might be, but he had come to admire him in a way. It was possible he might even think of him once he disappeared along with all the others, but he could never tell with such things.

Indeed, it would not be long. Pushing up air from his lungs and vibrating the flesh-cords in his throat, the mortal loosed an animal growl. There was one desperate hope left to him, but he recognized how futile it was. The man who called himself the supreme priest of the Way, though he believed in nothing the title implied, had offered to take the burden from the mortal. Joruman had his own selfish motives behind the offer, though he was trying to convince himself he was acting on behalf of life itself in his quest to defeat death.

The fool did not know what life was. It could not exist without death, just as light could have no birth without darkness. But the supreme priest was a mortal he could understand. Full of delusions and an inflated sense of his importance and purpose. Full of grasping fear. It was true that Joruman's interactions with the Prophet were changing him, but his real reasons for wanting the power had not altered. Still, as a last desperate tactic before the crumbling dam in his mind shattered forever, the mortal was preparing himself to consider Joruman's offer. As for him, he cared not. Had he been in control of the mortal's body at that moment, he would have given an indifferent shrug for all the difference it would make.

The mortal, who had learned others had once called him Dayraven but felt no attachment to or recognition of that name, made tight balls of his fists and squeezed his eyes shut. He was slipping away, hardly even able to recall what he was fighting for. Like a tiny pulse that faded with each throb, he winked in and out of awareness, and there was little left save his stubborn resistance. The mortal grimaced and dug in, and once again he admired such a heroic yet futile effort. He consoled the mortal with one thought: Soon it would end.

As he approached the locked door, Joruman gasped at the power rushing forth from the room and battering him as an almost physical force, like he was wading against a deep river's current. It was not something he had grown accustomed to even after all his interactions with the Prophet of Edan, and the power seemed to be intensifying. He took a breath and fumbled at the pocket in his robe for the key. Inserting it into the hole, he turned the lock and then opened the door, pushing it inward to reveal the Prophet's cell. Within on the pallet sat Dayraven, staring at the floor with his hands grasping his hair. He did not seem to notice when Joruman entered and closed the door behind him.

The supreme priest cleared his throat. "You needn't stay here in the dungeon, you know. I can have more fitting accommodations prepared for you."

Dayraven trembled, and he slowly lifted his head until he found Joruman with his gaze. The supreme priest almost stumbled backwards when those cold eyes pierced him, laying him bare and leaving him dangling over an endless, lightless abyss. His mouth hung open, but he found he could utter no word.

The eyes blinked, and a shudder passed over Dayraven's face. He shook his head before releasing a long sigh. "No. I must stay here." The young man's voice grated as if every word required an effort.

Returning to the waking world, Joruman forced a smile and stepped forward, but he could not repress the shiver that ran like a current along his body. He approached the table and gestured toward one of the chairs. "May I?"

Dayraven's head hung lower and did not rise again.

Taking that for a nod, Joruman grasped the chair and pulled it from the table so that he could sit facing the young man. After easing down onto his seat and pressing his palms together in a posture meant to convey solicitude, he waited for a long while, during which Dayraven did not stir. The supreme priest pursed his lips and nodded. "Not long now, is it?"

The Prophet sat motionless, but at length he looked up with half-lidded eyes that exuded despondency far beyond physical exhaustion. He gave a weary nod and continued to gaze at Joruman.

The supreme priest cleared his throat. "There's little choice, I fear. Before it swallows you forever, you must allow me to take the burden from you."

Dayraven's dull eyes continued to stare at him. He did not move.

Joruman waited a long time, and then he craned his neck forward as he narrowed his eyes. "Can you hear me?"

The Prophet blinked twice. "Yes. I hear you. I'm considering . . . your offer."

Hope sprang to life in Joruman, and his breathing quickened even as his chest tightened, but he tried to stifle the elation in his quivering voice. "Your suffering is needless. I could perform the spell at a moment's notice. And I will keep my promises to you. You know that. Caergilion and Adanon shall be free. I will do everything I can to lift up all people and all kingdoms, if such things will even continue to exist. And you may return to what life you had before. Even now, should you . . ."

"You don't know."

"Pardon?"

"You don't know."

"I don't know what?"

"What you're asking for."

Joruman closed his mouth, and then he stroked his beard and sighed. "That is true. I realize that now more than ever. I know you've searched my mind. You know my motives. My ambitions. I am subject to the limitations and desires of my kind. We are more than half animal, but *something* is emerging. The animal struggles toward it, crawling over hundreds and thousands and who knows how many untold years. What I seek: Is it not for the ennoblement of all? Is it not the natural progression of life? To want to *live*. And not only live, but to live enlightened, for as long as possible. Mayhap forever. Is that not the end of all this struggle? The one thing that could possibly give it purpose?"

The Prophet stared at him, but he did not offer any answers.

Joruman nodded again. "Death exists for a reason, I know. Up until now, our greatest minds have counseled us to accept it as the one inevitable thing. To lie down meekly when it is our time and go in peace. But what if death's purpose is to challenge life? What if death is calling to us, commanding us, saying, 'Conquer me if you dare'? Should we not rise to this challenge, no matter how puny our efforts may be at first? Is it not the ultimate mystery? Is it not what gives motive to everything our kind has achieved, all we've groped toward, blind creatures that we are, over the course of our benighted existence? And when we solve death, when we taste immortality, we will have left behind the animal and embraced the god. Can you not see it?"

The supreme priest was gasping for breath, and he relaxed his hands, which he had at some point made into tight fists. His voice calmed to something nearly as gentle as a whisper. "Can you not see it, my friend? This power that dwells within you — it offers the ability to peer behind the mystery. The elves, so far as we know, live forever. They are manifestations of eternity in time. My studies had convinced me of this, but after spending this time with you, I know it for true. Should we prove able to unite with them and use their power, we would share in that eternity. I know not whether I will master the power that it is in you. But you've carried this burden so far, and it has burned you down to almost nothing. It's time. Let me try. Let me at least *try*. There may never be such a chance again."

Dayraven glanced at the floor for a moment and then returned his gaze to Joruman's eyes. "The people. What do they fear?"

"What?"

"The people above. In Torrhelm. Their fear is spiking."

Joruman thought for a moment, and he looked up at the cell's ceiling, over which loomed so many layers of rock and soil. It was miraculous that the Prophet could feel what was happening on the surface. A shudder twitched his shoulders as he thought of such power. "The Ilarchae. A large horde of the barbarians is making its way to Torrhelm."

"What will they do?"

"The Ilarchae?" The supreme priest shrugged. "Destroy the city if they can. Kill everyone. Enslave any unfortunate survivors. But the walls should hold them back. We still have enough soldiers to defend the walls." An idea seized him, and he leaned forward. "And that is exactly the sort of thing we could move beyond. All the killing and dying and fighting. I know these barbarians, and there's little to distinguish them from wolves. We must leave behind the animal to enter a new world, one without such needless pain and loss. Only the conquest of death could achieve that."

Dayraven stared at him, and then he cocked his head as if he were weighing something he saw in Joruman.

Squirming in his chair, the supreme priest grew uncomfortable under that gaze and the constant pummeling of the power behind it. "What is it?"

The young man surprised him with a sad smile, and from his blue eyes radiated something that was larger than pity. It was an understanding, a connection that leapt out between them, giving Joruman a strange chill. Dayraven sighed. "I've seen her."

"Who?"

"The woman. You think you've forgotten her face. But you haven't. It's there, in the deepest parts of your mind. You've only hidden it from yourself."

Joruman's skin tingled, raising goosebumps all over his flesh, and he trembled as his mouth hung open. His mind groped toward a memory of his mother, slipping off the ring from her gaunt hand. The one he wore on his little finger. He was a boy again, longing for some way to save her, already missing her warmth that would be stolen from him. He looked up from her hand to her chest, which labored with its wheezy, shallow breaths. The veins protruded from her neck, veins in which the blood still feebly trickled, nudged along by the dwindling flutter of her heart. He took a deep breath before he began to lift his gaze higher . . .

Joruman started, flinching away as if he had grazed red-hot iron. The memory fled and slipped away into darkness. The supreme priest shook his head to recover from his daze. "I . . ." He looked at the Prophet, who still gazed at him. Conjuring up a hard smile, he composed himself. "Yes. You know. That is as it must be. But it changes nothing."

Dayraven nodded.

"The matter at hand. It grows more urgent with each passing moment. It will win, and you will lose. You know this."

The young man nodded again.

"You'll need to accept my offer before the end. You must see that."

Dayraven's body trembled, and he winced as he squeezed his eyes shut. The power that ever flowed from him surged with such violence that Joruman almost tipped backwards in his chair, but then it returned to its former strength. Joruman's heart was still skittering when the Prophet opened his exhausted eyes again. Almost the young man's face seemed to betray the cracks in his fragile being, behind which the vast energy and light loomed and waited for imminent freedom. Dayraven released a long sigh and regarded the supreme priest. "I will consider your offer. You'll have your answer soon."

21

A LIGHT FOR THE WAY

Abon feigned interest in the coppersmith's wares by picking up a pot from the cart and inspecting it with a critical frown, the sort that keeps a vendor from asking questions. Not that this vendor was going to ask any. He was a skinny, nervous-looking young man, mostlike an apprentice sent out to sell what he could before the storm unleashed its wrath. As if copper pots would be of any use against the invading horde. The fellow licked his lips and swallowed, the knob in his throat bobbing up and down as he gawked at Abon like the scarred shaper might be an early arrival from the Ilarchae. Abon did not blame him. Everyone was looking nervous and skittish these days as Torrhelm was simultaneously shutting down, swelling with panicked refugees, preparing for a siege, and buzzing with rumors about the Ilarchae and what the barbarians were doing to the villages and countryside on their way to the chief city.

Of course, Abon had no interest in copper pots at the moment either. It was just that this apprentice had parked his cart at a convenient distance from the street leading into Sigseld, King Earconwald's royal palace. They needed reliable information, and so, in spite of the danger, they had come here to get it. Among the many rumors about the Ilarchae and the end of times and everything else, folk were passing around tales about the Prophet of Edan being inside Sigseld. Most of the talk seemed to focus on how the Prophet had come to save them from the barbarians, and how he would call down dragons and lightning to slay them. Abon shook his head. If these people knew what was inside the Prophet — what he himself had felt in the Torrlonder camp when Dayraven seized his mind like a hawk pounces on a field mouse — they would be more terrified of him than of the Ilarchae.

He put down the copper pot and stole a glance across the way, where Galdor in his tattered, patched-up robe leaned his back against one of the old elm trees lining the street leading to Sigseld. Doing his best imitation of a tired and harmless old man, he was rubbing one of his calves as if it were cramping. A couple hundred yards away from the wizard, with spears bristling and swords ready at their hips, dozens of soldiers in grey kirtles stood rigid at their posts. At times their commanders barked orders, and some of them broke off to march in formation along the well-guarded street.

Abon smiled. The wizard had wanted to come here alone, but Abon insisted on accompanying him. It was not a safe place, and even Galdor needed someone to watch his back sometimes. Besides that, ever since Dayraven had flicked aside the wizard's attempt to reach his mind, Galdor had been jittery. After Orvandil had carried the unconscious old man back to the inn in East Torrhelm, they had managed to revive him. Upon waking, Galdor had seemed so confused that he did not know who he was anymore, and Abon had grown concerned that the wizard's mind was beyond recovery.

But the old man's babbling began to take on meaning, and Galdor returned to them, at length growing quiet and only muttering every now and again about the vast extent of the power pent up in Dayraven. It had taken a great deal more time for the wizard to smile as he was wont, and a bit longer still before he roused himself to take action. Not once did Galdor speak of giving up on Dayraven.

And now they were here, in possibly the most dangerous spot for them in Torrhelm, a place becoming even more dangerous with every passing moment, while the others waited for them at the dockside inn. The rumors they heard at the inn and elsewhere were at least consistent on one point: The Prophet was in Sigseld. But Galdor wanted to know for certain, and, if possible, he wanted to know exactly where in the sprawling complex Dayraven was. Once they had that information, they would form a plan for rescuing their friend from the Torrlonders. And saving everyone from him.

The wizard had told Abon to wait somewhere within viewing distance but far away enough to remain inconspicuous. That was not easy since the streets were growing emptier each day as the city locked down, but there were still enough passersby that Abon did not stick out too much. He was glad for the coppersmith's cart, which gave him some cover on this street of mostly closed shops. Galdor had said he needed to get as close as possible to the guards to gather what he needed, but Abon was growing anxious. It seemed to him a couple of the soldiers were glancing the old man's way and taking more than a passing interest in his presence.

"You won't find no bloody way out of Torrhelm."

"What?" Abon looked up in surprise and returned his attention to the cart. It turned out the apprentice had a voice after all.

"I said, you won't find no better wares in Torrhelm." The young man squinted at the shaper and nodded toward the contents of his cart. "No one makes a better copper pot."

Abon's shoulders relaxed, and he let go of his breath. "Oh. Right. They're very nice. But I was thinking of something a bit . . ."

The apprentice threw up his hands. "I know. Who wants a pot right now? That's what I said, but Master Birhtwold said we should all be brave and act like nothing's amiss. How do you do that, I said, when ten hundred thousand Ilarchae are coming to burn down the city and eat everyone alive?"

"Not *that* many, and they don't . . ."

"But he kept right on insisting, you know. Said the more hopeless it might seem, the braver we must be. Might be that's alright for some warrior, but I make pots, if you take my meaning."

"I'm sure I . . ."

"Edan only knows if we'll be around on the morrow, but if you do need a pot, you won't ever find a better price than now. And they are solid. Take care of 'em, and they'll last your lifetime." The young man licked his lips and swallowed again. "Even if you do survive the morrow."

Abon blinked at him. "I . . ."

"He'll take this one." Galdor appeared at the shaper's side and grabbed a pot from the cart with one hand as he tossed a coin at the apprentice with the other. The wizard thumped the pot into Abon's chest, and the shaper grasped it by the handle as he gave Galdor a puzzled frown. "What?"

"Come along now. We've got our pot." Galdor winked at the shaper, put a hand on his shoulder, and whisked him away from the cart and the apprentice, who was still gazing at the coin in his hand.

Once they lost themselves within the maze of cobbled side streets and alleys, Galdor spoke without looking at the shaper. "We needed to leave in a hurry. The song of origin I used no doubt attracted some attention. The place is squirming with priests. We're lucky none were about when we arrived."

Abon glanced around to make sure no one was close enough to hear them. "Well? What did you find out?"

Galdor sighed and leaned close to the shaper. "He's still in Sigseld."

"Any idea where?"

"Somewhere in the dungeons, it seems. Deep beneath the castle."

"The dungeons? Are you sure?"

The wizard nodded. "I entered several of the guards' minds. It took me three tries before I found anything useful. Two more before another confirmed it. But we can be reasonably certain."

"Shit. Then he's a prisoner. But how?"

"Not quite. From what I could gather, it was Dayraven's choice to enter the dungeons. He hasn't come out since he first entered Sigseld. The regular soldiers know little more than that. It seems only a few of the temple guards have any specific knowledge of his whereabouts, and only the Supreme Priest Joruman sees him."

"Well, we're pretty much fucked then, aren't we? Dayraven lost somewhere down in the dungeons, possibly in the hands of the most ambitious and manipulative supreme priest ever, ready to explode and suck away the minds of everyone in the city, with only hundreds, if not thousands, of Torrlonder soldiers between us and him. Not to mention the fucking Ilarchae arriving any moment now."

Galdor pursed his lips and nodded. "That sums it up nicely."

Abon stopped in the middle of the alley. "What do we do?" He looked at the pot he was still holding and raised it. "And what am I supposed to do with this?"

The wizard looked down at the pot, raised his eyebrows, and shrugged. "I haven't the slightest idea."

GALDOR GRUNTED WHEN ANOTHER HURRYING PASSERBY JOSTLED HIM without a look backward or even a hint of apology. Even without the crowd, he found it hard to concentrate. He was still putting pieces of his mind back in place after the encounter with Dayraven. Such vast power, and without even the intention of doing violence, he had shattered the wizard's being with the slightest touch. *I knew the illusion of my existence. There is no "I". "I" never have been. "I" am only eternity pretending to be the infinite variety of beings in the mask that is the world of forms. But behind the mask there is only one. Eternity hiding from itself. What a sublime game.* It was still disorienting to think about, and Galdor wished, not for the first time, he could just be done with it all and return to that eternity. *Return to Edan. And Arna.* He sighed, but then his attention jerked back to the present as someone elbowed him and the throng thickened even more.

Ever since they had crossed the bridge from the splendor of West Torrhelm to the grime of the East, the city's fear had taken on a sharper edge. Folk filled the streets, many running and a few frantic ones screaming. One man wandered too close to a group of soldiers and shouted something at them. When he refused to quiet down, one of the soldiers punched his face, and after he fell they kicked him and beat him unconscious while a woman shrieked at them. That did little to calm the witnesses.

The mayhem could mean only one thing. "The Ilarchae have arrived within sight of the city," Galdor said aloud.

Abon, who huddled close to the wizard's side, frowned and grunted. "Aye. We've landed in another fine pile of shit."

Galdor wrinkled his nose. "I must admit that East Torrhelm does give off a rather fecal odor, and the present crisis doesn't make it any pleasanter."

Through the agitated crowds they wove their way until they reached the docks closer to their inn, where soldiers with their weapons out blocked access to the ships even as the gathered sailors scowled and cursed at them. Upriver and down, other soldiers were raising huge chains across the span of the Ea to block access into or out of the city by the waterway. Much of the filth and garbage floating on the river's surface was already catching and accumulating on the chains.

"We'd best hasten back to the inn." Galdor shouted into Abon's ear so the shaper could hear him over the din. "But don't hurry overmuch. We don't wish to draw any attention."

The shaper nodded and plunged into the crowd, making a gap for Galdor to follow into. The two of them pushed their way through the sweaty bodies until their inn's façade greeted them above the heads. Before they reached it, the crowd cleared and the muddy street appeared almost vacant, making their path much opener. It was puzzling but also a relief not to have so many bodies pressing up close. The entrance to their inn was just a little further.

Galdor took a deep breath and smiled. "Ah, that's bet. . ." Awareness of the gift came over him like goosebumps over his flesh, and he peered down the street. A large troop of grey-kirtled soldiers was clinking as they marched toward the wizard and the shaper, which explained why everyone was bustling to clear out of the way. At the head of the column walked two white-robed priests of the Way.

"Shit." Abon grabbed Galdor by the arm and pulled him into the nearest place to duck into, a filthy little alley between their inn and the brothel next door.

Though he did not think the priests had detected the gift in him yet, the wizard was glad the shaper had the presence of mind to lead them away. "Well done, Abon. Just a bit further in, though. No point in taking any chances. We'll wait them out in here." They crept further into the alley and watched as the troops began marching past its mouth. The soldiers' boots kicked up dust as they stomped in unison, and their byrnies jingled as their commanders shouted at people to clear the street. Even as their clamor receded, the presence of the gift in the two priests dimmed until they were too far away for Galdor to feel. The chaotic noises of East Torrhelm's panic took over once again.

The wizard released a sigh. The next hours and days were going to be difficult to negotiate, and he had no notion how to get inside Sigseld. He was hoping the chaos of the Ilarchac siege would create an opportunity or two. He would need to be vigilant and bold, and a good slice of luck would not hurt besides. Perhaps . . .

Something unfamiliar tugged at Galdor's awareness from behind. He turned around. The strange sensation was emanating from a pile of rubbish in the alleyway. It was a kind of sickness that mere garbage should never have exuded. No. Not a sickness. Rather, an unnatural lack of something, like a hole in the world that should not have been there. But it was not a hole in the realm of forms. This was a gap, a wrongness in the realm of origins.

"It's likely safe enough now." Abon stepped closer. "My lord?"

Galdor took a few cautious steps closer to the rubbish pile. It stank of rot, but far more offensive to his senses was the terrible feeling that some sort of nothingness had found a focal point and entered the world in that alley.

"The others will be waiting for us, my lord. We should . . ." Abon stopped short when the rubbish pile stirred. "There's something in there."

Galdor frowned at the rubbish pile. "Not something. Someone. With a sort of wound I cannot understand or ex . . ."

"Gaaahhhhh!" The rubbish pile exploded upwards, and a filth-covered, starved animal emerged. From its throat came a raspy shriek before it bolted in a shambling but swift gait away from Galdor and Abon.

Abon staggered back a step. "What the fuck is that?"

Galdor frowned and stared at the hunched-over creature, whom the tattered remains of a grey robe covered. "A man. Or so it once was." Needing to know what had wounded the wretch, he flung aside caution and uttered a song of origin. "Druanil ecthonias di andyon dimniathon. Abu mihil inghanias mi rakhyon inlorathon."

Even as Galdor floated in the realm of origins, the afflicted man shuffled farther away, holding one hand to his hip and emitting a terrified whine. The wizard repeated the song of origin, and just before the man reached the alley's end, he jerked to an abrupt halt. His body shivered all over, and he unleashed a long wail before Galdor silenced him with a command to his mind. The wretch collapsed into a fetal tuck and lay trembling on the ground.

"Come." Galdor did not look back to see if Abon obeyed, but he heard the shaper grumbling and cursing behind him as he stepped closer to the man whose mind he controlled. While the wizard neared the quivering wretch, he gently probed deeper into his mind to look into the nature of his wound. A piece of him was missing. Most people, Galdor knew, had either no trace of the gift or such a negligible amount that they were not even aware of its presence. This was different. This skeletal, filthy shell of a human being had a hole in him, an absence or darkness in his mind, as if the gift had once been there but had been torn from him. "Impossible," whispered the wizard.

Galdor reached further into the man's mind even as he attempted to soothe him with assuring messages. *I'll not hurt you. Perhaps I can help.* The only answer was raw terror, but the man was helpless to control his body as Galdor held him in place. *Keep still. No harm will come to you.* The wizard crept closer to the part of the man's mind where the chasm waited. He drew nigh it . . . and recoiled as it struck him with a cold force. The man's shaking grew more intense, and Galdor could not repress a shiver that shook his shoulders and ran along his spine. "Worse than darkness," he said aloud as he gawked at the poor wretch.

"What's wrong with him?" Abon's nose wrinkled as he stared down at the quivering mess that had once been a man.

Galdor shook his head and took a step back. "I can't say. To know, I must take a further look at his memories. This will be painful."

"Perhaps you shouldn't, my lord."

"Not to worry, old friend. No permanent damage will come to me. I think. And I must know what happened to him. I've never seen the like." And with that, he plunged further into what remained of the man's mind.

Loneliness. Pain. Anguish. Galdor flinched as he seemed to drown in a swirl of physical agony and mental torture. The earliest images from boyhood were filled with episodes of older and bigger boys bullying him in cruel, humiliating ways. They had taken their toll, maiming his confidence, stripping him of social graces, and feeding his fear of rejection. Manhood had given little better, with assignments that mocked his abilities and held him down. Somehow, due to circumstances beyond his control, his failures followed hard upon one another.

One chance had come, but it too had ended in disaster. As a result, his backside and entire spine were aflame with jolts that traveled down his legs. These were from old wounds, back in the Mark, when the hag had hurt him and destroyed his prospects. But these memories were remote and faded. Far larger loomed the more recent terrors. He was in a place of darkness. His grave. Cold stones and the stench of piss and shit. A ghost in a white robe with a bright light boring into his eyes. Water dripping from walls and ceiling. A long tunnel. Running along with cold feet that slapped on rough stone. Cruel men holding torches and chasing him. Deeper. Deeper. Chilly water sucking at him, tugging him in. Suffocating. Drowning.

Further into the man's mind Galdor dived, where he found memories walled off and locked away. A glass of wine spilling on him. Staining him with deep shame. Resentment and envy mixed with hate and fear. Waking up to sweaty horror. The ghost ripping at him. The terrible pressure pulling at his head. The smooth, arrogant voice chanting a spell and tearing his brain out of his skull. Scream.

Galdor staggered backward, not knowing if he had screamed or if it had been the man's memory. Just managing to maintain control of the wretch, he retreated to the periphery of his mind and held him in place.

Abon was at his side, holding his arm. "Are you well, my lord?"

The wizard was panting for breath. "Worse than any nightmare. This man has been to hell and back. And his robe. It was once white." He looked down at the man, who curled into a tighter ball. "Wasn't it? You were once a priest of the Way."

A whimper and moan emanated from the emaciated man, the sound of a wounded and terrified animal.

"I will heal you as best I can."

Abon shook his head. "Why? He's a pitiful creature, but we haven't the time just now."

"I'm afraid I must."

"But the Ilarchae are here, damn it. We've got to find a way to get to Dayraven."

Galdor looked at his friend. "That's precisely why I must heal this man. He has information we need."

Confusion and revulsion lined the shaper's brow when he glanced down at the man. "What?"

"He's been in Sigseld's dungeons. And somehow, he escaped."

"HE'S MAD. DERANGED. FELL-ON-HIS-HEAD-AND-CRACKED-IT CRAZY." Gnorn tugged on his beard and looked up at Orvandil.

The Thjoth shrugged and narrowed his eyes as if sizing up the trembling stranger the wizard and the shaper had brought into their sparsely furnished room. "Been in a dungeon. Lost something down there. Looks a bit better now he's clean."

Gnorn frowned and sniffed before crossing his arms in front of his chest. "Cleaner, at any rate."

Abon and Galdor were helping the man into the room's one chair while the Dweorg, the Thjoth, and Seren leaned on the wall by the window and watched. It had been a long and tedious process to get to this point.

After they fed the stranger, during which time Gnorn had suppressed the powerful urge to retch due to the man's pungent stench, the wizard had paid to use the inn's small bathhouse and brought him there like a stray dog. Abon, Gnorn, and Orvandil had scrubbed him down, using several tubs of water to clear away the grease and grime and stench. Each tub save the last had ended up filled with brown, filmy water. The Dweorg could still catch whiffs of the madman's stink in the air or on his own hands or clothes, and he wondered with distaste how long its traces would linger. They threw out the rag of a robe he had worn — Gnorn had urged them to burn it — and dressed him in one of Abon's spare tunics, which fit him like a loose sack, and a pair of breeches, which they tied onto the man's skinny waist with a rope. This was all possible only after Galdor had possessed the man's mind to calm him down and heal him. Before that, he had shrieked and cackled like a forlorn and tortured beast. Now, he was dazed and silent, not saying a word as he hunched in the chair. The Dweorg wondered if he even possessed the faculty to speak.

"Anyway, I didn't mean him." Gnorn pointed his thick finger at Galdor. "I meant *him*. Oh, to be sure, the other one's missing something in the attic, alright. But it takes a special sort of madman to follow a madman, if you take my meaning."

"Who cares?" Seren glanced at the Dweorg for a moment before returning her intense gaze to the stranger. "As long as he helps us find the Prophet. Dayraven." The girl still sounded quiet and unsure when she said Dayraven's name, like she was trying on a shoe to see if it fit.

But the Dweorg did not doubt her fierce devotion to their mutual friend for a moment. She would have carried the four of them past a thousand guards down into the dungeons beneath Sigseld if she thought it would help Dayraven. He grunted at the stubborn girl. "I suppose you may be right."

With the stranger seated, Galdor looked up from his ministrations and produced a toothy smile directed at Gnorn. "You don't approve, Master Dweorg?"

"What's not to approve of? We're in a city filled with foes who would love to part us from our pretty heads, which is in turn surrounded by a horde of crazed barbarians ready to burn the whole thing down, and we're trying to rescue our friend, who may very well annihilate everyone concerned at any moment — *and* we're throwing in our lot with a mute lunatic."

The wizard pursed his lips and, after thinking a moment, he nodded. "Well, when you put it that way . . . Perhaps we are a wee bit desperate just now."

The Dweorg raised his eyebrows. "A *wee* bit?"

Seren stepped forward, closer to the stranger, not taking her gaze off him. "How do you know he's mute?"

Gnorn frowned. "He hasn't said a word. Not one a human being could understand, at least." The man sat there shivering and staring into the air, as if no one else were in the room with him.

"Perhaps because we haven't spoken to him the right way." She took another step closer and turned toward Galdor. "May I?"

The wizard gave her a gentle smile. "I've done my best to heal his mind, but he hasn't yet responded to our questions. You may try, but I'm no longer controlling him, so be careful, my dear."

Gnorn held his tongue, but he inched closer and was ready to spring if the wretched man so much as looked at the girl cross-eyed.

Seren took another few steps toward the trembling madman, who continued to gawk at nothing. She crouched so that her eyes were level with his. "I'm Seren. What's your name?"

He jerked his eyes away from hers to gaze at a different spot of nothing, and his shivering increased.

"It's alright," said the girl. "You've been through something bad. I can see that. Mostlike you lost something important to you." She looked at the floor for a moment before nodding at the madman. "I've lost some things too. My home. My mother and father. Some people took them from me. I almost lost my life too. I wouldn't be here if some other people hadn't helped me."

Gnorn cleared his tightening throat when Seren spoke of her losses. He knew the girl had suffered, and he vowed to do what he could to keep her from future hurt. He also reckoned Dayraven must have been one of those who had helped her.

"That's what we're doing now, you see. Trying to help you." The girl sighed even as the madman continued to look away from her and tremble while half his face shuddered and his eye twitched. "And I'll tell it true. We need your help too. Someone important to us, someone we care about, is in the dungeons of Sigseld."

The man's shaking became more violent, and he whimpered.

Seren leaned in closer. "I know it must be hard to think about. I'm sorry to remind you of bad things. I don't like to think of the bad things that hurt me. But we need your help. Our friend may be trapped down there. If you've been there, and if you know a way out, we'd be grateful if you'd tell us about it. That's all. We just want to know that. Nothing else."

The man covered his face with his hands, and he whined into them as his fingers dug into his bald scalp. He huddled in the chair and tucked his body away from her as if he sought to disappear. She knelt by him for a while, but the only response she got was more of his trembling fits.

At length, Gnorn stepped up and put his hand on Seren's shoulder. "It's alright, lass. You tried. You did better than the rest of us could have."

The girl released a long sigh.

"You did very well, Seren." Galdor nodded. "I fear he's too far gone, though. Even were he able to speak, it's possible he has little conscious recollection of how he escaped. I'll have to enter his mind again and see what I can find. Based on the fragments I saw before, I can conjecture someone was chasing him in the darkness when he fell into some kind of water."

Seren looked up. "Will it hurt him?"

Galdor gave her a sad smile. "Not much. It will stir up his memories. I'll be as gentle as I'm able."

"I was there."

Everyone in the room started save the madman, who had been the source of the raspy voice, like rusted metal grating on gravel. They all gazed at him for a moment, and then they looked at each other, wondering what to do and afraid to do anything that might frighten that fragile voice away. Gnorn found himself staring into Seren's eyes, and he smiled before he nodded to her to signal she should be the one to speak to the stranger.

Seren made a couple slow steps toward the madman, who had stopped trembling but still held his face in his hands. She crouched once again to put herself on his level. "You mean the dungeons? Beneath Sigseld?"

The stranger's hands parted to reveal his scarred, bony nose, and he turned his deep-set eyes toward her. For the first time, he appeared in possession of his wits, but his was a bitter, fearful gaze. "Yes." He nodded.

Gnorn held his breath as Seren leaned closer to the stranger and asked, "And you escaped?"

A spasm passed over the man's face, and Gnorn feared he would fall back into a mad fit. But, after his eye fluttered a while longer, he regained control of his features. "Yes."

Seren breathed a sigh. "Can you tell us how? How you made it out?"

The man's tongue flicked out of his mouth to lick his lips, and he glanced at Galdor before returning his frightened eyes to Seren. "Are you foes of The Way of Edan?"

There was a brief silence before Galdor answered, "We are not foes of Edan. But many of the Way's priests as well as its hierarchy regard us as their enemies."

"You mean the supreme priest?" The man did not look at Galdor, but rather at either the floor or at Seren.

Galdor nodded. "Yes. Including the supreme priest."

The madman quivered, and his eye twitched before he grimaced and tugged at his wiry hair. Gnorn began to fear his moment of lucidity had passed. The wretch snarled and writhed in the chair, and then he stopped shaking. His vacant eyes once again stared into the air, and Gnorn's shoulders drooped with the disappointment that they might never get anything useful out of the fellow.

The wretch's eyes snapped toward Seren and gawked at her. "Then I will help you. But he must never take hold of my mind again." He jerked his head toward Galdor but did not look at the wizard.

Seren nodded at him. "He won't." She glanced back at the wizard. "Will you?"

"I gladly swear I will not." Galdor seemed to shudder. "Unless he wishes me to."

The madman squinted and stared at Seren, and then he nodded to her before grinning. "Very well. I'll take you to the place whence I emerged from my grave." He fell into a fit of cackling and coughing that might have been crazed laughter.

With a sense of dread, Gnorn knew beyond a doubt that, even if he could speak, the man was entirely cracked.

THE SIX OF THEM LEFT THE INN AFTER IT GREW DARK. AT LEAST IT would have been dark were it not for the huge bonfires the Ilarchae had lit outside the city's wall. They must have been massive, for their ruddy glow and thick plumes of smoke blotted out most of the stars. The stench of the smoke filled the night air and stung the eyes, and every once in a while the cries of frightened citizens of Torrhelm mingled with the distant roar of the flames.

Such were smells and sounds Orvandil knew well. His very blood seemed to respond to them with the old tingle that foreshadowed the lust and ecstasy of combat. As he paced at the rear of their small party, he fought back the urge to run out to the wall and climb it in order to gain a view of the besieging army. It was not his battle, but a large part of him longed for a place in it — enough of him that he gritted his teeth as he unclenched his tight grip on Seeker's hilt.

Ahead of him, the wretched madman who, according to Galdor, had once been a priest of the Way slunk and limped through the dimness as he led the companions along the docks lining the River Ea. Torches outside buildings gave some feeble light, but few other folk occupied the street in this part of East Torrhelm. A hush had fallen over the city as the Ilarchae burned and raved outside it. It was strangely peaceful and still within the walls, but Orvandil well knew what such calm foretold.

"Halt! Who are you, and what are you doing out here?" A patrol of Torrlonder soldiers materialized out of the darkness and clinked closer to them. The madman whimpered and collapsed into a shivering heap. Seren stepped backwards, behind Gnorn and Abon. Orvandil reached for Seeker, but Galdor raised a palm. The Thjoth relaxed and let his hand drift away from his weapon, just as Gnorn and Abon did.

Orvandil could not hear the words Galdor was muttering, but he knew they were part of the wizard's spell. By the time the soldiers reached them with their weapons drawn, the old man had ceased chanting and was pulling up the cowering madman by the hand. Galdor smiled at the soldiers. "Good evening, gentlemen. We're seeing about the defenses, and we're quite gratified by your promptness."

The puzzled soldiers glanced at each other. The one at their head, however, gave a slow nod. "Oh. Right. The defenses." His words and movements were a bit sluggish as he turned toward his fellow soldiers. "Leave them be, and let them go about their business."

The other soldiers gazed at their leader, a sergeant. The torchlight from a nearby building yellowed the red stripe over the king's ensign on the man's shoulder, and its sputtering flames gleamed from the helm that hid his shadowed features. As the sergeant turned for a moment, the ruddy light caught his eyes, which appeared expressionless and vacant. Orvandil allowed himself a crooked smile at Galdor's cleverness.

Before any of the other soldiers could say a word, Galdor bulled forward. "Thank you, men. Be wary, and stay alert. Blessed be the Eternal." The other companions followed the wizard, who pulled the cringing madman along with him. Orvandil came last, giving the Torrlonders one backward glance before the darkness swallowed them. He had itched to fight them, but he recognized the stupidity of his desire. Galdor's way was far better.

They continued on their way under the cover of night, none of them even whispering as they followed the shuffling madman along the stinking river, which was a deeper darkness oozing through the murk. Their wretched guide had recovered enough courage to lead them once again, though he hunched even lower and muttered to himself after the encounter with the soldiers. Something large appeared up ahead, spanning the river. As they drew nigh, it resolved out of the darkness into one of the stone bridges connecting East Torrhelm with West Torrhelm. The madman stopped when they reached it, looking all about him and making snuffling noises as he stooped over and shivered.

"Well?" Gnorn's gruff voice broke the silence as the Dweorg faced their guide. "What are you sniffing for? All I smell is the putrid river, whose odor you shared not so long ago, and the smoke in the air."

Their guide whined and cowered away from Gnorn. "The foolish Dweorg doesn't know," rasped the madman. "He doesn't know where we are."

Gnorn scoffed. "We're in Torrhelm risking our necks on a wild goose chase in the darkness, you miserable stick of a . . ."

"Quiet." Seren held up her palm and stepped closer to their guide. "Where are we, then?"

In the dim, ruddy light, the madman's remaining teeth flashed in a crazed grin. "The place whence I emerged." A giddy, high-pitched laugh trickled out of him. "From my grave."

"Here?" Abon pointed down at the ground. "On the bloody street?"

The madman shook his head even as the rest of him trembled. "No, scarred man. Not *here*. Under the bridge. In the river." He cackled as if laughing at some especially clever jest he had told. "I came out of the water."

Galdor stroked his beard. "On which side of the bridge?"

Their guide grunted and winced as he clutched his backside with one hand. With the other hand he pointed across the river, to the other side of the bridge.

The wizard nodded. "Yes. You would have come from West Torrhelm, of course. It begins to make sense. But how, my friend, did you enter the water in the first place?"

The madman lapsed into a fit of cackling and coughing. When he recovered, he nodded at the wizard. "You want to know? I escaped from my grave. When the man came. I used the chamber pot." Here he swung a hand and grinned before he gave in to another bout of hideous laughter. They all waited for him to resume. "I ran. Cold hard stone. The voices came. They came for me. But I went down. Down, down, down. Deeper into the earth, further into the stone. All the while there was dripping. But when I reached the bottom of it all, the deepest darkness, there was water on the floor, covering the stone. Through the door I went, as quiet as I could. But the cruel voices came. With flames. Bright flames to hurt my eyes. They wanted to take me back, drag me back to him. But I fled. Through the door, and further down, where the water grew deeper and deeper, past my legs. It was cold. So cold. But they were coming. Closer and closer, with their bright flame. And I fled further, until the water crept over my chest. Up my neck it slithered. So cold. The ceiling came down, and there was nowhere to go. But I had to flee. So I went on. Until . . ."

The wretch stopped speaking, and he stared into the darkness without making a motion. Even his shivering ceased.

Galdor reached a hand toward the man's shoulder, but then, seeming to think better of it, he retracted it. "Until what, friend?"

The madman jerked out of his trance with a shudder and stared at the wizard. "The floor disappeared, and I fell. The water pushed me. Faster and faster. Through darkness. A narrow place. I could feel the rock around me with my hands, bumped my head on it. The water kept pushing me. I thought I would drown there, saw my bloated body trapped and rotting there until the long years and the water wore it away to nothing. But then there was no more rock. It was still dark, but I was floating now. Free. In the water. Floating. Up or down, I didn't know. Just floating. Until my head broke the surface, and I gasped and drew in air. Quite a surprise, eh?" He pointed across the bridge again. "There."

"You emerged beneath the bridge. Are you certain?" Galdor did not bother to mask the urgency in his voice.

The man nodded, and he did not seem so mad any longer, as if so much speaking had unlocked portions of his mind. "Yes. Though the river's current carried me further downstream and onto the eastern bank. But that is where I came out. There's a hole in the rock deep beneath the bridge. Very narrow." He shuddered, and his body succumbed to its tremors. "I don't think I could find it again. But it's there." He nodded and grinned at them all.

Galdor released a long sigh. "The dungeons beneath Sigseld are ancient caverns, carved out by water. Our friend here must have fallen into a natural outlet. Sigseld is on a hill, and the water would run downward."

"Until it reached the river," said Abon.

"Just so," said Galdor.

"So there's a way out. But is it a way in?" Gnorn turned to their guide. "This outlet. You said it was narrow. Could *I* fit through it?"

"You can't swim." Abon grinned. "Or even look at water without going weak in the knees."

The Dweorg waved away the shaper. "Never mind that, you daft singer." He turned back to their guide. "Would I fit?"

The man's eyes narrowed as he scowled at Gnorn. "You're too fat." He pointed at Abon. "So is he." He nodded toward Orvandil. "Too big."

Galdor pointed at himself. "Too old. And even were I not, the current is going the wrong way for us. It sounds as if it dragged our friend here out. Perhaps no one could swim against such a force, even if the outlet weren't so narrow." He released a long sigh, unable to hide his disappointment. "I'm afraid you might have a point, Gnorn. It's too dangerous to think of using except as a last resort. Perhaps not even then. We shall return to the inn and think this over carefully. Perhaps the morrow will show us another way."

The glow of the Ilarchae bonfires called to Orvandil as he turned his gaze outward, beyond the city wall. "The Ilarchae are knocking at the door."

"We must hope the Torrlonders will hold them back a while." Galdor shook his head, and for a moment the weight of his cares seemed to bow him down. "For now, let us return to our room and think on it."

The others followed, and Orvandil was about to bring up the rear when he noticed Seren had not moved. The girl was still gazing over toward the western side of the bridge. "Seren?"

She turned toward him, her determination clear in her eyes and in the set of her jaw. "We *will* find a way in."

Orvandil nodded to her. "Aye." The girl was more stubborn than any of them. He put a hand on her shoulder, and they walked back toward the inn together.

Seren lay awake on her sleeping pallet in the dark room, pretending to sleep. Other than the sounds of her companions' breathing and snoring, the inn was quiet. Too quiet. The late-night eating, drinking, singing, arguing, and boisterous conversations of a few nights before had come to an abrupt halt after the arrival of the Ilarchae, and the usual flow of patrons had dried up. Only a few other guests remained, all trapped in the besieged city, for the Torrlonders were determined to let no one in or out.

She was a long way from Caergilion and everything that seemed normal. Of course, after the Torrlonder invasion, her home kingdom would never be the same, even if she ever returned to it. Sometimes she thought of her brother and wondered if he was alive. She also wondered why she was in this horrible place, if she had not lost her mind in coming here. But then she thought of the Prophet and smiled, and she knew she had lost a great many things, but not her mind. She would find him. And if he needed her help, she would give it, the same way he had helped her.

Sleep had evaded her most of the night, though she thought she might have drifted in and out of it for a bit and even dreamed for a while after they returned to the inn. If they had come to her, she had forgotten her dreams, though they left her with a vague unease — or perhaps it was just the anxiety that accompanied this place. She listened to her breaths for a time. She was waiting for her turn at the watch. Among their many precautions, the companions had taken turns staying awake during the nights in Torrhelm, and they always gave Seren the last watch so that her slumber would be uninterrupted. These four friends of the Prophet thought of such little things all the time, and she both enjoyed and resented how protective they were with her. She was not a child any longer, but it was still somehow a comfort, a faint reminder of the security — even if it was illusory — that came with being part of a family.

She had decided she liked each of them in his own way. Gnorn pretended to be gruff sometimes, but his bright smile told another story, and sorrow always dwelled alongside the wisdom in his eyes. Orvandil had frightened her like a giant, shaggy wolf at first, but he also seemed to understand her the most easily, and he hid tenderness beneath his warrior's skin. Galdor was both an ancient, rugged rock buried deep beneath the soil and a leaf blowing and twisting in the wind — the strangest and most wonderful person she had ever met, the perfect grandfather. With Abon she shared the mysterious and unshakeable bond of song, which made them brother and sister. And they were all the Prophet's friends. By knowing them, she knew another layer of him. With a mixture of gratitude and guilt, she thanked each of them in her mind, wishing she could have given them a proper farewell.

The night seemed to drag on, and she was growing impatient with it. After giving up any notion of sleep, she stretched her body and then sat up. Faint light coming through the window outlined Gnorn's silhouette. The Dweorg was sitting in the room's lone chair, still and quiet. She slipped on her shoes, stood up, and walked toward him.

"Still early," whispered Gnorn when she reached him. "Go back to sleep."

"Can't sleep. I'll take the watch now. First light's not far off anyway."

The Dweorg hesitated. She could almost hear his mind working and dreaded whether he suspected anything. She put a hand on his shoulder. "Truly. It's alright. I've got some thinking to do, and I might as well do it sitting as lying down."

After another moment of silence, Gnorn sighed. "Very well. My eyelids are heavy just now anyway. If you're certain you won't sleep . . ."

"I won't."

When the Dweorg rose from the chair, Seren took his place and wrapped her cloak around her. She watched him tiptoe along the creaky floorboards to his sleeping pallet. A few moments after he took off his boots and lay down, Gnorn's usual snore began to accompany Abon's. Those two could sleep through anything. Galdor also was a sound sleeper, though he often woke early. It was Orvandil she worried most about. The slightest stir could awaken the alert Thjoth, and she sometimes wondered if he ever really slept. She would need to be silent. She already knew which floorboards to avoid, and she was not as heavy as the others anyway. She remained seated a while longer in case she and Gnorn had wakened Orvandil. It was hard to wait. Her heart squirmed harder in her chest as she felt its beats count out the moments, and her palms were clammy.

At length, she could bear it no longer. She slid her body up and off the chair. She gazed around the dim room to see if any of her companions budged. Raising one foot, she took a slow step, easing her toes and the ball of her foot onto the floor. She leaned and let her weight fall on that leg, and the floorboard did not protest. No movement from her friends. The other foot performed the same series of drawn-out movements with an identical result.

It seemed an interminable time for Seren to make her way to the room's door, and she worried the sun would rise and stab a ray through the window before she reached it. But darkness still cloaked the room when her trembling hand reached out toward the door's latch, which seemed to beckon to her. Her fingertips brushed the wooden latch, and she grasped it. She edged it up, all the while holding her breath.

A shadowy form rose and loomed over her, and Seren just stifled a frightened gasp. The stranger who had once been a priest stood next to her. Refusing to sleep by the others on the pallets, the skeletal man had curled up near the door. She had not reckoned on him in her plans, and now he was standing so close to her that the stench of his breath brushed her cheek. He said nothing, but his stare was hard and relentless, and his few teeth flashed in a mad grin. He put his hand over her hand on the door latch, and she almost recoiled from his touch.

Without a word exchanged between them, the stranger raised the latch the rest of the way, nudged the door open, and gestured with an outstretched hand for Seren to exit. She nodded at him and crept out of the room. When she looked behind her, the stranger had followed her out and was easing the door shut. He turned toward her, grinned, and tittered before he put his hand over his mouth.

Seren stared at him for a moment before deciding he could accompany her, if that was his intention, as long as he did not interfere. She communicated this with a nod, and then she walked down the silent hallway, which a lone lamp illuminated. They crept by all the closed doors until the hallway opened into the inn's large common room. The corners hid in grey shadows. Sending up a lone curl of smoke, a few dying embers glowed in the fireplace. Not a soul stirred, and the place seemed abandoned and desolate.

When Seren opened the inn's front door, the predawn's chill breath caressed her face. She shivered. Outside it was still and dark. The giant bonfires of the Ilarchae no longer glowed in the distance. She stepped outside, and the stranger followed.

As she walked along the docks, the stranger shuffled beside her like a loyal hound. He said nothing, seeming not to care what she was up to, and she did not care to explain either. They kept quiet, and Seren hoped they would meet no patrols of soldiers. She had no spells such as the one Galdor had used, and she could not fight them. Her defense was stealth, and even that might be difficult to maintain if her jangling nerves got the better of her.

Though he had a terrible limp, the stranger was as silent as she, and she reckoned the life he had been living had taught him enough furtiveness. As it happened, they met no one on their path, and Seren could see nothing moving in the distance. East Torrhelm was still abed, but perhaps the presence of the Ilarchae outside the city would have muted any activity no matter the time of day. A few ships tied by hawsers to docks creaked as they rocked, and the cold, damp wind soughed along the river, but there was little other movement. Seren forged ahead, trying her best to ignore how rapid her heartbeats were.

This time it seemed a shorter journey to the bridge. When Seren reached it, she did not hesitate. She turned onto the bridge and began to walk across its stones. It was a large, solid structure, wide enough for several carts to cross at the same time. She felt tiny on it. She looked behind her to see if the stranger followed her. He was there, but he had become agitated. There was a larger hitch in his limp, and his body was trembling. He was also mumbling in his raspy voice.

"Where's the girl going?" was the first intelligible thing he said.

Seren did not know if he was addressing her, but she turned to him and answered anyway. "You might have asked earlier. If you want to, you can turn back. You could tell the others where I've gone. It won't make a difference now." She turned away from him and continued across the bridge, sticking to the middle. The river murmured beneath her. The stranger hesitated for a moment, but then he hobbled behind her again.

"The girl is nicer company than they are."

"They did help you, you know." Seren did not bother looking back.

"But what is the girl doing?"

"What I must."

She reached the western end of the bridge, grasped the cold stone of its parapet, pulled her body up, wiggled over its side, and jumped down. She landed on her feet and began to climb down the steep bank, holding on to the stones of the bridge's support to aid her footing. The stranger started rasping and hissing above her. "What is the girl doing? It's cold down there. Cold and wet."

Seren looked up at his shadowy silhouette atop the parapet. Light was beginning to bleed into the dome of darkness overhead, and the stars were fading. She needed to hurry. "Tell them where I've gone, will you?"

"But the girl mustn't." He kept his voice to a raspy whisper. "Come back up, silly girl. Come back to the nice warm room."

"I can't. I told you, I must do this. I must help to free my friend."

"But how? There's no way back into that place. The tunnel is narrow, and the water is too strong. The old man said so. The girl heard him. Too dangerous. Not possible at all."

"Don't worry. It'll be just like Crag Isle back home."

"What is . . . ?" He shook his head. "It's not like anything, silly girl. It's dark and cold. The girl will drown and stay forever in the chilly water until her body rots. It will be her grave."

"You've never seen me swim. Len and Tob could tell you . . . Well, not Len anymore."

"Who is Len? Who is Tob?"

"Never mind. Just tell the others where I've gone. Alright?"

The stranger hissed, and to Seren's surprise, he began to clamber up and over the high parapet.

"What are you doing?"

The stranger did not answer, but he hauled himself over the stones with a series of grunts and groans. His legs dangled over the parapet's edge, and in an awkward tumble, he fell down on the other side onto the top of the bank, landing with a grunt on his back. After wheezing and spluttering and kicking his legs in the air, he managed to rise. He climbed down the bank, wincing and holding his backside with one hand as he clutched the support's stones with his other hand. Just before he reached her, he nearly tottered over and rolled into Seren, who caught him and held him up.

With heaving breaths, he looked into her face and grasped her hands. "The girl mustn't do this. She will die. Please. Come back. The room is nice. It is warm. There will be food. Down there is only cold and wet and dark. The girl will *be* food. For fish. They will suck at her bones. Come back."

Seren pulled her hands free. "I told you, I can't."

"But . . ." The stranger's mouth gaped open as if he were about to say something or scream, but no further sound came out. A fit of trembling seized him, and his eyes went wide before he jerked backwards and fell on his back. Seren wondered what she had done to frighten him, but then she realized he was not gawking at her, but rather at something beyond her. She turned around.

Across the river, on the eastern bank, dark forms crawled out of the water. They crept up onto docks, climbed upon the tied-up vessels, and clambered onto the street. Hundreds of them. Moving in silence. Enough light had leaked into the sky for Seren to tell what they were: men, and very large ones if she judged them aright. Her voice caught in her throat, and she did not dare even to breathe as more and more of them surfaced from the river and swarmed all over the docks, making their silent way into the city. They must have been the Ilarchae, who seemed to have no intention of conducting a long siege. Thank the Mother and Father they were all heading up the eastern bank and creeping into East Torrhelm, while she was under the western side of the bridge.

She thought of her friends in the inn and wondered if she should go back to warn them. But it was no good. The Ilarchae would catch her first, and they were between her and her companions. Besides, she could not, would not, give up on her present purpose. There was nothing else for it but to press ahead and hope Galdor and the others would manage for themselves.

Screams shattered the early morning stillness. To Seren's ears, they sounded like battle cries. Mostlike a Torrlonder patrol had encountered some of the Ilarchae. There would be fighting now, perhaps a pitched battle in the streets. At least that would waken her friends. It was time for her to go.

Seren turned again to the stranger, who was quivering and cowering on the bank. "You must hide. Here, under the bridge. Don't let them see you. Do you understand?"

He remained in a fetal tuck, and his whole body convulsed with his trembling as he whimpered.

"Don't make a sound. They'll find you otherwise. Stay here and hide. I'll come back for you if I can."

He went silent, but he remained curled up in a tight ball.

She had no time. Seren hastened down the rest of the bank until she reached the edge of the river, which rushed by in a growling babble. The growing light revealed the froth skimming along atop it, and she wrinkled her nose at its foul odor. She could not imagine what sort of filth floated within it.

"Better not think about it." Seren removed her shoes and then her cloak, which she dropped on the bank. Standing on the edge, she smiled. "Ready, losers?" She inhaled a deep, long breath of the chilly air to fill her lungs. Then, she leapt.

Cold slapped her flesh. Dark surrounded her. The world became a wet pulse that roiled and pressed in on her ears. She grasped on to the bank to keep the strong current from sweeping her downstream, and her clumsy, numbed fingers slid along slimy rock before they found purchase. She felt along the rock for the gap that would tell her where the outlet was. She should have been able to feel the flow of water emerging from it into the river. The pressure of the river was a vast force around her, squeezing her body and threatening to collapse her lungs. Its current grabbed and pulled her. It was so cold that her cramped muscles began to feel remote and detached from her. She would need to find the outlet fast.

HE LAY ON THE COLD RIVERBANK, PANTING WITH HOARSE BREATHS and unable to rise. The dim world around him slowed and spun, or perhaps it was his mind that grew sluggish and disoriented. His heart beat so hard that his ribs rattled. His skinny limbs felt heavy, almost impossible to lift. The girl had left him alone. He heard her splash in the river, and when he dared to look down at the water, there was no trace of her. She had told him to hide. Perhaps he should do that.

Suppressing his whimpers as best he could, he grunted and forced his weary, shivering muscles to move. Rolling over onto his stomach, he managed to crawl, scraping his knees and hands on the stone. Under the bridge lurked deep shadows. He did not like them, for they reminded him of something he did not wish to think about. But he knew he could hide better under there, and so he crawled further.

It took him a long time to skulk into the shadows, and all the while he expected a hand to seize his ankle and pull him back. No. He must not let them catch him. He must hide. The girl had told him to.

At length, the darkness beneath the bridge swallowed him, and he wedged his emaciated body into a narrow corner, pressing his spine against the stones and wishing he could disappear inside them. He must not let them see him. He refused to look across the river again, though he knew more and more of them were swarming out of the water. He shut his eyes, but he could still see their dark forms creeping out of the river and grasping onto the opposite bank. There was shouting and screaming going on in East Torrhelm, but he did his best to ignore all that. He did not want to think about them. He wished he could erase the vision from his mind, but it was lodged inside there, and he could not snatch it out.

There was no denying what he had seen. The dead were rising from the deeps. They had all escaped from their graves like he had, and now they had come for the living. He shivered and trembled as his face gave way to a spasm and his eye fluttered out of control.

22

THE BREAKING POINT

Munzil's head broke the filthy water's surface, and he gasped for breath, sucking in air with a hoarse rush. After his ears popped, the cries and clashes of battle surged from somewhere within the city. The Torrlonders had discovered them, but he and his fellow warriors had made it without detection further than he could have hoped. Thus far the gods were with them.

He smiled. Surt's ploy with the bonfires had worked, proving an effective distraction to keep the Torrlonders from seeing the movements of the warriors when they marched upstream under the cover of night. In darkness they had plunged into the River Ea, swimming with its current. The trickiest part had been passing through the lowered portcullis of the river gate. They had approached it underwater in small groups, and the bars — wrought to keep out ships but not swimmers — were just wide enough to slip between. An attack on the wall not far from the river gate provided an additional distraction to prevent the guards atop it from noticing the groups of swimmers passing beneath them in the dark, murky water. It was a bold, improbable move, one of many the great War-leader had made, and it was working. It would work. Munzil could feel the will and the cunning of the gods in it.

When Surt had asked for strong swimmers for this mission, Munzil knew he would be among them. He was one of the few representing the tribes of the inner Wildlands, for the folk of the islands, like Marg and his Broad Eagles, half lived in the chilly waters of the north and throve in them. For them, had it not been for the filth in the water, this dip in the river would have been a pleasure. Munzil knew he was no match for their best swimmers. Among the Grey Wolves, though, he had won many swimming contests. But he had been younger back then, and, from the lack of company, it appeared he was one of the last to exit and leave behind the river. "Well, at least I'm still alive," he muttered to himself.

Still breathing hard, he grasped the wooden support of a dock and pulled himself out of the River Ea. He clambered up until he was able to clutch onto the dock's edge and haul his body over. Once there, he stood for a moment to gather his breath and take his bearings. The water dripped from him and pattered onto the dock's wooden planks, which were wet where his fellow warriors had already stood. He wore only his kirtle with his sword in the scabbard around his waist. No shield. No helm. No mail. No boots. Almost naked. That was all well for swimming, but soon he would be in the midst of fighting, and he doubted the Torrlonders would forego their shields and mail, let alone their boots. His teeth chattered, and he shivered in the early morning breeze, which probed him with its cold fingers. In spite of his exertions, goosebumps broke out all over his body.

Before him, the early morning light revealed a row of shabby structures across the muddy street. As a trader, he had been in East Torrhelm before and knew its squalor. He also knew it would be less well protected than West Torrhelm, which was why he had advised Surt that they should head east for their attack. So far it was working, but the grey-kirtled soldiers had come, and soon the whole city would be alerted. The Folk of the Tribes would need to smash through any resistance and get to the gate they had chosen as swiftly as possible. If the Torrlonders slowed them and gathered enough troops to surround them, the hundreds of warriors who volunteered for this mission would die without accomplishing their purpose.

The screams and din of battle rose to a higher pitch up ahead. A few other remaining warriors ran past him and disappeared into the streets and alleys heading into the city. He smirked when he thought of how Skuld would mock him for standing there dripping. "Right. Time to move."

MUNZIL GAZED UP AHEAD. BETWEEN THE ROOFTOPS OF THE LEANING buildings on either side of the alley, the ruddy glow of fire invaded the purple of the early morning sky, and the acrid scent of smoke wafted by him. Somewhere nearby, crackling sounds snapped over the dull rumble of hungry flames. The screams and ringing of steel were not far away either, and though he was eager to join the fray, he paused in the alley, where the recent fighting must have been hard.

Fresh corpses littered the ground. Blood pooled on the cobblestones and spattered the walls. Several of the dead were warriors wearing nothing but their kirtles, like Munzil. But others were grey-kirtled Torrlonder soldiers. Those that died on their backs stared upwards, gawking in wide-eyed surprise at the brightening sky. Munzil wondered why death almost always took folk unawares. Everyone knew it was coming at some point, and even the gods could not escape it.

He wasted no time entertaining this thought and bent over one of the dead Torrlonders, a man about his size with a nasty gash that bit more than halfway through his neck. Grabbing the man's still warm leg, Munzil grunted and tugged at the boot, wriggling it until it peeled off, and then he repeated the process on the other leg. He pulled on the boots, which resisted only a little before slipping into place, and smiled at how well they fit his feet. *Good leather*.

Pondering a moment about the man's byrny, he shook his head. It would take far too long to don. He did not pass over the soldier's shield, however, even though it had the Torrlonders' ensign painted on it. It might come in useful in a moment or two, so he pulled it off the dead man's arm and gripped it. He also slipped the man's long dagger from its sheath, but he paused before tucking it into his belt. Something — a small movement and a squeak — warned him to turn around, and he sprang up and spun with the shield up and dagger ready.

A smudge-faced child in a simple frock gawped at him from a doorway, with the door cracked open far enough for her to peek out. She could not have been more than five, and though her hair was blonde, she put him in mind of his daughter, his lovely Inga who had been gone for so long. Eyes wide and unblinking, she was taking in not only him, but also the whole scene of carnage outside her shabby little alleyway home. Munzil froze for a moment, and their eyes met.

A woman wailed from somewhere within the home. "Elba! Come in at once!"

The girl did not move.

Munzil lowered the shield and the dagger and frowned at her. "You'd better listen to your mother, little girl," he said in the Northern Tongue. "But then tell her there's a fire nearby. It'd be best to run for West Torrhelm. Clear out of the city if you can."

The girl's head snapped back inside, and the door slammed shut.

He stood there a moment staring at the closed door, imagining what the girl's eyes must have seen. If she lived beyond this day, she would not soon forget the fierce barbarian standing over the dead bodies and looming over her. Shaking his head to break the spell, he turned and hastened towards the sounds of battle.

MUNZIL SPRINTED THROUGH A BLUR OF MUDDY ALLEYS AND STREETS, scarcely glancing at the ramshackle buildings of East Torrhelm. More and more screams erupted all around him, some in fury and some in terror, but the citizens appeared to be burrowing inside the imagined safety of their homes. He flew by them as his heart pounded with desperate urgency.

The streets were not empty, of course. Knots of soldiers engaged in fighting with pockets of warriors from the Folk of the Tribes. Keeping his destination at the forefront of his mind, Munzil avoided them and hastened on. Once he tried to join a frenzied melee that was happening in his path, but it was over by the time he reached it, with all the combatants dead or wounded. He left them behind, forcing his lungs to keep huffing. Nothing mattered more than reaching the gate.

At last the narrow alley he ran along opened onto a broad avenue, whereupon the roar of battle escalated to a fevered pitch. He gazed over the heads of the combatants at where the avenue ended. Thitherward waited a large gate in the vast, crenellated wall surrounding the city. It was a looming, formidable structure. East Torrhelm's Carcass Gate was so named since it was the main route through which the butchers and tanners carted out the remains of the beasts they slaughtered. Even from a distance, Munzil could see the lowered portcullis on the gate's inner side. Past the portcullis was the stout wooden gate, reinforced with bands of iron. Surrounding it was the gatehouse, wherein no doubt many soldiers guarded the winch for raising the portcullis. Arrow slits dotted the gatehouse, and a wall of grey-kirtled troops surrounded the structure on the ground, spears bristling between their long shields. Somehow, Munzil and his ill-protected fellow warriors had to take and open the Carcass Gate. Its name was apt enough for the present occasion.

Piles of bloody and ruined bodies lay on the street cobbles. Too many of them were his brother and sister warriors. Not a few were Torrlonders, but the foe had the advantage of raining missiles down on the Folk of the Tribes from the height of the wall, making it nigh unfeasible for them to storm the gate. Not only that, but his fellow warriors had arrived with little defense other than their swords. Almost all were still barefoot. But many had taken shields from dead Torrlonders to fend off the arrows, and these were beginning to form a shieldwall facing the gate.

Fortunately, the soldiers up on the massive wall were also busy engaging with the scores of thousands of warriors commanded by Surt on the other side. The tribes were all concentrating their attack, which should have begun as soon as the fighting started within the city, on this gate. Still, it was only a matter of time before Torrlonder reinforcements arrived, and it was unlikely — mayhap impossible — the Folk of the Tribes could take the well-fortified gate from the outside without help from within. Munzil and his brothers and sisters inside the city had to rally soon. The alternative was death.

Not waiting to catch his breath, he rushed forward to join the shieldwall. It had become solid and well formed, but it seemed the warriors were waiting for commands as the arrows rained down upon them. When he found a place and held his shield before him, Munzil recognized a man of the Broad Eagles next to him. "Does Marg yet live?" he yelled over the din.

"Aye." He pointed toward a knot of warriors engaging with a troop of Torrlonders across the street.

"Go to your war-leader. Tell him to gather a line of warriors to ward our backs from the Torrlonders that are arriving. Tell the rest to follow behind us, and when we fall, take up our shields."

The warrior nodded and left his place in the shieldwall to run toward Marg. Munzil faced the warriors nearest him. "Folk of the Tribes! Stay together! Stay behind the shieldwall! We storm the gate! As one!"

Munzil's heart raced as they moved forward in lockstep, something the Folk of the Tribes never would have done not so long ago. Other warriors crouched and followed behind them. Closer to the gate they marched. "Stay together!" bellowed Munzil. "Steady!" He peeked over the rim of his shield. A score of archers atop the wall had turned to face them, arrows nocked. "Shields up!" A moment later, a hail of missiles punched into the line of warriors. Most thunked into the upraised wooden shields. At least two bit into Munzil's, the tips of their heads poking through the wood. A few cries of agony went up from the line of warriors, and others rushed forward to replace the wounded or slain.

"Forward!" shouted Munzil.

Arrows rained down on them twice more before they closed on the line of spearmen surrounding the gatehouse. Munzil gritted his teeth. "Take the gate! Hew them down!"

War cries surged, and the warriors of the Folk of the Tribes screamed as they hurled themselves at the bristling spears. The man next to Munzil jerked backwards with a steel point embedded in his neck, and blood gushed from his mouth. The long weapons impaled many, ending their screams in wheezes and grunts, but their deaths gave their brothers and sisters a chance to move inside the spears and hack at their wielders. More warriors came from behind to join the melee.

Munzil ducked under a spear thrust and leapt forward to ram his shield into a Torrlonder, who grunted and fell. At the same time, a thunderous crash accompanied the groan of wood, sweeping over the battle like the death scream of a huge tree when it tumbles. Surt and the others were smashing the gate from the outside with a battering ram. Even if they succeeded, it would do little good with the portcullis still down.

"Take the gate!" Munzil cried over the din. "Take the gate!"

Hope surged as a few warriors broke through the Torrlonder line and rushed the gatehouse. Arrows poured down on them from window slits, filling their shields and piercing their limbs. They rolled in agony before more missiles silenced them.

"As one! Forward!" Munzil cracked the face of the Torrlonder before him with his shield's boss. He stepped toward the gatehouse, and, holding his shield high, waved on the Folk of the Tribes with his sword. "Take the gate! Now!"

More warriors broke through the wavering Torrlonder line, and they formed another shieldwall. The buzz of arrows filled the air, and they thudded into the shields like hailstones. Munzil screamed and pushed forward until the storm came to an abrupt halt. He was directly beneath the gatehouse, staring at a thick wooden door. His hand reached for the door's latch, and he shoved his shoulder into the wood. The door did not budge. More warriors arrived next to him, one a big fellow with an axe. Munzil nodded at the axman. "Hack it down." He turned to the others. "Form a circle around him and see that no foes get through."

The large warrior swung his weapon, which thudded as it bit deep, but the wood was thick and banded with iron. The other warriors defended him as grey-kirtled soldiers attacked, but the axman paid them no heed. It took many blows before the door began to shiver and splinter. The warrior raised his axe for another swing, but before his axe descended, a shower of ash and sand bathed him from above, and he began screaming within the dusty cloud enveloping him. Munzil understood the screams since a few of the grains of sand had drifted to land on him and burn into his skin, stinging wherever they touched him. The shrieking axman's kirtle blackened and shriveled away. The flesh on his face and body had turned first bright red and then darkened and crisped, and it was flaking off in large pieces to expose the raw meat beneath. The poor wretch flailed blindly before collapsing to the cobbles and going silent. Munzil winced and looked above the door to the top of the gatehouse, where soldiers stood with another barrel of heated sand and ash to pour down on the warriors.

A warrior took up a spear from a fallen Torrlonder and, with a loud bellow, cast it at one of the two soldiers preparing to tip the barrel. It landed true, striking the man in the chest and hurling him backward. The remaining soldier tried in vain to keep the barrel from tipping too soon, and he toppled along with it from the top of the gatehouse. Man and barrel shattered on the cobbles, and Munzil jumped back as hot sand and ash scattered everywhere, forming another deadly dust cloud. Like the others, he shrank back from its heat until it dissipated. Blinking at the grit in his eyes, he cast aside sword and shield to rush forward and take up the fallen warrior's axe. The handle was still hot, but he ignored the pain on his palms. He screamed as he swung with all the ferocity he could muster against the door. Wood cracked as the axe sank in through the already splintered door. Three more blows shattered it, and he kicked in the pieces.

Munzil twisted aside just before arrows whistled out the doorway to pierce the warrior behind him, who groaned and crumpled. "Take the gatehouse!" Munzil yelled, and warriors poured inside, roaring and grunting as arrows punctured their bodies. More tribespeople dashed in. Steel clashed amidst the screams, and Munzil took up his shield and sword once again before rushing in.

Bodies lay everywhere inside the stone gatehouse, and a few warriors still wrestled down and hacked at dying soldiers. Munzil ran by them. "The winch! Take the winch!" He dashed up wooden stairs made slick with blood to where several bodies lay at the top of the staircase. With a loud thud, an arrow burrowed into the wall next to his face, and its shaft quivered there. Munzil roared as he rushed toward the bowman, whose hands trembled while he tried to nock another missile. The edge of Munzil's blade sliced through his helm and clove his head in half down to his teeth, which clattered on the floor before his body dropped like a sack.

Several other warriors ran up the stairs to join Munzil, who dropped his shield and sword to grasp the wooden spokes of the large wheel that turned the winch. "Help me turn this. You others, ward us." Two warriors joined him while the others watched the staircase and the ladder leading to the rooftop, at the top of which was an open hatch. From the roof came screams and the clashing of steel. If any Torrlonders came down that way, Munzil and his fellow warriors would need to slay them one at a time and hold the gatehouse long enough for Surt's army to pass through.

The three of them at the wheel grasped the spokes and threw their weight into it as they turned it. Chains beneath the floor clanked, and the planks under Munzil's feet vibrated from the rising portcullis. A massive crash shook the gatehouse from outside, startling Munzil and punching into his ears. Surt and the others were still ramming the gate. Munzil smiled through his grimace as he pushed. If the Folk of the Tribes broke through the outer gate, they would find the way open to them.

The warriors warding the ladder to the roof tensed, and Munzil looked up in time to see a pair of boots on the rungs. One of the warriors rushed forward with sword aloft to meet the newcomer.

Munzil screamed, "Hold!" Everyone froze in place. "What tribe is yours?"

The warrior descending the ladder turned around and grinned. "I'm of the Raven Eyes. You just beat us here, but we've had a hard fight of it on the wall, so I reckon we'll share the glory. The gate and wall around it are ours, friends."

Still gasping for breath, Munzil breathed out a long sigh. The first phase of their plan had worked. *Now for the hard part.*

THE RAVEN EYES, WHO HAD SCALED THE WALL NEAR THE GATE AND fought hard to take it, stayed with the surviving Broad Eagles and other island tribes at the Carcass Gate to hold it. The islanders had taken heavy casualties in the assault within the city, and the Raven

Eyes had also suffered great losses, and so those tribes, having won their share of the day's glory, stayed behind while the rest of the Folk of the Tribes swept through East Torrhelm to attack West Torrhelm. Munzil too remained at the Carcass Gate until everything there was in order. He decided to accompany Marg, war-leader of the Broad Eagles, and Bolverk, war-leader of the Raven Eyes, when they departed to report and seek new orders from Surt. After all, his place was with the Fire Dragons, and most especially with Skuld.

With a band of about thirty warriors, Marg, Bolverk, and Munzil walked westward through East Torrhelm. In the wake of Surt's army, the poor half of Torrlond's chief city had become a silent wasteland. Detritus covered the streets as if the place had endured a fierce windstorm. Corpses lay in clusters everywhere, most of them Torrlonder soldiers, while few were warriors of the tribesfolk, as if the Torrlonders had died in full retreat. Also, a fair number had been ordinary citizens, mostlike caught up fleeing with the soldiers. Some were children. Such was war's cost. Munzil knew this all too well, but he could not help sparing a thought for the girl he had seen in the alley. He wondered if she had heeded him and fled. Likely not. A few buildings also burned, crackling with flames and churning out dark smoke. All of East Torrhelm, with its rickety wooden structures squeezed together, would light up if no one tamed those fires.

"These are the Torrlonders' vaunted piles of stones?" Marg spat. "Such hovels aren't worthy of even slaves."

Munzil nodded. "East Torrhelm is a wretched place. But the western half of the city is different. It's there you'll see the largest *buildings*, as they call them. They are indeed sights to marvel at, though they seem cold and cheerless to dwell in."

The tall war-leader's brow wrinkled in puzzlement. "Why would the two halves be different?"

"The rich and powerful among them live west of the river. In these parts dwell their poor folk."

"They keep them apart?"

Bolverk smirked. "Yes. And that's why their leaders left this half ill defended. And also why they abandoned it so easily. They care nothing for their people, having no bonds as we do save for coin. Their division is their weakness."

Munzil glanced at the one-eyed war-leader of the Raven Eyes. He had never trusted or liked the man, who was among the most cunning he had ever met. "Aye. I reckon the Torrlonder soldiers have pulled back to the bridges to defend West Torrhelm. That's where the day's heaviest fighting will be."

Marg grunted and frowned. Munzil could see it did not sit well with the big war-leader that the Broad Eagles would miss the main battle. But they had nothing to be ashamed of. Winning the gate had been a great feat, and it had cost the tribesfolk much blood. Folk all over Eormenlond had considered Torrhelm's wall unbreachable. Bolverk, on the other hand, stroked his iron-grey beard and grinned like a wolf, or like a man who enjoyed knowing more than others, calculating the day's gain.

They said little as they walked along the abandoned streets, for the din of battle grew louder as they made their way westward. Closer and closer they drew to clashing steel and shouts and screams, and in spite of his exhaustion, Munzil found his heart responding to the noises with an eager beat. Over it all soared the death chant of the Folk of the Tribes, who sang to give themselves over to the gods and put fear in their foes' hearts.

Munzil, Marg, Bolverk, and their party took a turn from a street onto a broad avenue, at which point the battle noises surged. Up ahead, thousands of warriors crowded together where the avenue seemed to end, the site of one of the seven stone bridges spanning the River Ea to connect East and West Torrhelm. In the far distance, beyond the broad river, loomed some of the stone buildings Munzil had spoken of to Marg. The tall war-leader was gazing upward at them with his mouth hanging open, his scorn for shabby East Torrhelm forgotten.

The massed warriors were facing westwards, away from Munzil and the others, and they seemed to be waiting for something to happen, though somewhere beyond them steel clashed and smoke rose into the air amidst the general clamor of voices. Clouds of arrows whistled and filled the sky, speeding from west and east in opposing directions before raining down. No doubt a fierce but narrow battle was taking place on the bridge while the soldiers on one side and the warriors on the other awaited their turns to join the slaughter.

It was only a matter of time before the Folk of the Tribes smashed their way through one of the bridges. Once that happened, the Torrlonder resistance on the other bridges would give way swiftly, and the Folk of the Tribes could pour into West Torrhelm to complete their conquest of their foe's chief city.

Marg and Bolverk strode straight toward the bridge, and Munzil kept pace with them. The others stayed close behind them. The press of warriors hid the bridge from view, and no Torrlonders were visible, but there could be no doubt about the ferocity of the fighting going on. The clamor grew so loud that Munzil's chest vibrated, and his pulse quickened as the battle lust stirred his blood and drew him in. He could almost forget his blistered hands and the sore muscles in his chest and shoulders from the swim and the combat.

Marg approached a warrior and shouted to be heard over the din. "Where is the War-leader Surt?"

The man turned and took in Marg and Bolverk. He also glanced at Munzil and smiled in recognition. He gave a slight bow before pointing. "Two bridges northward."

It was too loud for conversation, so Marg nodded, and they headed back into East Torrhelm since the streets close to the river were clogged with warriors. From there they walked north and passed by the first knot of warriors they encountered. Upon reaching the second throng of waiting combatants, Marg and Bolverk told their followers to wait for them, and then they plunged into the roiling crowd. Munzil followed them, and as they passed through, he recognized most of the warriors as belonging to the Fire Dragons. However, he said nothing to any of them since it would have been difficult to speak over all the shouting.

Ahead, the bridge rose into view above the heads of the warriors. It was a massive thing of stone, a monument to the Torrlonders' building skill. Today, like a strong hand of the gods reaching into the world, the Folk of the Tribes were there to destroy and humble, but Munzil reflected that one day it would be a fine thing to be able to work such things as that bridge. They would learn from the people they conquered and become greater still. Somehow, though, they must avoid becoming soft and corrupt like them.

But first, they needed to take one of these big bridges. Surt would accomplish this feat. He knew it.

And as if in confirmation of this thought, the great man appeared ahead, surrounded by his chieftains and warriors, one of which was Skuld, the sight of whom lifted Munzil's heart. He suppressed the urge to rush to her and embrace her. She and the others were standing nigh the battle just out of bowshot, and beyond them rows of warriors stood in narrow shieldwalls, ready to march forward onto the bridge under the hail of arrows. Surt was wearing a byrny and held a massive shield on one arm. He was giving orders to the chieftains when he looked up and greeted Munzil with a bright smile. Munzil sensed something decisive was about to happen.

The War-leader of the united Folk of the Tribes nodded as he hailed them with his booming bass. "Munzil. Bolverk. Marg. You are welcome. How fare our defenses at the Carcass Gate?"

Bolverk stepped forward and grinned. "All is well, my lord. We left our warriors with firm instructions to stay alert. They will hold it better than the Torrlonders did."

"Good. Your tribes have done well this day, opening the door for us. It was a great deed, and the singers will tell of it."

Marg bowed. "Thank you, my lord."

Bolverk gave a nod, and his grin widened.

Surt eyed them both, and he glanced at Munzil before returning his gaze to them. "You've done much, but I have another task for you today."

Marg's bright blue eyes lit up with fervor. "We're ready, my lord."

Bolverk appeared less eager as his grin disappeared.

Surt's eyes narrowed, and his blade-like gaze commanded full attention. "Keep warding our backs by holding the Carcass Gate. In addition, send some of your warriors to put out the fires and round up the Torrlonder survivors in East Torrhelm. See that no harm comes to them. They are our thralls now."

Marg's face fell. "But, we could join you here, my lord. Those tasks are . . ."

"Necessary." Surt's frown cut off Marg, but then he favored the war-leader of the Broad Eagles with a hard smile. "Your morning's work won you great glory, and the rest of us have much to do to catch up. What's more, your tribes took great losses, and I'll not have you lose more until the rest of us give blood as you have. We shall try to match your courage. Does that sit well with you?"

Marg frowned for a moment, but then he nodded. "Aye, my lord. We shall do as you say."

Bolverk's grin had returned. "We'll put out the fires and round up the Torrlonder slaves, my lord."

"And see that no harm comes to them," finished Surt. He turned to Munzil. "I heard of your deeds this morning, brother. The Fire Dragons take pride in them."

Munzil bowed and just managed to hold back a huge grin. Surt's words were more than praise. He was acknowledging Munzil's place in his tribe. "Many sacrificed more than I, but I thank you, my lord." Munzil stole a glance at Skuld, who did not hide her smile as she beamed at him.

Surt placed his huge hand on Munzil's shoulder. "You too have earned rest, but I wish you to go back with Marg and Bolverk into East Torrhelm to help in their tasks. You know the Torrlonder's tongue, and so you will speak to our thralls and tell them if they obey, they will live."

Both relieved and disappointed not to witness the battle, Munzil nodded. "Yes, my lord." He paused a moment, and then he glanced toward the fighting before turning back to Surt. "Before we leave, will you tell us what is afoot here?"

The screams and shouts on the bridge spiraled into a frenzied maelstrom as steel rang out and arrows keened.

Surt smiled at Munzil. "Bring word to those who wait back at the gate: Before you return to them, we will have taken this bridge."

"You'll lead the attack, then?"

"I am War-leader. That is my place."

Munzil nodded again. "May the gods be with you, then, my lord."

Surt's smile disappeared, and his gaze threatened to bore a hole through Munzil. "They are, brother. You among all others know that. Go now."

Almost overwhelmed with the pride surging in him, Munzil put his fist over his heart and turned to leave, but Skuld's voice broke out over the din. "Not yet, little man." He turned to face his lover.

Skuld broke away from the others and approached him. She held a large shield, but she grasped him behind the head with her sword arm and pressed his lips to hers for a long kiss, during which she bit his lip. When she released him, she showed her teeth in a fierce grin. "Tonight, we'll celebrate our triumph in our tent."

The men around them chuckled, and Munzil too smiled even as his face reddened. He did not voice his worry for her. He did not tell her to stay safe in the struggle for the bridge. He did not speak of the chill that ran up and down his spine, a cold premonition that crept under his flesh along with the nerves and the thrill of being near such divine chaos as a battle. He knew the contempt with which she would have greeted such concerns. "Yes, chieftain. I'll be ready. Come back to me then."

She nodded and turned from him. Munzil gazed after her, Surt, and the others a little longer before leaving with Marg and Bolverk. The crowded warriors parted to make way for them. Before they left behind the streets nigh the dock, a war horn wailed, and a vast, collective shout erupted from the Folk of the Tribes. Surt was leading them to victory.

ON THE BALCONY OF THE QUEEN'S CHAMBER, WHEREIN HE OFTEN took cover from prying eyes but could not hide from the ghosts haunting his mind, King Earconwald hugged himself and gazed far out at the plumes of smoke rising above East Torrhelm. The same cold wind that plucked at his nightdress swept the dark smoke into a hazy mass that gathered over the city. Unblinking, Earconwald gawked eastward and shivered from more than just the wind. The end had come.

Torrlond had been the greatest of kingdoms. This city — *his* city — was the pinnacle of civilization. Generations of strong kings — *his* ancestors in a long line of unbroken succession — had built it over the long centuries into its present state, expanding and strengthening it into the mightiest and wealthiest center of life known in all of Eormenlond.

Until this moment.

On the cusp of certain ruin, the city and all the achievements rolled into it were about to slide into the abyss, whence there was no escape, not even the prospect of lingering in memory. This brutal fact defied everything the king had not long ago known to be true. The undisciplined Ilarchae should not have been able to fight their way across Torrlond with no effective opposition until they arrived at Torrhelm. The barbarians never should have been able to breach the city's wall, the mightiest defense ever to have shielded any dwelling place. They should not have been there at all. They belonged far off in the desolate Wildlands, or invading some other, weaker, more corrupt kingdom.

Yet here they were, teeming within the city, having taken the eastern half the morning after their arrival, without even the need for a siege. All that stood between the proud edifices of West Torrhelm and complete destruction was the defense of seven bridges. On such a thin thread hung everything. It would snap.

The Torrlonder soldiers fighting at the bridges would fall. The triumphant Ilarchae would rave and burn. Like the kingdoms of Sildharan and Golgar in the east, Torrlond would turn to dust. It was not how it was supposed to be. *He* was supposed to have been the ruler of all of Eormenlond, not some nasty barbarian with no notion of what civilization meant — who probably could not tell the difference between a fine wine and a flask of horse piss. He would have been the center of the most magnificent empire, throughout which the people would have worshipped him. What would the wanton Ilarchae put in his place? Desolation. They knew nothing else. He would have built great monuments and tall buildings, but now of his magnificent city there would remain only ruins.

The saddest thing was he did not give a damn. Not about any of it. All he wanted was to rid his mind of the voices and images that were his constant companions. They haunted him within his shredded psyche, bequeathing him their nightmares and pain. The slaughter and rape and violence and anguish and dying again and again and again until there was nothing else. How many times had he died, only to find the nightmare beginning anew? How many horrors had he witnessed? Not only witnessed, but *experienced*, so that they were part of him now.

And these damned Ilarchae had come to create more of it. It was too much to bear. He pressed his hands against his temples and groaned as he trembled at all the imminent suffering. It would all worm its way into his skull, taunting him with his impotence and bleeding into his memories until he lived every agonized moment over and over for eternity. He had to stop it. But what could he do? What could one man do against so much brute force gathered into one place? It would take a man of supremely commanding stature, one with the minds of the multitudes in his grasp, to halt the advance of the barbarians. He squeezed his eyes shut, and he whined as the tormented voices wailed and the images of horror loomed before him. He groaned and growled, and the growl grew in volume until it became a long, hoarse scream that the howling wind seemed to carry over the whole city.

And then it happened. At the end of that scream, it flashed in his mind — the insight he had been unknowingly groping toward through all the endless layers of anguish. Stillness asserted itself all around him. For the first time, freedom and victory appeared like a pinprick of light at the end of his vast, dark misery.

Earconwald's mouth hung open, and his hands drooped to his sides. He stood on the balcony with a vacant stare on his face, and his trembling left him for a short time. The minds of the multitudes. Were they not within him? Perhaps this was the reason the Prophet had inserted them. It was for this moment. He was the conduit, and he would channel all the suffering, so that they could see. He would show the Ilarchae how wrong it was to create such pain. He would come before them, and he would give commands. *See. Learn from me. You must not do this thing, else it will haunt you forever.* Was he not still king? Could he not give commands? Who better to speak for the people of Torrlond? He would save them by becoming the protector he was always meant to be. He must save them.

He stood straight and stared out at the plumes of smoke across the River Ea. Gritting his teeth, he nodded and made balls of his fists. By Edan, he would end it.

It felt good to come to a resolution, as if he were more than half free already, and though his chilled body resumed its quivering, he managed to walk erect as he left behind the balcony to enter the queen's chamber. A sense of rightness seeped into him and radiated from his chest into his whole body. His vision cleared. He was more in command of his faculties than he had been in a long time. This would be his act of redemption. Perhaps, he dared to hope, it would even end the nightmares that pounded and echoed in his skull.

Through the bedroom he strode until he reached the door. Without thinking about it, he pushed the latch and shoved the door open, whereupon the two guards outside started and stood at attention. Earconwald said nothing to them, jogging in his haste to carry out his decision. The hallway was a blur behind him, and he could hear the two guards clinking in their mail to keep up with him. When he came to the broad staircase, he leapt down it, taking two or three steps at a time. Since his nightdress was an encumbrance, he hitched it up around his thighs as he flew down the stairs with his bare feet flapping on the cold stone.

His palace felt quiet and abandoned, strangely alien to him. Fewer than the usual number of guards stood in their posts throughout Sigseld, and those few watched him pass without making a move to interfere. Only the two that had been stationed outside his door panted in their byrnies as they ran to keep up with him. He also was laboring to breathe when he reached the bottom of the stairs and arrived in the main entrance hall, where something closer to the usual number of people milled about. Yet they moved with great tension and seemed under the cloud of some deep disturbance. Most of the activity emanated from one place. There, surrounded by soldiers, was a man he recognized by name.

Captain Nothelm was speaking to the others as he was walking in some haste on his way somewhere. He appeared to be giving orders to the soldiers, who were taut and silent until he addressed them. When he halted to face one of them, the entire group came to an abrupt stop.

Once he finished talking with the soldier, the man ran off, only to be replaced by a newcomer who cried out as he rushed toward the old captain and kept him from resuming his course.

"Captain Nothelm! I've just come from Captain Helmred." What appeared to be specks of blood covered the soldier's smudged face and grey kirtle. He was sweaty and short of breath as well. "High Bridge is in danger of falling to the Ilarchae, my lord. Captain Helmred requests reinforcements."

Captain Nothelm closed his eyes for a moment, and he appeared older and wearier than Earconwald had ever seen him. When he opened his eyes, he gazed at the soldier and shook his head. "We have none to send, lad. Go back to Helmred and tell him he'll have to hold High Bridge as best he can. I'll send word to the other bridges to see if any troops can be spared. Don't hold up your hopes."

The soldier stood for a moment with his mouth open in disbelief, but then he nodded and turned to depart.

Another of the soldiers surrounding Nothelm stepped closer to the old earl. "My lord, we should retreat to Sigseld. Abandon the bridges. It's our best chance to hold out until Duke Ethelred arrives."

Nothelm slowly turned toward the man and blinked at him with a blank expression on his face, as if he were too tired to reply. "I told you, the bridges are our *only* chance. We protect more people by holding them. West Torrhelm is filled with refugees from the east. And what of the merchants and priests and nobles who cower in their splendid homes? Should we abandon them as well? More to the point, Sigseld is not defensible. Once, a century ago, it might have been. But the kings of most recent years have built for splendor, not for defense. The old walls would have served, but they are pulled down to make way for new ones with carvings and statues upon which our enemies may climb with ease. In Sigseld lies no security. What safety we had here was in the illusion of power."

The soldiers around Nothelm all stood in stunned silence. The old captain turned toward Earconwald and gazed at him with the same resigned look. "Speaking of the illusion of power, why are you here, your Majesty?"

The rest of them turned toward Earconwald, seeming to take

notice of him for the first time and staring with something like distaste and even repugnance curling their lips. But those gazes were momentary. The soldiers turned away from him as if in shame or embarrassment, and they did not bother any further with him, taking up conversations about the city's defense as if he, the king, had no stake in it. Only Nothelm continued to look at Earconwald, awaiting an answer.

The King of Torrlond shivered, and an inexplicable giggle arose in him that he could not suppress. "I'm going to end it."

The wrinkles around the old earl's eyes deepened as they narrowed. "End what, your Majesty?"

The voices. The screams. The anguish. "The Ilarchae invasion, of course. I am the king. I will give commands. They must obey me."

Nothelm gazed at him without saying a word.

"I will save us all."

Nothelm's blank stare met him with perhaps a hint of sorrow at the edges, but the sorrow could not break through the thick mask of weariness.

Earconwald favored him with a large grin. "Don't try to stop me."

The two soldiers who had pursued the king from the queen's chamber stepped forward and reached toward the king, but Nothelm held up a palm, and they froze. The old captain returned his dull-eyed gaze to the king, and he nodded.

And that was all.

A noise escaped Earconwald, half laughter and half whimper. He waited for Nothelm, or anyone else, to say anything. No one moved. The other soldiers carried on with their conversations. The king showed his teeth in a broad grin, and then the whining laughter took him, shaking his body so that he could no longer tell why he trembled. He walked past them all, cackling all the way to Sigseld's high front gate, where a soldier unbarred and opened the small side door and stood out of his way.

Giddy with laughter, Earconwald stepped through.

23

STRANDS IN THE WEB

Shouts. Screams. Frantic prayers. Hurrying boots. Clanging metal. The panic and chaos consuming Sigseld receded more and more as the Supreme Priest Joruman descended further into the dungeons until they became the barest whispers tugging at the edges of his mind. He succeeded in ignoring them. Once, he would have been beyond distraught at the wanton destruction of civilization and the threat to his life. But now the turmoil far above was a mere distraction. The Ilarchae invasion, the fall of Torrhelm, and even the end of Torrlond: None of it mattered in the face of the revelation awaiting him. He was teetering on the precipice of something vast. He could not quite see it yet, but he knew it was there, and when he fell into it, he would know it for what it was. All his ambitions and work over the long years had led to this moment. Every inch of him was aquiver with the mounting expectation. He was on the cusp of either his fulfillment or his destruction, and the next moments would determine which.

As usual, the immense power emanating from Dayraven's cell bludgeoned him, and he waded into it as he walked down the torch-lit corridor deep in the rocky bowels of the earth. But it was no longer just the elf or the promise of its power calling him here. Something had grown in him — a thing so unexpected that its strength caught him by surprise. No, it was not the elf but rather Dayraven who drew it out of him. The young man had a quality of inspiring one to bring out the best of oneself, to want to be better, and to feel shame at one's shortcomings, of which his own had grown more evident of late.

Joruman shook his head at the thought, and a smirk curled his lips. His interactions with the boy were changing him. Perhaps the elf lent power to Dayraven's personality, magnifying it and its effects, but he recognized the quality itself as being part of the young man. Not long ago, he would have scoffed at the naivety of such a notion. Joruman had always taken pride in being a practical man — sentiments interfered with the growth of knowledge — but he could not suppress the affection that had sprung to life in him for Dayraven, not least because the boy understood him to the core of his being. *Perhaps better than I understand myself.*

Along with such feelings came insights. The world unfolded itself in ways that had previously eluded him. Somewhere in all this, Dayraven was offering him the key to mastering the elf. The young man should not have been able to live with it for even a moment, let alone bend it to his will for so long. It would be like an ant perching between a wild horse's ears and steering the beast. In fact, the difference in power was far greater than that. So, how did the lad do it? The supreme priest had his suspicions, and if he was right, then it was possible his approach to this matter had been wrong all along.

Lost in such thoughts, he started when two figures appeared before him in the corridor, their white robes tinted a soft orange in the torch light. Joruman composed himself and frowned at the High Priests Edulf and Morcar, the former squinting and the latter wearing a nervous smile. "Ah. Still here, then? Have you emptied all the cells?"

Edulf cleared his throat. "The prisoners are all gone, my lord. The guards conducted them up to serve in the castle's defense, as you instructed." The man pouted in a sulky expression, like a child disappointed at losing his playthings.

"Good. We couldn't leave them to die down here, could we?"

Morcar shrugged. "They'll die up there as well when the Ilarchae break through."

Joruman nodded. "But at least they'll have the chance to fight up there."

Morcar gave a slight bow. "As you say, my lord. What now?"

"Now?" Joruman gestured with one hand pointed down the hallway whence he came. "You may leave." He kept a stony expression on his face as he stared down the two men.

Morcar and Edulf glanced at one another, their fear widening their eyes for a moment. Morcar licked his lips and forced an oily grin. "Leave, my lord?"

"Yes."

"But, where should we go?"

"Wherever you wish."

Edulf's face contorted into a snarl, and the keys looped on his belt jingled as his hands balled into fists. "You led us to believe you had a way out of this mess."

"I do."

Morcar pressed his palm to his chest. "And what of us?"

Joruman stared at him for a long while, and then he released a sigh. A part of him pitied these loathsome, pathetic creatures as he recognized that the contempt with which he regarded them sprang from the fact that they reminded him of what he had been. Yes, he too had been so full of petty ambitions and even cruelty, or at least callousness. He could see it and admit it now: He had been small-minded in his self-centeredness. "If you flee up to the surface, you will likely meet your deaths at the hands of the Ilarchae."

Edulf began to stir, but Joruman cut the air with his hand to silence him. "You may remain down here, but you must stay out of my way. Guard the entrances to the dungeon if it makes you feel any safer. Use wizard's fire to defend yourselves. You are, I believe, the last two priests in Torrhelm other than myself capable of wielding it. In that manner you may hold the dungeons for some time should the barbarians approach."

Morcar's lip quivered. "And what will you do?" The man had always been such a simpering coward.

"What I must. But I warn you, you *must* stay out of my way. Any interference could result in your deaths or a far worse disaster. Stay well away. If I succeed, I will procure your safety. It's even possible I'll be able to save what's left of the city."

Edulf frowned. "And if you fail?"

Joruman raised an eyebrow and smiled. "Then we'll all die." His smile fled as his face hardened again. "Now get out of my way. There's little time."

In spite of the steadiness of the force emanating from behind the door, the dread that he was too late gripped Joruman. All traces of the young man might be gone, devoured by the elf. By proceeding any further, he could be bringing himself face to face with a being capable of ripping away his mind and energy with a mere thought and sending him in myriad pieces to oblivion. For a moment he dared not budge. The notion was absurd, of course, as if the barrier of a simple door would make any difference if Dayraven had already succumbed. Had it wanted to, the elf could have taken him long ago, door or no door. Dayraven must still be there, holding it in check. He smiled at the thought of the lad, whose courage and goodness had carried him so far.

Still, Joruman's palm was clammy as he fumbled the key out of the pocket in his robe. The shaking of his hand prevented him from inserting the key in the lock until the third try. He took a deep breath. The key turned, and the lock clicked. His thumb pressed on the latch. Heart hammering in his chest, the supreme priest grimaced as he pushed through the river of power to open the door to Dayraven's cell.

He released a long sigh. The soft glow of the candles on the table revealed an almost placid scene. Dayraven was lying on his back atop his sleeping pallet with his eyes shut and hands folded across his stomach, appearing outwardly at peace and showing no physical sign of the immense power rushing forth from him. With slow, deliberate steps, Joruman walked further into the room and eased down into the chair, which stood where it had been when he last visited, facing the pallet. There he remained seated for a while, watching the slow movement of Dayraven's chest as the lad breathed. A sad smile crossed the supreme priest's face, and he knew all the cares and worries he struggled with were nothing next to the thing that burdened Dayraven, whom he dared to think of as his friend. He wondered if the young man enjoyed any peace when he slept.

Dayraven stirred and sat up. The veneer of placidity vanished, and Joruman flinched from eyes that pierced him and held him in place like a helpless insect. But the voice that came from the young man exuded an eerie calm. "In truth, I no longer sleep."

Joruman's eyes fell to his lap. "You hear all the thoughts passing through my mind, don't you?"

"Yes. That must feel strange for you, I suppose. There's little . . . barrier between what is left of me and the world any longer."

The supreme priest's face grew hot even as a hollow pit opened in his chest and his breaths became shallow. He was too ashamed to speak, too humiliated by the foolish arrogance that had ruled his life all these years. Dayraven knew everything about him. How he had used so many people, always assuming he had a right to simply because he was cleverer than they were. All the women he had slept with and discarded in a vain attempt to prove he did not care. People he had crushed because they were in his way, including Dayraven at one time, when he arranged for the assassin Crida to slay him during the Battle of Iarfaen. Even poor Colburga and wretched Bagsac. They had possessed lives with desires. What right had he to steal them? What he had done to them was worse than murder. After ripping the gift from Bagsac, he had greeted the augmentation of his power with such ecstasy, but now it sickened him, as if a festering wrongness were lodged inside him.

Joruman shook his head in a vain attempt to dispel such emotions, a sure sign of weakness when he needed single-minded strength more than ever. He had never bothered to care about anyone since his mother's passing, but something had changed since finding Dayraven. All his deeds were open to this young man, the Prophet of Edan, and the idea of him weighing them made him squirm with shame.

He clenched his teeth. What use was shame? On the verge of his destiny, he needed to focus on his task. Attempting to muster up some anger, he prodded himself to recall his ultimate goal, for which he had sacrificed all morals, emotions, and other inconveniences. But he could kindle nothing, and his resolve melted away. He swallowed and closed his eyes, trying to collect himself. He hardly dared speak for dread of what his lips might give vent to.

Dayraven spared him the need to say anything with a new observation. "The city is falling."

Joruman looked up, almost wincing as he forced himself to look at the young man. "Yes. The Ilarchae will soon sweep away the remaining defenses."

"I too am falling." Only in the young man's eyes was the desperate battle evident. His serene voice and bearing betrayed none of the turmoil consuming him within. It was almost over.

Sorrow and pain stabbed Joruman's chest, working their way up into his throat, which tightened so much that he had to clear it. He tried to rein in his breaths, but he could not master the damnable emotions assaulting him. He shook his head again and swallowed. "I don't understand why I . . . I'm so sorry. For your ordeal. For everything I've done."

"You did not cause this."

"No, but . . ." Joruman could not fathom what was happening to him. Why did he feel such a connection with this young man? *Damn him and his sentiments!* How did his pain leap out at him and mingle with the innermost recesses of his being? He growled and clutched his head. "I came here . . . I arranged all this so that I could . . . But it's not as it should be. I sorrow for you. Damn me in my weakness. This is the moment, and all I can do is . . ."

He took a deep breath. He rolled his eyes and shrugged in his helplessness, and something like a laugh or a sob escaped him. "I never had a brother. Not even a friend, to speak soothly. Mayhap I thought myself above such things. Mayhap it would have been too painful to lose someone close. Again. Whatever the case, I believed I was sufficient unto myself. That was my greatest folly. I understand that."

Dayraven slowly nodded. "Do you still wish to take the burden?"

A sharp intake of breath, and Joruman released it as a long sigh. This was the moment. This was what he had worked toward for so long, the key to his quest to defeat death, and all he needed to do was grasp it. He swallowed, blinked, and licked his lips. *Now! Take it! Seize it! There'll never be another chance.*

Joruman prepared to tell Dayraven he wanted the elf's power more than he had ever wanted anything — even more than he had wanted his mother to live. But something welled up from deep within him, and it broke him into pieces of uncertainty that he could not fit back together. There was no denying it. Everything he had believed before this moment was a vast mistake. His entire existence had been a pursuit of futility. He barked a laugh at the absurdity of it. The biggest surprise was the lack of disappointment. In its place was only grim resignation and sadness for all the waste and the lives he had hurt. *I deserve this.* Before he knew what he was doing, he was shaking his head and straining to suppress his tears. "I'm unworthy. I have done such things." He meant to say more, but those were the only words he could choke out.

A fleeting smile crossed Dayraven's face, and for the briefest instant his anguish disappeared. "It is good. You have learned."

A tremor from Joruman's chest shook him, and he gave a rueful laugh. "I fear I have too much to learn. It's over, isn't it?" The elf would soon burst free of Dayraven. When it did, it was certain to enact its will. What Dayraven had described left little room to suppose anyone nearby would survive. This was the moment of his destruction after all. He would die along with Dayraven. But why did that leave him feeling suffused with something like giddy happiness, as if a great burden had slid away from him and left him free? None of this made sense.

A sudden inspiration took him. He stood up from the chair and knelt on the cold stone floor. "I would remain with you, here in this cell, if you will permit me. If there is time, before the end of it all, I would learn from you. I've always sought to know. I cannot change that. Teach me. I'm ready to learn."

A shudder crossed Dayraven's face, and he winced. "A little time remains. Not much. What do you wish to learn?"

Joruman thought for a moment. If he was going to die soon, to be consumed by the elf for eternity, he needed to ask the right questions. The first was obvious enough. "What is the elf?"

Dayraven did not hesitate. "A window to Edan."

The supreme priest nodded. He had expected such an answer from the Prophet. His next question he would have once dismissed as a waste of breath, but perhaps it was the most important now. "And what is Edan?"

The young man paused. "What is Edan?" He closed his eyes for a moment and took a deep breath. "The thing we long for, chasing all our lives, sensing just beyond the horizon. Yet it's with us all the time, all around us, if we could but open our eyes and minds to it." He stopped and seemed to look somewhere far away.

Sensing something more was coming, Joruman waited in silence.

The Prophet's eyes gazed at him but seemed to look straight through him. "There is a vision before me. A memory, mayhap, of the one you call Dayraven. A village of folk stands nigh a river, which winds among grassy hills. Near those hills a vast forest enshrouds the land. Every tree of that forest, every leaf of each tree, every creature dwelling in it, the deer and the bear and the fox, the hawk that glides above it, every wildflower spotting those hills, every fish in that river, and every man, woman, and child of that village: All are strands in the eternal web of being."

As Dayraven spoke, the vision bled from him into Joruman's mind so that it seemed his own memories were flashing by. He beheld those hills, the river, the forest, and even the people of the village. And though he knew none of their names, the supreme priest felt each of those vivid lives as if he merged with them, became them. All their yearnings and fears, their loyalties and their sorrows, the little joys illuminating their days, and the losses that tugged at their hearts in the night and wore them down: Each of them in their beauty and grief was a thing of intricate wonder. And the birds flitting and flinging themselves in the air, the creatures burrowing and hiding in the forest shade, the elk pounding over the meadows, the fish darting in the river, the trees with their translucent leaves as they trembled in the sunlight, and the very blades of grass that overspread the hillsides — Joruman forgot who he was as he dwelled in all these things, and the expansion of his essence was a thousandfold beyond anything he had ever experienced when using the gift.

Beyond the scenes of Dayraven's memory he magnified into the lives of people and creatures the young man had met and seen in other parts of Eormenlond — in the Mark and Torrlond, on the rugged coast of Caergilion, in the ancient dwelling places of the eastern kingdoms, and on the shores of the Isle of Asdralad where they met the jewel-blue waters. From peasant to queen, from folk scattered across the green hillsides to cities teeming with denizens, from the smallest of forest dwellers to the swiftest of steeds, from aglaks of the swamps to creatures of the sea, from mountain wolves to the mightiest and eldest of dragons: All of them in their beauty and wonder swirled and stirred in the hidden depths of his mind, beyond his recall yet still part of him.

The sublime wonder of it propelled Joruman into the surpassing bliss that transcends time. Outside the present he travelled until all the lives of Eormenlond and the world were as uncountable stars drilling their light through him, and he partook of the light while the immensity of it all shattered him, and he drifted beyond the stars to eternity, at peace with the knowledge that it was all one. And *he* was of it.

The young man's eyes did not shift, but they seemed to return to the present and take in Joruman, who crashed back into his own tiny, frail body within the dungeon cell that seemed so dim now with the absence of sun. "That eternal web is Edan. They are all Edan. As are you. What you do to the least of those strands, you do to yourself."

Just realizing it was hanging open, Joruman closed his mouth. "You are Edan? I . . ." The beauty of the revelation stole his breath away, and he believed at that moment he could face the end, however it came.

"Yes. You are Edan, my friend." Dayraven smiled. "My brother. And you will return to Edan. We all must."

"You mean death."

"Yes. Life returns to Edan, Edan manifests as life in an eternal pulse, a cosmic dance beyond the passage of time. Like all other dualities, death and life are illusion, the breakage of eternity into time, but beyond time there is only Edan." Dayraven's head tilted to the side, and he asked in his calm voice. "Do you see the necessity of death?"

Joruman gave a slow nod, and his body trembled as a thrill ran through him and goosebumps covered his flesh. "Without death, there is no beauty, no pain, no sorrow, no joy. No loss. No life. When *she* died, I was so afraid. I wanted never to fear again. I see now. There was never a need to fear."

The Prophet's head drooped to his chest. "Yes. You understand. And now we're out of time." The power beating at his fragile body swelled as it emanated from him like a beacon, and his flesh began to appear like a thin veil over a bright light.

Joruman nodded in acceptance. His breaths came fast, and he swallowed in his dry throat. "It's taking you. It's finished."

Dayraven looked up and gazed at him, and his eyes narrowed and hardened. "Not yet. Say your spell."

Joruman froze in place, not sure which of the vast emotions swirling within him to give vent to. "What do you mean? You would have me . . . ?"

"Say it before I'm gone. You're as ready as you'll ever be."

"But . . . But I'm not worthy."

Dayraven winced. "You're all we've got." His voice roughened like gravel. "Say the spell."

"But if it fails . . ."

"What difference will it make? At least let us try." Dayraven nodded. "You're ready." He grimaced and bent over, clutching his stomach as he squeezed his eyes closed. "Be swift. Say the spell. I can't . . ." He grunted, and his breathing grew quicker and louder.

Joruman blinked at his friend. "But I . . ." He swallowed as he watched the young man buckling over and groaning while light pulsed from him. The suffering. Life was so full of it. Why? Was there something redemptive in it? Could *he* redeem himself? At the very least, he could try to help Dayraven. He could share in the suffering. He could accept it, even embrace it, as he had never done before. All that he had lived through, everything he had endured and afflicted, came to him in a new light.

He nodded. "Alright. But I fear I must . . . There might be need for restraints due to some . . . violent movement." He glanced at the chains near the sleeping pallet. "I'm sorry. I'll need you to be still. And you could hurt yourself elsewise."

Dayraven stopped groaning and nodded. "Chain me," he said between clenched teeth. He lay down and stretched out his arms and legs, which trembled as bright cracks of light webbed over his flesh and bled from him. When he opened his eyes, they were no longer human, but were white points of luminosity. "Hurry."

Joruman bent down and trembled as he lifted the cold, clinking chains. His heart squirmed in his chest, and his flesh itched and tingled as it broke out in a cold sweat. When he grasped Dayraven's arm to place the manacle around his wrist, he half expected the metal to pass through the translucent flesh lined with veins, so bright was the light throbbing beneath it. But when he clasped the metal together, it held there, and he took out the key in the pocket of his robe to insert it and lock the manacle with a click. He repeated the process on Dayraven's other limbs, shaking and almost succumbing to the tears building in his eyes and clouding his vision. "I'm so sorry, my friend."

The two points of light where Dayraven's eyes had been seemed to gaze at Joruman. "Begin the spell." The pleading voice was strained and distant.

The Supreme Priest Joruman cleared his throat and released a long sigh. So. This was the moment after all. After he renounced any claim to this power, it was to come to him. A chill ran through his body, and he shivered. *I will try to be worthy of it, as he was.* One last look at Dayraven. A deep breath with his eyes closed, and he slipped into the realm of origins. He opened his eyes and began:

Druanil ecthonias an dharian gadalathon,
Abu mihil inghanias ni rakhyon abhularon.
Vardas diagol im parthas akwinway,
Shardas inkhathol an ghalas khalithway.

Retaining the peace and acceptance the Prophet had shown him, Joruman repeated the spell he had learned from Ishdhara's volume. Even as he did, the light suffused Dayraven's form, which grew so bright that it banished all shadows from the dark womb of the cell. The young man's body writhed, and the chains that held him down clanked as they went taut and slackened. The supreme priest squinted and continued to chant. Blue sparks twinkled into existence as his energy began to coalesce with the energy inhabiting the Prophet.

Joruman released a long breath as he kept up the spell. The blue sparks increased in number until their brightness vied with the light emanating from Dayraven, whose growls escalated into screams as his body continued to thrash. The sparks morphed into waves of bluish light that warped the air. Beyond the cell the light stretched, glowing through the rock and failing to recognize the boundaries of the realm of forms. Joruman's vision in the realm of origins beheld the light as it reared up and swelled, heaving above and beyond the city of Torrhelm like a vast dome reaching for the heavens. The power confronting Joruman was immense beyond imagination. His own was a paltry thing before it, and he wondered how he could keep from being swallowed by it, let alone draw it into him, as his energy entwined with it. Yet Dayraven had taught him his oneness with it, and he did not flinch as he bathed in the calm of the realm of origins. He kept chanting the song of origin even as he shifted his focus onto tugging the power of the elf towards him.

All four chains on Dayraven's limbs tightened, and then his back arched up as he released a scream that morphed into a wail. Even within the impassivity of the realm of origins, Joruman sorrowed for his brother. *I will take on this burden. I will free him at last.*

Joruman let go and embraced his sacrifice, the most liberating act of his existence, like diving into the abyss and finding he could fly. As if he were pulling on the Great Sea, he willed the elf's power to enter him. The blue waves of light intensified and loomed still higher, and then, from the place of brightness where Dayraven's body had been, light exploded.

The supreme priest gasped and staggered as the flash of light punched into him like a physical force, and then it was all gone, swallowed in sudden darkness.

In the absence of light, understanding blossomed and unfurled at first like a small flame, and then with a dizzying rush. For a long while he stood and blinked in the darkness. His eyes began to adjust, and the dim, candle-lit little cell deep beneath the earth reappeared before him, but he needed no physical senses to tell him what had happened. Within him whispered millions of tiny voices, entities of consciousness all connected on the great web of being and partaking of the same ultimate source. His body seemed numb, or rather to belong to a different realm from the one wherein his expanded mind floated. It was just like the taste of eternity Dayraven had given him, only the sublime presence was within him now as well as all around him, and so its bliss was beyond expression.

The spell had worked. He had done it. There was no possibility of denying it. The transcending power of the elf dwelled in him. Eternity filled him.

His mouth hung open as he gawked at the palms of his hands in wonder. That fragile flesh harbored the power of the stars. It had worked. He could still not wrap his mind around the fact. And yet, a bewildering ocean of energy lay before him — no, within him — and Dayraven had shown him the way, else the spell never would have worked. He knew that. The young man had given him that final gift along with the terrible burden. Joruman gazed down toward the floor.

Dayraven's body lay on the pallet, his limbs unmoving, his eyes shut. Something that had animated him before was gone, and he seemed cold, like long dead ashes where a fire had consumed its fuel. Finally at peace.

Joruman stared at what remained of his still friend for a long while. At last, he clenched his hands into fists and released a sigh. "I will honor you for as long as I can." He steadied his breaths as he tried to grow accustomed to the disorienting reservoir of energy centered in him. Many things were happening all around him, and he needed to learn how to focus his attention. Once he felt steady enough, he would decide what to do next.

A click behind him seized his attention, and even as he turned around, he recognized the proximity of two specific presences among the thousands swirling within his awareness. The door swung open, and two white-robed men stood cowering in the doorway.

"My lord, we felt . . ."

Before the words left Morcar's lips, before Edulf withdrew his key from the hole, a too familiar companion erupted within Joruman, dragging him from sublimity back to humanity: anger. How dare these filthy vermin desecrate the place where Dayraven lay? Had he not instructed them to stay away?

With gristly pops, their two heads exploded at once, ending Morcar's utterance and spraying a wet mist of blood along with larger chunks of bone and brain all over the cell and the hall behind them. From Edulf's gaping neck hung his bearded jaw by a flap of glistening flesh, its rotten teeth still embedded in it as it dangled. Expanding islands of red splotched and dotted their white robes. Edulf's keys clinked on the stone floor as the headless bodies swayed backward and thumped to their final resting place. Spattered blood and bits of flesh and pinkish-grey matter dripped and slithered down the cell's walls.

It happened so fast that at first Joruman did not realize it had been the lash of his will. He had slain Morcar and Edulf with less than a thought. Again he looked down at his hands. Fine, wet spots of red covered them as well as his white robe. With his index finger he smudged a line of the blood on the back of his other hand, which began to tremble even as a chill voice from the shadows of his mind hissed like desiccated leaves in a winter wind. *Yes. It begins. Give them all peace.*

Joruman's eyes widened just before the power of the elf surged within him and shattered him, flinging the pieces of his panicking identity to the furthest reaches of the realm of origins, whence they could never regather. *I'm sorry, Dayraven. I failed.* Such was the last thought belonging to his scattering consciousness, and the man who had called himself the supreme priest knew no more as brightness consumed him.

THE ELF-DWOLA GAZED DOWN AT THE NEW BODY IT INHABITED. A white robe with fresh blood speckles clothed it. The man who had dwelled in this body and thought of it as his had convinced himself he had not wanted the power, at least for a fleeting moment. He had been quite skilled at deluding himself. But he was not like the other one, the one that had been so puzzling. This one the elf had understood immediately. Though he had thought himself different, cleverer, in truth he was like the thousands of others the creature had encountered and liberated over the countless span of its existence. They were always fooling themselves. At any rate, his body would suffice for the present occasion.

Traces of the mortal's anger, contempt, and fear still echoed within him, blending with and giving impetus to his purpose. He — he was not in truth a "he" or a "she," for he belonged to no such dichotomies, though the body he was using had been a male's, and so "he" would do — he looked up at the ceiling of the little cell, and through the tons of rock vibrated the presence of all the people on the surface. Worms consumed by rage and terror. Diseased life torturing itself. Delusional beings clinging to masks and forms, and in the process twisting the life all around them. He would end it. He would give them all the peace they longed for without knowing. Deliverance from fear.

He glanced back at the chained body lying on the sleeping pallet and paused a moment. Yes, that one had been intriguing. In truth, he had never belonged here. It was all such an interesting accident. Like life.

He turned away and walked out of the cell, stepping over the two headless bodies on his way. The fulfillment of his purpose had arrived. He would return whither he belonged. And they would come with him.

24
SURVIVING THE DARK

Orvandil waited by the door to their room, fidgeting with Seeker's hilt and cursing himself for not waking earlier. As soon as he had opened his eyes, he had felt something was amiss. Upon scanning the room and finding Seren and the madman absent, he had roused the others. Dawn's dull glow would soon seep through the window, and he wondered how long the girl and the madman had been gone. He clenched his fist and ground his teeth as he watched Gnorn and Abon struggling to hurry on the rest of their gear. Galdor stood next to the Thjoth, ready to leave.

"By the ancestors' beards, I can't understand how they slipped out." Gnorn tucked his axe into his belt. "I should've heard them. I should've heard *something*." The Dweorg had been berating himself since Orvandil woke him. "When she took her turn at the watch early, I should've suspected."

"It wasn't your doing, Gnorn. None of us heard them leave, and you had no reason to suspect anything." Galdor stroked his beard. "The question is not how they slipped out, but why? And *where* did they go?"

The Dweorg grunted as he pulled on his boot. "If that weasel-faced lunatic harms her, I'll bash out what's left of his brains."

"You needn't threaten our new friend," said Galdor. "He's fond of her, in his own way. Like as not, he's gone after her, perhaps with the intention of protecting her."

"There was no struggle." Abon slung his green sack on his back. "We would've heard that."

Galdor shook his head. "No. No struggle. It's clear Seren wanted to leave. But why?"

Orvandil frowned. "She was going to take a risk. Didn't want us to know. We would've stopped her."

Galdor squinted at the Thjoth. "What sort of risk?"

"She set out for Dayraven." Orvandil knew it in his gut. But exactly where the girl went, he could not guess.

The wizard nodded. "Yes. Of course. She's heading for Sigseld, then."

"But what route is she taking?" Abon pulled on his second boot and stood up.

"And how do we find her before she does something foolish?" Gnorn fastened his cloak. He too was ready.

Galdor sighed. "I wish I knew. I only hope we're not too late. Let's head down and look for any signs of them. Quietly, though. The city feels too still. Something's in the air, and we mustn't attract attention."

They crept down the stairs, making as little noise as possible, though Orvandil winced every time a stair or a floorboard creaked under one of their boots. No one else was about in the inn, which was nearly vacant anyway. They reached the dim and empty common room, each of them scanning it for any clues as they fanned out. Orvandil saw nothing of note, and when he looked back at the others, they shrugged and shook their heads. Thus, they approached the door none the wiser as to Seren's whereabouts.

Galdor nodded and put his hand on the door's latch. "We'll take a peek outside." He kept his voice to a whisper. "Try not to be noticed. We don't want to run into any Torrlonder patrols."

The wizard pressed the latch and eased the door open, and then he crept out. Abon followed him, and then Gnorn. Orvandil came last.

When the Thjoth emerged, the grey tones of early dawn greeted him outside. His three friends stood motionless facing the docks across the way. Opposite them were gathered scores of soaked people wearing only a kirtle or a loin cloth. They were massing without making a noise on the street that ran along the docks. Most were men. Almost every one was big. All were armed with at least one weapon — sword or axe — tucked into a belt, and more of them were clambering onto the docks as they emerged from the River Ea. The Thjoth knew one thing for certain: What they lacked in defensive gear they more than made up for with courage and grit.

Orvandil gave a half smile in admiration of the Ilarchae — for these bedraggled, panting warriors could be none other — who had swum the river to enter the city and attack it from within. But, at the moment, he and his companions were the objects of their confused stares, as if the barbarians were taking a moment to figure out the correct way to greet them.

"Fuck me." Abon shook his head. "Seems we've been noticed."

Gnorn put his hand atop his axe. "At least they're not a Torrlonder patrol, eh?"

Orvandil's hand drifted toward Seeker, and the old thrill leapt alive all over his body, the grim joy that accompanied battle.

As if he heard the Thjoth's thoughts, Galdor shook his head. "Too many. Run!" The wizard turned and bolted down the alley next to the inn. That was the signal that sent everything into motion. The companions hastened after the wizard, and scores of frenzied Ilarchae rumbled off after them, roaring and shouting battle cries.

Orvandil almost gave in to the temptation to stop and fight, but he recalled his purpose for being in Torrhelm, and in addition to helping Dayraven, he needed to find Seren too. The girl was in terrible danger, and he could not help her if he died fighting throngs of Ilarchae. Still, it was more likely than not that the barbarians would catch them at some point. This day would not pass without him testing Seeker, and there were good odds he would be little help to anyone after that.

Scurrying and gasping for breath, Galdor led them through a maze of alleys and streets, where the screams of citizens of East Torrhelm began to rise above the clamor the Ilarchae were raising behind the companions. From windows above them in the alleyways, a few faces frowned down in curiosity before shrieking or disappearing when their barbarian pursuers pounded closer. Windows and doors flashed by in a blur, and the few folk who were about dropped whatever they were doing to scuttle indoors for cover.

Orvandil glanced back down the alley they were flying along. A pack of red-faced Ilarchae sprinted after them, growling and shouting in their eagerness to fight. Orvandil was no less eager, and he nearly turned around to encounter them. The narrow alley would have made it impossible for more than two to approach him at once. Good enough odds, especially with their lack of mail. Of course, should more Ilarchae pour into the alley from the other end, he would have to fight them on both sides, a losing proposition.

He did not heed the urge to turn and fight. Instead, he allowed the wizard to drag him along with Gnorn and Abon through the alleys and streets, keeping just ahead of the yelling Ilarchae horde as the city jerked awake with terror. He and the others were panting and sweating even in the cold of early morning, and Galdor began wheezing. The old fellow was fit for his age, but he would not be able to keep it up much longer.

Galdor emerged from the alley ahead of him and stopped so abruptly that Abon nearly crashed into the wizard before Gnorn collided with the shaper with a loud grunt. When Orvandil arrived, he understood why the wizard had halted. A large company of grey-kirtled Torrlonder soldiers stood before them, shields up and ready to attack. "Advance!" shouted their commander. "Kill the savage scum!"

The wizard, who was panting hard, held up his palms. "We're not Ilarchae! They're just behind us!"

The line of Torrlonders kept advancing, shields up and swords ready.

"Orvandil, ward our backs!" shouted the wizard before he began chanting a song of origin.

The Thjoth showed his teeth in a smile as he turned about and paced back into the alley. The first of the Ilarchae were almost upon him. A moment after Seeker leapt out of its scabbard, Orvandil swung the blade, deflecting the blow from the large warrior before him. A quick riposte sent Seeker into his foe's face, slicing it open in a spray of blood a moment before the Thjoth kicked his groaning foe in the stomach. The Ilarchae toppled backward, crashing into his nearest companion. Before the second warrior could gain his balance, Seeker had cloven through his skull, dropping him onto the cobblestones. The third Ilarchae leapt over the first two, straight into Seeker's tip as Orvandil thrust it through the man's chest. A fountain of blood trailed the blade when he tugged it free before the skewered body fell backward with a wheeze.

A loud crack and bright flash behind the Thjoth announced that Galdor had unleashed wizard's fire on the Torrlonders. Even the Ilarchae halted with shock widening their eyes. But they came on a moment later with renewed ferocity. Orvandil dodged an axe that crashed into the wall of a building, sending chips of brick flying. Seeker parted the axe wielder's arm from his body, releasing a gush of blood from the meaty stump. Orvandil danced back from the next blow, caught his unbalanced foe by the neck with his free hand, and smashed the woman's face into the wall. He shoved the stunned warrior into the oncoming group, slowing them for a moment.

"Orvandil! Come!" shouted Galdor behind him.

The Thjoth tore himself from the melee, loth to turn his back on so many untested foes. He dashed out the alley again to meet a haze of smoke, whereupon someone grabbed his arm and yanked him aside. He raised Seeker before realizing it was Gnorn.

"Come on!" yelled the Dweorg.

Orvandil followed Gnorn along the building at the alley's end until they met Abon and Galdor, who were panting as they pressed their backs to the wall. The Dweorg assumed the same posture even as Orvandil thought he understood what they were doing. He glanced back at the mouth of the alley, out of which poured the obscured forms of the Ilarchae. When they emerged, they ran straight into the Torrlonders. The two sides roiled and roared as they engaged in bloody melee in the midst of smoke from Galdor's wizard's fire. On the other side of the building, more Ilarchae gushed out of another alley in a seemingly endless stream. The Torrlonders would cut them off if they could push the barbarians back, but the Ilarchae had the numbers, and more of them were joining the fray. Orvandil reckoned their warriors would soon overwhelm the Torrlonders.

"Let them have at it," yelled Galdor over the din of battle.

"And what do *we* do?" Abon clutched his stomach as he tried to catch his breath.

"We must return to the river."

"Why? It may still be seething with Ilarchae." Gnorn's brow wrinkled as he frowned.

The wizard winced as he panted and faced the Dweorg. "Something occurred to me while we were running. I think I know where Seren went."

It hit Orvandil at once. "The place where the madman washed out of the dungeons. Under the bridge."

Galdor nodded. "Precisely my thought."

"Might be tricky to make our way back." Gnorn glanced over at the alley they had run from, whence more Ilarchae dashed into the melee.

"What about this way?" Abon jerked his thumb at the other alley. No one was coming out of it at the moment. The fighting was receding from the companions as the Ilarchae pushed back the Torrlonders.

"Let's go." Galdor led the way once again. The wizard disappeared into the alley, followed by Abon and Gnorn. Orvandil brought up the rear.

They did not get far before another group of bellowing Ilarchae emerged at the alley's distant end, heading their way.

"Curse the savages," said Gnorn. "How many of them swam into the city?"

"More than enough, it seems." Abon readied his blade. "What now?"

Orvandil looked to his right, where there was a pair of double doors in the wall. He pressed the latch and pushed, but a draw bar on the other side kept them shut. Stepping back a couple paces, he thrust his body against the doors shoulder first. A loud crack preceded the sound of wood clattering on the floor, and the doors stood ajar. He pushed them the rest of the way open. "In here."

"What if they follow us inside?" Gnorn frowned at the Thjoth as if he thought him mad.

"They won't. Get in." He shoved the Dweorg through the dark doorway.

The companions hastened into a dim, musty hall past which

nothing was visible in the darkness. His friends' shadowy forms disappeared when Orvandil slammed the door shut, but a bit of weak light leaked beneath it, illuminating only a few inches of space at the Thjoth's feet. The darkness seemed to augment the sound of their rapid breathing. Galdor mumbled something under his breath, a song of origin no doubt. Orvandil stood with Seeker ready, not nearly as sure as he had sounded about the Ilarchae not pursuing them. A moment later, yells preceded hurrying footsteps that sent fleeting shadows across the bar of light at the bottom of the door. After a while, there was silence without.

"How'd you know they wouldn't follow us in here?" asked Abon's voice from the darkness.

Orvandil kept Seeker ready. "They're headed for one of the gates on the eastern side of the city wall."

"Of course," said Gnorn. "To let in the rest of their friends."

The Thjoth nodded, though no one could see his face. "They'll need to take it fast. Once they do — and they will — the lot will come back this way."

"What makes you so sure the Ilarchae will win?" asked Abon.

"East Torrhelm is ill defended. The Ilarchae will take it if they're swift. But they won't *win* until they fight into West Torrhelm."

"But, to take the western side of the city . . ."

Orvandil finished Gnorn's thought. "They need to cross the bridges. The Torrlonders will defend them."

"Seren." Abon needed to say no more to express what they were all fearing.

"Time to move on, gentlemen," said Galdor.

Orvandil released a sigh, hoping they would somehow find the girl before she ended up in the midst of the battle for Torrhelm.

GALDOR PEEKED OUT FROM A CRACK IN THE SHUTTERS OF THE window. The dockside warehouse he and the others had taken shelter in afforded a good vantage point from which to witness the battle raging for control of the bridge. Arrows flew, screams erupted, and steel clashed. Fires burned on both sides of the bridge, sending up billowing smoke that at times obscured the wizard's view. The Ilarchae were making a huge push, led by an immense warrior dressed in black. Bodies, or pieces of bodies, flew away from him as he swept his big blade in lethal arcs. The grey-kirtled Torrlonder soldiers, dead or alive, plummeted from the bridge into the river or disappeared beneath the boots of the scrambling barbarians. It was only a matter of time before the Ilarchae won this bridge, and once they gained it, the others would mostlike fall in rapid succession.

Torrhelm was doomed. The tide of battle was with the Ilarchae. And most especially with the one leading them. Galdor thought he knew who that tall warrior in black must be. "Surt, I reckon. The one they all speak of."

"Aye," said a deep voice above him.

Galdor glanced up. Next to the wizard, Orvandil stared out another crack in the shutters. Light seeping through the crack made a bright band across the Thjoth's icy blue eyes, which kindled the way another man's might were he staring at a heap of treasure beyond reckoning. Galdor well knew what Orvandil Dragonbane was fixing his gaze on. It must have been a rare thing for the Thjoth to witness a warrior who could rival him.

"How long before it's over?" asked the wizard.

"Not long."

"And what will be there for us once it's finished?" said a gruff voice behind them. Gnorn was pacing and fretting. "Assuming we can get to the bridge?"

They had arrived too late. None of them said what they all dreaded, but the implication lurked beneath the Dweorg's words. Galdor tried to shake away the image of Seren's still and mangled body amongst all the other corpses on and around the bridge.

"We'll get there somehow or other." Abon was leaning his back against a stack of crates. "It's the only lead we've got."

"After the Ilarchae break through and fight their way further into West Torrhelm, we'll have a moment." Galdor tried to sound more confident than he felt. "We must act while there's still chaos, before they think to post guards at the bridge. With luck, they won't bother. Our moment will be brief, but we will seize it. We'll find her." *And may*

Edan grant we'll find her alive. We led her into this. Damn me. I *led her into this.*

Gnorn stopped pacing and tugged at his beard. "If only we'd arrived before the Torrlonders. We might've had a chance then."

No one had the heart to answer him.

They had tried and failed. The companions had woven their way back to the river, taking care to avoid the stray bands of Ilarchae still smashing their way through East Torrhelm. By the time they made it to the bridge, the Torrlonder troops were in the midst of staking out their position defending the western end. The place where they had needed to seek Seren had been swarming with grey kirtles. So, Abon had picked the lock on the door of the warehouse, and the friends awaited the arrival of the Ilarchae, who came in their thousands and wasted no time in attacking the bridges.

The Torrlonders had made the barbarians fight for every inch, but it would end soon enough. Once they moved on, Galdor would do everything he could to find Seren. *And we'll still need to find Dayraven after that. Before he loses control to the elf.* It all seemed more impossible than ever. *Mustn't give in to despair.* The wizard sighed. *Perhaps we're doomed, and a cataclysm will swallow this city.* He glanced at Abon and smiled. *But the shapers all say there's nothing nobler than fighting for a doomed cause.*

A massive roar swelled from the battle, and Galdor turned his attention back to the desperate struggle on the bridge just as the Ilarchae punched through the last of the Torrlonder ranks. As soon as the few remaining soldiers in grey kirtles fell to their deaths or disappeared beneath the barbarians' flashing blades, the Ilarchae spread like a river bursting free of a dam into West Torrhelm. Thousands waited behind them to cross the bridge. They would seek out the other bridges one at a time and attack the Torrlonders from the west. The city's defenders would not last long.

Galdor frowned as he watched it unfold. "Ready yourselves. We leave in a moment."

. . .

MANGLED CORPSES LITTERED THE BRIDGE'S BLOOD-SLICKENED flagstones. Galdor did not relish gazing at them, but he inspected the slain, hoping all the while not to find what he sought as the companions crept along the bridge with their weapons out towards the western side. The battle here had been fierce and bloody. So many lives had ended in that small space. Men — and not a few women among the Ilarchae — had drawn their last frantic breaths in a primal rage and crush of bodies, stabbing and clawing and bludgeoning until someone ended their fury with a swift deathblow or a life-seeping wound, but either way their part was done, and they succumbed to join the carnage. Some must have suffocated in the press. Others were trampled underfoot, with bones cracking and snapping under the immense pressure.

No Ilarchae remained save the dead. Only the roar of distant battle interrupted the silence. Thus far there was no sign of Seren, yet the tension built in the wizard the further he tiptoed among the dead. *We're more likely to find her on the western side.*

A moan leaked out of one of the corpses, startling Galdor. *Not quite gone.* The Torrlonder's blood had gathered in a sticky pool where he lay face down. The wizard was glad he could not see the man's face. He moaned again as if appealing for help or perhaps just voicing his agony and misery and abandonment. Did he sense Galdor's presence? One of his arms ended in a raw stump with a piece of bone jutting out. A broken spear shaft protruded from his back.

Galdor wondered whether or not he could save the man. It was absurd in a way. This dying man could have been one of many Torrlonder soldiers the wizard had just slain with wizard's fire back in East Torrhelm. Perhaps it was the guilt over their deaths he was feeling. *That was different. They were about to mow us down. This man is helpless.* He bent down next to him and winced as he shook his head. Too much blood lost. It was a wonder the man was still breathing.

"Best move on, my lord." Abon crouched next to him. "He's gone, or near enough to it. We've got to find her."

Galdor's gaze did not move from the dying soldier until he glanced at the shaper. *Once you were not much more alive than this man, my friend. Perhaps I could . . . But no.* He would need to expend almost all his energy to save the soldier, who would most likely die anyway. Every moment lost meant further danger for the girl, for whom he felt responsible. Not to mention the matter of Dayraven. He nodded. "Yes, of course. Keep moving."

It felt like a betrayal to leave the dying soldier lying in his blood. *Yet another act I shall have to live with.* There was no consolation in the fact that hard choices always seemed to fall in his path. Thus had his life always been: no clear roads leading to right and wrong, no white and black to mark the way, only grey riddled with regrets. Yet he had always embraced what came, as he had vowed to do so long ago with Arna.

He permitted himself a sigh before returning his attention to the massacre on the bridge. They were approaching the western end, and still no sign of Seren appeared. Orvandil stalked ahead of the others, and as he reached the end of the bridge, he gazed downward over the parapet. The Thjoth looked back toward Galdor and pointed below the bridge.

The wizard held up a palm in response, and when he and the others caught up to Orvandil, the Thjoth whispered, "We must check underneath. Many slain down there."

Galdor's heart beat faster and his skin itched. Her ruined, discarded body appeared in his mind, down there among the cold, unmoving dead. He nodded to Orvandil.

"I'll go." The Thjoth clenched his jaw.

"Me too," said Abon.

Gnorn crossed his arms. "You won't leave me behind."

Galdor looked at them each in turn. "We ought to set a watch." The Dweorg opened his mouth to object, but the wizard held up his hand to cut him off. "Yet, I think we will face what we find down there together. Someone help me over the side. We haven't much time."

After Abon climbed over the stone and swung down to the other side, Orvandil lifted the wizard with seeming ease and set him on top of the parapet. The shaper steadied Galdor as he eased down and planted his feet on the riverbank. The Thjoth came next, and Gnorn scrambled over after him.

Galdor held on to the bridge's massive stone supports as he toddled down the riverbank, stepping over several corpses on his way. There were almost as many dead here as there were on the bridge above. Though the wizard paused a moment upon seeing one of the smaller female Ilarchae with her head twisted back in an unnatural position, none of the dead resembled Seren's size and darker skin and hair. Still, he could not help but imagine she might be under the bridge, or perhaps tossed into the cold river along with so many others only to emerge later, bloated and unrecognizable.

It was then, as he approached the foul-smelling, corpse-littered river's edge, that a familiar disturbance crept into the wizard's mind. A deep wrongness, a negation that should not have existed in the world. In spite of how it sickened him, the wizard smiled upon detecting that unsettling presence.

Galdor turned to Abon, who stood next to the wizard to steady him. "Our ex-priest friend is here. Alive, I think."

The shaper's eyes narrowed. "Where?"

"Under the bridge. Tucked as far into the shadows as he can get, I should think. She might be with him."

"I'll fetch him."

Galdor held Abon's arm. "Be careful. And be gentle."

The shaper nodded.

Gnorn and Orvandil waited alongside the wizard, whose heart pounded as Abon ducked and disappeared into the shadows beneath the bridge. Galdor swallowed and stroked his beard as he waited. The Dweorg fidgeted next to him, while the Thjoth stood staring under the bridge with his big arms crossed.

A hiss came from under the bridge, and a moment later, Abon's voice emerged, indistinct and mumbling but urgent in tone. There was a silence, and then Abon said something again. A few moments later, a scuffling noise preceded the shaper, who emerged from the shadows crouching. "He's here. Won't budge. You'll have to come under."

"And Seren?" Galdor's voice cracked like a weak old man's, betraying his anxiety.

Abon paused a moment and looked down at the ground. "Hard to say. He won't talk sense. But I think, from what he's gibbering . . . You'd best come hear for yourself."

The wizard's stiff back and knees protested with aches when he crouched and shuffled along, following Abon deep into the shadowy recesses beneath the bridge. Eagerness for word of Seren competed with dread of her fate, and his breaths came loud and fast. Gnorn and Orvandil made scuffling noises close behind him.

When Galdor could move no farther unless he crawled on his belly, the shadow that was Abon stopped and turned back. "Just up here, behind this support."

Galdor squinted in the dimness but could see nothing behind the stone. But the wrongness, the absence of the gift, emanated from there. "Hello? Hello, friend."

A long silence followed, but at length, the dark outline of a head poked out, and a whimper emitted from it. "I tried."

"You tried what?"

"I tried." The voice trembled. "I tried to stop her."

"To stop her from what?"

"The dead. They were coming. All over. First, over there. And I waited for her. I was brave. I waited. Here."

"You waited here for Seren? Where did she go?"

"But then they came here. To the bridge. It was terrible. They were howling and shrieking and dying. Again and again. Dying and falling. Falling like rain. With grunts and crunches. Again and again. The noise. It was unbearable. I tried not to listen. Put my fingers in my ears. But their wails reached inside my skull. The dead. They're all around. All around."

"And Seren? Where did she go?"

"She . . . she leapt in."

"Leapt in?"

"To where the dead come from."

Galdor's heart stuttered and nearly stopped. "You mean the river. She leapt into the river. Where you came out of the dungeons. The place you showed us."

A long pause. "Yes."

Galdor sat stunned for a moment. His guess had been correct. If only he had reached here sooner. If only he had read her intentions. He should have known. And it was he who had brought her to this doomed city.

"I tried to stop her," said the madman's voice from the darkness. "The girl would not listen."

The wizard gathered his voice, first clearing his throat before he spoke. "She's not come out again, then?"

"No. And I have waited. Like she told me to. I waited. Very brave."

Galdor slumped and released a long sigh. Everything he had done until this moment had been wrong. *Edan help me make the right decision now.*

"What do we do?" said Abon.

The wizard shook his head and tried to summon his wits. "We have no good choices. If she's alive . . . If, by some miracle, she comes out again, it will be here. We can't go in after her, and we will *not* abandon her. For the moment, I suggest we follow the example of our friend here: Try to be brave and wait."

WATERY SILENCE FILLED HER EARS, AND DARKNESS SURROUNDED Seren. Utter blackness sealed her vision whether she opened her eyes or not. But her hands clung to the slimy rock surrounding her on all sides. She clutched onto slippery fingerholds in it, pulling her body against the current as she kicked with her legs.

It had taken her several tries — she lost track in her franticness — to feel out the fissure in the rock of the riverbank. Mossy and weedy plant life had partially covered it, but she had found it. After surfacing from the chilly river and drawing as much air as she could into her lungs, she had dived down and pulled herself into the crevice, telling herself it would be just like Crag Isle.

It felt like a long time ago. *Just like Crag Isle.* But this tunnel was longer, and there was still no sign of light or anything but rock closing in all around her. The idea of turning back sprang up within her and clung to her. But she had come so far, and she was not sure she had enough air in her lungs to make it back if she turned around. If she *could* turn around — there was so little room even to wiggle in this tunnel. No. She would find the Prophet. She would reach him and help him. *Just like Crag Isle.*

The pressure on her lungs was painful, and her head was feeling heavy and dizzy. Little sparks of light began to swim before her vision. The relentless current shoved against her, and the pounding of her heart pulsed fuzzily in her ears. The idea seized her that she was going nowhere, that she had made no progress, that she was kicking and pulling as the current pushed her back until her lungs would give out and she swallowed that filthy water and it slithered into her body, drowning her in that place where light had never shone. She could not see it, but she could feel her bloated body floating in that darkness forever. Her limbs flailed, and she lost her grip on the rock. The current tugged her backwards until her palms scraped on the rock and her fingers dug in. She gritted her teeth. She could not afford another mistake like that. *Just like Crag Isle.*

She pulled her body forward and felt around, her hand sloshing through the water in slow motion. Hard, unyielding rock surrounded her with bare inches to spare, and the passage seemed to be narrowing, as if the rock sought to constrict around her. Water thrust against her, trying to pry her lips open and fill her. This had been a mistake. Like rushing into Len's home. Like trying to run into her burning farmhouse after the Torrlonders killed her parents and left. *No! Just like Crag Isle. Just like Crag Isle.*

She grasped another handhold and pulled. Her faint, sluggish head began to spin, or perhaps it was the dark tunnel that was spinning, and the sparks in her vision brightened. The pressure on her lungs was nigh unbearable. Her hand lunged forward again to grasp for another hold. But it closed only on water.

She reached out again and willed her fingers to clutch. Nothing. No rock. Only darkness. Her lungs were giving way, and she could hear the bubbles exploding out of her nose and mouth. She did not know whether it was up or down, but she plunged into the nothingness. She kicked and flailed with her arms, kicked and flailed.

Cold air slapped her face, and she sucked it in with a hoarse wheeze. Something sharp jabbed the top of her crown, jarring her entire head, and pins of light flashed before her vision. She sank back down and burbled before realizing her head had breached the surface of the water and smacked into something hard, probably a low rock ceiling. A dull pain throbbed in her tongue, which she must have bitten. Without hesitating, she kicked back up, taking care not to hit her head this time.

The water peeled away from her face, leaving her free to suck in the blessed air. There were only a few inches between the surface of the gurgling water and the rock. She tilted her face upward, and her forehead scraped the gritty ceiling as she took deep, gulping breaths. The water lapped her face, but the current no longer tugged at her body. Her sore and tired arms and legs kept treading water, and she thanked the Mother and Father for this cavern. In the utter darkness, she could not tell how long it was. Perhaps it was the beginning of the dungeon. "Just like Crag Isle," she said between heavy gasps.

But when she swam on her back in the direction she thought was further into the dungeon, the water crept back up over her face to the ceiling. She pulled back to where she could take in gulps of air, wondering if she had lost her sense of direction and had gone back towards the river. She swam the other way only to meet water lapping the rock once again. She tried every direction, but, meeting the same result, she soon determined she was in a small cavern in the midst of the tunnel.

So. Not the dungeons after all. Only a small breathing space along the way. She would have to dive back down and continue. Panic stabbed her as she realized she had forgotten which way she needed to swim. It was impossible to orient herself in this thick darkness. She was blind and buried deep within the bowels of the earth, where there was no up or down, left or right. What if she chose the wrong way and ended up sucked out to the river? She could not possibly find the nerve to try this again. Ignorance had given her false courage that had all but dissipated, and her body was shaking with cold and fear. And she still did not know what lay before her. What if she chose the right direction, but the tunnel went on too long?

She could still turn back. If she went back down the shaft, she would be swimming with the current and could make it out to the river easily. She could go back to look for Galdor and the others. If anyone could find their way out of the fighting that must be taking place between the Ilarchae and the Torrlonders, it would be her friends. But, even if she could escape this darkness, how would she find them in a city gripped by invasion? Would she be able to see anyone ever again? Panic surged in her, and she spun around as she treaded water. She sobbed in between her quickening, erratic breaths. Realizing she had no idea what direction to swim in this narrow space of darkness, she could only think of the vast amount of rock all around her, threatening to close its jaws and crush the life out of her.

She took a deep breath. And then she realized her foolishness. All she needed to do was swim against the current. That was the way up. The way to the Prophet. She would help him. "Just like Crag Isle." She smiled in the darkness, waited until her breathing steadied, and sucked in as much air as she could. Then she dived.

THE PASSAGE NARROWED JUST AS SEREN'S LUNGS WERE MOMENTS from giving way again. She clawed her way forward in the watery darkness, but the current fought her with more ferocity than ever, punching her chest and jerking her head back so hard she thought her neck might snap. She reached for a handhold, and her fingers found a crevice in the slimy rock. She grunted and pulled with the little strength remaining in her weary arms. Up her body inched. Up. Up.

And her head gained freedom from the current. It still sucked at her legs, but a sudden stillness in the water surrounded her upper body. At the same time, she realized she was no longer sealed in a narrow passage, for she could move her arms freely. Straddling the sides of the tunnel, her feet found solid rock, and she kicked with her legs. As if breaking loose from bonds, her body floated free of the current, and she swam upward.

Her face breached the water's surface, and this time she raised one hand, which slapped against another low rock ceiling, to keep from banging her head. She sucked in air, stale and foul-smelling like moldy wood and yet the most delicious she had ever taken into her lungs.

"Damn me." Heavy gasps escaped her as she sucked in the beautiful air in the darkness. "This is *nothing* like Crag Isle."

Treading water, she felt ahead with a hand that trembled half in weariness and half in fear that the water would rise up to the rock again, and she had a vision of an endless watery tunnel with small caverns like the previous one interspersed along it. But this time the gap between the water's surface and the ceiling expanded until she could keep her head out of the water with no difficulty. The gap continued to grow until the tips of her wrinkled, water-laden fingers lost contact with the ceiling, which she could not see for the utter darkness. For all she knew, the rock ceiling soared a hundred feet above her, and she was in a huge hollow below the earth. Yet, by the deadened sounds of the splashing water and the lack of an echo, she guessed the ceiling was not far off, and that there was a gradual slope ahead of her that would open up further. Perhaps her feet could touch the floor.

She took a deep breath and plunged beneath the cold water. When her bare feet sank into the slime-covered bottom, she reckoned her head was less than a foot beneath the surface. She swam farther along and surfaced, and this time, she could stand on her toes with her face tilted above the water. She swam still farther, hoping she was keeping to a straight line and proceeding with caution in the darkness lest she bump into a wall. The next time she stood, her entire upper body surfaced. The air was cold, and she shivered as goosebumps covered her flesh. Drops from her hair and from the ceiling plopped into the water all around her, making her feel like she was standing in a pond while it was raining on a starless night.

Seren squinted ahead in the darkness. Perhaps her eyes were playing tricks on her, but she thought there might be a dim glow up there in the distance. She sloshed through the water and kept her hands before her as she headed toward the dull, ruddy glow. Her left hand brushed against a wet stone wall, and she let it trail there to keep her bearings. After a moment, however, her hand slid along something with a different texture, smoother and softer than the stone. Wood. A door. The stone returned as she sloshed forward, and not long later, more wood. *Doors. The entrances to cells.* She smiled. *The dungeons for sure. He's here somewhere.*

She wondered if the remains of some unfortunate prisoners lurked behind these old doors, rotting beneath the water. She tried not to think about it as she waded toward the dim light. It seemed to glow a bit brighter as she approached it, but it was so feeble that it was hard to tell. The water dropped down to her thighs, then to her knees, and her soaked body shivered more as she emerged. When the water's surface licked her ankles, the rust-colored light took the shape of a bar floating just above her.

Her hand touched something hard, and she jerked back. She reached forward again and slid her palm along the smooth, damp wood. A door just before her. The weak light was leaking in from the top, where there must have been a gap. Seren took a deep breath. She had almost bumped into the door without realizing what it was. She knew nothing of what lay beyond it, except that it was the way to the Prophet.

Feeling the surface of the door, she found a latch and pushed. It seemed to be locked. She tried pulling. It would not budge. For a moment, her breathing quickened as she imagined remaining trapped in the darkness behind this door. She worked the latch and pushed again, this time harder. A bit of movement, and water sloshed as the door gave way and more of the ruddy light forced its way into the widening gap.

Seren breathed a sigh. Looking down at her body, she thought she could see her hands as dim shadows. It felt like ages since she had been able to use her eyes. She stepped forward and realized there was a wall before her, so she turned right, whence the source of the weak light came. It was somewhere high above her. She headed toward it.

A stab of pain jolted her toe as hard rock greeted it, and while it throbbed she cursed and realized there were stairs in front of her. Keeping her left hand on the cold, wet wall to steady herself, she began climbing.

LIKE THE DARKNESS, THE STAIRS SEEMED TO GO ON FOREVER. IT DID not help that she crept along to avoid missing her footing on the slippery, wet rock. All the while, she shivered from the cold and her dread as she climbed higher. Save for the dripping water, the dungeons were as silent as they were dark, the most lifeless thing she had ever encountered, and she almost longed for the sound of any voice as much as she feared the Torrlonders discovering her.

At length she came to a landing, upon which there stood another door, which she felt with her hands. Seren found the latch and pulled the door open, whereupon a stale, musty draft brushed against her face. Within that door abode complete blackness, like a yawning hole in the world, whereas the weak source of light still beckoned from somewhere above her. She debated a moment and, feeling the lifelessness emanating from the dark doorway, turned and ascended more steps.

Hunger began to pinch Seren's belly, and her shivering increased until her teeth chattered. Climbing the cold stone stairs grew more difficult, and her tired muscles ached, so she made frequent pauses while leaning a shoulder against the wall. But the light seemed to gain some strength, and she decided to focus upon it to keep her mind away from thoughts of the Torrlonders, or something worse, grabbing her in the darkness.

The light grew in intensity until it became a definite glow. As Seren drew near the glow, she understood what it was. The stairs ended, and to her right was a door, beneath which leaked the light. She looked down at her hands tinged brownish-red in the glow. It was strange and wonderful to be able to differentiate her body from the darkness.

At last. An end to the long night. Even if the Torrlonders found her, it would be a joy to leave it behind. She released a deep breath, found the latch, and pushed. The door's hinges squeaked. She squinted at the flood of brightness that bathed her, and she blinked for a while. After her eyes began to adjust, she realized what the source of the light was: a simple torch in a sconce on the wall. It showed her a long corridor carved through the rough rock, along which other interspersed torches revealed closed doors. Unlike the lower levels, there was a presence about this place, as if someone had recently dwelled in it.

Yet it was silent. Nothing stirred. Still shivering, Seren took a few tentative steps forward, beyond relieved at least to have her vision restored.

Her relief did not last long. The silence was a weight pressing in on her, a threat of something dreadful about to happen. She crept down the corridor, all the while keeping her distance from each closed door, behind which she knew not what lurked. Yet she would need to investigate if she wanted to find the Prophet. He was down here. He had to be.

Seren took a deep breath, chewed on her lip, and approached one of the doors. She tried the latch, but she could neither push nor pull the door. Locked. She hesitated, and then she gave it a gentle knock. No answer but a hollow echo. She knocked harder. Nothing. If it was a cell of some sort, it seemed to be empty. She could not beat down the stout door with her bare fists, so she decided to move on to the next one, where she met the same result. She tried several more before deciding they were all empty.

She continued until another corridor branched off the one she walked along, which presented her with a choice. Standing and shivering, she looked one way and then another. "Now what?" Her voice sounded tiny and weak. The silence was smothering her. She glanced toward each corridor, unable to decide which to take. What if there were more corridors? There must be. Would she be able to walk down them all without growing lost in a maze? Where were all the Torrlonders? The prisoners? Most of all, the Prophet? Was there no one down here but her? Was this some cruel trap she had fallen in? She was alone. Her shivering grew almost violent. Leaning her back on the rough, damp wall, she put her hand in her hair and tugged at it. "What to do? Help me. Someone help me."

The silence swallowed her words. No one would help her. She knew that. Her hands fell to her sides, and she clenched them into tight fists. "Well, then. I'll have to help myself."

Seren took a few deep breaths, and then she looked up in defiance of the silence. Before she realized she had decided to do it, she began to sing. At first her voice was thin and weak, and the Ondunic words croaked out of her throat. But they brought to mind the mournful sound of her father's fiddle and the flitting strings of Abon's harp, and they began to gather their own strength, which fed Seren until her quivering voice steadied. She stood there and sang, not caring who heard her, or if no one heard her. Pouring all the sorrow and beauty she had known in her short life into the song, she filled the silence, and it yielded to her, retreating in tatters as her voice echoed in the corridors.

Her fears dissipated as Seren sang with complete freedom, and even her shivering ceased. Beyond the dungeons her song soared, back to the rugged, wind- and rain-swept coast of Caergilion. In her song she wove her parents, her brother, her friends Len and Tob and the others she grew up with, Edge and the other Torrlonders who had befriended her, Galdor, Abon, Gnorn, and Orvandil. And the Prophet. She sang for no one and yet for everyone she had ever known. And since it was an Ondunic song, it was, of course, both melancholy and full of wonder, and it spoke of loss, which Seren understood to her core.

She drew a deep breath to prepare for another verse, but her voice faltered and fell silent. Had she heard something? A distant cry? She thought she had heard a man's voice. It had been faint, so she could not be certain, but it seemed to have come from somewhere ahead of her, along the corridor she had been walking down.

Whether she had imagined the cry or not, she made her decision. She walked down the corridor until she came to the entrance to another hallway branching off the main one, down which torches lit the way and illuminated the closed doors. "Another choice."

Seren hesitated. She began to think her imagination had supplied the man's cry. It had been so indistinct and weak. Perhaps her ears were so ready to hear any sign of life that her mind had conjured up the sound. "Only one way to find out."

She sang a verse of the same song, projecting her voice first down the main corridor and then turning toward the hallway branching from it. Then, she stopped and listened.

A thin cry. This time she was sure she had not imagined it. It had come from the side hallway. She crept into it and kept her gaze on the shadowy spaces between the torches lest something leap out of them to surprise her. Up ahead there was something on the floor. It glowed orange-red in the torch light, but she thought it would be white in the sunlight. As she neared the object, she saw there were two of them lying on the damp rock of the floor. Bodies. Wearing white robes. The kind the Way's priests all wore. But something was not right about them. When Seren came within a few feet of them, recognition came with a startled gasp, and she jerked backwards.

Instead of heads, the two bodies' necks ended in meaty stumps with vertebrae protruding in the middle. One still had a jaw attached, but the rest of their heads were gone. Blood pooling beneath them glistened in the torch light, and red speckled their white robes. The light also revealed little gobbets of flesh stuck to the wall behind the two corpses.

Seren's whole body was trembling, and her stuttering breaths came hard and fast. "Mother and Father have mercy." Her voice quivered, but she had to speak, to say something in a futile attempt to combat the overwhelming silence and fear looming all around her, creeping in on her, threatening to steal her breath away. "Something . . . Something tells me neither of *you* said anything." But if they had not, who had? Who or what had done that horrible thing to them, and was it still around?

"Seren?"

She screamed and leapt backwards, eyes locked on the dead men. But then she collected herself enough to look at the open door near the two headless corpses. The voice had come from in there. It had said her name. She had not imagined it. And she knew that voice.

The desperate hope that blossomed in her gave her the courage to step forward and tiptoe around the bodies in her path. She entered the doorway and stepped into a small cell containing a table and two chairs. Atop the table were candles melted down to stubs, small islands amidst a pool of wax. Their flames were fitful, but they still emitted enough soft light to illuminate the cell.

Behind the table lay a man on a pallet, his arms stretched above him. Recognizing the brown robe, dark breeches, and white tunic as well as the silver hair and beard, Seren rushed over to him. Even as her vision blurred with tears and sobs began shaking her body, she knelt down and embraced the Prophet. Unable to say a word, she clutched on to his warmth as her body convulsed.

"Seren." His voice was gentle. "It's alright. You're here. You came. How in Eormenlond you got here I could never guess. But I'm so happy to see you."

She nodded into his shoulder but could say nothing as her tears flowed.

"It's alright, little Sister. You're here. I was dreaming of a girl child when your singing woke me. It seemed so real, like a true-dream. No. Perhaps it was not you. Much younger."

She sniffled and nodded and then looked at his kind blue eyes. It was then that she noticed why he was not returning her embrace. His wrists and ankles were locked in manacles and chained to the wall.

"Yes. They're quite snug. We'll have to think of something. Which song of origin could I use? I must recall them. I don't suppose there's a key lying about?"

Seren froze. The sight of the two corpses outside the door had been so overwhelming that she had taken in few details around them, but she recalled a metal loop with a bunch of keys on the floor next to the one with his jaw still attached. "Wait here."

She wiped her eyes with her sleeve, and then she rose and walked back out of the cell. Doing her best not to glance at where the head should have been, she stole up to the body. Not far from its blood-speckled hand lay the bunch of keys. Seren edged toward them and then snatched them in a quick motion, darting away from the stained white robe.

She returned to the Prophet and held up her jingling prize. "These were outside on the floor."

"Excellent. But was there no guard?"

Seren swallowed. "Two men in white robes. Without heads."

"Without . . . ? But where are their heads?"

She glanced at the walls of the cell. "All over. I think."

His eyes widened. "Gods be good. That means . . ." He glanced up at the ceiling, and then he returned his gaze to her, whereupon he gave her a sad smile. "But that must come later." A pained look took over the Prophet's face. "Oh, Seren. You must have gone through such horrors to find your way here. How can I . . ."

"It's alright. I found you."

He smiled at her. "Yes, you did. You must tell me everything. But first, let's see if one of those keys will free me."

She took the bundle of keys and, approaching a manacle around one of his ankles, tried inserting them one at a time. Some fit in the hole but would not turn. Others were too large. By the time she tried about a dozen, she began to fear none of them would work, and her cold, clumsy hand was trembling. But when the next key slipped inside and produced a click, she released a long, relieved sigh. She pulled apart the manacle, which opened up and clanked on the floor after she dropped it. She tried the same key on the other ankle, and that manacle too fell away. Soon enough his wrists were free.

The Prophet sat up with a groan, smiled at Seren, and embraced her. She returned the embrace and sniffled as more tears came. They remained thus for a long time, and a wide grin took over her face as the bliss of that moment chased away all the fears and terrors.

At length, the Prophet broke away from her. He took her by the shoulders and looked in her eyes. "You're soaked and freezing. Here." He reached for a blanket next to the pallet and swept it over her, draping it on her shoulders. He rubbed her shoulders and then embraced her again. "I can't believe you're here. I heard your singing, and I thought it must have been part of my dream. There's only one voice like that. Of all the people, I never expected . . ." He broke off the embrace and gazed in her eyes. A slight smile betrayed his look of mock severity. "You broke your promise."

"So did you. Or you meant to."

He held up his palms in surrender, and the smile took over his face. "So I did." A concerned frown replaced the smile for a moment. "But you must have had quite a journey from Caergilion."

She grinned and nodded. "I came with Galdor, Abon, Gnorn, and Orvandil."

He looked somewhere far away. "Galdor . . . Yes, I remember. It's all come back to me. I remember." He smiled again, wider than ever, and his eyes sparkled. "It's gone, Seren. Gone. I remember everything. From before. My name is Dayraven."

"I know." She smiled. "They told me."

He looked about him and smiled, but it was a weary smile and perhaps tinged with regret. "It's gone."

"What's gone?"

"The elf. The power that was in me. But where are they? Galdor and the others?"

"I left them in East Torrhelm. I don't know if they . . . The Ilarchae are invading the city."

He nodded. "I know. Don't worry for them, though. They'll manage." His eyes narrowed, and he hesitated a moment. "Was there anyone else with them? A woman?"

"A woman?"

"Yes. A southerner. From Asdralad. A sorceress."

Wondering who this woman could be, Seren shook her head. "No."

He looked disappointed for a moment, but then he smiled. "Well." His eyes widened, and his smile grew. "But there's something that can't wait. You once told me about your mother."

Seren frowned. "My mother?"

"Yes. I'm sorry if I'm bringing up painful memories."

"It's alright. I don't mind thinking of her."

He stared at her and then nodded. "You said she was born in Adanon. She was brought to Caergilion as a . . ."

"A slave. Yes. Before she wed Da."

He waited a moment and looked at her with such intensity that she wondered what about her mother was so important to him. "If I may ask, what was her name?"

"Her name? Ria."

"Ria? Just that? It's not short for something else?"

"I never heard her called anything else. It's a common name in Caergilion and Adanon."

"She never mentioned a different name? Like 'Riall'?"

Seren shook her head. "Never."

"Did she ever say if she had any brothers? Back when she was in Adanon?"

"She never spoke about her girlhood. When I was little, I asked once or twice about it, but she got angry, and I never dared to again." She paused a moment. "I wish I could now. There's so much I'd like to know."

Dayraven smiled sadly. "Of course."

"Why do you want to know about her?"

He looked down at the floor and swallowed. "Before I lost my memories in the struggle with the elf, I was going to search for someone named Riall in Caergilion. Somehow the idea of going there survived in my mind. I think that's how I ended up there."

"What did you want with her?"

"She was the sister of . . . my friend. He's like a brother to me. I had promised him we would find his sister. I had thought she might be your mother. I reckon there's no way to know. There must be many Adanese slaves in Caergilion. Still . . ." He looked at her with a smile that could not disguise the weight of the memories passing through his mind. "But it matters little now. I found you instead." He shook his head in disbelief. "And you found your way here."

Seren did not think she could respond without crying again, so she simply nodded.

Dayraven released a long sigh. "I don't suppose you know a way out?"

She nodded again and gained control of her voice by clearing her throat. "Yes. It'll be easier than the way in. But not pleasant. Can you swim?"

"Like a fish."

"Good. We'll have to race sometime."

He laughed. "I'll take that challenge. But first perhaps we'd best find our way out."

She rose and tugged the blanket further over her shoulders. "Follow me."

She led the way out of the cell, taking care to look away from the two headless corpses in the doorway as they stepped around them. Behind her, Dayraven said, "I've an idea who they were."

Seren did not want to talk about them. "We might want to bring along a torch. It's dark where we're headed."

Dayraven walked toward the nearest torch and lifted it from the sconce on the wall. He nodded at her.

"We'll have to make sure it doesn't go out. It's *really* dark."

He smiled at her. "It won't go out." He gazed at the torch with a peculiar intensity in his eyes, and then he mumbled some words in a strange language. At once, the torch flared, flooding the corridor with brightness. Dayraven sighed as he nodded. "Yes. Still there. He must have left the gift that was native to me when he took the elf's power. I suppose it was more than enough."

Seren was used to the Prophet's miracles, but she still gawked at the torch in wonder. She was about to ask him what he was talking about when his gaze jerked upward at the ceiling. He looked back at her with widened eyes. "Did you feel that?"

She shook her head. "What?"

His mouth hung open, and sudden dread seemed to fill him. "I'm afraid I made a terrible mistake." He looked at her. "We might find something very unpleasant above in the city."

"You mean something besides the Ilarchae?"

"Something far worse. We must be careful, but I must hurry. I may still be able to help. Lead us out of here, Seren. But you must hide when I ask you to."

She nodded. "Alright. Let's go."

25

THE RECKONING

His bare feet flapping on the cold cobblestones of a street leading to Great Cheaping, King Earconwald giggled at his liberation and sense of purpose as he panted and jogged toward the commotion. Tall buildings on either side of the street cast long shadows with narrow strips of sunlight illuminating the spaces in between. He had hitched up his nightdress so that he would not trip on it. From the sounds of the yells and shrieks, a large crowd was approaching from up ahead.

A few of his people were already heading his way, running by him with panicked faces and dismayed cries. Wearing shabby and dull clothes, they appeared to be the poorer sort, mostlike refugees from East Torrhelm. The eyes on their smudged faces were bulging with fright, and their wide-mouthed screams exposed their yellowed teeth. With their hard lives, they were not the most beautiful specimens of humanity, but they were his people. Yet none of them seemed to recognize him. Or even notice him, for that matter. *Too busy fleeing. No matter. I will save them.*

The visions of suffering and dying still assaulted his mind. But he embraced them now, knowing they gave him the power to defy and command the Ilarchae. He showed his teeth in a wide smile and released a long laugh. His moment grew nigh. He would reckon with the Ilarchae and save his city, redeeming the memory of his kingship. They would sing of this deed. He might even go down in the annals as one of Torrlond's greatest kings. Earconwald II, the savior of Torrhelm.

More and more citizens rushed toward Earconwald, and, though the street was wide, it grew more difficult to avoid them. He needed to calm them so that he could reach the barbarians. "Fear not, my people! I've come to save you! I, your king. I must . . ." He grunted when a man elbowed him. As he collided with another body, someone shoved him. He staggered and, after he found his footing, looked back in vain to see who had done it. There were too many fleeing people. Their screams were growing louder, blending with the horrors running through his mind. *How dare they?* Perhaps he should have worn his crown. *Well, no matter. The kingship rests in my body, not in the trappings of power.*

He turned back toward the source of their panic. Smoke rose above the distant buildings, darkening the sky. Behind the fear-laden screams of the citizens loomed the furious roar of the Ilarchae, growing louder by the moment. There must have been scores of thousands of the savages, and they were not far away. He would need to reach them before they massacred his subjects. He had to act to save Torrhelm from destruction, but all these commoners were in the way. "Make way! Your king commands you! I have come to save you all!" The bodies pressing in around him stank of sweat and terror. They seemed spurred by some blind instinct, like animals stampeding without a rational thought to guide them.

He held up his palm and assumed a commanding pose, legs spread wide. "Move aside! I am your king!"

"Out of the way, damned fool!"

"I command you to . . ." Earconwald wheezed and buckled in half when the large man punched him in the gut. He leaned over and clutched his stomach as the man pushed him out of the way and ran on. When he could find his breath, he croaked at the man, who had disappeared, "Peasant. Slave. How dare you even touch me?"

A crack vibrated his skull, and bright shafts of light erupted in his

vision. A moment later came the sharp pain on the top of his head. Earconwald grasped his head and reeled. Someone had struck him with something hard. Or collided with him while he was bent over. He glanced at his palm, on which glistened a smear of blood. He tried to get his bearings, but there were bodies crowding all round him, shoving him and suffocating him with their stink. And the piercing screams assaulted him, both around him and within his mind. “I am your king. I must save you.”

But the words slurred from his thick tongue, and more shoves threw him off balance until the cobblestones hammered into his bare knees, skinning them and sending a bruising pain stabbing up his legs. The street tore open his hands when they slapped it to break his fall. “I am your . . .” When he tried to push himself up, a heavy boot stomped on his right hand, shattering bones with a crack. Earconwald wailed in anguish.

Another boot turned his wail into a muffled grunt when it slammed into his jaw, sending him sprawling as the iron tang of blood filled his mouth. The side of his face throbbed, and several small objects — white with smears of red — clattered on the cobbles when he spat out blood. *Teeth*, he realized with a mixture of curiosity and consternation. Red stains spattered the front of his nightdress, and he whimpered and wheezed through his ruined mouth as more boots and shoes surrounded him, heedless of his pain and vulnerability.

Agony radiated in his side when something bludgeoned his ribs and splintered them, thrusting the air from his lungs and making it impossible to breathe as he lay face down on the street. He writhed and tried to get up, but the pain nailed him to the cold, hard cobblestones. He needed to address the Ilarchae. To banish the voices. To save his people.

More feet stomped on him, tearing open flesh and cracking bones. Bloodstains blossomed all over his shredded nightdress. No one stopped to help him. The screams were taking over everything. He could not draw in air. He was suffocating beneath all the feet and the cries. The pain suffused him, so ubiquitous that it became an abstract thing, a state of general torment impossible to assign to one location. His legs and arms shattered in multiple places underneath the horrible pressure, and he could no longer even twitch. Blood — his blood — was staining the street and running in the cracks between stones, and the boots that stomped over him left red prints on the cobbles.

Something heavy came down hard and swift on the back of his neck where it entered his skull. There was a terrible crunch accompanied by a flash of red, and then darkness. The voices that had so tormented him winked out forever.

Flames growled, steel clashed, and the fleeing Torrlonders screamed out their terror. Warriors among the Folk of the Tribes shouted their triumph over the silent dead, whose bodies littered the cobbled streets. Spattered with the blood of her foes, Skuld slid her blade out of the soldier's limp body, which shuddered and went still. He had fought well, facing the Folk of the Tribes even as most of his fellow soldiers bolted.

After the bridges fell, the rest of city had succumbed with token resistance. Most of the citizens scurried away in a frenzied panic, even though Surt had given orders not to harm anyone not bearing a weapon or putting up a fight. They would need thralls, after all.

But first there was a little more fighting to do, which made Skuld grin as she marched in the vanguard of Surt's army toward the hall of Torrlond's kings. In truth, the conquest of Torrhelm had been much easier than she expected. These stone-dwellers were ill disciplined and, for the most part, cowardly. Especially their women-folk. Most could not defend themselves, which elicited a growl of contempt from her. She was weary of hearing their helpless shrieks. A small number of the soldiers were capable fighters, but even they suffered from a lack of strong leadership. And this was the most powerful kingdom of Eormenlond. The vaunted prowess of Torrlond seemed like mere wind to Skuld now, though she had to admit the piles of stone around her were impressive enough. And soon she would get a look at the greatest of them all.

A few grey-kirtled soldiers stood in the path of Surt's army, which filled the streets leading to the king's hall. Most threw down their weapons and ran. Bowmen shot them down, piercing their backs with

arrows, for they had cast aside their honor and deserved such a fate, to be shot like a hunted animal. The few who stood their ground gained more honorable deaths. Surt himself led the warriors who fought them. The war-leader carved through the ranks of Torrlonder soldiers, wielding his sword with more strength and speed than any other warrior could imagine. He was the greatest leader the Folk of the Tribes had ever produced. But it had taken Munzil to recognize Surt's full potential and bestow a greater vision upon the Folk of the Tribes. *Her* Munzil. She wore a fierce grin when she thought of her lover. Once they finished sweeping away the Torrlonders, she would reunite with him and celebrate the wondrous victory he had foreseen.

Warriors filled the streets, and the Torrlonder resistance melted away. The Folk of the Tribes followed Surt toward the hall of the Torrlonder king, of which Skuld gained her first view. Her mouth hung open and her head tilted as far up as her helm allowed while she took in the majestic heights of the massive structure. Stone piled on stone and carved into pinnacles like the tops of trees lining the peak of a mountain. It was so vast that she wondered if the gods had aided these Torrlonders in the making of it.

But she had little time to ponder this, for the warriors were shouting their battle cries as they surged toward the wall surrounding the king's hall. Racing ahead, she vowed to be one of the first over that wall. When she reached the stone barrier with panting breaths, she slid her blade into its scabbard and grasped the first handholds she could find. The wall proved easy to scale, for there were many carvings upon it. Skuld climbed up a large statue of some bearded man wearing a robe like the ones that covered the Torrlonder priests. His expression was stern, but it mattered naught to her as she planted her boot on his face.

Her fellow warriors clambered on every section of the wall. They overwhelmed the few grey-kirtled soldiers awaiting them atop it, hacking them to pieces and throwing their bodies down. Skuld swung over the other side and, after climbing down a few feet, leapt and landed in a crouch on the cobbled courtyard. Awaiting their deaths, a couple hundred soldiers stood in a shieldwall between the Folk of the Tribes and the massive open doors of the king's hall.

One in the center of the Torrlonder shieldwall shouted commands, and the soldiers assumed a defensive stance. Surt sprinted ahead of his followers straight toward the commander, and the other warriors knew well enough to keep out of his way. Skuld smiled as she unsheathed her blade and ran toward the fight.

The Folk of the Tribes dashed against the shieldwall, producing a terrible din of crashing steel and screams. Splinters flew from shields, blood spattered from bodies, and the Torrlonder line reeled back. Skuld leapt and kicked a shield held before her, sending the soldier behind it sprawling on his back with a grunt. Before he could rise, her blade skewered his chest, forcing out the man's last breath in a wheeze as his limbs shuddered. She looked up from her kill to see Surt engaging the Torrlonder commander, whose helm had fallen off. Blood ran from the man's nose onto his grey beard. His shield was gone, revealing the three red stripes on his shoulder that marked a captain among the Torrlonders. And though he was an old man, he moved with deadly grace, as a trained soldier should. Against Surt, he had no chance.

The huge war-leader dwarfed the old man, who yelled as he leapt forward and swung. Halfway through his swing, he changed his grip on the sword and altered the arc of the blow — a skillful feint that Surt easily read and countered with a strike so hard that the Torrlonder staggered back. The old man managed to parry Surt's next thrust, but he could do nothing to block the massive fist that hammered into his face. His head snapped backwards, and the rest of his body followed as his limbs flailed. A groan wheezed out of him when he landed on his back, and his sword clanged on the cobblestones.

The Torrlonder commander stirred, which impressed Skuld since Surt had slain many with a single blow such as that. The greybeard's body trembled as he rolled over and raised himself to his knees. A moan escaped his bleeding mouth, and he staggered up to his feet. Only for Surt's blade to carve through his neck, which spewed blood as the head spun in the air before smacking into the cobblestones. Holding his dripping blade, the war-leader stood over the body as it swayed and thudded to the ground. The commander had been the last defender to fall.

Skuld's gaze turned to the open doors of the king's hall. They loomed higher than any structure ever conceived of in the Wildlands. For a moment, there was a strange silence as the thousands of warriors filling the courtyard and the thousands more still outside the statue-lined wall gawked at the massive building before them and waited for Surt's command. The great war-leader smiled and stepped forward, but then he halted as his face hardened at something he beheld.

Skuld looked back at the doors, whence emerged a lone figure from the shadows within. Her eyes narrowed as the man strode into the sunlight, which revealed the white robe he wore. So, one of the Torrlonder holy men. And not just any one. A sharp grin of recognition crossed Skuld's face, and she locked her gaze onto the man pacing toward the Folk of the Tribes. The smiling fool. The liar. The one full of such glorious promises and poisonous words. He had become the chief of the Torrlonder holy men, she had learned. She had never liked Joruman, who fancied himself so clever and powerful. It would be a pleasure to watch him die.

It was Surt's right to slay the deceiver and betrayer, but Skuld's sword arm twitched all the same as the little man drew nearer. She expected Joruman's usual smirk, but instead his face wore a blank expression. Yet that was not the strangest thing about him. A weird light flickered in his eyes. Skuld recognized it as a sign of him unleashing magic, and since no one else was acting, she leapt forward with her sword raised.

Except that her body did not move. It refused to obey her. She stood frozen like all the other warriors of the Folk of the Tribes. Even Surt was motionless, his struggle visible only in his uncomprehending eyes.

A vast shadow swallowed the entire city as the sky darkened, as if the moon covered the sun at that moment, promising the cataclysmic end of times, including the death of the very gods. Warmth and light bled away from the air, leaving a cold vacuum, a looming darkness that stole away all glory, joy, and meaning. At the same time, where the monster wearing Joruman's face stood, a bright light rent the world asunder, and cold emanated from that tear. The chill pierced Skuld deep down in her guts, seeped right into the marrow of her bones.

Seldom in her life had she known fear, and even seldomer had she acknowledged it, but if she could have spoken or uttered even a sound, she would have wailed in abject terror.

The otherworldly creature in the guise of Joruman's flesh blazed with a blinding brightness and gazed at Surt's army, the assembled Folk of the Tribes, with eyes that robbed them of their clan, their tribe, and their selves. Looming before her with the threat of annihilation, those eyes filled Skuld's vision. Her mind swiftly followed the path her body had taken: helpless surrender. While her capacity for thought disappeared along with every memory and all else she had ever been, the light behind the eyes was consuming her. They shredded her until the warmth within her diminished and flickered. Just before the chill snuffed it out, one final thought stirred within her. *Stay away, Munzil.*

IT HAD BEGUN.

Of course, it always had been.

In a sense, all that was needed was to allow them to see the truth, the illusion of their painful existence. They had never existed in the way they thought of themselves, clutching onto the tiny bit of energy concentrated within them and blind to the vastness of the life all around them, from which they were never truly apart. They thought themselves so self-aware, but they were sightless worms with little idea of anything beyond the narrow desires of their bodies and sickened minds. They had blinded themselves in the interest of prolonging and accumulating, worshippers of the ephemeral with no ultimate purpose. It was the strangest madness life had ever produced, this clinging to self and to the empty tokens that conferred the delusion that one self was more important than all others.

An absurdity. How could one piece of life be more important than another? Take away the mask that existed only in the world of forms, and the illusion disappeared. All was one. It was this desperate cleaving to themselves that produced such agony, both to themselves and to the life all around them. Among all mortal creatures, only the humans could not see or accept the truth. They were a disease in the world of forms, a kind of twisted life that consumed itself and all else around it in a madness born from greed and fear.

Tens of thousands of them stood before the flesh it inhabited, cleansed and now part of its will, extensions of it dwelling in the fragile bodies the former owners had so grasped onto in their foolish delusion that such was their ultimate form. They had been warriors. Their bodies were muscled and scarred and hard, though just as fleeting as all other flesh forms. It would not release those bodies just yet, for an important insight had come to it. The insight had derived, perhaps, from the one who had dwelled in this flesh-home before it did, for that man's memories were part of the fabric of the body and so part of it. So were the man's rage and his terror, now amplified a thousandfold within the far mightier storm of its power. The rage and terror it had inherited from the one who had used the title of supreme priest were the source of his realization.

It was fitting. Here was the perfect weapon to enact its will. There were many other humans in this dwelling place awaiting their liberation, cringing and hiding in their desperate desire to cling to what they thought was life. This mortal army had existed for the glory of battle, and the echoes of the warriors' hunger still stirred within it, though the energy that had animated them was gone. While alive, they had begun the process of freeing the people of this place, and now that their thousands of bodies were vessels of its energy, they would finish it with its will guiding them.

Beneath the bridge Galdor stood and waited with his companions, trying to nurse his wavering hope that he would find Seren alive, and that he would be able to do something about Dayraven. None of them spoke. So thick was their despair that any attempt to voice courage would have seemed transparent and pathetic. And so they kept their dread to themselves, lest in speaking they should acknowledge it and smother what little hope remained.

Foam skimmed along the greasy surface of the River Ea, and every piece of refuse that floated by gave a start to the wizard's heart. All of them save the madman locked their gazes on the river. The former priest of the Way quivered and whimpered in his hiding place in the shadows, refusing to come out. Galdor gave an occasional glance in the poor wretch's direction, though he need not have since he could feel the horrible gap in the man's mind, whence the gift had been ripped from him. In the distance, the din of the Ilarchae roaring and fighting their way through West Torrhelm grew dimmer, though the screams and shrieks seemed to never cease. Another tragedy the wizard could do nothing to avert. *And far worse is yet to come. I've failed.*

As if in cruel and horrible confirmation of this thought, an eruption of vast power shook Galdor to his core even as the sky darkened, deepening the gloom beneath the bridge until it was almost like night. The wizard shuddered and stumbled, and he would have fallen to his knees had Abon not caught him and held him up. Orvandil assisted the shaper in getting Galdor to his feet.

Abon's widened eyes peered at the wizard. "What's happening, my lord?"

Galdor swallowed, recognizing the terrible chill invading his bones. He had first felt it at the Battle of Thulhan in Sildharan. Then, he had been mere feet away from the source of that power. Even at a distance, it terrified him to his core, for it seemed to have a more sinister edge to it this time, a malicious intent that boded ill for anyone close enough to feel it. He struggled to find his voice. "We're too late. Dayraven. He's gone. The power of the elf is free."

His companions blinked at him with their mouths open, but no words came from them until Orvandil shook his head. "Are you sure?"

Galdor stared at the Thjoth. "Yes. We've lost. Something terrible beyond words is happening. The elf's power. It has some desire. It will consume all within the city, I fear. Perhaps there'll be nowhere to hide."

"Shit." Abon released a long sigh. "What do we do?"

The wizard sighed. "If you would live, your only chance is to flee as fast and as far as you can. East. You must head east. This power is far beyond me. Go."

"And what of you?" Orvandil frowned at Galdor.

It's time. I'm so weary. And I miss you, Arna. More than ever. "I'll remain here. To wait for Seren. But there's no point in all of us staying. You must leave now."

"No."

Galdor turned to face Gnorn, whose voice had rumbled and shaken when he said the lone word.

Tears welled in the Dweorg's eyes, and he shook his head as he spoke through a pained frown. "I will not leave. I stay here. For Seren. And for Dayraven. Until the end."

The others bowed their heads, and no one moved. Galdor looked on them with a sad smile, and he nodded. The end would come soon enough.

MUNZIL GLANCED UP AT THE SKY AGAIN. SOMETHING FOUL AND wrong had drained the color from the world. It was more than just the sudden and unnatural darkness. It was a dreadful cold that enfolded the entire city and leached beneath his skin into his bones, stealing the warmth from him. He shivered as he marched along with the others across the bridge into West Torrhelm. The screams and shrieks coming from up ahead did not surprise him. But something else did. Something was lacking. There were no war chants and no shouts of triumph. This was the sound of slaughter, but not of victory.

It had not taken much to persuade Bolverk and Marg to accompany him, for they found the darkness as worrisome as he did. He was inclined to agree with Bolverk that some sorcery was afoot, of a sort they had never encountered. Munzil would not believe anything could defeat the Folk of the Tribes, especially with Surt at their head and the gods behind them. But the dread in the air was so thick that it was best to make sure all was well, even though Surt had sent no word for help. There were enough warriors waiting in East Torrhelm to make a difference should the main body of Surt's army need them for reinforcements.

The two war-leaders had picked a dozen warriors each to join this scouting party. Just managing to hide their suspicions of each other behind a mask of courtesy, Bolverk and Marg were careful to bring the same number of followers. Munzil did not blame Marg for suspecting the war-leader of the Raven Eyes, and Bolverk seemed to trust no one as a matter of policy. Fortunately, Surt was strong enough to hold the various tribes and factions together, and victory had a tendency to buy loyalty. As did a common threat.

The shadows cast by tall buildings enveloped them as they hastened at a quick march closer to the screams, which spoke of pure terror. Munzil wished he could see further ahead. Fighting in a city was not the same as honest battle on an open field. It was full of surprises, and a warrior had to be ready for anything around the next corner. He gazed up ahead, where the noises grew louder at once. A score of Torrlonder citizens burst into the street and ran towards them in wide-eyed panic. Women of every age, old men, and children. There were no soldiers among them.

The Torrlonders jerked to a halt when their eyes met Munzil's scouting party, and they looked left and right for some means of escape. Their hesitation cost them.

Raising no battle cry and giving no warning, several dozen warriors from the Folk of the Tribes caught up to them from behind. Wielding their blades with no mercy, they carved into the helpless Torrlonder citizens. The latter shrieked as their blood sprayed all over cobblestones and buildings, and before Munzil could blink twice, the Torrlonders were all dead. It was shameless and profitless murder, and he was outraged that his brother and sister warriors could commit such an atrocity, even in the heat of battle.

Marg stormed forward, and his men followed. "What have you done? These were no soldiers! Surt gave orders not to slay them. I am Marg, war-leader of the Broad Eagles. Of what tribe are you? Yours will be claiming fewer thralls than the rest."

Munzil thought he might have recognized a couple of the blood-spattered warriors as belonging to the Cleft Skulls. But none of them answered Marg. Instead, they met him with silent gazes and strode closer, holding out their reddened weapons.

Steel whispered as Marg drew his blade, and his warriors as well as the Raven Eyes followed suit. "Did you not hear me? Are you cowards who will not name your tribe?"

Munzil turned to Bolverk. "Something's not right. What ails them? Why don't they speak?"

Bolverk was squinting at the oncoming warriors with his one eye. The war-leader's blade was out, but he hesitated and gave no commands to his warriors, who held back behind the Broad Eagles.

The silent warriors stepped closer, and an eerie chill ran along Munzil's spine, causing him to shudder. But Marg let loose a loud and defiant laugh. "Fools! You won't find us as easy to kill as those helpless Torrlonders."

Even as Marg waded forward, several of his warriors belted out war-cries and dashed ahead of their war-leader. Steel clanged, and the Broad Eagles pressed forward for only a moment before the greater numbers of their opponents pushed them back. Two of them went down, and their foes hacked them to pieces. Marg roared and swung his big blade, swiping the head from one of his attackers in a spray of blood.

Before the tall war-leader could strike again, his body jerked, even though no weapon had touched him. The silent warriors that had been about to strike him froze in mid-swing and then left Marg alone to fight the remaining members of the Broad-Eagles. Their war-leader stood unmoving for a moment, turned about, and, with the same blank expression the silent ones wore, thrust his blade to pierce one of his own warriors through the back.

Munzil shared the dying man's shock. Why had Marg turned on his own people? It happened again when another man of the Broad Eagles slew a woman, went rigid, and, as stone-faced as the others, began attacking members of his own tribe. The cold was seizing Munzil's body, seeping away his strength and courage. Rooted to where he stood, he jerked his gaze toward Bolverk. "We must do something."

Just then, another group of panicked Torrlonder citizens spilled into the street from an alley, seizing the attention of the group attacking Munzil's party. The silent warriors pivoted toward the easier prey. The Torrlonders' shrieks grew in pitch and desperation when the possessed ones began hewing them down, and another group of tribes-people emerged from the alley to join in the slaughter. All the silent warriors of the Folk of the Tribes wore no emotion on their faces, and none of them bellowed a war cry or said a word.

The one-eyed war-leader of the Raven Eyes gawked at what was unfolding with his face wrinkled in an expression like disgust. "Something possesses them. Some magic. It takes us when we slay them." He sheathed his blade and stepped backwards. "We can't fight this. Away!" The last word was an order to his warriors, who followed Bolverk's example when he hastened back the way they had come.

With deep shame and horror burning inside him, Munzil ran alongside Bolverk and the Raven Eyes. He glanced back at the slaughter and picked out Marg's tall form chopping his blade down onto a prostrate Torrlonder. He had no doubt Marg and the others would come after them once they finished massacring the hapless citizens of Torrhelm.

Munzil's heart pounded and his breaths came fast as they fled through alleys and streets. More than ever he misliked the tall buildings that hid potential foes from his view. He looked over his shoulder again. Fortunately for him and the Raven Eyes of his party, there seemed to be plenty of citizens of Torrhelm to kill, for there was no immediate pursuit. That did not prevent Bolverk and his Raven Eyes from sprinting east until they reached one of the bridges over the River Ea. Having little choice, Munzil stayed with them. Once they crossed the bridge, Bolverk held up a hand and halted. His warriors stopped. They were all bent over and panting for breath, and they kept glancing back west. "What in the name of the gods happened to them?" said one in a quivering voice.

"I know not, but could you not feel it?" said another. "When I saw them, it was like ice in my guts. There's some demon magic at work here. It's taken them."

"Aye. But has it taken them all?"

Silence met the warrior's question, and they all looked at one another.

Bolverk looked up and gathered his breath. "It has."

More silence followed, and guilt stole into the warriors' eyes as they glanced around. They all knew what their war-leader was saying.

Munzil shook his head in horror. Skuld was back there. So was

Surt, and everyone else. "We don't know. We can't just leave them to the magic. They're our brothers and sisters. The Folk of the Tribes."

Bolverk scowled at him. "What would you have me do? You saw what happens when we slay them. We join them. How would you fight such magic? It takes anyone who stands against it."

"But, we can't . . ." As if losing his voice in a nightmare, Munzil looked on them all with his mouth stuck open. None of them save Bolverk would meet his eyes.

Thc war-leader of the Raven Eyes smirked. "Your gods have failed or fooled us, Munzil of the Grey Wolves. Don't be a damned fool. You don't wish to say what you fear, but you feel it just as I do: The dark magic has taken them all, and it works its will through them. You feel it stretching out towards us even now. Tell me you don't hear its whispering call. It wants us all, and there is but one defense: to flee."

"No." Munzil spoke through clenched teeth, but with little conviction.

Bolverk shrugged. "They're all as good as dead. I care not if you stay to die as well." He began to turn away.

Munzil watched him take several paces. "Where will you go?"

"East." The war-leader stopped but kept his back to Munzil. "I'll gather the Raven Eyes from the Carcass Gate and flee from this cursed place. The remaining Broad Eagles may accompany us, unless they too wish to perish. Perhaps we'll return to the Wildlands. We don't have the numbers to hold the lands we conquered." He turned to look at Munzil. "Your dream was a lie. You've killed them all." Bolverk raised his fist. "Let's move!"

The Raven Eyes ran behind their leader and soon disappeared behind a building. Munzil stared after them and, for a moment, considered following. *No.* Clenching his fists, he remained alone, rigid like one of the Torrlonders' statues at the end of the bridge. "I must find her." He would not abandon Skuld. He needed to discover if there were other survivors like him. Perhaps there would be a way to free the Folk of the Tribes from the magic ensnaring them. It was impossible that it could have taken Surt. The gods had given him a vision, and they were not so cruel as to lead them to this. "It cannot be. It cannot."

Screams arose in the near distance. His bewitched brothers and sisters were killing everyone in the city. The slaughter was drawing closer to him.

Munzil roused himself and looked about for a place to hide. He would need to watch his brothers and sisters unobserved. At all costs, he must not engage in combat with them. Stealth was the only way he could help. He would discover what he could, and he would not give up until he freed them or died trying.

Impenetrable blackness filled his vision. Water churned and bubbled in his ears. The pure darkness was a constricting force all around Dayraven, and a tautness rose in his chest the longer he could not draw breath within the force of the current propelling his body. He kept his arms stretched out in front of him, and though his hands at times scraped along the slimy rock of the tunnel wall, he had no need to pull his body along. For the tenth time he wondered if his lungs contained enough air to make it, even though Seren had assured him he would, but then he grew aware of a sudden change in his surroundings. When the current ejected him headfirst from the dark, narrow passage, a shaft of light from above pierced the muddy river, and he could move his limbs freely. He kicked his legs and swam hard for the Ea's surface.

The dirty water parted from his face as it breached the surface, and he sucked in a hoarse breath. He blinked the water from his eyes. As Seren had said, he emerged from the narrow passage leading out of the dungeons beneath a bridge, but the river's current was carrying him downstream. Though the ominous, darkened sky seemed to frown down upon him, the daylight was a welcome change from the dimness of the dungeons and the blind darkness of the tunnel. For a moment, his relief at surfacing chased away Seren's instructions, but then he recalled that he should swim for the western bank.

While he swam towards his goal, the river lugged him farther downstream, and the intermittent sound of distant screams reached his ears as half his face rose above the water between his splashing strokes. His dread at the immense release of power he felt earlier prodded him like a blade in his chest. A chill enveloped the whole of Torrhelm, and it pricked his flesh as he swam. When he neared the bank, his hands, knees, and boots sank into muddy silt, and he stumbled the rest of the way out of the river through the muck, which stank of rot. The weeds and mud pulling at him made it slow going.

At last he stood on the bank, hands on his knees as he panted, and drops from his hair pattered on the ground beneath him. There was no sign of Seren, who had gone before him. Her words echoed in his mind. *Meet under the bridge.* He would need to get her out of the city somehow before he confronted Joruman, or the being that he hoped still inhabited the supreme priest's body. He had no plan, but he had known the moment he felt the exertion of vast power that he must atone for his mistake somehow. *But what other choice did I have? Had it not been Joruman, it would have been me.*

As he struggled farther along the riverbank, the dirty water kept dripping from his clothes and hair, and he trudged toward the bridge with heavy breaths. Like the water, the crisp air had a cold edge to it, but it was the elf's power and the shadow it cast over the city that made him shiver. There was no sign of Seren, and as he looked about, his fear for her spiked, especially when he noticed unmoving bodies lying all over the riverbank near the bridge. She had gone ahead of him in the narrow tunnel, and so she must have emerged before him. Surely if she had been lodged in the passage somewhere, he would have bumped into her. He quickened his pace for a few steps as he neared the stone bridge, but then he stopped short and held his breath.

Several shadows moved in the murk beneath the bridge. The slender one in the middle was Seren. Someone had found her before he did. One of the other figures crowding round her put something over her head. He was a big man. Dayraven resisted the urge to cry out, and he gritted his teeth as he crept closer. He was not powerless. He still had the gift, and as much as he hated to inflict any harm, he would use it to defend Seren. He began to think of which song of origin he should use when their excited voices reached his ears.

"Are you certain? He was right behind you?"

Seren's response was muffled.

"Where in damnation is he, then?"

"Hasn't come up yet."

"You don't think he's stuck down there, do you?"

In spite of the dark influence of the elf's power in the air and all his fears, a smile broke out across Dayraven's face. After placing the voices, he recognized their forms, and he also felt the presence of the gift in one. Galdor, Abon, Orvandil, and Gnorn had been waiting under the bridge for them. "No," he called out. "I'm no longer stuck anywhere."

Their gazes jerked in his direction at once.

"Dayraven!" Gnorn was the first to hurry over and surround him in a rough embrace. "Ah, you led us on quite a chase, my lad." The Dweorg's voice was choked with emotion.

Dayraven nodded. "I'm sorry. I wasn't myself."

"We know. But you are now." Galdor's eyes twinkled in a knowing smile, and he held out his arms. Dayraven accepted the embrace, and then he hugged Orvandil and Abon, who laughed and clapped him on the back.

"Yes. I am myself now. But I wouldn't be here if it weren't for Seren." Dayraven looked toward her. Surrounded by the cloak Orvandil had been using to dry her off, she hung back and gazed at him. He nodded at her and gave her a smile, which she returned with a shy one of her own.

"She told us what she did." Galdor shook his head and smiled. "The most foolish and bravest thing I've ever heard of."

"More brave than you know. She could give each of us lessons in courage, and I reckon I might be in trouble when we have our swimming contest." Dayraven looked at the girl, whose smile wavered as she wiped her eye and peered down at the ground. A sob shook her body, and he wondered if her tears came of relief or some memory that nudged her. His other friends took a sudden interest in their boots.

He smiled as he approached her and enfolded her in an embrace. Her body quivered, and she sniffed. He stroked her wet hair. "Little Sister. I don't know how you made your way inside the dungeons — up the tunnel and against the current. I hardly made it out when it was behind me. Another moment in that darkness . . . It was . . ." He was going to say *like death*, but then he thought better of it as it reminded him of the elf's power loose in the city. "But we haven't time." He released Seren and held her by the shoulders. "You must all leave the city."

She collected herself and looked up at him with her wet eyes, which seemed to plead for something. "Don't leave me again."

"We'll leave." Gnorn frowned at Dayraven and crossed his burly arms before his chest. "But only with you."

"You can't fight it, Dayraven." Galdor shook his head. "The power is too vast. I feel the gift in you, and you're a strong wizard, just as Urd said you'd be, but even combined we would be like a firefly challenging a conflagration. I don't know how you survived, or how the elf's power left you, but it's here in the city, and it's exerting its will."

"Joruman." Dayraven sighed.

Galdor's brow furrowed. "The supreme priest?"

"He discovered a song of origin that enabled him to seize the gift from another. I allowed him to . . . It was a terrible mistake, but I convinced myself I had no other choice. Perhaps I . . . I thought I couldn't carry the burden any longer."

The frenzied shrieks and screams Dayraven had heard earlier grew louder, and Galdor looked up to the bridge above them. "It might be best to tell us of this as we make our way out of the city. We'll put our heads together to see what might be done. But we must leave here alive if we're to do anything about it." He glanced deeper under the bridge, where the shadows behind a support were darkest. "We must gather our friend as well."

Dayraven grew aware of another presence, which he had ignored amidst the larger malignance of the elf's power. Emanating from the shadows behind the support was a wound, a gap in the realm of origins that had somehow manifested in the realm of forms.

Galdor turned back to him. "Yes, you feel it, don't you?" He continued speaking as he edged toward the shadows, bowing his head in the narrowing space. "We may know a bit more about Joruman's spell than you think. Though it seems to have rid you of the elf, its effects are not always so benevolent." He stopped and addressed the place whence the terrible absence emanated. "Hello, friend. We must leave here if we're going to survive. Please come out of your hiding place. Seren has returned to us, along with our other friend, thanks in great measure to you. Your information about the exit from the dungeons proved invaluable. We'd like to help you in return, but we must hasten just now."

"The girl has returned?" The raspy voice seemed strangely familiar to Dayraven.

"Yes," said Seren behind Dayraven. "I'm here. Come out. It's safe for now. But Galdor's right. We must leave the city."

A head peeked out from behind the support. Then the rest of the body slunk out of the shadows, and after he crawled forward, the man raised himself to his feet. But as he stood, his body seemed to submit to a spasm, and he grunted and clutched his backside. His emaciated face grew visible as well, and one of his eyes twitched as half his face convulsed.

Dayraven squinted at the fellow. "Bagsac?"

The twitching ceased, and Bagsac's eyes widened. "You?"

Galdor stepped closer. "You two know each other?"

Bagsac released a terrified shriek.

Dayraven held up his palms. "It's alright. I bear you no hard feelings. I won't harm . . ."

But the former priest of the Way shrieked again as he pointed at something behind Dayraven, who pivoted around.

"Company." Orvandil's blade rasped out of its scabbard, and the Thjoth assumed a defensive stance as he pushed Seren closer to Dayraven and Galdor.

Gnorn and Abon too drew their weapons, and Galdor began chanting a song of origin. Surrounding them on both sides were dozens of large Ilarchae warriors holding bloodied weapons. They were pouring down the corpse-strewn riverbank and making their way under the bridge. They had drawn up in silence, and still they said no word as they prowled closer. Stranger still were the expressionless, uncanny faces they wore, as if they had no purpose but to slay. The chill pervading the city found a focal point in each of the barbarians. It was a whisper that formed no words, but it was intimately familiar to Dayraven, who well understood what it said. As if a link between him and the elf somehow remained, he knew its intention as clearly as though its thoughts still welled up from his mind. He held up his palms. "Wait! Don't fight them. They're creatures of the elf, parts of it. Elf-dwolas. If you slay one, the elf will take you, and you'll become one of them."

"So we let them cut us to pieces?" Abon held up his blade. "Fuck that."

"No! Fall back. I can still hear it. It could have slain me earlier, but it didn't. I think I know what it wants." A sudden wild and desperate hope took hold of him. "Let me try something first."

"We've little choice." Galdor grasped Seren by the shoulders and backed up a few paces, closer to where Bagsac was cowering and trembling, and the rest of Dayraven's friends followed.

"I will enter your minds. You must not resist." Dayraven did not wait for his friends to answer him, and he slipped into the realm of origins as he chanted: "Druanil ecthoniae di borolin ar doranae. Varadil ingharonae im govalin ni hurodae." His energy radiated outward, leaving behind his body to seek the energy dwelling in his friends behind him. The blending of these energies was swift, and even as he mingled with each of them, he knew them to be one. At once his vision shifted, and he perceived the world from six minds in addition to his own. They saw what he saw: the dwolas in Ilarchae bodies stalking closer, with faces indifferent to the slaughter they were about to commit. Shock at his presence and naked fear roiled in each of his companions, especially in Bagsac, yet in the others there was also determination, fierce loyalty, trust, and love. They were ready to die for him. Even as he remained impassive in the realm of origins, he took heart from them. At the same time, he imparted as much bliss to them as he dared, showing them a glimpse of the bewildering, sublime energy underlying all forms.

He stepped forward, closer to the Ilarchae, with his palms still raised. "Joruman. Can you hear me?"

The silent warriors kept creeping towards him, their faces blank masks. The hiss of the elf's power pulsed in Dayraven's mind, whispering of eternal shadows and rest. There was no other response.

"Joruman will no longer speak, I think. It's what you would have done to me, isn't it? But his influence is still with you. This murder. It comes of his fear. And the desire of the Ilarchae for vengeance and glory. Does it not?"

The elf-dwolas strode nearer, none of them showing a trace of emotion in the faces gazing at him from the shadows under their helms. They were closing in.

Dayraven shook his head. "It's enough now. The anger has been unleashed. Spent. This murder: It's no solution. Our kind does enough of this on our own, and, as powerful as you are, you cannot cleanse this world. We, or something like us, will always return." He took a breath. The elf-dwolas slowed their advance but pressed closer. He hardly realized what he was saying until the words spilled out of him of their own accord, as if he were a mere vessel for the thoughts flowing forth. But he began to speak with more conviction, and understanding bloomed within him.

"You're not a window, but a reflection. This death comes not from you, but from us. From Joruman. His fear and anger. From the Ilarchae. Their vengeance. Their lust for honor and glory. Even the desire to show mercy. It was mine all along, not yours. All those are our futile answers to the darkness awaiting us. But you . . . You show us we belong to that darkness as much as the light. We are blind, as you say, but we are part of life's path as it comes into being, grows, and succumbs only to begin anew from its own decay. We are always groping toward awareness of that path, but to find it, we need you. In the world we inhabit and destroy, the only hope is for you to show us what we are. What we belong to. But to do this, you must return whence you came. You know where I mean."

The elf-dwola closest to Dayraven, a huge man, brandished his reddened blade above his impassive face, and then he swung it down.

Dayraven remained standing before the dwola's descending sword. It halted inches from him, as he knew it would. The rest of the silent attackers stopped advancing, and their arms went limp and hung at their sides.

From the throat of the foremost Ilarchae warrior came a rough voice, but Dayraven recognized the thoughts behind the words as belonging to the power wielding that body. And though it used the warrior's throat, it spoke in the Northern Tongue, employing an inflection that reminded Dayraven of Joruman. The whole time, the man's eyes remained vacant of expression. "Had I wished to kill you, I would have done so in the dungeon."

Dayraven nodded. "I know."

"There is no need to free you."

"No. I have seen what you wish to show. And so have these others, for I am in them, just as you are in all the Ilarchae."

The elf-dwola's eyes flicked toward Dayraven's friends for a moment, and it gave a curt nod before repeating, "There is no need to free you."

"Because of what you showed me."

"You are . . . different from most of your kind."

"Not so different. But living with you in my head gave me an altered, perhaps truer, sight. The rest of my kind . . . They need to know what I've seen. If they know, they'll do less harm. To themselves, and to the world around them. They may even make it better."

"I do not share your faith."

"You must at least wonder about the possibility, else you would have slain me by now."

"Perhaps."

Dayraven seized his chance while the elf-dwola hesitated. "You've shown me what some call Edan."

"A word. Mere air expelled with lungs and manipulated with throat, teeth, and tongue. This thing you call *language* is inelegant and imprecise. Even deceitful." The dwola sounded more like Joruman than ever.

"Yes, a word. A clumsy tool. A symbol. For something we cannot wrap with words. And yet, we can experience it. We *must* experience it. There is no other meaning. No other purpose. We are here for experiencing. For *living*. You have shown me Edan. Let them see it and live."

"I am Edan. They are Edan. As are you."

Dayraven nodded. "Yes. This is the wisdom we mortals need. We must know there's something beyond our narrow idea of what we are, not just the image of ourselves most of us worship as we seek to lord it over all else. Something we belong to. Something we return to. But first we *live*. It's the only way. This," and he gestured with his hands towards the ruined city, "is not the answer. There's a better way."

"What way is that?"

"You know. You must return whence you came. There you must remain, coming to those who are ready for you. I will prepare them as best I can. I swear it."

"The Prophet of Edan."

Dayraven gave a half smile. "So they call me."

The elf-dwola hesitated, giving no hint of thought on its blank face. Finally, it answered. "We will return to the place whence we came. But if any of your kind interferes in our journey, we will release them as well."

"I cannot think any would wish to interfere. And the Ilarchae? The bodies you dwell in?"

"Bodies only. Those who called them theirs are all gone. Released from their pain and desire. We will take the bodies with us."

This surprised Dayraven, but there was no need to bargain if the Ilarchae had all succumbed to the elf. Once it left their bodies, nothing would animate them. So many lives in one stroke. It was too much to dwell on, and he needed to help where he could. He nodded. "Then you're finished with Torrhelm. This city."

"Yes. Be sure none of your kind comes in our way before we have returned to our home. We never belonged away from it."

The elf's chill stabbed Dayraven, and a shiver shook his body even as he dwelled in the realm of origins. It had given a warning, though he did not quite understand the need for it. "I think no one here will try to stop you. But I'll do what I can to keep my kind away from you."

"Then it is agreed. Farewell, Prophet." The elf-dwola nodded, turned around, and walked away, heading up the riverbank. The others followed suit, departing in silence.

Dayraven's shoulders sagged, and he released a long sigh as his energy returned to his body, leaving his friends and bestowing upon him once again his own single vision of the world. The shreds of their fear and awe lingered a moment before they dissipated. He looked over at Galdor, whose eyes were still bulging as they followed the last of the Ilarchae heading up to the bridge. His other companions were all frozen in place, gazes locked on the departing elf-dwolas, except for

Bagsac, who shivered in a fetal tuck on the ground. They were all gasping for breath.

Still wide-eyed and gape-mouthed, Gnorn turned to Dayraven and blinked. "How did you . . . ? What did you do to us?"

"I entered your minds. So that it would spare you. In a sense, it thought I was you."

"Aye. So did I." The Dweorg shook his head and then wiggled his fingers in front of his face, gawking at them cross-eyed.

Orvandil hid his wonder behind a controlled gaze. "The Ilarchae. Need we fear them?"

Dayraven nodded. "They'll leave the city. We must get the word out to anyone still alive in Torrhelm: Stay away from the Ilarchae. And there'll be many in need of healing. We have work to do."

Galdor turned toward him and, trembling slightly, nodded. "Yes. As soon as my breath returns."

26

MEETINGS AND REUNIONS

Beneath the westering sun, dark plumes of smoke rose and drifted from dozens of places over Torrhelm, deepening the redness of the sky. The wails of the bereaved drifted in the wind, telling a tale open to any who heard them. The city's survivors had witnessed many deaths, and death still hung in the air.

As Sequara rode ahead of Elfwy and the other Ellonders on the road leading to the city's southernmost gate, she squinted into the distance. There was one presence, vast and unmistakable, that she missed. The closer her steed cantered to the city, the more she felt its absence, and the more her dread increased. She knew it had unleashed itself on the city. The echoes of the elf's power vibrated all around her, and a hint of its chill still lingered in the air. She reckoned many within those looming walls up ahead had met their end when the elf erupted from Dayraven.

Her shallow breaths came with great difficulty, and though a numb helplessness seized her, her arms and legs followed through with the motions of urging her horse on. Recognizing the shock that precedes the loosing of grief, she observed herself as a healer would a patient: She had begun to mourn. That was all she could do because she was too late. She had failed all of them. She had failed Dayraven. He was gone.

Despair sank its claws deep into her mind. There was but one response she could think of to keep herself from falling into the pit of madness awaiting her. *I can be of use. They'll need healing.*

And so she rode closer to Torrhelm, taking care to stay ahead of Elfwy and the others lest they see her grief written on her face. When she reached the open gate, she alighted from her steed and motioned for Elfwy to keep his men well back. She approached an old man standing outside the gate and leaning on a spear as if he were a sentry. He was no soldier, but he appeared to be the only person minding the gate, and not a single Torrlonder was patrolling the high wall. The old man squinted at Sequara as she walked up to him.

She stopped a few feet away. "Are you the keeper of this gate?"

"Aye. I am today, for lack of a better one."

"The city has been attacked."

The old man looked behind him as if checking to make sure the city was still there. "Aye. That it has. The Ilarchae." He spat. "But they're gone."

"And was there magic here as well?"

"Was there magic? Begging your pardon, my lady, but it was the damnedest thing I ever beheld, and I've been around a good while, mind you. The sky went all dark, and it near froze my bones. I thought it was going to suck the life out of every living soul. Still not sure how it is I'm alive. Luckier than most today, I reckon. But they asked me to mind the gate, and that's what I'm doing."

Sequara released a long sigh. So. The old man had confirmed her worst fears. She stood before him a long while, unable to force her jaw to work. Asdralad in ruins. Dayraven gone. It was too much to bear, and she had been able to save no one. Not even herself.

The old man frowned at her as if beginning to wonder if she was mad.

She shook her head and, remembering her own words to Queen Rona outside the ruins of Palahon, resolved to keep going somehow. *One stone at a time. I mustn't give in.* She put her hand on her stomach.

Perhaps life will return. She gazed at the old gatekeeper. "Are there many wounded in the city? I am a . . . healer."

The old man gave her a slow nod. "Aye. Plenty of wounded." His gaze shifted behind her to Elfwy and his men, and he raised his eyebrows at them as he scratched his beard. "Would they be healers too?"

"No. They are men of Ellond, led by Earl Elfwy. They're here to help."

He nodded, though his wide eyes expressed his incredulity. "Well, I reckon we could use some help."

"May we enter the city, then?"

He shrugged and glanced at the spear he was leaning on. "Not likely I could stop you anyway. They're bringing the wounded to Sigseld, the king's palace. I reckon you could help there. Just head north after you pass through the gate, and . . ."

"I know the way." She began walking toward her horse and then remembered something and turned back to the old gatekeeper. "I have some welcome tidings for you. An army of Torrlonders is behind us. They've come from the south, from Caergilion and Adanon. Led by one Lieutenant Edgelaf. They should arrive soon. Perhaps then you'll be relieved of your gatekeeping duties."

The old man smiled for the first time and bowed to Sequara. "That is welcome news, indeed, my lady."

SEQUARA LEFT HER HORSE WITH TWO OF ELFWY'S MEN WHEN SHE and the earl entered Sigseld's open gate. All the other Ellonders were already assisting the Torrlonders in gathering the dead and wounded in the city. She and Elfwy crossed the stained cobbles, upon which blood had pooled in places into red puddles. They made their way to the open doors of the main entrance hall, whither surviving citizens were carrying and carting the wounded. The people were also arranging the torn and bloody bodies of Torrlonder soldiers in neat rows near the wall. Some grey-kirtled corpses still lay strewn about the courtyard, a mute testimony to the ferocity of the battle here. A few Ilarchae dead lay neglected.

The sorceress accosted a citizen on his way out of Sigseld, a well-dressed young man with blood staining the front of his kirtle. The blood did not appear to be his own. "Would you tell me where they're bringing the wounded within? I'm a healer."

The boy assessed her with weary eyes, and he glanced once at Elfwy. "In the Great Golden Hall, my lady." He gestured with one hand. "After you enter the main doors, turn right and proceed down the hallway until you reach the gilded doors." He swallowed, and Sequara waited since he seemed to want to say something more. On the verge of tears, he choked out his words. "They can use you in there." He nodded and bit his lip as his eyes watered up.

Sequara returned his nod. "Thank you. I'll see what I can do."

She left the boy behind and entered Sigseld, reminding herself she was not the only one to have lost someone on this dreadful day. As she paced down the hallway with Elfwy at her side, the sorceress reflected on the irony of her presence here. She had hated this city and everything she thought it represented. Not so long ago, she had been slaying Torrlonders with almakhti and flames on Asdralad. When she encountered the grey-kirtled soldiers in Adanon and Caergilion, followers of the Prophet of Edan who had surrendered their claim to the conquered kingdoms, she had accepted their humanity. And here and now, she felt not just pity but empathy for the people of this city, who had suffered losses not unlike the ones their armies had inflicted on Asdralad and other kingdoms.

Suffering recognized no borders. She recalled something Urd had said to her long ago back on Asdralad, when the old woman reminded her that the Torrlonders were not so different from the Asdralae. Dayraven too had seen beyond the loyalties and passions that blinded people everywhere to the deeper bonds they shared with those who differed from them. But, like Urd and Queen Faldira, he was gone, and nothing could bring him back. At least she would try to honor their vision. Somehow, she would turn her grief into action.

Moans of pain and cries of loss emanated from the open doors at the end of the hallway. Sequara paused to compose herself.

Elfwy put a gentle hand on her shoulder. "My lady. After such a swift and long journey, I confess to some weariness. Perhaps you're feeling the same. You might do these people more good after some rest."

Sequara mustered a smile to answer the earl's courtesy. "I *am* weary. But not too weary to be of use here. It will do me good to help them." She did not tell him how she wished to keep busy to prevent thoughts of Dayraven from overwhelming her.

Though she had not shared with him what the release of the elf's power meant, the earl's concerned gaze suggested he saw through Sequara's stoical face. At length, he nodded. "Alright. I can bandage wounds and carry water. I'll aid you as I can."

"Thank you."

When they entered the Great Golden Hall, Sequara did not need to guess where its name came from. In the last rays of light streaming through the intricate western windows, the gold covering the back wall and ceiling glowed with a ruddy radiance. Torches were also lit throughout the hall, their flames reflecting on the vast black columns. The wounded lay everywhere, many groaning in their agony, some lying still. The haunted eyes of all the others reflected their recent trauma and loss. A few unhurt citizens and healers — several white-robed priests and priestesses with little power in the gift among the latter — attended to them.

Sequara took a deep breath and prepared to begin her work when the presence of the gift in a far greater amount nudged her awareness. She looked about for a priest of the Way but saw instead an old man in a patched brown robe with his back to her crouched over one of the wounded. Recognition stole the sorceress's voice from her for a moment. Of course, he would be here. He and the others had been seeking Dayraven, after all.

"Lord Galdor?" Elfwy had spotted the old wizard too.

Galdor stood up and turned around in response to the young earl. He appeared older and frailer than Sequara remembered him. "Earl Elfwy? Has King Fullan come, then?"

Elfwy bowed. "No, my lord. I and twenty-five of my men are here in the company of Lady Sequara."

The old wizard turned to Sequara, and his green eyes shone in a kind smile. "My dear. You're here. That is good."

Galdor must have known what happened to Dayraven too. The sorrow and pity in his smile were too much for Sequara to bear, and her composure began to crumble. "Too late. I realized . . . I came too late."

The old wizard shook his head, and his smile remained. "What happened here was not your doing. And you're not quite as late as you might think." He gestured with a jerk of his head toward the other end of the hall.

Sequara followed his glance until her eyes fell on another of the healers. At first, because of his silver hair, she took him for an old man. But when he turned toward the dark-haired girl standing next to him, the sorceress saw that his face was that of a young man. *Just as I saw him in the true-dream.* The brown robe and dark breeches fell into place along with the face, and Sequara covered her mouth with her trembling hand. The gift in great measure emanated from him, but it was not the monstrous power that used to awe her.

Sequara's boots felt like lead, and her heart hammered so hard in her chest that it seemed to pulse in her ears as she stepped toward Dayraven. She turned around once to see Elfwy standing next to Galdor, who beamed a smile at her. The young earl wore a sadder smile, but he too watched her with kindness in his eyes. Sequara stifled a laugh or a sob — she knew not which — and walked closer to Dayraven, who still had not noticed her. He was speaking to the girl, who appeared to be a southerner. He seemed to be giving her instructions, and when he finished, he smiled at the girl before placing his hand affectionately on her shoulder. Sequara froze where she stood.

Dayraven's face turned toward the sorceress, and his eyes widened as his hand fell away from the girl. The girl followed his gaze and stared at Sequara. She glanced once back at Dayraven, and then she looked again at Sequara before she stepped back a pace as if sensing she should not intrude.

Skirting around his patients, Dayraven took slow steps toward the sorceress, who stood rooted to the floor. All the while he kept his unblinking gaze on her. When he was within three feet, he stopped and stared at her. His mouth opened as if he would speak, but no words came out. He blinked a few times and shut his mouth. It was the same startled, awkward look he had often displayed when learning Andumaic from her back on Asdralad.

Sequara mustered a fragile smile. “I came here looking for you. I thought . . .”

He smiled back. “You found me. Again. I’m glad.”

“As am I.”

He glanced at the floor and scratched his beard. “What news of Asdralad?”

She nodded. “Asdralad is free. Much needs doing there. Rebuilding. Healing. I will return after . . . I was hoping . . . There’s so much I want to tell you.”

His grin broadened. “And I you.” The smile faded as his eyes glanced around the hall before returning to her. “There’s work here, and we could use your skill.”

“Yes. That’s why I came. *Here*, that is, after I thought . . .”

He took a deep breath. “When we’ve finished, perhaps we could find . . . There are rooms here in the palace. Somewhere quiet where we could . . . speak.” His face flushed.

She nodded. “Yes. I would like that.”

His smile returned. “Good. Shall we get to work, then?”

THE HOURS OF HEALING HAD BEEN EXHAUSTING, BUT THE satisfaction of saving many lives gave Sequara a sense of renewal and an aura of hope that accompanied her after she finished. She and Dayraven had agreed to depart from the Great Golden Hall only when Galdor assured them there was no more they could do for the present, and that he would see to any new arrivals, should there be any. A few more priests and priestesses of the Way with some skill in healing had also arrived. Even the one Dayraven called Bagsac had come out of hiding to help haul water. Many of the wounded Torrlonders expressed their gratitude to the sorceress and to Dayraven, who left hand in hand.

In the privacy of a small and simple sleeping chamber in Sigseld, a room normally given over to servants of important guests, Sequara waited while Dayraven lit a candle and then turned to face her in the flame's ruddy glow. He smiled and walked toward her. She closed and bolted the door behind her. When she finished, he was standing before her, gazing down into her eyes. His hands reached toward her face, and her skin tingled as his fingertips brushed her cheeks. Her arms reached around his waist and pulled him closer until their bodies pressed against one another.

As he bent to kiss her, she tilted her head up. His warm lips touched hers, and she squeezed him tighter while he enfolded her in his arms. A rush of pleasant dizziness accompanied the kiss. When it ended, his blue eyes looked down at her. "I think I have enough energy for one last spell tonight."

She cocked an inquiring eyebrow. "Which spell would that be?"

He paused a moment as he stroked her hair, brought a strand of it close to his face, and inhaled its scent with a long breath. "When you saved my life at the Battle of Iarfaen, we shared . . . everything. It was frightening, but also the most beautiful thing that ever happened to me. To know you in that way. To see your memories, which became part of me. Even if I had never seen you afterwards, I would have longed for you for the rest of my days."

She looked down at the floor for a moment, and then she reached up to trace the scar on his neck with her fingertip. "That would have been a cruel fate, to long for someone you could not have."

His hand caressed her neck, sending a thrill through her body. "Perhaps. But it is better to have longed, even if for something out of reach." His gentle smile gave way to a slight frown. "In the time we've been apart, I sense you've passed through a great ordeal. I want to know it all, and I want you to know everything that has happened to me. Some terrible things came to pass. And some wonderful things. They're all wrapped together. But I want to share them all with you. We don't need words. With your consent, we could . . ."

"Yes."

His eyes widened in mild surprise for a moment. "You agree?"

"We'll say the song of origin together."

He smiled. "Yes. Now?"

Returning his smile, she slipped into the realm of origins, and she sensed him following her. She nodded, and they chanted together:

"Druanil ecthoniae di borolin ar doranae. Varadil ingharonae im govalin ni hurodae."

Like a gentle breeze, his energy probed the boundaries of her awareness, and she opened her mind fully as they began to mingle. Their bodies in the realm of forms held each other in an embrace, and they gazed into one another's eyes as they succumbed to this ultimate act of trust and sharing. Even as they floated in the realm of origins, their bond grew in intensity as more of their energy coalesced. Gaining his view in addition to hers, she saw her own dark eyes reflecting his blue ones. The full array of his personhood struck her as a thing of intricate and awesome wonder. His beauty, compassion, and loyalty permeated her, and she surrendered to the cleansing and miraculous ecstasy of knowing another being. What was more, she knew he was sharing in that bliss.

Images and impressions blossomed within them, memories of events during their weeks apart. Since their two minds were one, it was often hard to tell whose memories were surfacing. But they sorrowed equally at her agony as she sacrificed her identity to cleanse Asdralad of the Torrlonders and his pain at the suffering in Caergilion as well as his incessant battle to stifle the elf's desire to end it all. They shed silent tears at the beauty of the friends they shared, such as Imharr and Jhaia, and the friends they had made, such as Queen Rona, Earl Elfwy, and Lieutenant Eanred, or Seren, Edge, and Tob. The transfer of the elf's power from him to the Supreme Priest Joruman was a matter of grave concern, as was the subsequent destruction of Torrhelm by the possessed Ilarchae. But the most wondrous and powerful thought was the one they both smiled and wept over as her hand rode his while it caressed her belly.

"We'll take care of her."

Sequara realized only moments later that it had been his lips that said the words. "*Her*? How do you know?"

He smiled. "Because I do. She'll be as beautiful as her mother."

Remaining in the realm of origins, she tasted his bliss as well as her own when they kissed again. They interrupted the kiss to pull off their boots, and the cold stone floor sent a pleasant shiver from the bottom of her feet up her body. He removed his robe and kirtle as she took off her tunic, throwing the garments onto a chair to join their cloaks. Goosebumps arose on their flesh when their bare chests came together, and they kissed as their hands explored each other. Waves of pleasure throbbed within their bodies, and their linked minds intensified each other's ecstasy. Here was the home each had yearned for all their lives.

They smiled at each other, and Sequara grasped Dayraven's hand to guide him over to the bed.

EARLY THE NEXT MORNING, DAYRAVEN OPENED HIS EYES. ENOUGH light leaked under the doorway for him to make out the silhouette of Sequara's form lying next to him under the blankets. The thrill and bliss of his union with her rushed into him, and he smiled in the dimness of the little chamber.

After a moment, however, his smile faltered. It was almost too much. He realized that such happiness exposed him to the possibility of loss. How could he ever bear to lose her again? What of their child? The world was full of threats and pain and suffering. Was it right to bring someone into such a precarious existence when the final outcome was inevitable?

He gritted his teeth. Resisting the rise of such paralyzing fear, he calmed his breaths and shook his head at his foolishness. Urd's sensible voice came into his head, and it told him to live now and not borrow trouble from the future. *Yes, there will be later loss, but without it, you couldn't have this moment.*

Sequara's steady breaths told him she still slept, and he took comfort from the nearness and warmth of her body. Unable to resist, he stroked the curves of her body. When she stirred and groaned, he kissed her. She returned the kiss and buried her hands in his hair, which she pulled on until she was finished kissing him. She held his face in her hands, and her breaths were heavy. "If we keep going, I won't want to leave this chamber all day."

He grinned and nodded. "There'll be more work for us in the hall. Afterwards. Tonight."

"Yes."

They held each other a little longer before rising to light the candle and dress. He fetched a basin of water for them to wash up, and when they were ready, they set out hand in hand for the Great Golden Hall to see if more wounded had come in for healing.

When they arrived in the hall, the first thing Dayraven saw was Orvandil, Gnorn, and Abon speaking in urgent tones to Galdor near the entrance. Seren was standing behind the wizard, keeping quiet and unobtrusive but listening to every word. The Thjoth, the Dweorg, and the shaper had been out riding with other volunteers to warn the people in the countryside to clear away from the path of the Ilarchae army. He had not expected his friends to return so soon.

Galdor, who no doubt felt the presence of the gift in Dayraven and Sequara, turned toward them, and the gazes of the others followed. "Lady Sequara," said Abon with a bow, and Gnorn and Orvandil followed suit. Seren kept an intent gaze on the sorceress, but she said not a word.

Gnorn took in Dayraven and Sequara, who were still holding hands, with a broad grin. He jerked a fat thumb towards Galdor. "The old fellow was just telling us of your arrival. It's good beyond words to see you, my lady." Abon too was smiling, and even Orvandil cracked a half-smile as they all beamed at the pair.

Sequara released a light laugh, which lifted Dayraven's heart. "And it gives me joy to see you, my friends."

Dayraven noticed the dust on their faces. "You've just returned, it seems. What news do you bring?"

The smiles gave way to concerned frowns. Gnorn tugged at his beard. "The army of Ilarchae is still on the move."

Dayraven looked toward Galdor, whose eyes fell to the floor. His other friends stared at him and seemed to await some answer from him.

"It hasn't . . . No one else has been hurt?"

Gnorn looked at Dayraven with a pained grimace and sighed. "I'm sorry, lad. We were just telling Galdor about one of the villages in the dwolas' path. The messengers tried to convince them to leave, but they refused. Said they would defend their soil from any threat. The messengers just escaped. They saw . . . The dwolas were feeding upon the villagers' corpses."

"Oh, gods." Dayraven's mouth hung open, and it was only when Sequara squeezed his hand, bringing a little warmth back into him, that he felt able to speak again. "Of course, they're still bodies. They need food to keep moving. But why? Why does the elf continue to possess them?"

Gnorn shrugged and shook his head.

Galdor frowned. "We had hoped you might have some idea about that."

"I'm not sure. I had thought it would return to the realm of origins and release all the bodies soon after leaving Torrhelm." Dayraven turned back to Gnorn. "Were there any other villages like that?"

"Only the one thus far, thank the ancestors. Our messengers are staying ahead of the dwola army. Since it's afoot, the horses outpace it. Anyone that listens and gets out of the way is safe."

Dayraven breathed a sigh. "At least there's that. But I hadn't expected the elf to keep possession of their bodies for so long. Once it returns to its natural state, they'll all be lifeless." He thought of the scores of thousands of dead warriors lying somewhere on the plains of North Torrlond. The Ilarchae had suffered more losses than anyone, and he wondered how their loved ones back in the Wildlands would fare without them.

Abon's eyes squinted in thought. "And why keep them on the march?"

Dayraven scratched his head. "I don't know. But we must continue to make sure folk stay out of their way. We'll have to keep sending messengers ahead of the dwola army. Where's it headed?"

"Northwest." Gnorn's frown deepened. "Towards Etinstone."

Dayraven's thoughts leapt to the remnant of the Dweorg's people dwelling in that city among the tens of thousands of Torrlonders. "We must send word to Etinstone, then. Tell them to abandon the city. We'd better start now since it won't be an easy task."

Gnorn nodded. "We already sent fresh riders there in case."

"Good."

"Something else you should know." Gnorn crossed his arms in front of his chest. "We captured one of them on our way back into Torrhelm."

"One of . . . ? An elf-dwola?"

"An Ilarchae. This one's still got his brains, as far as I can tell. Speaks the Northern Tongue too. Popped out of nowhere and came straight up to us with his hands in the air. No weapons on him. The Torrlonders wanted to rip his head off right there, but he got to us first and surrendered. Took some grumbling from Orvandil before they backed off."

Dayraven thought for a moment. "He must have been away from the other Ilarchae when the elf took them."

"Aye. So he says. And he wants to speak to you."

"To me?"

"Aye. Kept asking to see you. Described you pretty well." The Dweorg chuckled at that.

Dayraven could not recollect meeting an Ilarchae warrior other than the dwolas they had encountered under the bridge. "Let's see what he has to say, then."

Sequara squeezed his hand and then released it. "I'll remain here. I'd like to speak with Seren." She turned to the girl. "If you have a moment."

Seren looked up, her eyes betraying her surprise. She gazed at the sorceress and managed a nervous smile before nodding. "Alright."

Dayraven smiled at Seren. "I'll meet you back here when I'm done." He nodded to Sequara before following Gnorn and Orvandil out of the hall.

SEQUARA SAT DOWN ON A BENCH IN THE HALL AND GESTURED FOR Seren to sit next to her. Staring at the sorceress, the girl paused before complying.

It was quiet since most of the wounded were sleeping. A few healers and priests moved among them, and Galdor was off in a corner speaking with Abon and Earl Elfwy. Sequara waited a while before turning to Seren with a tentative smile. "Dayraven shared a lot about you with me."

Seren looked at her and then nodded, but she said nothing.

The sorceress cleared her throat. "I wanted to thank you."

"For what?"

"For helping him. And I don't mean just in the dungeons. He needed you in Caergilion too."

"He saved me first."

Sequara nodded. "Still. You helped him when others were not there. Including me."

A quick, shy, and gracious smile crossed the girl's face. "You had other things to do. Galdor told me about it. Sometimes we have hard choices. None of us can be in two places at once."

It was Sequara's turn to pause and stare. This girl had endured much hardship, and still she managed to transform her pain into understanding for others.

Seren frowned for a moment. "At least, I don't think even you can be in two places at once. Is it true you're a sorceress? And the queen of Asdralad?"

Sequara nodded. "I am a sorceress. And, it seems, Asdralad's ruler, at least for now."

The girl smiled again, this time with more confidence. "Hard choices. I suppose they never end."

The sorceress sighed. "You're likely right."

"The way I see it, the important thing is to keep close to good friends to help you get through the hard things." Seren pursed her lips in a sagacious nod.

Sequara's mouth hung open for a moment before she smiled back at Seren, this girl who understood a piece of wisdom she had only just learned. "I hope *we* can become good friends."

The girl's smile returned, brighter than ever. "I reckon we could."

"I am Munzil of the Folk of the Tribes, born into the Grey Wolves, honored by the Fire Dragons. You are the one they call the Prophet of Edan."

The red-headed Ilarchae blinked up at Dayraven as he sat on a stool with manacles around his hands and feet, chained to the wall of a small chamber in Sigseld. It was not in the dungeons, which made Dayraven thankful since he would not have cared to return there, but it seemed to be a holding cell in the part of the castle where the king's guard quartered.

Dayraven stood inside the open doorway, whence light streamed in the dim little chamber. Orvandil and Gnorn waited outside alongside the Torrlonder guard posted there. "I am." He released a sigh. "Let me say I'm sorry for what happened to your people. It's not a fate I would wish on anyone."

In response, Munzil stared at him for a long while. His gaze was hard, but there was a wild edge to his eyes, the look of a man who knew recent and terrible loss. At length, he nodded.

Dayraven stepped closer to the man. "My friends tell me you would speak with me."

The Ilarchae nodded again. "I was hiding under the bridge, on the eastern side. I saw what you did over on the western bank."

"You mean with the elf-dwolas? That is to say, your folk after the elf possessed them."

"Aye. If that's the cold magic that took them and turned them into witless murderers." He shuddered. "I know not. Yet they didn't fight *you*. You spoke to them. I couldn't hear what you said across the river. But you spoke to them. They listened, and they all left the city after that."

"Yes. They're headed northwest."

"I know. I snuck out of the city and followed them, but I came back to speak to you."

"Why to me?"

Munzil paused but did not turn his intense stare away from Dayraven. "Can you save them?"

Dayraven blinked at the man, and his mouth hung open for a moment as words failed him.

"Tell me. Can you save them?"

He shook his head. "I'm sorry. They're all gone. The elf dwells in them all. Only their bodies obey its commands. Once it leaves them, the bodies will be empty. Lifeless. The folk you knew . . . They're all gone."

Munzil's jaw quivered, and he sniffed as he fought back tears. "What does it want with their bodies?" He spoke through clenched teeth.

"I wish I knew. I thought it would abandon them sooner. All we know is they're headed northwest, towards . . ."

Dayraven's skin tingled as a chill crept under it, and his heart seemed to stop when a realization fell on him like a massive weight. For a moment he forgot about Munzil. He stood with his eyes widened and mouth hanging open until he managed to force out the words. "The warning it gave me. They're not going to Etinstone. They're headed back to the Southweald. To the Mark."

27
IN THE HORDE'S PATH

With Bagsac cowering at her side, Seren stood in the palace courtyard. Placing her hand on her brow to shield her eyes from the sun, she watched the procession of grey-kirtled soldiers marching into Sigseld. Boots stomped, byrnies clinked, and shouting and swearing punctuated the din. The renegade Torrlonder army from the south had arrived, followers of the Prophet of Edan. Relieved at their presence and the restoration of military strength and order to the city, the surviving citizens of Torrhelm expressed no concern that these troops had defied King Earconwald and the nobles by abandoning the kingdoms of Caergilion and Adanon. In fact, they were inclined to praise them for it. And, at the moment, no one could even find King Earconwald, who was rumored to be dead.

Seren bit her lip as she scanned the passing faces. She was not happy about staying in Torrhelm, but Dayraven had made her promise. Of course, she had considered breaking her promise again. Even though the army of elf-dwolas inspired paralyzing dread deep in her bones, she hated the idea of being left behind while her friends all hurried off to pursue it. But, as Dayraven had pointed out, someone had to take care of Bagsac, whom Sequara had tried in vain to heal, and the Prophet wanted her to convey some important messages as well.

And so, with a mixture of nervous dread and joyful anticipation, she was looking for the person in charge of all these troops fanning out across the city.

At last a familiar face appeared amongst the ranks of soldiers. She turned to Bagsac. "Come on."

The former priest shrank in on himself as his eye twitched. "Does the girl know someone? Is it safe?"

"It's safe. Should be for you, anyway. You're not in any trouble." She sighed. "Not sure about me, though." She walked toward the column of soldiers to head off the one she knew. Probably too nervous to stand alone in the courtyard, poor Bagsac had little choice but to follow.

When she was close enough to be heard over the din of the marching troops, Seren cupped her hands around her mouth. "Sergeant Hulm!"

The bluff sergeant's face snapped in her direction, and then a wide smile lit it up. "Seren!" He broke away from the column and approached her. "By Edan, it's good to see you."

"And you. How's Edge?"

Hulm chortled. "Miserable. Hates being in command. Says he's going to retire as soon as someone proper takes over." His eyes narrowed as he frowned and looked closer at Seren. "And he's been worried about you, lass."

Seren glanced at the cobblestones. "I know. I'm sorry."

"Tell him, not me."

"I was hoping you could take me to him."

"That I will." Hulm looked at Bagsac. "Who's your skinny friend?"

The former priest's eyes bulged as he cowered and shivered under the sergeant's glance.

"That's Bagsac. He's harmless. And he's part of the message I've got to give to Edge."

"Is that right?" Sergeant Hulm's eyes narrowed with suspicion. "Looks a bit nervous, doesn't he?"

"He's been through a lot. Been a great deal of help too. Even the Prophet reckons he owes him."

The sergeant lifted his eyebrows. "Well, then. The two of you better follow me. Mind you, Lieutenant Edgelaf might be a bit grumpy just now."

Seren fell in behind Sergeant Hulm, and Bagsac limped behind her as they exited the gates, squeezing through against the stream of troops marching into Sigseld's compound. They walked along several streets filled with more grey-kirtled soldiers until they came to a large market square where many congregated and talked around a cart. Sergeant Hulm turned to address Seren and winked. "Stay close behind me, now."

"Coming through! Make way!" The sergeant pushed his way through the crowd, and Seren stayed in his wake with Bagsac tailing her like a nervous hound. At last the bodies parted to reveal Lieutenant Edge standing behind the cart, his big hands grasping its sides as he gazed down at a map while giving orders about where the troops should station themselves in the city. He scratched his blond beard, which seemed to have more grey peppering it than before.

Hulm elbowed through to stand across from Edge. "Sergeant Hulm reporting, my lord."

Edge scowled and did not look up from the map. "Didn't I tell you to bring the 130th and 212th Companies to Sigseld?"

"Done, my lord."

"For Edan's sake, stop calling me that. You know I hate it."

"Hate what, my lord?"

"That! I'm no damn lord, and you know it."

"As you say, my lord."

Edge released a long sigh. "Oh, hang it, man, what do you want?"

"Brought someone to see you." Hulm stepped aside with a cheerful smile on his face, putting Seren directly in the lieutenant's view.

Edge looked up from the map. His eyes widened for a moment, and he stood up to his full height. He crossed his arms in front of his chest and scowled. "You."

Seren shrank back and glanced down at the ground. She would have backed up further if Bagsac had not been whimpering behind her and clutching onto her arm. She made herself look back up at Edge, unable to force her jaw to work just yet.

"You stole my horse." One of the big lieutenant's eyebrows shot up as if demanding an answer to the accusation.

"I . . . borrowed it." She sighed. "I'm sorry, Edge. I had to follow him. He asked me to stay here. To tell you everything. There's a lot you need to know."

"First thing's first, young lady. Come here." He glowered at the other men around the cart. "Out of the way, you lot."

Sergeant Hulm began pushing the others away. "You heard the Lieutenant. Get going."

The grumbling soldiers scattered away, and when no one else stood around the cart save Edge, Seren shuffled over with Bagsac still clinging to her arm. She stood before the lieutenant, who towered over her. His thick arms were still crossed in front of his big chest, and his glare grew tighter. He released a long breath. And then he opened his arms wide, causing Bagsac to flinch and whimper. But Edge only wrapped Seren in his arms, smothering her in a long embrace. "I missed you, my lass." His rough voice was a mere whisper.

Seren returned the embrace and sniffed. "I'm sorry, Edge. I had to."

He ended the hug and grasped her by the shoulders. His scowl had transformed into a bright smile. "Well. You're alright, aren't you? You've seen the Prophet here in Torrhelm?"

She wiped her eyes and nodded. "Yes. He wanted me to stay here to tell you what's happened and where he's going."

The lieutenant squinted and peeked behind her. "Who's the jittery fellow?"

Seren smiled. "That's Bagsac. He's helped us."

"Has he? Well, then. I reckon the two of you had best come with me and tell me everything."

Captain Ludecan rode with some of the other captains and Duke Ethelred of Etinstone at the head of the troops as they marched southeast through the dukedom of Rimdale on their way to Torrhelm. A wide grin was spread across the captain's face. For the hundredth time, he was recalling the peace council, wherein he played a key role. But it was not the favor he had gained with Duke Ethelred by advising him about the wergeld that made him smile. That was, of course, a great victory for him, for good standing with a man as powerful as Ethelred was sure to help his prospects. Rather, it was the enraged face of Duke Siric that he chuckled over again and again.

When word had come of the Ilarchae approaching Torrhelm to attack the kingdom's chief city, Duke Ethelred had resolved to end the conflict against the Norfasters and Thjoths with the utmost swiftness. The kingdom needed every soldier to deal with the invading barbarians. Duke Siric, however, had insisted that they massacre the entire populace if necessary to gain the dukedom of Norfast for him.

The trouble was that, even if everyone had been as enthusiastic as Siric for his rather dubious cause, the Norfasters and the Thjoths were not going away quietly. Any soldier with half a brain could have seen that the campaign would have taken weeks or even months longer to succeed, and there was no guarantee of success even then. Ludecan had concluded that Duke Siric's whole brain had turned to lard, and he was no soldier, just a grasping nobleman. Ethelred, and everyone else save Siric, understood the necessity of reaching Torrhelm as swiftly as possible to defend the realm. But he had no way of extricating his troops from the conflict with the Norfasters and Thjoths, for the Thjoths had sworn to avenge King Vols until they were all dead, or until every Torrlonder soldier was no more.

However, having known one Thjoth as well as anyone knows a fellow soldier, Ludecan had a notion about what to do. He sought out Duke Ethelred to tell him he would need to do two things if he wanted to end the conflict in Norfast: recognize Durn, son of Durathror, as duke of Norfast, and pay the Thjoths an enormous wergeld for Vols.

Duke Ethelred had needed to use every coin he had laid aside to pay his troops. In addition, since Rimdale was the closest town, he had ordered his soldiers to raid Siric's treasury — over the violent objections of the pudgy little duke. But, with a few exceptions, Siric's own captains refused to obey him, having transferred their allegiance to Ethelred out of disgust for the unchecked greed of their lord when the kingdom was in peril.

Thus, Duke Ethelred had come to the peace council with cartloads of treasure, most of it from Duke Siric's personal hoard, to hand over to the Thjoths as wergeld for the death of King Vols. No one among the Thjoths, noble or king, had ever warranted such a payment, but Vols had been much beloved. The leaders of the Thjoths hotly debated whether or not to accept the treasure in compensation for the loss, but in the end, the one who had become their temporary leader, Duneyr, persuaded them it was enough. Duneyr also warned them that King Earconwald would need to honor the bargain to recognize Durn, or they would return with vengeance.

Duke Ethelred gave his word to convince Earconwald, and he swore to support Durn no matter what. Knowing Ethelred's reputation for honor, the Thjoths agreed. Duke Siric, on the other hand, rode off in a fury with a few hundred loyal soldiers, heading to Torrhelm with the greatest possible swiftness to inform King Earconwald of the outrage Ethelred had committed. Before he left, he had delivered an incomprehensible, spluttering rant, going so red in the face that Ludecan had wondered if the duke's head would explode. He chuckled as he once again envisioned the fat little man's crossed eyes and the spittle flying from his mouth.

Ludecan was more grateful than ever to be serving under Ethelred's direct command again. The duke's army was heading south on the road from the town of Rimdale as fast as it could march, sending up a cloud of dust in its wake. Glad for the most part to be at the head of the march, Ludecan sniffed and pulled his cloak tighter around his neck with his gloved hand. With the chill in the air, he almost wished he was working up some heat by walking among the troops instead of riding. Up on his horse, he was more exposed to the wind, which was watering up his eyes. The leaves on the trees interspersed alongside the road and in the fields were changing color, with green yielding to reds, oranges, and yellows. Winter was well on its way, but at least the bright sun overhead was still there to warm his body. The captain glanced over at Duke Ethelred, who happened to be looking his way and gave him a confident nod. Ludecan nodded back before returning his gaze to the horizon.

For the first time in a long time, his prospects seemed to be improving. With Ethelred supporting him, he might even be able to get something back from his brother. But, most of all, he just wanted to enjoy the memory of that garlic-slathered toad Siric when he was fuming and unable to vent all his rage in a coherent fashion. He chuckled once again.

A horse's neigh in the distance interrupted his thoughts. The beast sounded distressed. A moment later, three grey-kirtled riders appeared up ahead, galloping hard toward them and waving. One of the men was screaming, his voice thin from so far away, "Duke Ethelred! My lord! Duke Ethelred!"

Ethelred's personal guards rode closer to the duke, who held up a hand and gestured to signify he would halt by the roadside but that the troops should keep marching. Driven by curiosity and having no contrary instructions, Ludecan followed the duke and other captains to await the three riders a little distance from the road.

As they neared, the three slowed their steeds only a little, and their hooves clattered as they rushed closer. When they came within thirty feet, they yanked on the reins, and the lathered beasts made an abrupt halt. The lead horse neighed in a weary groan and seemed to stumble before gaining its footing. Its rider leapt off along with the other two, and they all knelt before the duke, who remained on his horse, frowning down at them. The lead rider was none other than Captain Grimulf, who had been one of the few captains loyal enough to Duke Siric to ride off with him. Kneeling before Ethelred with sweat running down his face and tremors shaking his body, Grimulf appeared far less confident and sneering than he had when he departed with Siric.

Duke Ethelred's lip curled in distaste. "You've killed that horse, man."

"Your pardon, my lord." Grimulf and the other two men were panting hard. Flecks of blood stained the kirtles of the two soldiers, but Grimulf had no spot on him. "But you'll understand when I tell you."

"Tell me what?"

"The messengers tried to warn us, but Duke Siric wouldn't listen. He was mad with rage. He would hear of nothing but riding for Torrhelm with the greatest swiftness. He wouldn't listen." Grimulf shuddered and emitted something like a frightened whine.

"What is it? Pull yourself together, man. What messengers?"

"Oh, blessed Edan spare us. They sent them from Torrhelm. To warn us."

Ethelred squinted down at the captain. "Warn us of what? Speak clearly."

"The Ilarchae army."

"What of it?"

"It's coming. This way."

Other than the din of the troops marching in the distance, there was a long silence as the captains all glanced at each other. Ludecan watched Ethelred to note the duke's reaction. The only change to his face was that his jaw muscles bunched as he ground his teeth for a moment. "I take it Siric and his followers met with the Ilarchae."

Grimulf's first answer was to tremble with his teeth chattering. "Oh, Edan. Oh, Edan. Yes. We met with them. We came upon them suddenly. Siric rode straight into their midst before he knew what he was doing. Tried to turn back. Too late. The horses were exhausted. They had surrounded us. So many, and their faces. Oh, Edan."

"What happened, man? Where is Duke Siric?"

Captain Grimulf blinked up at the duke and seemed unable to say a word or make a sound until he buckled over and retched. Holding his stomach, he managed to recover enough to speak. "Dead."

"Are you sure?"

"Yes. I saw it myself. They . . . *ate* him."

"What? The Ilarchae are savages, but they don't eat . . ."

"I saw it. The messengers tried to warn us, but Siric didn't listen."

"Warn you?"

"The Ilarchae. Their eyes . . . They're dead. And some of our own are among them now. There's some sorcery enthralling their bodies. The messengers told us. Siric didn't believe. But it's true. You can't kill them without becoming one of them. And they eat the slain."

Captain Ludecan suppressed a grim chuckle. *Siric must've made a decent meal, at least. Especially if they like garlic.*

The rest of the captains gaped with horror and disbelief at Grimulf. Duke Ethelred narrowed his eyes and scratched his beard. "How large is the Ilarchae army? How far is it from us? And where is it headed?"

Grimulf's eyes darted around, and he appeared confused. "My lord? I'm not certain . . . I was too busy . . ."

"At least one hundred thousand strong, my lord," said one of the soldiers kneeling behind Grimulf. "And at least ten leagues away, I'd say. A day's march on foot, leastways. They're not on the main road, though. They're stomping across the countryside in no particular formation, and they're headed toward us. If they continue on their course, they'll skirt Etinstone to the north. They don't seem to trouble anyone who stays away from them, just as the messengers from Torrhelm told us. But when they come across anything living . . . Well, they kill and eat whatever comes their way. It's just as the captain says, my lord. They're not human anymore. Not even beasts. They're cold." The man shivered. "Heartless and mindless."

Ethelred frowned in concentration. "There's some good news at least if they're staying away from Etinsone." The duke nodded at the soldier before returning his gaze to Grimulf. "And how did you three get away alive?"

Grimulf licked his lips and blinked for a moment. He glanced toward the other two men and seemed to consider his response. "I . . . held back after the messengers from Torrhelm reached us. I urged Siric to consider their warning, but he didn't listen. His rage drove him like a madman. He would hear of no delay. So, I . . . took to riding in the rear of our company, in case. It saved my life." He glanced again at the two soldiers. "These two escaped from the combat."

Ethelred turned his gaze to the soldier who had spoken earlier. "How did you escape?"

"My lord, we slew no one, else we would have become one of them, as several of the others did. More were killed around us by the Ilarchae spears and arrows. My horse took a spear, but I found another mount whose rider was down. We galloped away. Just the two of us managed to get out. Met the captain further along the way and fell in with him."

"I see." The duke turned to one of his guards. "Find fresh mounts for these two." He looked again at the two soldiers kneeling before him. "You will ride with me. I have further questions for you." Then he gazed at Grimulf again. "Captain. Some would call you a coward, some wise, for preserving your life in such a manner. I'll refrain from judgement. However, since you prefer the rear of the formation, that's where you will march now."

Grimulf's head hung lower, and he stared at the ground. "Yes, my lord."

Another of the captains surrounding the duke asked. "What of the Ilarchae, my lord?"

Ethelred sighed. "We haven't the numbers to meet them head on, even were they not bewitched in the manner these men describe. But we must by any means lure them away from Etinstone. We'll take no chances that they mean to skirt the city. Perhaps we can entice them further north. Let's learn what we can first, and then we'll decide."

A wise approach, thought Ludecan. Had it been only Captain Grimulf, he would have dismissed most of the man's report as a craven's exaggerated fantasy. But he deemed the other two were solid soldiers and not prone to let their imaginations run away. *So. Bewitched, man-eating Ilarchae. And I thought fighting Thjoths was a jab up the arse.*

For the hundredth time on the journey, Dayraven worried about Seren back in Torrhelm. At least he hoped she was there. *She'll find Edge.* It had not been easy leaving her behind again, but he had no desire for her to be anywhere near the danger he and the others were riding towards. Putting her in charge of Bagsac and the messages to convey to Edge had been a wise ploy since it gave her a purpose for staying behind. *As long as she's safe.*

In fact, it had been his desire to go into this without company. Dealing with the elf was his task, his duty alone, and there was no need for the others to involve themselves. But Sequara refused to listen. So did Gnorn and Orvandil. And Galdor and Abon. Along with Galdor came the Ellonders that had accompanied Sequara. At least Imharr was safe back in Adanon and, according to Sequara, happy there. He imagined sharing the news with his friend that he had found Seren, whom he suspected — but could not be sure — was Imharr's niece. But he would also have to share the tidings of how Seren's mother died, and he had no wish to add to his friend's grief.

He sighed and shook his head as he glanced at all his companions riding around him. In truth, part of him was glad for the company. Had he not been worried for their safety, he might even have been happy.

Having friends nearby gave him great comfort after the ordeal of wandering without his memory, and he was loth to be out of their sight. Especially Sequara. Even the Ellonders, who regarded him with a measure of awe since most had witnessed the Battle of Thulhan, were welcome. Earl Elfwy was a good man, exactly the sort of soldier he might have wanted to become before the elf stole his old life away. A man of honor and a strong leader, like Dayraven's father had been.

As they rode closer to the kingdom of his birth, a feeling like the ache of an old wound arose in him, and he found himself thinking more of Edgil. Had he been alive, what would he have thought of his son? *He would have loved me no matter how strange I had become.* It hurt to think of his old home without his father and Urd there. He felt disconnected from the place, yet a melancholy yearning for the land and its folk still stirred within him. The one person he thought he understood more than ever was Urd. She would have known the sort of longing that prodded him. *I miss her.* He wondered how the people of the Mark would view him, an exile and an outcast. But the Dayraven they had known was long gone. In his place was someone a bit more battered and weary, but also wiser, he hoped. Transformed in the heat of his trials. *Yet the Mark will always be part of me.*

He understood what it was to lose his people. That was why he had insisted on allowing their last traveling companion to accompany them over the objections of the others. Munzil the Ilarchae rode apart from everyone else, perhaps wishing to be alone in his grief, perhaps sensing they had not wanted his company. He spoke seldom, and then only to Dayraven. He looked even more intimidating with his weapons, which he had picked up from where he hid them outside Torrhelm. Dayraven did not know what Munzil hoped from this journey, but he believed he should be allowed to witness whatever happened to the bodies of his kin.

He left his thoughts to survey the landscape. The few trees on the rolling plains of North Torrlond were changing color. A couple leagues back, Gnorn had informed him they were not too distant from the crossroads where he and Hlokk had first met Dayraven and Imharr, and that the old Dweorg barrows where his ancestors had buried their dead on the way to Etinstone were not far away either. Riding with good speed and taking care to maintain their distance, they had passed the army of elf-dwolas, which was now south of them. It had been a relief to get ahead of the Ilarchae, but with every league covered, his sense of dread swelled since he knew he had been right about their destination: They remained on a direct course for the Mark.

Releasing a long sigh, Dayraven pondered again how he should speak to the Markmen. He hoped to gain an audience with King Ithamar in Wolvendon before he, his earls, his thegns, and all his warriors set out to confront what would appear to them an invading army. It would not be easy to convince them they should abandon their homes to allow the Ilarchae to march through unchallenged. Knowing his people, they would stubbornly defend their kingdom from any threat no matter the odds. To do anything else would shame them. Dayraven guessed that, once the dwolas reached the forest, the elf would abandon their bodies. But he did not know this for certain. He hoped. Regardless, he would somehow need to persuade the folk of the Mark to keep away from them.

Riding to the top of a swelling in the land, he gained a view of a place in the distance where two dark lines intersected each other amidst the rolling sea of green. He turned to Gnorn, who rode nearby, and smiled at the Dweorg. "It's the crossroads where we met."

The Dweorg nodded, and his grin did not quite reach his melancholy eyes. "Aye. So it is. Seems so long ago." He would be remembering his brother, Dayraven realized.

"We're not the only ones headed for it." Orvandil pointed north of the crossroads, where the telltale glints of steel and dust cloud revealed the presence of an army marching towards them.

AFTER ALIGHTING FROM HIS STEED IN THE MIDDLE OF THE FAMILIAR crossroads, Dayraven walked between two filing columns of Torrlonder soldiers, who seemed to be something between escorts and guards. Sequara, Galdor, Abon, Elfwy, Gnorn, Orvandil, and Munzil accompanied him. The rest of the Ellonders waited by the horses. Several of the Torrlonders conducting them stole nervous glances at him, and he supposed some of them had been at the Battle of Thulhan. All of them would have heard of the Prophet of Edan. He was not about to tell them most of the power that had dwelled in him was gone. He needed all the authority he could muster.

The looks the Torrlonders cast toward the others in his party were almost as curious, and Dayraven saw how outlandish he and his friends must appear to the Torrlonders. An Asdralae woman, an old wizard, a scarred shaper, a nobleman of Ellond, a Dweorg, and a large Thjoth. But the most hostile stares came Munzil's way. The Ilarchae locked his stony gaze straight ahead as if he did not notice them.

The soldiers steered the companions away from the main body of the army toward a small party awaiting them in the shadow of a familiar outcrop of rocks. Dayraven remembered it well as the spot where he and Imharr had come to an abrupt halt in the rain. It was a different scene now. Several Torrlonder captains, all of them directing their open stares at Dayraven and his party, stood around an imposing man he recognized. Duke Ethelred of Etinstone had spoken to Dayraven at the Battle of Thulhan. It was he who had fetched King Earconwald, his cousin, for the peace parley. The duke had made a strong impression that day as a man of integrity and strong principles, and Dayraven hoped that impression had been correct. At the moment, Ethelred kept his face neutral and impassive.

Scanning the men around the duke to assess their mood, Dayraven squinted as his eyes lingered on one of them, and then the man fell into place. Among the captains gazing at him and his companions was a familiar face: Lieutenant Ludecan, at whom Dayraven directed a quick nod. Ludecan, who wore the three red stripes of a captain on his shoulder, bared his teeth in a smile.

The guard of soldiers stopped in unison, and Dayraven took that as the signal that they were close enough to the duke. Ethelred frowned at Dayraven, seeming to weigh him. "Welcome. We are honored to meet you again." He turned to Galdor and Earl Elfwy. "The wizard Galdor, if I'm not mistaken. You too are welcome." He paused as Galdor gave a slight bow. "And Earl Elfwy. My wife's kin is always welcome, though when we last met, we fought on opposite sides. How fares your mother?"

Elfwy bowed. "Well, my lord, when I left her."

"And why do men of Ellond ride in this company?"

Elfwy glanced at Dayraven before speaking. "I and my soldiers have come with my lord Galdor to aid the Prophet of Edan. Insofar as my word has weight with you, I urge you to heed what he must say."

"Very well." Duke Ethelred returned his gaze to Dayraven. "What brings the Prophet of Edan and his companions here? I fear we are in haste, so I beg you to forgive my lack of ceremony."

"Duke Ethelred. I thank you for your welcome. We too are in haste. We have come to warn you against marching on the army of Ilarchae headed this way. Not only do they far outnumber you, but they are no longer human. They are the vessels of an elf, a power that possesses their bodies with sorcery much greater than we can match, though there are three strong in the gift among us." He glanced at Sequara and Galdor, who stood erect as they faced the duke. "Even if you had the numbers to fight them, the moment a man among you slays one of the elf-dwolas, he becomes one of them: a soulless shell, a mere part of a creature with a mysterious and dangerous will. You must not engage with them."

The duke gave a grim smile. "So I've heard. But I can't let this horde of demons march through Torrlond unopposed. Even now, we have little time to spare. I must ensure that the Ilarchae come nowhere near Etinstone."

"You needn't fear for Etinstone. We sent messengers to tell all folk there to abandon the city and flee southwest, toward Woodburg."

"All these messengers across the countryside were your doing, then?"

"Yes. My friends and I sent them from Torrhelm. But the ones we sent to Etinstone were a precaution only. The dwolas are not headed for that city. They're on their way to the Southweald, in the kingdom of the Mark."

Several of the Torrlonder captains murmured to each other, and Ethelred squinted at Dayraven. "How do you know this?"

For a moment, Dayraven considered telling the duke the whole truth. He decided part of it would do for now. "The Supreme Priest Joruman summoned the elf for its power. He wished to protect the kingdom from the Ilarchae. But he could not wield it, and it took him ere it claimed them."

Duke Ethelred scowled. "That sounds like Joruman."

Dayraven continued, inwardly regretting his role in surrendering the power to Joruman and struggling to voice the most convincing version of events for the present need. "I have spoken to the elf. It comes from the Southweald, and it is of the forest. It wishes to return. It will not go out of its way to harm anyone, but, like a vast storm, it will devour any in its path with complete indifference. The wisest course for you would be to allow the dwolas through without standing in their way." He took a deep breath. "What is more, Torrhelm has need of you. The Ilarchae wrought much destruction there. The kingdom needs you in Torrhelm, in the seat of power." He paused a moment, and then he spoke his next words with emphasis. "King Earconwald is no more."

The murmuring of the captains exploded into exclamations and excited chatter.

Ethelred let them continue a moment, and then he cut the air with his hand. Silence followed, and the duke stared at Dayraven with a rigid expression as he took in those tidings. "Are you certain of this?"

"We believe it from the accounts of surviving witnesses, servants within Sigseld. While the Ilarchae were destroying the city, Earconwald in his madness ran from the palace towards the invading army wearing naught but a nightdress. He's not been heard from since."

"Was his body recovered?"

"No. When we left, no one had discovered it. Torrhelm is full of the dead. Surely, though, were he living, he would have come forward. But, whether he is mad or dead, the city needs you. You are the heir to the throne, and you must be seen there as soon as possible. There's a Torrlonder army, a much larger force than this, back in the city now, the one that had occupied the kingdoms of Caergilion and Adanon. It's led by a lieutenant called Edgelaf. He and the men following him have brought some order and stability, but they need you. They're waiting for *you*. They're good men, faithful soldiers, loyal to Torrlond."

The duke clenched his broad jaw and frowned at Dayraven. "Why? Why would you come here to tell me all this?"

Dayraven returned his stare and smiled. "To spare lives. There's been enough death everywhere. Torrlond needs a strong king now more than ever. A good king. You can do nothing here. Go back to Torrhelm."

"And if I heed your counsel, what will you do?"

"We're on our way to the Mark to warn King Ithamar to keep out of the way of the dwola army. The Southweald is its goal. Once it reaches it, the elf will release all the bodies it wields. If we can keep the Markmen away from the elf and its dwolas, no one need come to harm." Dayraven tried to appear more confident about these assertions than he felt.

Duke Ethelred kept his gaze on Dayraven as he stroked his beard. "Your answers satisfy me thus far. One last question, then." He glanced at Munzil. "Why does one of the foe stand among you? Is that man not an Ilarchae?"

Some of the Torrlonder captains grumbled and directed hostile sneers Munzil's way.

Dayraven nodded. "He is Munzil of the Grey Wolves. An Ilarchae. He avoided the fate of his folk when the elf slew them and seized their bodies. He wishes to see those bodies at peace. The elf has slaughtered all that have come in its path, but in the end, no people will have lost more than the Ilarchae."

Anger flared in Ethelred's eyes, and his frown deepened. "Had the elf not taken them, those same Ilarchae would have utterly destroyed Torrhelm. Women, children, the elderly: They would have left not a soul alive."

Munzil scowled at the duke. "Our war-leader bade us to slay no one unarmed, and we obeyed his command. There's no right in murdering the helpless. It was the dark magic — the elf, as he says — that turned the Folk of the Tribes into mindless killers."

The duke ignored him, whereas the captains around him grew louder and angrier in their remarks, and one could be heard above the others: "We should kill the bastard now!"

Dayraven held up his hand, and he was relieved when the captains went quiet. "He speaks the truth, Duke Ethelred. And it is also true that the Ilarchae came to Torrlond to wreak revenge and destruction.

Yet one may have compassion on a fallen foe. Especially one that fought with honor."

"What of the deaths he caused? Must he not answer for them?" The duke glared once again at Munzil.

"If you kill every soldier who slays in battle, there will be no armies left. And has he not answered for them? What worse fate can you imagine than losing all your people?" Dayraven shook his head. "Slay him, and you do him a kindness."

Ethelred paused and stroked his beard, but the fury remained in his eyes.

Before anyone else could speak, Dayraven seized the moment. "As I said, there has been enough death. Here is my counsel: Compassion will free you and set you on the path to healing. That is the need of the moment. What is more, this man is here under my protection. No one will harm him with my consent, and he will do no harm to Torrlond or anyone in it. You have my word." Dayraven glanced at Munzil, who stared at him before giving a deep nod.

Ethelred gazed at Dayraven for a long while with his jaw clenched tight. At length, he took a deep breath and nodded. "Very well. I place my faith in you, Prophet. I will follow your counsel. But you must answer for anything that man does. And I ask that you allow a company of my soldiers to accompany you as witnesses. We Torrlonders should be represented in whatever happens. They will report back to me, and they will ride for Torrhelm should anything go amiss. Do you agree?"

Dayraven gave a slight bow. "I do. It is fitting that Torrlonders should ride among us."

Ethelred turned to his captains. "Which of you volunteers to accompany the Prophet and his companions?"

Most of the captains looked down at their feet, and none met Dayraven's eyes save one. Ludecan directed a crooked grin at him and then at Orvandil, Gnorn, and Abon in turn. He stepped forward. "I do, my lord. Less than half of my company remains, however."

The duke nodded. "That will do, Captain Ludecan. Procure horses for your men from the quartermaster. Report to me afterwards. I shall give you your orders before you depart. The rest of you, prepare to march for Torrhelm."

Dayraven let out a quiet sigh.

Sequara approached him and communicated her approval with a nod.

On his other side, Galdor stepped up next to him and smiled. "Well done, Dayraven." His voice was a near whisper. "Prophet of Edan, indeed."

As Dayraven and the others were returning to the twenty-five Ellonder soldiers and their horses, a voice called out behind them. "A word, if you will."

Dayraven and his companions halted and turned around, and Ludecan approached them. The Torrlonder captain was still displaying a fierce grin. "Fitting, isn't it, that we should meet here?"

Dayraven nodded. "So, you remember."

"How could I forget my brush with the bloody Prophet of Edan?"

Gnorn growled. "Mind your tongue, captain."

Dayraven held out his hand. "It's alright, Gnorn." He looked at Ludecan. "Why did you volunteer to accompany us?"

The captain shrugged, and he glanced at Orvandil, Gnorn, and Abon before speaking to Dayraven. "For old time's sake, I suppose." He paused and shook his head. "No, that's a lie. See, we were there at Thulhan. The Mercenary Company of Etinstone. The fucking bastards you four abandoned."

Gnorn opened his mouth to object, but Ludecan continued before he could speak. "No doubt you had your reasons. And I don't blame you. But here's the thing. Ever since Thulhan, half of us who knew you — those that are still alive, anyway — believe you're holier than Edan's fucking fart. The other half can't think of you as anything other than that idiot boy who turned up in this very spot."

Dayraven smiled. "Which half are you in?"

Ludecan raised his eyebrows. "Can't make up my mind. *That*'s why I volunteered. Figured I'd get to observe you real close. The boys'll thank me for it, I promise you."

"I'm not sure they will, but I'm glad of your company all the same."

Ludecan gave him a gentler smile and he nodded. "Something else I need to tell you. Orvandil Dragonbane, in particular." He turned to the Thjoth, who leveled a hard gaze at his former lieutenant. "Yes, we heard all about your deeds too." The captain shook his head and grinned. "If anyone was going to kill a fucking dragon, it had to be you."

Orvandil's face did not change. "What do you wish to tell me?"

Ludecan's grin faded, and a serious frown replaced it. "We were up north fighting the Norfasters and your folk. Not much fun. The thing is, King Vols — your cousin, I believe . . . He died during the fighting."

Orvandil's hand went to the pommel of his blade, and his fierce eyes narrowed at the captain.

Ludecan backed up a pace as he held up his palm. "Duke Ethelred paid your people the biggest damn wergeld in all of the annals. And he recognized Durn, son of Durathror, as Duke of Norfast."

Orvandil's hand drifted away from his sword. "The Thjoths agreed to make peace?"

"Aye. That's how we got out of there."

"Who led them after Vols's death?"

"Red-headed fellow. Duneyr. He was in favor of settling things."

Orvandil gave a slow nod. "Then I too agree."

Ludecan peered more closely at Orvandil. "I also got the impression Duneyr didn't fancy remaining in charge for too long. He spoke of some sort of moot back in Grimrik."

The Thjoth sighed, and his eyes looked somewhere far away. "In the Thingvang they'll choose a new leader."

Dayraven put a hand on Orvandil's shoulder. "I'm sorry, my friend. Vols was a good king."

Gnorn bowed his head. "A good king, and a good man."

Orvandil nodded.

Though Dayraven could not tell what thoughts passed through his friend's mind, he sensed strong emotions behind his stony face. "If you need to return to Grimrik . . ."

"No." The Thjoth gazed at him and shook his head. "We finish this first."

28

THE EXILE

The road hugging the Withweald River led Dayraven and his large party, now swollen with the forty-eight survivors of the Mercenary Company of Etinstone, ever closer to Torrlond's border with the Mark. They met few travelers along it, and to them Dayraven gave warning of the approaching army of dwolas. Most gawked at him as if he had spouted gibberish, but, even though he and his friends had no time to linger to convince them of the threat, he hoped they would stay far from the road all the same. He reckoned the elf and the bodies enthralled to it would veer south of the river and away from the road on their way to the Southweald, but he was taking every precaution he could think of. Thus the leagues passed, and he hoped they were far enough ahead of the dwola army to head off King Ithamar before he set out with his warriors to encounter it. They hastened with as much speed as they thought the horses could bear, with Dayraven, Sequara, and Galdor healing the steeds every time they rested.

Just as the river was beginning to broaden, the road dwindled into a wide dirt track, marking the beginning of Dayraven's native kingdom. He grew silent. Images of his journey out of the Mark with Imharr swam in his mind, and, though he felt the melancholy of his friend's absence, he was glad for the knowledge that he had found his place in Adanon with Queen Rona. Sequara rode next to him, and when he glanced at her, her sad smile told him she guessed his thoughts. He drew a deep breath and let it out as a sigh before gazing around him at his onetime home.

The Withweald cut through a lush valley, shimmering and snaking between green knolls that grew higher and more rugged as they receded afar. In the distance, both north and south of the river, forest blanketed the rolling hills. Beneath the crisp blue sky with a few thin wisps of cloud streaking it, the trees of both the Northweald and the Southweald were afire with color. In waves undulating over the landscape, an endless conflagration of reds, purples, oranges, and yellows mingled with patches of green where there were pines and firs, but the leaf-bearing trees far outnumbered the evergreens.

"Now I know what Urd meant." Sequara gazed off into the distance as her horse trotted next to Dayraven's. "Though I've seen this forest in so many of your memories, I'm glad for a sight of it with my own eyes."

Recalling the evening in Kiriath, Asdralad's chief city, when his great aunt had spoken of the Mark's changing leaves and the rampage of color as life retreated before winter with a final flourish, Dayraven smiled and nodded at the sorceress. No longer his kingdom but still lodged in his heart, the Mark was more beautiful than ever.

"It's strange."

Sequara tilted her head toward him. "What is?"

He sighed. "I'm where I began, but I feel I know the place for the first time." He thought for a moment as the horses clopped along. "Yet it's not the Mark that's changed, of course. I have. I'm not just older. Having had the elf inside me, and the memories of so many. It feels like I've lived so long. Stretched over a thousand lives."

Sequara listened but said naught. With no need for words between them, she conveyed her understanding with a gentle smile.

Up ahead a troop of twenty riders cantered toward Dayraven's much larger party. The young wizard turned in his saddle and held up his hand, indicating his friends should await him while he approached the Markmen. He urged his horse forward at a trot until he deemed it best to stop and allow the oncoming group of warriors to approach as close as they saw fit.

They wore byrnies and helms, and most carried ash-shafted spears with glinting tips. Their swords lay in their scabbards, but Dayraven had the feeling their hands were ready to draw the weapons at the slightest hint of ill will from him. These were not simple farmers or even ordinary warriors. They were thegns, trained fighters attached to earl or king, and such men were the doughty backbone of the Mark's strength. Dayraven's father had been one of these men, and he had always thought to become one himself.

He raised his palms in token of peace. The Markmen halted their steeds save one, who rode until his horse stood ten feet from Dayraven's. "I am Thegn Tiowulf of Mere's End. Who are you, and why do you bring such a large company into the Mark?"

The man's familiar manner of speaking the Northern Tongue, another reminder of Dayraven's former home, drew a quick and subtle smile from him. "Greetings to you, Thegn Tiowulf. I am the Prophet of Edan, once Dayraven, son of Edgil of Kinsford. I and my companions come to offer our help and to warn King Ithamar and the folk of the Mark of an approaching army."

The rider gazed more closely at Dayraven's face. "You speak of the Ilarchae army crossing Torrlond."

"Yes. I have good reason to believe it's coming here. To the Southweald. And it is no ordinary army. It's many times larger than any force the Mark can muster, but that's the least worry. There are things I must tell King Ithamar to spare the folk of the Mark many deaths, and thus we have ridden with great speed."

"Son of Edgil of Kinsford, you say? How do we know you are who you claim?"

"There are those here who will know me. Earl Stigand of Kinsford, for one. Since you know of the Ilarchae, I gather King Ithamar has called his warriors to Wolvendon."

"Aye. He has."

"If he remains there, I would hasten to him."

The warrior gave Dayraven a hard smile. "Might be you are who you claim, Prophet of Edan, and might be you're here to offer help. I was at the Battle of Thulhan. Saw the dragon. Wasn't close enough to see your face. But let's say I believe you. For now. I still can't let such a large armed party ride into Wolvendon."

"Most of our party are soldiers of Ellond and Torrlond, men serving Earl Elfwy, who is here with us, and Duke Ethelred. The soldiers needn't come with us." Dayraven did a quick calculation. "They'll remain here with you while nine of us ride to Wolvendon."

The thegn scratched his beard and narrowed his eyes, which never left Dayraven's face. "That suits me. Nine of you may pass."

Dayraven nodded. "My thanks. I'll tell my companions, and we'll depart. I fear we must reach the king as soon as possible." He began to turn his steed, but he stopped when the thegn called out.

"One last thing, Prophet."

"Yes?"

The man grinned. "Welcome back to the Mark."

Dayraven nodded and smiled in return. "Thank you."

AFTER GIVING FIRM INSTRUCTIONS TO THE ELLONDER AND Torrlonder soldiers to stay well away from the army of dwolas should it arrive at the border of the Mark, Dayraven rode in the company of Sequara, Galdor, Elfwy, Abon, Gnorn, Orvandil, Ludecan, and Munzil until they reached Mere's End, which was little more than a village perched nigh the place where the Withweald yielded its waters to the lake. Thence they took a ferry bound across the glittering Folkmere to Wolvendon. Dayraven had beheld the vast lake but once before, and it still awed him how one could not see one end of it from the other, as if it were an inlet of the Great Sea.

Bucking a little as the gentle, wind-driven waves nudged it, the ferry plied the water at a steady rate, for the ferrymen knew their work. At length, the western shore took form as a dark smudge on the horizon. A bit later, shapes grew distinguishable, revealing the presence of a large settlement. As they approached Wolvendon from the water, Dayraven stood closer to Sequara and put an arm around her. He pulled his cloak tight to keep out the cool lake breeze and gazed toward the seat of the Mark's kings.

A network of docks webbed out over the lake's far margin, and behind them on an upward slope rose the town's sturdy wooden homes, shops, inns, and storehouses. An obvious change marked the town from his previous visit. At first they appeared as small white points flecking the green hills, like grazing sheep. But it did not take Dayraven long to realize what they were. Surrounding the docks and buildings on the further hillsides were thousands of tents arrayed in encampments, the mustered forces of the Mark.

Each of the Mark's four earls would have brought his warriors at King Ithamar's summons. Earl Hadulac from the rugged Hemeldowns, Earl Haereth from distant Farwick, Earl Ranulf from Mere's End, and, of course, Earl Stigand from Kinsford. To judge by the tents dotting the slopes on the town's outskirts, it was an impressive army. Yet it could not hope to match the oncoming horde, even were the bodies of the Ilarchae not the elf's vessels.

Upon reaching the shore, they stabled their weary horses at an inn near the docks. Wolvendon's streets were crowded with the influx of people, and along with the sounds of the bellowing merchants, barking dogs, clucking chickens, clinking warriors, shouting children, and general clamor, the scents of fish and burning wood were heavy in the air. One thing lacking was a sense of panic or even foreboding in the town, and Dayraven reckoned the folk of the Mark either knew little of the oncoming horde or placed great confidence in their lords to deal with it.

He guided his friends along the muddy streets past the many well-wrought wooden structures towards the king's hall, Widuru. It was a large enough town to host frequent visitors from other kingdoms, but there were still many whispers, lingering gazes, and fingers pointing toward the companions. Suppressing a resigned grin, Dayraven reckoned he and his friends must have been one of the odder parties to pass through. He decided the best response was to look as much as he could like the prophet he was supposed to be, and so he strode on the streets with a fixed gaze, as if no one should question his presence or purpose. The matter of his exile, he hoped, would remain unremarked.

When they arrived before Widuru, he spared a glance down the street at one of the few stone structures in the whole of the Mark: the Temple of the Way. He smiled as he realized he no longer feared that place or its white-robed inhabitants as he had when he journeyed through here before. It seemed so long ago, and he had felt so much younger and wide-eyed then. But the temple did not hold his attention for long, not with Widuru's breathtaking façade to gaze at.

Just as he remembered them, skillful carvings of the ancestral gods lived upon the tall doors of the ancient hall of the Mark's kings. With one at the peak of each door, Regnor and Hruga reposed on their thrones surveying the others from above. The bull's eyes bulged from its face, and veins protruded from its muscles as Bolthar wrestled it. From opposite doors, Syn and Logan waged their eternal battle with their weapons of frost and fire. The gentler Dyna opened her arms wide in a gesture of blessing over the earth's fruits. Halmar stood on the back of a vast creature emerging from the rough waves of the sea, while lovely Glora flew above him perched atop a sleek swan, her long hair streaming behind her. In his own corner, Sithfar stood apart, his face concealed beneath the hood of his cloak. To judge by the staff he pointed in warning, the god who conveyed the dead to their final place of rest was gazing straight at the onlooker.

Dayraven turned to Sequara, who stood next to him observing the carvings. He sensed how the old gods of his people must have seemed to her: primitive and wild, full of rough power and energy, like the folk who created them in their stories. "Most in the Mark still worship them, though the priests of the Way have won many followers for Edan, especially in the farmsteads around Mere's End and here in Wolvendon."

Sequara kept her eyes on the façade. "They are beautiful." She gazed more closely, holding a hand toward the carvings as if she would touch them. "And strong."

"Strong enough to last more winters than we can reckon." Abon, who sang of the old gods and their ancient stories, smiled up at the carvings.

"We worship these same gods." Munzil stood on Dayraven's other side with his mouth hanging open in a stunned look.

Dayraven nodded. "Yes. Our ancestors were the same people once, long ago. Before they settled in this part of Eormenlond, the folk of the Mark, Torrlond, and Ellond came from the Wildlands. Before that, from the frozen islands northeast of Eormenlond." He nodded toward Orvandil. "The Thjoths too came from the Wildlands before they took Grimrik from the Dweorgs."

Orvandil nodded and glanced at Gnorn, who released a quiet sigh.

His mouth still hanging open, Munzil turned to Dayraven. "Then you too are Folk of the Tribes."

Galdor stepped up and smiled at Munzil. "In a manner of speaking, we are indeed, though most of us have forgotten it. Whatever tribes we belonged to are long gone, their names not even a memory. However, I suppose to the Andumae or the Dweorgs, we're still more or less Ilarchae with a smattering of what they call civilization."

Gnorn chuckled. "A smattering, mayhap."

Munzil stared at the old wizard. "I've seen what civilization does. Those who have it count themselves better than others, but they are only more corrupt and arrogant, cleverer at finding ways to make others work for them until they become soft and lazy."

Captain Ludecan barked a bitter laugh. "The savage has a point."

Munzil curled his lip in a sneer. "Better a savage than cowards who run from battle and leave their allies to fight alone."

Ludecan's smile became a glare as his hand shot to the pommel of his sword.

Dayraven held up a palm. "Enough. Save your insults and quarrels for later. Or better yet, bury them for good. We don't have time for them."

Munzil and Ludecan gave each other hard stares, and Dayraven wondered if he would need to intervene with more force. People on the street began to gawk at their party with frowns on their faces. They were already outlandish enough. The last thing they needed was to draw more attention by fighting amongst themselves.

Just then, Widuru's small side door opened, and everyone's face turned to the thegn who emerged, an armed man with a craggy face, greying beard, and keen eyes that took them all in. He stepped toward them with a slight limp. "Why do you wait before Widuru? Do you have dealings with King Ithamar?"

Dayraven walked toward him. "I am Dayraven, the one many call the Prophet of Edan. I was born in the Mark, son of Edgil of Kinsford. We've come to warn King Ithamar about the Ilarchae army approaching the Mark. There are things we must tell him that would spare many lives."

The thegn's eyes narrowed as he peered first at Dayraven and then at each of his companions. His gaze returned to the young wizard, and he grinned. "I'm Thegn Athelgar. I knew your father well. Fought alongside him in Torrlond long ago. You have something of his look." He nodded. "Ithamar has called a moot this day to speak of the Ilarchae. Come with me, and I'll bring you to the king. You may seek a seat at the table to give us your tidings."

IN THE SMOKY SPACE WITHIN THE GREAT HALL, TORCHES ADDED TO the sunlight streaming in through the louver high above. Carved upon the oak columns and the network of beams supporting Widuru's lofty ceiling were fanciful creatures and intricate knot patterns with curling plants and foliage. In the center of the long hall was the stone fire pit, and behind the columns were the raised platforms upon which folk gathered and feasted at tables. At the hall's far end stood a table long enough to seat fifty, and around this table King Ithamar held his moot. The king occupied the high seat at the table's head, and his four earls sat closest to him, two on each side.

Dayraven had never met Ithamar or the earls other than Stigand, but he had heard of them many times, and it was not hard to put names to their faces. Tall and handsome with a noble bearing, Ithamar seemed born for the role of king, though still young and perhaps somewhat untried. Red-haired Earl Hadulac's gruff face seemed fixed in a permanent scowl, and it was said he and the folk of the Hemeldowns were most devoted to the old ways. Earl Ranulf of Mere's End stroked his grey beard as he studied the others around the table. Dayraven reckoned his appearance accorded well with his reputation for caution. But it was Haereth of Farwick whom most thought the cleverest of the earls. With his greying hair and lined, tanned face, he looked every bit the seaman he was said to be. And, of course, there was Stigand. The big Earl of Kinsford, his father's old lord and friend, had locked eyes with Dayraven once and ended it with a nod, giving no hint of emotion. Dayraven had always liked Stigand, but it was he who had pronounced his exile what seemed so long ago.

Others seated around the table included many of the king's thegns. But a number of them stood around the table or leaned on columns nearby, some having given their seats at the behest of Ithamar to Dayraven and his friends, who occupied a bench at the end of the table opposite the king's. In addition, many more of the earls' thegns joined these in standing groups around the table, crowding the hall and filling it with the murmur of their conversations.

Among these thegns were those of Kinsford. There were Eanmund, Halga, Baldred, young Alwyn, and others, often glancing with narrowed eyes at Dayraven. There too was Guthere, who had been Edgil's closest friend and the man Dayraven had once expected to be his father-in-law. Ebba's father pointedly refused to look at him. Standing by him, his son Guthmund, who had been Dayraven's friend, once directed a weak smile his way. At the table too sat a white-robed man whom Dayraven recognized as the priest of the Way who had tried to accost him when he was last in Wolvendon. The man glared his way, making it clear he also remembered their encounter. *At least I didn't kill him.*

King Ithamar held up a hand, silencing the murmurs at once. "I have called this moot to speak of what we must do about the army of Ilarchae marching across Torrlond and heading toward the Mark. Word has come to us from Torrlond. To begin, we will hear what the one called the Prophet of Edan has to say of this invading army." He gestured with an open hand toward Dayraven, who nodded in acknowledgement and opened his mouth to speak.

"My lord," said a stern voice before the young wizard could get out a word. It was the priest of the Way, to whom all eyes turned. "If I may." He directed a scowl toward Dayraven and pointed an accusing finger. "This man claiming to be the Prophet of Edan is known to me. The Way does not acknowledge him or sanction the title he so sacrilegiously wears, and therefore he has no authority. There is but one Prophet of Edan: the blessed Aldmund, founder of our faith."

The fleeting look of reverence on the priest's face when he mentioned Aldmund gave way to a sneer as he pointed again at Dayraven. "Furthermore, I once caught this imposter skulking about Widuru with dangerous power dwelling in him, a dire threat that needed containing. Not only that, but in his company is a notorious heretic." He jabbed his finger at Galdor. "*That* is Galdor of Ellond, ever a foe of the Way. And who is the southern woman? She too is strong in the gift, I can tell you, and I doubt she is a friend to this kingdom. This is a dangerous company you've welcomed through your doors, and I counsel you to cast them out without delay."

Most of the eyes in the hall studied Dayraven and his companions, and they were not friendly.

Galdor cleared his throat and directed a smile toward the priest. "You are Bertric, head priest of the Temple of the Way here in Wolvendon, I believe. As I've heard, you were ever faithful to the Supreme Priest Bledla. A devout priest and a true man. So, tell us now: This dangerous power you spoke of, this dire threat . . . Do you sense it in this man at this very moment?" The old wizard cocked an eyebrow and gestured toward Dayraven.

The priest Bertric frowned and licked his lips. "Well, no, not now, but . . ."

"There is one charge laid to rest, then." Galdor grinned. "As for my supposed heresy, unless I'm mistaken, the Way is not the kingdom's law in the Mark."

"It is not," rumbled Earl Hadulac, and he gazed around as if challenging anyone to disagree. "Especially after the mess those white-robes led us all into back in Sildharan." Many disgruntled mumbles of agreement followed this assertion, and the priest Bertric sat straighter on his bench as he frowned.

"There we are." Galdor's grin grew larger. The old wizard had scored an important point since the Way and Torrlond's standing was at a low after Bledla and Earconwald dragged the Mark into what most saw as a deceitful and foolish war.

Galdor put his finger to his lips in mock concentration. "Now, let us see. Your objection to Lady Sequara is that she is from the south? Asdralad, to be precise. As far as I'm aware, it's no crime to be born on that island. And, like the rest of us, she is here to lend her aid to the Mark." He gestured with his palms spread out as if suggesting the matter were settled.

Bertric sneered. "Don't play innocent with me. Everyone knows you're a foe of Torrlond and therefore of the Mark. It's not in our interest to heed anything coming from your deceitful lips."

"Wrong again, priest." All eyes turned to Ludecan, who had spoken.

"And who are you?" Bertric glanced toward the ensign and three red stripes on the shoulder of the captain's grey kirtle.

"Captain Ludecan, here to witness on behalf of Duke Ethelred of Etinstone. It would indeed be in the interest of this moot to hearken to the Prophet here. There's nasty business coming your way, and if you don't listen to what this man is trying to tell you, you'll be far the worse for it."

The priest looked surprised at the mention of Duke Ethelred, but then he grinned at Ludecan. "Captain Ludecan, you say? What company do you command?"

Ludecan held his head high. "The Mercenary Company of Etinstone."

Bertric chortled. "A mercenary company? You expect us to take your word?"

Ludecan glared at the priest and leaned forward in his seat, but before he could answer, someone else spoke. "You're wasting time we don't have, Bertric. An army's on its way here. If these folk say they've come to offer help, let them have their say, and we'll judge the matter at once." It was one of the thegns at the table, a large, middle-aged warrior Dayraven did not know. He glanced at Dayraven and nodded.

Dayraven returned the nod and then looked to King Ithamar. "With your leave, King Ithamar?"

The king, who was older in years than Dayraven but still seemed young, thought for a moment before replying, "You may speak if there are no other objections."

"I have three objections."

Recognizing the voice, Dayraven closed his eyes for a moment before turning towards Guthere. His father's friend glared at him, his face red with anger. "First, this man is an exile from the Mark and has no right to speak at this moot. Second, he keeps company with one of the foe." The thegn's rough voice was strained with emotion as he pointed at Munzil. "Third, and worst of all, he keeps company with the slayer of his own father, whom he ought to *avenge*." Guthere growled out the last word as he pointed at Orvandil. "Do you deny you are the Thjoth they call Dragonbane, who slew Edgil of Kinsford at the Battle of Thulhan?"

Orvandil looked down at the table before engaging Guthere with a steady, hard gaze. "I don't deny it."

Angry voices erupted in the hall, a chaos of babble. Some of the thegns put their hands on the pommels of their swords. Dayraven ground his teeth. The moot was not going at all as he had hoped. *Too stubborn in their ways. I must find a means to make them listen.*

King Ithamar stood from his seat. "Silence!"

Quiet seized the hall.

Ithamar gazed around with lowered brow at his warriors. "My own blade will strike off the next hand that touches weapon in this sacred hall."

The warriors' arms fell to their sides.

"I have taken these guests under my roof. No one is to threaten them while they are here." He sat down and turned to Dayraven as if there had been no interruption. "How do you answer the charges we have heard?"

Dayraven took a deep breath as all faces turned toward him. "Orvandil Dragonbane has paid me many times over for my father's death through his friendship. It is true: He slew him in battle, warrior against warrior, though he tried to avert it. My father mistook him for my murderer, and in his grief he did not heed Orvandil trying to tell him he was my friend, and that I lived. In the end, he had but two choices: fight or die. What man among you would not defend himself in such a place?"

Dayraven gazed around the hall, stopping as he faced Guthere, who scowled and looked away. No one responded. *I must bring them round. They* must *see the coming danger.* He gestured towards Munzil with one outstretched hand. "This man is an Ilarchae. One of the few to survive. What is marching toward us is *not* an Ilarchae army, not even a *human* army any longer, and thus he is no foe of the Mark and never was." A few murmurs broke out, but Dayraven held up his palm to silence them. "All will be made clear. But you must listen first if you value your lives and the lives of your kin." The hall went quiet again.

Dayraven let out a long sigh. It was time to tell them. "As for me, I *am* an exile from the Mark. This kingdom was my home, and the love for it and its folk still runs deep in me. Even were it not so, I would have come here to tell you what I must. You will hear the whole of the truth, and this truth will reveal your present danger."

He paused a moment, fighting down despair and panic at the thought that they would not listen. *I must keep calm.* He swallowed, took several breaths, and, when he knew he had mastered his voice, began. "As you have heard and many of you know, I was born Dayraven, son of Edgil of Kinsford. From my mother, Eldelith, I inherited the gift. But that power was small next to what came to dwell in me when I met with an elf in the Southweald. I know not how or why I lived, nor can I tell you how the elf's energy became lodged in me. I never asked for it." He faced the priest Bertric, whose eyes narrowed with suspicion. "That is the vast power you felt when you stumbled upon me here in Wolvendon."

Dayraven paused a moment, and he nodded at Earl Stigand. "The folk of Kinsford were right to exile me. Though I did not wish to accept the truth, I was a danger to them. At first I tried to run away, and I feigned that I could shut the elf inside my mind. Later, I tried to turn the elf's power to good. I used it to help stop the Supreme Priest Bledla's mad war, which most of you witnessed at Thulhan when, with the elf's energy, I wrested the dragons from him."

Many in the hall nodded and murmured at these words before Dayraven continued. "But the elf was far too strong for me, and at last it robbed me of my memories in its quest to follow its will. It is no creature bound to flesh, though it can wear a body when it wishes. It is cold, and it cares not for our yearnings any more than the wind would. And yet, this elf, interwoven as it has been with the lives of mortals, seeks to deliver our kind from pain. It believes it is a mercy to steal our lives away. I fought its purpose for long, but every day I grew more lost, and my end was coming."

He shook his head. "In my desperation, I agreed to permit the Supreme Priest Joruman to attempt to take the burden of the elf's power from me. I believed I could strive against it no longer. It might be I was right. To avert the many deaths that would have followed the end of my struggle, I allowed the supreme priest to convince me he could wield it. But he could not."

Whispers and murmurs broke out, and the priest Bertric's eyes widened with keener interest. King Ithamar held up a hand, and silence blanketed the hall once again.

Dayraven sighed. "Joruman is no more, but the elf walks in his body. The army on its way here is under its sway. The Ilarchae are no longer human. They're gone. But the elf dwells in all their bodies, using them as extensions of its will. They are an army of dwolas."

The silence was thick enough to suffocate on. Dayraven gazed at the faces around the hall and stopped at King Ithamar, whose eyes betrayed his intense curiosity. *This is the moment. They must listen. I must make them understand.* "Heed me now. You cannot fight them. If you slay one of the dwolas, you will take its place. The elf will seize you with complete indifference, and you will be no more, though your body will be a tool the elf wields against your kin."

The priest Bertric scoffed. "You can't expect us to believe . . ."

"I saw it happen in Torrhelm." Munzil glowered at the priest, and then he turned to the king. "Some of us were away when the elf took the Folk of the Tribes, my brothers and sisters. When we met those under the sway of the dark magic, they turned on us with no recognition in their faces, slaying several before we knew what was happening. Those who fought back and killed them became dwolas and began attacking us in their turn." His jaw muscles bunched as he paused a moment and glanced down at the table. "It shames me to admit it before you all, but the only to survive were those who fled. I give you my word: It's just as he says."

Bertric rolled his eyes. "The word of an Ilarchae."

"It happened to some of our soldiers in Torrlond too." Ludecan nodded. "I spoke to three witnesses, survivors who told the same tale."

The Torrlonder captain and Munzil glanced at each other and nodded as if in silent agreement to put aside their previous quarrel.

The priest shook his head. "This is ridiculous."

King Ithamar stared at Dayraven. "You say we cannot fight this army. What would you have us do instead?"

Dayraven looked back at the king, once again holding in check his roiling emotions and desperation to convince the Markmen lest they think him mad. He needed to sound confident and firm. *They won't like this, but they must see it's the only way.* "Back in Torrhelm, I spoke to the elf. I believe it intends to return to the Southweald, whence it came. When it reaches the forest, it will release the bodies it holds in its power, including Joruman's. Do nothing to oppose the dwola army, and it will not harm you. You must stay out of its way."

"This is madness." Earl Ranulf of Mere's End, whose folk were closest to the approaching army, frowned at Dayraven. "You would have us allow a horde of Ilarchae to invade our kingdom without lifting a finger to defend ourselves."

One of the thegns pounded the table with his fist. "He leaves his father unavenged, and he would have us dishonor ourselves too."

"They must be in league with the Ilarchae," shouted the priest Bertric. "They've come to fool us into letting down our guard."

Angry shouts broke out, too many to hear at once.

Near Dayraven, Gnorn growled under his breath. "These fools aren't listening." He shouted over the rising din of voices, "If you try to fight that army, you'll *all* die, and yours may be the hand that slays your kin."

But they were not listening, and more joined in the yelling.

King Ithamar raised his palm, and once again the hall went still. "Enough. We've heard what our guests have come to say, and there's little time. Warriors of the Mark: Let us hear your will, then. Who here wishes to heed the counsel of the one called the Prophet of Edan, once Dayraven of the Mark, and allow the army of Ilarchae to enter the Southweald unopposed?"

No one raised a voice.

Dayraven's stomach squirmed as he gazed around the table at them. The shock of his failure numbed most of his mind even as some remote part of him screamed inwardly that he must convince them somehow. *If I could begin anew* . . . With a cold dread, he felt powerless to prevent what he knew must come.

King Ithamar waited a moment longer before speaking again. "And which of you would fight the Ilarchae army should it cross into the Mark?"

A resounding chorus of shouts followed. A few, such as Earl Stigand and the thegn who had earlier spoken in favor of letting Dayraven have his say, had refrained from joining in, but the other earls and almost all the thegns had made their will clear. A large smirk crossed the priest Bertric's face.

Ithamar looked across the table at Dayraven. "You have heard our will. You may leave this hall in peace and go where you wish whilst we decide how to fight this threat. Let no one hinder or seek to harm them, for they have guested in Widuru."

The entire moot stared at Dayraven and his friends, their faces stonier than ever.

Ludecan was the first to rise. The Torrlonder captain shook his head. "He tried to warn you. At least there's plenty of wood around here for your funeral pyres, assuming anyone will be left to care for the dead."

The others rose from their seats, but Dayraven remained rooted to the bench, unable to move or think of anything he could say to persuade the Markmen. He had failed.

Sequara put her hand on his shoulder. "Come."

His body rose, and though he shook his head at King Ithamar, still no words would come. He allowed Sequara to guide him out of the hall.

LIKE BEGGARS TURNED OUT OF THE HALL, DAYRAVEN AND HIS companions stood outside Widuru on the street, where folk began staring at them again. The young wizard was still trying to think of the right words to convince the Markmen at the moot that they must allow the dwolas to pass into the Southweald unhindered. But he knew he would not gain entry through those doors again. "It's over. I failed."

Sequara's hand squeezed his shoulder. "They wouldn't listen. It's no fault of yours. There'll be another way. We must think."

"But the folk of the Mark . . . The needless deaths." He looked around at the people on the street: men, women, and children. He shook his head. "There must be something I can say."

"Mayhap the elf will release the bodies of the Ilarchae before they reach the Mark." Abon did not sound convinced, and no one responded to the suggestion.

Gnorn frowned at Dayraven. "What do we do now?"

Dayraven shook his head again, and his voice trembled when he spoke. "I don't know."

"If they prize their bloody honor more than their lives, there's little you can do." Captain Ludecan shrugged. "You warned them. Best thing now is to stay out of the way and clear out of here."

"I will remain." Munzil crossed his arms in front of his chest and thrust out his jaw. "I must witness."

"Whatever you decide, we're with you." Gnorn clenched his hand in a fist and nodded at Dayraven.

Orvandil too nodded. "Your path is ours."

Earl Elfwy spoke up. "If my lord Galdor agrees, my men and I will see this task to its end."

The old wizard smiled. "Yes. We're here to help as we can. We'll not give up hope. Eh, Abon?"

The shaper gave a crooked grin. "Aye, damn me. We're too fucking stupid to give up."

Dayraven turned and gazed into Sequara's eyes. The sorceress took his hand in hers, and she gave him the slightest nod.

So. They were with him, which gave him some courage. The only problem was he still had no notion what he would do.

"Dayraven."

He turned at the sound of the woman's voice, which tugged on strands buried deep in his memory.

The woman stood outside Widuru's small side door, which she closed behind her. She held a sleeping babe in her arms. Though she seemed older and a bit more filled out, everything about her, from her braided blonde hair to the flushed cheeks on her pale face to her blue eyes, was intimately familiar. He thought he recognized even the blue dress she wore. It had always been her favorite color.

"Ebba."

Ebba gazed at him for a long moment, seeming to struggle with finding her words. She glanced at Sequara, who still held Dayraven's hand, and then at his other companions before her eyes turned back to him. "A word with you, if I may?"

Dayraven swallowed and stared back at Ebba. He released a long sigh. "Of course." Turning to Sequara, he nodded. The sorceress gave him a gentle smile and nodded back, and then she and the others turned away and moved a few paces from Dayraven and Ebba, out of earshot.

Dayraven stepped closer to Ebba and tried to muster up a smile. He glanced at the babe. "Yours?"

She nodded and directed an affectionate grin toward the bundle she held. "My son." She lifted the blanket so that Dayraven could see the child's face. His eyes were closed, his nose small and delicate, and his tiny pink lips were pursed as if he were dreaming of suckling. The hair atop his head was so blond it was almost white.

"He's beautiful." Remembering how often they had talked of the children they would have, Dayraven looked into Ebba's face. "Ebba. There's no time. You must leave here. Take your son and go. Back to Kinsford, perhaps. That might be far enough, but if not . . . There's an army of . . ."

"I know. I heard everything."

"You did?"

"Yes. There are chambers behind the king's high seat. Many of the women were listening there. I live here in Wolvendon, you know."

He looked at the ground for a moment, recollecting the day on Asdralad when he had learned from Kulva of Ebba's marriage. "I had heard."

"My husband, Leofwin . . . He's the one who spoke for you."

Dayraven pictured the thegn who, in spite of the priest Bertric's warnings, had insisted on letting him have his say to the moot. He nodded. "You must thank him for me, but I fear I failed to convince them. Ebba, listen to me. Tell your husband . . ."

"I told him I believed in you." She nodded, and tears began to fill her eyes. "I made him promise to listen."

"And he did. But I failed."

She smiled as one tear spilled down her cheek. "Silly." It was a good imitation of how she used to speak to him when she was being sensible. "You can't always make folk see what you see. It's not your doing if they don't heed you."

"Yes, but people will *die*. Everyone in the path of that horde will perish. You believe me, don't you?"

She nodded and sniffed before wiping her cheek with the back of her hand.

"Good. You must flee to . . ."

Ebba shook her head as more tears tracked down her face. "This is my home. I won't leave."

"But you . . . Your babe . . . Surely you . . ." His mouth hung open, but he snapped it shut when he saw the familiar stubbornness in her eyes. "Ebba, please . . ."

"I'll share my people's fate." She glanced down at her son's face. "So will he. Might be we'll win somehow. Don't give up on us. Either way, I wanted to thank you, and to say . . . goodbye." She stepped back, but her wet eyes were still locked onto him. "I'd best get back inside." Her face trembled as she sobbed, and she turned away from him to open the door and disappear inside Widuru before closing it.

Dayraven stood gazing at the door. "Goodbye, dear Ebba. I won't. I won't give up on you."

He clenched his teeth and made tight fists with his hands before nodding to himself. He understood what he must do. And, in spite of his friends' loyalty, he would need to do it alone. There was no need to risk their lives, for the elf was his task alone. Sequara especially must remain safe. And the child growing within her, the daughter he felt sure he saw in the true-dream back in Sigseld's dungeon before Seren found him. Somehow, he would have to convince them all to stay away. He would think of what he must say to them on the way back to the ferry.

. . .

"Not a chance," growled Gnorn, whose arms crossed his broad chest. His posture was weakened, however, as he wobbled and caught his footing. They were on the ferry back across the Folkmere. The waves were not too choppy as the breeze was mild, but the Dweorg had always been most uneasy on water.

"Told you already." Orvandil glared at Dayraven. "We're with you."

Dayraven stared in disbelief. "Will no one heed me this day?"

Sequara put her hand on his shoulder. "Listen. We can be of help."

Dayraven stared at her and then glanced down at her stomach, but he said nothing of their child aloud since they had not told their friends yet. "No. You can do naught. I alone know the song of origin Joruman used to take the elf's energy from me. If it fails, there's no need for any of you to be nearby."

"You're wrong. We can get you out."

Galdor nodded. "She's right, Dayraven. Remember the song of origin you used when you shared your mind with us in Torrhelm? We can do a similar thing. Together, Sequara and I might have just enough power to enter the minds of all our companions. We can shield them from the elf, at least for a short while."

"Long enough to get you out if Joruman's song of origin has no effect." Sequara stared at him with defiance in her dark eyes and shook her head. "I'm not asking permission. We'll be with you. I won't leave you again."

Earl Elfwy placed his hand on his sword's pommel. "My men and I will stand ready to ward you."

Ludecan stepped closer and squinted as he cocked his head at Galdor. "Are you saying you can sing one of your spells, and it'll keep that elf thing out of our heads? We'd be able to fight the dwolas without becoming one of them?"

The old wizard nodded. "At least for a little while. I think. Especially if you're willing to let us in, and if Dayraven is distracting the elf with his song of origin."

The captain gave a thoughtful frown. "Sounds interesting."

Dayraven glared at Ludecan. "I thought *you* at least had more sense. What about staying out of the way?"

The captain shrugged. "Duke Ethelred wanted me to witness what happens here. Might as well be of some use while I'm at it. And if there's some way to shield us from that thing's sorcery, I won't say no."

"You may lay your magic upon me." There was a fierce light in Munzil's eyes. "I welcome the chance to free as many of my kin as I can with my blade."

Sequara took a deep breath and faced Dayraven. "You'll not do this alone. If Joruman's song of origin succeeds, you may need help casting the elf back into the forest. I will be there by your side."

Dayraven looked around at them all and shook his head. Past them, beyond the lake, and far out on the eastern horizon, darkness tinged the sky, and there was a chill in the wind skimming across the lake from that direction. His shoulders dropped in resignation, and he took a deep breath before he gazed at each of his friends in turn. "Alright, then. But you will all stay well out of harm's way, and you must do exactly as I say."

29

RETURN TO EDAN

Ghostly tatters of morning mist floated amongst the outlying trees of the Southweald, clinging to the branches as the rays of the rising sun burned them away. In an explosion of vivid and fleeting color, oak, ash, elm, beech, maple, birch, and sundry others stood in the light, which tinged the brilliant reds, oranges, and yellows of the leaves with dawn's golden hue. The gaps between the trunks revealed the dim shapes of other trees and the unending sylvan shadow deeper within.

Just outside the eaves of the Southweald stood an army several thousand strong. Facing away from the forest and fixing their eyes towards the east, the warriors of the Mark had gathered to defend their kingdom. The main strength of that army was the thegns, but farmers, huntsmen, and tradesmen stood by them, many grasping the long bows with which they hoped to whittle down the invading foe. Every man among them had come to keep his home and his kin from harm. They were grim but determined, and they placed great faith in their earls and king, who stood at the forefront of their formations.

A much smaller force waited several furlongs further from the Southweald. Fifty-nine individuals sat astride their horses, facing away from the Markmen and the Southweald. Most of their number were soldiers of Torrlond and Ellond, but among them too was a sorceress of Asdralad, a Dweorg of the Fyrnhowes, a Thjoth of Grimrik, a wizard and a shaper of Ellond, and a warrior of the Folk of the Tribes.

Two furlongs past them a lone rider gazed east, his back to the smaller force and, beyond them, the army waiting before the Southweald. No kingdom was his, but he chanted a song of origin again and again in the desperate hope that it might safeguard all the folk behind him.

Even as he chanted, darkness bled into the sky and spread like a miasma until it blotted out the sun. Shadow cloaked the land. Greyness swallowed the vibrancy of the leaves, and the warmth too fled as a chill sliced the air. The sharp cold penetrated the bodies of all the gathered mortals, and even the bravest of them shivered.

The lone rider kept chanting as he squinted and gazed east. On the horizon, a vast, silent horde appeared.

Earl Elfwy clenched his jaw and sat straighter atop his horse. The beast whinnied, and he supposed it too felt the terrible chill threatening to steal away all will and life. Ready on their steeds, twelve of his men were arrayed behind him, while the other twelve waited in a row behind Lieutenant Eanred, who was next to him. He knew his soldiers, each a fine horseman and capable of fighting from the saddle. There was no doubt the Ellonders were the ablest and swiftest riders among the Prophet's party.

While Elfwy did not suspect the Torrlonders' courage and effectiveness as fighters, he had observed them during the journey and knew them for foot soldiers, not cavalry. As for Dayraven's other friends, the Ilarchae never fought on horseback, and he had no reason to believe Munzil was different. The Thjoth was no doubt the most dangerous among them all with a blade, but he was too big to be a fast rider. The Dweorg could hardly sit in his saddle. Abon would stay by Galdor, who remained with Sequara as the wizard and sorceress kept chanting their spells to maintain their presence within the minds of everyone in the party. Thus, it fell to Elfwy and his soldiers to be the first to defend the Prophet should things go amiss.

It was the old wizard who occupied the minds of all the Ellonders. Elfwy winced at the thought that Galdor might detect his regret that it was not Sequara who protected him from the elf's power. It was undignified to think such things. Besides that, it was likely best this way, for the idea of her reading his thoughts brought color to his cheeks.

Of course, Galdor would know everything running through his head, but he had faith in the wizard's discretion. The old man's presence in his mind was a strange thing, gentle like the stroke of a feather, and it gave rise to the feeling that someone was standing right behind him. At first, he had even turned around several times just to make sure. At the same time, it was comforting. Galdor's quiet wisdom and love of life sparked a warm flame inside him even as the elf's chill stabbed at him and its looming shadow threatened to smother him.

Elfwy glanced at Lieutenant Eanred. The old veteran stared forward with a look of fierce determination, and then he seemed to notice his lord's gaze as he turned to face him. The earl nodded. "Remember the commands."

"Aye, my lord. I'll follow your lead. The lads will be behind us. If it comes to that."

Elfwy looked toward the Prophet, alone on his horse. Past him, the massive army of dwolas began to take shape in the far distance, blotting the horizon. "Let's hope it doesn't." He could not quite keep the quiver out of his voice.

"Aye, my lord."

Captain Ludecan spat as he sat on his steed. It was meant to be a gesture of defiance, or at least an expression of unconcern, but it struck him as in fact pathetic as he looked toward the advancing horde of dwolas and the uncanny darkness looming above it. *Shit. Trying to fight them all would be about as effective as spitting.* A shiver he could not suppress shook his shoulders.

More than ever, he reckoned the men in his company who had chosen to return to Torrlond were the sensible ones. He had given them all the choice of whether to stand here and witness or, in the likely event that everything turned to shit, ride back to Duke Ethelred and bear a message about what happened. Twenty-six had decided to stay, and the rest were gone. Of those who remained, most had known the Prophet back when he was just Dayraven, the green boy who had been part of the Mercenary Company of Etinstone. "At least we'll settle this business about the Prophet of Edan."

"How do you reckon that?" Lieutenant Irling sat astride his horse next to him.

"Well, if we're all dead after this, we'll know he was no damned prophet. Right?"

Just past Irling, Utred squished his face into a puzzled frown. "We won't know nothin' if we're dead, Cap'n. Will we?"

Sergeant Mull stroked his beard. "I reckon that's a question for the priests, Utred."

"Least we got the pretty one, eh?" Bernred stared ahead at the army of dwolas with a forced grin that his chattering teeth belied. "I'd hate to have the old man mucking around in my head."

"Not much to muck around in." Hewald directed a wink and a wicked smile at Bernred, who glared at his fellow soldier.

Ludecan chuckled. With the cold seeping into his marrow, he was glad for the chance to grin at something. The sorceress's presence was a comfort too, and her beauty was more than just physical. Without it, he might have turned his horse and galloped away already. Perhaps it gave them something to stand for, which was an embarrassingly sentimental thought he kept to himself. He nodded and returned his gaze to the oncoming horde. "As long as she keeps that bloody elf thing out of our minds."

"OH, FUCK. FUCKING BLOODY FUCK." ABON SWALLOWED, AND IN spite of the chill that made his body shiver, he was sweating all over. No song in his hoard of tales told of anything like this. If he survived, he was not sure he could put it into song, or if he would even want to.

He clutched his unsheathed sword in one hand, which was awkward for him since he was not used to fighting from horseback. His throwing dagger was ready in his belt. Stationed behind the soldiers from Torrlond and Ellond, he guarded Galdor and Sequara, who sat motionless atop their horses. The wizard and the sorceress stared ahead with vacant eyes, all their concentration pouring into the song of origin they both chanted. The shaper felt the old wizard's presence like a playful whisper in the back of his mind, and he was more than glad for it. Had it not been there, he was certain he would have run away screaming and cursing.

Likely sensing the ominous aura from the approaching horde and its otherworldly wielder, Abon's horse whickered. The shaper's nose wrinkled as he caught a whiff of something foul in the air. No wonder the horses were spooked. It was the horde's reek, a corpse-like stench that the cold wind carried out in front of it. He squinted up at the sky, where the darkness clotted as the dwola army neared them. He almost wished they would make some sort of noise, but they marched toward the Southweald in eerie silence.

Soon enough, however, the sound of their scores of thousands of stomping boots arose as a dull rumble. Not long later, the very earth seemed to vibrate, and his nervous horse began neighing and tamping the soil with its hooves. Not a cloud dotted the morning sky, but it was as if the sun were westering on a deeply overcast day. The gloom stole the color from the world, and, sitting in the midst of it, the shaper wondered if it would all end in utter darkness with all of them stumbling blindly until they perished under the blades of the horde. It was not the mere prospect of death that was so overwhelming, but that the vast and indifferent shadow would wipe away all trace and memory of their brief existence, as if they had never been.

Louder grew the din of the approaching dwolas, like a ceaseless thunder. Galdor and Sequara kept up their chant, but their voices seemed thin and small and fragile. The thought of fleeing screamed in the shaper's mind, but he clenched his jaw and tightened his grip on his sword. He would never abandon his friends. Better to drown in the darkness. Dayraven needed his chance. Up ahead, a dark silhouette atop his steed, the young wizard stood alone against the oncoming hoard.

. . .

Scores of thousands of dwolas covered the hillsides, crawling over the darkened land as far as Dayraven could see like an endless plague of locusts. Their marching shook the earth, and the sound was like huge drums pounding in his ears. He imagined the vast path of destruction they had carved leading all the way back to Torrhelm. The horde seethed nearer and nearer, and even in the gloom he began to make out the individual forms of the ones closest. He could not see Joruman's body, but somewhere amongst them all, he knew, a white-robed corpse walked. Though the elf dwelled in every one of the dwolas, he detected a concentration of its presence somewhere up ahead, the center of the storm. In that center, he did not doubt, he would find the former flesh-home of the supreme priest.

He focused on that knot of power, hoping that the closer it came, the greater the chance his spell would take effect. Even as he floated in the realm of origins, near-paralyzing fear leaked like rising water into the young wizard's mind. He recalled the folk of the Mark behind him. His friends. Sequara. *I cannot fail.* Steadying his breaths, he kept rising above the terror. Straight ahead the nearest dwolas of the massive army drew within bowshot, yet, unblinking, Dayraven continued to chant the song of origin again and again:

Druanil ecthonias an dharian gadalathon,
Abu mihil inghanias ni rakhyon abhularon.
Vardas diagol im parthas akwinway,
Shardas inkhathol an ghalas khalithway.

Like the wind soughing through the dying leaves, an answer came as a familiar hiss in his mind. *I warned you.*

"Spare these folk. They don't understand."

They stand in the path.

"They defend their homes. Their loved ones."

It matters naught. I will release them all. They will know peace.

"No. You must not. Come to me. To me alone."

The center, the heart of the elf's power, was drawing nigh. Dayraven opened his mouth to chant the song of origin again, but that center of power shot toward him first, its energy thrusting out and seizing him with sudden strength, like a giant invisible fist. His mouth froze open, and he found he could not move the rest of body. Cursing himself, he realized he could not give his friends the signal to ride away. They might linger until it was too late or, worse yet, attempt to save him. His horse too seemed immobile beneath him.

I warned you. Now you must witness.

The foremost of the dwolas began to run, setting in motion the entire horde, which roiled as it rushed like an avalanche toward the Southweald. Dayraven struggled to free his mind, to move even a finger, but he was helpless. He had been a fool to attempt this, and an even greater fool to allow those he loved to come with him. Within, he screamed his thoughts. *Flee! Leave me!* His friends were behind him. They had no way to hear him. They would see him helpless, and they would come to rescue him.

The dwolas sprinted yet closer, their impassive expressions growing visible. Dark stains streaked their lower faces and chests, the blood of whatever they had feasted upon to carry their bodies this far. Their very stench was overpowering, a foul odor of decay. They uttered no war cries, yelled no screams of fury, but their running steps and their rapid breaths seemed loud enough to crumble mountains to dust.

Dayraven strained with all his being to free himself so that he could scream at his companions to ride away, but to no avail. He could not even turn to see what they were doing. The dwolas pounded closer. Some of their dead eyes looked toward him, and he hoped they would slay him rather than force him to see all his friends and the Markmen perish. They were almost upon him. Just a few more strides. They brandished their reddened blades. *Finish it, damn you.*

A moment before the foremost dwolas reached him, another sound battered Dayraven's ears. Before he understood what it was, something large streaked by from behind him on both sides. Clods of earth flew up in their wake — men riding steeds that galloped into the teeth of death. Earl Elfwy led his Ellonders in a wedge formation, charging straight into the horde.

They struck the first of the dwolas with a sickening crunch. Shattered bodies flew away from the screaming horses. The riders swung their blades downward, and spatters of blood trailed them. The wedge of horsemen carved a small gap in the horde around Dayraven, who labored and strained to gain mastery of his voice so that he could scream at them to ride away. Instead, with his eyes pried open, he could only watch as they drove deeper into the ranks of the dwolas. Against the endless bodies, the momentum of the charge slowed and then stopped.

"Regroup! Protect the Prophet!" yelled Elfwy as he wheeled his horse about and chopped his sword into a dwola's face.

It seemed Galdor's presence in Elfwy and his soldiers was protecting them from becoming dwolas at least. But they were encountering another pressing problem. Bodies swarmed the Ellonders, grasping and climbing onto the screaming horses while stabbing and chopping with their weapons. Several of the struggling soldiers fell from their steeds and disappeared beneath piles of thrashing dwolas. Some of the shrieking horses went down as well. Dayraven sorrowed and railed at each of the deaths, but still he could not move, and the dark presence of the elf hissed in his mind. *No more fear. No more desire. No more pain.* The surviving Ellonders extricated themselves and followed Elfwy as the earl ordered them into a half-circle around Dayraven.

At the same time, other riders arrived. Most were Torrlonder soldiers, but among them was Orvandil's tall form and Munzil's long red hair. And one rider tumbled off his horse as soon as he appeared, landing and rolling only a dozen feet from Dayraven. Gnorn sprang up and tore his axe from his belt, brandishing it as he roared in defiance at the horde.

No! More helpless than a newborn babe, Dayraven shouted and fought within his mind, but he might as well have tried to defy the wind or the Great Sea's waves. The elf's merciless grip on him did not falter, and it whispered of release.

Making no sound, he screamed, *Get away from me!*

Galdor cried out, winced, and gripped his rein tighter as another of the Ellonders whose mind he shared died beneath the dwolas' blades. As with the others, he experienced the man's pain and terror, saw the memories rush through his mind with his dying breath, and said farewell to loved ones forever. Each death was a sharp blow to his mind. An agony.

The old man's body trembled, and tears ran freely down his wrinkled cheeks. It was like saying goodbye to Arna again and again. The old wounds of the spirit split open and bled freely, and he relived the parting moment with the man he loved like no other along with the final wail within each soldier's mind. A long groan escaped his throat, and it became difficult to see through his tears.

But his blurred vision showed him enough. The horde of dwolas was swallowing them. Above the melee, Dayraven sat unmoving on his horse, and Galdor did not doubt the elf had enslaved the young wizard's body. A few of the Ellonders, including Earl Elfwy, remained on their mounts, hacking at the dozens of hands reaching for them. The outcome was inevitable.

Another burst of pain in his mind buckled him over in his saddle, and he screamed as he grasped onto the horse's neck to keep from falling. At the same time, he clung to the realm of origins with equal desperation. Yet another of the Ellonders had succumbed. For the sake of those remaining, he clenched his teeth and held on. He sat up and gave a fierce smile as he thought of Arna. *It's a good day to join you, my friend.*

The dwolas pressed closer, surrounding Dayraven and his remaining defenders and closing them off. Some of the elf's creatures began to sprint towards him and Sequara, their grim weapons flashing before them. Abon started to urge his horse forward and brandished his sword, their lone protector. The faithful shaper would die only a moment before they did. Galdor glanced at Sequara, whose face showed the tremendous strain she was under as she shielded the minds of the dying Torrlonders and Gnorn and Orvandil.

No. I'll not let them have her. The old wizard growled under his breath and wiped the tears from his eyes. Almost all the Ellonders were dead. *One last act of defiance.* "Hold, Abon! Sequara, you must flee now! Both of you get behind me and flee back to the forest!"

. . .

Blood spattered from the dwola's nose and mouth when Seeker clove through helm and skull, and another body dropped to the ground. Five more took its place, rushing in from all sides and jabbing their weapons into the rippling, straining muscles of Orvandil's screaming horse. Bone crunched and one went reeling when the horse's flailing back hoof smashed its face in, and the beast bit another's shoulder, after which its arm dangled at its side. Ropes of gore trailed his blade when the Thjoth severed another's arm at the shoulder as it reached up to hack his mount's neck. But more and more came, tearing and ripping and jabbing. The steed snorted and bucked, sending one who had climbed on its rump flying, and Orvandil just managed to stay in the saddle.

But when the beast reared, a large dwola's spear pierced its chest. The steed screamed and tottered. For one slowly unfolding moment, the Thjoth could not free his right foot from the stirrup, but he jerked it out and leapt just before the horse collapsed into a wall of dwolas. Orvandil grunted when the ground smacked his shoulder and hip, and he rolled before bounding to his feet with his sword ready. Even as the dwolas hacked it, his horse thrashed and kicked one, shattering its ribs and caving in its chest. The Thjoth waded into them with Seeker, swinging so hard that blood and bowels exploded when he sliced one in half. Another swung at him, but he dodged the blade and chopped off the dwola's arm, snapping the bone above the elbow with a loud crack. In two more breaths, Seeker lopped another's leg short and claimed another's head. Covered with the blood of his endless foes and knowing they would overwhelm him, Orvandil Dragonbane grinned at death.

All around him the dwolas swarmed over the grey-kirtled soldiers of the mercenary company, who were all unhorsed. Bleeding from several wounds, Bernred went down under a pile of bodies. With blood streaming over his face, Ludecan grimaced as he clutched his wounded side with one hand. His other hand seemed hardly able to raise his sword at the group of dwolas about to attack him. A thin Torrlonder whom Orvandil did not know moved with deadly grace as he carved through the dwolas to get at his captain, but he would likely be too late.

Orvandil turned to look for Gnorn, but instead he caught a glimpse of Elfwy, the last of their party to remain horsed besides Dayraven. The earl yelled as he hacked downward, and his steed kicked and bit at the dwolas. He was a skilled fighter, more adept at wielding his blade while in the saddle than Orvandil was. He commanded his steed with superb control as well, and though the dwolas attempted to swarm him, he gave them no chance as he directed his horse in darting circles and swung his bloodstained sword.

But then, moving with incredible swiftness, a massive dwola garbed in black rose up next to the earl and scythed his huge blade down. Blood spattered from the horse's neck, and the beast had no time to scream as its severed head dropped to the soaked earth. Elfwy managed to fling himself free of the horse's falling body, and he leapt to his feet in a fighting stance just before the giant dwola pierced him through the middle with his blade.

Elfwy wheezed and dropped his weapon. With gore dripping from it, the tip of the dwola's sword protruded from the young earl's back, and his limbs slumped like a discarded puppet's as the huge dwola lifted him from the ground. It yanked the blade free, and before Elfwy's lifeless body could fall, it swept its blade through the earl's neck, sending the head spinning.

The earl's death happened in a few swift moments, and when it was over, Orvandil recognized the dwola, which gazed at him with impassive eyes. The body of Surt, former war-leader of the Ilarchae, pounded closer to Orvandil, shoving away several of its fellow dwolas to get at the Thjoth.

Orvandil assumed a fighting stance with Seeker held before him. Surt was bigger than he was, and he was faster than he had any right to be. Becoming a dwola had not slowed him either, and if he had ever possessed any fear in life, the massive body rumbling closer felt none now. The Thjoth clenched his teeth in a fierce smile just before locking blades with the greatest warrior he had ever seen.

Steel keened when Seeker clashed against the huge blade, and Orvandil stumbled back a pace. The dwola charged forward, its sword blurring in a series of blows the Thjoth just managed to parry. Never had any warrior so outmatched him in strength. Another dwola came from his right to attack him. Orvandil dodged the newcomer's blade and pivoted behind him, putting the smaller dwola between him and Surt.

The smaller dwola turned to attack, but its arms flailed when the former war-leader's huge blade burst through its chest from behind, sending out a spray of blood. The reddened tip almost grazed Orvandil, who lunged back as Surt ripped his sword free of the falling corpse and advanced again. Looking in vain for a weakness, Orvandil parried another series of rapid blows, but the last grazed his left shoulder, and then Surt's massive fist cracked into the Thjoth's face.

Orvandil spun back as white flashed in his eyes, and the breeze of Surt's sword caressed his neck as the tip just missed him. He wheeled Seeker in front of him, and steel rang out again as it met Surt's oncoming blade. The Thjoth's bleeding nose throbbed, and his breaths came rapid and hard. But when Surt lunged at him, he sprang forward and collided with the huge dwola. Their swords clanged and then screeched together, and Orvandil growled as he tried to keep his footing. The war-leader shifted his weight and moved to stomp on the Thjoth's leg. Orvandil saw it coming and dodged the boot, only for white to flash before his vision again when Surt's elbow caught him in the face. He ducked as he heard more than saw the huge blade whirl over him, and he thrust Seeker forward.

The massive dwola dodged his blade and sliced Orvandil's ribs as he leapt away. Clenching his teeth in a smile, the Thjoth glanced down. The sword had parted his kirtle and byrny and left a stinging cut as well as an aching bruise, but he had no time to wonder how much damage there was. With his sword aloft for a massive blow, Surt was upon him. But so was the sweet curse and blessing of his battle rage.

Orvandil spun away from Surt's blow and swung Seeker, which clove through the byrny deep into the flesh of the huge dwola's back, releasing a trail of blood in its wake. Surt jerked away and pivoted. The giant's shoulders shuddered as he faced Orvandil, and the two sprinted at each other again. Orvandil slipped under Surt's swing and took his foe low, slicing a bloody line in the meat of the war-leader's thigh as they passed one another.

The former war leader of the Ilarchae jerked to an awkward stop, favoring the wounded leg, and swung around. His dead eyes locked onto the Thjoth, and he raised his huge blade.

"Come on!" yelled Orvandil at Surt's animated corpse, and he raised Seeker in one hand as he beat his chest with the other. Almost too late did he sense the presence behind him, but he ducked just in time for another dwola's blade to pass over his head. Orvandil jerked around and stabbed the new attacker through the stomach. The dwola buckled over, but the Thjoth knew he would be too late to stop Surt, a massive blur and flash of steel coming from behind and above.

MUNZIL SPARED ONLY A GLANCE AT THE THJOTH FIGHTING AGAINST Surt's body. On any other day, he would have stopped everything to witness that struggle. But with so many of his former brothers and sisters attacking him, it was hard even to stay alive, and he had caught sight of the one dwola he sought above all others. He had taken several small but stinging wounds in the course of freeing more than a dozen of them, but *her* body was the one he most wanted to put to rest. Thank the gods he had been right: She was at the forefront of the dwola horde.

The thing wearing Skuld's flesh yanked its blade from a dead Torrlonder. Munzil swiped a dwola across the face with his sword, sending it spinning to the earth, and yelled toward the thing that had taken the body of his former lover, "Here! Fight me!" He sprinted toward her moving corpse, which looked toward him with its dead eyes and launched at him. They met in a flurry of steel, and Munzil backed up with each blow. Their swords clanged again and again, and, grunting with every clash, Munzil knew right away he would never get inside its guard. Just as Skuld had been, this dwola was too fast, and its greater strength would wear him down. He also knew he would need to act before the thing killed him. *It's time.*

He ducked low under the sweep of the dwola's blade and, with his free hand, grasped the hilt of the dagger placed in his boot. When he rose from his crouch, he lifted his sword just a little too high in a defensive stance. Lunging forward, the dwola in Skuld's flesh did not refuse the invitation.

Red-hot pain such as Munzil had never known seared through his guts when Skuld's blade pierced his stomach to emerge out his back, and he wheezed as it drove the air from his body. The stench of the dwolas gave way to the overwhelming iron taste of blood in his mouth, and his pain-racked body needed so much to fall and writhe on the ground, but he focused on the one thing he must do and forced his limbs to comply with his will.

Munzil dropped his sword and grasped the front of the dwola's blood-stained kirtle to pull himself closer, sliding the sharp steel further through his body. With his other hand, he plunged his dagger into the dwola's neck. Blood pumped out of the wound onto his hand, warm and satisfying. As Munzil gritted his teeth, he twisted the blade and gazed into the dwola's eyes, where there was no recognition of either him or its end. The dwola choked and hacked out blood, and drops of it pattered Munzil's face. They wobbled and fell next to one another, and the sword lodged in his stomach sent a jolt of agony through him when he landed. He could draw no breath, but, as his vision blurred and faded, he managed to smile at Skuld's lifeless form. She at least was free, and he would no longer be the last survivor.

Unable to look away or flicker the smallest muscle of his eyelids, Dayraven abided the unfolding slaughter of his friends. He could not even scream out his anguish, which swelled in him and pushed him to the brink of madness. The elf's chill voice still whispered its wordless thoughts in his mind. *They will suffer no more.* Casting its shadow over everything, it was so vast and strong that its will seemed undeniable, and he had been a foolish, naïve child ever to oppose it.

He witnessed the deaths of Earl Elfwy and all his soldiers. Only a few of the Torrlonders still stood. Gnorn had disappeared beneath a pile of dwolas. Orvandil struggled with a massive dwola dressed in black. Munzil was nowhere to be seen. Sequara, Galdor, and Abon had been behind him. He entertained the desperate hope that those three at least had ridden away upon seeing his failure and the hopelessness of their situation. Yet he knew it was not so. Even amidst the vast power of the elf, he sensed the presence of the gift behind him.

There was nothing he wanted more than to turn around and scream at them to flee. It was impossible that Sequara could perish. Had he not seen their daughter in the true-dream? He felt uncertain now, and he did not trust his memory. Perhaps it was some other girl child. Perhaps it had not been a true-dream at all. He grappled against the elf, knowing all the while that struggle was futile, just as when he first encountered it in the Southweald.

A memory of that day flitted through his mind. When he met the elf and it stripped him of everything, there had been a brief moment of letting go, during which he surfaced and the world presented itself to him with uncanny clarity. If he could have moved, he would have gasped at the sudden spark of hope in his mind. There was no time to think about it. Forcing himself to forget all his anger and fear, Dayraven surrendered.

As soon as he ceased fighting against the elf, more memories sprang to life, unfolding before him as if he lived them once again. He followed the ghost raven on a warm summer day into the Southweald as it hopped from tree to tree, leading him to his fate. On the island of Asdralad, he watched Urd sacrifice herself amidst ruin and destruction, sending forth her energy in an outward-seeking rush from her body by means of some spell or force of will. And, as the straining muscles of his sweaty, blood-slickened fingers and hands clutched onto rock on an icy cliff somewhere on the Wyrmberg, the ghost raven came to him once again, peering into his eyes before showing him the way up to the eldest of dragons.

Born from these memories, an inspiration came to him. With a sense of awe, Dayraven gathered himself. He thought once more of Sequara and the folk of the Mark, and he knew what he must do. But where was Joruman's body? The young wizard could not move his eyes, but he sensed the center of the elf's power somewhere up ahead, and he concentrated there.

. . .

Letting loose a feral roar, Gnorn rammed against the wall of dwolas with his axe held before him. They had tried to bury him, to stab him and claw at him as their sweaty, putrid-smelling bodies smothered him. He had gone down on one knee, choking on the stench as darkness swallowed him and more piled on. He had suffered numerous bruises and cuts and scratches, but his byrny and helm had warded him from the worst, and the sheer number of dwolas on top of him prevented the others from wounding him or getting at him.

The real danger had been suffocating. But somehow, a chink of light had appeared through the roiling press, and he shoved with all his might into it. To the Dweorg's surprise, the bodies gave way, tumbling over each other and scrambling to get at him, and he kept pushing until they fell off him, tearing at him to the last. One strong grip held the sleeve of his kirtle, but he pivoted and chopped off the arm, exposing a meaty stump that spurted blood. As with all the others Gnorn had slain and hewn, the wounded creature's lifeless eyes did not change, and it did not scream. The Dweorg stumbled three strides away from the mob of tangled dwolas and clenched his teeth at what he saw.

Orvandil had just stabbed a dwola through the stomach with Seeker, but another with a frame more massive than the Thjoth's raced at him from behind with sword aloft. Gnorn did not take time to think. He lunged one more step and launched his axe, leaving himself weaponless.

The axe sailed true. Just before the huge, black-garbed dwola brought its blade down on Orvandil, Gnorn's weapon crunched into its face, yanking its head back with a violent jerk and a spray of blood. The dwola dropped its weapon and crashed onto its back, where its limbs flopped once before going still.

Gnorn just had time to grin at Orvandil before several sharp pains pierced his torso from behind and the dwolas leapt all over him. Even as he toppled forward, a brief, bright flash in his skull preceded darkness.

. . .

Standing among the warriors of Kinsford where they were arrayed among the ranks of the Mark, Guthmund gripped his spear tighter as he watched the Ilarchae swallow Dayraven's small party. In spite of the chill in the air and the darkness blotting out the sun, sweat was running down his back. It was his first battle — his first *look* at a battle. The prospect of fighting that massive horde made it hard to breathe, but his fear was still not as strong as the sense of disgrace closing in on him.

He glanced next to him at his father again, but, as before, Guthere did not return the look. Instead, his father kept his stony gaze straight ahead and frowned at the ones who were dying for their kingdom — outlanders and the exile who had once been Guthmund's friend and his sister's betrothed.

The young man shook his head. He looked around at the other warriors of Kinsford, and in their faces burned the same shame he felt. Some looked at each other for a brief moment as if they would speak or at least grumble, but they did not gaze for long lest they see their dishonor reflected in the eyes of their fellows. Guthmund ground his teeth, swallowed, and took a deep breath. "I'm sorry, Father." And then he stepped forward a few paces, abandoning his place in the shieldwall, and pivoted around to face his folk.

Heads turned, and the thegns of Kinsford stared.

Guthere scowled at him. "What are you doing, boy?"

He ignored his father and yelled at the top of his voice to the warriors of Kinsford and the Mark. "Are we cowards that we would watch them die for us? Can we not fight when they fight for us? I will no longer watch." He brandished his spear. "For Dayraven!"

"Guthmund! No!"

But his father was too late. Guthmund had already turned and was sprinting towards the battle. From behind him, another yell reached his ears.

"Kinsford for Dayraven!" It was Earl Stigand's voice, and a giant roar of hundreds followed it.

In spite of his terror of the shadow he was dashing towards, Guthmund smiled. He did not need to turn around to know the warriors of the Mark were running behind him.

. . .

KEEPING A TENUOUS GRIP ON THE REALM OF ORIGINS WHILE sharing in the sharp anguish of so many deaths, Sequara cried out when Gnorn fell. It was almost impossible to think through the maelstrom of loss, despair, and horror. Dayraven was in the midst of the horde of dwolas, helpless in the elf's grip. Though the urge to turn her horse around and gallop away was nearly overwhelming, she and Abon had ignored Galdor's command to flee. She would not leave Dayraven or the others. But the old wizard had prodded his horse forward all the same, and he was intoning a song of origin.

"He's left my mind. What's he doing?" Abon gawked at Sequara, his bulging eyes betraying the same paralyzing powerlessness she felt.

But she could only shake her head. She did not know the answer since she could not hear what song of origin Galdor was chanting. She devoted what strength and courage were left to her to remaining in the realm of origins and maintaining her shaky hold on the minds of the surviving members of their company. The elf was a vast presence biding its time to enter any that might live. Sequara had to keep it out. Forming any other coherent thought was well-nigh impossible.

A moment later, there was no need to guess Galdor's intention. Bright and jagged tendrils of almakhti sprang to life around the old wizard's hands, which he raised aloft as he sat atop his screaming and rearing horse. Sequara's panicked steed too neighed and bucked, and the sorceress clutched onto the rein as she struggled to master the beast. The energy around Galdor crackled and writhed, outlining his form in bluish brightness. When the old man thrust his arms forward, a monstrous explosion tore asunder the air, and a tremendous flash of energy stole away all color, unveiling a stark world in shades of grey. All was light and shadow, and the deadly stream of wizard's fire erupted toward the oncoming horde of dwolas.

Crackling and buzzing, the massive current of almakhti flowed from Galdor's outstretched hands, which the wizard swept in a wide motion. Seared bodies flew in the air, and Sequara marveled at both the size and duration of the lethal energy the old wizard was unleashing. Holding her hands up to shade her eyes, she tried to glimpse further away to see Dayraven, but the almakhti was blinding.

And then the brightness winked out, returning the landscape to dimness and leaving a large red streak hovering in Sequara's vision. His arms still outstretched, Galdor leaned to one side and toppled from his horse, landing with a thud on the ground. His frightened steed emitted a high-pitched whinny and galloped away.

"My lord!" Abon leapt off his mount and rushed toward the old wizard's motionless body.

Keeping hold of her neighing horse and blinking her eyes to regain her vision and seek Dayraven, Sequara squinted as she tried to gaze through the smoke and beyond the hundreds of smoldering corpses strewn all over. But then a huge roar of thousands of voices erupted from behind her, and she jerked her head around. Long ranks of warriors were sprinting towards her, brandishing swords and spears. The Markmen were coming, rushing to their deaths.

THE FLASHING AND CRACKLING OF GALDOR'S WIZARD'S FIRE CEASED behind Dayraven, and, as smoke and the sickening stench of burnt hair and flesh filled the air, he knew the old wizard had spent himself. Soon after came the war cries of thousands and the rumble of their rushing boots, telling him the Markmen were joining the battle. He had to act now.

He knew what he must do. At last Dayraven understood. It was the final deed Urd had wrought back on Asdralad when she saved him and his companions from Bledla, his high priests, and the Torrlonder army. As she trained him in using the gift, Queen Faldira had warned him about drifting too far into the realm of origins and the need to maintain a line of connection with his body lest he never return. Diving into the realm of origins, Urd had severed the tether and allowed her spirit to spread beyond her mortal form, surrendering the energy that animated her back into the world. Given the vastness of the elf's power, Dayraven did not know if the energy contained within him would suffice for the present need, but there was no other choice. He had to focus it all on the center of the elf's presence, which loomed somewhere ahead.

And then, amidst the sea of dwolas, a patch of white appeared in his line of vision. Joruman's robe. That was all he needed. An image of Sequara and the little girl he had seen in his true-dream, his daughter, flashed in his mind. One last tug at his heart, a silent keen that he would never see her grow, knowing this was the only way he could protect her and her mother. He bid them farewell.

He could not move his body, but Dayraven was able to let go of his mind and drift further into the realm of origins. He left behind his trapped flesh. As if from above, he gazed down at the scene of the battle with the scores of thousands of dwolas covering the earth. But they receded like insects and disappeared altogether as he floated outward. The trees of the Southweald blended into a vast blur of red, orange, yellow, and green. The Folkmere appeared as a gleaming streak on the land. Beyond the Mark he soared, taking in the contours of Eormenlond with its rugged, snow-capped mountain ranges, its smoother plains, the veins of its rivers, and the pools of its lakes.

Still further into the realm of origins he willed his awareness to journey. Outward he sought, and as darkness surrounded him, he gazed down upon the orb of the world, half in shade and half bright with blue and brown and green and airy swirls of white. Outward he sought, joining the cold stillness and immensity of the dark, which the clear points of the shimmering stars dotted all around him. And then beyond them he soared to where massive glowing discs swirled with an incomprehensible number of lights and giant gaseous clouds sparked with explosions that were vaster than worlds.

So far did he travel that, back in the world of forms, his body shuddered when the distance grew too great. His consciousness stretched a little further, and then, like a drop of dew falling from the tip of a blade of grass, his energy's connection to his body slipped away.

Dayraven's last act was to focus his departing energy and fling it toward the elf's power, which dwelled in the white-robed form. Even as the young wizard's lifeless husk of a body slumped in the saddle, the force that had animated his flesh shot toward the elf's center in the world of forms. And it seemed to his fading consciousness that his energy took the shape of the ghost raven, flapping its wings and glorying in the flight as it streaked straight toward the focal point of the elf. He was the raven.

In the realm of origins, the eternal present, the raven made three flights at once. It journeyed to the Southweald on a fine summer day to encounter a young man waiting for a party of his fellow villagers, who were slaying pucas within the forest. Without realizing it, the young man awaited his fate, which the raven well knew since it dwelled where all fates were and are and will be. Left alone, the young man would have remained in his home and lived a life more or less like the one he expected, filled with many moments of fleeting contentedness. Cocking its head, the raven gazed at him from its perch on an oak branch and, knowing the loss it would mean, called out to him. He was the raven.

Simultaneously, it sported in the currents over the Wyrmberg, seeking the same young man as he clutched to the face of an icy cliff with his weary hands, upon which the veins stood out like tree roots, his legs dangling in the air beneath him. The struggling young man did not yet know it, but this was another mark on his life journey, a moment of great decision. The raven saw all decisions and where they led. It considered the young man and, in spite of knowing the pain he would endure after this moment and how much easier it would have been for him to let go and fall, it fluttered down to him to show him the way. He was the raven.

And it sped like an arrow toward the white-robed flesh-home wherein dwelled one of the great powers, more ancient than time, a reflection in which all things saw the one source within and without them in accordance with their readiness. Vast, beautiful, terrible, wonderful, monstrous, ethereal, demonic, sublime: It lay beyond light and dark, beyond life and death. The elf was the path to return to Edan. He was the raven, and he took that path.

Flitting by hundreds of dwolas, the ghost raven flew into the chest of the white-robed body, which absorbed it in an instant. Its face impassive, the elf glanced down at its chest, which glowed with brightness where the raven had entered. The light expanded to illuminate the entire body, whence it exploded outward to wash over hills and forest and all the astonished creatures in its path.

Within that explosion of light was both a moment and an eternity in which the raven spoke to the power, the thing the mortals conceived of as the elf. It spoke not in words but in images and thoughts, and the elf listened.

Return to the forest. To the trees and their swaying, intertwining branches. To the glimmer and play of light and breeze on the trembling leaves. To bark rough with grooves and smooth like skin. To roots tangling and grasping deep in dirt. To the soil with its centuries of musty decay. To the bubbling of streams that trickle and flow from the secret depths of the earth. Be the presence in these things, the mystery that lingers on through uncountable births and deaths, through untold summers and winters. Be at peace. Return to your slumber. Return to the forest. To Edan.

Who are you? asked the elf.

I am the raven, Edan's messenger.

A slight shift occurred in the power, subtler than a nod and quieter than a breath, but clear all the same. *As you wish. We return. You have stood in their place. Come with me.*

And the light splintered and surged with a vast rush toward the forest, flattening the mortals in its path and leaving a whisper of its presence as it streamed and ghosted through them. Scores of thousands of empty bodies fell lifeless, and thousands of the living cried out as the light blinded them and they fell on their backs.

The raven scattered into the light, becoming one with it as it bathed the land and the trees and spread its presence throughout the forest. The raven was the light, no longer a creature of warring parts, but one, and it left the barest echo of itself in all the mortals through which it passed. And though it was no more, it lingered in them, and in all things it touched.

Blue had returned to the sky, and the bright sun shone overhead. The chill was gone from the air. Orvandil blinked and groaned as he forced his stiff body up. The wounds and cuts that the dwola in Surt's body had inflicted on him ached and stung, especially the one across his ribs, slowing his movements. It was difficult to grasp his thoughts, and he shook his head to clear the bleariness surrounding it.

All around him were bodies. The Ilarchae. The entire horde was lying on the field of battle, limbs askew, mouths agape, eyes empty, still and lifeless. A few grey-kirtled Torrlonder corpses joined them along with the Ellonder soldiers. Orvandil gazed around him with his mouth hanging open. "He did it." Though he somehow knew his friend was gone, Dayraven's presence tugged at the corners of his mind, a tiny pulse that whispered of peace and bathed the rest of the Thjoth, giving him the courage to live. A moment ago the darkness had seemed so right. But Dayraven had wanted him to live, and he grasped onto that thought.

He sheathed Seeker and turned to look for Gnorn, and then clarity returned to his head along with a sense of dire urgency. The Dweorg had saved his life at the cost of exposing his back to the dwolas.

The Thjoth rushed to where he thought he had last seen Gnorn. The Dweorg's stubby boot poked out beneath a pile of bodies. Orvandil grunted as he tossed the corpses away until there was only Gnorn lying on his stomach. Several deep wounds where blades had penetrated his byrny bled out of his back. His helm was off, and his hair was wet and matted with blood.

Orvandil knelt next to his friend and gently rolled him onto his back to check for signs of life. When he saw the Dweorg's ashen, bloodied face with closed eyes, the Thjoth spoke to him. "He did it, my friend. It's finished."

To his surprise, Gnorn groaned, and his eyes cracked open. His grin exposed the blood on his teeth. "Good. Go back." His voice was a bare croak.

"Keep quiet. I'll patch you up." Orvandil looked about for something he could use to bind the Dweorg's wounds.

Gnorn closed his eyes, and the Thjoth feared his friend was gone. But the Dweorg slowly opened them again. They seemed to have trouble focusing, and he stared somewhere past Orvandil. "Go back to her."

"Be still."

The Dweorg lifted a trembling hand. "They'll make you . . . king. Go back."

Orvandil took the hand and gripped it in his own before sighing. "If they do such a foolish thing, I give you my vow: I will seek out the Dweorgs of the Fyrnhowes in Etinstone and invite them to return to their ancient home. And you will come with me."

Gnorn made the barest movement as he shook his head, but he smiled all the same. He shut his eyes and said no more.

SEQUARA'S HIP ACHED WHERE SHE HAD LANDED HARD ON THE ground, and her wrist was sore as well. She shook her head, trying to recall what had happened. The explosion of light had knocked her off the horse, which must have galloped away. It had also severed her connection with the two or three remaining minds she had been protecting. She was so tired, but something was tugging at her thoughts, something more important than all the pain and weariness in the world.

Her breath caught, and her eyes widened as she gazed up at the blue sky. *He* was within her. Not gone. Not that. Never that. He would always be with her. As much as she wanted to wail and cry out the grief welling up inside, she could not, for he was within her, soothing her with his beautiful presence. She hugged herself as if she were embracing him, as if she could hold him, the sensation of him, there forever. He had done it so she could live. She and their daughter, and all the others.

Sequara nodded. She raised her tired and stiff body from the ground, gritting her teeth through dizziness, and the first thing she saw was Abon, who was kneeling by Galdor's still body.

The shaper turned toward her. Tears streaked down his face, and he gave Sequara a weak smile. "He's gone. Finally at rest."

Abon had placed Galdor's hands at his sides and arranged his body as if he were slumbering on his back. His eyes were closed. There was no presence of the gift in the old wizard's body. No life. The loss hit Sequara like a blow that stole the air from her lungs. She shook her head. "I'm so sorry," she choked out.

Abon smiled again, a smile so forlorn Sequara nearly sobbed. He glanced down at Galdor's peaceful face. "I wish he could have known. Might be he felt it before he left us. Dayraven did it. You felt him, didn't you? In the light, when he . . ."

"Yes." She could hardly breathe, let alone speak.

Seeming to realize he should say no more, the shaper blinked at her. He gave her a quiet nod. "Might be his body's waiting over yonder. I'll stay with the old fellow a moment."

Numb with shock and exhaustion, Sequara nodded and began limping toward the place where Dayraven had sat atop his horse. The steed was gone. She thought she had seen him fall from it just before the explosion of light. As she walked among the corpses littering the ground, she spotted some of the bodies of the Torrlonders and Ellonders who had aided them. She grieved for them all, and she thought with a pang of Earl Elfwy, who also had given his young and noble life for others.

A grey-kirtled Torrlonder staggered to his feet. He was a thin man, one she had noticed fighting with grace and fierce tenacity. He turned toward her as she hobbled up to him. Sequara winced at a twinge of pain in her leg and then spoke to him. "Are you hurt?"

He squinted at her as they stood among the thousands upon thousands of dead, which lay upon the land into the distance beyond Sequara's vision. Speckles of blood covered him. "I reckon I'm in better shape than you are just now. Am I the only one left?"

"Of your company, yes." She shivered. She had lived every one of their deaths, and the grief for them was raw and fresh.

"Captain Ludecan's gone too?"

"Yes."

He spat and shook his head. "Damn."

"You'll need to report what you witnessed here to Duke Ethelred. What is your name?"

He made a slight bow. "Hewald, my lady. I'll do as you say."

"Thank you, Hewald. Now I must find someone."

He nodded and held back. But there was still a question in his eyes. "My lady?"

"Yes?"

"I felt . . . When the light washed over us . . . *He* was in it."

She nodded and held back her tears. "His presence passed through us. He is in the world now."

Hewald frowned and nodded as if he had expected such an answer. "Was he truly the Prophet of Edan?"

Sequara mustered a quick smile. "I suppose he was." She turned and left the Torrlonder to seek what remained of Dayraven.

A few more hobbling strides, and she stopped. There it lay up ahead. There was something familiar about the form sprawled on the ground, and that familiarity was at once jarring, frightening, and painful even though she had loved that body. *His* body. Even from that distance, she sensed something absent from it. It was the absence that felt so wrong, and a desperate, futile longing for the restoration of what had animated that flesh took hold of her. *He is within me,* she reminded herself.

His brown robe and white kirtle were visible above the grass. He was lying on his back. She could not see his face yet, but she imagined it pale and strange with the lack of life and with his eyes shut. She moved closer to him, almost counting her sore hip a blessing since it excused her slow steps.

Before she reached Dayraven's empty form, however, she glanced nearby toward one of the living. Since she had protected Orvandil's mind until the eruption of light, she had known he survived. He was hunched over a body, and Sequara also knew whose it was. She both dreaded and ached to gaze upon Dayraven, and though it seemed to her the most important thing she could do, there was still a chance Gnorn might be alive. If he was, he would need her help, whereas Dayraven was beyond her.

She tore herself away and promised she would grieve in due time. As she limped closer to him, the Thjoth turned his head. "Lady Sequara. Are you too hurt to help him?" Orvandil could not mask the strain and urgency in his voice.

"He lives?"

"He's as tough as a rock. And as stubborn. He yet breathes, but not much longer, I deem."

"Let me see what I can do." She knelt next to Orvandil and looked down at Gnorn. “The worst wounds are in his back. I felt the blades enter him.” They had been like heat slicing through her flesh. “Turn him over.”

“Aye.” Orvandil nodded at her before he carefully rolled the Dweorg’s body over.

Sequara placed her hands over two of the largest stabs. She was beyond exhausted, but, amidst all the loss and devastation, she was also glad to be healing once again. Especially a dear friend like Gnorn. It kept her grief from overwhelming her, at least for a moment. She whispered the song of origin again and again, and as she did so, she imparted her energy to the Dweorg’s body so that it could heal.

A sudden warm breeze caressed her face and toyed with her hair, dispelling the last remnants of the chill in the air and seeming to promise life’s eventual return. It almost pushed her over, so weary was she. But she continued her spell and poured all her concentration into the healing. It was far from easy, yet at length Gnorn’s wounds ceased to bleed, and the gashes in his organs and flesh closed. She broke off the song of origin and returned from the realm of origins. Though the Dweorg did not stir, she knew he was alive.

Her breaths came hard, and her shoulders slumped. Her eyelids were so heavy that she could hardly force them open. “I must stop for now. Too weak. He’s lost much blood, but he will live, I think. I must gather strength. Heal him again later.”

Orvandil nodded, and then he reached for her as she tottered over. The Thjoth caught her with his large hands and gently eased her down. Sequara’s worn out mind and body seemed to float as everything around her spun. The deep blue sky arching above her dimmed. It all fell away, even the looming sense of the duties awaiting her in Asdralad. She closed her eyes and began to drift, welcoming the sleep that flowed over her as it offered the solace of temporary forgetfulness. Just before she succumbed, thoughts of Dayraven and of their child growing within her flitted through her, and she knew she had much to live for.

30
HOME

Sequara, Orvandil, Abon, and Gnorn stayed with the folk of the Mark for three days to rest from the wounds of the body, helped along by the priest of the Way, Bertric, who used the gift to heal the sorceress and speed the Dweorg and the Thjoth's recovery as well. The wounds of the mind would take much longer to mend, and they were beyond even the gift's influence. The lone surviving Torrlonder, Hewald, set out for Torrhelm on his own on a horse King Ithamar provided to report to Duke Ethelred.

During those days of mourning, thousands of the Markmen set about burying the dead Ilarchae within several huge mounds just outside the Southweald. Among the corpses was Munzil's, which lay in one of the mounds next to the body of Skuld. It was a massive undertaking, and everyone reckoned those earthworks would serve as a reminder of what happened there for generations.

According to the customs of the Torrlonders and the Ellonders, who for the most part followed the Way, the folk of the Mark buried Captain Ludecan and the men of the Mercenary Company of Etinstone as well as Earl Elfwy and his soldiers in private graves. The surviving four companions spent time at each of the graves to say their farewells. If any of the friends thought it strange that Sequara should linger for a moment at Elfwy's grave, they said naught of it.

Not far from the Ellonders in his own mound reposed the body of Galdor, wizard of Ellond. When his final resting place was readied, Sequara and the others said their goodbyes to the old man, dearest and truest of friends. In a row, they stood before the mound for a long while in silence.

Gnorn cleared his throat. "The world's lost some of its color without the old wizard."

"Aye." Orvandil nodded.

Sequara released a long sigh, refusing to dwell on the years of grief ahead. "He labored long to make the lives around him better and brighter. He'll live in our memories. We must honor him by making sure the world understands who he was."

Abon stared at the mound, seeming lost in his thoughts. "That we will. He would have wanted no monument, but I'll craft one nevertheless."

Gnorn nodded. "The Song of Galdor. I hope to hear it someday."

The shaper turned to him and smiled. "You will."

They left Galdor's mound to bid goodbye to King Ithamar, who had stayed to watch over the digging. The king had supplied the four of them with horses and provisions for their journeys. When they found him, Ithamar broke away from a group of his warriors as soon as he noticed them. Followed by Bertric, head priest of the Way for Wolvendon, he strode over to Sequara and nodded. "You're leaving, then?"

"Yes. We came to give our farewells, and to thank you once again for the horses."

"It's the least I could offer after your sacrifices." Ithamar glanced down at the ground once before looking again at the sorceress. "In truth, it is we who owe you thanks. And our apologies." He glanced at Bertric, who lingered a couple steps behind the king.

The priest stepped forward and bowed to Sequara. "I am . . . very sorry, my lady. Both for your loss and for my grievous error."

Remembering how the priest had come to help heal her and her friends, Sequara suppressed her anger and nodded at him. "Thank you."

He swallowed and seemed to gather courage before speaking again. "He truly was the Prophet of Edan, wasn't he?"

In the priest's eyes Sequara saw a certain longing. More than the desire to allay guilt, it was a need to put a name to the ineffable even while knowing it was too vast for the mind to capture. She decided to give him what he desired. "Yes."

The priest's mouth hung open with awe, and he nodded in stunned acceptance.

King Ithamar cleared his throat. "Are you sure you won't stay longer?"

"We have pressing errands, I fear." Sequara stood straighter and gazed into the king's eyes. "But if you would thank us, then let it be known throughout your kingdom and beyond what happened here. Tell your people of the Prophet's deed. He might have been an exile, but he still loved this kingdom and its people. Tell them what Dayraven of the Mark did here."

Ithamar nodded. "I will let it be known. As long as I and my descendants rule this kingdom, the folk of the Mark will remember the deeds of the Prophet of Edan and his friends."

Sequara made a slight bow. "It is well." She turned and left the king, followed by her friends.

After taking leave of the king, there was one last stop. Gnorn, Orvandil, and Abon waited apart, allowing Sequara to approach Dayraven's barrow alone. The Markmen had burned his body on a large pyre, and Sequara had watched the flames devour the empty husk that had once housed her beloved. Gazing in silence, she had not wept then, for she did not feel his presence in that lifeless body. When the flames died down and only ashes remained, they piled a massive mound over them. Thousands of the Markmen had tossed their swords and jewels and ornaments into the mound. Though part of her found the gesture futile, she had not protested the honor they did Dayraven. She watched it all until they finished, when darkness had descended.

Now she stood before the mound in daylight, wondering what to say.

Her mind still preserved his memories, the fleeting evocations that became part of her when she healed him a lifetime ago and those he shared with her afterwards. Such images and their child were all that was left her. She smiled, though the smile did not reach her eyes, and she stared at the mound. "How can I say goodbye to you? You're not here within this soil."

She looked up at the blue sky and then gazed toward Orvandil, Gnorn, and Abon, and behind them at the laboring Markmen and the vast forest beyond them. She faced the mound once again and placed her hand on her belly. She tried to smile again, but instead a sob broke from deep inside her, and she collapsed onto her knees and shook as the tears flowed from her eyes. Grief racked her body with sobs, and the only thing to interrupt her tears were sharp intakes of breath. Whether from a desire to afford her a moment of privacy or because their hearts could not bear to look, the Markmen turned away from that outpouring, though not without their own tears. Long she wept, but not alone. Gnorn, Abon, and Orvandil approached her, and each put his hand on her shoulder as she mourned. They wept with her until they all fell silent. No one spoke.

At length, Sequara rose. She did not look back at the mound as they departed. Feeling the loss of their missing companions as a weight pressing upon their shoulders and hearts, the friends set out together in heavy silence, riding for Torrhelm the way they had come.

DURING THEIR JOURNEY THEY FOUND THEIR VOICES. AS THEY RODE and made camp, they recounted stories to each other, at times telling of their trials and ordeals and other times speaking of older, less painful tales wherein they lost themselves with no thought for the present. But, at last, there came a time when their paths sundered. They arrived there with great reluctance to relinquish the pleasure and comfort of each other's company, feeling that, after all they had been through together, no one else in Eormenlond or in the wide world could understand them or their losses the way these few could. Perhaps too they did not wish to face their grief alone.

They alighted from their steeds and spoke their farewells at the crossroads where Dayraven and Imharr first met Gnorn and Hlokk, a fact that the Dweorg remarked upon with a heavy sigh. Abon was to head east to Ellordor, his kingdom's chief city, where he would report all he had witnessed to King Fullan, most especially the deaths of Earl Elfwy and Galdor. The loss of those two would be a terrible blow to the kingdom of Ellond, and he vowed to make sure all knew of their sacrifices.

After the others, Gnorn embraced the shaper. "You're sure you wish to ride alone? The last I was here, bandits were waylaying travelers on the road east."

The shaper gave him a crooked smile and adjusted the green sack slung over his shoulder. "In Torrlond folk have forgotten many of the old ways, but most still deem it ill luck to harm a shaper. Even bandits. I'll be safe enough, provided I give them a song or two. I've played for them along this road before."

Sequara nodded. "Farewell, then, friend. May our paths cross again soon."

"You must visit me in Ellordor. King Fullan will welcome you, and the old schools in the city hold much lore."

Sequara put a hand on the shaper's shoulder. "I accept your offer. I've been in your beautiful city, but not for long enough. Asdralad may have need of its lore in the days to come."

"I await your coming, then." The shaper mounted his horse and rode off, waving once before leaving the others to say their goodbyes.

Orvandil and Gnorn were riding north. They planned to depart from the road and head for Grimrik, stopping by the Dweorg barrows of Gnorn's ancestors on their way. Unable to meet Sequara's gaze, the two of them looked down, and the Thjoth fumbled with his sword's hilt.

Sequara smiled at Orvandil. "When will your folk choose a new king?"

Orvandil looked up with a pained expression, the struggle for words evident on his face. "The funeral feast for Vols will last at least a fortnight. Then they'll gather in the Thingvang." He glanced down at the ground again. Sequara knew there was much on her friend's mind, but she had no wish to pry further.

She took in Orvandil and Gnorn with her gaze. "I hope you both find what you seek in Grimrik."

Gnorn nodded. "A sight of those old hills again will be a good start for me. Wherever I end up, I'll be needing plenty of ink and vellum. Someone's got to set down everything good and proper. For the big fellow," and he jerked his fat thumb at Orvandil, "it's enough to be heading home. For now."

The Thjoth directed a half smile at the Dweorg and nodded.

Gnorn stared at Sequara, and his grin faltered. "Are you certain? It's just that, perhaps you oughtn't to be alone."

The sorceress took a breath and stood taller. "We've discussed this already. I'll be fine. There will be much to occupy me. But I expect you two to visit Asdralad at the first chance, once things are settled."

Orvandil nodded. "We will."

Gnorn exhaled. "Well. I suppose we ought to . . ." But he stopped short as he sniffed and tugged on his beard. The Dweorg's lower lip trembled, and he looked down and shook his head.

Sequara embraced Gnorn and Orvandil. In the end, words failed them all, but in each other's eyes they saw the depth of their friendship and the knowledge that they would seek each other again.

"Don't forget to greet Seren for us," the Dweorg finally managed to say as he clambered up his horse. "Help her understand. And tell her to stay out of mischief."

He and Orvandil looked back several times as they rode away. Their forms grew blurry through her quiet tears. There would be many more of those in the days to come. Only when they were too far off to see any longer did Sequara release a long sigh before climbing on her horse and riding south.

THE JOURNEY TO TORRHELM PASSED SWIFTLY, AND WHEN SEQUARA reached Torrlond's chief city, there were already many signs of the rebuilding taking place there. Fresh graves dotted the land outside the walls, but there was also much activity, including carts and caravans of stone, timber, and workers for the repairs. The city had suffered much, but the eyes and faces of the survivors showed a grim determination to grow it again.

It did not take Sequara long to gain an audience in Sigseld with Ethelred, who had become king of Torrlond after soldiers found Earconwald's body. True to his word, Hewald had preceded her to the chief city and given his report, and thus the court expected her arrival. What was more, the tale of how the Prophet of Edan set out with a small company to banish the powerful demon that had afflicted their city and defeat its army of dwolas was already all over the streets in various colorful forms.

After a meal and a bath, the sorceress sat at a table with King Ethelred in a small, private room. She told him of everything that passed. At the end of her tale, Ethelred favored her with a gruff smile. "Well, I admit I had my doubts when that soldier came with his tidings, but your account matches his. Still, if I hadn't seen what I saw, it would've been a lot harder to swallow." He hesitated for a moment. "I'm sorry for your losses. The Prophet . . . He was a good man. I always felt it."

Sequara sighed. The pity in the king's eyes nudged her out of her composure, and she could not speak of Dayraven just then. "Many sacrificed to keep the elf from doing further harm."

The king folded his hands before him. "Aye. Ludecan and his lads. A fine soldier. Earl Elfwy. The queen took it ill to learn of his passing, I promise you. As did I. He was a true nobleman, that one, and I don't mean by birth."

The sorceress nodded. "He was indeed."

Ethelred released a deep sigh. "Enough death and destruction for a long time, I say."

Sequara cleared her throat. "On that we agree. I was hoping we might speak of Caergilion and Adanon."

King Ethelred gazed at her and frowned. "The kingdoms you helped to rebel against Torrlond?"

Sequara opened her mouth to speak, but the king's frown turned into a sudden grin. "Fear not. I spoke at length to Lieutenant Edgelaf about these matters. Good man. Seems to think rather highly of the Prophet. I've pardoned him and the rest for their treason, and thank

Edan they committed it. You'll be glad to know I've renounced all claims to the southern kingdoms, and I've offered them aid in rebuilding as well. The last bit was the lieutenant's idea, though he insisted the Prophet would have wanted it." He took a deep breath and bowed to Sequara. "And I offer you the same. I can't undo the destruction and deaths we wrought in Asdralad, but I hope you'll accept this gesture of peace between our kingdoms. Ships will sail for your island filled with supplies and craftspeople to help you rebuild Kiriath. With your permission, of course, my lady."

She nodded and favored him with a serene smile. "I give it gladly. Once I reach Asdralad, I'll send word of what we most need." Prodded by a hope for the future she could not have predicted, her smile broadened just a little. "You show great wisdom, my lord, and Torrlond is fortunate to have such a king."

Ethelred frowned. "We'll see about that. I never believed in my cousin's mad war, especially after he murdered Bledla. Things will be different in Torrlond now, I assure you. Among other matters, we're in need of a new supreme priest. A good man. A true follower of Edan."

Sequara thought a moment, and a memory of Dayraven's stirred within her along with the emotions and sensations associated with it. It was from a time before he met her, not long after he left the Mark. She looked upon the king with a true smile. "Just west of the crossroads on the east-west road, there's a village on a hill. I cannot tell you what it's called. But there's a priest there. A good man, as you say. I believe he's the sort you're seeking."

SEQUARA LEFT HER DISCUSSION WITH KING ETHELRED WITH A strange hope in her heart and anticipation for her next meeting. Through the king she learned the man called Edge had retired from the Torrlonder army as soon as he handed over power. Before leaving Torrhelm, Edge and Seren had found a place for the former priest Bagsac in the Way's monastery, where the High Priestess Gida had given him a comfortable cell and the task of looking after the library's books and scrolls. Taking the girl with him, the retired lieutenant had gone back to his home village, which lay a couple leagues south of Torrhelm.

Sequara rode to the village, which turned out to be almost a small town, and, after asking around, arrived at a modest but comfortable looking home with a timber and stucco exterior and a low stone wall around it. Next to the home was a small shop, whence a loud banging noise emerged. Sequara opened the gate and, after she stepped through into the yard, closed it again. She approached the shop, which had an open front.

Inside the shop was a large man clad like a tradesman, with a leather apron that had large pockets bulging with tools. The big man was hunched over a shelf and surrounded by pieces of wood and shavings. There was a chair, a chest, and what seemed to be a cradle in various stages of completion. The source of the banging turned out to be the man driving in a dowel with a wooden hammer to attach an arm to the chair he was making.

As she approached, he glanced up in mid-stroke. His eyes widened at Sequara just as he brought down the hammer, which he dropped as he cried out and waved his hand around. He grimaced and squeezed his thumb with his other hand. "By Aldmund's hairy left ball, that hurt."

Sequara stepped closer. "I can help you with that if you like."

He shook his head. "No. It's not too bad, and it'll serve as a reminder to heed what I'm doing."

"Lieutenant Edgelaf?"

"Edge. No longer lieutenant."

"You're a carpenter now?"

"Aye. Like my old Pa before me. This was his shop." He shrugged. "I was never much good at it. That's why I took to soldiering, I reckon." His face broke out in a sad smile. "I know who you are, my lady." The big man took a deep breath and sighed it out. "Is it true about the Prophet?"

Sequara nodded. "He is gone."

Edge swallowed and looked down at the ground. "I'm right sorry."

"So am I. But he gave up his life so that I and many others might live. I intend to honor him by doing that."

The big man looked up and smiled, but his eyes glistened with wetness, and his voice broke when he spoke. "They say he sprouted wings and chased away some demon and its horde."

Sequara shook her head. "Not quite."

Edge chuckled and wiped one eye. "Well, I suppose there's a true tale or two behind all the stories. You'll be staying a while to tell them, I hope." He looked at Sequara, and he favored her with a gentle smile. "That is to say, you would grace my home, simple as it is, with your presence, my lady."

Sequara inclined her head. "I thank you for your kind welcome. Your home is lovely."

The old soldier's smile broadened, and he shook his head. "It's a wonder to see you standing here, and no mistake. Seren won't stop talking about you."

"Truly?" The sorceress smiled. "And Dayraven told me much of you. It's an honor to meet you."

"The honor's all mine. From what Seren's said . . ." He stopped short, and his brow wrinkled in a suspicious frown. "You've come to fetch her, haven't you?"

"I'm afraid so. Her home's in Caergilion. She has a brother who may be alive. And . . . possibly an uncle in Adanon."

Edge scowled as if he were about to argue, but his big shoulders dropped when he sighed. "I reckon I knew it was coming. Still, it's a shame. She and my Ardith were becoming fast friends. Like long lost sisters, they are. They're of an age, you know." His smile returned, though it was not quite as bright as before. "Well, come inside, then, and meet the family. There's Nelda and Ma making supper just now. I'll see if I can find where the girls have run off to. Mind you, she's taken the tidings quite hard. She's a tough one, our Seren, but she's devoted to him."

"I know."

They walked toward the house, and Edge opened the door. Just as Sequara was entering, she heard Seren cry out, and she opened her arms wide to embrace the girl.

. . .

After a short stay with many tales exchanged and tears shed, Sequara and Seren rode many leagues, having bought a horse for the girl and winter cloaks for both of them in Edge's village. Over the Marar Mountains they passed, where the snows had crept down into the lower elevations and foothills with the coming of colder weather. When they reached Balnor Pass, one member of the small Caergilese garrison recognized Sequara from the days when she aided the rebellion against Torrlond, and they greeted both travelers like heroes. Since none of the Caergilese spoke the Northern Tongue or Andumaic, Seren served as translator for Sequara.

After passing through the mountains and skirting Iarfaen, they journeyed west by the Rivers Gilion and Glas, and then they headed south, bypassing the town of Gadomiel to ride the swiftest way to Culvor Sound. At length, under a grey sky and in a chilly drizzle, they approached a landscape of rugged green hills with the sea's scent heavy in the air. Sequara deemed it best to ask for tidings from one of the small farmsteads, and so Seren guided them to Tob and his family, where they had word of Seren's brother Allon. Tob broke the news gently, telling Seren how her brother had died defending Lord Imrys. She took in the tidings with a stoic face and a nod. "I will see my home now."

Sequara laid her hand on Seren's shoulder and nodded.

They rode in silence along the coastal trail, where the wind-driven droplets stung their faces and the waves moaned against the rocky cliffs and hillsides plummeting into the sound.

When they turned their horses along the path leading to the farmstead, Sequara kept a careful watch on Seren. The girl looked forward in stubborn concentration, and she decided not to ask her if she wished to turn back. Soon enough, they approached the place where Seren grew up and her parents died. There appeared the wet, charred remains of the farmhouse and barn, the forlorn wreckage of destroyed lives.

Seren alighted from her horse, and Sequara followed suit to walk behind the girl as she approached the ruins of her past. The only sounds were the keening of seagulls, the moaning of the sea in the distance, and the soft patter of the rain. Seren halted and gazed for a time at her former home, though her eyes seemed not to take in anything.

She began to quiver, and a sob broke the silence, crumpling the girl as she folded her body and then sat in the mud. Sequara rushed to kneel by her and embrace her. There they stayed for a long while, saying nothing as they both wept.

After Seren's convulsions gave way to gentler tears and sniffles, she turned to Sequara. "I'm alone."

Sequara held her tighter. "I'm here." She looked the girl in the eyes. "You are always welcome to stay with me. But there is someone I can take you to. Someone who might need you as much as you need him. Dayraven believed so."

Seren stared back at Sequara for a long time, her eyes dull as if something within her had broken. The sorceress wondered if the girl had understood her. At length, however, Seren nodded. "Alright."

THE WEATHER CLEARED SOON AFTER SEQUARA AND SEREN CROSSED the River Gilion into Adanon, but the girl remained silent unless the sorceress spoke to her. And yet, as the two mourned their absent loved ones, an occasional gentle smile confirmed the comfort they took in each other's company. Feeling the loss of Dayraven, Galdor, and so many others like a weight sinking her down, Sequara did her best to put on a brave face for Seren. Somehow, she reckoned, they helped each other just by being in the presence of another who understood their loss. The company of a fellow survivor made them feel a little less alone.

Once they reached the outskirts of Palahon, they beheld the efforts that Queen Rona had already set in motion toward rebuilding the chief city. On the plain before them, carts drawn by oxen and horses carried debris away, while others loaded with stone, wood, and other building materials crawled toward the city from barges all along the River Maranant. New walls and structures were already creeping upward, with the tiny forms of workers swarming on and around them. The clinking of hammers on stone punctuated the shouts of busy work crews, and everywhere the two travelers looked, there were laborers and those who came to support them beneath a cloud of dust and smoke from forges. Occupying the plain around the resurrecting city were thousands of tents laid out in neat rows. That was where Sequara would find Queen Rona, and not far from her would be Imharr.

Leading their horses afoot through the bustling camp, Sequara and Seren inquired about Queen Rona's whereabouts, with Seren doing the speaking in Ondunic. Most eyes, however, lingered on Sequara, and word of her presence spread as many recognized the sorceress of Asdralad. Many bystanders began to bow as she passed, and whispers followed in her wake.

Seeming ill at ease at all the attention, Seren began to frown.

"Don't worry. We'll find the queen soon." Sequara put an assuring hand on the girl's shoulder.

"Queen Sequara!"

Still unaccustomed to the title, Sequara nevertheless breathed a sigh of relief at the sound of the familiar voice addressing her. She turned around and accompanied her nod with a smile. "Duke Imharr."

Imharr smiled in return at her, but his smile gave way to a concerned frown. He turned to the men surrounding him, engineers and architects by the look of their robes and the bundles of maps and parchments they held. "Proceed to the planning tent and try to work out the issue with the palace walls," he said in the Northern Tongue. "I'll join you there shortly."

They all bowed, and the eldest among them said, "Yes, Lord Silverhand."

The men dispersed, and the rest of the crowd also took that as their signal to go back to their business, though many still sneaked looks at Sequara.

Imharr gave the sorceress another smile, though this one appeared tired and perhaps forced. "It is good to see you." His smile faltered. "Is it true about Day?"

Sequara's throat tightened. She nodded and managed to get two words out. "I'm sorry."

He shook his head. "No. I'm the one who should apologize. We had messages about what happened, but I . . . They say . . ." His eyes watered up, and he brushed away a tear. "They say he saved the Mark."

Her own eyes clouding with tears, Sequara nodded. "He did."

"More than just the Mark." Seren looked down as if unsure whether she should have spoken, but she faced Imharr when she continued. "Caergilion and Adanon too. Some would say Torrlond as well. And the East . . . Though I wasn't there to see that part." The girl stole a look at Imharr's scarred hand before turning her gaze downward again.

Imharr looked at Seren and smiled. "Nor was I. But I can see we have some tales to exchange." He glanced at Sequara. "However, first, will you introduce me to your companion?"

Sequara took a deep breath in preparation. "In fact, that is my main purpose here."

Imharr's brow wrinkled in puzzlement. "Oh?"

The sorceress put her hand on Seren's shoulder again. "This is Seren. She was . . . is Dayraven's friend. She served as his translator in Caergilion. And she saved his life before the end."

"Truly?" Imharr's eyes narrowed, and he seemed to be reassessing the girl standing before him. "Then, we all owe you a great debt."

Seren looked down at her feet. "He saved me first."

Imharr waited, seeming to expect more, and then he smiled gently at Seren. "If you are willing to tell me, I would hear of his days in Caergilion."

Seren smiled back before returning her gaze to the ground. "I . . . I would be glad to . . ." She looked at Imharr and seemed to struggle to say more. "There is so much . . . I don't know how to start." She shook her head, and she hugged herself as she began to tremble.

Imharr glanced at Sequara with a concerned frown.

The sorceress looked around at the laborers milling about them, all engaged in the rebuilding of Adanon's chief city. No one was paying them special attention any longer. "I was going to wait for somewhere more private, but I think it's best to spare Seren further delay."

Imharr's frown deepened in confusion, but he recovered with a quick grin. "There's little privacy to be had around here anyway."

Sequara nodded, and she took Seren's hand in one of her own. "When Dayraven healed Seren, he saw many of her memories. Took them into his mind. Later, he shared them with me."

"I see." Imharr nodded, but he still appeared confused.

"That is how I have come to possess an image of Seren's mother in my mind."

Imharr looked at Seren, but the girl was still staring at the ground, seemingly locked in a battle to keep control over her emotions.

"With your permission, I will share with you a memory of Seren's mother. One that Dayraven wanted you to see."

The duke's eyes widened. "You mean . . .?"

"Yes. I would use the gift to enter your mind and let you see this memory. If Dayraven's guess was right, it will explain everything, and it will erase any doubt."

"I . . . Very well." Imharr glanced at Seren before nodding to Sequara. "You may share it with me."

"This will require that we remain calm and trust each other."

"I trust you. How could I not?" He held up his scarred hand.

Sequara nodded. "Good." She reached up with her free hand and placed her palm on Imharr's cheek, with her fingers resting on his temple. "Be at ease. Deep, slow breaths will help. I will keep the contact as brief as possible, but you may feel disoriented for a moment. It will pass."

"I'm ready."

Sequara nodded again and then, after releasing her mind to the realm of origins, began intoning the song of origin beneath her breath. "Druanil ecthoniae di borolin ar doranae. Varadil ingharonae im govalin ni hurodae." When she was ready, she focused on the memory she wanted to share with Imharr, who took deep breaths as he watched her.

Like tendrils of mist on a breeze, Sequara's awareness drifted toward him. It probed until it met the energy that constituted Imharr, who gasped but put up no resistance to what felt like seeing from two pairs of eyes at once, one focused on himself. More of their energy coalesced, but before it went very far, Sequara judged he was ready to see the memory, and she nudged it toward him.

Imharr nearly staggered, but he held himself upright as the image formed in his mind just as it existed in Sequara's: A beautiful woman in the sort of dress found on farms throughout Caergilion and Adanon was wearing a lopsided smile and holding her arms out in invitation for a hug. She was standing in what seemed to be a stable or a barn, but Imharr was likely paying little heed to her surroundings.

His eyes widened, and he shook his head. His mouth hung open, and his lower lip trembled before he could form a word. "Mother?" Tears sprang to his eyes, and he shook his head again before beaming a smile. "No." A sob choked his voice. "Riall." He whispered the name, but there could be no doubt that he recognized the woman his sister had grown into.

Sequara broke off the contact, and Imharr brought his trembling hands up to grasp his head. He gasped several times before managing to calm himself enough to focus his eyes back in the world of forms. He turned to Seren, who looked at Imharr as if unsure what to do. "She is your mother?"

Seren managed a timid nod.

A look of pure wonder and joy illuminated Imharr's face. "She is your mother? Riall? My sister?"

The girl nodded again and sniffled as tears began to spill down her cheeks. "Was." She could manage no more.

Imharr too was weeping. "I'm so sorry." A wince of pain passed over his face, and he shook his head. "I see that you have suffered." Amidst his tears, he summoned a smile, one of joy and sorrow in equal measure. "But we will have each other now. That is, if you would like that?"

"Yes." The word came as little more than a whisper, and Seren's face crumpled as she wept.

Imharr leapt forward to embrace his niece. "Welcome home," he said as she buried her face in his chest.

They held each other while Sequara placed a hand on each of them, joining her tears and smiles to theirs.

THE DAY ARRIVED WHEN SEQUARA WAS READY TO BOARD A SHIP THAT Queen Rona arranged to carry her from Adanon's coast to Asdralad. On a sandy beach with guardsmen surrounding them, she said farewell to the queen and to Imharr, embracing them each and parting with vows of friendship between themselves and their peoples. The sorceress then turned to Seren before they smiled at one another and wrapped each other in a long embrace.

"I'll visit as soon as I can," whispered Sequara before they broke off the embrace.

"Dayraven once broke a promise to come back." In spite of a tear or two, Seren smiled at Sequara. "Don't you do the same."

"I won't." The sorceress kissed the girl on the cheek. "Don't worry. I'll come. And I expect you and your uncle to visit Asdralad as well."

After one last embrace with Seren, Sequara climbed aboard the rowboat that was to convey her over the choppy waves to the ship waiting at anchor for her. The sailors splashed their oars in the water until they reached the larger vessel, which they and Sequara boarded with a rope ladder and the assistance of other sailors.

Standing in the stern, the sorceress peered back at the shore and waved to the distant party there while the shouting Adanese seamen prepared the sail and weighed anchor. The sturdy ship clove through the waves, and the groaning of the water lapping its sides joined the soughing of the sea breeze and the occasional luffing of the sail. Once they had sailed too far to see Seren and the others any longer, Sequara looked down and held her hand to her stomach. "So. We too are headed home at last."

The salt-laden wind toyed with the sorceress's dark hair. Pulling her cloak tighter about her and hugging herself, she gazed back at the land and gave it a wistful smile.

THE END

ABOUT THE AUTHOR

Rather than write about myself in third person, allow me to thank you for reading my book, dear reader, and to introduce myself. A medievalist with special interests in Old English, Old Norse, and various mythological traditions, I teach English composition and literature and run a YouTube channel ("Philip Chase" or "PhilipChaseTheBestofFantasy") dedicated to the exploration of the fantasy genre. Feel free to visit me there and join the wonderful fantasy literature community that exists on YouTube. I can also be found puttering around on Twitter (philipchase90), and if you would like to hear from me occasionally about writing updates or whatever ponderings I might happen to be tapping out on my keyboard, you could wander over to my website, PhilipChaseAuthor.com. Until next time!